Penny Vincenzi is one of the UK authors. Since her first novel, *Ol* she has written sixteen bestselling novels, most recently *A Perfect Heritage*, *The Decision* and the *Sunday Times* number one bestseller *The Best of Times*.

Her first 'proper' job was at the Harrods Library, aged sixteen, after which she went to secretarial college. She joined the *Mirror* and later became a journalist, writing for *The Times*, the *Daily Mail* and *Cosmopolitan* amongst many others, before turning to fiction. Several years later, over seven million copies of Penny's books have been sold worldwide and she is universally held to be the 'doyenne of the modern blockbuster' (*Glamour*).

Penny Vincenzi has four daughters, and divides her time between London and Gower, South Wales.

For exciting updates and the latest news from Penny visit
www.pennyvincenzi.com

Reading a Penny Vincenzi novel is . . .

'Pure pleasure, Vincenzi-style' *Woman & Home*

'An addictive experience . . . Penny Vincenzi dazzlingly
combines the old-fashioned virtues of gripping storytelling
with the up-to-the-minute contemporary feel for emotional
depth and insight' Elizabeth Buchan

'Marvellously engrossing . . . perfect for curling up with'
Barbara Taylor Bradford

'Oh, the bliss . . . I was shamefully glued, as if to the best gossip'
Kate Saunders, *Saga*

'Glamorous, weepy, indulgent and at times heartbreaking.
Oh, and it has some racy bits, too. Hooray!' *Heat*

'Like a glass of champagne: bubbly, moreish and you don't
want it to end' *Daily Express*

'Spectacular . . . utterly captivating' *Closer*

By Penny Vincenzi

Old Sins
Wicked Pleasures
An Outrageous Affair
Another Woman
Forbidden Places
The Dilemma
The Glimpses (short stories)
Windfall
Almost a Crime
No Angel
Something Dangerous
Into Temptation
Sheer Abandon
An Absolute Scandal
The Best of Times
The Decision
Love in the Afternoon and Other Delights (short stories)
A Perfect Heritage

PENNY VINCENZI

An Absolute Scandal

headline review

First published in 2007
by HEADLINE REVIEW
An imprint of HEADLINE PUBLISHING GROUP

First published in paperback in 2008
by HEADLINE REVIEW

This edition published in 2014
by HEADLINE REVIEW

12

Cataloguing in Publication Data is available from the British Library

ISBN 978 0 7553 3680 7

Typeset in New Caledonia by Avon DataSet Ltd,
Bidford-on-Avon, Warwickshire

Printed and bound in Great Britain by Clays Ltd, St Ives plc

Headline's policy is to use papers that are natural, renewable and
recyclable products and made from wood grown in sustainable forests.
The logging and manufacturing processes are expected to conform
to the environmental regulations of the country of origin.

HEADLINE PUBLISHING GROUP
An Hachette UK Company
338 Euston Road
London NW1 3BH

www.headline.co.uk
www.hachette.co.uk

For Paul. For endless support and patience,
and incredible generosity.

Acknowledgements

This has been one of the most demanding books I've ever written, in terms of required and acquired knowledge; I owe a huge debt to a large number of people.

The most outstanding contribution of all came from Gordon Medcalf, whose knowledge of Lloyd's and attention to detail was only matched by editorial inventiveness, and without whom certain chapters would have been sad and sorry affairs. It is with incredible sadness that I find myself unable to thank him properly, for he died just before the book was finished; I would like to express my gratitude therefore, for his huge input, to his wife Julia and his family and to tell them what of course they know, that he was a dear and brilliant person and a privilege to work with.

Many other people gave most generously of their time and expertise too; Jay and Nick Upton, Peter Carvell, John Mays, Victor Sandelson, John Rew, David Durant, Nigel Symons Jones and James Lotery all shared their experiences of being Names at Lloyd's with me; Geoff Spencer gave me invaluable financial background and a vivid insight into life as a banker at the time; Mark Spash, Michael Drake and Lionel Rosenblatt all provided fantastic (and frequently inspired) legal input; and step forward Edward Harris, who alerted me to the existence of male entail and then spent many hours working out the logistics of its relevance to the plot. Jillie Hardie proved herself a fountain of knowledge on sailing and sailing races; Duncan Brown managed to make life insurance of various kinds not only comprehensible but hugely interesting; and Sandi Meisner instructed me so fully and efficiently on the conduct of inquests that I feel I could almost set up as a coroner myself. Charlotte Taylor gave me the most brilliant and witty account of her early life as a star hairdresser, and a patient but anonymous person at Vodafone spent hours in her archives in order to confirm that mobile phones were indeed able to offer voicemail in 1990. And Clodagh Hartley once again provided me with some valuable inside information on the conduct of newspaper reporting; and on the subject of newspapers, much gratitude to the staff in the archive library at the *Daily Mirror*, who dug out one huge dusty volume after another.

Detective Superintendent Dermot Keating gave me a crash course in the conduct of sundry complex police procedures; I would like to thank Anthony Saxton, who tirelessly enrolled so many people to talk to me with a capital T, and also of course the amazing Sue Stapely who once again shared her encyclopaedic knowledge and contact book with me.

And thanks to my amazingly informative and engaging guide around Harvard, and on the Duck Tour of Boston.

Adam Raphael's brilliant book, *Ultimate Risk*, provided invaluable background information.

I couldn't have got by without the almost daily input from Simon Cornish on City matters; and I would especially like to thank David Short, aka Shorty, who not only gave me a particularly vivid view of life as a trader at the relevant time, but provided the name for Blue, who turned out to be almost everyone's favourite hero.

I want to thank all those wonderful people at Headline: working with Harrie Evans, my editor, has proved an absolute delight; her input was both creative and judicious and we managed to finally and triumphantly reach The End without exchanging a cross word, which was undoubtedly more to her credit than mine; I would also like to thank her for crying so appropriately and whole-heartedly whenever the plot required it. Emily Kennedy has seen to the marketing in the most marvellous and creative style (and also managed to cry over the book quite satisfactorily), and Kerr MacRae and James Horobin have been their wonderful whizzy selves selling it, as has Peter Newsom, trundling it round the world (although none of those three cried much, I believe). Thanks to Georgina Moore, there cannot be many people in the country, or indeed on the planet, who haven't heard about the book; and I am deeply indebted to Justinia Baird-Murray for designing yet another ravishing cover, and of course Joan Deitch, the copy editor, who made neat sense of my wilder sentences and statements and made sure all the 'i's were dotted and the 't's crossed.

And then I must also like to pay a big tribute to my agent, Clare Alexander of Gillon Aitken, who is so wonderfully, permanently and instantly supportive.

Lastly, but most certainly not leastly, I want to say thank you so, so much to my four daughters, Polly, Sophie, Emily and Claudia, who have all in their various ways and from their various viewpoints and areas of expertise helped me a great deal; and have been always there for me, cheering and encouraging me along what must have seemed to them, as well as me, a rather long road.

Penny Vincenzi

Legal Disclaimer

In this novel, I have aimed to draw an authentic portrait, which necessarily, as context, makes reference to Lloyd's and the scandals surrounding the organisation such as those relating to asbestosis claims. However, as will readily be understood, the novel is from start to finish entirely a work of my imagination and the characters, companies and their actions in the story are entirely fictional.

Characters

Simon Beaumont, *a merchant banker*
Elizabeth, *his wife, the managing director of Hargreaves, Harris &*
    Osborne (H₂O) advertising agency
Annabel, Toby and Tilly, *their children*
Florian, *a hairdresser, and Annabel's best friend*
Madison and Fallon, *Tilly's best friends*
Martin Dudley, *Simon's chairman*
David Green, *an old friend and sailing companion of Simon's*
Felicity Parker Jones, *a friend of Simon's*
Neil Lawrence, *a client of Elizabeth's and Lloyd's victim*

Lucinda and Nigel Cowper, *Sloaney couple living in Cadogan Square*
Eric and Margaret Worthington, *Lucinda's parents*
Lydia Newhouse, *Nigel's secretary*
Steve Durham, *Lucinda's tough lawyer*
Graham Parker, *her boss*

Blue Horton, *a market trader in the City*
Charlie, *his best friend*

Flora Fielding, *a glamorous widow*
Richard Fielding, *her son, a teacher*
Debbie Fielding, *his wife*
Alexander, Emma and Rachel, *their children*
Anna Carter, *Debbie's boss*
Morag Dunbar, *a headmistress*
Colin Peterson, *a property developer*

Joel Strickland, *a financial journalist on the* Daily News
Hugh Renwick, *his editor*

Catherine Morgan, *a young and pretty widow and Lloyd's victim*
Freddie and Caroline, *her children*
Phyllis and Dudley Morgan, *her parents-in-law*
Mary Lennox, *her babysitter*
Dominic Mays, *Freddie's best friend in London*

Jane-Anne Price, *Caroline's best friend in the country and her posh parents, the Honourable Mark Prices*
Patrick Fisher, *an admirer of Catherine's*

Jamie Cartwright, *dashing young lawyer from Boston*
Frances and Philip, *his parents*
Kathleen, *his sister, married to Joe*
Bartholomew ('Bif'), *his brother and his wife Dana*

Gillian Thompson, *a piano teacher and Lloyd's victim*
May Williams, *her neighbour*
George Meyer, *leader of an action group, mounting a legal challenge against Lloyd's*
Fiona Broadhurst, *a solicitor*
Tim Allinson, *man about town*
Robert Jeffries, *a coroner's officer*

Prologue

August, 1990

So the person you loved best in the world had killed themselves. Had felt so desperate, so absolutely hopeless that it seemed the only option.

How could you live with yourself, how could you ever come to terms with it, knowing that, in the end, even you had not been able to help, to offer comfort of any kind?

And, even though you knew it was not directly your fault, that the blame could be very arguably laid at the door of that gleaming, futuristic-looking building in the heart of the City of London, currently wrecking so many lives, you would still blame yourself every hour of every day for the rest of your life.

It wasn't the first such death of course and nor would it be the last. People had been lured by the promise of an easy, apparently risk-free wealth by the tenants of that building, basing a luxurious lifestyle upon it – a lifestyle of beautiful houses, of expensively educated children, of lavish grown-up toys, and all the other powers and pleasures of wealth – only to discover the foundations of it were built for a while at least on shifting, albeit golden sands rather than solid rock. And yet the promise had been far from empty, based as it was on a background of three centuries of economic success, the success of a great financial institution. But for a time in those darkly turbulent years at the end of what has now been labelled the Greed Decade, that promise seemed not only empty but also a terrifying vacuum; and it was not just the houses and the educations and the toys that were lost, but frequently the most basic of life's requirements, and for many, pride, self-respect, and indeed, hope itself.

1

Part One

Part One

Chapter 1

22 April 1988, morning

She wasn't even going to think about having an affair. She simply wasn't.

It was something she totally disapproved of; it wasn't only immoral and selfish, it was deeply dangerous. She was married, very happily, to someone she not only loved, but admired, and there was no way she was going to break her vows (and risk breaking Nigel's heart), and put her marriage and her very happy life at risk. So that was that. Absolutely that. And if he phoned – which he almost certainly wouldn't, he'd been drunk and probably hadn't meant a word of what he said – but if he did, she would simply say that, say, 'No, I'm sorry, it was lovely meeting you, but I'm happily married and well, I'm happily married.' That would be enough. Surely. She wouldn't have to go on. He'd know what she meant and he'd probably come out with some jokey reply and that would be that. And if she had to spell it out – well, she would. That would be the end of it. A fun encounter: that's all it had been. She might have been a bit silly: she had been a bit silly. But that was all. Blame the champagne. And luckily Nigel hadn't noticed anything . . .

He came into the bedroom now, from their bathroom, offering his wrists to her so she could put in his cufflinks; as she did so, her fingers unusually fumbly – blame the champagne for that as well, she seemed to have a bit of a hangover – she suddenly found herself looking at him as if she had never seen him before. Was he really, as HE had said so rudely – *so* rudely – a bit of a caricature? She supposed, honestly, he was: tall, blond – well, blond-ish, going just slightly grey now – very slim, pretty good-looking really, perfectly dressed, in his Turnbull &

Asser shirt, his pinstripe suit, his Lobbs shoes. (HE had been wearing Lobbs shoes, he told her: 'Only posh thing about me. I get a real thrill going in there, them getting the old last out.')

'Lucinda! Do concentrate, darling, I can't stand here all day.'

'Sorry. There you are.'

'Thanks. You having breakfast this morning?'

'Oh – no.' The thought made her feel sick.

'Hope you're not overdoing the dieting?'

'Nigel, of course I'm not. I'd have thought you only had to look at me to see that.'

'Well – you look pretty good to me. Anyway, I'm hungry. Not enough to eat at that thing, was there?'

'No, not really. Gosh, it's late, I didn't realise.'

She mustn't be late for work today, of all days. She worked for Peter Harrison, the publishers, as secretary to Graham Parker, one of the editors, and he had an important meeting that morning with some Americans, who were coming over on what Graham wittily called 'an acquisition mission'. Being Americans, they had suggested an eight o'clock meeting; Graham had managed to persuade them forwards an hour to nine, but she'd have to be there well before then, coffee brewed, biscuits and the best cups on a tray, and herself ready to greet them. It would be fun.

One of the things Lucinda loved most about her job was the social aspect; there was always something going on – book launches, marketing meetings, sales conferences, press jaunts, and the famous Frankfurt Book Fair where the entire publishing world packed itself under one enormous roof. She'd been working for Graham for a year now; she was hoping to be an editor herself one day, but there were so many people with that particular ambition, and to be absolutely honest, hers was slightly half-hearted; she didn't intend to go on working after she'd had a baby. That was something else she disapproved of: working mothers. She intended to be like her own mother, always there, putting her children first. Of course, the baby was hardly a reality: bit far from it, actually. But – come on, Lucinda, don't start thinking about that now. You've got to get to work.

*

She was ready twenty minutes later: she caught sight of herself in the hall mirror and tried to see herself through HIS eyes: long-ish full-ish skirt (Laura Ashley), blue shirt with a turned-up collar (Thomas Pink), and her twenty-first-birthday pearls, of course; navy sleeveless Puffa jacket, flat shoes (Charlie Jourdan), blond hair scooped back in a velvet band.

There really was no way she could possibly appeal to HIM, not really, not if he was sober. He'd like one of those sharp eighties girls in short-skirted suits with padded shoulders, girls with big hair and big ambitions. He wouldn't even be able to remember her this morning, never mind ringing her . . . and as she stood there, checking that she had her wallet and her keys, the post came through the letter box. A couple of quite nice-looking things, clearly invitations, a bill or two, a postcard from Verbier, from the ski-ing party she'd wanted to join and Nigel hadn't, and a letter from Lloyd's. Lloyd's of London. One of the whiter-than-white envelopes that arrived once a year, containing a statement of their account and followed in due course by a large cheque. Nigel was a Member of Lloyd's; it was one of the things that had pleased her father most when he and Nigel had had their Little Chat, just before they got engaged.

'Not only all that land, down in Norfolk, but he's a Name as well; that'll stand you in good stead in the years to come.'

One of her uncles had been a Name in quite a big way, apparently. When she was young, she'd heard her mother talking about it, and asked her what it meant: 'Well, darling, it means you become a sort of sleeping partner,' Margaret Worthington had said rather vaguely. 'They insure things, big things I mean, like ships and buildings, and they make a big profit on it. If you're a Name, you get a share in those profits.' 'What happens if the ships sink?' she'd asked, and her mother had said, well, there was more than enough money to deal with that. 'They still make a profit. Ask Daddy about it, he'll tell you more, I don't really understand it. Except that it pays all your cousins' school fees,' she added.

It hadn't sounded interesting enough for Lucinda to ask her father; but she did know now that there was enough money coming in from Lloyd's every year for Nigel to boost their income quite a bit. Which they didn't need at the moment of course, Nigel's salary as Chairman of the family business was perfectly adequate, and he had quite a big portfolio of stocks and shares, but it would be wonderfully helpful when they wanted to move to the country and buy a house.

That was the plan, to move as soon as they had children. Not to Norfolk, that was too far and the last thing Nigel wanted was to run the farm, but he didn't want to spend the rest of his life in London, he said. Nor did she; she'd grown up in the country herself and loved it.

'Where did you live when you were a child then?' HE had asked last night. 'Some pile in the country, I s'pose?'

And, 'Well,' she'd said, 'not exactly a pile, but quite a nice house, yes, in Gloucestershire, near Cirencester.'

'Oh yeah? Ponies?'

'Yes. Yes, I did have a pony. Actually.'

'Very nice,' he'd said, 'very nice indeed. I'd like my kids to have all that, ponies and boarding school; you go to boarding school?'

'Yes, when I was thirteen.'

'Like it?'

'Quite. I got awfully homesick and missed my pony. And Mummy, of course, and my sister and brothers.'

'And where were they at school? Eton or Harrow or some such?'

'Um – Eton, yes, actually.'

'And Hubby over there, he go to Eton?'

'Yes, he did.'

That was when he'd said Nigel was a caricature. And— stop it, Lucinda, stop thinking about it.

She started ripping open the envelopes to distract herself. Invitations: oh, fantastic, Caroline's wedding. And that looked like Philippa's writing (it was) – brilliant, party in the country – and Sarah's baby's christening, so sweet to ask them and— damn! She'd opened a letter addressed to Nigel by mistake, half-pulled it out. Not that Nigel would mind – at least, she didn't think so. He always said he had no secrets from her. She'd just say she was sorry and— now the letter wouldn't go back into the envelope. Lucinda pulled it out to refold it and couldn't resist reading it. The letterheading was *Jackson & Bond, Members' Agent, Lloyd's of London*, and the letter itself was quite brief:

Dear Nigel,
I thought I should warn you ahead of the final account
that, as I feared, you did make a loss for the year just
closed. Not a big one, just a few thousand pounds . . .

A loss. A loss! How extraordinary. That had never happened
before. Never. She didn't know how many thousands of pounds
Lloyd's would regard as 'just a few'. Maybe ten thousand, or
even more? Surely not. But she did know they dealt in very big
numbers. Nigel would know. They'd have to talk about it
tonight.

God, she was late; she must go. She left the letters on the
hall table and slammed the door behind her.

She found herself suppressing a rather strong feeling of
nausea as she half-ran down Sloane Street towards the Square
and the tube. She managed to just catch a train, and then sank
weakly into a seat. She couldn't face the change this morning;
she'd get out at Temple and take a taxi up to Russell Square.
She knew it was lazy but she really did feel rough: and she
simply couldn't be late. Graham would kill her . . .

Despite her resolve, as the train jerked and swayed along, she
began to think about HIM again: him and the night before. He
really had had the most profound effect on her. She wasn't sure
why. Partly, she supposed, because she'd never met anyone
quite like him before. It had been at a publishing party, to
celebrate the publication of a book edited by Graham Parker
about the financial markets just before and just after Big Bang
– that extraordinary day in October 1986, when the Stock
Market became totally computerised and a free-for-all, rather
than the gentlemanly domain of the traditional stockbroker.

Lucinda organised and attended all the editorial
department's parties; it was part of her job and she enjoyed it.

The guest-list had looked like a *Who's Who* of the Square
Mile. Nigel had been invited, not because he worked in the
City, he didn't; he worked for a large manufacturing company
that had been founded by his grandfather, but he had a large
share portfolio and Graham had kindly suggested to Lucinda
that it might be interesting for him. HE on the other hand did
work in the City.

9

HE was one of that entirely new breed of traders, the market makers, sprung not from the great public schools, but the East End of London. 'I'm one of your electronic barrow boys, so called,' he said, grinning at her, as he allowed her to refill his glass for the third time in what seemed about five minutes. 'Not the sort the City used to give the time of day to, unless we was in our proper place in the back office.' He held out his hand. 'Gary Horton. Known these days as Blue. Pleased to meet you' – he peered at her name badge – 'Lucinda Cowper.' He pronounced it wrongly as people so often did; it always annoyed her.

'It's pronounced Cooper,' she said briskly, 'the W's silent.'

'Yeah, I see,' he said looking mildly amused, and then, his dark eyes moving over her, 'are you really called Lucinda?'

'Yes, of course. Is that so unusual?'

'Well, where I come from it is. I mean, that is a posh name, isn't it? Seriously posh.'

'I – I don't know,' she said.

'I don't s'pose you would. Don't s'pose you know anyone who isn't posh, do you?'

'Well, of course I do,' she said, rather helplessly.

'Oh, OK. What, like Daddy's chauffeur and Mummy's cleaner?'

'I think you're being rather rude,' said Lucinda, 'if you don't mind my saying so. Now if you'll excuse me, I—'

'Sorry,' he said, putting out an arm, stopping her. 'I was out of order. Sorry. It interests me, all that Eton and ponies stuff, not sure I know why. Probably because I can't understand how they – *you*'ve – done it.'

'What do you mean?' she said, reluctantly interested.

'How you've survived so long. I mean, most dinosaurs die out, don't they? Oh, shit. Now I've been rude again, haven't I?'

'Yes. Very,' she said coolly and moved away from him, right across the room. She felt unduly upset by him, unable to laugh it off; she looked for Nigel, went over and refilled his glass.

'You all right?' she said, giving him a quick kiss. 'Got enough people to talk to?'

'Oh yes, of course. Jolly good party, Lucinda, well done.'

'I can't take any credit,' she said.

'Nonsense. Of course you can.' He smiled at her; it was one of his more endearing characteristics, that he enjoyed life enormously; his work, his social life – although he got a bit irritated with her more giggly friends – his tennis, his shooting. He was seldom out of sorts, always cheerful, almost always good-tempered. He was quite a bit older than she was, forty-two to her twenty-four, but it had never been a problem. She rather liked it; it made her feel safe.

She moved away and was in earnest conversation with one of the other editors when Blue Horton appeared at her side again. She smiled briefly at him and then ignored him.

'Look,' he said, waiting patiently until the editor moved away, 'I just wanted to apologise. I've got a real gift for saying the wrong thing. Can't help it, really.'

'It's all right,' she said. 'Now if you'll excuse me, I really have to go and talk to some more – what did you call them? – oh yes, dinosaurs . . .'

'No, don't go,' he said, putting his hand on her arm, 'please. One of the reasons I got carried away was because I felt – I don't know – thrown by you.'

'Thrown? Why?'

'Well, because you're so bloody gorgeous,' he said. 'I just totally forgot myself. Looking at you.'

Lucinda felt a blush rising up her throat; she blushed easily and she hated it.

'Don't be ridiculous,' she said.

'I'm not being ridiculous. I'm a shy, retiring sort of a fellow.'

'Now you are really being ridiculous.' She smiled in spite of herself. 'You're about as shy as – as –' she struggled to think of someone suitably self-confident, 'Mrs Thatcher.'

'Ah, now there's a lady I admire,' he said, surprising her.

'Really?'

'Yeah, course. She's responsible for all this –' he waved his arm round the room '– all this enterprise; she's freed up the market, she's made it possible to do whatever you want, given enough ambition and energy and that. It's getting more like the States every day here, and I like it. I think that's what I was really trying to say,' he added with a grin, 'when I said your lot were dinosaurs. I meant, everything's changed and you've managed not to. And still done well. Very admirable.'

'Well, all right. I'll try to accept that.'

'Good. So how long you been married then?'

'Three and a half years.'

'And kids? Got any kids?'

'No. Not yet.'

'OK.' He paused in his inquisition, as if digesting this piece of information, then: 'And where d'you live? Don't tell me, somewhere not too far away from Sloane Square.'

'Well, yes. Actually. In dinosaur country.'

'You're not going to let me forget that, are you?'

'No, I'm not. Now I really do have to circulate a bit more.'

'I'll come with you.'

'Blue—' She stopped suddenly. 'Why Blue, when you were christened Gary?'

'It's a nickname,' he said. 'We all have them and they all got some sort of reason. I mean, there's Luft, short for Luftwaffe, he's got blond hair and blue eyes and very, very right-wing views. And Croydon, because his surname is Sutton, and Harry, he's one of your coloured gentlemen, so Harry as in Belafonte, and Kermit who looks like a frog, and—'

'Yes, I get the idea,' she said, laughing, 'but why Blue?'

'You heard of Blue Buttons?'

'No.'

'They were the runaround boys on the old Stock-Exchange floor. Looked after the brokers, kept them supplied with tea and coffee – and info, of course. You'd hear people shouting for them: "Where's the Blue? Hey, Blue, over here!" I was one of them, before Big Bang. In fact, I got to be the head Blue Button. So the name stuck. I quite like it. Don't you?'

'I – well, yes, I think so,' she said doubtfully.

'Good. Anyway, it's a better name than Gary. Come on, let's do some of this circulating then. You introduce me to some of these people. And your husband, if you like.'

She hadn't introduced him to Nigel; it didn't seem a very good idea, she wasn't sure why. For the next half-hour he followed her round the room, listening respectfully while she talked to people, shaking hands when required, eventually carrying a bottle of champagne himself to assist with the glass refilling. And then, somehow, she had found herself alone with him, in the little kitchen; a lot of people had gone, the catering people were packing up glasses and he said suddenly, 'Would you have lunch with me one day?'

'No,' she said, staring at him, quite shocked, feeling the wretched flush rising again, 'of course not.'

'Why of course?'

'Well, isn't it obvious?'

'Not really, no.'

'Mr Horton,' she said firmly, piling up glasses, sorting empty bottles from full. 'I'm – well, I'm married, you know that.'

'And married ladies never have lunch with gentlemen? Is that right?'

'Not – well, not like that.'

'Like what?'

'You know—' She stopped. 'You know perfectly well what I mean. Perfectly.'

'No, I don't.'

'Yes, you do. Oh, this is silly.'

'Yes, it is,' he said, 'just a bit.'

And then he leaned forward and kissed her. On the mouth. Only very briefly, but it was enough; enough to create the most extraordinary sensations, somewhere deep inside her, a lurch, a sort of stirring. She pulled away, stared at him; he smiled at her. He had, she noticed, even in her confusion, extraordinarily nice teeth. He wasn't very tall, only a little taller than she was in her heels; his dark hair was close cropped, his eyes a deep, deep brown. He had long, almost girly eyelashes, a very straight nose and quite a wide mouth (showing the very nice teeth). He wasn't fat, but he was very solidly built, broad-shouldered, with rather large hands and feet, and he seemed to emit a lot of energy; he was restless, permanently fidgeting. It was oddly attractive.

He leaned forward and kissed her again; for just a fraction longer. She could feel herself responding to him, feel her lips parting, moving just a little; it was terrible, scary—

'Please stop it,' she said, 'I really must go.'

'OK,' he said, 'that's absolutely fine. I'll keep trying, though. I'll call you in a day or so, see if you've changed your mind.'

'Blue – I mean Mr Horton – I won't. Honestly.'

'You might. You never know. I don't give up easy. Bye, Lucinda.' And he was gone.

13

Thinking about him now, as the train clattered along, about how he had disturbed her, how funny he had been – how really rather nice – she completely forgot about the letter from Lloyd's.

In the trading room at McArthur's Bank, Blue Horton was telling his best mate, Charlie, over a bacon butty and page three of the *Sun* that he had met the girl he wanted to marry.

'Oh yeah? What's she do then?'

'Works for a publisher. And her husband's a—'

'Her husband? Blue, don't be daft, mate. You don't want to get mixed up with a married woman.'

'Charlie, she was just sensational. Posh, dead posh, you know how I like all that, and beautiful. I mean really beautiful. Blonde, blue eyes, legs like a racehorse, and really sweet, still waters running really deep – you know the sort of thing. No idea how sexy she was. I reckon she's never had a good fuck, and I reckon I could give her one. Correction, I'm going to.'

'You're crazy,' said Charlie, returning to his study of the page three girl, whose breasts were now studded with crumbs from the bacon butty. He flicked them off. 'You're heading for trouble, mate, you go down that road. And if she's got any sense, she won't let you.'

'She hasn't got a lot, I'd say,' said Blue, 'that's what I'm banking on. And she fancied me,' he added modestly, 'I know she did. You can always tell.'

Elizabeth Beaumont was becoming obsessed with her upper arms. It was an absurd obsession, she could see that; she had far more important things to be obsessed about, like her career and her relationship with her husband, and her eldest daughter who was turning into something of a nightmare, but she still found herself returning to the arms. They were the one bit of her body that she didn't seem able to get the better of. She could work the rest of it into submission, with the help of her personal trainer, the gym and her own self-discipline, could make sure her stomach was flat – who would think now it had submitted to three pregnancies – and her bum taut, and her thighs cellulite-free – although several of her friends had told her that was luck rather than anything more scientific. And her

14

bust was mercifully small and therefore pretty firm still. But her arms – above the elbows – were beginning to sag. She fought it, of course, with weights and swimming and the special exercises recommended by the trainer and indeed Ms Fonda, but it didn't quite work. If she relaxed them, they sagged. Only a bit: but she was beginning to feel they had to be covered up, that sleeveless tops were not a good idea. She had worn a sleeveless top this morning, a black one under her red suit, and as she dressed after her workout in the gym, she realised it had been a mistake, that she wouldn't really want to remove her jacket during the meeting. Which was a pain, as the meeting room was always too hot, and the suit, in thick ribbed silk, was quite heavy . . .

Oh, for goodness sake, Elizabeth, she thought, reaching for her bag, ready to leave the gym and go to the hairdresser, you shouldn't even be thinking about your arms, you should be thinking about the meeting. Which was going to be tricky; it was with one of the agency Account Directors who was anxious about a forthcoming presentation to one of their major clients, Hunters, a big-spending over-the-counter medicinal and toiletries brand. He didn't like the work the creative team had done and had refused to present it, said he knew the client wouldn't like it either. Both the Account Director and the creative team had dug their heels in; the Client Services Director backed the creative team, and the presentation was in two days' time. In fact, the situation was more than tricky, it was looking pretty dangerous. It had to be sorted. She walked out of the building, got into the cab waiting for her outside the door and turned the full force of her formidable brain onto what lay ahead of her that morning.

Elizabeth had a Very Big Job. She was Managing Director of one of London's leading advertising agencies, Hargreaves, Harris & Osborne, known in the business as H₂O. Her boss had once called her the embodiment of eighties have-it-all woman: with her gilt-edged life, her three perfect children, her handsome charming husband, her high-profile career; the compliment had pleased her immensely. She adored her work, and was immensely good at it; she loved the constant striving for excellence, the ferocity of the competition – so much greater than in the glory days of advertising in the sixties and seventies – loved urging and coercing her staff into the better-than-best work she knew they were capable of, even enjoyed the schmoozing as the essential tool it was in getting what she wanted. She enjoyed her large salary, not only for what it could buy her, but what it represented: success and on a major scale in the part of the industry that traditionally had been male-dominated. She didn't mind the long hours, the panics, not even the occasional savage disappointment when an account went to another agency; it was all part of a cut-and-thrust industry that she had worked in all her adult life.

Viewed from the outside, indeed, she was an absolute success; admired and fêted, self-assured, in complete command of herself and her life. From the inside, it was a little different, and a diffident, almost anxious, Elizabeth looked out, managing, but only just, to display the glossy confidence, the sense of order both at home and at work, the cool, calm enjoyment of it all. From the inside, she very well knew, she was rather less of a success. And her upper arms seemed to symbolise the whole thing.

Simon Beaumont had never been remotely jealous of his wife's success; indeed, he was extremely proud of it, generous both emotionally and practically. In this he was a little ahead of his time. It helped, of course, that he was a success himself, a Board Director of Graburn & French, merchant bankers, working in Investment Management, and spent his days in the heady world of global stock markets, managing portfolios for private clients. He combined an ease of manner with a brilliant mind and a sharp financial instinct, and was a well-known figure in the City, much sought-after for after-dinner speaking.

Just the same, colleagues at a comparable level would not have dreamed of doing what he was doing that morning: which was getting his eldest daughter back to school for the summer term. Or what he had done on a hundred, possibly more, occasions, attending (on his own) school plays and carol concerts, parents' evenings and even, once or twice, sitting by sickbeds when for various complex reasons, neither the nanny nor the housekeeper were available and Elizabeth had had a crucial meeting. For which he enjoyed, it had to be said, a great deal of cooing from various other wives of their acquaintanceship who told Elizabeth she had no idea how lucky she was. And Simon was rather afraid she did not.

He enjoyed the cooing, though; he enjoyed most of what came his way from the women in their social circle and also the ones that he worked with. He enjoyed women altogether; they were as essential to his happiness and sense of well-being as his excellent health, his work, the fine wines with which he had filled his cellars, his two beautiful houses, one in London, one in Sussex, the long days sailing his boat, the *Lizzie*, and his children, with all of whom he was besotted. He flirted with women and charmed them, and even gossiped with them – it was well-known that Simon Beaumont was a fine keeper of secrets – and basked in their admiration. He enjoyed Elizabeth too: when she would allow it.

And that morning, in Elizabeth's absence at her meeting, he was seeing his eldest daughter Annabel off to boarding school. Which he was happy to do; it provided an opportunity to admire both the girls and their mothers.

He really was a father to be proud of, Annabel thought, looking at him as he appeared in her bedroom doorway. He was very good-looking, tall and slim, with loads of hair still, even if it was going a bit grey; and he did dress well. He was wearing a great suit this morning, light grey, and really, really nice shoes. He always had nice shoes; she supposed it was having them handmade.

It was great to have a father you could be proud of. She looked at some of her friends' fathers, paunchy and balding, and wearing really naff things sometimes, specially at weekend exeats, and wondered how they could bear it.

Her mother always looked good too; her clothes were great. Annabel thought it must be because she worked, knew what was what. She had never been inside Marks & Spencer, for instance, Annabel was sure. A power-suited mother. A powerful mother altogether. Annabel was proud of her too: intensely so. When she had been little, she had wished that her mother could be at home, of course, but that had passed and their relationship was far better, she knew, more genuinely

17

friendly and mature than those a lot of her friends had with their mothers.

'Come on, we're going to be late.' Her father's voice was less tolerant than usual.

'Well, we'll have to be late. I can't find one of my essays. I know I brought it home, and now it's just vanished . . .'

'Have you been working on it? What about your desk?' he said, carefully patient, obviously stressing. God, he stressed. They both stressed.

'I've looked there, Daddy. Obviously. And yes, I have been working on it, actually.'

She hadn't, of course; she'd been much too busy seeing her friends, having fun. She'd only brought it home with her to look good.

'Shall I have a search? Often a fresh eye . . .'

'No,' she said sharply. She didn't want him rummaging in her desk. She kept her pills there; of course, she'd got the current pack in her bag, but there were a couple of empty ones that she kept meaning to throw away. They weren't the sort of thing you could just chuck in the waste-paper basket.

'Well, all right. But if you can't find it, we'll just have to go or you'll miss the train. I'll have a good look when you've gone and send it on to you.'

'Daddy, I know it's here. Just give me five minutes. And I can always get a later train.'

'Sweetheart, you have to get the school train. You're booked onto it. I'm sorry, I've got a big meeting later this morning and—'

'I can perfectly well get myself back to school,' she said, trying to sound patient. 'I'm sixteen, for God's sake, I can get a cab across London and buy another ticket and read a timetable all by myself.'

'You're not actually sixteen yet, Annabel. Not for another three weeks. And I want to see you safely onto that train. It's ridiculous, you should have got everything ready last night.'

'Yes, all right. Sorry.' She went over to him, gave him a kiss. 'I was busy last night.'

'Busy?' He smiled down at her, unable as she had known he would be, to stay cross with her.

'Yes, very busy.'

18

'Hmm. Partying until after midnight.'

'Well, it was the last chance before we all go back to prison.'

'All right, all right. So what do we do?'

'You wait, I go on looking. That's what we do. If I haven't found it in five minutes, we can go. Promise. Just leave me in peace, Daddy, please. I'm much more effective on my own.'

He sighed and turned out of the room; she smiled briefly after him. He might be an old fusspot, he might stress a lot, but he was a sweetheart.

She was right, of course; as soon as he had gone out of the room, she did remember where the essay was: in her bathroom, in the magazine rack. She'd been glancing at it two days earlier, as she waited for the bath to run, thinking she really must do something about it. As, of course, she hadn't. She retrieved it, pushed it into her leather Gladstone bag and rushed out into the hall.

'I'm ready.'

'Good. Well, off we go then. Any more luggage?'

'No. I travel light. Apart from my trunk, and that's in the car. Bye, Josie.'

Josie was the Portuguese housekeeper.

'And you've rung Mum?'

'Yes, I've rung Mum. Come on then let's go'

There was a pile of letters on the hall table, placed there by Josie.

'Want those?' said Annabel.

'What? Oh, maybe. Grab them for me, darling, will you. I'll look at them in the car.' Simon pulled the door shut behind them, ran down the steps in front of her. 'Morning, Carter. Paddington Station, please, here's Annabel's bag, and then I'm going on to the office.'

Carter opened the door for them both; Annabel smiled at him as she slithered in, tugging her extremely short skirt down.

'Hi, Carter. Off we go again.'

'Indeed,' he said primly. She could see him trying not to look at her legs; it amused her. Men amused her altogether; they were so bloody predictable. She might not be quite sixteen, but she did know that.

19

She sank into the corner of the car, looking back at the house briefly, then at her father as he sorted through the letters. It had been a very good holiday; they'd all had fun. Even dinner, the whole family number, had been all right. Bit of a waste of a Saturday night, but Toby had been on great form, he was an OK brother really, and it was lovely to see little Tilly so happy. She had just passed the exam into St Mary's – couldn't wait to get there, she said. She was so sweet and so pretty; most of her friends were terribly impatient of their little sisters, yet Annabel really loved Tilly. But then everybody did.

She met Carter's eyes in the driving mirror and winked at him; he frowned and hooted at a cyclist. Silly old fart; still, he'd been jolly patient when he'd taken her shopping last week, her and Miranda, sitting for hours in High Street Ken as they trekked from shop to shop.

Now should she have her hair cut, she wondered, bobbed like Miranda's? It was getting a bit long. Shame to lop it all off though, and she wasn't at all sure a bob would really suit it. Maybe she should just have some highlights put in . . . 'You all right, Daddy?' she said. A subdued 'Fuck!' had escaped him in a tone that was half-exasperation, half-groan.

He looked at her rather oddly, as if he had forgotten she was there; then managed a weak smile.

'Sorry, darling. Yes, I'm fine.'

He didn't look fine; he looked a bit flushed. She hoped he wasn't having a heart-attack or something.

'You sure?'

'Yes, yes, fine, just – just remembered something I should have done, that's all.'

'Oh, good.'

He was pushing a letter back into its envelope. She couldn't see what it said; the only words she recognised were *Lloyd's of London* at the top. She didn't know much about them, except that they were something to do with the City, and her father had once pointed out a rather amazing building to her and Toby, all blue glass and steel and external lifts and pipes.

Well, if it was only business it couldn't be that serious. She had complete faith in her father and his ability to run the world, or at least the City of London.

She looked at him again: he was reaching for the carphone

now, rummaging in his briefcase at the same time; he seemed flustered. Which was unlike him.

And then they reached Paddington Station, and she saw Miranda's mother pulling in just in front of them, and hooting, and after that in the hassle of getting her stuff out and assuring her father that there was no need to come to the platform with her, and hugging him and telling him she loved him, and saying goodbye to Carter, and waving and blowing her father kisses, she put it right out of her mind.

Back in the car, Simon read and reread the letter, and then sat staring out of the window. Carter watched him in the rearview mirror with interest. Such silence was unnerving; normally his employer either chatted to him, or talked on the carphone, or read the papers. Something was worrying him, that was for sure.

'Eat your breakfast, Emma, there's a good girl. Otherwise you'll be late for school.'

Debbie Fielding said this every morning and at exactly the same time (8.15), just as she said, 'Have a good day, both of you,' to Alex and Richard, after giving them both a kiss (at 8.05), and, 'Yes, Rachel, you do have to go to playschool,' (at 8.40).

Sometimes she thought she might as well have made a recording and just let it run each day, apart from the kissing, for all the notice anyone took of her or the response she got. Well, Richard smiled and said thanks, and plonked Alex's cap on his son's head, but Alex said nothing, just heaved his school bag onto his back, Emma continued not to eat her breakfast and Rachel continued to argue and say she didn't want to go to stupid playschool. Just the same, by 9.30 Debbie was usually safely back at home on her own, apart from the dog and the cat.

It was her favourite moment of the day, that, the house briefly hers, nobody arguing with her or asking her for things or saying could she discuss something with him – that was Richard and usually when she was absolutely frantic and trying to get Emma off to ballet or Alex to judo or Rachel out of the bath. She often wondered how a man whose job was looking after children – well, looking after their education anyway – could possibly not realise how much time and attention they required.

What she did next was have a bath; she knew this was recklessly extravagant, in terms of time, but it helped her cling onto her sanity; she would lie there for exactly five minutes, sloshing the water over herself, listening to the silence, planning exactly what she would do for the rest of the day. Quite why she found it so hard to remain sane she wasn't sure; she often said if there was a prize awarded for the most boring family in the British Isles they would win it. Three children, one boy and two girls, one cat, one dog, one car, house in the suburbs – well, she clung to the thought that Acton wasn't quite the suburbs, it had a London postcode, after all – father Headmaster of the local junior school, mother fulltime at home, editor of the Neighbourhood Watch newsletter, Deputy Chair of the local National Childbirth Trust.

And how had that happened, Debbie wondered. How had the Debbie who had been the ground-breaker of her year at school, first to go to a music festival (Glastonbury in 1971 in its second year, at the age of sixteen and without telling her parents – that had resulted in what she called house arrest for a month and which she swore was worth it), first to sleep with a boy, first to go on the pill, first to smoke pot, and who had been so excited on the morning of her first job, that of runner for a local TV station, that she had been literally sick – how was it she had turned into this dull and dutiful person?

She had been clever, although not brilliant, and had got two As and a B for her A-levels – and moved from her grammar school in Kent to Birmingham University to read English. Where she found herself less of a ground-breaker but blissfully happy, released finally from the claustrophobia of only-childhood in her aggressively suburban home, into a paradise of like-minded, free-thinking, pleasure-seeking contemporaries. She joined the Debating Society and several more ridiculous ones, like the Druids, partied furiously and almost failed her first-year exams. Sobered by that experience and a warning that she might lose her place unless her performance improved, she attached her nose firmly to the grindstone, and apart from a much-reduced social life, worked harder, and wrote endless pieces for *Redbrick*, the student newspaper.

And in that calmer, better-behaved phase she had met Richard. Richard Fielding, who was the antithesis of everything she liked or admired: public school, modestly good-looking, painstakingly polite, absolutely decent – it was an old-fashioned word, but suited him perfectly – bit of a swot, a reject, as he put it, from Cambridge, as if it mattered, Debbie thought, and who indeed for a while she regarded with some disdain. He was reading English as well, and he was awesomely clever, regarded as a near-certainty for a First. Debbie found herself listening to him, unwillingly impressed as he talked and argued in tutorials and in the student union and in debates, and gradually she became intrigued by him. He was very intense, very serious; that intrigued her too, used as she was to boys taking nothing very seriously at all, except sex and drink and various attendant pleasures, and he was able to surprise her too: a bit of a rock music buff, where she would have written him off as a classics lover, and the proud owner of a Harley Davidson motor bike, on which he took her out occasionally. Sitting behind him, holding him round the waist, as the world was reduced to a throbbing, scary blur was oddly erotic; after only the second outing she went to bed with him. He wasn't fantastic at sex, indeed rather dull compared to some of the boys she had known; and was slightly daunted by Debbie's enthusiasm for it, greeting her frequent propositions with a rather sheepish smile, which she found engaging. But he had given the matter of her pleasure very careful attention and worked hard on it, as with everything he did, and that seemed rather engaging too.

By the end of the second year they had become accepted as a couple, albeit a rather unlikely one, and he took her to meet his parents one weekend; it was a shock. They lived on the Gower Peninsula in south-west Wales, an astonishingly lovely piece of countryside, unspoiled and untamed: where wild ponies roamed the moorland and lanes, where hawks hovered over the hills and sheep grazed the grassy cliffs high above the sea. Broken Bay House was a great heap of a place, quite isolated, high on the cliffs with an incredible view of the sea. It was large and rambling (and very cold), badly in need of painting, full of battered old rugs on stone flags, and lumpy sofas and jugs full of dried flowers everywhere, and real fires blazing, which only warmed your front and left your back freezing. The kitchen was the only cosy room, because of the Aga, and they ate there, at a wooden table which was so big it could seat eight and still leave quite a long expanse at one end to be covered with letters and newspapers and books and catalogues of things like agricultural shows and art auctions. There was a vast garden – well, it seemed vast to Debbie – with a large population of hens at the vegetable end and a stableyard with three horses: and an old Rolls tucked into one of the stables. They were obviously rich, Debbie thought, and wondered why they didn't get central heating put in. She liked William, Richard's father, he was sweet and old-fashionedly courteous, but his mother frightened her a bit, she was so sure of herself and rather grand. She wore long flowing skirts and shirts and very large sweaters, and her hair was always tumbling down from the knot she tied it in; she was nice to Debbie, but slightly patronising. Debbie could tell she thought she was common.

'How interesting you should say that,' she would say when Debbie ventured an opinion on anything (which wasn't often), clearly implying it was not a view she would ever hold herself. Richard was their only child. 'Do you remember so and so?' she'd keep saying to him, recalling some event. 'Wasn't that fun?' And it made Debbie feel somehow excluded, as if Flora was an ex-girlfriend, rather than his mother.

She came away freshly anxious about a relationship with a person and a life so alien to her, and indeed called a trial separation; but then missed Richard so much she found herself apologising and begging him to take her back. She often thought that if she had been really in love with someone else, she would never have got involved with him; but she wasn't, she never had been, and she was rather used to being treated badly by boys. Richard's gentlemanly thoughtful behaviour was a novelty, and she liked it.

By the time they graduated, they had agreed to live together; only six months into her new life with the TV company, which she had absolutely loved, she was pregnant. It was the result of a reckless weekend away when she forgot her pills, and with only a brief backward glance at her putative career in television, she declared herself astonishingly happy about it, and they agreed to get married.

And it was only now, her questing spirit tamed and subdued by family life and routine, and cast in the role of Head Teacher's wife, that she looked back and realised how much she had changed. She had made one very brief break for freedom when she ran away to join the women at Greenham Common with her two elder children, in order to protest about the arrival of American Cruise Missiles, and returned cold and filthy after four days to a rather smug Richard, but that was all.

As she lay in the bath that morning, Debbie knew exactly what she had to do that day, every moment of it prescribed: cooking a lasagne for an NCT quiz event tonight; writing her newsletter, collecting Rachel from playschool and taking her to a party, first getting her to sign the card herself because all the other mothers did that, it seemed to be a point of pride (and hugely time-consuming), meeting Emma and Alex from their prospective schools, taking Emma to the dentist and Alex to judo – more snooty, unfriendly mothers to face down – and then tea, supervising homework (while wishing Richard could at least do that instead of disappearing into his study to do paperwork), and then the bath round, and getting Rachel into bed, and being ready, complete with lasagne, to go out, all by 7.30. And, as she lay there, she realised there didn't seem to be a single moment in all this for attacking the high wall of ironing awaiting her. Oh well.

She could never work out quite why she found it all so difficult; surely running such a life required neither talent nor brainpower? But ever since Alex's birth, she had lived in a chaos above which she never seemed to be able properly to surface. She often said she only had to walk into a room to make it untidy; she was always late, the fridge was always empty of everything except some rather doubtful-looking small foil parcels.

She studied her friends in their smoothly organised, neat homes and lives, and tried to copy what they did: without a great deal of success.

As she pulled on her bathrobe, the phone rang; she'd been

waiting for some news of a recent series of break-ins from the Neighbourhood Watch Chairman for her newsletter.

'Hi, John,' she said, but it wasn't nice John Peters, it was Flora. She still had an extremely uneasy relationship with Flora; she made her feel inadequate, and thus touchy and perverse, and she knew Flora didn't really approve of her and considered Richard had married beneath himself. She was an appalling snob.

'OK,' Debbie said to her best friend, Jan, 'she may not be the mother-in-law from hell, but I'd certainly call it purgatory. How would you like it if Mike's mother thought you were common? It's horrible.'

Flora Fielding had been widowed five years earlier, when William had died suddenly of a heart-attack, but she had taken widowhood in her stride as she did everything else, and while genuinely grief-stricken and shocked, she went on determinedly and bravely with her life, refusing to move out of the house, as Richard felt she should, continuing to ride and hunt, and returning to her career as a photographer.

She was actually very good at it, Debbie could see that from all the many examples scattered around the house: she worked only in black and white and specialised in seascapes and architectural photography. She didn't get a great many commissions, apart from a local Christmas card company, but it didn't matter, it absorbed her – along with her horses and an extremely active social life – and she certainly seemed to have no money worries. William had been a very successful accountant, as well as having family money, and he was also a Name at Lloyd's, Richard had explained to Debbie; she didn't really understand what that meant, except that it appeared to be a club for posh, rich people and was very financially desirable.

One of the things Flora insisted on was paying for the children's education: 'I really want to do this,' she said to them firmly, when Alex was coming up for seven, 'I can afford it, and I don't want them going to some useless place where they can indulge in free expression or whatever the latest fad is and come out at eleven with ghastly accents, not able to read.'

Debbie was not even made part of this discussion, which enraged her; it seemed not to occur to Flora that Richard

26

was the headmaster of what she would certainly consider 'a useless place'; and indeed he would not have been, had he not failed to beat two other contestants at a prep school in Chiswick.

'First rejected by Cambridge, then rejected by Grange House,' he said to Debbie, trying to make light of it. 'What next?'

Debbie told him he would be much more use to the community at St Luke's Junior; she would have greatly preferred Alex to be going there as well. She hated Flora paying the school fees. It meant two very uncomfortable things: permanent gratitude, and the right for Flora to interfere constantly in the children's progress. Not that, to be fair, she often did: although she did insist on doing spelling tests and tables in the car which made Debbie want to scream.

In any case, Debbie didn't approve of private education, the social divisiveness it created, and she had done fine in the state system herself. She often looked at Emma in particular running into her snobby little school in her blazer and boater, greeting other snobby little girls dropped off by snobby mothers, not one of whom Debbie wanted to befriend, and wished passionately that Emma was wandering along the road to St Luke's herself, with all the other local children. It already caused problems, with the children in the road not really wanting to play with Emma; but Richard was adamant, it was much better for them both, and they were very lucky that Flora was so happy to pay for them. And certainly they were both doing very well, roughly a year ahead of their state-educated counterparts; Debbie tried to concentrate on that and to feel genuinely – rather than resentfully – grateful to Flora.

Flora was still beautiful, tall and slim, with wild dark curly hair; the children found her huge fun to be with, playing endless games of tracking and hide and seek with her and clambering over rocks and up cliff paths; she had said they would all go pony-trekking in the summer, and she would start teaching them to surf. This actually worried Debbie, as she felt that Flora wasn't as careful with the children as she should be. 'You mustn't mollycoddle them,' she would say to Debbie, as she fretted while they climbed on a particularly hazardous pile of rocks, or waded screaming into the freezing Easter sea, their wellies filling inevitably with water. 'Children have an inbuilt sense of self-preservation.'

Debbie didn't feel any amount of self-preservation could save a small child of seven from falling off a pony or getting swept out to sea in a rip, but she wasn't allowed to say so; it annoyed Richard. He had grown up doing all those things, and he liked the idea of his children doing them too.

Flora did other annoying things, like keeping the children up hours beyond their bedtimes: 'Rules are made to be broken,' she would say, ignoring Debbie's request for a cooked tea for them, and serving dinner up for everybody at half-past eight. 'It does them good to eat with the grown-ups, teaches them far more than just lying upstairs in bed,' and even suggested after-supper games of Scrabble to keep them up later still. Of course, it didn't matter in the holidays, but it did make the children overtired and overexcited, made them question Debbie's own rules and argue with her endlessly.

And she just wished it could be her mother sometimes instead, that they rushed to the phone to speak to, or begged to be allowed to stay with; but then her mother was a hopeless grandmother, always full of excuses about her arthritis and her husband's blood pressure preventing her from having them to stay.

'Debbie, it's Flora,' she said now, her plummy voice brisk. 'How are you?'

'I'm very well,' said Debbie, feeling instantly wrong-footed; the children still hadn't written their thank-you letters after their visit at Easter, and it was ten days since they had all got home. 'How are you? Flora, I'm sorry the children haven't—'

Flora cut in. 'I'm fine, thank you. Absolutely fine. I'd like to speak to Richard, please. Is he there?' There was a moment's pause, then she said, 'Oh, stupid of me, he must have left for school.'

'Yes,' said Debbie, 'yes, he has, I'm afraid. I'm sorry. You could try phoning at break, but they—'

'No, no, it's not that urgent. Perhaps you could ask him to ring me. What time does he get home? Around four, isn't it?'

'Yes. Is it anything I can help with?' Which of course it wouldn't be.

'Oh – no, thank you. No, it's fine. Thank you Debbie. Such fun at Easter, wasn't it?'

'Wonderful,' said Debbie, 'and like I said, I'm so—'

But Flora had rung off.

Sometimes, Debbie thought, making a face at the phone, she really did feel like the hired help.

Chapter 2

The thing to do was tell Nigel. Tell him she was going to have lunch with one of the traders at McArthur's who had phoned that day at lunchtime and issued an invitation which she had found it impossible to refuse. Which had been rather silly of her: but surely if she told Nigel that would make it all right. In fact she could more or less ask him if it was all right, if he minded. He'd want to know why, she supposed, and she could say that Blue had helped with the Big Bang book and now he – he what? Wanted to know more about publishing? Not likely. Graham wanted to know more about life as a trader for a spin-off book? Bit better, but surely he'd take him to lunch himself. Graham had asked her to take him to lunch to say thank you for his help? But then he'd been asked to the party, and that had been by way of thanks. Perhaps she'd better not tell Nigel at all. The best thing would be just to have the wretched lunch and that would be that. No, the best thing would be to cancel the lunch: not go. Or—

'Lucinda, you're not listening.'

'Sorry, Nigel.'

He had been quite cross – or as near as Nigel ever got to being cross, which was more like extremely irritable – about her opening the Lloyd's letter. She wasn't quite sure why. She supposed it was the contents. They had visibly rattled him.

'It's fine, of course,' he said, 'we can afford it. In actual fact, it won't cost us very much at all, I can write it off as a tax loss. It's one of the joys of Lloyd's. And given how much we've had out of them over the years, it's – it's fine.'

'Oh, good. Well, that's all right then.'

'Yes.'

She looked at him, as she ladled out the lasagne. 'So why are you worried?'

'I'm not worried. Not at all.'

'Yes, you are.'

'Well, it's just that I've never known it happen before. I suppose it was inevitable, sooner or later, although one was rather led to believe that it never would.'

'Really?' She thought about this for a bit. Could anything ever be that safe? Surely the whole thing about any money-making enterprise was that sometimes you did come unstuck. Otherwise none of them would be better than any others, and everybody would be extremely rich. 'But surely they must have warned you it might?'

'Well, they did,' he said irritably, 'obviously. And of course it could happen in theory, but it never has, that's the point. Well, not since the mid-sixties, anyway. They're too clever, too ahead of the game.'

'Yes, but—'

'Lucinda, please. I do know what I'm talking about.'

She suddenly felt fiercely cross with him. 'It seems,' she said, 'that maybe you don't.'

He stared at her. 'Well if that's going to be your attitude, I find it rather unhelpful.'

'Nigel, it's not an attitude. It's a simple statement of fact. Surely nothing can be absolutely one hundred per cent certain. It can't be, you can't just know that you're going to get x thousand pounds every year, no matter what happens.'

'Lucinda, you really don't know what you're talking about.'

'Yes, I do,' she said, stung. 'Well, not exactly, I don't know anything about Lloyd's, but I haven't been listening to Daddy for years and years, talking about the stock market, without taking some of it in. You seem to think I'm a complete idiot. And how much is it anyway? Obviously enough to worry you, I can tell.'

'I think we'd better stop this conversation,' he said. 'It's going in a direction I don't really like very much. I've been a Name for over fifteen years, and my father was for twenty years before that, and it's served us very well indeed.'

Even she could see he wasn't talking a great deal of sense.

'But that's the last thirty-five years or whatever. This is now. It seems to be changing.'

'Lucinda, please. Can we stop this?'

'I don't see why. You started it. I mean, you started wanting to talk about it. And I really want to know what the problem is.'

'There isn't a problem. I've spoken to my Members' Agent, and he assures me it's a one-off. In fact he actually advised me to push my underwriting limit as high as I could for next year. He said it was a bit like the casino.'

'Well, there you are. Clearly it isn't as safe as houses. So—'

'That was only a joke,' Nigel said irritably.

'Not very funny. When it's your money he's talking about, not his.'

He ignored this. 'Of course I wouldn't do that, it would be a little reckless, but there is absolutely – absolutely nothing to worry about.'

'Well, good,' she said, after a brief silence. She raised her glass and smiled at him. 'And here's to next year's cheque.'

He clearly was having difficulty smiling back at her; he was obviously still annoyed by her arguing with him. And he hadn't told her how much it was. It was definitely not the moment to tell him she was going out to lunch with another man. In fact, she'd better cancel it first thing in the morning.

'Your mother phoned,' said Debbie, as soon as Richard came in. 'She wants you to ring her.'

'Oh. OK. Mind if I do it now?'

'Of course not. Why should I?'

'Well, you do tend to hang onto the phone this time of day, as if it was some sort of lifeline.' He grinned at her, gave her a kiss to show he didn't mean it. Not too much anyway.

'I—' She stopped. There was no point rising to this bait. No point explaining that the phone was literally a lifeline, trawling through the chaos of arrangements. 'No, that's fine, you call her.'

'Did she say what it was about?'

'No. The summer, I expect.'

'Right. I'll just make myself a cup of tea and – want one?'

'Please.'

He disappeared into the study; she heard the phone on the

extension click as he picked it up. Twenty minutes later she needed to call Sue at the NCT about cutlery for the evening, see if she might want any of theirs; she picked it up. She could hear Richard's voice.

'Sorry,' she said, and put it down again. Twenty minutes was a long call, even for them.

Another ten minutes later, he came into the kitchen; he was looking very serious.

'Sorry about that,' she said.

'What? Oh, the phone. Don't worry. You busy? I need to talk to you.'

'Richard! Can't it be later, please? I really could do with some help.' She was hurling spaghetti bolognese onto the children's plates; Emma was tapping her arm, asking her to test her spellings . . .

'OK. Sorry. Can I do anything?'

'You could fetch Alex. That'd be great.'

'Debs, I can't do that. I don't have that sort of time, I've got a heap of marking to do and I've already lost half an hour. Sorry.'

'You seemed to have plenty of time to talk to your mother,' she said, driven beyond endurance.

'Oh, for God's sake,' he said, and went out, slamming the door. She looked after him, surprised. He had many faults, but a bad temper wasn't usually among them.

Later, as she was changing, he came into their bedroom.

'Sorry about that,' he said. 'I was a bit worried. Look, do we have to go to this thing?'

'We do really, yes. I'm off to get the babysitter in about three minutes and I've cooked a lasagne for our table. We can't not go now.'

'I really do need to talk to you,' he said. 'It's quite important.'

'And so is this evening to me. I helped organise it, I have to go.'

'Oh, all right,' he said wearily, 'but let's get away as soon as we can, maybe go for a drink?'

She looked at him; he really did look distressed: drawn and rather pale. She felt a pang of concern, and put her arms round him.

'Whatever it is, it can't be that bad. And of course we'll leave the minute it's over. Promise. I'll duck out of the clearing up. I usually do it, they won't mind.'

Flora had a problem, Richard said, settling uneasily into a chair in the corner of the pub. 'Which could affect us.'

'Really? How?'

'She's – well, she's made a loss at Lloyd's this year. Not much, but enough to worry her.'

'Oh dear. And – what's not much?'

'About six grand.'

'Six grand? My God, Richard. I'd call that quite much. But – well, I suppose she can afford it.'

'She can. But she says it could leave her a bit short.'

'Short?' Debbie thought of the big house, the Rolls, the new horse Flora had just bought, the portfolio of shares she was always wanting to discuss with Richard. 'Can't she sell some shares or something?'

'She could. Of course. But the market's not good at the moment; she feels it would be short-sighted.'

'Oh. Well, that's her decision. Obviously.'

'Well, it is. And it isn't.'

Debbie began to feel uneasy. Just a bit. It was like the niggle of heaviness before indigestion struck.

'How isn't it? Richard, you'd better get this over. You're not suggesting it might affect us, I hope?'

'Yes. It might. Not badly, but she wonders if we could take on the school fees, just for this year. It's almost exactly that sum. Six thousand, for the two lots.'

'Well, we can't,' she said. 'It's perfectly simple. We don't have six thousand to spare. Do we?'

'Well, we do,' he said. 'Actually.'

'What? What are you talking about?'

'There's the money my father left me.'

'The— Richard, I cannot believe I'm hearing this. You invested that, very carefully, you told me. We agreed it was for the future, our security, in case something awful happened, or we wanted to do something really special with it, put the children through university or—'

'Yes, well Mother says she'll pay us back when she can.'

'Which is very kind of her, of course,' said Debbie, thinking, If they'd consulted me, we wouldn't even be having this conversation. 'But, Richard, I just don't like it; it feels sort of dangerous. Not what we thought that money was for.'

'I know. But don't forget Father left the children some money in trust for things like their further education.'

'Well I know. But there are other things to spend it on. Don't forget our dream, to take the children out of school for a term, and travel with them. I think that would be much more valuable, actually. I'm sorry Richard, but I'm just not going to give in on this. I mean, your mother undertook to pay the school fees. I never wanted her to, I was never asked about it.'

'I seem to remember you being fairly articulate on the subject. At the time.'

'Very briefly,' she said, feeling her temper beginning to surge. 'And then it was made clear my views were of no interest to either of you. You'd both decided. And now, she's asking us to use up our precious savings, to do it instead. Well, I'm not going to. Sorry. They can leave those bloody schools if she's not going to pay for them, and go somewhere sensible, like St Luke's instead. I'd far rather.'

'You're so hostile to her, aren't you?' he said. 'You don't like her, you're jealous of her, you don't understand her. Or appreciate what she does for us. For the children.'

Debbie stared at him. 'That is so unfair,' she said.

'No, it isn't. And I happen to know she finds it very hurtful, your hostility.'

'My hostility! What about hers?'

'She is not hostile to you,' he said flatly.

'Well, I don't know what else you'd call it. I feel like some sort of intruder half the time. Or the hired help. And anyway, how do you know it's hurtful? Has she told you? Pretty bloody shitty of her if she has. Emotional blackmail, I'd call it. Driving a wedge between us.'

'Oh, don't be absurd,' he said, 'she's doing nothing of the sort. And no, she hasn't said anything. She's very loyal to you, as a matter of fact. I can just – just see it. For myself.'

Debbie was silent.

'It's not much fun, her life, you know,' said Richard. 'Living alone in that great house.'

'She could sell it. That would solve lots of problems.'

'She doesn't want to sell it. It's her home, where she was happy. It doesn't stop her feeling lonely. And she has to cope with everything on her own, the admin, any financial problems. Including this. And I want to help her.'

'Well, I don't. Not in the way you suggest, anyway. I don't and I won't. We can go down there, talk to her about it, help her sort things out, of course. Hold her hand. But I will not agree to use that money to pay the school fees. Any of it. And that's all there is to it.'

'I'm afraid we have to,' he said, and he looked very drawn suddenly, 'some of it anyway. Or get a bank loan. Or re-mortgage.'

'But why? I don't understand.' There seemed to be a grip on her lungs, squeezing them, making her breathless.

'Debbie, you can't just not pay the school fees at the beginning of term, take the children away. You have to give a term's notice in writing. It's a legal requirement. So at the very worst, we have to find two grand.'

She digested this. 'And she won't even do that?'

'No. She says she can't. She's very, very upset about it.'

'Oh, for God's sake –' She was about to say more, rail against Flora's snobbishness, the absurdity of her plea of poverty. Then she looked at Richard again; his distress was clearly greater than she had realised. He was grey and drawn, his fingers twisting helplessly together; when he picked up his pint of beer, his hand shook. He met her eyes over the glass; his were suspiciously bright. He couldn't be in tears, could he? Could he?

'Have you any idea,' he said, his voice shaking, 'any idea at all how humiliating this is for me? To have my mother know that after all they did for me, all my fine education, I can't even afford to pay my own children's school fees, give them what I know they need? It's pretty bloody hard, Debbie, I can tell you.'

Shocked out of her anger, her heart suddenly aching for him, for the lack of confidence that consumed him – and why, why, she often wondered, when he was so clever – and often thought too that Flora was responsible for it. She would not have liked to grow up with Flora as a mother, with her crushing conviction that she knew best, her impatient dismissal of any other point of view. And she heard herself saying that she was sorry, that of course, if that was really the only way, they would take on the school fees for the year. 'But it is only the year, isn't it? You're not suggesting we do more than that?'

'Only the year,' he said, 'I swear. We can't do more anyway, unless I get some amazing new job. Which is—'

'Absolutely possible,' she said, 'in fact, quite probable. The only thing that's keeping you from an amazing new job, Richard, is that you've stopped applying for them, OK? Now I know you love St Luke's, but if it's not really what you want, you must – *we* must – rethink. You're a bloody good teacher, and a brilliant head, and there are lots of schools which would be just desperate for you. You just start buying the *Guardian* on Wednesdays again, OK? And I'll do some applying for you, if you won't do it yourself.'

'Oh, all right. Maybe.' He smiled at her. He had a wonderful smile; brilliant and sudden. And irresistible. It was Flora's smile; everything else about him was his father, the thick dark brown hair, the rather square jaw, the dark eyes. Except perhaps his sweaters; she teased him about those sweaters, large and shabby, the arms too long, exactly like Flora's.

'I love you Debs,' he said. 'I'm so lucky to have you. I still think that, you know, every day of my life. And I'm sorry I said that about Mother and you. I do understand – she is quite bossy and overbearing; I can see it, you know.'

'You can?' she said, astonished. He had never so much as hinted at such a thing; she had always assumed Flora was perfect in his eyes, that the fault was all hers. She felt a rush of gratitude, and of affection for him, suddenly wanted desperately to make him feel better. She leaned forward and kissed him.

'You mean that? You can see it, you don't think I'm imagining it?'

'Of course I can see it. I'm not completely stupid.'

'Well,' she said, 'if it took Lloyd's crashing—'

'Not crashing, just making a few small losses—'

'All right, making a few small losses, to get you to tell me that, it was worth it. Ring her in the morning and tell her we'll do it. But like I said, it must only be this year, OK?'

'OK,' he said. 'It will be. Bless you Debbie. Let's go home, I want to show you how much I love you.'

Elizabeth was talking to Peter Hargreaves in her office, dissecting the presentation of the morning – the successful presentation – when Simon rang.

'Hello. It's me.'

'Hello Simon.' Her voice was cool. She didn't mean it to be, it was just that she found interruptions hard to cope with, always had. Simon on the other hand always sounded warmly welcoming, even if he was in a really tough meeting.

'I wondered if we could have dinner tonight?' he said.

'Any particular reason?'

'Does there have to be?'

'No, not really. But I'd sort of thought I'd work on for a couple of hours. I've got a lot on—'

'Elizabeth, please. I want to talk to you.' About what, she wondered with a stab of fear: surely not *that* again, surely –

'And we might as well do it over a good dinner. It can be late if you like. Around nine.'

'Oh, OK. Yes.' She paused then said, almost as if prompted, 'It'd be nice anyway, of course.'

'Right, I'll book at Langan's. See you there.'

They ate at Langan's. Elizabeth was late. She often was. Simon sat waiting for her, drinking first one, then a second martini, his patience slowly fading. Why did she do this to him? When she knew he wanted to talk to her, that a table had been booked, that he might be hungry? Was it deliberate, to make her point, that she had her own life, that she was not at his beck and call – and given the events of the past two years, was that actually justified, did he deserve it? Or was it that in her hectic, high-powered schedule, time simply disappeared? She often seemed quite surprised that he was irritable when she arrived; and today he had felt spectacularly sidelined, both ends of the day shaped around her and the demands of her life.

And then he saw her, walking across the restaurant, kissing him briefly before slithering into the chair the waiter had pulled out for her. She was immaculate as always, in a red short-skirted suit, with the ubiquitous padded shoulders, not a dark hair out of place in her gleaming lacquered bob, carrying the unmistakable aura of success and power.

And he remembered fiercely, briefly, the other Elizabeth, the one he had fallen in love with, so beautiful his heart had turned over the very first time he had seen her, neither successful nor powerful, a secretary indeed, at the advertising agency his bank was considering at the time; her dark eyes serious as she greeted him in Reception, shook his hand, asked him to follow her to the boardroom. Even then, she had dressed the part: no seventies flowing skirts for her, no wild layered perm, but a narrow black calf-length dress and high-heeled boots, her dark hair clipped into a neat page-boy. He had liked her voice: rather low and calm, a well-educated voice, and her thoughtful good manners, taking his overcoat, offering him, as they went into the boardroom, coffee and orange juice. She said that he was the first to arrive – Simon was incapable of not being early – and indicated the presentation folders on the table, suggesting that he might like to look at his before the others arrived.

'Will you be at the meeting?' he asked hopefully, and yes, she said, she would but in a very menial capacity, purely to take notes, 'And refill coffee cups,' she added with a quick smile.

'Very important,' he said, 'and you'll be refilling mine a lot. I run on caffeine.'

'Me too,' she said. 'They say it's very bad for you.'

'Oh, I have a lot of bad habits,' he had said. 'I'm awfully good at them. I like drinking and smoking too,' and immediately she had offered him the cigarette box that was on the table and lit his cigarette with the big silver lighter.

The others had arrived then, including her boss; and all through the meeting, he had been aware of her, sitting there, taking notes, filling cups and glasses, a quiet, efficient presence.

After the third meeting – for the agency had won the account – he had asked her out; she had given him the same serious look and waited for a few moments before saying, 'That would be very nice, but I don't think my boyfriend would like it.'

And he had said he would hate to upset her boyfriend, and that might have been that, had not Simon and his colleagues been invited to an advertising awards ceremony where their campaign was on the shortlist, and there she was at the lavish black-tie dinner, wearing a modestly sexy dress, smiling at him across the pre-dinner drinks party.

'How nice to see you again,' he said, taking a glass of champagne. 'And how is the new firm?'

'Very good, thank you,' she said, 'and I'm now a junior Account Executive, which is very exciting.'

'Indeed it must be. We miss you a lot, though. Your successor is much slower on the uptake with the coffee jug.'

'I'm sorry to hear that.'

'And—' He had been about to ask her about her boyfriend, but a colleague from the bank came over and invited him to join his party; he gave her an apologetic grin and moved away.

But later, much later, when they were milling about before the actual presentations were made, he managed to bump into her. 'Can I get you a drink afterwards,' he said, 'at the bar? Or would your boyfriend not like that either?'

'I don't think he'd mind at all,' she said, 'since he's not my boyfriend any more. I'd like that very much, thank you.'

After several drinks – mostly orange juice for her – they danced; she danced well, giving it the serious attention she gave everything. At two in the morning he offered to take her home in his cab; she refused, saying she had one of her own booked.

'Then promise to have dinner with me very soon. I don't want to lose you again.'

'That would be lovely,' she said, 'thank you,' and the very next night they had dinner at L'Escargot in Greek Street, and after that, it was all very simple; they were together all the time and fell mutually and very passionately in love.

Elizabeth was only just twenty and in the style of those days, there was no question of their living together; she shared a flat with two other girls in Earl's Court, and Simon, only twenty-five himself, lived in appalling and expensive squalor with three other young men just off the Brompton Road. But they met several nights a week, and started sleeping together after a very short time; she put up a brief fight, claiming to be not ready and 'nearly a virgin'.

'You can't be nearly a virgin,' he said, twisting a strand of her dark hair in his fingers. 'It's all or nothing.'

'Well, I know, but I only slept with Tony twice and I didn't like it very much at all.'

'You'll like it with me,' he said. 'Promise.'

And she did.

He had wanted to marry her, quite badly, quite soon. 'I know we're very young,' he said to her, when he asked her, 'but I like the idea of being married to you so much. It'd be fun. And we could buy one of those houses you were admiring the other night in The Boltons.'

'Simon, you know that's nonsense. They cost about a quarter of a million.'

'OK. I'm an up-and-coming young man. We'll get one next year. Or when we have our first baby.'

'I don't want to have a baby,' she said, 'you know that Simon, not for quite a long time. I've got my career to take care of, no time for babies.'

Even then she was ferociously ambitious, determined to do not just well, but superbly in the profession she loved: 'I want to be successful and I want to be a force to be reckoned with. I want to do the sort of thing women don't usually do in advertising, I don't want to be some dappy creative, well, I couldn't be anyway. I want to run things, have them done my way.'

She wasn't sure why she wanted it so much, she said; it was just important to her. 'Terribly important. I shall be miserable if I fail.'

And it was the reason she hadn't gone to university in spite of some very impressive A-levels; she regarded it as a waste of time, self-indulgent even, when she could have been starting on her journey in the real world.

Simon had his own theory that she was righting the wrong in the only way she could for a mother who had been crushed in her own very modest ambitions (to teach music) by a domineering husband, who told her her place was at home, looking after their children. The fact that Elizabeth had turned out to be an only child seemed to her to make her mother's situation worse.

'I know she'd have loved lots of babies, it would have justified the sacrifice. But – just me – it's such a waste.'

'Not at all,' he had said, kissing her. 'Raising you, making you the person you are could never be termed a waste.'

They did get married, six months later, when she was just twenty-one. Her father was delighted with the charming, handsome and successful young man who wanted to be his son-in-law, and they moved into a very pretty little mews house in Kensington.

She had meant it when she said she didn't want a baby; but Annabel was born just the same, eighteen months after they were married. There had been a scare about the pill, Simon had ordered her off it – she had done everything he wanted in those days, trusted him absolutely – and, 'That seems to be that,' she said to him, half-happy, half-tearful when she got the result of her pregnancy test.

He had been overjoyed; he loved children, loved the idea of being a father. She was less certain.

'I can't give up work,' she said, 'you know that. I've just got this new job.'

'I do know it. Of course you can't. We'll get a nanny, don't worry. We'll have to move, maybe not into The Boltons this time, maybe next—'

'And you'll have to help, have to support me.'

'I will, I promise. I'll be the most supportive husband in London. In the world. I love you, Elizabeth, very, very much. And I'm so proud of you.'

That had been the beginning of the glory years; of dizzy success for both of them. He was made a Director of Graburn & French at an extraordinarily young age, her new job was at H_2O, as an Account Executive – and Account Director two years later – they bought first a bigger house in Kensington and moved finally into Bolton Place just before Tilly was born. They were successful, rich, good-looking, high-profile, with far more than their fair share of life's goodies. They had had fun together too; wonderful extravagant holidays, sometimes with the children, but sneaking off too for long weekends on their own to Paris, Rome, the South of France – happy pleasure-drenched times, free from everything except one another, the early sexy days brought back to life. 'I wonder how many married people have actually made love three times in twenty-four hours,' Simon said, raising a glass of champagne to her in their very splendid bed at the Crillon in Paris. 'Oh, probably quite a few, let's make it four,' she said, falling on him and laughing at his protests.

They entertained lavishly, in the splendid Boltons house, bought another in the country, gave parties that were legendary; they were sought-after, admired, on every smart guest-list. And he had adored her: absolutely. And she had adored him. So where – and why – had things gone so dreadfully wrong?

'Sorry, Simon.' She kissed him briefly. 'So sorry. Had a crisis, it went on all day, and then I wanted to debrief Peter Hargreaves tonight—'

'What sort of crisis?'

'Oh – clash of egos. Management versus creative. Over Hunters, and a presentation in two days' time.'

'I'm sure you handled it well,' he said, and his tone was rather dry.

High on her success, her head still half in the office, she didn't notice. 'I think I did, yes. I backed the creative team, anyway. It was the only thing to do. Especially as Michael Warner, he's the Creative Director—'

'Yes, Elizabeth, I do know, I do listen to you. Quite a lot.'

'Yes, I know you do. Anyway, he was refusing to call for a revise . . . and I liked the campaign anyway. It was very clever. But I had to smooth a lot of ruffled feathers. Peter was very relieved and—'

'I'm sure,' he said again, and this time she pulled herself away from her work, back to him.

'Sorry, Simon.'

'Never mind. I've ordered a Sancerre, all right for you?'

'Fine.' She smiled up at the waiter as he poured it and then at him. 'Good day?'

'Not very, no.'

'I'm sorry. Annabel get off all right?'

'Yes, of course. Anyway, she should have rung you from school, I told her to.'

'Well she didn't. But there's such a scrum for the phones. Toby rang this evening though. And Tilly did too. She's all settled in again. She's been made House Captain, bless her.

She's really happy there, Simon, you don't have to worry about her.'

'Good.'

He hadn't liked Tilly going away to school so young: at the age of ten. But Elizabeth had argued she would be lonely at home, and that she'd be able to take her horse to school, ride right through the term, not just the holidays. What she really meant, he'd known, was that with all three children away from home, her own life would become much easier.

'I can't believe Toby's in his second year,' she said. 'He does love it.'

'Just as well,' said Simon shortly, 'given the cost.'

She looked at him curiously. 'Simon! That's not like you.'

'Well, I don't feel quite like me. Actually.'

'Is that why you invited me to dinner?'

'Well – I wanted to have dinner with you, of course. But yes, so we could talk.'

'We could have talked just as well at home. With none of the children there.'

'Except that you probably would have been about three hours late, rather than nearly one. With no table booking to put pressure on you and—' He stopped suddenly, looked at her very sadly, then said, 'Oh Elizabeth. What's happened to us, why do we have to quarrel about everything?'

'I would have thought,' she said, the pain hitting afresh, as it still did sometimes, 'you should know that very well.'

'Yes,' he said quietly, 'I do. But—'

'But what? There doesn't seem a but to me, you know—'

'Oh, for Christ's sake,' he said and stood up suddenly and walked away from her across the restaurant. She wondered, half-frightened, if he was going to walk out, leave her there; but after a couple of minutes, he was back, smiling ruefully at her.

'Sorry,' he said, 'it's difficult to be always in the wrong. I am trying, Elizabeth, so hard.'

And suddenly she felt remorseful, that she was not trying too; and she reached across the table and took his hand, said, 'I know you are.'

'Oh God,' he said, and looked away from her. She felt alarmed.

'Simon, for heaven's sake, what on earth is it?'

'I've had a bit of bad news,' he said, looking up, and his face was very bleak.

'What sort of bad news? Is it the bank?'

'No, no. It's Lloyd's.'

'What's the matter with them?'

'I'm not sure,' he said slowly. 'It's more what's the matter with me.'

'Which is?'

'They've made a loss on several of my syndicates this year. Including the major one.'

'Oh,' she said. 'Oh, I see. And – what's the damage?'

'About – about fifteen thousand pounds.'

'God. God, Simon, that's a lot.'

'Yes, I do know that. I mean, we can afford it, obviously, it's fine this year, but—'

'But?'

'I have a horrible feeling,' he said, 'that this is only the beginning.'

Chapter 3

Christmas, 1988

'Oh my God. Oh, God. Oh – my – God!'

She could hear herself shouting, she was somewhere outside herself, yet still there, inside it, inside the pleasure, the wonderful, soaring, bright, dark pleasure, riding it, savouring it, on and on, as long as she needed.

And then it was over. Gently, sweetly over. She collapsed slowly, back into normality: her body, fractured by delight, by the shock of it, easing together again. The tears that always came then were hot on her face; her hair, sweaty and tangled, seemed everywhere, in her eyes, across her mouth. He pushed it back, smiled at her, licked at her tears.

'Salty. Sweet. Like you.'

'Oh dear,' she said.

'Why d'you say that?'

'You know.'

'No, I don't.'

'Blue, you do. I mean, oh dear, that was so lovely and now it's over –'

'I could do it again.'

'You couldn't.'

'I could. Want me to try?'

'No,' she said, laughing, 'because I certainly couldn't. Anyway, that wasn't what I meant. I meant our lovely Little Christmas is over.'

'Doesn't have to be. I'm sure they'd let us keep this room over Christmas. They're not fully booked, I asked.'

'Blue, don't be silly.'

'I'm not being silly, I'm being sensible. Look, you got to do it sometime. Why not now? Then we could enjoy Christmas.

I'm not looking forward to it either, round my mum's with about a hundred kids.'

'It sounds lovely to me,' she said wistfully.

'Well, we could go there together instead. They'd be pleased to see you.'

'I bet they wouldn't!'

'No, they probably wouldn't,' he said cheerfully. 'They'd feel they had to be on their best behaviour with a princess in their midst. No, much better stay here.'

'Oh, how I'd love to,' she said, 'how I'd love it. This lovely place and you, and – oh dear.'

She looked round the room. He had booked it for just twenty-four hours, 22 December it was; in a charming hotel in the Cotswolds, full of wood fires and leather chairs and flouncy chintz blinds. She wasn't staying, even for the night: it was impossible. But she'd invented (for Nigel) a booksellers' Christmas party that she'd had to go to; had left London very early in the morning and she and Blue had had a late breakfast, gone for a (very short) walk, come back and had champagne in bed and then a room service lunch (just smoked salmon and caviar) and then more champagne in bed and so much lovely sex. And now she had to go back to London somehow (she probably wasn't fit to drive, although she'd only had about three glasses altogether), collect Nigel and all the presents from the flat and be driven down to his cousins in Norfolk for a very long cold Christmas.

'Well,' said Blue, 'like I said. You got to do it, Lucy girl. Go on, bite the bullet.'

'I can't. Not at Christmas. It would be too cruel.'

'So it would hurt less at Easter, would it? Or August Bank Holiday? I don't think so.'

'Actually, I think it would,' she said very seriously. 'Christmas is special. It's about family and being together, and—'

'Yeah, well, why can't we?'

'Because we can't. It would be very wrong.'

'And what you've been doing so far is very right, is it? I don't know, Lucy, seems to me you've got your morals in a twist.'

'I know. I'm sorry. I'm totally awful.'

'Not totally,' he said, and slithered down the bed, started lazily tongueing her.

She tried to push him away, laughing, 'Blue, no, no, oh God, Blue, no, I mean yes, yes . . .'

Driving very slowly and carefully down the M40 (while telling herself the police had better things to do just before Christmas than chase respectable-looking young matrons in Peugeot 204s), she looked down on the black Chanel box with the white ribbon he had presented her with, holding a watch, a diamond-studded watch on a pink strap, absurdly vulgar and beautiful, that she could hardly ever wear: she had said that, even as she kissed him over and over again. 'You can wear it when you're with me,' he said, kissing her back. 'It can be your fucking watch, for telling the fucking time.'

She wondered, as she was always doing these days, how she could possibly have become this dreadful, deceitful, totally amoral person. Who regularly had sex with her lover, who lied to her boss as well as her husband (she had an idea that Graham suspected what she was actually up to and was rather amused by it), who was actually now seriously beginning to contemplate leaving her husband for her lover (and would that be more or less amoral, she wondered: less, probably, at least it'd be honest).

That had been quite a new thing, the contemplating; for several months she had just told herself she was having an affair, that it was terribly wrong of her, but at least Nigel had no idea, he wasn't being hurt, rather the reverse since she was so naughtily, dreadfully happy and in consequence incredibly nice to him. Although, of course, she'd always been pretty nice to him, had thought herself perfectly happy and content, indeed: so that didn't quite wash as an excuse. But anyway, he wasn't being hurt, and he wasn't going to be, she would never allow that; the only person to be hurt would be her when she ended it, which she would, and she'd deserve it and it wasn't for long anyway. She'd end it and go back to being a respectable wife and have a baby – only of course that was one of the worst things she was doing; she was taking the pill. Which she hadn't for nearly two years, ever since she and Nigel had decided to try and have a baby. Trying being the operative word; they certainly hadn't succeeded, had begun to get anxious and edgy, and she was beginning to try to persuade him to have some investigations of various sorts, which he'd resisted totally, seemed to find it very insulting.

She'd gone to her doctor of course: who'd examined her, got her taking her temperature, making sure she was ovulating, all that sort of thing. So they'd just started stepping up their efforts, as Nigel called it, at the right time, still unsuccessfully, when she'd met Blue. And after a shockingly short time, started to have an affair with Blue. And obviously, going back on the pill. She was so terrified of Nigel finding them that she kept them in the office.

She still wasn't sure how Blue had done it: persuaded her into bed. She'd had that first lunch, and it had been totally respectable really; they'd gone to Claridges, 'Thought I'd better bring you somewhere you'd feel at home,' and afterwards he had kissed her in the taxi, but not too much, and she'd told him it had been lovely, but she couldn't possibly have lunch with him again, and he'd said bollocks, course she could, and somehow very weakly, she'd agreed to just one more. Well, it was so exciting and it made her feel so different, sort of sleek and confident and properly grown-up, and surely everyone should have one fling in their lives; in no time now she'd be living in the country with a small baby, and as flings went, two lunches weren't that serious, and she'd been absolutely resolved it would be the last.

Only he'd spent the next lunch – at the Dorchester this time – doing the most disturbing things to her legs under the table, and she'd been positively squirming with pleasure – and embarrassment – by the time they were in the taxi, and then he'd turned his attention to her breasts, his hands inside her shirt, inside her bra, teasing, stroking, smoothing her into a state of acute excitement and she'd only objected in the most feeble way because it had just been so – so lovely. And she'd said no more lunches and he'd said that's OK, dinner then, and she'd said don't be ridiculous, and he'd said OK, we'll cut the eating, just go to bed.

And she'd said of course not, of course not, she wouldn't even dream of it, and he'd said, I think you will. Dream of it anyway. So she'd agreed to yet another lunch; and then the night before, she and Nigel had had a row, quite a bad one, about not going skiing – again – and she'd been really cross

49

with him and she'd told Blue about it: 'He doesn't like ski-ing, you see. And I love it. And he'll never ever agree to go. It's not fair, I go on his beastly shooting weekends, which I really don't like and—'

'How old is he, your old man?' said Blue suddenly.

'Oh – he's quite a bit older than me. He's forty-four next year. Blue, please don't do that –' (one of his hands was under the table, moving relentlessly and determinedly up her thigh), 'but I do sometimes feel it's all give on my part and no take.'

'Sounds like it,' he said. 'Lucy, why haven't you had no kids? I'd have thought it high on the agenda, specially hubby getting on a bit.'

'We just haven't,' she said, blushing. 'It hasn't – well, it hasn't happened yet.'

'Oh right.'

'Blue, please,' she said, for his fingers had now moved into her knickers. 'Please don't, we'll get thrown out.'

'No, we won't,' he said, 'but maybe we should move upstairs.'

'Upstairs? What do you mean?'

'I got a room up there,' he said. 'Booked it.'

'What for?' she said, shocked.

'What do you think?' he said, giving her his widest grin. 'For us. For us to have sex in, to be precise.'

'I don't believe you. They wouldn't let you book a room here for – for just the afternoon.'

'I didn't – I booked it for twenty-four hours. I thought we might go to my place, but then I thought that'd be a bit compromising for you.'

'And this isn't?'

'Well, not so much. Don't look scared, you don't have to stay the full time. Come on, finish your fish. It's good for you. Then I tell you what, we'll go up there, just have coffee and a brandy, and I swear I won't do anything you don't want. How's that? Your call, you know you can trust me.'

For some reason – curiosity, a desire to appear sophisticated – she did; and discovered that she couldn't even trust herself.

'You never come before?' he said, as she lay, wide-eyed, wild-haired, sweating, almost shocked, after her baptism into pleasure, and, 'Yes, of course' she'd said indignantly; but she hadn't. Not properly. She absolutely hadn't. What she had known with Nigel – compared to this – was like – well, it was like dutifully plodding away at scales rather than conquering some breathtaking arpeggios, like pedalling earnestly uphill rather than flying down, with the wind in her hair, like being stuck in first gear rather than shooting away into fifth, like—

'I don't know what you're thinking about,' he said, grinning at her, 'but I could tell you liked it. Am I right or am I right?'

'You're right,' she said feebly. And grinned back.

So of course she'd had to go on the pill; because obviously it was going to go on for a bit. And when it was over, as it absolutely would be, she would come off it again. She had heard that quite often, actually, people had babies very quickly when they came off the pill; all your hormones went into overdrive or something. She would just have this quick, wicked fling and then . . .

Only she had to go and fall in love with him. And he with her.

She really did love him; she loved everything about him and she could see that what she felt for Nigel wasn't love at all. It was fondness, a desire to be settled, in a life she was happy with, a deep affection, a recognition that Nigel was exactly the sort of man with whom she wanted to spend the rest of her life. What she felt for Blue was wild, uncomfortable, disturbing, exhilarating – and absolutely wonderful. And it wasn't just sex; he made her laugh, and he made her feel more confident. He clearly and genuinely found her interesting, he was always asking her opinion on all sorts of things, and listened carefully to her answers – unlike Nigel, who only seemed to ask her out of politeness. They had quite fierce political discussions – Blue was a rabid Tory, found her watery liberalism extremely amusing – and he was fascinated by her job, the people she met, the books Peter Harrison published. 'I'm totally uneducated,' he was always saying. 'Don't know nothing. You know what Princess Diana said, about having a brain the size of a pea? Mine's a petit pois.'

She had laughed at that and told him it was rubbish; and it was true. He might only have two O-levels, might have left school at sixteen, but his brain was like a razor – quick, considering, uncompromising. Given an education, she told him, he could have been a professor. 'No thanks. They don't make half a million a year, professors don't. Least, not when I was last looking.'

'Do you really make half a million a year?' she'd said awed, and he'd said well maybe this year only a third, due to the crash, but usually, with the bonuses added in, yes, easy.

She in turn was fascinated by *his* work: he had told her only that he played what he called 'racing demon' with the Stock Market every day; she had pressed him further and he said well it was like this, he bought and sold shares, and got paid a commission. 'I work solo, in a manner of speaking. The bank just backs me. I make a lot of money for them, and a fair bit for me.'

'And – I thought you all got sacked after the crash?'

'Some did. Some didn't. If you was making enough money, they kept you on. I make them a lot of money. And you know something, Lucy? For every loser there's a winner – that's my philosophy. And so far I've lived up to it.'

'And – is it fun?'

'Fun? Not sure. Sort of. Shit scary at times. It's a bit like being able to sing in tune,' he added, 'which I can't, I might say. But I know when the market's flying; I can feel it, I can almost smell it. No one can teach you that.'

He certainly seemed to have limitless money. He had a small house in one of the new developments near Limehouse, with pale polished wooden floors and a lot of leather and chrome furniture; he had a Ferrari, he went off on ski-ing weekends to the French Alps, and he had a windsurfer and a Jet Ski, which he kept down at Poole, and 'one leg of a racehorse', the other three being held by colleagues in the trading room. He had a roomful of incredibly expensive designer-label clothes of which he was absurdly proud: 'Got this at Gucci on Saturday,' he would say, doing a fancy pose in a leather coat, 'and d'you like this suit, Armani, bought it twice, once in black, once in navy.' He spent a fortune on drink, he and his fellow traders; where their manual labourer or market stall-holder fathers would go to the pub after work, their sons went to places like Corney & Barrow or the Colony Wine Bar and got through countless bottles of champagne and then bought hundreds of pounds' worth of wine to consume over their dinners as well. Lucinda, raised in a culture that considered the overt display of wealth not only vulgar but close to immoral, was fascinated by the whole thing. They were all the same, Blue's colleagues, it seemed to her, for she heard a great deal about them; and it was a kind of City club they belonged to, just as Nigel and her father did, but the entry requirements were not a public-school education and a good address book, but an awesome capacity for work, a lightning brain, a cheerful disposition and an iron nerve.

But Blue wasn't just clever and successful, he was sweet-natured and thoughtful and insanely generous. And he loved her.

It had never occurred to her that he might be genuinely fond of her, that he saw her as more than a nice bit of skirt, as he was so keen on saying, a notch in his gun; until one early evening, when they had gone back to his apartment (she had left a publishing party after about twenty minutes, praying no one would notice) and were lying in his vast bed sipping champagne. They had just had some rather good sex and she was tired and a little sad, bracing herself to return to Cadogan Square and Nigel, sipping half-heartedly at the vintage Cristal he had just produced, when he suddenly said, 'You know what, Lucy?' And, 'No,' she had said, 'I don't,' and he said, 'I love you more every time I see you. Wouldn't have thought it was possible, but there you go.'

She had been so shocked, she had dropped her glass and the champagne went all over the bed; she was amused at how bothered he was, dabbing at it with endless Kleenex: 'This is Russian linen, you know, none of your Percale rubbish.'

'What did you say?' she said.

'I said it was Russian linen.'

'No, before that.'

'Can't remember. Oh, except I loved you. Yeah. Yeah, that's it.' He leaned forward, kissed her.

'You love me?' she said very slowly, a long pause between each word.

'Yeah, course I do. Come on, Lucy! You must've realised

that. Why d'you think I've been doing all this, taking me annual holiday in days off, missing out on trades—'

'Be serious.'

'I am serious. You daft cow. Of course I love you. I love you more than I'd ever believed I could. Well, I hope you love me. I've been wasting me time otherwise. And quite a bit of money as well.'

And, 'Yes,' she said, bursting into sudden, sweet tears, 'yes, I suppose I do. I hadn't realised – yes, I must do.'

'Better bloody well make sure,' he said. 'I'm well hurt now. You'll have to make it up to me, the only way you know how. OK?'

'OK,' she said, lying back on the pillows, staring at him. 'Sorry. So stupid of me.'

'So stupid,' he said, mimicking her accent, starting to kiss her shoulder. 'So jolly stupid.'

And now, a couple of months later, she knew she did love him. Terribly. And being married to Nigel was beginning to seem rather pointless. Whether she had the courage though to give it all up – and it would mean all: friends, family, job possibly – she really didn't know. She'd think about it properly after Christmas.

Elizabeth always cursed having to spend Christmas in the country: it had begun eight years earlier when Simon had bought Chadwick House, on the strength of a spectacular bonus, and had said that it was made for Christmas, with its huge fireplaces for hanging stockings, a great big hall for a really show-offy tree, and a hedge-lined drive that was made for stringing fairylights along, and – just about everything really.

It was a beautiful house, redbrick, early seventeenth-century, with an orchard and a walled vegetable garden. There was a tennis court and a swimming pool, and a stable-block and paddock to house the love of Tilly's life, which at that time was a sturdy little New Forest pony and now was a beautiful bright bay gelding called Golden Boy.

It was just off the Chichester Road, tucked into the South Downs, and convenient for Bosham where Simon kept his other favourite toy – his sailing boat, a 22-foot Seal called the

Lizzie. Chadwick House was a huge extravagance, as not only a housekeeper but a gardener-cum-groom had to be employed to look after it. Simon was very fond of telling people they went there every weekend, but they didn't, especially now Tilly was at boarding school, but it was a glorious bolt-hole; they all moved down there for the whole of the summer holidays – Simon and Elizabeth commuting – and indeed for Christmas as well. And sometimes even Easter.

Annabel was already beginning to find it boring, as her friends were all in London, but for Toby who played tennis rather well and was learning to shoot, and Tilly who could ride every day, it was a small slice of paradise.

And Elizabeth did like it and enjoyed it; especially the summer; loved giving big garden parties and barbecues, and having friends to stay. But Christmas was different: and however magical it was, it did mean, for her, doing everything twice.

The house in London had to be decorated, you couldn't live in a house through December and give a party in it, as they always did, without making it look festive, having a tree, all that sort of thing. Then on about the twenty-third, the cars had to be packed up with all the food and presents and crackers and driven sixty miles down the road to Sussex, where she had to set about transforming Chadwick House into something out of Dickens. Mrs Ford, the housekeeper, did a lot of course, and made the puddings and so on; but her idea of decorating was not Elizabeth's and she had to tactfully redo it. But somehow, in the end, it was worth it. From the moment they arrived, to be greeted by Mrs Ford on the doorstep, and Mr Ford inside lighting a huge log fire in the drawing room, Christmas began.

However much Elizabeth said every year that they would arrive for lunch, they never managed to drive away from London until after two, and so they got there as dusk was falling, and while Simon and Mr Ford got the tree up, and Toby and Annabel strung the lights along the hedges, and Tilly had a rapturous reunion with Boy, Elizabeth unpacked the endless clothes and presents and food and wine, and tried to enjoy it too. And by the time they had eaten their first dinner, in the kitchen, in the glorious bone-warming glow of the Aga and had their first Christmas bottle of champagne, she did.

It made Christmas much more special, giving it its own setting, as it were. And there were all the lovely traditions – midnight service in the village church, the long tramp over the fields on Christmas Day, carol-singing on the green, the Boxing Day meet. And this Christmas especially she felt it was wonderful to get away. It hadn't been an exactly easy year . . .

It was well known that advertising was the first budget to be cut when a company was feeling the pinch: and there was a lot of pinching going on. The economic climate was not good, whatever smooth story was being put out by Nigel Lawson. But with an agency the size of H_2O you could afford to lose a bit; it was the little boys, the creative hot shops that went under, where losing one account could make all the difference between profit and loss. Just the same, everyone was on edge, every account review carrying an implied threat, and everyone told to economise where they could. Even the Christmas party had been a more modest affair than usual, held in the office rather than at their 'local', as Peter Hargreaves, their very hands-on Chairman, called the Ritz. 'I think there are better things to spend twenty grand on than that. Especially since after an hour or so nobody can remember where they are.'

And she really felt she was beginning to recover from what she had managed to think of as The Other Business. Painful and humiliating, far more than she would have imagined: she would have thought, had she been asked, that she could have dealt with it somehow – not shrugged it off of course but managed to accept it, for all their sakes – that of course it would have hurt, certainly have made her angry but not destroyed her as a person, not wrecked her self-confidence in a way she would never have dreamed. But – she'd survived it. Hadn't she?

Thank God Christmas was over, Annabel thought; it was the first one she hadn't properly enjoyed, which seemed a bit sad, really. But it was true. Her father seemed edgy, and kept on and on about money, it was so boring; their mother had been hyper-bossy and control-freaky – if you didn't want to play games, for God's sake, why should you, it was everyone's Christmas, not just hers – and even Toby had been kicking the furniture a bit. Only Tilly had been really happy, earnestly practising her jumping and her dressage every day on her beloved Boy. She was staying on at Chadwick with their father for another week; he always took a long break at Christmas as the money markets went dead. She and Toby were going back to London with their mother the next day.

She was just longing to see Dan. They'd had a long phone conversation on Christmas Eve, and another rather shorter one on Boxing Day, but that was about it. She was starved of him; she'd only seen him once since she'd got home from school as a matter of fact, and then only for an hour. She wanted to see him properly: all of him. She wanted to be in bed with him.

It was fantastic, having a boyfriend who was older, who had his own place, so that sex was possible. It just wasn't with younger boys. You were limited to upstairs at parties, or hotel rooms on holiday while the parents were sailing or playing tennis or ski-ing; rushed and nervous, not ideal. Whereas she and Dan had whole long evenings while she was supposed to be shopping or out with friends; the result was that sex was utterly wonderful. Utterly. He was terrifically good at it; of course, she didn't have any comparison, but she could just tell, from what other people said, that he was. Well, he should be, he'd had lots of practice.

He was twenty-two, and working for his father's stock-broking firm and he had his own flat. She'd met him at a party and just fallen for him, absolutely. He'd told her he felt exactly the same about her, that she was utterly special and he'd never known anyone quite like her, so she supposed she was doing all right. Things had moved pretty fast; she'd been in bed with him only ten days after she met him. She'd been quite nervous, it had been the first time, but he'd made it really easy for her, had kept reassuring her and telling her how lovely she was, and she was so happy about him she couldn't quite believe it was all true.

And tomorrow, New Year's Eve, she would see him; she had already spent hours trying on different outfits, experimenting with her hair; she might try doing it up again now, with the bits falling loose at the sides, she'd liked that best, but she hadn't quite got it right –

'Annabel! I thought you wanted to go for a walk?'

It was her mother; she'd agreed to the walk at breakfast, thinking it would pass the time, but now she'd rather stay in, in case Dan phoned. But then – he probably wouldn't.

'Yeah, I do.' She headed in the direction of the utility room to get her wellies; halfway across the hall she heard an odd sound coming from the drawing room. Going in, she found Tilly sitting huddled onto the window seat, her long skinny legs tucked under her, sobbing as if she would never stop. Annabel sat down beside her, put her arms round her.

'Angel, don't cry, whatever is it?'

'I heard Daddy on the phone. He was talking about selling Chadwick, saying that we didn't use it as much as we used to, and it was an appalling waste of money. Just think if he did, I couldn't keep Boy in London, I'd have to sell him too. I couldn't bear it. You don't know anything about it, do you?'

'Of course not. I'm sure you heard wrong, but I'll ask Mummy anyway. She'll obviously know. He was probably just trying to get an idea of its worth or something; you know how obsessed he is with that sort of thing.'

Tilly was doubtful. 'It didn't sound like that. Yes, could you ask Mummy, please? Daddy'd just fob me off with some stupid story, I know he would; he still thinks I'm about seven years old.'

'You're not thinking of selling this place, are you?' Elizabeth had cornered Simon in his study; the children were all upstairs, watching television.

He looked awkward, then said, 'I am, as a matter of fact. Thinking about it.'

'Simon! Why, for God's sake? We all love it here. And don't I have any say in it? It's mine as well, or so I've always thought.' She felt a rush of anger, that he had not discussed it with her, not told her even; this was what happened now, each new injustice, added to the seething, dangerous past.

'I know, I know, I'm sorry. But I do have to meet the cost, which is inordinate. We could all go for a holiday to the Bahamas three times a year for what Chadwick costs to run.'

'Well, I'd rather have Chadwick.'

'Elizabeth,' he said, and his expression was very serious, 'this

58

is not a matter of either or. I'm sorry. It will probably have to go.'

'Well, thanks for telling me,' she said. She felt extremely upset suddenly. 'Tilly's been crying – she overheard you talking about it. I told her it must be a mistake, that you'd never do it without discussing it with me. Which you shouldn't.'

'You're not exactly available for discussion,' he said, 'very often.' This was always his excuse for not consulting her; as usual it annoyed her.

'Simon, that's not fair. You know it's not.'

'It may be. It's true.'

She felt near to tears herself: she loved Chadwick, and not just for itself but what it represented, those carefree years when she had been what seemed now unimaginably happy. And thought how she longed to be back there, or at least in what they had given her, those years, the warmth, the closeness, the sense that she and Simon were at least travelling in the same direction. Now they seemed lost to one another, in some cold, uncharted territory.

'Simon, I do have time to talk,' she said. 'When it's important.'

'Do you?'

She knew what he meant; precisely. Her lack of time for him had been the excuse. With – as she knew – a degree of justification. She became defensive. 'And in case you hadn't noticed, I'm doing quite a big job and running quite a big family.'

'Yes, and don't we all know it.'

'You bastard,' she said slowly, 'and don't you dare sell Chadwick. I won't let you.'

She went upstairs to pack; half an hour later he came into the room.

'I'm sorry,' he said, 'very sorry. I shouldn't have said that.'

'No, you shouldn't.'

'You're doing a fantastic job, and I don't deserve you. Oh, Elizabeth.' He reached out and took her hand. 'It's all very sad, isn't it?'

'Yes,' she said, 'very sad.' Knowing he meant more than the loss of Chadwick, more than the distance between them; and then because he looked so wretched, she managed to push down her own hurt. 'You're really worried aren't you?' she said. 'Is it this Lloyd's thing?'

'It is. Yes.'

'Is it really so bad?'

'It will be,' he said, 'I'm afraid.'

'And you can't just – just get out? Now?'

'Absolutely not,' he said. 'If I could, Elizabeth, I would. Believe me.'

The children said it had been the best Christmas ever; Debbie found that hugely annoying, thinking of all the ones she had slaved over, struggled to make perfect, consigned to a sort of 'could do better' in her mothering report book.

They'd gone down to Wales, to stay with Flora. Debbie hadn't exactly wanted to – of course – but the others all had, and Flora had said she'd love to have them, it would be a way of saying thank you, and Debbie's own parents had gone on a cruise, so there was no excuse there and – no way out, really.

And it had been lovely: Midnight Mass at the beautiful little church above the sea at Oxwich, a Christmas-morning walk down onto the beach at Three Cliffs Bay, where the children had played for hours on the stepping stones, Christmas dinner by candlelight – and yes, all right, the children had been tired next day, but it had been rather special, something they'd remember always. And Flora was clearly making a great effort to be less overbearing and bossy; Debbie did wonder if Richard might have said something, but he swore he hadn't.

'I told you, she's very very fond of you. And she does know her own faults. Thank you for coming, darling, I know it wasn't what you most wanted.'

He was very good at that: properly appreciating what she did for him. It was one of the things she had fallen in love with him for.

Flora had sold one of her horses, the younger, feistier one.

'Well, I was getting a bit old for him,' she said with a quick smile, 'and I'm giving up hunting next season, it costs so much – another bit of belt-tightening, you know. Every little helps.'

As belt-tightening went, it didn't seem too stringent to

Debbie, more of a token really; but it was somehow soothing to think that Flora was prepared to do it. On the other hand, she was slightly alarmed that there was a need for further economies; she hoped they had both been speaking the truth when they had told her that the last time had only been a blip.

It had been a very jolly Christmas indeed at the Diamond Bay Hotel in Barbados. The place was booked to capacity, in spite of the much publicised recession going on in England. The clientèle weren't quite the crème-de-la-crème crowd to be found at the Sandy Lane; and indeed would not have met with a very warm welcome, had they strayed onto the private beach or golf-course of the crèmes. The Diamond Bay was mostly full of the Thatcherite newly rich, survivors of the 87 crash – who would have agreed wholeheartedly with Blue Horton's doctrine that for every loser there was a winner – people who had gone public with their companies in the early to mid eighties and walked away with millions, or ridden the wave of the property boom and then surfed off it with skill – all wearing their money in the form of cars and speedboats and jewellery, and taking suites at the Diamond Bay for Christmas and the New Year.

Tim Allinson, who was occupying one of the slightly smaller suites, would probably not previously have wished to join them; Tim was Old Money, Harrow, Guards, a resident of Belgrave Square; tall, blond, always impeccably dressed, hugely charming. Since leaving the Guards he had worked for one of the blue-chip estate agents, mostly engaged in finding clients from his impressively large circle of friends and acquaintances in both London and the country. Finding clients or, as he preferred to express it, 'making introductions' was his métier; a very pleasant second income had been earned over the past ten years by introducing people to Lloyd's. Or, to be more precise, to one of the Members' Agents. His commission on it was a very modest-sounding percentage, but the large number of new Names on which he earned it had certainly financed much of his lifestyle.

Time could be running out now, of course. The Lloyd's shore was getting just a trifle rocky. But there were still plenty of outsiders who didn't share that knowledge, and many of the revellers at the Diamond Bay, greedy for social cachet as well as financial security, were among them.

He had gone as the guest of the hotel's owner, who had appreciated what someone of Tim's class would add to the tone of the place; thus they suited one another very well. And by New Year's Day, as he packed to go home with some relief – the conga he had found himself dancing onto the beach last night in the company of a rich industrialist from Manchester and his much younger girlfriend had been one of the lowlights – he reflected on at least two and possibly three new introductions. Including the rich industrialist.

Chapter 4

April, 1989

'I can't tell him this week. I just can't.' Lucinda's voice was shaky on the phone. 'It would be too cruel, Blue. I'm sorry. He got a letter from Lloyd's this morning. It really upset him, he—'

Blue had been reaching for his cigarettes; he was trying to give up smoking, Lucinda hated it and he never smoked when he was with her, but he wasn't doing very well so far . . . He pushed the pack away again, sat bolt upright in his chair and started easing his tie, his other reaction to stress.

'Lloyd's of London? He's a Name, is he? I didn't realise.'

'Yes, he is. And it all seems rather bad.'

'Yeah, well, it would be—'

'Last year his main syndicate made its first loss ever. Nigel had to write a cheque for – gosh, I can't remember, but quite a lot, about ten thousand pounds. And this year it's about double that. He's terribly –' She paused. 'Blue, what did you say?'

'I said it would be. Would be bad. It's obvious.'

'Why is it obvious? And how do you know? Nigel says getting information out of them is like getting blood from a stone.'

'Sweet, you only have to keep your ear to the ground. And your brain working. You never heard of asbestosis?'

'No. Whatever is it?'

'Dear oh dear. Very nasty thing. Contracted by workers in the asbestos industry. Or rather, workers in the industries that use asbestos. Like construction. Cars. Furniture. Leads to cancer, all sorts of horrible things in your lungs.'

'I don't see what that's got to do with Lloyd's.'

63

'My darling Lucy, all companies insure with Lloyd's. They cover things like bodily injury, I think it'd be called. Year after year now, starting in the States, people have begun to claim huge sums of money. And the companies bloody well deserve all they can possibly get. They've acted disgracefully, tried to wriggle out of it, hush it up. Shocking story. Anyway, the floodgates could start to open here now. Billions and billions of pounds' worth of claims, I reckon. So course Lloyd's is affected. Horribly.'

'But – but I'm sure Nigel didn't know any of this. I don't see how—'

There was a silence then Blue said, 'You know, there's something about being a Member of Lloyd's. I don't know what it is. Head becomes disengaged from brain. They all seem to think it's God given nothing'll ever go wrong. Something to do with a public-school education, maybe.'

'Blue, don't. That's not fair.'

'Sorry.'

'That is so frightening. God. So – it could get worse?'

'Not could, sweetheart. It *will* get worse. And worse. Maybe you should get this thing over now, quickly, before it does.'

'Blue, I can't. Not just – just yet. He's so upset. Just let me have a tiny bit longer. I'm not chickening out, I couldn't do that now. I love you much too much. But not for a few more days.'

This was a terrible indictment of her motherhood, Elizabeth thought. That she'd had no idea, no idea at all what was going on, and—

She heard the front door slam. Simon. He'd been on a business trip to France for three days. She was going to have to tell him, and quickly. He'd be pretty shocked. And he'd probably cast a lot of the blame at her.

There was a pause while he checked the post. She heard him ripping open a few envelopes, heard a suppressed groan and a, 'Shit. Holy shit,' and then he walked into the drawing room, went straight over to the drinks table without seeing her, and poured himself a very large whisky.

'Hello, Simon,' she said.

'Elizabeth! What are you doing home at,' he looked at his watch, 'teatime? Are you ill?'

She shook her head. 'No, I'm fine. You?'

'Oh – OK. Bit tired. So – why are you here?'

'Simon, we need to talk.'

'I was about to say the same thing to you. You first.'

'It's Annabel.'

'Annabel? What about her? Boy trouble, I s'pose. She's not pregnant, is she?'

'No,' said Elizabeth, 'it's worse in a way, we could have fixed that. No, she's – she's been expelled.'

'Expelled! Annabel? Jesus. I don't believe it.'

'I'm afraid you have to.'

'But for God's sake, why? What's she done? She's only been back at school a week.'

'Bit less,' said Elizabeth, 'actually. She bunked off, spent Saturday night in London.'

'Jesus. What was she doing?'

'I've only spoken to her briefly. She came up to see some boy. Who,' she hesitated, he really wasn't going to like this, 'who she's been seeing for a while, apparently.'

'Oh my God.'

'Yes. Anyway, we have to go down, bring her home.'

'No way we can talk them round?'

'No. None. Her headmistress was absolutely clear on that one. She's broken about every rule in the book. It's pretty bad.'

'Why in God's name didn't they ring us? When they found her missing?'

'They didn't know about it. Her friends covered up for her beautifully, it's not difficult over a weekend. They caught her coming in last night, it seems, complete with bottle of champagne in her rucksack. Oh, and some reefers.'

'Dear God! So why the hell didn't they ring us then?'

'I was told they wanted to conduct a full enquiry first. Make sure they'd got everything straight, that it really was necessary to expel her.'

'Well,' he said, 'I can see it is.'

'So – come on. We're going down now.'

'Now? To Somerset?'

'Yes. We have to bring her home. She can't stay there another night. I – thought it best if we went together.'

'Of course. Let me just change my shirt and I'll be with you.'

As the car pulled onto the Cromwell Road, he said, 'I've got some more bad news. If you can take it.'

'Of course I can.'

He looked at her and half-smiled for the first time. 'I have to say, Elizabeth, you're very good in a crisis. Always were.'

This was true; she never panicked, never cried – just stayed calm and positive and clear-thinking. Not even when Toby had gone missing at the age of eight, for several hours – and was found blissfully happy riding the milk float together with the milkman's little boy, with whom he had made friends – nor when Tilly had been thrown by Boy and quite badly concussed; even *then*: she had met the news with dignity, bravely cool. It was her way of coping; holding onto herself and her image of herself.

'Try me now,' she said.

'It's – it's Lloyd's. Second year. Much worse. As I said at Christmas, Chadwick may have to go, I'm afraid. Correction. *Will* have to go.'

'Oh Simon, no. It must be very bad. How much this time?'

'Well, about forty-five thousand.'

'My God.' She was stunned. 'That's huge. Absolutely huge. I don't understand, how has it happened? What's gone wrong? And I thought you said you'd built up a hedge-fund to deal with this sort of thing.'

'I –' He didn't look at her, busied himself with the traffic. 'Not enough there, I'm afraid.'

'Can't we borrow the money from the bank?'

'Well – no. We can't. I'm already quite heavily in hock to the bank.'

'What for?'

'I made a loss on the Stock Market. In the crash. It's not good at the moment.'

'Yes, I know, but that was just a loss. Bit of a shame, of course, but—'

'More than a shame. I'd made that other rather unfortunate investment.'

'What?' she said sharply.

'I put a lot of money into that overseas hotel business. Set up by Ted Rayne, remember?'

'What, in the Bahamas?'

'That's the one. It went belly up, earlier this year.'

'You didn't tell me that. Well, not that it had gone bust.'

There was a silence, then: 'I know,' he said. 'I'm sorry, I should have done. But I couldn't see much point worrying you. I thought things would sort themselves out, that the market would recover.'

'Which it has.'

'Not enough. Not nearly enough. The country's in a hell of a mess, and Lawson seems set on taking us into the ERM, which would be disastrous in my view. And his policy on inflation isn't helping. Businesses are going under right left and centre. He's at loggerheads with Thatcher over that. Anyway, I thought that real estate was a cast-iron certainty. I was wrong. That's why Chadwick's in hock. I should have discussed it all with you, I know. I'm very sorry.'

She was silent. Then she said, 'Not a lot we can do about it, it seems. It's OK. Do you think we can squeeze one last summer in at Chadwick before it goes?'

'Yes, I should think so. Just about.'

'Well, that's something. After that it won't matter quite so much. Except for Tilly, of course. Let's keep it from the children for as long as we can.'

'OK.' He looked at her, smiled his sudden sweet smile, reached out and briefly took her hand. 'Thank you, darling.'

'What for?'

'For not blaming me.'

'It's not exactly your fault, is it?'

'Well,' he said, with a sigh, 'it's kind of you to say so, but I fear that to a degree it is. I didn't look very far before I leaped, I'm afraid.'

'But you didn't leap alone, did you? You had lots of company. And don't forget, we had some awfully good years. We wouldn't have had Chadwick at all without Lloyd's.'

'Oh, I know. But—'

'I would say,' she said, realising that she felt closer to him than she had for a long time, able to comfort him rather than rail against him, 'this thing with Annabel rather puts it in perspective. And it's not as if we're starving.'

'Well, not yet,' he said.

And in the days that followed he struggled to be his positive upbeat self; but it was hurting him badly, the erosion of his personal heritage. Simon was not Old Money; his father had been a grammar-school boy, and had scrimped and saved to send his bright, handsome, and already charming son to public school, wanting him to have as if by right the confidence, the accent, the manner that he himself had been at such pains to learn. Simon had left Charterhouse and then Oxford and moved straight into the City, a shooting star; within a very few years he was making a fortune. But as a boy, he had loathed the comparison between his schoolfriends' lavish houses and his own modest one, had been miserable at not being able to return invitations, to offer hospitality. He had loved his parents dearly, but he had suffered what all children in his position suffer: at best embarrassment, at worst shame. And the symbols of his own wealth, taking him further and further into the sleek confidence that he wore now like yet another perfectly tailored suit, had been doubly important, doubly precious because he had secured them for and by himself.

And he found the contemplation of their loss – and the effect of it on his own children – almost unbearable. He felt guilt at his own lack of judgement, and foolish too. 'It's my own bloody fault,' he would say, with a forced cheerfulness, to sympathetic friends and colleagues. 'Absolutely no one to blame but myself. Should have seen it coming.'

Flora sat staring at the letter. It had happened again. Lloyd's wanted more money: possibly twice as much. How could she have been so stupid: *how*? Why had she let William do this to her, make her a Member?

'I'm persuaded to become a Name,' he had said, fifteen years before. 'It seems an excellent idea. But there are risks, and I think with your agreement, I'd rather it was you. That way, they can't bankrupt us. You've got no money and the house isn't in your name, so it'll be pretty foolproof. I'll make over just enough money to you to do it. And it'll be a nice pension for you when I'm gone. How would that be?'

She hadn't actually been very keen; she'd always been slightly suspicious of the whole Lloyd's thing, the assumption that you could get something for nothing, and her visit to Lloyd's when she'd been admitted as a Member had done nothing to make her feel better. She'd been unimpressed by Edward Trafford Smythe, the Members' Agent who had talked William into this (as she saw it); he was some kind of distant cousin to William and seemed to her very second-rate; and she'd heartily disliked most of the members of the Rota committee who'd made such a hoo-ha about the honour of being admitted, and their rather pompous threats that while it was of course extremely unlikely that she would be called upon, she must understand that this was an unlimited liability she was getting into and that she would be in it down to her last cufflink.

'Don't you talk to me about cufflinks,' she had said. 'I haven't got any.'

They hadn't liked that, she could tell, hadn't liked a woman answering them back; but they managed to laugh it off and say the family silver would do very nicely.

And she had absolutely hated the business of the 20 per cent deposit of the assets they had shown, even though William had explained that it didn't have to be cash, that it could be share certificates if they preferred. There was altogether too big an element of smoke and mirrors for her commonsense turn of mind.

But, uneasy or not, she had to admit that for the past decade and more it had been an excellent source of income. Every June or July the cheque arrived; not vast, because they'd only written the minimum amount, but extremely welcome. It had funded the purchase of stocks and shares, their horses, their hunting, wonderful trips to South Africa and India; and then the house soaked up money of course, they'd had dry rot one year, needed a new roof another; the stables had needed rebuilding . . .

'Good old Lloyd's will see to it,' William always said, and indeed it had. And land had come onto the market, adjacent to the house, which they had bought, including one huge field sloping right down to the top of the cliffs at Broken Bay – so called, it was said, because of the way three huge, jagged rocks lay in the centre of the beach, as if they had been dropped from a great height, fracturing the smooth curve of the bay.

Flora loved that field; she called it The Meadow and she refused to put sheep on it, or graze the horses; she kept it in its natural state, filled with wild flowers and grasses. It had three dilapidated stone buildings on it, once cow sheds, but they in no way spoiled it, rather they adorned it, accessorised it even, the flame-red climbing roses of Gower half-covering one, and ivy and honeysuckle the others. When she walked through The Meadow in early summer, butterflies rose in great clouds about her, and at night she would hear the owls cry as they hunted the voles and mice that lived under the surface of the grasses. She would lean on the gate sometimes for hours in the darkness, holding William's big flashlight, watching the badgers that had established a run across it, and take photographs in the early morning of the hawks that hovered above it patiently, watching and waiting for their prey. And in the autumn she and the children would gather baskets of blackberries from the hedges that marked the boundaries of the field and she would turn them into jam and jelly and blackberry crumble.

But now she was a widow and on paper at least, a much wealthier woman, it was all rather different. She could never understand why William hadn't thought of this, when he willed her everything. The house was hers, William's pension was hers, his stocks and shares were hers, and most of his capital was hers; and they would all go, into the admittedly small but unpluggable hole in the dyke that was Lloyd's. The day the letter came, that second April, she went for a long walk, scrambling down the steep path from The Meadow to Broken Bay, and then, because it was low tide, making her way along the beaches as far as Tor Bay. She sat on the rocks there, looking out at the sea, and wondered how much of this treasure of hers she would have to lose. Her happiness was absolutely bound up in this place; in the roaring sea, the rolling surf, the wind, the storms, the huge brilliant skies: it was her lifeblood, she could not survive without it.

Of course, it wouldn't happen yet. She could manage this year; she would have to renege on the school-fees agreement again, and she would have to sell all her shares, albeit at a loss, and perhaps a couple of pictures, but she could do it. But then – what of the next? And the next? How much would they take from her? The land? The house? All her money? Where would she go, what would she do?

Suddenly Flora, inexhaustible lion-hearted Flora, found herself frightened: frightened and terribly tired. She couldn't lose all this; she really would much rather die.

Chapter 5

May, 1989

'I've decided what I want to do.' Annabel smiled at her parents over the dinner table. She had especially requested they ate together; it was rare enough during the week to have to be arranged.

Simon was delighted; some positive steps at last.

'Darling how exciting. What?'

It had been a difficult few weeks since her expulsion from school. First there had been her tantrums – anyone would have thought it was the school at fault, not her. She'd refused to accept that what she'd done was worthy of expulsion, apologising for upsetting them but insisting that the school was run by a mass of dreary old cows who had never come into the real world. 'I'm seventeen, for God's sake. Why should we all live like nuns? It's pathetic.'

Useless to point out – although Simon and Elizabeth did, of course – the dangers of girls wandering off at will, staying with strange men in strange houses in London, nobody knowing where they were, the folly of breaking the law, of risking a criminal record at the age of seventeen . . . 'What, for smoking a bit of grass! Please! The law should be changed.'

She had been all for moving in with Dan at first; 'He's got a really nice flat in Pimlico, by the river.'

'Where you spent last Saturday night?'

'Yes. I did.'

'And how long has this been going on?' said Simon.

'You know that, perfectly well, Miss Bollocks—'

'Don't call her that.'

'Sorry, Miss Balls told you, I thought, when we all had that cosy chat.'

'Annabel!' said her mother sharply. 'We're trying to understand. If you're not going to cooperate at all, we really will get angry.'

'How would I know the difference?' she said.

It had got better; she had tried to explain how she felt suffocated boarding at an all-girls' school, how she loved Dan, how he was really special, how she would have told them but she knew they'd disapprove, how she'd felt they didn't have enough time for her anyway, how she could never talk to either of them properly. Guilt-stricken, both of them, they hadn't even tried to deny it; later, she came in to see them before she went to bed and apologised, said she hadn't meant that, at least, and they told her again how much they loved her, and cared what happened to her.

She'd volunteered to get a job, 'Pay for my keep,' and she'd actually worked in Jigsaw for a while and hated it, nearly died of boredom. Elizabeth had let her hand over £10 a week (which hardly covered her phone calls), thinking it was good for her.

They'd suggested she went to some sort of crammer, so she could take her A-levels next year; she said she'd think about it, but she didn't really want to.

'I just want to get on with my life.'

Simon had said rather briskly that most people had to work in order to get on with their lives; and that more interesting work was available to those with qualifications; they had reached stalemate on that one.

The relationship with Dan had fizzled out; robbed of the glamour of an illicit affair, she had begun to find him boring and even rather silly. Something at least had been accomplished, Elizabeth said to Simon.

'Well, don't keep us in suspense,' said Simon now. 'What is it? Do you want to go to the Sorbonne, like Miranda, fun for you, or—'

'No. No, this won't cost you anything at all.'

'Really? That sounds pretty good to me.'

'I – hope so. Well, the thing is, I want to be a – a . . .' She stopped.

What on earth could it be, Elizabeth wondered, did she want to do nursing or physiotherapy, something like that? Might be all right: at a good hospital.

'Darling come on. Tell us.'

'I want to be a hairdresser,' she said, and the words suddenly tumbled out, very fast, as if she was afraid they might stop again if she let them.

'A hairdresser! Annabel, you can't be a hairdresser.'

'Why not?'

'Well, you just – can't. It's not – not the sort of thing you'd – we'd . . .' Elizabeth's voice tailed away.

'Not the sort of thing you'd what? Mummy, you make it sound like I wanted to be a prostitute. What's wrong with being a hairdresser?'

'Well, nothing darling of course. It's just—'

'It's just what? Look, you should be pleased. I've found something I really want to do.'

'How do you know you really want to do it?'

'There was a fashion show at Jigsaw the other night; I was talking to the guy who did the hair, he was great. It's such a fun thing, I know I'd like it. And I'd be good at it. I love doing my hair and Tilly's, and I used to do it for people at school—'

'Annabel, you are not going to be a hairdresser.' Simon's tone was final. 'I haven't spent a fortune on your education so you can spend the rest of your life brushing people's hair.'

'But it isn't just brushing people's hair. It's making it look good, making them look good, making them *feel* good. I think it's a great job and it's what I'm going to do. It won't cost you anything, and I just can't see what's wrong with it.'

'Darling,' Elizabeth said again, 'there's nothing wrong with it. But there's nothing right with it either. Not really I mean, it's not a very – very . . .'

'Very what? Oh, I get it. Not a very socially acceptable job. Is that it? Not like working for an advertising agency, or a bank. Not something you could tell your friends about. Well, you're going to bloody well have to, because it's what I'm going to do.'

'Annabel—'

'You really are pathetic, you know that? You are such snobs. And I don't see that your wonderful jobs have done you much good. Daddy worried to death about losing everything, Mum worried to death about losing clients and accounts. Listen, the world's changed. People don't just follow the same paths as their parents any more. There are loads of hairdressers making fortunes, people like Nicky Clarke and John Frieda, not that you'd have heard of either of them—'

'I certainly have,' said Elizabeth, stung.

'Well, good. You should be pleased I'm going to get out there and do something, instead of sitting around for another four years studying a load of crap that doesn't interest me and won't do me any good at all.'

'Of course we're pleased,' said Elizabeth, 'and it is a very interesting idea. But we just think, darling, you could do better for yourself than that. It might seem very exciting now, but it's an incredibly boring job, you know. You'll want more than that, I promise you.'

'How do you know it's boring? You've got no idea what you're talking about. Anyway, I'm going to do it and that's that. I've got an interview tomorrow, and if they offer me a job I'm taking it, OK? God, you are so – so unimaginative. I give up.'

And she was gone, with a slam of the door.

'I must go.' Lucinda looked fretfully at the watch on her wrist: the pink-strapped diamond fucking watch that she could only wear – to her sorrow – when she was with Blue. 'Sorry, but I promised I'd be there when Nigel got home and—'

'And when are you going to be there when I get home?'

She looked at him, startled. 'What do you mean?'

'I mean, how much longer is this going on? I'm getting a little bit tired of it, Lucinda; a man can only take so much.'

'Oh darling, I'm sorry. I'm so, so sorry. But I told you, he's so worried about all this Lloyd's business, so upset, he's not sleeping . . .'

'Yeah, yeah, I know the script. Why, I ask myself, doesn't he get off his arse and do something about it? Sell all those bloody acres, auction the family silver, just face up to the fact that the good times are over. It happens in the real world, you know, so why not to your lot? He's had it pretty good up to now.'

'Blue, that's horrible.'

'I don't see why. Listen, I had mates lost everything in the crash two years ago: their jobs, their cars, their houses. D'you think they sat around whining and saying they couldn't sleep? They did not. One of them took a stall on the Porto, got a very nice little business there now, selling rubbish to tourists, another's gone into the gardening business – well, window-boxes, actually – sells them, keeps them looking nice, and another's making a fucking fortune already out of sandwiches, cycling round delivering them to offices – whole fleet of them he's got now. I mean, please, Lucinda. Tell your old man to grow up.'

She stared at him. 'Why are you being like this?'

'Well, it's bloody pathetic. You seem to think your husband has a God-given right to having it easy.'

'I don't.'

'Yes, you do. Otherwise why not tell him to get a different act together. It's over, tell him, move on, do something different.'

She was silent for a moment, contemplating this.

'Yes, well, it might just be possible if – if things between us were different. But they're not. How am I supposed to say all that and then wave him goodbye and go off into the sunset with you? It's impossible.'

'Yeah, well, you should've done it earlier. I kept telling you.'

'I know you did. But Blue, can't you begin to imagine how unhappy he's going to be? How lost and lonely and—'

'Oh spare me. How about you imagine how unhappy *I* am, lot of the time? I get fucking lonely, Lucinda, but that's different, isn't it? I just have to get on with it, spend weekends on my own, most evenings on my own, just being grateful for the weekly fuck. Usually pretty rushed at that.'

He pulled open a drawer by his bed, took out his cigarettes and lit one. It was a very aggressive gesture.

'Don't be so horrible,' she said, and then started to cry. 'I can't believe you're talking like this.'

'Well, you'd better believe it. It's going to go on, until you do something about it. I can't stand it much more, Lucinda. It's over a year now, and as far as I can see we're no nearer getting it sorted. I love you more than I can ever tell you, but there are limits, I'm not made of fucking stone. What do you think it's like for me, thinking about you in bed with him, for God's sake? Bloody horrible. So make your mind up and make it up fast, OK? Get it fucking sorted, I want to fucking be with you. You'd better go, this isn't getting us anywhere.'

She stood up, pulling on her clothes frantically, crying, tears pouring down her face.

'I never knew you could be like this,' she said, 'so hard and – and cruel.' She wiped her nose on the back of her hand.

'It's you that's cruel,' he said, 'I'd say.'

'And how dare you talk about – about our relationship like that?'

'We don't have a relationship,' he said, and he got up now, pulled on his bathrobe, stubbed out the cigarette, glaring at her. His face was very white, his dark eyes almost black; he was literally shaking with rage. 'We have a weekly fuck. Like I said. Now, are you going to sort it out or are you not?'

'No,' she said, 'I'm not. Not in the way you mean. I'm certainly not going to be blackmailed into it. If you can't wait for me, if you insist on holding a – a sort of gun to my head, then – then it's over. It's not fair, Blue, you've got me into this and—'

'Oh really? I seem to remember a fair bit of cooperation now and again.' He began mimicking her voice. ' "Oh, I don't love him any more. Oh, I want to be with you." Well, come and be with me, Lucinda, or just get out for fucking good. OK?'

'I'm going,' she said, 'for good. And don't you dare ever come near me again.'

'Don't worry,' he said, lighting another cigarette. 'I wouldn't dream of it.'

Nigel was buying dinner for his accountant, an old schoolfriend, to see if he had any suggestions to make about the ghastly mess he seemed to be in. He'd asked Lucinda to join them, but she'd had to go to a publishing function somewhere in the City, and couldn't get away in time, she said.

'But I'll be jolly interested to hear what he has to say, darling. You never know, he might have some ideas. I'll wait up for you.'

'Bless you. But if I'm late I want you to go to bed, you're looking so tired.'

'I'm all right. Honestly. You don't look so good yourself.' She sighed. 'This is really worrying you, isn't it?'

'Just a bit. Not too serious though.'

'I mean, you can always sell the land, can't you? We're not exactly using it on a day-to-day basis.'

'Lucinda—' He stopped. How could he sell the land? For a

start it was a working farm; it might not exactly produce much of a profit, but it provided a living for quite a few people, and there were cottages on it – some of which he had turned into holiday cottages.

But far more serious was the fact that it was worth a million or so on paper – which was presumably why Lloyd's had accepted it as one of his assets, but it wasn't worth half that on the open market. Not at the moment anyway. Of course, one of the supermarket giants, like Tesco, might buy some of it and build one of their superstores; but it was bloody miles from anywhere, not on the edge of some market town, which was what they liked. And could he live with himself, selling his birthright to someone like that, land that had been in the family for five generations? He supposed those sorts of scruples were a luxury if the alternative was bankruptcy, but . . .

The accountant was late; Nigel ordered himself a second gin and lime. He hoped Lucinda was enjoying her party at least. And that Graham Parker appreciated how hard she worked.

Lucinda sat in the taxi, willing it to go faster. What if she arrived home after Nigel? If he saw her swollen face and streaming eyes? She absolutely couldn't stop crying, terrible tearing sobs; she could never remember anything like it. She knew now what people meant by having their hearts broken; it was a very apt description. There was a place she could almost feel physically, somewhere in her centre, that felt as if it had been hacked into pieces: a huge, bleeding, gaping hole. How was she going to bear it, how was she going to get through the night, never mind the next day and the next week and . . .

Don't think about that, Lucinda: one day at a time. Wasn't that what alcoholics were told to do? She felt like an alcoholic, in her need for Blue; she had developed a total dependency on him, a physical craving, not just for sex, but for being with him, talking to him, listening to him: he phoned her several times a day, how would she get through an hour without that? Without the promise of him, the hope of him, the remembering of him.

That was almost the worst thing; she had such horrible memories now, of him being cruel and harsh and angry. She must concentrate on that, try to tell herself at least she had found out what he was really like. It might help. Sweet, funny, infinitely nice Blue wasn't that at all; it was an act, a sham. Cling onto that, Lucinda, try to think you're fortunate.

At last: Sloane Street. Nearly there. As they swung right and then round into Cadogan Square she took a deep breath, got out her wallet. It had been hugely expensive: nearly twelve pounds. Never mind; she'd made it. The lights weren't on in the house.

'There you are,' she said, stifling her sobs briefly, handing over fifteen pounds. 'Keep the change – no, it's fine.'

'You all right, love?' said the driver curiously.

'Yes, I'm fine, really absolutely fine, thank you.'

'Had a row with yer boyfriend? They're not worth it, darlin', take it from me.'

'No,' she said, and a new wave of grief rose in her throat, 'no, I don't think they are. Thank you. Good night.'

God: a taxi had just followed her in. Nigel? Please not! But it was, she could see him bending back into the cab, picking up his bags. She pulled out her keys, just got in in time, slammed the door. She didn't put the lights on, because she knew he'd see, just raced upstairs in the dark, kicked off her shoes and climbed into bed, pulled the covers over her head, buried her face in the pillow. She heard him opening the front door, then closing it again, very carefully; moving about quietly, going into the cloakroom. She'd better move or he'd find her like this, fully dressed, crying . . . She got up again and tiptoed along to the spare room, climbed into bed there. She could just say in the morning that she'd had a terrible headache, had had to have some peace and quiet.

Inside the darkness, buried beneath the duvet, the pillows muffling her sobs, she gave herself up to unhappiness.

Debbie watched Richard surface from the bottom of the swimming pool, gasping for breath, laughing, Rachel clinging to his hair. He was the most amazingly good father. He never got cross with the children – in fact, that was his only fault in that direction, he was too lenient with them; they had no idea what a cross Daddy looked – or sounded – like. She had said as much to him once and he said he used up all his disciplinary impulses at school; there was nothing left over for his own children.

'That's all very well, but it makes me the bad guy,' she said plaintively, but she didn't really mind. Her own style of mothering was a quick snap and then it was over; she couldn't have lived with all that 'you wait till Daddy gets home' stuff.

They went to the swimming pool every Sunday morning, and then in the summer for a picnic to somewhere like Richmond Park or Kew Gardens, in the winter home for a game of Monopoly or Cluedo while Debbie cooked a (very late) lunch. She could never work out how anyone could manage to get Sunday lunch on the table by one o'clock; she had tried quite hard over the years, even doing the vegetables the night before or very early in the morning, but it was still somehow nearer three before they all sat down. Which meant at least that supper could be something really lazy, like French toast or baked beans.

Today was the first picnic day of the year; and they were going to Regent's Park, 'But not the zoo,' Richard said firmly, as they all got into the car.

'Oh Daddy, why not, please please . . .'

'I said no, I need a rest.'

'A rest? What do you want a rest for?' said Emma.

'Emma, I've spent the entire morning like some primeval creature from the swamps—'

'What's primeval?'

'You ought to know that,' said Debbie. 'I thought you were doing a project on dinosaurs.'

'Well, we are, but no one's said anything about primeval.'

'Really?' said Debbie. 'Well, they should have done.'

'I know, I know,' said Rachel, 'we did it at my school, it means really really long ago, before there were any people.'

'Hmm,' said Debbie, 'St Luke's one, Hadley Hall nil.' She grinned at Richard. 'That's a good school you're running, Mr Fielding. Don't let anyone tell you otherwise.'

'I won't.'

He hadn't got a new job yet, but he'd been shortlisted for two, one boarding prep school in Oxfordshire, which would have been wonderful for him, but dreadful for Debbie, and one very posh little establishment in Richmond. She'd been so dreading him getting the Oxford one and having to move there and leave all her friends and disrupt the children that when he didn't, she'd burst into tears; he had assumed she was upset for him, and kept telling her she was sweet and it was all right and he really hadn't wanted it, he'd much prefer Richmond. He didn't get that either, but they were terribly nice and said it was only because he was so young that they'd given it to the other, more experienced chap; he was now applying for several more with greatly increased confidence.

'And it's all because of you,' he said, giving her a kiss, 'making me go for it. What would I do without you Debbie? Best thing I ever did, marrying you.'

It was slightly chilly for a picnic; they sat by the boating lake and fed the ducks, and the children kept asking to go to the zoo. Debbie was afraid Richard would give in, but he didn't, nor to their demands to go to the Planetarium; he organised a relay race round the lake, which Debbie and Emma just managed to win – 'although the fact I was carrying Rachel on my shoulders might just have had something to do with it,' Richard said – and then they went home quite early.

Debbie was just loading up the washing-machine with the swimming things when the phone rang.

'Debbie, hello my dear, this is Flora.'

'Oh, Flora hello. How are you? Do you want Richard?'

'If you don't mind. I won't keep him long, I expect he's very busy.'

'Not really,' said Debbie briskly, looking at Richard who was nodding off over the Monopoly board. 'Richard, it's your mother.'

He got up, took the phone from her. 'Hello? Of course not, it's fine. We've just been for a picnic, I'm— Look, let me take this in the study, it's quieter there.'

He was gone quite a long time, about ten minutes; when he came out he smiled at Debbie rather distractedly.

'Sorry, darling.'

'What was that about then? The summer?'

'No, no, she just wanted to tell me about a meeting she's going to have. With her Members' Agent.'

Members' Agent, like Managing Agent and Names and Syndicate were all words from the Lloyd's dictionary; Debbie didn't understand any of them. Richard had told her more than once that everything was better at Lloyd's now, and that was all she cared about.

'I see. Good.'

'And she did mention the summer, yes, of course. Says she's looking forward to it. I said we couldn't wait either.'

Flora was going to have all three children on her own for a week in August; Debbie and Richard were to have a whole wonderful seven days on their own; they were driving up to Scotland. They'd wondered about going to Florence or somewhere, but it would be terribly hot there and expensive, and if anything happened – Debbie tried not to think what that might be, drowning, broken limbs – and they had to make a dash to Wales, it would be much easier.

'She's not still worried about Lloyd's, is she?' said Debbie suddenly, pausing in her potato peeling; and there was an imperceptible pause before Richard said, 'Good Lord no,' and at that moment Rachel managed to fall off her chair and hit her head on the edge of the table, and Debbie forgot about that pause until much, much later when everyone was in bed; and then decided she must have imagined it and that Richard, who was the most painfully honest person she had ever met, would never be deceiving her about something so important.

Chapter 6

June, 1989

She was trying to see it as a sort of project. It helped, made something positive of it all, rather than just struggling through endless days of awful aching misery. She had to do it, after all; had to get over it, put her life back in order. Their lives. Hers and Nigel's.

She clung determinedly to what she had told herself at the very beginning, when she had first begun the affair with Blue; that it was just a little fling, very naughty and dangerous, but nothing more. It had only been later, when they had fallen in love with each other that it had got so complicated and – well, so important. Important-seeming, anyway. What she had to concentrate on now was the fact that until she had met Blue and had the fling, she had been perfectly happy. She had been married to someone she loved, they had had a very nice life, with lots of friends, she had a job she really liked.

That couldn't really all have changed. Nigel was the same person, their friends and their social lives were the same, her job was the same. Nigel hadn't turned into someone harsh and unpleasant (as Blue so shockingly had), her friends were still fun and nice and invited them to jolly dinner parties, and her job wasn't dull and boring. Everything was exactly the same as it had been, when she had been perfectly happy. She just had to settle down again and pull herself together. And thank her lucky stars, of course, that she'd never been caught. Suppose she had? Suppose Nigel had found out, and been totally furious and shocked and told her he wanted a divorce, and then she'd found out about Blue, about the sort of person he really was. And he must be pretty vile; it had been ten days now, and he hadn't called her. She'd sort of thought he would, the first few days; every time the phone rang she'd expected to hear his voice, saying, 'Sorry, Lucy, didn't mean it, love you.' But – nothing. He was a complete – well, bastard. Not sweet and kind and good like Nigel. He hadn't really cared about her at all. He'd just used her. He'd told her he'd always wanted a posh bird, and she'd been just that, a sort of trophy. He'd probably told all his mates at McArthur's about her; what a pushover she'd been, how he'd had her in bed in no time . . .

Now don't start crying again, Lucinda. Just concentrate on your project. Move forward. Be a good wife again. Think about Nigel. Making him happy. He deserves it. He deserves you, looking after him.

And she had done rather well, actually, she thought. Somehow got through the worst, the early days. She must be a terrific actress. She had managed to smile at him over breakfast that first morning, pretend to think she was getting some bug – felt a bit rough but she'd be fine. It was quite clever that, explaining as it did her swollen eyes and runny nose. She'd gone to work, concentrated really hard on a particularly boring manuscript Graham had asked her to read at least three weeks ago, even managed to make a few suggestions about some jacket copy he was struggling over; she'd gone into Marks & Sparks on her way home and bought Chicken Kievs for supper, Nigel's favourite, and suggested they listened to some extremly boring concert on the radio instead of watching *Howard's Way*, which she'd known would distract her. Every so often, all through the day, the pain kept coming back; she'd feel her heart contracting with it and know the tears were about to come and had to run to the Ladies and hide. Crying helped, it seemed to let the misery out in a strange way, but it was also a bit dangerous, because it seemed to take a hold on her and it was terribly hard to stop.

It hadn't been too bad at work, no one had noticed, but it happened over supper; she'd had to rush away from the concert and sit on the lavatory, a towel clutched to her face to muffle the noise, and fight to get it under control again. She'd made much of running the tap and washing her face and hands; when she went back, fearful of being questioned, Nigel was deep in an article in *The Times* about Kenneth Clark's reforms to the NHS.

'You all right?' he said, rather vaguely, and, 'Yes, I'm fine,' she said, 'I told you, got some sort of a flu-ey-bug, so silly in May.'

The worst, the absolutely worst thing of course was when they went to bed; she'd been petrified he'd want to have sex, and she sat up reading for ages, willing him to go to sleep, but he just wouldn't and then finally he'd said, 'Darling, can we please turn the light out?'

God, she'd thought, please, please no, and she could feel herself physically shrinking from him as he put his arms round her; he'd kissed her a couple of times and said, 'I missed you last night, don't like sleeping on my own.' He put a tentative hand on her breast, always his first move, and she felt completely panic-stricken; it was hideous, almost as if he was a total stranger, a rapist or something, far, far worse than all the times over the past year when she'd just lain there and tried to enjoy it until it was over, which was usually pretty soon. But this was infinitely worse; she simply couldn't go through with it, not that night, and she had feigned a coughing fit, said she had to go to the bathroom and get some water.

'You all right, darling?' he'd called, and, 'Yes, I'm fine,' she said, going back into the room, fighting down the tears, the awful treacherous tears. 'Sorry, got a bit of a tummy upset as well.'

'Poor love. Look, it's all right, why don't you go into the spare room again? To be absolutely brutal, I need some sleep myself, got a big meeting tomorrow. Come and give me a kiss and I'll release you from your marital duties.'

He often talked about sex like that, always had; it was a sort of joke, obviously, but for her recently it had come to seem a pretty sick one . . .

Thankfully, she kissed him and crept away. It would happen again, but for tonight, the very worst night, she was safe.

Two weeks later and she was feeling just a little better; crying less, hurting quite a bit less, able to find just a little pleasure in a few things: shopping (she'd got a really nice pair of shoes from J.P. Tod and a bag to match, terribly expensive, but she reckoned she needed to spoil herself a bit), planning a dinner party for the following Saturday (always fun and the more she didn't have to be alone with Nigel the better at the moment), and – long-postponed chore – making some new curtains for their bedroom. She'd actually wanted the ruched Austrian blinds, they were so pretty, but Nigel didn't like them, said they were like having a wedding dress hung up at your window. So it was just curtains, but lovely pale-blue silk, and she did enjoy doing things like that, and it was certainly in keeping with The Project. Being a Good Wife; that was what she was once more, and what she would always be from now on.

A very busy weekend lay ahead: Saturday lunch with friends at the Pheasantry in the King's Road, a fortieth birthday party for one of Nigel's oldest friends – that might be a bit dull, but she always got spoiled on such occasions, being (usually) quite a bit younger and prettier than anyone else; and then on Sunday afternoon, a christening at Chelsea Old Church, and the consequent tea party. So lots of distraction, not much time alone with Nigel, and she could give the new shoes and bag an airing. It was going to be all right; she was getting through it – and thank goodness she and Blue inhabited such different worlds socially: imagine if he'd been part of their crowd and every single party and dinner a minefield in prospect.

She took a bit of a long lunch-hour – well, she'd been working so hard for the last ten days she felt entitled to – and took a bus to Selfridges to buy a christening present and some smoked salmon for the evening: coming out of the store she caught sight of herself in the window and saw what she seemed to have become once more, a virtuous, busy young wife, and felt rather pleased with herself. It had been hell, it was still hell for a lot of the time, but she was winning, she was making her way back to where she belonged. She was certainly never going to leave it again; she would never be so stupid again . . .

She had just sat down at her desk and stowed the salmon in the small fridge in the company kitchen when her phone rang.

'Lucinda? Lucinda, it's Blue. Don't, please don't ring off. Look, I'm so, so sorry. I behaved like some kind of moron. I can't cope without you. Can I see you soon? Please, Lucy, please?'

Annabel had never really thought about her feet before. They had been there to put shoes on, the prettier the better, to get her about, to look at when she was lying in the bath; suddenly they were the dominant thing in her life. They felt literally tired, as tired as she was; she remembered her grandmother saying her feet were tired and wondering what on earth she meant. They ached, endlessly; her heels especially throbbed. They felt as if she had become extremely heavy, not the seven and a half stone of reality; she would look at herself sometimes in one of the salon mirrors, and be surprised to see herself exactly the same, rather pale and tired-looking, perhaps, deprived of fresh air as she was so much of the time, her own hair blonder by the week, as she allowed it to be used as a model for highlighting, caught back in a ponytail. She was dressed in the salon uniform of black and white, usually black leggings, and white T-shirt, the feet, the aching tired feet in white or black jazz shoes from Anello & Davide in Covent Garden. She had actually bought them to wear for classes at the Dance Centre in Covent Garden, and at the Pineapple Studio, in a somehow unimaginable time when she had had energy to spare.

Her hands were terribly sore with the constant immersion in water, she could only keep a rash at bay with a steroid cream, and her back ached quite a lot of the time as well; it started in her shoulder-blades as she stood at the backwash, shampooing endlessly, and slowly spread down her spine: and her head too, towards the end of her sessions – nine or ten hours long, illegally long she was sure, but who was counting or looking; she was sure she must be keeping the manufacturers of paracetamol going, she swallowed so much, and when she was really tired her ears buzzed as well, so that she could hardly hear the endless loop of George Michael's *Faith* and Michael Jackson's *Bad* that filled the salon.

She had got a job as a trainee at Miki Wallace, one of the top salons in London, and knew how lucky she was; some days she did love it, some days she hated it, but quitting was never an option. In the first place she knew her parents would have been delighted, and in the second, she was determined to make a success of it. She had never forgotten that heady evening at Jigsaw in Kensington High Street, watching the two

87

stylists twisting and brushing and pushing hair into all manner of wonderful shapes, and how it had transformed the models from fairly ordinary girls into exotic creatures, works of art almost; and at a slightly less dramatic level, how quite plain girls would come into Miki's and get themselves turned into dazzling beauties for an evening, or a day, or a wedding. Hair, she had discovered, wasn't just something that grew on your head, a flattering adjunct to a face, it was a powerful statement about its wearer, more important even than make-up or clothes. The styles of the day were so disparate, yet as absolutely and recognisably stylish as the padded shoulders and killer heels of the age; the sleek bob of the careerwoman, the long layered curls of the free spirit, the big bouffant of the lady who lunches, they all walked out of the salon hour by hour, day by day, perfectly, yet imaginatively exercised. One of the most important things she had learned was that a stylist first masters a style, and then personalises it.

Most of all Annabel loved watching Miki work, as she did sometimes, from her position at the backwash or as humble passer of foils to one of the colourists; he would stand behind a client, staring intently at her in the mirror, asking her questions, holding her hair in his hands, easing it forwards, drawing it back, piling it up, creating his vision for her without even taking so much as a comb to it; her greatest ambition was to be sent as assistant on one of the photographic sessions for the magazines, that he excelled at; but she knew she had a very long way to go before that was a possibility.

She wasn't even sure how good she was; whether she had hairdresser's hands as they were called, or not; she only knew she wanted to.

The salon was in Belgravia, just off West Halkin Street, small enough to feel exclusive, large enough to get a buzz going, and near enough to the West End to draw its clients from the working community of London, not merely the lunching ladies; the female stars of the advertising, business and the magazine world were on its books, even a corporate lawyer or two, busy women who nevertheless knew they must invest some time at least on their looks. One of Miki's promises was that no one was ever kept waiting for more than ten minutes, and for the most part he managed to honour that.

Styled in time for today was the rather complex promise made in his advertising material.

He was acknowledged to be one of the greats, on a par with Michaeljohn and Daniel Galvin and John Frieda; he was clever and funny and Annabel adored him. He wasn't very tall, only a couple of inches taller than she was, with rather long dark hair and burning dark eyes, and he had a longstanding boyfriend, but he managed to project something heterosexual at the same time; conversations between Miki and the women lucky enough to be his clients were not giggly and gay and gossipy, but rather intense. The other boy stylists were more flippant and fun; some were gay, some not, but Annabel loved them all.

'You can't love them all,' Tilly had said, 'there must be some nasty ones,' but Annabel said no, there weren't, not really. 'Well, some are a bit bitchy, I suppose, but they're all so – so pleased to be there and they all work so hard, and care so much about what they do. And they make me laugh,' she added, 'and they're really kind to me, and that's the most important thing.'

She was something of a curiosity in the salon, she knew; from the very first day when she had arrived, acutely nervous, and rather formally dressed in a red dress and jacket from Jigsaw, and announced herself in her unmistakably expensive voice, she had been studied closely. For the first few days, she had been sniggered at, and when she had survived that with a display of unshakable good nature, she had been teased relentlessly, called 'Posho' or 'Sloane-y'.

'You sure you're not a client got into the wrong side of the salon?' Carol, a sharp little thing from Croydon, had asked her; and, 'Quite sure,' Annabel said firmly. 'My mum might come here, not me.' She and Carol became best friends, sharing snatched sandwiches, swapping shifts, covering up for one another's mistakes, practising on one another's hair; a world apart in background and education, they were identical in ambition, a streak of deviousness and a capacity for extremely hard work.

Tania, the Salon Manager in charge of the juniors, tall, languid, red-taloned, came forward and hustled her into the staff room that first day: 'You have brought something else to wear, haven't you?' she said. 'Of course,' Annabel said, and produced not one but three black and white outfits from the large Way In bag she carried. She had been introduced to the others, then given a crash course in salon behaviour: 'Be welcoming, smile, don't draw attention to yourself, defer to the stylists, do what they say without question,' and, 'The client is always right and that means *always*: if she throws a brush at you – and that has happened – just smile and say thank you.'

Tania said she should call herself Bel, that Annabel was a bit of a mouthful, and sent her to change, saying that she'd be in at the deep end, they were three juniors short that day. Dressed in her black trousers and white shirt, she was handed a broom and told to sweep the floor. 'But it looks perfectly clean,' she said, staring at it. 'Give it ten minutes and it won't be,' said Tania, and indeed, at the first drops of the waterfall of hair which flowed onto the floor every day, Annabel realised her problem would be keeping up with it, for as fast as she cleared the area round one client, another filled up.

At twelve o'clock, Tania called her over. 'I'm going to give you a quick lesson in gowning up, Bel,' she said.

'In what?' said Annabel.

'Gowning up. It's extremely important to get it right. Here, take this,' handing her a black nylon cape, 'and imagine I'm the client. Now you greet me, tell me your name, say you're taking me to the backwash, or over to whoever the stylist is, and help me into the gown. Make me feel welcome, pleased to be here, be polite but not pushy . . .'

Annabel smiled meekly; she supposed there might be some people who needed to be taught such things, but it seemed very unlikely. But she could see also that it was absolutely essential not to say so.

After three days, she stayed on for school, down in what was known as the Academy, and learned shampooing. 'Don't think you know how to do this,' Tania said to her and two other new girls, 'because you don't. There's a procedure and you must follow it. Now you start with the temperature, check and check again, then spray it gently on the client's head and say, "Is the temperature all right for you?" Always do what he or she wants: if it feels cold to you and she says it's hot, make it colder, all right? Then very carefully soak the hair and . . .'

Next day, Annabel began putting this newfound skill into

practice: confident that she'd be able to do it, she settled the client (a man) at the backwash, carefully adjusted the level of the basin, checked that the water temperature was all right for him – and proceeded to soak the back of his shirt. She had forgotten to place the towel round his neck.

Fortunately he was middle-aged, not too self-important and clearly fancied first himself and then her; when she offered to dry his shirt with the hair dryer (official emergency procedure for such a gaffe) while the stylist cut his hair, he winked at her and said could he keep it on while she did it. Luckily for her, Tania was not witness to any of this.

Her worst moments were when her friends' mothers or indeed her own mother's friends came in and recognised her: 'Annabel, darling, what on earth are *you* doing here?' they would shriek across the salon, often beckoning her over and occasionally and most dreadfully insisting on jumping up and kissing her. This was not only embarrassing and against the rules ('never kiss or hug a client, even if she seems to want it'), it immediately lost her a great deal of street cred with the others.

'Annabel, dah-ling,' they would chant as she went into the staff room, or, 'I say, yah, it's Annabel, sweetie.'

But for the most part, they seemed to like her, and apart from a clear and acute curiosity about how and why she came to be there at all, accepted her. She had planned not to explain about being expelled from school but she confided it to Carol in strictest confidence, who spread it swiftly around. Annabel's reputation and popularity were immediately greatly enhanced.

'Lulu, wake up. I said, had you decided yet?'

'Oh – no, sorry. Um, just give me a moment . . .'

Of course she hadn't decided. How could she have, she wondered, sitting in the restaurant, studying the menu, desperately forcing her mind onto a choice between quiche and lasagne, knowing she would not be able to swallow either. And how was she supposed to make a choice now between seeing Blue again and not seeing Blue again? It was horrendous. If only, if only he hadn't rung. When she was just beginning – but it had only been beginning – to feel better, to miss him a tiny bit less. If only she'd been able to go on thinking he was horrible, instead of listening to him saying he was sorry over and over again, that he was a bastard, that he didn't deserve her, that he'd understand completely if she never wanted to speak to him or see him ever again. When the only thing in the world she really wanted *was* to speak to him and see him, and be held by him, and – it wasn't fair; it just wasn't fair . . .

Simon was at his desk, engrossed in the Nikkei – the Japanese stock market – and its seemingly unstoppable progress, when the phone rang.

'Simon Beaumont?'

'Yes.'

'Look, you don't know me, but your wife said you wouldn't mind me ringing. My name's Neil Lawrence and—'

'Oh yes, of course. I remember. Nice to hear from you.'

Elizabeth had told him about Lawrence. 'I saw him at an advertising bash, that one at the Hilton the other night. Marketing Director of Maxwells – you know, the confectionery people; we pitched for their business two years ago, didn't get it. Anyway, he's normally very buttoned up, but he was terribly drunk in the bar after dinner, and he mentioned that he was having "fun and games" as he put it, with Lloyd's. I said you too, and that was it, I couldn't stop him. Had to sell a lot of shares, and a house in Italy, all that stuff, scared of having to take the children out of school even. He's desperate. I told him about you and so on, and he thought he might like to talk to you. He'll ring you. He's very nice.'

Simon invited Neil to have a drink with him. He liked him, he was quiet, almost shy, deeply embarrassed at what he had done.

'I can't believe I was so bloody stupid,' he said, drinking a large glass of red wine at great speed, holding it out to have it refilled. 'I came into some money, Father died, met this chap at a drinks party, we got talking, he asked me if I'd ever considered becoming a Name, I was rather—'

'Don't tell me,' said Simon, 'flattered.'

'Well, yes, for Christ's sake. Totally pathetic.'

'What was his name? Just so I can avoid him. Or alternatively, kick him in the balls.'

'Allinson. Tim Allinson. Classic old Harrovian, Guards, terribly charming. Ever come across him?'

Simon shook his head.

'Well, he introduced me to someone there, I was impressed, thought it would help with the school fees, all that sort of thing – I've got four small children, I could see it was going to be very expensive, and – Jesus. I don't know. My wife has no idea,' he added, picking up a handful of nuts, cramming them into his mouth. He was very thin; Simon wondered if he ate enough.

'What, you haven't told her?'

'No, I can't. She's a rather anxious person, and I know she just couldn't handle it. I've managed to keep them at bay so far, but – anyway, I'd never told a soul about it at all until I met your wife. She was talking about you and – well, it was a huge relief somehow.'

Simon was shocked into silence. He sat staring at Lawrence, wondering what on earth his midnight crises must be like. At least he could talk to Elizabeth: when she was there.

'Yes, you see, your wife, she's so capable and obviously a huge help financially. It must be bloody marvellous. Amanda's never worked, and—'

'But surely she'll have to know soon. I thought you'd had to sell a house in Italy?'

'Well, it's on the market, just haven't had any offers. Bad time of year, of course. I think I'm going to throw up, every time I even contemplate the next letter. That chap Allinson has a lot to answer for. But – well, it might be all right, don't you think? My Members' Agent was very reassuring.'

'Mine, too,' said Simon. He called the waiter over and ordered another bottle of wine. It seemed about the only thing he could do for Neil Lawrence.

Alan Richards had been working as a clerk at Jackson & Bond, Members' Agents at Lloyd's, for five years now; he was very ambitious and he had been told that within another year or so, he could well have his own portfolio of Members to look after. He loved his job, he loved the whole business of insurance; people thought it must be terribly boring and looked at him with great sympathy when he assured them it wasn't. He tried to tell them how it felt to be there at the heart of things, the heart of global insurance, where you could almost smell the money summoned to staunch the ever-increasing flow of claims, drawn in from all over the world, money that no one ever actually saw, not even at Lloyd's, presenting itself only in the form of letters of credit and bankers' documents, and then materialising by some almost magical process not only to service the claims but as hard cash in the bank accounts of the people who had brought it – by way of the letters of credit – to Lloyd's in the first place. Alan had often tried to explain this to Heather, his girlfriend, especially after a particularly dramatic day when some awful tragedy had taken place – like the PiperAlpha explosion just over a year ago – but she failed to find it even remotely interesting and certainly not in the least exciting. She worked in a bank in Esher and said she could understand that, it was straightforward; people actually brought money in there, either in the form of cheques, or quite often actual cash; the bank looked after it for them and paid them interest on it while they had it; and if they wanted it back, they got it.

'But your business, Alan, it's a bit like a conjuring trick, isn't it?'

Alan said not really, but he could see why it might seem like that. He loved going into Lloyd's; it felt a bit like walking into a history book, with brokers queuing up at the under-writers' desks to talk to them and sell them propositions, and the waiters, as they were called, in their red coats, ushering people about, and the great Lutine Bell still standing on a podium at the centre of the main room. It was still rung on ceremonial occasions: 'But it was once rung to alert under-writers of an overdue ship,' he told the underwhelmed Heather, 'once for bad news, twice for good. And losses are still recorded in the ceremonial loss book – with a quill pen,' he added. He felt a distinct pride in being associated with such an institution.

Alan's work had never presented him with much personal pressure; of course he was very busy at times, especially once a year when calculating which Members had made money and which had lost, but for the most part his work proceeded at a fairly steady pace. He never questioned the machinations of

94

Lloyd's; he knew that things were pretty difficult at the moment, and that the Names – some of the Names – were having a bit of a hard time, but then they had had a pretty easy one for the past couple of decades, and you had to take the rough with the smooth in life. He was beginning to develop the slightly patronising, even cynical attitude towards the Names that some inside Lloyd's had; they had come into it for profit, after all, they'd succeeded for a long time and now that things weren't quite so easy, they shouldn't complain. It was like betting on the horses, as he'd also said to Heather; you put your money on a horse in the full knowledge of what you were doing, and if the odds weren't good or the horse lost, that was hardly anyone's fault except your own. Heather said she had never understood all that stuff about odds either, even though she worked practically on top of Sandown Park racecourse. Alan couldn't quite see what that had to do with it but he was too polite to say so. He was a very polite young man.

He was very polite to Gillian Thompson when she came into the office, asking to see someone in authority. It was a filthy, unseasonal day, raining hard; Miss Thompson had walked to the offices of Jackson & Bond, which were just off Bishopsgate, from Liverpool Street tube station, and she was very wind-swept and wet, her neat brown shoes stained from stepping in puddles, and her umbrella, as she explained to Marion, the girl in Reception, completely ruined. 'Like my hair.'

Marion came into Alan's office and said that Miss Thompson wanted to see someone about her syndicates, and that she seemed rather upset. 'Make her a cup of coffee, Marion, please,' Alan said, 'and I'll be out.'

He came out a few minutes later, smiled at Miss Thompson who was twisting her handkerchief in her fingers and asked what he could do to help. 'I don't know,' Miss Thompson said, and burst into tears. Alan was rather alarmed; he suggested to Marion that she showed them into the small conference room and brought another cup of coffee.

'I don't want any more coffee,' Miss Thomspon said, blowing her nose. 'I want to talk to someone about my syndicates.'

'You can talk to me,' Alan said soothingly – he had learned to soothe middle-aged women when his mother had had The

Change – 'and we can sort something out, I'm sure. Why don't you begin at the beginning? Always a good place, I think.' And he smiled at her encouragingly.

The beginning had been just a few years earlier – seven, to be precise – when Miss Thompson had been approached by the son of an acquaintance of her parents – 'such a nice young man', and he had suggested, having learned of the modest fortune bequeathed her by her father, that she became a Name at Lloyd's. 'I can arrange everything for you,' he said, 'introduce you to someone there and he'll take care of everything for you.'

Lonely and unmarried, Gillian Thompson had been grateful for such kindness, and felt the weight of her financial affairs lifting from her shoulders; three months later she was admitted as a Name: 'And it was such a lovely day; I was taken up to that beautiful room, in the old building that was, of course, and these extremely charming gentlemen welcomed me. It was like having a sort of second family suddenly. I felt very secure. And I hadn't even had to hand over any money, apart from the deposit, of course. Sinclairs, they were my bank, simply provided a letter of credit and I was in. And for the first few years it was wonderful: I got a cheque every July, and I was able to do up my little house and buy a small car. And then – then . . .'

'Yes?' said Alan gently.

'Then it all began to go wrong. The first year wasn't too bad, they only wanted four thousand pounds. I could manage that. Of course, I was worried, but my agent told me it was simply a hiccup. The next year it was eleven thousand, which was a shock, but again I paid up, and now this year, they want forty thousand. Well, I just haven't got it, Mr – Mr –'

'Richards,' said Alan.

'Mr Richards. I mean, I could sell my house, but then I'd have nowhere to live, and I've sold my car, but I only got just over a thousand for it. I could sell my mother's jewellery, which is very precious to me, but of course it's all antique and what I'd get is nothing like its true worth. I just don't know where to turn. And the gentleman I saw on that first day, from this office, he was so charming and helpful and I'm sure he'd know what to do.'

'What was his name?' asked Alan.

'Ferguson. Donald Ferguson.'

'I'm afraid he has left,' said Alan carefully. 'Retired.' Rather hurriedly and mysteriously, Alan just happened to know. Ferguson was now living in the South of France in a villa of considerable splendour.

'Oh dear. I was afraid of that. Well, someone else must be doing his job.'

'Indeed. And I shall certainly take your case up with him.'

'But – can't I see him now? I've come up from Hampshire, specially.'

'Didn't you make an appointment?'

'Well, no. But I had other appointments today, with Sinclairs as a matter of fact, and my lawyers, and when I telephoned your office late one day last week, someone said if I was coming anyway, I might do best to just drop in.'

Alan mentally cursed whoever that person had been – Jackie the telephonist, probably, wanting to get away quickly at the end of the day. He said how sorry he was.

'But I will look very carefully at your syndicates – I've got the numbers here – and make sure everything is in order. And then I'll write to you.'

'But – I need rather more than that,' said Gillian Thompson, the tears rising again. 'You don't seem to understand, I'm absolutely desperate. I haven't got forty thousand pounds and I can't possibly pay it, it's out of the question. I need some kind of advice or reassurance that I won't have to, otherwise I just don't know what I can do.'

'Well, the first thing to do is to make sure everything's in order,' said Alan, 'and I will see that your underwriters are fully informed about your case. And then I will write to you. Please try not to worry. Now can I get you a taxi or—'

Gillian Thompson suddenly became less pathetic. She stood up and faced him, the tears drying on her face.

'You haven't been listening to a word I've said, have you?' she said. 'I face absolute ruin. I'm a woman completely on my own, with no assets of any kind and no support, with a demand from Lloyd's for forty thousand pounds – and you suggest getting me a taxi. I could hardly afford my train fare up from the country. Good afternoon. I have found this conversation deeply insulting and totally unsatisfactory.'

And she stalked off, dumping her ruined umbrella in the waste-paper bin in the corner of Reception.

Alan found himself rather bothered by the vision of Gillian Thompson: by her rage even more than her weeping. She had seemed such a mild, sad little woman; her outburst had clearly been driven by absolute desperation. Looking up her biggest syndicate alone, Westfield Bradley, from the trend in asbestosis-related claims, it looked as if it might literally wipe her out, a dread phrase not heard at Lloyd's for over twenty years. What was she doing in such a syndicate at all? She had trusted them completely, and they had failed her equally completely. Surely they could have found some way to do a better job for her? She was not that profitable a client, and maybe a few years ago they could have suggested quietly to her that she start the three-year rundown and get out. Even the greediest fishermen know enough to throw the tiddlers back.

He tried to put it behind him, but when after three days he could still see her pale puckered little face streaked with tears and hear her quiet anxious voice suddenly rising into attack, he went to see his boss, reported Miss Thompson's visit, her distress and her complete inability to pay.

When he started to express his concern for her, and the duty the agency owed her, Norman Clarke interrupted him.

'Alan,' he said, 'everybody who comes to Lloyd's wants the same thing: risk-free investment – little old ladies included. And there is no such thing, as you and I both know. Lloyd's is above all a repository for dreams. Rather greedy dreams. Everyone's warned, it's incumbent upon us to do so, they know perfectly well what they're getting into. Don't worry about it. Certainly don't worry about Miss Thompson. She'll be all right, I'm sure. Remember, she must have shown at least seventy-five thousand to get in, she's hardly a penniless widow.'

'She's not a widow, Mr Clarke. I told you, she's unmarried, she has no family, no one to support her in any way, and—'

'All right, penniless spinster then. They often have neurotic fantasies, spinsters, you know.' He smiled at Alan, a dismissive, impatient smile. 'Now I suggest you get on with your work, and leave mine to me. All right?'

Alan's grandmother had had a saying about putting something in your back tooth and chewing on it for a bit. Hardly aware of it, Alan did exactly that.

Chapter 7

July, 1989

Lucinda had agreed to have lunch with him. Well, that was all right. They could talk things over, she could explain that really she couldn't go on seeing him, that it was wrong, and so unfair to Nigel, who most certainly didn't deserve it, and she could see now that she did love him, but that it had been lovely and she'd always remember Blue, and the wonderful time they'd had together. And then they could part friends instead of enemies; which was important. It was what she'd always hoped, from the very beginning – well, hope was the wrong word, planned might be better – anyway, that if she had to do this very, very naughty thing, and she wasn't exactly proud of herself for doing it, of course, then at the end of it she would go back to being a good wife, and Nigel would never have to know about it, and any unhappiness she might feel would absolutely serve her right.

So – that's what she'd done; met him for lunch.

And been really firm about it not being any more than that . . .

'I really, really will tell him tonight. I promise. Blue, don't do that, please. I can't concentrate on what I'm saying, it's important.'

'Sorry. It's just that you do have such incredibly beautiful breasts. Would that be breeding, do you reckon? Are they posh breasts?'

'I don't know. I really don't know. Anyway—'

'You could get on page three, you know. No problem at all.'

'Page three of what?'

'Lucy! I sometimes despair of you. You don't live in the real

100

world at all, do you? Page three of what?! The *Sun*, girl, the *Sun* newspaper.'

'Oh Blue! That's so awful. It's really disgusting, the way they do that—'

'Why? Giving innocent pleasure to millions, what's wrong with that?'

'But it's not innocent, is it?'

'Isn't it? Why not?'

'Well – it exploits women, that's why not.'

There was a silence, then, 'You never cease to surprise me,' he said, bending to kiss the objects under discussion. 'You're much cleverer than I thought, first time I met you.'

'I know,' said Lucinda with a sigh. 'I mean, people are always saying things like that, that I'm not such a dumb blonde as they thought. I think that's how Nigel sees me though. He really doesn't think I've got a brain at all.'

'Which is one of the reasons you're leaving him for someone who appreciates you. All of you. Now, you going to come straight to me tonight, or what? After you've told him?'

'Oh Blue, I suppose so. I'm so scared.'

'Want me to come with you?'

'No, of course not. I'm not scared in that way. He won't do anything to me. I'm scared of what it'll do to him, that's all – how upset he'll be.'

'Well, I expect he will be upset. And it's a measure of what a lovely person you are that it's worrying you so much. But he'll get over it, sweetheart. He really will.'

'You said you never would. Get over me.'

'Yeah, I know that. And I wouldn't. But that's because you love me, which makes me love you even more, which makes you love me more and so on; it's what you might call exponential growth.'

'What's that?' asked Lucinda, genuinely intrigued.

'It means the growth curve is disproportionately steep. It's like two reproduces itself to four and then four to sixteen and so on. Basic law of mathematics, I think.'

'You're really clever, aren't you?' she said, looking at him curiously.

'Not really, no. Got a good memory, that makes up for a lot. Now then, come on, what about tonight, what you going to do?

I could come, park round the corner, wait for you. How'd that be?'

She considered this. 'Yes. That might be good. I'll – I'll tell him, and then just – leave. I couldn't stay anyway, not once he knows, and he won't want me to. I mean, however upset he is, he'll want me to leave. Once he's convinced, that is. Oh poor, poor Nigel. God, I feel so bad.'

'Did you feel that bad about me?' he asked. 'When you left me?'

'Of course not,' she said. 'You told me to get out, don't forget, and it never occurred to me that you'd be miserable. And then I was so unhappy for me, there wasn't room for even thinking about anyone else.'

'Is that right?' he said, and his face was very tender suddenly. 'Did you feel that bad?'

'I felt that bad. I remember kneeling in the church at Merlin's christening and thinking, I just can't bear this, it's too awful, and—'

'Who's Merlin?'

'Sarah Cope-Brown's baby. She's one of my best friends. I'm his godmother, and—'

'Sometimes, Lucinda,' said Blue, and his face was absolutely serious, 'sometimes I do wonder if you realise quite how different your life is going to be.'

'I think I do,' she said, and gave him a kiss. 'And even if I don't like all of it, it'll be worth it because I'll be with you.'

'Oh fuck,' he said, and flung himself back on the pillows, staring up at the ceiling, and she realised he had tears in his eyes. 'You shouldn't say things like that, I can't cope with it. I don't deserve you, and that's all there is to it.'

'Nor does Nigel,' she said very earnestly. 'He doesn't deserve anyone so awful. Now look, I must go now, but I'll see you tonight. Keep thinking of me, Blue, won't you? It's going to be so hard.'

'Course,' he said, 'and I'll be waiting. I'll be parked in the Square.'

'Oh, all right. Do you know where it is?'

'Of course I know where it is. I've sat there for bloody hours, thinking about you and wondering which was your house and what you was doing.'

102

'You didn't, did you?'

'Course I did.'

'Now you've made me cry,' she said. 'I love you, Blue.'

'That's all right then,' he said.

Quite often these days, Annabel found herself thinking about Dan and marvelling that she could have ever liked him so much. Or indeed a lot of her old friends. The new world she was in now seemed to suit her much better, inhabited as it was by people who had genuine ambitions – to make money, sure, not merely to enjoy life but to carve out a way for themselves; they didn't mind how hard they worked, and for how long, provided it was taking them in their chosen direction. In this they reminded her of her mother.

And they were all so funny, so irreverent, and so extremely cool. Her favourite among the stylists was a beautiful boy called Florian; he was tall and very thin, with a cap of golden-tipped brown curly hair, huge blue eyes and an extremely full, girly mouth; he wore rather loose clothes, wide black trousers and floppy white shirts and a lot of rings. He had been at the salon for three years and was one of the top three stylists. Annabel assumed he must be gay, and formed a wonderfully chatty, gossipy relationship with him; she was outraged when Carol told her he was a 'fantastic stud, girls lined up from here to Fulham where he lives'.

'I don't believe you,' Annabel said. 'How do you know?'

Carol shrugged. 'Ask one of the other boys.'

Annabel didn't want to do that, she felt it would mark her out as naive and silly; but she found him one morning in the staff room, his head in his hands.

'Whatever's the matter?' she asked, genuinely sympathetic.

'Oh God, Bel, I've got such a hangover,' he said, 'combination of red wine and other naughty stuff, never mix it darling, very silly.'

She had rushed out to the pharmacy in Sloane Street for him and bought him some Revive and fed him with that and orange juice all morning. 'You're sweet,' he said, 'so sweet. Let me buy you a drink this evening, say thank you.'

Which he had; after an hour or so, she had felt one of his long legs pressed unmistakably against hers, and shortly after that, his hand eased her face round to his and he kissed her.

'You are utterly lovely,' he said, releasing her, 'and I totally adore you.' Shaken more with surprise than anything, she had smiled feebly at him. 'I bet you thought I was gay,' he said, smiling back.

'Of – of course I didn't,' she said.

'Of course you did. Everyone does. Well I'm not, sweetie, not in the very least. I don't even swing both ways, which is the other erroneous theory about me. My wrists are as firm as my cock is right this minute. Promise. Where would you like to go next?'

A strong instinct for self-preservation told Annabel to have an important dinner at home with her parents. It was the one thing she felt confident he wouldn't want to gatecrash; and she was right, which was a huge relief. She wasn't sure that she should get involved with him, much as she liked the idea. It was certainly too soon in her career at Miki Wallace. She was the most junior member of staff, teetering on the edge of unpopularity and ridicule because of her background; it wasn't going to endear her to the rest of the staff, and especially people like Tania, if she started going around with one of the senior stylists. And they would certainly all get to hear about it; Florian's best friend couldn't call him discreet.

She found herself half-wishing, rather sadly on the way home, that he was actually gay. It had been less complicated that way. And then fell to wondering how her parents would react if they knew she was having a relationship with a hairdresser. It was almost worth risking, just to be able to tell them.

This was what made her so angry, Elizabeth thought, still did; and why did he have to do it, under her nose, when he knew it upset her so much? She watched him standing in the centre of the room, listening to some woman, she had no idea who she was, listening very carefully, smiling then laughing, and then, God, here was another, coming over, interrupting, joining the two of them, reaching up to kiss Simon briefly. And he returned the kiss, said something in her ear, clearly some small shared intimacy, and then introduced them to one another, took a glass from a passing tray to hand to the newcomer, and then, then worse than all of it, pulled out his wallet, took one

104

of his cards out, gave it to the first woman who studied it, smiled up at him, said something, and then tucked it into her bag . . .

At moments like this, Elizabeth's success, her power, her much-acknowledged brilliance meant nothing to her whatsoever; it was simply a wife who stood there, an anxious, jealous, fearful wife, unable to concentrate on what anyone else might be saying to her, watching her husband operate in his acutely polished way . . .

'He's such a charmer, your husband, isn't he?' said their hostess, a new neighbour from The Boltons whom Elizabeth hardly knew, and turning to look at her, seeing that she was pretty too, pretty and young and beautifully dressed, and therefore yet another source of danger, further prey for Simon, suddenly she couldn't bear it any longer, thought that she might go over to the small group and throw her glass of champagne in Simon's face, just to take the smile off it, and she did indeed go over, but only to say, 'Simon, darling, I'm sorry to break up the party, but we really do have to go.'

And he was immediately responsive, saying yes, of course, and he kissed the first woman, the one he had given his card to, and followed her over to their hostess so that they could say goodbye, and he kissed her too, waved briefly at her husband and then they were out of the door and it was over.

'What was that about?' he said, clearly genuinely baffled as they walked away.

'I think I might ask you the same thing,' she said. 'What was *that* about? Who was that woman, why did you give her your card?'

'She was a very nice girl,' he said, 'an American who's come to live here with her husband. He's looking for a tennis partner, apparently, and I said I might just be able to fill that brief.'

'And you expect me to believe that?'

'Oh Elizabeth,' he said wearily, shaking his head. 'Please, please don't do this.'

'Do what?'

'You know very well what. Pursue me with that insane jealousy of yours. It's so destructive—'

'Insane! You call it insane, Simon? Given what happened, what you did . . .'

They had reached their own house now; he unlocked the door, ushered her in.

'Elizabeth, this just isn't helping,' he said.

'Helping what?'

'Our relationship, of course.'

'We still have one, do we?' she said, stalking into the kitchen, reaching into the fridge for a bottle of water. 'I hadn't realised.'

'Oh, for Christ's sake. Of course we do. Well, we could if you would give it only half a chance. You've got to learn to trust me again. I know it's difficult, I know I was a bastard, but it was over a year ago – more. I promised you and I've kept my promise.'

She was silent, fiddling with the top of the bottle.

'Please, Elizabeth. Otherwise there's no point our being together. I might as well clear out.'

'And go back to her, do you mean?'

'No, of course not.'

'Well . . .' She paused, then, 'It's so easy for you, Simon. Saying these things now. Telling me it's firmly in the past, when you'd been lying to me for years.'

'Not years.'

'Years, Simon. You just don't know how much it hurt.'

'I – I don't suppose I do,' he said.

'You can't just expect someone to start believing you, when you've been lying to them for a long time.'

'No, I suppose not.'

'I mean, every time I hear you saying a woman's name, I wonder.'

'Look,' he said, pouring himself a glass of wine, 'I made an appalling mistake. I'm terribly sorry. But I can't wipe it out. It's there. And really it's up to you now. To try and make it work.'

'Yes, I know,' she said very quietly.

'We can survive – I know we can. Other marriages do.'

'Simon, you're doing it again, talking as if it was just a fling. It wasn't.'

'Oh, for fuck's sake,' he said. 'I'm tired, I've got some work to do. Look, we've been over this a hundred times. I'm a bastard, I did you terribly wrong. But I've been eating humble pie for a long time now and the taste's pretty ghastly. I can't do more. Good night. I'll see you in the morning.'

106

She sat there, staring at the closed door, too angry, too proud to meet him halfway.

It was quite true, what he had said: there was nothing more he could do. It was up to her now. Otherwise there was no point staying. Staying in this chill, comfortless place where she took two steps towards him and then at least one back.

She had to start trusting him – somehow. Or at least mistrusting him less. It couldn't be impossible. It was just that – well, as she said, it hadn't been just a fling. That would have been bearable. But it hadn't . . .

She had found out in the age-old way; he had told her he was somewhere one night, one of the children had been taken ill, she had phoned the hotel where he was supposed to be at a conference, and they had said, clearly embarrassed, that he wasn't there, had never been there.

Confronted, he had confessed: said he was sorry. She had said it must end, at once. He said that was impossible, he couldn't give her up.

'Then get out,' she said. 'Get out, now. Tonight.'

He had, for a while, not to live with the other woman but to bide his time, try to decide what to do. Elizabeth refused to learn her name even, didn't want to know who she was – 'even if she's a friend of ours'.

'She's not,' he said.

She said she'd never take him back, but she did. They talked and talked; he said he couldn't after all walk out on his family, his beloved family, that if she would take him back he would like to come.

She said she would: and expecting to feel better, she felt worse. Jealousy tore at her; what did she have, this woman, that she, his wife, had not? What had she given him?

'Time,' he had said. 'Time and attention.'

'Simon, that is grotesquely unfair. Our whole relationship has been built on both of us working, both of us having careers, big ambitions. We agreed, right from the beginning, we'd shape our lives and our families around that.'

'Yes, I know. And yet, Elizabeth, when you really need me, I manage to be there for you. Somehow I don't feel you do that for me. I quite often feel completely abandoned. I long to talk to you, to consult you, just to be with you, and quite often you simply are never there. And I don't mean just physically. How often have I sat talking to you, trying to discuss something important with you, and felt you were actually at the next presentation, the last sales conference.'

Clear-sighted about herself, she recognised this. Her work, her career consumed her; but how could she change that, something so central to her? And then she felt ashamed, that she was prioritising her career above her marriage, above Simon whom she did – astonishingly – still love. She promised to try to spend more time at home and with him, but it was difficult; her job was not one that could be fitted into prescribed hours. But she did struggle to be more attentive, to consider his needs, to do more to please him. It seemed to have been in vain.

She sighed, picked up her glass and the bottle of water and walked up the stairs and into her own study. Where she had work to do and where for a while, she would feel in command and control once more. For a while . . .

Nigel had got home early, so that Lucinda couldn't possibly beat him to it. He had some champagne on ice, and some strawberries to dip into it, and he'd booked a table at San Frediano for later in the evening. It was going to be so special and she was going to be so pleased, and relieved too: he was sure she'd been worrying quietly about Lloyd's, that it had contributed to her stress. And then he wanted to tell her about his other decision; that would make her happy too. He knew she felt it was time, time he got himself checked out babywise, as she put it (although she hadn't said anything about it lately); he didn't exactly want to, and he knew there were all sorts of unspeakable trials to be gone through, but he was prepared to do it for her – and so that they could become a family, of course. She— there was the door now.

She came in looking rather strained; she kissed him briefly, put down her bag and then said, 'Nigel, could I possibly have a drink?'

This was unlike her; he really hadn't wanted to open the champagne until he'd told her what he'd done, and it was

Bollinger Premier Cru; it needed to be appreciated, not drunk as a sort of tranquilliser. He went over to the fridge and got out the bottle of Sancerre they'd started on last night.

'This all right?'

'Yes, fine. Thank you.' She took an enormous gulp, then as if she'd only just noticed, said, 'You're very early.'

'Yes,' he said, 'I know. I wanted to talk to you about something.'

'Oh yes? Me too. I mean, I wanted to talk to you. Nigel, you have a drink too.'

'I will in a minute, darling. Actually I've got something a bit special for us. In the fridge. Some Bolly.'

'Oh Nigel, how lovely. But—'

'It's to go with what I've got to tell you. To celebrate it.'

'Oh.' She didn't look quite as he might have hoped, she didn't have her sweet, excited expression on. She looked almost frightened.

'Nigel, I think I'd better go first. If you don't mind.'

'Poor darling. You're really in a bit of a state, aren't you? It's that wretched job. You've been working much too hard. Well, I think – if you want to – you can give it up.'

She stared at him. 'Give it up? But – why should I? And I thought you said we needed my income. In case Lloyd's got worse.'

'Well, darling, I've got that all sorted. It's not going to be nearly such a problem now.'

'What? Really?'

'Really.'

'Oh Nigel, that's wonderful news. I'm so glad. So you're feeling much better? Much happier?'

'Much.'

'Right. Well,' she looked at him rather nervously, 'well then, my news. Nigel, I—'

'Lucinda, let me finish. I've hardly begun.'

'But—'

'Please, darling. Please.'

She sat down, her eyes fixed on his face. 'Go on, then.'

'Right. You are, from this moment – well, from this morning anyway – a much richer woman.'

'Nigel, what are you talking about?'

109

'I've transferred all my assets to you. Well, everything I could. Into a trust fund for you. The contents of our deposit account, a few hundred thou, I've sold most of my shares and put that money in too; and the deeds of this house, and the deeds of the farm; they'll all be in your name too, once it's been legally cleared. So, you'd better not leave me, darling, all right?'

She looked a bit odd then. 'But – but Nigel, why? I don't understand.'

'It's quite simple really. If all one's assets are held by the person in the family who isn't the Name, I'm not explaining this very well, they can't claim them. Apparently. So – we're safe. Isn't that wonderful?'

'Well, yes.' She was very white. 'Is it really so bad, Nigel?'

'Pretty bad. I talked to a couple of people who were getting out, and . . .'

'But why can't you do that as well?'

'Darling, it's not as easy as that. In the first place, liability is unlimited – literally. It can go on when you're food for worms. And anyway, as I've told you before, the accounting is three years in arrears. So even if I resigned tomorrow, and I am trying very hard to do that, I'd still be liable for another three years' underwriting. At very best.'

'So – how bad is it?'

'Well, it isn't any more. But it could have been. I could literally have lost everything. I'm in pretty deep, I'm afraid. I've underwritten about a million, and frankly I'd be hardpressed to put my hands on half of that. And they'd want twice that. That's how it works. I – we – really would have been bankrupted. As it is, they can take all I've got, which is very little really, and you can look after the rest.'

'But – but are you sure it's this simple?'

'Seems to be. Someone suggested it to me – dear old Chris Paige, remember Chris?'

Lucinda did; he was a sweet, rather jolly friend of Nigel's, about ten years older than he was, who worked, like Nigel, in his family business. She wouldn't have taken any financial advice from him more complex than not keeping money under the bed.

'Yes, well, he's doing it, seemed a brilliant idea to me.'

110

'And what about legally? Is it all right?'

'Well,' he said, looking slightly less confident, 'it might be necessary if it went to court, which it wouldn't, for you to say you had no idea I'd done this. But as you didn't – that's fine. It's true. So as I say, you'd better not leave me.'

'And – if I don't want it?'

'Darling, why on earth should you not want it? I promise it won't make any difference, day to day. It'll just be – yours. And please do want it, because otherwise I'm up the creek without a canoe. Honestly, Lucinda, it's the perfect solution. Now before I get the champagne out, I want to tell you something else. Something on the baby front. I think I've been rather selfish and . . .'

Blue had been waiting for about half an hour when Lucinda came out of the house. She walked very slowly over to the car and got in. She seemed very calm, very composed; she turned her head to look at him.

'Hello.'

'Hello, lovely. All right?'

'I – suppose so,' she said.

'He took it well, then?'

'I . . . Blue, I'm sorry, I'm so sorry, but I can't do it. I can't come. He's – well, he's sort of trumped us. Without meaning to, obviously.'

'What the fuck are you talking about, Lucinda?'

She sat there, ice calm, being very, very careful not to touch him, and told him.

In his modest flat in the less smart area of Putney, George Meyer was patiently addressing envelopes. The envelopes which were to contain a letter from him to everyone appearing on his list of clients of the Jackson & Bond Members' Agency. It was a long job, but George Meyer had time on his side, a lot of empty evenings, and he was hopeful that the time was being well spent.

The letter took the form of an invitation to a meeting at the Grenville Club, Pall Mall; and was, George hoped, sufficiently intriguing and attractive to ensure a high acceptance rate.

Chapter 8

August to September, 1989

'Good Lord,' said Simon. 'Have a look at this. Very interesting.' He handed Elizabeth a letter; she was reading in bed, a book for once rather than a report. They were spending a week in London, worn out by the grind of commuting in the hottest summer of the decade, leaving Tilly and Toby at Chadwick House in the care of Mrs Ford.

She reached out, took the letter, read it, then said, 'Goodness. That is quite – interesting. I agree. He sounds eminently sensible.'

'More than that, I'd say. Impressive even. He's obviously done his homework. Do you think I should go?'

'Oh definitely, yes.'

'Would you come with me?'

'Simon, I—' and then she stopped. She should go. It would be a supportive thing to do. The sort of thing that might help. And it was only one evening, after all.

'Yes,' she said, 'yes, I will. I'd like to.'

'Thank you. And I promise to stay by your side all evening and not even speak to anyone who isn't wearing a three-piece suit and stout shoes.'

She managed to smile, picked up the letter and read it again.

Dear Simon Beaumont,

*As a Lloyd's Name, a client of Members' Agent Jackson &
Bond and a major participant in the Westfield Bradley
Group of Syndicates, I have become increasingly
unhappy with what I am sure many of us regard as a
deplorable state of affairs. I have been looking into the*

112

situation in some depth and I have come to three very disturbing conclusions.

The heavy losses we have all experienced recently are almost certain to get worse rather than better over the next few years.

Many of us may well be bearing a disproportionate share of these losses. I have heard it estimated (though I cannot vouch for the figures) that 70 per cent of the losses are being borne by only 30 per cent of the Members!

I fear the possibility cannot at this stage be eliminated that as a result of (at best) bad management, there have been some serious irregularities in the way our affairs have been handled. More than this I am reluctant to commit to paper at this point, but I am inviting a number of people in a similar situation to get together for an informal exchange of views and ideas, and I would be delighted if you would join us in the Large Meeting Room at the Grenville Club, Pall Mall, on Friday 9 September at 6 p.m.

Yours sincerely,
George Meyer

Nigel was very intrigued by the letter. He showed it to Lucinda.

'Interesting, darling, wouldn't you say? Of course, I don't think we have much of a problem any more, but it would still be a good idea to go, I think. We'd meet some people in the same boat, have an exchange of views and ideas, as he says. I don't know any other Names at the Westfield Bradley Group and I'd like to. That'd be my main reason for going.'

'Can I go too?'

'You? Lucinda, why on earth would you want to go? You're not a Name, I don't think you understand it very well and—'

'Nigel, I understand it perfectly well, thank you,' she said, stung, remembering sharply the conversation with Blue about Lloyd's. 'I know there are big problems with claims over—' She stopped.

'Over what?' he said. He looked almost shocked, as if she had shown a knowledge of sex shops or smoking pot.

'Oh, I've read quite a lot about it recently, as a matter of fact.' Careful, he'd be wondering how she knew so much about it. 'Something about asbestos – is that right?'

'In a way, yes. Asbestosis is what you're probably thinking of. Well, you can come if you want to, but I think you'll be very bored.'

'I'm sure I won't.'

It was getting better. She knew it was getting better. Of course, the agony had been horribly prolonged by the re-encounter with Blue, and her decision then to leave Nigel and go and live with him; it was as if the skin had begun to grow over the gaping wound that was centred somewhere where she supposed her heart to be, and now it had been flayed off again. But – well, that had been three, no nearly four weeks ago – and gradually, day by day, she could feel herself recovering. It was a pretty feeble recovery; she still had dreadful, or rather wonderful dreams where she was with Blue and woke up smiling to the wretched reality, she still saw him on every street corner, she still half-expected to hear his voice every time the phone rang, and she was very far from feeling emotionally well. But at least she didn't want to die any more. And Nigel had been utterly sweet, of course, and so happy, released from his own dreadful anxiety. He kept telling her she looked washed out – which she certainly did, and felt it too – and suggesting they took a little holiday.

'Just a few days, darling, in the sun somewhere. Greece is lovely in the autumn, or maybe Italy, put a bit of colour in your cheeks – think of it as a second honeymoon. Of course if you don't want to take me, spend the money on me . . .'

This was his favourite joke at the moment and it made her want to scream: that she was the financially dominant partner in their relationship and he the poor dependant. 'I'm a kept man,' he told everyone. 'Sort of a toyboy, if you like. Rather an elderly one, of course, but still . . .'

Lucinda still found it hard to be alone with him anywhere at all, let alone on holiday, with time to think about Blue; her only salvation lay in surrounding herself and Nigel with their friends and keeping terribly busy. She entertained feverishly, one dinner party and one kitchen supper every week, in spite of feeling dreadfully tired and not actually very well; she had bought what

114

seemed to be miles of material to make curtains (not only for their bedroom – the torture chamber as she thought of it) but the drawing room and the dining room as well.

The other thing she had done was take on some extra work, reading some manuscripts for Graham. She'd made this offer before, and it had always been refused; she hadn't been considered experienced enough to make even a preliminary judgement on submitted manuscripts. But this time he'd smiled at her and said yes, that would be great, and asked her to do a short report on each of them; she had felt pleased and excited and as near to happy as she had been since she had said goodbye to Blue that night. Maybe she was a careerwoman at heart, after all . . .

It had been so terrible, that parting; she still couldn't think about it without her eyes filling with tears. He hadn't argued much. He told her she could give the money back again, but she wasn't at all sure that she could, from what Nigel had said, and anyway, if that was the way for Nigel to avoid bankruptcy, then clearly she shouldn't. It would be a double whammy, as Blue had said, if she exposed him to it again.

'But there are other things he could do, sweetheart. Like putting some offshore, or—'

'Yes, but Blue, he hasn't, has he? He's done this. Because he trusts me. If ever there was a total expression of trust, this is it. I can't do it to him, darling darling Blue, I just can't. I'm sorry.'

And she had got out of the car, without even kissing him and run, run as fast as she could, to the door of the house; the last thing she saw of him was the Ferrari, the absurd flashy thing that she had once accused him of loving more than her – 'If only you knew,' he had said, very serious suddenly, 'how horribly wrong you were, you wouldn't even think of joking about such a thing, Lucinda' – anyway, that was the vision that had stayed with her, of seeing it disappear very slowly round the corner, taking him away from her for the rest of her life.

The other thing Nigel had done for her, and she knew what an ordeal it must have been for him, was to have a sperm test. He had gone off to the fertility clinic alone – he'd said he preferred

115

it that way – and come back rather quiet and said that it'd been fine but that he didn't want to talk about it. 'They'll let me know in a week or so. Can't think why it takes so long. Suppose they want to be sure. Too jolly important to make a mistake.'

Lucinda hoped desperately that the news would be good. More than anything now she longed for a baby; a baby would make sense of life again, help to mend her heart, recreate her marriage. And help ease the misery of the torture chamber . . .

Flora Fielding was quite excited by the letter from George Meyer. It was completely against her nature to accept misfortune without a great deal of questioning, and so far the only questioning she had been able to do had been contained in a few, extremely unsatisfactory conversations with her Members' Agent. Here, perhaps, was a chance to discuss things with other beleaguered people, and even find a way to fight back, rather than just lie down and accept whatever it was Lloyd's wanted her to do. Starve, quite possibly, she thought; although she knew that actually they wouldn't like that, adverse publicity being the last thing they desired. At worst, the meeting would be a way of establishing contact with other Names in the syndicate, of pooling knowledge and experience. But, like Simon Beaumont, she sensed that George Meyer had more in mind than an evening of waffle. She rang Richard.

'I wondered if I could stay with you next Wednesday?'

'Of course you can, Mother, you know you're always very welcome. The children will be thrilled. And Debbie, of course,' he added hastily.

'Thank you. I'm going to a meeting in the evening, in Central London.'

'What sort of meeting?'

'Well, it's rather exciting. It's a meeting of Names in Westfield Bradley, my major syndicate at Lloyds. I had a letter from someone called George Meyer, who sounds very interesting. I was very impressed by his letter anyway.'

'Well, it'll be lovely to see you,' said Richard, smiling down the phone. 'Will you come here first?'

'Oh, I don't think so, darling, no. I've got a meeting with

a gallery in Mumbles, they're talking about giving me an exhibition, and that's not till midday. No, I'll go straight to the meeting. And I'll leave quite early in the morning too; there's a talk at the Gower Society in the early afternoon, which I don't want to miss.'

'Fine. I'll tell Debs. Oh, and Mother . . .' His voice was slightly anxious suddenly.

'Sorry, Richard, I have to go, the blacksmith's just arrived.'

He put down the phone, thinking how grateful he was, they should be, that Flora led such a dynamic life, and thought that he must ring her again as soon as possible, and certainly before the next Wednesday.

Debbie said carefully that it would be lovely to see Flora and then added: 'But I don't quite see why she wants to go to a meeting with lots of other Lloyd's people when things are better for her. It seems like a waste of time to me.'

'Well, they're very complex, these syndicates,' Richard said, and had she not been sorting out whites from coloureds and wondering how it was that Rachel and Emma's white ballet socks always looked slightly dingy when those of all the other little girls were in a state of dazzling Persil whiteness, she would have noticed that he flushed suddenly, then started busying himself with folding up the papers.

'No two Names have quite the same underwriting, you see,' he said, 'and you know what Mother's like, always ready to go up to the wire and beyond.'

'Yes, I suppose so. Well, it's fine anyway.'

And all might yet have been well, had Flora not phoned again the very next day and before he had been able to have the conversation – which was clearly going to be difficult – with Debbie. She had answered the phone, and Flora had said that she wondered if Richard might be free to come to the meeting with her: 'And you too, of course, darling, if it would interest you. See what we're all up against. I could certainly do with Richard's support and advice, and get his reaction to what's been said. The man who's called the meeting definitely sounds as if he means business.'

'Well, I'm sure he'll come if he can,' Debbie said. 'He's very immersed in timetable-ing at the moment, but there's nothing on that evening, as far as I know. I'll get him to ring you.'

'Thank you, Debbie.'

And then, as the proper weight of Flora's words worked into Debbie's brain, and a dreadful, wormlike suspicion began to form, she asked the question. The question – and its answer – which, as she saw it, altered her life for ever.

'What I don't understand though, Flora, is why you're going to this meeting, and why you need Richard's support, when everything's so much better.'

There was a silence; then Flora said, 'But Debbie, it isn't so much better. I don't quite understand why you should think it was. It's worse – much worse.'

'You lied to me. Don't try to deny it, you did. I can't believe you could have done anything so awful. God, you're disgusting. The pair of you.'

'It's got nothing to do with my mother.'

'I'm sorry, but I find that very hard to believe. Don't speak to me, don't come near me. I'm going out now, to try and think what to do. You can stay here and look after the children. And maybe you'd like to sort out some more things you're going to tell me. Only don't expect me to believe anything either of you ever says again.'

'Debbie, I swear to you, Mother had no idea what I'd told you. And I'd meant to tell you—'

'Tell me what? Some more lies. I don't know that I can stay married to someone who's done something so disgusting. I need to think. And you might as well start writing letters to those schools now, tell them the children are leaving. They're not getting any more of our money than I can help.'

Richard stared after her as she stalked away from the house; it was beginning to rain and she only had a T-shirt on. Maybe that would bring her back. But it wouldn't. He knew her better than that. She'd walk all day, get soaked to the skin, before she'd give in. And she was terribly angry. And hurt. He knew that was actually her greater emotion – hurt. Trust was a huge thing for Debbie. Naturally prickly and wary, her confidence was not easily won. As for what it would do to relations between her and his mother . . .

*

Debbie was crying so hard, she didn't notice the rain for quite a long time. She walked for miles along the Uxbridge Road and then down Gunnersbury Avenue, and into Gunnersbury Park, careless that she was soaked through, that people were looking at her curiously, then past the Boating Lake and across to the Potomac Fish Pond where she and the children and indeed Richard had spent many happy hours. There she sat on a bench, staring into the water, blinded by her tears as much as the rain. How could he have done that, deceived her like that? They were supposed to trust each other, completely; that was what marriage was about. She wanted to blame Flora, and she did – a bit; she hadn't quite believed Richard when he said she had no idea, but Richard was thirty-five, for God's sake, he ought to know right from wrong by now. Know what a lie was and what it meant. She felt their relationship had been shaken to its very heart: a quake off the Richter scale. She would never trust him again: never. It was just as bad as if she had discovered he was having an affair – worse, in fact. This wasn't just about the two of them, it was about their family. Him deciding what was best for the children and then lying about it, in case she didn't agree.

'I hate you!' she shouted into the wet grey skies. 'I hate you so much!' And in spite of the fact that she was very cold now, she stayed on her bench and buried her head in her arms and wept.

She reached home again well into the afternoon, cold and soaked to the skin; she stalked upstairs, ran herself a bath and locked the door. The children, who had watched her come in in silence, didn't follow her, but Richard did, and started first knocking tentatively, then banging on the door.

'Debs, let me in. Please.'

'No. Go away. Leave me alone.'

'I'm not going anywhere. I have to explain.'

'There's nothing to explain. Just – just leave me alone.'

Finally she came out, walked into their bedroom; he was there, looking pale and wretched.

'Oh, just go away,' she said. 'I told you to leave me alone.'

'Debbie, please—' He put his hand on her arm.

'Stop it. I don't like being lied to and I don't want to talk about it now.'

119

'Oh, for God's sake,' he said, 'you're overreacting. I haven't committed a crime, for God's sake, I haven't been unfaithful to you, I just wanted to spare you any anxiety, and the children any distress, for that matter. It would have been dreadful for them to have to change schools now, they're doing so well, and you'd have hated seeing them disrupted and upset. And I know I can do the fees another year at least. I'll get a new job and—'

'Oh, do shut up,' Debbie said, 'and as far as I'm concerned, I think I'd almost rather you had been unfaithful to me. At least that's an uncomplicated situation. Anyway, I have decided one thing: I'm going to come to that meeting with you, hear it all for myself, find out exactly what is going on. I wouldn't trust a word you told me about it. Or your mother, come to that. Now just piss off, why don't you, and take the children to the cinema or something.'

Richard did as he was told.

Very few of the Names who were to attend George Meyer's meeting at the Grenville Club slept particularly soundly the night before.

George Meyer himself was very anxious; he had staked a great deal on this, invested a huge amount of time, some money – only a few hundred, but that he could ill afford – and he was nervous as well about people's reactions to what he had to say, and that he would end up back where he started. It had given him a purpose in life for a few months, as he researched his original idea, took legal advice, and then went about writing the letters, arranging a venue – he was even anxious about that, whether it would be as suitable as he had first thought – and composing his speech. It would be very sad if it all came to nothing for lack of interest.

He was hopeful, however, that it would not.

The uptake on his invitation had been encouraging: a very large number of the Names approached had accepted. Among them surely he would find not only recruits to his cause, but other prime movers, associates with areas of expertise other than his own, who could help him progress the whole thing. What was that quote from *Henry V* before the Battle of Agincourt? Oh, yes: '*stiffen the sinews, summon up the blood'*. It was hard to do much sinew stiffening on your own. Time for some companionship and some support.

A former Marketing Director of a medium-sized company operating from Greater Manchester, Meyer had been a casualty of first the recession – 'terribly sorry, George, we're going to have to let you go' – and then of Lloyd's, and he was still reeling at the change in his circumstances from being well-heeled and successful, living in a large house in Cheshire with a rather glamorous wife and three children, to hard up and a failure, living in a small flat in Putney without his wife, who had left him. For most of which he blamed Lloyd's.

Simon Beaumont was very hopeful; apart from a natural attraction to new ideas, new causes, he could see that, without some plan such as George Meyer might be offering, he faced a future of increasing unpleasantness. One that he had no real means of fighting.

Elizabeth was rather less hopeful; she was acutely realistic, and she couldn't imagine what a few individuals could possibly do, pitted against the might of Lloyd's. But she was touched by Simon's excitement, she saw him more hopeful and positive about the situation than he had been for some time, and she was anxious to be supportive. Things had improved between them recently, since she had promised Simon to try to be less clinging – how absurd, she thought, that a woman in her professional position should be clinging – and her accompanying him to the meeting clearly meant a lot to him. It would be boring and almost certainly a waste of time – but it was only one evening. She rather hoped.

Nigel was trying not to pin too many hopes on the meeting. He wasn't feeling quite as bullish about his situation with Lloyd's as he had been. And he felt unable to talk to Lucinda about it. He didn't want to worry her, she was rather tense herself at the moment; he had a feeling it was this baby business. She had got very thin and was certainly not eating enough; and she was working so hard which couldn't possibly help her to get pregnant. He had tried several times to suggest she gave up work, but she had got quite cross and said what on earth would she do, sitting around at home all day, with nothing to do, watching the calendar.

He had been so excited about his plan, the transfer of his assets to her, that he had effected as much as he could simply by instructing his bank manager. But his solicitor, who had had to be involved in the transfer of the properties to Lucinda, had been most unhappy about it.

'The transfer of assets in the full knowledge of outstanding debts could well be deemed illegal, Nigel. I would advise very strongly against it. How far are you along this road?'

Nigel said that he had only transferred the contents of his bank account and his share portfolio to Lucinda.

'I should leave it at that, if I were you. A lot of people are getting into trouble over this. And Lloyd's aren't fools, they'll prosecute. Even money put offshore isn't safe. I really think you're on very dangerous ground, Nigel. You'd be committing perjury if you denied your knowledge of the situation a year or so down the road.'

And so he had left it at that. And fallen prey once again to the dreadful anxiety that gnawed away at him in the middle of the night, his stomach churning, his head throbbing. It would be wonderful to meet and talk to other people in his situation.

Lucinda was quite looking forward to it; anything that served as a distraction was welcome at the moment. Anything that saved her from sitting alone at home with Nigel.

Flora was also looking forward to it very much, but was acutely anxious about Debbie's emotional state and how it would affect their relationship. She felt furious with Richard; not just that he had told a stupid lie to Debbie, but failed to think it through properly, how much it involved her and indeed, to warn her about it. She felt pleased in a way that Debbie was coming to the meeting: although hardly in a state of mind to be properly supportive, she might understand more clearly what they all were up against. And it would be awfully good to meet some other people in her situation; Flora had been feeling increasingly overwhelmed lately.

*

Richard was simply terrified of one thing: of Debbie making another scene. Which seemed to him altogether possible since, after well over a week, she was still hardly speaking to him.

And Debbie, quietly furious, with absolutely no intention of making a scene, was simply determined to find out the truth: and how bad for everyone the whole business threatened to be. And almost more importantly, for how long.

Chapter 9

September, 1989

'Do you mind if I sit here?'

'Of course not. My son and daughter-in-law are coming shortly, but they can sit here on my other side.'

'Thank you. And I have to keep a seat for my wife. She's working late.'

Flora smiled at the young man as he settled in the chair beside her, well, he was fairly young, young men were getting older these days. He was in his late thirties, early forties maybe, very well dressed, with a public-school accent: he seemed charming. A good person to have as an ally in adversity. William had always said that was one of the best things about Lloyd's – you knew you were with the right sort.

'Nigel Cowper,' the young man said, holding out his hand.

'Flora Fielding.'

'And – where do you live, Mrs Fielding?'

'I live in Wales.' She smiled at him. 'And call me Flora, please. Mrs Fielding makes me feel old. Which I am, of course.'

'May I say you don't look it.'

'Thank you.'

'And that's a long way to come for a meeting.'

'Oh, I'm sure others will have come just as far, if not further. It certainly seemed worth it to me. Things are rather ... worrying. And getting information really is the allegorical blood from a stone. I thought Mr Meyer's letter promised at least a little blood – if you follow me. I presume that was him, greeting us at the door.'

'I gathered so, yes. Well, he's got a good turn-out.'

'Very good. But then we're all rather in need of him, aren't we?'

'I hope so. I mean, I hope he's the answer, that he can do something for us. Ah, here's Lucinda now. Hello, darling.' He stood up, gave her a quick kiss. 'Come and sit down. This is Mrs Fielding, Mrs Flora Fielding. She's travelled all the way up from Wales. Mrs Fielding, Lucinda. My wife.'

He spoke with great pride: and no wonder, Flora thought, this really was a very pretty girl, blonde with big blue eyes, and her voice was pretty too, very light and attractively soft. She thought of Debbie's voice, tinged with her London accent, slightly throaty and, when its owner was annoyed, quite raw, and then chided herself for her disloyalty. No one could help their voice.

'I love Wales,' said Lucinda, shaking Flora's hand. 'We used to go there quite often when I was little – to Abersoch, do you know it?'

'Oh, it's lovely,' said Flora. 'I haven't been there for many years though. I live in South Wales, on the Gower Peninsula. Anyway, do come and join us. Oh, and there are my lot. Debbie, Richard, over here . . .'

This was even worse than she had expected, Debbie thought, absolutely full of braying posh people. Flora must be in heaven. She'd already homed in on a couple of her own; that girl was just ridiculous, an absolute cliché, more like Princess Diana than Princess Diana herself. As for that chinless wonder she was with . . .

'Hi,' she said briefly to Lucinda and Nigel, after kissing Flora rather perfunctorily. 'Sorry to disturb you. And sorry we're late, Flora, the babysitter let us down.'

'Oh, have you got a baby?' said Lucinda. 'How lovely.'

'Sometimes,' said Richard. 'I mean, sometimes it's lovely. And actually we've got three. Well past the baby stage, unfortunately.' He smiled at Lucinda; he was clearly very taken with her.

'That's a matter of opinion, Richard,' said Debbie. 'Personally, I'm very glad they're not babies any more.'

'No, I should think they're pretty hard work,' said the chinless Nigel. 'My brother's got a couple and they're permanently exhausted. Jolly little things though.'

Jolly little things! thought Debbie. How was she going to get through this evening? If these were Lloyd's sufferers, they deserved all they got. And then she saw a rather pale middle-aged woman, very neatly dressed, sit down just in front of them and take her husband's hand. He gripped hers; he appeared very distressed. Debbie felt suddenly less sure of herself.

The room had filled up considerably. Simon looked round, amazed – and slightly comforted – at the extraordinary mix of people there: representatives of the chattering classes, earnest women with no make-up and worn-corduroy-jacketed husbands, bellowing City types – he hoped he wasn't as much of a caricature as many of them – others equally near-caricatures, of the huntin', shootin' and fishin' community, a few who were clearly theatricals, luvvie-ing away, and a lot of anxious middle-aged couples.

The man who had been greeting everyone at the door walked towards the platform at the front of the room. He was quite short, with neat dark hair; he was probably about forty-five, Simon thought, watching from where he was still standing at the door, waiting for Elizabeth. Couldn't she just this once, just for him, be on time? And then the door opened and she slipped in. 'Sorry,' she whispered, 'did my best. Is that George Meyer?'

'Think so. Wearing an Old Carthusian tie. Bodes well, doesn't it?'

She smiled at him. 'You are such a snob, Simon. Can we sit down?'

'Sure. I can see some seats over there . . .'

George Meyer got up onto the platform, went through the usual rigmarole of microphone tapping and testing, and then raised his hand. Everyone stopped talking and cleared their throats. The middle-aged couple in front of Debbie grasped one another's hands more tightly.

George Meyer smiled at them all.

'Thank you for coming. I'm George Meyer and I'm very pleased to see you all. I've talked to a few of you already and it's clear we've all been hit very hard financially, some of us desperately so, by the steeply escalating Lloyd's losses of the last few years.'

A general murmur of affirmation ran through the room.

'Another thing we have in common is that we all share the same Members' Agent, Jackson and Bond. In my case, and I'm pretty sure in all of yours too, our massive problem has been greatly exacerbated by what was – with hindsight – a disproportionately heavy participation in the Westfield Bradley Group of Syndicates, whose performance has been particularly disastrous.'

Another murmur; Debbie shifted on her seat. This could get tedious. George Meyer obviously liked the sound of his own voice. He was asking questions now, requested a show of hands in answer to each one. She tried to concentrate. There was no point her being here otherwise. He asked how many of them had been introduced to Lloyd's by someone they had not met before; how many got a specific suggestion from Jackson & Bond that 1986 was sure to be a very good year and that the best way to recoup any losses from 1985 (the first year there had been any, it seemed) was to increase their premium income limit – whatever that was – by as much as possible; and how many had been told by Jackson & Bond that they were recommending heavy participation in the Westfield Bradley Group, because they never took any big risks and were therefore 'as safe as the Bank of England'.

There was some edgy laughter at this, and a great many hands went up.

'And I wonder how many of you have since had your exposure to Westfield Bradley reduced at the recommendation of Jackson and Bond? I see. None. And no doubt when you got the "down to your last cufflink" speech, you were told that apart from two people in 1963, no one could remember any Name losing a lot of money.'

More laughter; this time braver and louder.

He's good, this chap, Simon thought, really good. Better even than he'd hoped. He could see he would be good to deal with, and he could also see that Elizabeth was impressed.

'Now,' said Meyer, 'how many of you think that at the time you were recruited, there was no one, absolutely no one, working at Lloyd's who had any idea there was serious trouble ahead.'

Not a hand went up.

He paused. This was terrific, Lucinda thought; it was like watching a programme on TV.

'Right,' Meyer said, 'I'm not a lawyer, but if Lloyd's knew there were big problems looming and they deliberately withheld that information when they recruited us, then I believe we've been the victims of deliberate fraud. And therefore have some legal redress.'

People were sitting up straighter now; the silence was intense.

'I am, I suppose, raising the flag of rebellion, saying in fact that I intend to take urgent and, if necessary, drastic steps. Heaven knows how difficult it will be to collect evidence that will stand up in a court of law, but I'm determined to have a bloody good try.

'Now, before I talk any more, I'd like to hear from you. If anyone has a story which they would like to tell, please go ahead. I think it's important we share experiences, get to know what others are up against. After which I suggest a coffee break, and then we can move on to the next key question, which is – where do we go from here? So . . . anyone want to speak?'

There was the usual awkward silence while people looked at their feet, round the room, up at the ceiling – and then Flora stood up. She would, Debbie thought; she would be the one to break the silence, the one to have that sort of hyper-confidence. Why didn't Richard have it, she wondered. Why was he so diffident? Should Flora bear the blame for that, or perhaps his father . . .

'Yes, the lady in the blue jacket,' said George Meyer, smiling across at her. 'Do you want to come up here, or . . .'

'Yes, if you like,' said Flora, and she made her way onto the platform and stood there, looking at them all, pushing back her wild hair. She was wearing a blue embroidered velvet jacket over her long skirt, and high-heeled black boots; she looked wonderful, Debbie thought, with an unwilling stab of pride.

'Hello,' she said, 'and can I first thank George Meyer for having this marvellous idea in the first place. And for being good enough to contact us all. I simply wanted to tell my story very briefly; it's in no way unusual, I fear, but it will probably explain why I for one would like to explore his idea further.'

And she went on to talk about how her husband had made her a Name, so that their assets were limited, and then when he died four years earlier, she had inherited everything anyway.

'It was a double whammy,' she said with her wonderful smile. 'I'm alone and I've got a lot more to lose. So, Mr Meyer, I'm with you.'

She went back to her place; after a pause a grey-haired man came up, probably in his mid-fifties, rather redfaced, dressed in a very shabby tweed suit. He was, he said, a farmer, with a 'thousand acres or so in Suffolk'; he had become a Name twenty years earlier, 'and I must admit, several of those years were good. But now – well, I would seem to be destitute. Almost.'

Destitute, Debbie thought, with a thousand acres? Honestly . . .

'They're really taking me to the cleaners,' he said. 'Everything I had and valued is going. The farm, which my family has owned for generations, my livestock, my horses; in theory, of course, we could keep the house, but the farm'd be worth much less without it, so my wife and I are moving into a small cottage, with no income except our state pension to look forward to. I simply don't know what we're going to do. And what angers me most, and I agree totally with Mr Meyer, is they must have known this was happening, must have seen it coming, and at no time did my agent warn me of anything. In fact, he had the gall to encourage me to *increase* my underwriting for next year if I could find the assets.'

Nigel thought of his own land in Norfolk, very much under threat, and felt sick.

And then the line of people wanting to tell their stories grew longer: a couple in late middle age stood up. They'd become Names just ten years ago in the late seventies; if things didn't get better in the next year, they said, standing on the platform together, they'd have to sell the family home, sell all they had; the wife actually started weeping at this point, clinging to her husband's arm. George Meyer gently ushered them off the platform.

And then there was a young widow. She'd been living out in Hong Kong, her husband had died, and left her enough money to allow her to become a Name at Lloyd's, which had been suggested to her by a charming and helpful young man.

'I met him when we got home. He was connected with my husband's business in some way, and he said Lloyd's would see me and the children through. Now they're asking for more than I can possibly give them. I really don't know what to do.'

And so it went on. Debbie sat there, struggling to retain her conviction that they all deserved anything they got, while listening to story after story of broken lives, of ghastly fear, of lost homes, of what had seemed secure futures wiped out. She felt very shaken, and oddly ashamed of herself; she avoided Richard's eyes. Finally, Meyer came back onto the platform and thanked everyone who had spoken for their honesty and courage.

'Coffee break follows. All are welcome to that, but could I ask anyone totally out of sympathy with my proposition to leave afterwards.'

Coffee was served at the back of the room. Everyone moved in that direction, smiling rather awkwardly at each other, especially at the ones who had spoken. Nigel found himself in the queue behind the young widow: she was rather pretty, he thought, with light brown hair and large, anxious grey eyes. He held out his hand to her.

'Nigel Cowper. Well done for speaking. Don't think I'd have had the bottle, quite honestly.'

She smiled back at him, a rather pale smile. 'Catherine Morgan. I wouldn't have expected it either, but suddenly I felt I had to. People need to know. And what's the point of us all being in it together, if we're not honest?'

'You look awfully tired,' he said. 'Why don't you sit down there, with my wife,' he waved at Lucinda, called, 'we've got company, darling,' and returned to the coffee queue.

'Come and join me,' said Lucinda. 'Jolly brave of you, that. And what an awful story. I'm so sorry, I never realised how bad things could be.'

'Oh well,' said Catherine, 'I'm not the only one. As you heard.'

'No, but . . . well, anyway, I'm Lucinda. So nice to meet you.'

Nigel passed Flora Fielding on his way back to the table; she smiled at him.

'Hello. My lot are over there. Do you want to join us?'

'No,' said Nigel, 'but thank you for the invitation. We've set up camp on the other side of the room. With that poor girl, the widow.'

'What a nightmare for her. I don't know when I felt sorrier for anyone.'

'But you're a widow yourself,' said Nigel, surprised at his own bluntness.

'Yes, I know, but I'm a tough old bird and I haven't got a young family. I feel so sorry for her. Perhaps I'll see you later. I don't know how much good this has actually done, but I feel much better.'

Catherine Morgan smiled at Nigel and Lucinda over her coffee. 'It's jolly nice to be with people, you can't imagine.' She had a rather schoolgirlish turn of phrase. 'It's pretty lonely, my situation. This is the most fun I've had for ages.'

'Oh dear,' said Lucinda, 'that doesn't sound too good. I've had better evenings out. I'm so sorry. How old are your children?'

'Caroline's six and Freddie's eight. Long way to go, I'm afraid. Oh Lord, now look what I've done.'

Her coffee cup was lying on its side, the contents spilling out across the table and dribbling down onto the floor. Lucinda's bag lay in its path; she snatched it up.

'Don't worry,' she said. 'Nigel, why don't you go and see if you can find some paper napkins.'

Nigel went obediently off; Catherine smiled awkwardly at Lucinda, and tried to dab some of the mess up with a couple of small tissues.

'I shouldn't worry,' said Lucinda. 'He'll be back in a minute.'

'Oh, but I get so cross with myself, it's so embarrassing. I am just awfully clumsy. And accident-prone, come to that. My dad always said I was a walking disaster.'

'Nonsense,' said Lucinda. 'Of course you're not. You can make wonderful speeches, for a start. And here's Nigel now, with a great stash of napkins. Well done, Nigel.'

'There, that's better,' he said, mopping rather ineffectually. 'No harm done. And – where do you live, Catherine? May we call you Catherine?'

'Of course. I've got a flat in Fulham, but I'm afraid that'll have to go if things get any worse. It's my only asset.'

'Well – let's hope,' said Nigel without much conviction.

'Indeed.'

'Tell me, Catherine,' said Lucinda, 'do you work?'

'Oh yes. I work part-time as a secretary at a local estate agents. It's pretty tedious, but they let me leave at three-thirty each day, in time to get the children.'

'And – and when did your husband die?'

'Oh, just over four years ago. We'd been living abroad, he worked for one of the big oil companies. I was still getting myself sorted out, trying to cope with everything when this chap approached me, obviously saw me as an ideal victim for Lloyd's and their merry men, an innocent from abroad. I can't imagine now how I could have been so stupid, but I suppose I was still a bit shocked . . .'

'That is terrible,' said Lucinda. 'I think you're just so, so brave. God, they should all be strung up. More coffee, Catherine? To replace the other? I'll go, Nigel, you stay and talk to Catherine.'

She headed over to the queue; it had certainly been a very distracting evening.

Simon sought out George Meyer, leaving Elizabeth talking to some poor woman who was almost in tears.

What he had seen of Meyer, he liked very much. Apart from his great clarity of thought, he had obviously done a good deal of research. He held out his hand.

'Simon Beaumont. See you went to my old school.'

'Charterhouse? Yes, I was there from fifty-four. What about you?'

'Bit later.' He was surprised; George Meyer was obviously older than he'd thought.

'Nice old place, wasn't it?'

'Absolutely. Now I just wanted to say I've been very impressed indeed by what you've had to say so far. Can't wait to hear the rest, in fact. You've had a terrific turn-out. Well-earned, I'd say. Well done.'

'Thanks,' said Meyer. 'And I must say I'm delighted by the uptake. I hadn't expected to get so many.'

'Well, we've all got our backs to the wall. It's nice to see something that holds out some promise of a move forward. However slight.'

Simon made his way after that to the coffee queue and found himself standing next to – or almost next to – the most stunning girl. She was dressed in full Sloane regalia: white ruffled shirt, Liberty print skirt – bit too long, Simon thought, covered most of what were clearly the most glorious legs – pale beige Gucci shoes with a chain, hair held back with a velvet band. Amazing how girls like that were still around: Elizabeth was very scornful of them, of the whole Sloane tribe, said they were dinosaurs. Simon had always thought the girls at least were lovely.

'Hello,' he said.

She smiled at him. 'Hello.'

'Have you sampled the coffee yet?'

'Yes, unfortunately. I'm having tea this time. I'd advise you to do the same.' She held out a small hand, complete with gold signet ring (naturally). 'How do you do? Lucinda Cowper.'

'Simon Beaumont. Extremely nice to meet you, Lucinda. Er, are you here with your husband?'

'Yes. We've been fairly lucky so far, but goodness, what terrible stories we've heard. Come and meet him – we're over there, see, with that dear girl, the one who told her story, the widow.'

'Oh, thank you. Yes, I will. May I collect my wife, bring her over?'

'Of course,' she said pleasantly, 'it's not my party.'

She had a sweet, rather careful smile, showing very pretty teeth; there was something altogether careful about her, he couldn't quite put his finger on it, she was slightly subdued, not as bubbly as her breed usually were. But lovely and so sexy . . . Oh, for God's sake, Beaumont, get a grip.

He went over to Elizabeth; she was relieved to be rescued.

'Come and meet some new friends,' he said.

'I saw you talking to one of them. She didn't exactly seem to be wearing a three-piece suit and stout boots.' But she smiled and followed him just the same.

Simon studied Nigel with some interest. Here was a classic

133

Name, very public school, tall and slim, fair-haired, not quite good-looking, very formally dressed, possibly a bit dim – and a most unlikely husband for the delicious Lucinda.

He liked Catherine Morgan very much; she was rather pretty too, he thought, with her great grey eyes, and very sweet, and in spite of looking exhausted, she managed to chat to him quite cheerfully, about what she was doing and how she was coping. Which wasn't very well, she said; she had had to make a decison to take her children out of their private schools the term before, and send them to the local state primary.

'Of course, I know that's not exactly the end of the world, and most people would feel very little sympathy, but they both loved their other schools and were doing so well, and had lots of nice friends, and it's very different for them. Especially Freddie, he's quite bright and wants to do well, and he's constantly teased for being a swot. It's so hard on them, and it's certainly not their fault. I feel so guilty.'

Simon said he couldn't imagine anything worse.

'And at that age, it's so hard for them to understand. God, what a mess. Do you work?'

'Well, I do. But it's very, very low calibre work, I'm afraid. And terribly badly paid, not nearly enough really. It was the only job I could get that let me be home after school. But at least it's something. It gets me out of the house, and it helps a bit.'

'How old are your children?' asked Elizabeth.

'Freddie's eight and Caroline's six.'

'How lovely. Perfect ages, I always think. They must be such a comfort to you.'

'Yes, they are, of course. Er . . . what about you, what do you do?'

'Oh, I work in advertising.'

'Goodness, how interesting.'

'Yes, it is sometimes,' she said, and Simon loved her in that moment, for making it sound nothing special, a run-of-the-mill job, in front of this sweetly unfortunate girl.

'And Lucinda, what do you do?'

'I work in publishing. Nothing important, I'm just a PA, nothing the least bit clever.'

'Oh, come on, darling, don't put yourself down,' said Nigel, adding rather pompously, 'she's always doing that.'

'I'm not,' said Lucinda, and her voice was intensely irritated suddenly. 'And don't talk about me as if I wasn't there.'

Ah, discord in paradise, thought Simon, catching a glance of something less than devotion from Lucinda to Nigel.

'Sorry, darling. Sorry.'

'And where do you live?' said Catherine.

'Oh, Chelsea. Yes. Cadogan Square.'

Simon couldn't remember when he had met anyone quite so delicious.

Debbie, still feeling rather shocked, was sitting with the nice hand-holding couple from the row in front. They had remained in their seats at the start of the coffee break, looking quite shell-shocked, not moving. It was Flora who had smiled at them, invited them to join their party for coffee; the woman had been pleased and said how nice that would be, but her husband said nothing, simply followed her. He would clearly rather have stayed where he was.

Flora and Richard went off to get the coffee; Debbie smiled rather awkwardly at the couple.

'Hello. I'm Debbie Fielding.'

'Mary and Michael Gardner,' said Mary.

'So – what did you think?'

'About going to court, do you mean? Oh, I don't know. We were quite impressed by Mr Meyer, weren't we, dear? But we don't think we'd contemplate any further risks. Trouble enough already.'

'Yes, I can understand that,' said Debbie.

Michael stood up. 'I'm just going to the cloakroom, Mary. Won't be long.'

'All right, see you later.' She looked after him anxiously, then confided in Debbie, 'He was very reluctant to come, but I said we should. See if we could gain anything from the evening.'

She certainly wasn't what Debbie had expected; her voice was pleasant, but in no way posh, and she wore a twinset and a pleated skirt, and rather old-fashioned, highly polished court shoes.

'And you?' she said to Debbie. 'Are you and your husband Names?'

'Er, no,' Debbie said. 'We're here with my mother-in-law, Flora Fielding, the first to speak.'

'Yes,' said Mary Gardner. 'What a remarkable woman. You must be very proud of her.'

Debbie longed to say that she wasn't, but it seemed necessary to be polite.

'Yes, of course,' she said.

'Well, you're very fortunate,' said Mary Gardner, 'not to be directly involved. It has been so dreadful for us.'

'I'm sure.'

'And the worst thing— Oh, I do hope you don't mind my talking to you, but it's such a relief. I've been bottling it up for so long – Michael won't let me talk about it.'

'No,' said Debbie. 'No, of course I don't mind.'

'The worst thing of all has been his pride. The loss of his pride, rather.'

'His pride?' That hadn't occurred to her.

'Yes. He was so proud of being invited to become a Name. His parents were quite – quite modest people. For him it was a great honour, a bit like getting his MBE . . .'

'Oh really?' said Debbie politely.

'Oh yes. Perhaps not quite as good; that was really wonderful, going into Buckingham Palace, sitting in that wonderful room, watching Michael actually being spoken to by the Queen, and you know, she pins on the medal herself. I always thought some – some lackey would do that.'

'Really?' said Debbie again. 'Yes, that is very nice.' Her own views on the Royal Family were not too much like Mary Gardner's.

'Isn't it? Anyway, Michael was invited into Lloyd's when his firm went public. He was Managing Director, you see, and there was a lot of publicity in the paper about it, and someone who'd known someone on the board, had rung him up and said he was a Members' Agent at Lloyd's and had Michael ever considered becoming a Name. Oh, he was so excited! The day he joined, he came back terribly impressed. He said they'd really made him feel someone, and he'd seen the underwriting room, and Lord Nelson's telescope, and then they served him lunch and congratulated him on becoming a Name. They gave him a certificate and, oh dear, he was so proud of that, he hung it on the wall of his study. I don't need to tell you it's not there any more.'

'No, I'm sure not.'

'And of course they told him the risks were negligible. I'd been a bit worried, to tell you the truth, but he assured me the last person to be ruined by them was in the mid-sixties. Just as Mr Meyer said.'

Silly to believe them, Debbie thought, there must have been some way of checking – and then thought of the fatal vanity that had led Michael Gardner into Lloyd's and realised it would have been easy to pull flockfuls of wool over his – and many other people's – eyes.

'So,' she said, 'then what happened?'

'Well, what happened was that for several years, we did get quite a lot of money. I have to admit that. And I must also admit that Michael liked to boast about it a bit. I'd hear him saying, "Oh, I'm a Name at Lloyd's, you know" when we were entertaining and it seemed quite harmless to me. But that's what I mean about his pride. When they started demanding money – oh, two years ago – he didn't even tell me at first.'

'He didn't tell you!'

'No. He couldn't bring himself to. That must sound very shocking to you. But it wasn't just that he thought I'd worry, he thought he'd look foolish. I only found out when he was ill and I discovered he'd cancelled the medical insurance. By which time he owed a lot of money. Almost as much as our house in Guildford is worth. It was a dreadful shock. But that didn't matter to him nearly as much as having to confess to me. And he won't talk about it to anyone else, he won't even tell our children. I had a terrible time getting him to come here this evening.'

'So – what are you going to do?' asked Debbie. She felt genuinely sympathetic.

'Well, we can sell the house and buy somewhere much smaller. But that will only be this year's debt. Goodness knows how we'll manage next time.'

'It's awful. I'm so sorry.'

'Thank you, dear, that's kind of you. Oh, I see your mother-

137

in-law coming back now. She's more the sort of person I think you'd expect to be a Name – obviously very well educated and so on. But you know, there are an awful lot of people like us, much more ordinary people, who should never have been brought in in the first place, but who were – well, dazzled by it all. As Michael was.'

'Yes,' said Debbie. 'Yes, I hadn't realised that.'

George Meyer was back on the platform. He smiled into the room; he had a very nice smile, Elizabeth noticed, it transformed his rather severe face.

'Right. Back to business. I can see almost no one has gone, which means that everyone wants to explore the fraud possibility. Our very first task must be to find a good solicitor, preferably with a sound knowledge of Lloyd's, who can confirm whether or not we have a case.

'Now, as far I can see, there is one very difficult decision to be taken. Who, precisely, do we sue?'

He had everyone's attention; the silence in the room was absolute. Looking round, Flora was impressed that she was the only person doing so; everyone's eyes were fixed on Meyer. She felt profoundly glad she had come to the meeting; if nothing else, it had created a camaraderie in a shorter time than she would have believed possible. And it was a very positive, almost excited camaraderie. For two years, they had all felt isolated, helpless, absolutely wretched, and this meeting was providing a marvellous break from that.

'Anyway,' Meyer was saying, 'I discussed the problem with my accountant, who came back to me with an interesting idea. "I don't think you should sue Lloyd's as a whole," he said. "The law protects the Council and all the others are like stallholders in a marketplace. Your best bet is to concentrate on the specifically named companies which have let you down." I think that is very good advice. And that, of course, is what we should do – in my view. Step forward, therefore, Members' Agents, Jackson and Bond. I don't know if we could ever prove conclusively that they knew there was big trouble brewing yet failed to warn us when we joined. But it's worth a damn good try. They certainly piled us recklessly into the Westfield Bradley Group, probably the worst loss-making syndicate of all time. And unlike some other agents, they did little or nothing to switch us out of WBG into syndicates with a better track record, which I believe it was their duty to do.

'I'd dearly like to know how it came about that the allegedly safe WB Group took on so many more open-ended asbestos and pollution risks than virtually anyone else; risks which turned out to be hundreds – maybe thousands – of lethal time-bombs which are now threatening to destroy our lives.

'Now there is clearly much more to be said; but there is one other crucial thing. This is going to cost us a great deal of money. But in my view, if the lawyers don't get our money, then sooner or later Lloyd's will. So, to all intents and purposes it will be Lloyd's money we are spending, which I find a comforting thought. Anyway, that's quite enough from me; you are invited to stay for further refreshment and I shall be delighted to talk to anyone personally. Thank you all so much again.'

There was a silence; then a spontaneous burst of applause. Simon stood up and said, 'I'm sure you would all like to join me in thanking George Meyer for all his hard work, and for a most inspiring evening. I for one will undoubtedly be signing up.'

He might have asked me, Elizabeth thought. It was so typical of Simon, leaping in without looking for even a nano-second, taking a leading part in the drama. And it wasn't actually Lloyd's money that he'd be using, whatever Mr Meyer might say; it was his – theirs – and she felt suddenly and fiercely angry.

'We're going,' whispered Lucinda. 'Lovely to have met you both. I can see your husband's going to be a very leading light, marvellous of him. I think he and Nigel have swapped cards. Bye!'

'Bye,' said Elizabeth, forcing a smile, and then she caught up with Simon in the queue to talk to George Meyer and said she was sorry, but she had to go; she had a lot of work to do still, and she'd get a cab home.

'Fine,' he said, clearly so taken up with his new cause he was unaware of the edge in her voice. 'See you later, darling, thank you for coming.'

'Oh, it was nothing,' she said, and left; had she stayed she would have been still more annoyed, for Simon, having talked

139

very briefly to George Meyer, pledging him his support, giving him his card, was now pushing his way through the crowd, trying to catch up with Catherine Morgan.

He had been very moved by her story, and her obvious loneliness, and he had been impressed by her courage in getting up to speak. She was no Lucinda Cowper; she was nervous and shy, but very sweet; he felt that here was one victim at least he could help. He tapped her on the shoulder; she turned round, flushed as she saw him and dropped her bag – the contents went all over the floor.

'Oh gosh, I'm so sorry,' she said, as Simon dived down to recapture lipsticks, biros, small change, a diary. 'Thank you very much.'

'That's perfectly all right. Think I've got everything. There you are. Look, here's my card. I was thinking, I might well be able to find you a job. We employ a large number of secretaries, in my department alone; two of the girls are leaving next week. Come and see me if you're interested.'

'Golly,' she said, staring at him, 'how terribly kind. Of course I'd be interested. But I don't think you realise, I can only do school hours.'

'Yes, I do,' he said, 'I realise it very well. I really mean it, come and talk to me. I'm sure we can work something out. I'd like to help. As one Lloyd's victim to another.'

'Well, thank you,' said Catherine, her big grey eyes brilliant as she looked at him, 'that is extremely kind. I – well, I don't know what to say.'

'You don't have to say anything now,' Simon said. 'Oh, God, I must go back, I've left my scarf on my seat. Bye, Catherine, see you again, I hope.'

Debbie and Richard had gone home, to rescue the emergency babysitter; Flora had been delayed talking to the nice Mary Gardner; she was buttoning up her coat and found herself near to Simon as they made their way to the door. He held it open for her.

'Thank you. Quite an evening, wasn't it?' she said.

'Quite. Extremely interesting, I thought.'

'Me, too.' She held out her hand. 'Flora Fielding. Are you on your own?'

'Yes, I am, as a matter of fact. My wife's just left.'

'Not permanently, I hope?'

'I hope not too. No, she had some work to attend to. How do you do, Mrs Fielding. Simon Beaumont.'

'Flora, please. My family have left too. I'm on my way out.' He smiled at her; he was very attractive, she thought, with his thick greying hair and smiling brown eyes. And his suit was beautiful – and his shoes. Nothing ready to wear about Mr Beaumont.

'Now tell me,' he said as they headed for the main door. 'What did you really think? Will you be joining him?'

'I thought there were shades of group therapy, but nothing wrong with that. I also thought he was very good. And yes, I'll come on board. For a while at least.'

'Oh, I'm delighted. Me too. I was pretty impressed by him, I must say. And I enjoyed your little speech.'

'Thank you.'

'Where do you come from? Are you a Londoner?'

'No, thank God. I live in Wales.'

'Wet Wales.'

'Not my bit,' said Flora firmly. 'We have lovely weather. We get the Gulf Stream.'

'You know, I always think,' he said, holding the door open for her, 'that the Gulf Stream is quite extraordinarily energetic. Gets everywhere. People are always claiming it as a near-neighbour. You're not going back to Wales tonight, I hope?'

'No, I'm staying with my son and his family. In – in Ealing.' She could never quite bring herself to say Acton, it sounded so dreadful.

'And have you met any of our fellow-sufferers? My wallet's stuffed with cards. You must give me yours.'

'Yes, I met several. A rather pathetic couple; he hadn't even told his wife he owed a fortune – she found out by accident, can you imagine?'

'I'm afraid I know of another case. It's quite standard, alas. I talked to that sweet girl, the one who spoke – you know, the widow?'

'Oh yes. What a ghastly story. One finds it hard to believe, the ruthlessness of people.'

'I don't, I'm afraid.' He looked at his watch. 'Bit of a trek to Ealing. Have you got a car?'

'Yes, but I don't know if I'll ever find it again. I left it in a multi-storey car park near Leicester Square.'

'Mine's there too,' he said, smiling at her again. 'Look, why don't I escort you there, make sure you do find it. I hate to think of you wandering those dangerous streets on your own.'

'That's very kind of you, but—'

'No buts,' he said. 'I never leave a damsel in distress.'

'I'm far from being a damsel, I'm afraid.'

'Nonsense. So – impertinent question, but it's been a night for truth-telling. How bad are your losses?'

'Well, I'm doing pretty nicely so far. At losing, I mean. Where do you think it will end?'

'God knows,' Simon said.

Part Two

Part Two

Chapter 10

Autumn, 1989

It seemed to go on all night, the crying. He got up three times to try and comfort her, to take her in his arms; she shook him off, told him she hated him, buried her head in the pillow and wept on. Finally, somewhere near two o'clock, it stopped; in the silence he lay and hated himself.

How had it happened, that with the very best of intentions he had brought this upon her, his beloved younger daughter, forced her – as she saw it – to bid farewell to a pony that was more dear to her than anything else in the world. Simon's remorse and guilt were huge; he would have taken and borne all her grief if he could.

Should he have investigated further before he risked so much of his money, dug deeper into the apparently limitless fortunes of Lloyd's, ripped off the smiling masks, applied acid to the silver tongues? Should he have recognised that nothing could be quite so safe, so risk-free as they purported it to be? Should he have acknowledged his own greed in the affair, and yes, his own vanity, in wishing to join this gilt-edged brotherhood, sitting at the high table and smiling down just slightly contemptuously on the less fortunate who lacked the means and the capability to join them. Had he not enjoyed saying, as he went into lunch at the Savoy Grill or the Reform Club or the boardroom at the bank, 'Got the Lloyd's cheque this morning,' almost as much as he had enjoyed what it brought: the country house, the horses, the cars, the holidays, the best schools, the finest clothes.

Well, if that was so, if he had indeed committed not just one but two of the Seven Deadly Sins, those of Pride and Gluttony – and God, what about a third: Lust – he had committed that

145

fairly frequently as well – he was being punished for it now. Not by being cast down into the fires of hell, but by a fiercer, more agonising pain: by hearing the sobs of his daughter, and knowing he had caused them, as surely as if he had taken her pony and shot it himself.

'Can't I keep him in London?' she had said. 'There are livery stables here, aren't there? I could see him more probably than now.'

And he had said, yes, she could; but asked her to consider how would he feel, her beautiful, free-spirited Boy, used to the hills and valleys of Sussex, of going out hunting on frosty mornings, taking fences, half-flying across fields; how would he be, confined to a stableyard in Kensington, say and limited to a neat and tidy canter across Hyde Park?

They had investigated livery stables in the country too; less expensive, but how could she ride him, without a home to go from, without the means to get there?

'I'd take you when I could, darling, and so would Mummy, of course, but it could only be just a day here and there.' He had stopped, silenced by the dislike in her eyes, the hurt in her voice. She would get over it, he knew, to a degree, but she would never forgive him. It wasn't exactly easy to live with.

It was terrible, the creeping tentacles of this thing: the unhappiness taking hold of more and more people, innocent people. So he had only been acting for the best, a decade before, thinking to improve his lot and the lot of his family, to bring happiness, security, pleasure to all of them. Of what value was that to them all now?

'I'm going back to work,' Debbie said. This was something of an exaggeration, but she wanted to upset Richard as much as she possibly could. She could see she'd succeeded; they were having supper and he put down his knife and fork and went rather pale.

'Debbie, you can't do that. You know we agreed—'

'We agreed lots of things, Richard. Like we'd always be honest with each other.'

'Debbie, please. It really doesn't help, raking that over endlessly. I've told you so many times how sorry I am . . .'

'Yes, you have. Funnily enough, I don't seem to feel much

better about it. Anyway, never mind, don't you want to hear about my job?'

'Well, I'm not sure. I mean, what about the children? Who's going to look after them?'

'After school, you can. You're here, aren't you, and it's not rocket science. Rachel's at school now, and you can pick her up quite easily, before you get the others. That's what I do. After that, it's pretty straightforward, just giving them their tea and making sure they do their homework. And then bathing them, of course. I'll be home long before supper and I can still do that. I think you're getting off pretty lightly really.'

'Debbie, I can't do all that! I have work of my own to do, you know that.'

'Yes, well, you'll have to do it later in the evening. Or something.' He looked so alarmed, she suddenly gave in and grinned at him. 'Oh, and I did say, didn't I, it's only two days a week. Monday and Wednesday. So that really won't be too difficult, will it?'

They had settled into a truce; like all truces it was uncomfortable, but it was either that or leaving him, and she could see that wasn't any kind of answer.

She was still desperate about the school fees; she had told Richard to make sure the children could leave their schools as soon as possible; he hadn't argued, but when Emma came back on the first day appointed Form Captain and Alex had won a place by the end of the week in the under-10s rugby team, he had asked her very mildly if she was quite sure that leaving would be best for them.

'I really can do at least two terms, and I know I'll have a new job by the summer so, for their sake, Debbie, couldn't you—'

And of course, after furiously arguing, she had given in; the only concession she won was that Rachel at least would start at the local primary with all her friends from playschool. But she was left hurting, and very badly; she had not been exaggerating when she had said she would never trust Richard again. Something had been broken between them, and nothing seemed quite right any more. They were not exactly unhappy, but they were less happy; it was as simple as that.

'It's a bit like having permanent indigestion,' she confided to

Jan, 'but all over. And especially when Richard wants to have sex. I just lie there seething and willing him to stop.'

Jan said she did that most of the time anyway. 'Well, willing Mike to stop, so I can go to sleep. Honestly, Debbie, remember when we couldn't get enough? What happened? Babies, I suppose.'

'Babies and housework,' sighed Debbie, 'and predictability. Sometimes I think if Richard says what I know he's going to say just once more I shall scream. And especially in bed. My God, how do we let them get away with it?'

'So what does he say?' asked Jan with interest.

'He says "I hope you've got a bit of energy left for me" when he puts the light out. I mean, how erotic is that?'

'Better than Mike. He says, "How are you feeling?" One of these days I shall tell him.'

'No, you won't,' said Debbie.

＊

The job Debbie had got was with a PR company. It was one she had come across when she had worked for the radio station; they did a lot of book promotion, but they had recently moved into the health and fitness area, still enjoying a boom against all the odds, and as well as a couple of health clubs and a range of dancewear, had taken on a line of what they called 'body cosmetics' – shower gels, body lotions, scrubs and some special shampoos. The new venture wouldn't pay for a fulltime person, but two days a week was just about affordable; Debbie got to hear about it when she was chatting to someone at the radio station one day, trying to get a mention of a garage sale the NCT were holding.

'Be right up your street, Debs,' said Grant, her old boss. 'I always said you could sell oil to the Arabs.'

It wasn't exactly her ideal job, but it meant two days a week out of the house, getting dressed up, going into the West End – well, Earl's Court – and actually being with grown-ups. She was very excited. Equally importantly, it would pay her £8000 a year, which was almost as much as she had been earning when she had given up last time.

'OK, it's not a king's ransom, but it'll help, won't it?' she said to Richard. 'And if you do the childcare then it won't cost us anything.'

'Yes, but Debs—'

'Look, Richard, I'm sorry but I'm going to do it, so you'll just have to get used to the idea. Oh, and not one farthing of it is to go towards the school fees, OK?'

Richard was silent.

The company, Know How Promotions, was run by a husband and wife team, Anna and Peter Carter; Peter stayed in the back room and did the hard slog, and Anna went out and got the business. She was very good at it; Debbie, who was uneasy with any kind of hard sell, was nevertheless terribly impressed by her. Anna was tiny, with cropped dark hair and large brown eyes, and an energy that seemed to explode out of her. She did everything at the run; she ran round the office, she ran up and down the stairs, she even ran into restaurants. Her voice, which was swift and clipped, would fly through presentations, blinding prospective clients with facts and figures, finishing by telling them they couldn't afford not to employ Know How; she had a large portfolio of letters from satisfied clients, which she produced over the strong coffee which ended her performance. Peter was much more laidback and apparently rather slow on the uptake, but painstaking and astonishingly efficient; they made a formidable team. They employed four other fulltime people. 'We've never tried part-timers before, never quite believed in it,' Anna said to Debbie, 'and I'm still not sure, to be truthful with you. You've got to prove me wrong.'

Debbie was determined that she would.

'Mrs Fielding, isn't it? Are you all right?'

Flora had been hurrying through Leadenhall Market, anxious to get to Monument tube station; she hadn't been looking where she was going and caught her heel in the cobblestones. It snapped. She was standing balancing on one leg, trying to work out what she could do to effect a temporary repair, muttering furiously under her breath. She looked up and for a moment couldn't think who it was.

'It's Simon Beaumont. We met at the Lloyd's meeting, a month or so ago.'

'Oh – yes. Yes, of course. How rude of me, after you so gallantly took me to my car. I'm so sorry.'

'That's quite all right. Is there something wrong with your shoe?'

'Yes, I broke my heel on the stones in the market. That'll teach me to dress unsuitably. I should be in grandmotherly lace-ups, not tottering about two and a half inches above the ground.'

'I can't think of anything less suitable for you than lace-ups,' he said. 'Here, let me see. Ah, yes, completely snapped. Oh dear. Where are you heading for?'

'The tube station and thence to Paddington. I'll just have to hop. Bloody stones. They're very picturesque, but—'

'They are, aren't they? You know, this is where all our troubles started, just about three hundred years ago.'

'What do you mean?'

'This was coffee-house country. And Mr Edward Lloyd had the initiative to open one near Tower Wharf. All the ship-owners used to go there, as did the merchants, who dabbled in marine insurance. That was the beginning of Lloyd's,' he smiled at her. 'Still, this isn't getting you to Paddington. Look, I've got an appointment in Park Lane in half an hour's time. My driver's got nothing to do this afternoon except wait for me. He can take you on. And you could buy some slippers or something on the way.'

'I couldn't possibly. It would be much too kind.'

'Now how could something be too kind?' he said. 'Too cruel perhaps, but – anyway, come along. My office is a hundred yards away, so if you can just hobble there . . . I'd offer my arm if it wouldn't seem a little forward of me.'

'It wouldn't,' she said, taking his arm gratefully. 'So – where is your office? And what does it do?'

'It's a small merchant bank. Well, quite small. I'm one of the directors. Here it is. Now if you wouldn't mind just waiting down here in Reception a few minutes . . .'

He really was very charming, Flora thought, sinking into the deep leather sofa by the lift; the sort of man she had always instinctively mistrusted. God alone knew why. Possibly because William had been rather brusque; if you'd been married to brusqueness for thirty years, you inevitably began to regard it as the norm. And Simon was everything William would have disapproved of; rather ostentatiously well-dressed – his blue and white shirt had the Ralph Lauren logo on it, that would have earned him several black marks for a start, very good-looking – not that he could be blamed for that – the greying hair almost styled, rather than just cut, manners a bit showy. But he did seem genuinely kind – and amusing too. Well William wasn't here, so –

'Fascinating place, that market,' Simon said as the car passed it. 'Do you know, every so often they release a falcon into it, very, very early, to catch the pigeons. The tourists don't want to be showered with pigeon sh— poo.'

'Don't be ridiculous,' she said, laughing.

'It's absolutely true, I swear. What are you doing here anyway? Why aren't you in Wales?'

'You have a very good memory,' she said. 'I came up to have lunch with my Members' Agent; he had the gall to show me that bloody building, ask me to admire it . . .'

'They don't own it, you know,' said Simon. 'They couldn't afford to keep it, had to sell it to some Americans to whom they now pay rent. I find that very ironic. It is rather splendid though, isn't it, whatever goes on inside.'

'I suppose so.'

'Anyway, did he have anything cheerful to tell you?'

'Of course not. Another difficult year, he said.'

'Mine too. Oh well. Have you heard anything from George Meyer?'

'Not really. Have you?'

'I had a very good lunch with him, and I've volunteered to help him look for a likely solicitor, but he was waiting to get some more firm responses in before we went any further. Everyone might have expressed great interest that night, but a lot of it has evaporated, apparently. People are scared of further risk. So if you haven't written yet, do. I don't want to influence you, but it is at least something we can do.'

'Yes, I know. And I have been meaning to write. I will.'

'Good for you. I just think it's worth a shot. Although I'm a bit disappointed there's no action yet. I wouldn't mind if it was just me, you know, but it's hurting the family now. My twelve-year-old daughter, Tilly she's called, isn't speaking to me.'

'Isn't that par for the course, with twelve year olds?'

151

'It may be. But this isn't an adolescent tantrum, it's real grief.'

'About?'

'Oh, to cut a long story short, our house in the country has to go and her pony with it. We've had our last summer there, it's on the market.'

'Where is it?'

'West Sussex. Lovely place. And I keep a boat near Chichester – my wife calls her the love of my life.'

'My husband used to sail,' said Flora. 'I could never see the fun of it myself.'

'Oh, no, it's wonderful! Some of my happiest hours are out there with the *Lizzie*, that's her name, the nearest thing to flying on this earth.'

'Why *Lizzie*?'

'It's my wife's name. Well, she's Elizabeth, but . . . Anyway, back to Tilly and the horse. She adores that animal. No boy could possibly compare with him in her eyes and I must say, he is a rather fine chap. And I feel utterly wretched about it. She cries herself to sleep every night.'

'That is very sad,' said Flora, and meant it. 'Have you considered livery?'

'Yes, but it's not very satisfactory really. London would be ghastly for him, and – well, it's just not very practical, I'm afraid.'

There was a silence, then Flora said, quite casually, 'Well if it's a matter of not having anywhere for him to go, I have a couple of empty stalls at the moment. I've had to sell one of my hunters – thanks again to Messrs Lloyd's. I'd be very willing to have him. How big is he?'

'Fifteen hands. He's an eventer.'

'He sounds lovely. And I could ride him for her, keep him exercised. I'm quite light. Your daughter could come down in the school holidays, perhaps. It's quite a big house. The riding's a bit rough, it's not like Sussex, but I could keep him fit. And at least it wouldn't be that awful agonising farewell. I had to sell my pony at her age; it was at the beginning of the war, and I'll never forget it. I truly thought my heart would break. Think about it, I really mean it.'

'Daddy, oh Daddy, I love you so so much. Thank you, thank you . . .' Tilly was home at Chadwick House on a weekend exeat.

'Darling, don't thank me. Thank this very nice lady. It's she who's going to have Boy.'

'And this very nice lady is – who?' said Elizabeth when Tilly had gone off to get herself a drink from the fridge. Her voice was rather cold.

'She's called Flora Fielding. Remember? She was the first to speak on the platform at the Lloyd's meeting, and I got chatting to her later. After you'd gone off early.'

'It seems an awful lot to do for a complete stranger,' Elizabeth said, ignoring this.

'Do you know,' he said, 'she doesn't feel like a complete stranger. It's a very strong bond, this business. We're all in it together. It's the one good thing about it.'

'Yes, well, you certainly seem keen on sharing it with George Meyer.'

'Oh for heaven's sake. It's something I might be able to do, Elizabeth, rather than just chewing my nails to the quick and staring into the darkness.'

'Yes, but—' She stopped. They had had one row about his not consulting her; and he had been completely incapable of understanding her anger.

'It's my money, I'm not asking you to contribute.'

'Simon, any money you don't have, I have to find.'

'That's a filthy lie,' he said. 'I'm probably going to have to sell the *Lizzie*, and that would support me through this lawsuit. If we ever get it going. Oh, for God's sake, what is the point of this discussion! I thought you'd be pleased about Flora Fielding having Boy. Obviously I was wrong.'

He seemed very upset; she felt remorse suddenly.

'I'm sorry. I am really. And it *is* very good of her. I just feel – well, we should be giving her something for it. Towards Boy's keep.'

'I offered, obviously. She said at the moment it wouldn't be much – apart from vets' bills, of course. He'll be out a lot of the year. And she seems to have a fair bit of land.'

'And when can he go down there? Boy I mean?'

'Probably at half-term. When the sale of the house will be

153

complete.' As their daughter came back into the room: 'Now, Tilly darling, you do realise, don't you, that you won't be able to see nearly so much of Boy? Wales is a lot further away than this place.'

'Yes, of course. But at least he won't have to be sold, and he'll be happy and I can see him every holidays.'

'Tilly, not every holidays, darling,' said Elizabeth.

'Why not? Daddy said Mrs Fielding said I could go and stay in the holidays.'

'Yes, well, that won't always be easy. And you might not like her. She might not like you. I really think, Simon, we should perhaps take Tilly down to meet Mrs Fielding before we even accept this offer. And then we could check the place out. I mean, it might be some fearful dump, you don't know.'

'I think I do know,' said Simon, 'but yes, I agree, of course, that she and Tilly should meet. We could go down next weekend even, if it suited her. And if we could take Tilly out of school again.'

'Oh, they won't mind,' said Tilly blithely.

'Well, I'll ask. Toby's home next weekend, we could make a family outing of it. Anyway, what I think you should do first, Tilly darling, is write Mrs Fielding a very, very nice letter, saying thank you. And maybe send her some pictures of Boy, so she –'

'– can see how beautiful he is. Yes, I will. I'll go and write to her now. Oh I'm so happy. I can't believe how happy I am.'

She danced off; Elizabeth looked at Simon.

'I can't help feeling this is all a bit odd,' she said. 'I don't like the idea of Tilly just going to stay with this woman. We don't know anything about her and—'

'You might not,' he said impatiently, 'I do. But of course I wouldn't dream of sending Tilly down there on her own, not until she really knows Mrs Fielding well. I'll take her, we can stay in a B&B or something, and we can all feel our way.'

'Don't I get a say in any of this?'

'If you want to. And if you have time to make the trip. Don't be such a fucking wet blanket, Elizabeth. It's not perfect, but it's a lot better than nothing. Now if you'll excuse me, I've got a lot of work to do.'

*

It was on 10 October that it happened. Lucinda would never forget the date: 10.10.89, so easy to remember, it seemed somehow gouged out in her brain. In the months to come she would find herself repeating it over and over again like some hideous mantra, helping her to cling to calm, to sanity even, as her life swung into dizzy chaos.

She had actually had a good day. Graham had been very pleased with a report of a manuscript she had done, said she had made some really good points that he had missed; she had spotted a lovely lamp in the window of the General Trading Company, as she rushed past it on her way to the station, exactly the sort of thing she'd been looking for, for the dining room, and Justin, the Art Director, whom she'd always fancied, told her she was looking particularly tasty. She was wearing a new pale-pink V-necked sweater she'd bought herself as a present – she was buying herself a lot of presents at the moment, she felt she deserved them – and a much shorter skirt than she usually wore (another present). This made her think of Blue, who was always telling her she had the best legs he'd ever seen, and why did she keep them hidden under a series of tablecloths; but she managed to push that thought down and concentrate on Justin's compliment instead.

And then she had met her friend Katy for lunch. Katy worked for a small art gallery in Cork Street and had just become engaged. She was very excited, waving her hands about a lot and then spreading them on the table, as newly engaged girls do, the better to display the large diamond on her finger. The very large diamond. Clearly Tim, the beloved, was quite rich, Lucinda thought, studying it.

'So – when's the wedding? And where?' she said, surprised to find she could actually whip up a degree of interest at least.

'Oh, in the country. Mummy would die if it wasn't, I think. She's dreamed of it for so long, planned exactly where to have the marquee, who'll do the flowers in the church – oh, you know. They're all the same, aren't they? And next June – how corny is that? But it is the perfect month, don't you think, roses everywhere, and it might even be nice weather, you never know. Only thing that might be tricky is planning it round Ascot and Wimbledon, so we might switch to July –

only then people start going away. Daddy even suggested May, but that really is a bit early. And Lucinda, please please will you be matron of honour?'

Lucinda flushed with pleasure and said she'd love to, and thought how amazingly lucky she was to have such good friends, and how without even knowing it, they were all helping her get through her misery; and after an hour of discussing the wedding and its date, and whether Katy should get her wedding dress from the Chelsea Design Company, or have it made from scratch: 'I know exactly what I want, really over the top, you know, just loads and loads of frills and ruching – well, you only get to be a bride once, don't you?' she returned to the office feeling almost happy.

She and Nigel were going out that evening to see *When Harry Met Sally*. Going to the cinema was one of the things that worked best for Lucinda at the moment; a total absorption in the experience, an evening taken care of with no need to talk much, and then straight home to bed. Quite late: which meant Nigel usually went straight to sleep. He needed a lot of sleep; that was a big help as well.

He came to collect her from the office; they were going to eat at the Pizza Express in Museum Street. She was still clearing up and told Reception to send him along to her office; he came in looking very happy and kissed her.

'Something to celebrate,' he said, shutting the door and then lowering his voice. 'I got my results today. Of the – you know, the test.'

'And?' said Lucinda, suddenly nervous.

'And it's not too bad. Not too bad at all. I don't exactly have a high – you know, high sperm count, apparently, in fact, it's a little low – but there's no reason why we shouldn't be able to have a family. Isn't that wonderful?'

'It is, really wonderful,' said Lucinda, and meant it. It would be wonderful for her too she thought.

'Yes. So we just have to keep working at it, darling. Be fun, won't it?' He blushed. 'They suggested we went in to see them together, discuss other things, not sure what.'

'Nigel, I'm so, so happy,' said Lucinda, shrinking slightly from the thought of working at it. 'It's really good news. We must celebrate, maybe go somewhere a bit better than the

156

Pizza Express. Now look, I just have to go to the loo, make myself look a bit more presentable.'

'You look pretty presentable to me,' he said, 'but then you always do. OK, I'll wait for you here.'

'I won't be a minute. Help yourself to a book, there's that new one on the Ancient Egyptians you were interested in.'

She took her time in the loo; putting on some fresh lipstick, spraying herself with perfume, even gingering up her hair with her tongs, humming under her breath. One of the secretaries came in.

'You look nice, Lucinda. Going out somewhere?'

'Only to the cinema. With my old man. *When Harry Met Sally*. Have you seen it?'

'Yes, it's fantastic. So, so funny. Specially the orgasm scene. The fake one, in the café, you know.'

'Yes, I've heard about that,' said Lucinda, smiling. She had worried about that a bit: might Nigel start studying her own reaction in bed? And then decided he was simply too nice and too good to even suspect her of such a thing as faking an orgasm. She didn't deserve him; she really didn't.

She walked out, after smiling at herself in the mirror, thinking that things really were getting better, thinking that even the sex would be more bearable now, with the thought of a baby to help her along, and she did a little skip as she walked along the corridor into her office.

'Sorry I was so long, darling, I—'

And stopped. For he was standing with his back to her desk, white-faced and almost hollow-eyed, one hand in his pocket, looking at her with such intense hostility she was quite frightened.

'Nigel,' she said, 'whatever is it? What's the matter?'

'What the fuck are you doing with these?' he said, shaking something at her; he never swore, the strongest word he ever used was 'shit', and that only in the most dire situations. 'What the fuck have you been up to?'

She couldn't see for a moment what it was he was holding, thought perhaps it was the watch. And then she realised. It was what she had kept so carefully, so fearfully, in her desk drawer, only taking them into the house singly at the weekends, tucked into her wallet, wrapped in tissue: her contraceptive pills.

157

An analyst would probably have said, Lucinda reflected, that she had left Nigel alone in her office with the pills deliberately: seeking a way out, an escape from her unhappy marriage. She would have told the analyst that he or she was absolutely wrong.

Everything she had done had been to protect Nigel, to save him from unhappiness. All her own misery, and Blue's misery too, all her struggles to re-engage with her marriage, had been to that end. There was not one shred of desire in her to hurt him, to tell him about her affair. OK, she had been stupid not to think of it, and she kept going over and over that fatal five minutes in her head: if only she had been quicker, if only she had not decided to do her hair, if only the secretary hadn't come in, if only she hadn't had that conversation, albeit brief, then it was possible he might not have found them – but it had been simply a mistake, a completely unlooked-for, terrible mistake. And who would have thought anyway that Nigel of all people should go rummaging through her desk, for the pills were well hidden, inside the toilet bag she kept there? It turned out he had had a headache and was looking for some aspirin. It seemed an ironically dreadful time for him to have found them too: on the very day that he had been told he could father a child; he had been allowed perhaps a few hours of absolute happiness before being condemned to this dreadful shocking misery.

And it apparently increased her own perfidy; indeed, at the very first, he had assumed she had been taking them simply to avoid pregnancy, had been lying to him, had not wanted a child at all, had accused her of the ultimate selfishness. 'What were you worrying about, Lucinda? Ruining your figure? Giving up your job?' But even as she protested, tears of panic streaming down her face, the second horror hit him.

'You've been having an affair, haven't you? That's what you've been doing. All that working late, having to go away – I thought it seemed odd – you know, I'm not quite the simpleton you clearly think – but I kept telling myself you'd never do that, it wasn't in you. I thought you were incapable of it. That's it, isn't it, you've been having an affair?'

And yes, she had said finally, calm suddenly; and he became calmer too, said who was it, that he had to know. Was it someone at work, was it one of their friends . . .?

They were home now; after a totally silent cab ride – they could clearly not stay in the office. It had seemed endless, that journey, a nightmare of fear and guilt; he had sat with his back turned to her, looking out of the window, had paid the cab off in complete silence and stalked into the house, and they had continued in the drawing room, the new curtains that she had made to soothe her misery a reproachful backdrop.

'No, Nigel, it isn't one of our friends, it's no one you know,' she said.

'So – who then? I would rather know, Lucinda. I shall go mad otherwise.'

'Really,' she said, 'there's no point telling you. You've never met him, you'd have no idea who he was. Leave it, please.'

'Are you still seeing him?'

And, 'No,' she said, 'I'm not,' thankful for that at least, that she could claim it was over, that she had decided not to stay with him.

'And why was that?'

'Well, I—' She couldn't give him the real reason, that it was because of the money; it would sound terrible, so open to misinterpretation.

'When did it end then? Perhaps you'd be good enough to tell me that? It seems odd that you're still taking those – those things.'

'I'm not,' she said, 'truly I'm not, I stopped the moment I ended the affair. I felt I had to give our marriage every possible chance, and obviously having a baby, or trying to have a baby, was a huge part of that.'

'How good of you.'

She was silent.

'I do want to know,' he said, 'when it ended. I really feel I have a right to know. To know everything. I'm not sure why,' he added. He sounded bewildered, the old Nigel, gentle and good. And then he said, 'It wasn't the money, was it? You didn't stay with me because of the money? I did wonder where on earth you disappeared to that night, rushing out like that, coming back without the coffee.'

'What coffee?' she said.

'The coffee you said you were going to get.'

'Did I? I'd forgotten.' And indeed she had.

'So, was that it? When you decided to stay with me?'

'Well – yes,' she said, watching herself walking into his trap, absolutely unable to prevent herself. 'Yes, it was.'

'How very noble of you. So it wasn't loyalty that drove you back to me, or a desire to keep your marriage vows, or even love. It was money—'

'Nigel, please. You don't understand.'

'You are disgusting,' he said, and his pale, decent face was suddenly flushed and ugly, distorted with pain and rage. 'You are utterly disgusting. I cannot imagine how I could ever have loved you, been taken in by you. Just get out, would you? I don't care where you go, you can sleep in the street for all I care. Just get out.'

'Yes, all right,' she said, her voice very low, and she picked up her bag and walked towards the door.

'Of course, you could go and stay at Claridges or the Savoy, with the money I gave you. And take your fancy man with you. Why don't you, Lucinda, why don't you do that?'

And then he put his head in his arms and started to sob; and she looked at him, and thought she could hardly endure having put him in such pain, and she went over and placed her hand on his shoulders.

'Just go,' he said, 'just go away, please.'

'I'm so sorry,' she said, 'so very, very sorry. I do hope one day you'll be able to believe it.'

And she walked out, pulling the door to behind her.

Chapter 11

Debbie was trying very hard to be a good wife. She knew Richard deserved it, because he was being so great about her working; of course he still felt guilty about lying to her, but just the same, it wasn't exactly easy for him, having to leave all his marking and organisational work until she got home, making sure he wasn't late to collect the children, and that there was something for their tea, and OK, it was only what she did, what most mothers did, but it didn't come so easily to men. It just didn't. And it meant she could have this wonderful time, for two days every week when she was doing something so well that someone was paying her for it. It made her feel sleek and cool and clever, far far from the dithery Debbie who had become so familiar to her, always late, the house always in chaos. She was still like that at home, of course, but in the office she was a by-word for efficiency, with a slickly neat desk, a perfectly planned diary. She got more done in her two days, Anna often told her, than most people did in five.

'Well, it's so mind-concentrating,' she had said. 'I know I can't waste a minute, from the moment I hit the desk.'

It was actually when she hit the train that she changed from mummy to Debbie, when her mind sloughed off the woolly tangle of motherhood to reveal beneath it a perfectly ordered grid. School, food, dog, washing, ironing, ballet, judo, committees: all replaced by clients, schedules, press releases, presentations. It quite surprised, impressed her even, that change: that she could accomplish it so quickly and with such ease. Clearly it was her real self, lying asleep for years and years, and awoken now by something a great deal more satisfying than a kiss.

She loved it, loved the work; she enjoyed presentations and was going to be extremely good at them, Anna had said, having allowed her to assist on a couple; sensing when a cool prospective client became enthusiastic, picking up on what they liked and running with it. 'It's taken me years to learn to do that,' Anna said, slightly ruefully, after one particularly successful pitch for a series of books on finance for women. 'Who taught you?'

'My husband,' said Debbie briefly, and in a way it was true. She had learned to read Richard's mind and capitalise on the knowledge very early in their marriage.

And so she had suggested half-term in Wales, and of course everyone had been thrilled, especially Richard.

'I know I was against you working,' he said carefully, 'but I think I was wrong. It suits you. You seem different, somehow.'

'I feel different,' she said, giving him a quick kiss, 'and I enjoy being at home more as well. So thank you for making it possible.'

And she had been really nice to Flora, and found it surprisingly easy. And they had all been having a lovely time until . . .

'We have some visitors coming the day after tomorrow,' Flora said. 'I do hope you'll like them.' The visitors were the Beaumonts: 'He was at the Lloyds meeting,' Flora said. 'I met him after you'd gone. Charming, absolutely charming.'

Debbie knew what charming meant. Posh. Smooth. Public school. She managed to smile.

'And – he's bringing his wife and family. I've offered to have the daughter's pony here, they've got to sell their country house and . . .'

They arrived about midday, the man, yes, oh so charming, with his perfect haircut and smile and his Barbour and green wellies, pretending to be a proper country person, and his wife, who was actually rather beautiful, and turned out to have an incredibly high-powered job; in fact, she was exactly the sort of person Debbie would have liked to be. But the child, she was really ridiculous, a simpering, irritating little thing, with her long blond hair and her big blue eyes and a voice so plummy you practically needed an interpreter; she could see Flora thought she was absolutely wonderful, that she'd grow up into exactly the sort of girl Richard should have married, if Flora had had her way. And the boy, he'd just been a joke; he'd stayed in the Land Rover at first, had sat there listening to his Walkman until the man called him from the doorway, said, 'Come on, Toby, come along in,' and he'd reluctantly got out of the car and walked across the yard and into the house; and then shaken hands with Flora and everyone in sight, saying how do you do.

'And where are you at school, Toby?' Flora had said, and 'Eton,' he'd said (of course). Debbie studied him, with his floppy haircut and his blue and white striped shirt and blazer – a blazer, for God's sake, what sort of a boy these days wore a blazer? – and thought how much she'd hate it if Alexander turned out like that.

And they'd all stood there in the kitchen, drinking sherry, apart from the children who'd been given lemonade – 'Home-made, hope it's all right,' Flora had said, with her most annoying smile, while the visitors blah-blahed away, and the girl, Tilly – Tilly, what a name – brought out some pictures of her pony to show them.

'Oh, he's such a gorgeous chap. So beautiful,' Flora had said, gushing, 'sweet face' – as if a horse could have a face that was sweet or sour or anything really.

If only they'd all gone out for the day, but Richard had been rather keen on the idea of meeting these people, and Emma was just tipping into pony mode and said she wanted to meet the girl and hear about her pony who might be coming to stay, and Rachel had taken up the chant; and then, when the morning was wet, the outing which was to have been a picnic on Burry Holm seemed rather less attractive and the alternative, a shopping trip to Swansea, even less so. Debbie had decided to stay, to have lunch with them all and then leave them to their horsey conversations and go to the garden centre near Oxwich: she had plans to install a patio in the garden in Acton and they had some rather nice pots there.

Sherry finished, they all went out to inspect the stables; Debbie said she'd make the salad for lunch and was furiously chopping cucumber when Toby, the boy, came back in.

'Hi,' she said. 'Finished viewing the accommodation?'

'What? Oh yes, thanks.' He grinned at her, rather shyly. He wasn't so bad maybe. 'I'm not very horse-minded. Don't like them that much, to tell you the truth. In fact, I hate riding. How about you?'

'I've never tried it, but I'm sure I'd hate it too. Too far from the ground. What do you like doing? Want some more lemonade?'

'Thanks. Well, I like ski-ing.' He would, Debbie thought. 'And rugby. Oh, and tennis. I love tennis.'

'I like tennis,' said Debbie, 'but I never manage to play enough to get good. Only at uni, really.'

'Well, I play at school, of course. And rugby. I'm hoping to get in a team, but I'm a bit small.'

'And do you like school?'

'Yeah, I love it. It's great.'

'You don't get homesick at all?' she said.

'No way.' He looked quite surprised. 'I've been away since I was nine, so I'm quite used to it. It's fun, all your friends around you all the time.'

How odd they were, these upper-class people, she thought, sending little boys of eight or nine away from home when they didn't have to. What was the point of having them at all?

There was a silence. Really, Debbie thought, what am I doing here, struggling to make polite conversation with an Etonian? She returned her attention to the chopping.

'This is really kind of Mrs Fielding,' said Toby suddenly, 'having Boy.'

'I think she wants to,' said Debbie. 'She doesn't like the stables being empty.'

'No, maybe not. Still, jolly nice of her. Tilly is just so happy about it. She was crying herself to sleep every night.'

'Poor Tilly,' said Debbie politely. She thought of some of the people at the meeting, of the poor old couple weeping together, of anxious Mary Gardner, whose husband was clearly about to crack under the strain, and the loss of a pony didn't seem too terribly serious. Still, she told herself firmly, all things were relative.

'So, if she can still get to see him in the holidays, that's the answer,' Toby said. 'She can't take him to school with her, anyway.'

'I shouldn't think she could,' said Debbie, laughing. 'What school would take a pony?'

'Oh, some do,' said Toby earnestly. 'I have one friend, he plays polo, and he takes his ponies to school. He's at Millfield, they have a polo team, you know.'

'No,' said Debbie, 'I didn't know that actually. Pass me those tomatoes, would you, Toby, please.'

There was a lot of noise in the yard; and then everyone came back into the kitchen, talking and laughing.

'Let's have lunch then,' said Flora, 'hope nobody minds the kitchen. Oh, Debbie dear, how sweet of you to do the salad. Now Tilly, would you like to help Emma lay the table and Simon, you give Elizabeth another sherry and have one yourself. And Richard, you could open that wine.'

Dobbio had to admit by the end of lunch that she quite liked Simon Beaumont. She tried not to, but it was difficult. He was incredibly relaxed and easy to talk to, he flirted with her just enough to please and not embarrass her, and made her feel much more interesting than she really was. He asked her about her work, said it must be very difficult to combine it with running a family, and she'd taken a huge breath and said she couldn't possibly do it without Richard's help – while smiling across the table at Richard, who was clearly pleased by this acknowledgement – and then Elizabeth Beaumont had said rather unexpectedly that she could never have done her job without Simon's help when the children were young.

'He was marvellous, well ahead of his time; he could change a nappy when most men hardly knew which end of a baby it should go on, and he'd go to plays and concerts at school if I absolutely couldn't get there.'

'Very ahead of his time,' Debbie said, grinning at Simon; and then Elizabeth Beaumont started asking Debbie about her job, which she found almost embarrassing, given Elizabeth's own awe-inspiring status, but she seemed genuinely interested and said her agency had considered having a PR wing, but she'd given up the idea because she'd never found anyone of sufficient calibre to run it. 'Maybe you could do it for me in a few years' time,' she said to Debbie, and Simon said from what he'd seen of Debbie, she'd be running her own agency by then; and it was all rather fun in the end and she forgot about being cross and not liking people like the Beaumonts. And then Emma, who was clearly completely captivated by Tilly, as small girls tend to be by their just-slightly elders, asked her if she would come and see Flora's horses with her and Tilly was endlessly patient and led Emma up and down the yard on Becky, Flora's gentle old mare, for about an hour, while they continued to talk; and it wasn't until they had all gone and Flora had taken the children for a walk, that Debbie realised that Richard was looking very dark and brooding.

'What on earth's the matter with you?' she said.

'Oh, nothing. You seemed to be enjoying yourself.'

'Well, I was. What's wrong with that?'

'You don't usually like those sorts of people.'

'I know, but I liked them. I thought they were interesting.'

He was silent; then he said, 'I suppose that's the sort of set-up you'd like. Big smart house, with staff' – the existence of Josie had emerged – 'rich successful husband, so you could pursue your own career . . .'

Debbie stared at him. 'Richard,' she said, 'I don't know what you're talking about.'

'Yes, you do. You'd like all that and you've got me. Not rich, not successful, and a rotten little house in the suburbs.'

'Richard. Honestly.' She tended to forget this: how vulnerable he was, how acutely aware of his failure, as he saw it, how he had let her down, her and his parents and his education, by not achieving what he thought he should. She went over to him, where he sat at the kitchen table and put her arms round him. 'Richard, you are so very silly. You are not a failure and it is not a rotten little house, it's home and I love it. Except I wish you wouldn't call it the suburbs, it's West London. It's as bad as your mother calling it Ealing. And I've got you – do you really think I'd be happy with that smoothie?'

'You seemed to be pretty happy at lunch.'

'That is just ridiculous. OK, I was happy at lunch. But that's fantasy land. Lunch isn't a marriage. Is it? A marriage is what we've got and it's working pretty well, specially lately. I think we're doing pretty good.'

'Do you?' he said, and he put his arms round her waist, rested his head on her breast. 'Do you really?'

'Yes,' she said, 'I really do. And if you come upstairs with me now, I'll show you.'

He looked up at her, clearly half-shocked, half-tempted.

'But Debbie, they might come back, then what would we do?'

'What we used to do, get dressed mega-fast and one of us dive into the loo. Come on, it'll be fun. I really, really want to. Don't you?'

'Well – yes. Yes, I do. But—'

'Richard,' she said, pulling him up from his chair, slithering her fingers into his fly, 'Richard, I do really want to.' And it was true, she did, excitement rising into her for the first time in ages. 'Come on, then, what are you waiting for?'

But he shook his head, drew away from her, said, 'No, no, I wouldn't enjoy it. I'd be worrying all the time. Sorry. Maybe later, tonight?'

But later, her desire was stilled, disappointed, and although she let him make love to her, she was haunted by what might have been a few hours earlier and thought that it was not Richard's failure in his work that troubled her, but his failure to recognise what she really wanted.

Lucinda supposed a lot of people would have expected her to go back to Blue. This seemed to her absolutely unthinkable. She had entered into a relationship with him, let him fall in love with her and then broken his heart. According to Lucinda's code of conduct, it was simply unfair to then return to him because it suited her and expect him to be grateful. It was almost two months now since she had said goodbye to him; he had probably begun to recover, had found someone else. It would be monstrously selfish and indeed arrogant of her to say, 'OK, Blue, bit of a to-do with Nigel, I'm free now, come on over.'

His primary emotion towards her, she thought, was almost certainly dislike. And disappointment. Endless promises she had made to him, and then broken them all. He would simply expect her to do it again. No, she was on her own and she had to manage. Somehow. The only good thing about the whole mess was that at last she could wear the pink Chanel watch. All the time.

Her parents had been predictably horrified by her separation from Nigel. She had gone down bravely for the weekend following the dreadful Friday to tell them; at that point she was still staying in a boarding-house in Victoria. It had been even worse than she feared; her mother had burst into tears and her father had stalked out of the room without a word and shut himself in his study, slamming the door.

'You're making the most terrible mistake,' her mother had said, wiping her eyes. 'He's such a dear, and so devoted to you. Men like that don't grow on trees, Lucinda. What is it? What's gone wrong?'

'I – don't really know. It's impossible to say.'

'Is it the age difference? You were so sure it wouldn't matter . . .'

'No, Mummy. It's got nothing to do with it. I told you, the marriage just isn't working.'

'Marriages can be made to work,' said her mother, 'with a bit of determination on both sides. Of course, I always thought you should have started a family sooner. Children cement a marriage. A career isn't everything, you know.'

Her father stalked back into the room, glass of gin and tonic in hand, and glared at her.

'I really think you must have taken leave of your senses, Lucinda. You won't find another husband as good as Nigel in a hurry.'

'No, I'm sure you're right.'

'He hasn't been playing around, I presume? Because if he has, I'll speak to him myself.'

'No, Daddy, he hasn't. And please, whatever you do, don't speak to him. He's terribly upset and—'

'I expect he is. Well, in that case, what on earth is the matter with him? He's a thoroughly decent chap, pleasure to have in the family. We all like him. He's clearly very fond of you. I mean, what are you looking for, Lucinda, some sort of Prince Charming? Because I'm telling you, you aren't going to find him.'

More silence.

'Well, I'm lost for words. I really am.' If only, thought

Lucinda. 'I mean, for God's sake, think of your marriage vows. For better for worse, sickness and health, all that. And you go running away at the first little bit of – well, what? You don't seem to know yourself.'

'No, maybe not.'

'Look, you just go back to him and tell him you want to work things out. I daresay you think it'll be rather exciting, living in London on your own, a single girl again. Well it won't. You'll be lonely and miserable.'

'It's quite true, Lucinda.' Her mother leaned forward earnestly. 'I've a couple of friends who were divorced. Their lives were pretty good hell.'

'Truly,' she said, 'truly, I don't like the idea of being on my own.'

'Then why—'

'I told you. It just isn't working any more.'

'Well, I think it's a pretty poor show,' said her father.

From her sister Susannah came much the same. 'You're quite mad, Lucinda. He's such a sweetheart, and he adores you. So unless he's actually knocking you about, which he clearly isn't, I think you should go back to him PDQ. Work it out. Marriage isn't always easy, I should know. But it's better than not being married.'

Her brothers were slightly more sympathetic. John the baby just gave her a hug and said he was very sorry for her and Anthony, always her favourite sibling, said, 'I did always think Nigel was a bit – well, you know, not terribly exciting. But such a nice chap, Lucinda, and he seemed absolutely devoted to you.'

'Yes, he was.'

'I'm sure you know what you're doing. Don't let the parents bully you into something you don't want. I'm just afraid you'll be lonely, that's all. Wish I lived in London, then I could keep you company.' Anthony was in the Army, currently based in Shrivenham, about to be posted to Northern Ireland.

'Well, thanks, Anthony. You're the only person who's even tried to see it my way.'

And so it went: on and on.

'Shall we leave this lot, go and have a quiet drink in the bar?'

Elizabeth had been planning on sneaking off herself, going up to bed. She smiled rather cautiously at John Martin, World Wide President of Hunter Pharmaceuticals.

The sales conference had gone well; she had sat with Peter Hargreaves watching it, proud of the creative team, proud of all of them. It was the big one: the annual Hunter sales conference. Held at Boyle Park, the huge country-house hotel on the Gloucestershire/Warwickshire borders, that provided not only accommodation for the entire sales force and top management, and a magnificently equipped conference centre, but also a spa and swimming pool, a nine-hole golf course, and a boating lake.

John Martin always came over from the States for the conference, and Peter Hargreaves and Elizabeth always made speeches. It took place over two days, with one afternoon set aside for the delights of Boyle Park. The advertising work had gone down well, the sales figures, despite the economic downturn, were good and morale was high.

Elizabeth looked around her; the evening had moved into chaos phase, the pre-dinner flirty drinks and the four-course meal over. It was with the drinks that the change really began, as the men stood in groups, still serious, looking suddenly more handsome in their dinner jackets, and the girls began to join them, smiling and self-conscious, emerging like so many butterflies from their sober suits and neat shirts into brightly coloured silk and chiffon, their legs and bosoms well on display, their sleek hair teased into chignons and ringlets, and everywhere a myriad of bracelets and necklaces and earrings, dangling and swinging and teasing in a cloud of over-heavy perfume. Elizabeth always thought that most of them, except the real beauties, looked better in the suits, but the men most clearly did not agree, proffering champagne and compliments, smiling and joking, and with appalling unsubtlety, obviously lining up their prospects for the long night ahead.

Dinner saw the Rubicon crossed; from civilisation, good manners and a display still of personal ambition and the qualities required to fulfil it, to noise, drunkenness, and above all sex. In another hour or two, Elizabeth thought, the hotel would be rocking on its foundations; what exactly was it about conferences (she wondered at every one), that suspended normal moral judgement, that saw otherwise devoted and dutiful young husbands moving into beds and bodies where they had no business to be, and normally well-behaved and self-respecting young women encouraging them, luring them even, on their way. It wasn't just the alcohol, in fact, it was hardly the alcohol at all; it was a kind of moral moratorium, a sense of reckless freedom and sexual greed, created not so much by an absence from hearth and home, as a presence in a shared and oddly isolated country that offered, or rather almost demanded, as full an exploration as possible. And a return from which could be easily and safely accomplished, with the unspoken promise that no mention, or even acknowledgement of it need ever be made.

There was a disco in the room next to the dining room; sitting at her table, watching girls weaving their way rather unsteadily towards the dancing, dreading that someone would feel duty-bound to invite her to dance, Elizabeth was surprised as well as relieved by John Martin's invitation. The previous year he had been a most vigorous member of the disco team; she reminded him of it now as they settled in the comparative quiet of the main bar.

'Oh, don't,' he said. 'I can't bear to think what a complete moron I must have looked. My fourteen-year-old daughter explained to me in words of very few syllables how obscene it was for anyone over twenty to dance in public.'

'Well, she has a point, I suppose,' said Elizabeth. 'I don't think I'd go quite as far as obscene but our children certainly do a lot of heckling on the rare occasions Simon and I try it in their presence. Anyway, this is much nicer.'

'Simon is your husband? Yes, I remember. What would you like? Brandy? Whisky?'

'Oh, more champagne, I think. It ends the evening on such a high.'

'I hope it's not over yet. But – fine. I'm a bourbon man myself. I never can quite see the point of wine. You have to drink so much to take off. And it's all such bloody nonsense, what wine with what dish. I like my stomach lined and warmed and then kept that way. But I expect your husband is a great wine buff?'

'Well, he likes it. And takes a bit of interest in it, I suppose. Not as much as he did,' she added, thinking of the fast-emptying cellar in London, the decimated one that had left Chadwick.

'Oh really? Why is that?'

'It's an expensive hobby.'

'So?'

'Oh well, you know. Inflation, children to educate, all that sort of thing,' she said quickly. She certainly wasn't going to air their financial troubles with John Martin.

'Right. Well, how do you think it's gone?'

'Very, very well. There's a terrific spirit in the company. Not surprising, of course, it's doing extremely well. And this is a great venue – I really like it.'

'Me too. I almost brought my wife – she'd have loved it, the spa and so on, and she's a great golfer. But, you know, I don't really believe in mixing business with pleasure.'

This was not what Elizabeth had heard; John Martin took a great deal of pleasure along with his business. And he was actually very attractive; lots of the secretaries fancied him. He was tall and heavily built with a shock of blond hair and startlingly dark-blue eyes beneath a thatch of thick blond eyebrow. And he dressed well too, in cutting-edge suits. His dinner-jacket was particularly nice, with proper lapels rather than the shawl collar currently fashionable. He wasn't Old Money, indeed he had come up the hard way, but he enjoyed what he could buy of the Old Money life, a house on Long Island as well as an apartment in Manhattan, a yacht (motor variety, Simon had been deeply disapproving), and an impressive golf handicap. He was also on his third wife: 'Classic, she is,' Peter Hargreaves had said, 'blonde, big blue eyes, Permatan, extremely deep cleavage . . . and quite young.'

Elizabeth had shuddered. 'How can they do it, these girls?'

'Elizabeth, I'm surprised at you. You're usually more realistic than that. Think what she gets out of it: big house, big wardrobe, lots of baubles . . .'

'I know. But I still find it dispiriting. What were we fighting for in our youth, what are we still fighting for, if girls still just – sell themselves to men like that? It's such a cop-out.'

'Well, they're not all brilliant like you. There are easier ways to get life's goodies than fighting boardroom battles.'

'I know. I just hate that whole thing, it feels so – so retrograde.'

'They seem to be having a great time at the disco,' John Martin said now. 'Good to see them all letting their hair down. Helps.'

'Helps what?'

'Oh, you know. With company loyalty, that sort of thing. They'll all go back to their desks now, feeling good about us. Wouldn't you say so?'

He obviously required her agreement. 'Of course.'

The waiter arrived with the drinks.

'Cheers,' he said.

'Cheers John. Thank you.'

'Your team's presentation was very good,' he said. 'I like the new corporate campaign. Not sure about fannying around with the logo, but—'

'I wouldn't call it fannying around,' she said. 'I'd call it a strong new branding statement.'

'Yes, I know, I was listening. Don't look so indignant, everyone likes it except me, but it'll happen. I do occasionally bow to pressure, you know.'

'I didn't, no,' she said, smiling at him. 'I've never seen you even dip your head, let alone bow.'

'Well, you haven't known me long enough then,' he said. 'I know enough about running companies to give the experts a say now and again. And I'd call your agency experts.'

'Well – thank you.'

'That's all right. Tell me, Elizabeth,' he said suddenly, 'are you happily married?'

'That's an extremely impertinent question,' she said, trying both to keep her voice light, and not to let herself consider it seriously. It was too dangerous, too destructive . . .

'No, it's not. I find you interesting. I want to know.'

'Well, I don't think you're going to find out,' she said, smiling.

'OK.' He smiled back. 'That means no, I would suggest.'

'It doesn't actually,' she said coolly. 'It means I don't want to tell you, that I don't think it's relevant to the occasion.'

173

'Well, I think it is,' he said, and 'Why?' she said and was annoyed at the irritation in her voice; she should be keeping cool.

'Elizabeth, Elizabeth,' he shook his head at her, 'there's no need to be so edgy. You interest me, that's all. What makes you tick, what drives you.'

'Do you know,' she said, suddenly less annoyed with him, feeling this was safer ground, 'I often wonder that myself. I really have no idea. It's just – there. I was born with it. I mean, it's certainly not the money, or anything. In the beginning I worked for nothing. Well, I mean there wasn't any profit, after paying the nanny and so on. I was an only child,' she added. 'I often think that has something to do with it. My father was incredibly proud of me, urged me on, and I so wanted to please him. He desperately wanted a son, and my mother couldn't have any more children.'

'I was an only child too. The centre of my parents' world. Interesting, isn't it? I've heard that theory before, as a matter of fact. About only children. We're a very high-achieving lot. Well, whatever does it for you, it makes you very attractive.'

'Oh,' she said, suddenly confused, brought back to the present, back from the claustrophobic meals of her childhood, her father demanding to know every detail of her day, how she had done, what marks she had got for her homework, whether she had made the netball team, what she had to say about the national and international events of the day, her mother sitting quietly, of little interest to either of them, resentful of the fact. 'Oh – well, thank you.'

'No need to thank me. It's a fact.'

She was suddenly aware that one of his legs was pressing against hers, that he had moved closer to her; she moved, as subtly as she could, just slightly away from him.

'You are an extraordinarily fascinating woman,' he said, 'as well as successful and clever. I hope your husband appreciates you.'

'I'm sure he doesn't,' she said, and smiled at him brightly. 'What husband does?'

'That's a very dim view to take of us men.'

'Well, I wasn't being entirely serious. And I'm sure you appreciate your wife.'

'Of course I do. Lovely girl. But she isn't like you. She

174

doesn't . . .' She thought he was going to say that his wife didn't understand him, but: 'She has no idea what I do,' he said. 'Well, she knows what my job is, but she has no idea what it entails. She thinks I just sit in the office all day, giving orders; has no notion of how tough it is.'

'Well, it's hard to, unless you're actually there,' said Elizabeth fairly. 'I daresay she appreciates how hard you work.'

'The only thing she appreciates is how much money I bring home,' he said, and then, 'No, I'm probably being unfair. But I envy your husband; you must know what he goes through every day, how tough it is out there. It's important that, in a marriage.'

'Well . . .'

'And it's not the only thing I envy him,' he said, and she felt him move nearer to her again, felt the heat of him, smelled the whisky breath. 'You're very sexy, Elizabeth, you know that? Sexy and beautiful. How about we go and hit the dance floor? Since none of our children are present . . .'

Elizabeth felt two very conflicting things. A stab of panic: this could be dangerous. Professionally. He was the Chairman of their biggest client, not to be offended, and not to be led on, either. She also felt a strong desire to take him up on his suggestion, to go and dance with him; it would be fun, and he was very attractive. She could fancy him very easily. She did fancy him. And it was good to be thought sexy, declared so, by a man you fancied. Especially when your husband had demoralised you, hurt you so badly you knew you would never quite recover. How wonderful to be on the other side of that divide, the one who was out there and winning, not the one who had been left behind to lose.

She looked at John Martin and she not only quite literally longed to dance with him, but to talk to him some more, drink with him some more, possibly even go to bed with him, for she had no doubt that that could happen too, at the end of her little adventure. How wonderful to return to Simon, knowing she was still desirable, still desiring.

But: 'I'd love to, John, and thank you for the invitation. I really am tired – I'm sorry. I've enjoyed our talk though. Very much. And thank you for the champagne. It was lovely. I'll see you in the morning.'

For he was arguably the most powerful man she knew, and however attractive that made him, it also made him dangerous; she had seen too many such liaisons and the quicksands they created. She couldn't risk it. It would be an act of infinite folly.

And he smiled at her, regret in the astonishing blue eyes, and she could see he understood. All of it. Which made her at one and the same time want him even more and yet be absolutely sure that she had done the right thing.

Chapter 12

Christmas, 1989

'While shepherds watched their cocks by night . . .'

'Oh, do shut up, that is just totally disgusting.'

'Darling, such prudery. I'm surprised at you. Doesn't suit you. Now listen, I'm having a special little carol service tonight, all on my ownsome – why don't you come and join me? I could show you my version of the Immaculate Conception.'

'I'm sure you could. Sorry, but I'm busy.'

'With what, little angel? God, you'd look delicious in wings. Especially if you wore nothing else. Come on, come and enjoy yourself for once. I've got some special religious ecstasy I could share with you and—'

'I said I'm busy,' said Annabel. 'I've got some presents to wrap up.'

Florian was silent for a moment, then he said, 'You really are cross with me, aren't you?'

'You worked it out.'

'Darling I'm sorry. Look I keep saying I'm sorry. It's not a word that trips very easily off my lips. What else can I do – drag myself across the floor wearing nothing but sackcloth and ashes? I don't think that would suit me too well, although I suppose I could fake it with linen . . .'

'Oh Florian, stop it.' Annabel threw a towel at him and turned away, hoping he wouldn't see her smile, but he did. Hating herself, she agreed to have one quick drink with him after work, 'And then I've got two parties to go to.'

He really was – well, irresistible. Infuriating and exhausting and devious and self-centred beyond anyone she had ever met – and irresistible. She had managed not to go out with him for about two weeks after that first drink: then she gave in.

Her big anxiety, that the rest of the staff would be annoyed, proved unfounded. They all thought it rather amusing. Afterwards she realised that they'd seen it all before. Which was making her feel even sillier now. What she hadn't bargained for was getting involved with him emotionally.

For he was beguiling – in every sense of the word. He flattered, charmed and amused her; on their first proper date he told her she was beautiful, clever and talented. He took her to the Criterion where he bought her vintage champagne and then on to the Wag Club in Wardour Street. Annabel was competely overwhelmed by the place; it seemed to her like some kind of amazing film, full as it was of exotic creatures, models, actresses, rock stars, and a lot of beautiful boys like Florian himself, of slightly confusing sexual orientation, wearing make-up and jewellery. A great deal of dope was being smoked.

The place was rather like a theatre; they stood upstairs, drinking more champagne, watching the crowd below.

'Is that Naomi Campbell?'

'Could be.'

'Look, it's Jason Donovan – isn't it?'

'Looks like him.'

'And isn't that Prince?'

'Think so.'

Mick Hucknall wandered through, his great tangle of red hair falling down his back.

'We could do a lot with that hair, couldn't we, sweetie?' said Florian. A man appeared suddenly, dressed like Beau Brummel, in frockcoat and tall hat, with a crowd of followers. 'Philip Sallon,' said Florian. 'Isn't he amazing?'

'He is. Who is he? Can we meet him?'

'Darling, I don't actually know him. Sorry. He's a very famous man about the scene.' He seemed rather awed by Sallon; Annabel was amused; it was the first crack in his confidence.

Later they danced; Florian was an astonishingly good dancer. Confused now by the dope and the champagne, Annabel watched the evening blur into total shimmering fantasy; when Florian finally suggested they went home she followed him dutifully into a cab, into his flat in Fulham, into his bed. What ensued there was fairly amazing.

It went on like that for about three weeks; she discarded caution, allowed herself to think herself in love. They went out three or four nights a week; to all the London clubs, to the Fridge in Brixton, the Marquee, to a rock concert at the Camden Palace, 'Sorry, my angel, I know it's a bit naff now, but one of the guys is a friend, I promised we'd go.'

Annabel didn't find it at all naff. She was dazzled by Florian, caught in his headlights; naive in spite of her cool image, she believed him when he said he adored her, that she was the most beautiful girl he had ever known, that she was special, that what he felt for her was 'totally mind-blowing'. And then she had gone to his flat one night unannounced, to collect a sweater she had left there, and he opened the door to her in his bathrobe, and as she walked in, pulled the bedroom door to just a little too late. A completely naked girl was sitting on the bed, smoking a spliff and giggling and pouring champagne in a very slow trickle into her pubic hair.

'Just a little tasting,' Florian said airily.

He was never at a loss for words.

That had been three weeks ago; intensely hurt, she hadn't spoken to him since, unless absolutely forced to. She had seriously considered leaving the salon; then she thought it would be cutting off her nose to spite her face, and he – and her parents – would have won. She was doing rather well there; even Tania had told her so. She had graduated to removing clients' foils at the backwash, after highlighting; the first time she did it she felt like a master hairdresser, and she and Carol had almost cracked blow-drying: well enough to be let loose on the guinea pigs who came in to have their hair done at a fraction of the usual cost on model nights. That too was much more difficult than she had thought: her method on Tilly's hair and indeed her own, a haphazard journey from one side to the other, was completely wrong. 'You start at the nape,' Tania said, 'and work upwards. You have to section the hair off, and be really methodical. Otherwise you'll get into a terrible muddle, forget where you were.'

Sectioning was horribly difficult; clipping chunks of hair out of the way and then not getting it tangled or mixed up with the dry hair when you released them.

179

A lot of hairdressing, she had discovered, was down to being organised and systematic; it was hideously easy to get confused over coffee orders, to lead clients to the wrong chair after the backwash, to mix up the stylists' brushes and scissors. Even the dreaded sweeping up, which she still had to do, had a right and a wrong direction: 'Clients don't want to walk through heaps of hair as they go to the desk.' And as for giving the client the wrong coat . . .

'It's one of our little specialities,' Tania had said. 'Of course, you can ask the client which is her coat, but they really love it if you're waiting there with it. So hang them up systematically, according to which dressing-table they're sitting at. It's not rocket science.'

It wasn't, but several times she had brought out the wrong ones, a raincoat instead of a mink, a neat blazer instead of a chunky knit and was made to feel as if she had put ground glass in the clients' coffee.

She grew to hate the word 'client' and indeed, some of the clients themselves. Most – including almost without exception the men – were friendly, chatty, generous with their tips. Others were monsters, complaining about water temperature, uncomfortable chairs, five-minute delays, about coffee that was too cold, mineral water that was too warm, magazines that had been read the week before: pampered, demanding creatures who would plant their Hermès or Asprey handbags on the floor in everyone's way at the backwash and then glare fiercely or sigh heavily if they were asked to move them, who would insist on getting up and making long phone calls from the desk in the middle of having their colour done so that the timing was messed up. Or they would rush in late and demand to be out again within half an hour, or bring in their small children and smile indulgently as they raced about or played in the middle of the salon, tipped boxes of rollers or hairclips onto the floor, or made faces at the stylists in the mirrors.

But there was no client behaviour that could not be met with a smile and a, 'That's perfectly all right,' or, 'I'm so sorry.'

'Darling,' Florian once told her, 'if they spit in your face, you just say "that's absolutely my pleasure" as you wipe it off.'

And yet, still Annabel loved it.

And loved even more telling her parents so. And about Florian: omitting his bad behaviour. She could see that the only thing worse than being a hairdresser was going out with one.

Simon was dreading Christmas: the first time they wouldn't be at Chadwick. The rest of the family, apart from Tilly, were quite looking forward to it. Elizabeth because it would be easier, Annabel and Toby because they would be nearer their friends.

But for Simon it was yet another mark of a very public and high-profile failure: having been the golden boy all his life, successful at school, successful with women, immensely successful at work, he was having to watch as the symbols of that success – the lovely houses, the horses, the spectacular holidays – slowly but steadily whittled away. They were all going ski-ing early next year; at half-term. It might be the last year, he warned them, 'but let's bloody well make it a humdinger.'

And what he saw coming now, as they moved with sickening inevitability towards the next year, the third set of losses, was a reckoning of such vast proportions it was all he could do, especially in the middle of the night, not to panic totally, pull out, and run away. It was very frightening indeed: and it was an absolutely lonely terror, that he found hard to share, even with Elizabeth. Only his fellow-sufferers provided proper comfort, only they understood the pre-dawn terrors, the sense of dreadful impotence. Although the lawsuit promised some relief from that: if it ever happened. He was beginning to despair of that as well; there had been no further word from George Meyer . . .

Flora had become a great confidante: she seemed to understand his sense of humiliation and frustration, indeed shared much of it. He called her at least once a week, Boy providing the excuse, but actually to talk about things, his anxieties, his progress or rather lack of it in finding a solicitor, and had come to admire her, for her courage, her determined if rather doomy optimism. She was now housing Boy in her stableyard, 'And enjoying him, he's a wonderful ride.' Simon and Tilly were going down immediately after Christmas, staying at a 'really awfully good' B&B that Flora had told them about. She had invited them to stay with her, but Simon said she was already doing more than enough: 'And besides, having strangers in the house, bit much really.' Tilly could spend time with Boy; and if she felt comfortable enough with Flora, then he would leave and she would stay with her in the house for a few days. Flora had been immensely understanding about the whole thing.

'If she feels remotely ill-at-ease, or indeed you or Elizabeth do, then we can just forget it. But if she'd like to stay, just for a couple of days, then I'd love to have her. We can ride together, it'd be fun. My family aren't coming down this Christmas, so it'll be nice to have Tilly's company afterwards.'

Simon felt rather sorry for her; there had clearly been some tension with her daughter-in-law, that day they had been down. Bit of a spiky creature, not exactly pretty but very attractive. He could imagine that if you didn't get along with Flora, as she clearly didn't, she would seem very strong medicine indeed.

And then, just before Christmas, he got two calls that cheered him immensely.

The first was from Catherine Morgan: could she come and see him, if his offer was still open? Her voice was very tentative.

'Of course you can. It'd be lovely to see you.'

He invited her up to his office; she came in, clearly impressed by its grandeur, the deep leather sofas, his huge desk, the books lining the walls, the rather fine black marble fireplace. She looked tireder than ever; she was wearing exactly the same skirt and sweater as she had at the meeting. He wondered if she possessed anything else.

He sat her down, asked for some coffee for them both.

'How are the kids getting on at school?'

'Oh, just about all right,' she said, but her eyes were shadowy. 'That's why I'm here. I'm just so worried. Caroline isn't doing too badly, there are a few what you might call nice little girls there, but for Freddie it's pretty miserable really. He gets teased endlessly about his accent, and about being rather bright academically; it's so confusing for him, he still wants to try and do well, and the other boys just don't. He often comes home looking very upset and even with a few scrapes and bruises, but he's so brave and he refuses to admit there's anything wrong. I could kill those boys: I feel absolutely desperate about it. I just don't know what to do.'

'And you don't have any family?'

'No. Both my parents died while we were in Hong Kong and their legacy has gone to Lloyd's as well. And my in-laws are . . . well. Not very approachable. That's an understatement.'

Intriguing, Simon thought. How could they not help their grandchildren? Or indeed their pretty, brave daughter-in-law?

'So the buck stops with me rather,' Catherine said. 'Honestly, Mr Beaumont, I ask myself why I did it, became a Name I mean, over and over again, until my head feels as if it's going to explode.'

'I certainly know that feeling,' said Simon, smiling at her.

'I mean, I'm not at all that sort of person—'

'What sort of person?'

'Well, you know, sort of posh and grand. My family is really very ordinary, I grew up in the suburbs, went to a grammar school.'

'Catherine, as I would have thought you'd notice, there were all sorts of people at the meeting. It's a long time since Names were posh and grand. That's part of the scandal, getting people like you in who really can't afford it.'

'Well, yes, I suppose so. Anyway, that's why I've come to see you – because of Freddie, I mean. I thought if – well, if you were mad enough to take me on, then I could perhaps put him back in the independent sector. But then is that fair to Caroline? And I certainly can't pay two lots of school fees.'

'Well, if she's doing all right, I shouldn't fret about that, not at the moment anyway,' said Simon. 'It's Freddie we should be concerned about. Oh, don't worry,' he added, as she stirred the coffee over-zealously in her nervousness, and spilled some of it into her saucer. 'Now, tell me about yourself – professionally, I mean. How up on all the new technology you are, that sort of thing.'

It transpired that she was very up on it – the estate agents where she worked had embraced it rather fervently – and she began talking about spreadsheets and documents. 'I'm a very good typist, and I can do shorthand, and – well, I'm quite a good secretary although I say it myself. But I am tied to school hours, I can't possibly pay anyone to look after the children. The other thing I've thought of is selling the flat, moving into rented accommodation, that would provide a few terms' fees, but then I worry all the time about next year and how much money I might have to find then.'

'Catherine, don't sell your flat, whatever you do,' said Simon. 'The market's on the up again, it'll be worth more soon. I think your working is the answer. All you need is an enlightened boss. Like me.'

'Yes, well, it does seem pretty lucky. You've got children of your own, of course?'

'I have. Two still at school and one out in the big wide world, working.'

'Oh really? What does he do?'

'She. She's a hairdresser. Not what I'd have chosen for her, I have to say, but—'

'Why not?' asked Catherine, and she seemed genuinely puzzled. 'I think it's a really good job for a girl. You spend your days making people look better, which must be very satisfying, and then when you're married and have babies, you can still do it, working from home.'

'I suppose so,' said Simon. He felt rather ashamed of himself suddenly, presented with this blindingly sensible view of Annabel's job. All right, she might not be getting a degree, or using her education much, but what good had his fine degree and his high-profile job done him, now the chips were down? It was a genuinely good and useful career, and he resolved in future to say so.

'Right then,' he said to Catherine, 'you'll be wondering what I'm going to do with you, or if I've got you here under false pretences.'

'Of course not,' she said, and blushed violently.

'Well, obviously I have a personal secretary and she works pretty long hours, but we do need someone to help my assistant's PA; the current incumbent is leaving to have a baby. I'll call her in, in a minute, and you can have a chat with her.'

'It sounds too good to be true,' said Catherine, 'but won't she mind about the hours I can do?'

184

'No, she won't. I've had a word with her, and provided you can come in fairly early, make up the time a bit there – banking's an early-start business, or the sort we do – she thinks it'll be fine.'

In fact, the secretary in question didn't think it would be fine at all, but she had a cushy job and knew she'd put it at risk if she acted up. And she was rather dazzled by Simon Beaumont; all the secretaries were. Together with most of the female staff.

'Yes, I do think I could manage that – getting in early, I mean.'

'Good. Now, I don't know what you're earning at the moment . . .'

'Nine thousand. I know it sounds a lot, but it doesn't seem to go anywhere and—'

'It doesn't sound a great deal,' said Simon, thinking that this was roughly what Boy's vet's bills came to, 'and we can certainly improve on that. How does twelve sound to you? Twelve and your season ticket? There now. Take it or leave it.' He smiled at her. 'I think you'd suit us all very well.'

Catherine said she would take it, and had great difficulty restraining herself from hugging him.

And then, three days before Christmas Eve, he got another call.

'Simon Beaumont?'

'Yes.'

'Simon, it's George Meyer.'

'Oh, hi. I was beginning to wonder when I'd hear from you.'

'Yes, I'm sorry. The thing is, I felt we had to get the solicitor absolutely right and the first one I approached, who seemed so keen, fell by the wayside. As did yours, I seem to remember. And then I had to go to the Gulf for a month—'

'Yes, your office did explain. Doesn't matter.'

'Anyway, are you still with me?'

'Absolutely. Especially as I reckon I'll be in for well over half a million next year. The house'll have to go. I'm just bracing myself to contemplate putting it on the market, buying something smaller.'

'You should be grateful you've got a house. Mine is long gone. No, I'm sorry for you, there's something very – seminal about having to sell your house. The basis of the whole of one's life is there, deep within the bricks and mortar. Everything becomes very shaky without it. I don't mind admitting I shed a few tears the day mine went. Beautiful place it was, in a lovely part of Cheshire.'

It wasn't all he'd lost, Simon knew; his wife had left him for a man who 'seems to own half Chelsea', and his children, initially loyal, had been lured away by ski-ing holidays at the boyfriend's chalet in Mégève and sailing in his yacht in the Maldives.

'Why did we do, it, Simon?' Meyer said now. 'How could we have been so monumentally stupid?'

'Christ knows.'

'Well anyway, I do now have a solicitor for us. Absolutely top-notch, reputation as a fighter, willing at least to consider us and our case. Wants to meet as soon as possible.'

'Fine. Count me in. How are the others doing?'

'I think we've got quite a few.'

'Me too. Look, I'll have another ring-round, see if I can get some more in. Anyway, when do we see this chap?'

'Well, as I said, the sooner the better. Get your diary out. But – there's one thing, and I don't know how you'll feel about it.'

'What's that?' said Simon, reaching for his diary.

'It's not a chap.'

Alan Richards and Barry Grove were having lunch in the George and Vulture, a favourite bar with the City boys as well as the serious bankers and the Lloyd's people; it was extremely busy. The long bench tables, always cosy, were packed so tightly that it required a certain dexterity to move hand to mouth; lifting a pint glass was particularly hazardous. Those standing at the bar were so closely jammed together that, had one of them collapsed, he would not have fallen but remained upright, supported by his fellow drinkers. The noise level was also considerable; a newcomer to the scene would have considered speech out of the question. Alan and Barry were not newcomers.

'What you doing for Christmas then?' asked Barry, taking a large swill of beer. 'Spending it with Heather?'

'Splitting it,' said Alan. 'Her parents for lunch, mine for the evening. Not ideal, but there you go. And then Boxing Day I'm taking her to the races at Sandown Park. Really special, that is, and she said she'd always wanted to go. You?'

'Oh, going round my brother's. Him and his wife, they really know how to do Christmas. First bottle opened straight after breakfast and then it's non-stop till bedtime. Pretty good day on the whole. I've never been to the races, though. I envy you that. Do you put a lot of money on the gee-gees?'

'Not me. Cautious kind of bloke, I am. Maybe a tenner each way on the George the Sixth – that's the big race of the day. Hey – why don't you come with us? Heather won't mind – the more, the merrier.'

'Cheers, mate, I might just do that,' said Barry. 'But I probably won't bet. Haven't got the guts. I like a certainty, myself, with my money. Premium Bonds, that sort of thing.'

'Or Lloyd's,' said Barry. 'I mean, that's what they all thought; poor buggers.'

'Yeah. And it turned out to be more like the George the Sixth. Incidentally, I meant to tell you I heard someone talking the other day, round in the Jam Pot it was, saying that there are those that think it wasn't just bad luck got all those people into trouble.'

'Yeah? What was it then?'

'Well . . .' Alan leaned forward, took another swig of beer and set his glass down with huge difficulty, 'the word is – and it's only a rumour, mind – that there's a sort of conspiracy going on.'

'What sort of conspiracy?'

Alan looked around, and then thought no one could possibly hear a word he said, or know what he was talking about unless they were skilled at lipreading. 'Lloyd's needed more money and sharpish. So they hauled in a lot of new people, blinded them with science, didn't look too hard at their equity and bunged them in the dodgiest syndicates. Reckoned they'd never know the difference. Well, no one does, do they?'

Barry shook his head. 'Certainly don't. Most of them are like me at the races – don't have a clue, poor suckers.'

187

'But it is only a rumour,' said Alan again, 'and you didn't hear it from me – right?'

'Heard what?' said Barry. He grinned at Alan, then went on more soberly, 'But if it is true, then it's pretty bloody rotten, I'd say. You up for another one of those?'

'Yeah, why not,' said Alan.

He watched Barry disappear into the mob; it would be a while before he was back. He pulled his handkerchief out of his pocket, wiped his forehead. As he put it back, he knocked the arm of the man sitting next to him.

'Sorry, mate.'

'No, that's OK,' said the man. 'Wonder you can breathe at all in here. Someone's gone to get me a pint as well. If he's back before teatime I'll be impressed. You work in the City then?'

'Well, sort of. For Jackson and Bond, underwriters – you know them?'

'Yeah, course. At Lloyd's.'

'You in the business? S'pose you must be, or you wouldn't be here.'

'In a way. I'm a hack,' said the man, 'work for the *Daily News*. On the City pages.'

'That interesting, is it?' said Alan.

'Sometimes. Much of the time it's pretty boring. Look, I couldn't help hearing what you were saying just now. About Lloyd's.'

'Yeah?'

'I'd be really interested in hearing a bit more – if you felt you could talk. It sounded quite – well, it intrigued me. Let's just say that.'

'Sorry,' said Alan shortly, feeling a rush of panic rising in his throat. 'Never talk to the press. More than my job's worth. And I don't know what you heard, but—'

'Let's just say I've heard something a bit like it before,' said the man. 'About Lloyd's pulling a few fast ones on people.'

'No,' said Alan. 'No, you couldn't have heard me say that.'

'Oh, OK,' said the man, 'my hearing must be playing up. Well, don't worry about it. But if you ever did want to talk to me – in the strictest confidence, of course – just give me a bell. Here's my card.'

188

'Thanks,' said Alan, taking it rather gingerly, as if it might burn him. 'No offence or anything, but I don't think I'll be using it.'

The man shrugged. 'Fine. But you never know, there might be another story, one that you were less worried about . . .'

'Who said I was worried?' said Alan.

'I did. Look, I'm going to cut and run, my friend's got my pint and he's waving me to move outside. Nice to talk to you. Merry Christmas.'

'Merry Christmas,' said Alan.

He smiled rather warily at the man. He was quite young – about Alan's age, maybe a bit older, certainly no more than thirty – and Alan had an idea Heather would have considered him a bit tasty. He was dark, with fairly close-cropped hair, and he was wearing quite a sharp suit. Alan, who prided himself on his know-how about clothes and spent quite a lot of his salary on them, would have said it was Paul Smith. Not his idea of what a hack would wear, but maybe if they worked for the City pages, they had to look a bit more respectable. He looked at the card: *Joel Strickland*, it said, *City Editor, the 'Daily News', Butts Wharf, E.1. direct line 01–271–7913*. Well, that was one number he wouldn't be ringing. Just the same he put the card carefully in his wallet. You never knew.

Lucinda was to spend Christmas with her parents, together with her sister, Susannah, and her extremely pompous husband and rather dull children. It was not an attractive proposition.

Nobody knew what had happened to her, except a few people at work; Graham had more or less had to know and was predictably understanding and charming, without saying anything very much at all; and a couple of her very closest friends had been told: like Katy. She had hated telling Katy, who was in a daze of romantic happiness, but she had had to, Katy had said that Tim, her fiancé, wanted Nigel to be one of the ushers, and could they both come round for supper. She'd been very upset; she had cried and said if there was anything, anything at all she could do . . .

'But are you sure, Lucinda? Nigel is such a sweetie and he so adores you . . .'

She told nobody, nobody at all about Blue.

From everyone else she hid. She dodged invitations, avoided any suggestions of get-togethers, pleading an exceptional workload on account of Christmas. Weekends were the worst; she had always read of single people dreading the weekends, having to fill them somehow, and she knew now it was true. Her bedsit was pretty horrible; she had taken only the barest minimum of her things, feeling she had no claim on any of them, and from living in a cluttered, welcoming house, full of treasures, furniture, pictures, ornaments, either inherited or lovingly chosen with Nigel, she was in a drab room, all beige, the bed doubling as a sofa, the walls bare, dominated by a large television. She hated that television, it seemed to symbolise in a strange way her lonely state; but on the other hand it did help to fill the long hours, especially at the weekends.

She hadn't even spoken to Nigel; he had sent her a note, giving her some times when she could go and pick up her things, and asking her to leave the keys on the hall table. At least after that she had some clothes, and a few photographs, although most of them were of the two of them together. She had left her keys with a note, saying once again how sorry she was; there was no reply.

She felt totally ashamed; horribly remorseful at making him so unhappy, and very depressed. She seemed to herself a worthless, useless creature. She couldn't sleep, couldn't eat, lacked the energy even to read.

Blue Horton supposed he was dreading Christmas. He certainly ought to be, it was going to be pretty bloody awful, although his vast family did manage to make quite an event out of it, lot of eating, awful lot of drinking, and his mum did the best Christmas dinner in the world, she cooked a goose and a bloody great ham as well and they had it with all the trimmings, and his dad always dressed up as Santa Claus for the kids, and in the evening they all got completely hammered and the males tried to get a poker school going only it never lasted long because the girls rolled back the carpet and they had a good old knees-up. Twenty-four of them last year there'd been, counting the kids; they all went to his parents'

190

house in Chelmsford, not because it was the biggest in the family, his brother had a bloody great place in Romford, but because they knew no one would ever be able to do it half as well. From time to time, during what he thought of as the Lucinda period, Blue tried to picture her joining in; bit of a worry, but she'd probably get used to it, she was always telling him how adaptable she was, and anyway, he'd always thought that the first year, they'd spend it in his place. Just the first year. And the next could take care of itself. But he wasn't actually dreading it too much, because he was so bloody miserable all the time he couldn't imagine ever feeling any worse. Every day was horrible, and this would be another one just like it.

Two months it was now, just over actually, since that awful night, and he didn't feel the slightest bit better; his mates kept telling him he'd get over it, that she was only a woman, plenty more fish in the sea, taking him out, getting him plastered, and he didn't feel any better at all. Not at all.

For the first few days, he had hoped; she was a bit inclined to blow hot and cold, she might come round, decide she couldn't stand it, she could give all the money back, for God's sake, he'd kept suggesting that all through that hideous conversation in the car, and she'd said no, she couldn't, that would mean Nigel would lose it all to Lloyd's, quite apart from anything else; but there had been no call, nothing, and finally he'd faced the fact that he'd lost her. It was almost unbearable, that realisation: that he had to spend the rest of his life without ever seeing her again. He'd loved her so much, so very, very much – no, more than loved her, he'd bloody well worshipped her, he'd have died for her if she'd asked him, chucked himself out of the window of McArthur's without a moment's hesitation.

He'd told her that once and she'd sat looking at him, very seriously as she did, with her lovely eyes wide, and then she'd said, 'But Blue, if you did that, what would be the point of my living either? I'd just have to jump out after you.' And then she'd giggled and said, 'Bit of a waste, really, both of us gone.' God, he missed that giggle. And those eyes. And – well, there was nothing he didn't miss really, it was horrible.

*

191

'Now come on, mate,' said Charlie, as the screens went down on 23 December. 'You're going to come out with me and get properly pissed. And you're going to enjoy it. For real, OK? And you're not going home till I've made you laugh, at least five times. Come on, we'll start at Corney and Barrow and then go up West. I am getting a tiny bit tired of all this misery. She's only a woman, for Christ's sake. Plenty more where she came from. And don't tell me there aren't, because I'm getting well sick of that argument as well. There's girls everywhere, some of them bleedin' gorgeous. And you're not going to get over your bit of posh totty until you accept the fact. She's not the only fish in the sea, mate. She might have been a very tasty bit of caviar, but there's other stuff just as satisfying.'

By two-thirty in the morning, Blue had reached the sentimental stage. He had obediently followed Charlie from Corney & Barrow into Balls Brothers on Blomfield Street and thence to Stringfellows – 'Blimey, Blue, you'd have to be made of stone, not going for one of these little beauties.' And he had done his best. Had told jokes, laughed, drunk first beer and then champagne and then cocktails, chatted up at least three of the tutu-clad girls, shared a bottle of champagne with them, thrown up, and then started again in a strip club Charlie knew somewhere round the back of Marble Arch.

'You've done well, my friend,' Charlie said, as they staggered out into the street, 'very well indeed. Told you, it's just a matter of willpower. Plenty more what was it, yes, fish on the beach—'

'But not like her,' said Blue, suddenly sober again, 'not like Lucinda. There's nobody like her, Charlie, I tell you. You've never seen her, she's just in a class of her own . . .'

'Blue,' said Charlie, 'I don't know if I can take much more of this. If she's that wonderful, why don't you put up a bit more of a fight? This husband of hers, chinless wonder, I suppose . . .'

'Totally chinless, Charlie, wouldn't know one if it came up and hit him—'

'Or if you went and hit it. Well, go and do a dawn raid then. Get her. Or try. Instead of sitting down and snivelling—'

'I have never snivelled,' said Blue indignantly.

'You have snivelled, believe me. Go on in and get her. Think of those women, what was they called, in Ancient Rome, as I recall . . .'

'What do you know about Ancient Rome?' said Blue. 'Christ, I think I might be sick again.'

'Please don't. Deep breaths. That's better. What was I saying? Oh yes, Sabine women.' Charlie was a general knowledge buff, much in demand at quiz nights in his local pub. 'They all got raped, and then carried off, right under their men's noses – that's the way to do it.'

'I don't know what you're talking about. And I am not going to rape Lucinda,' said Blue.

'Course you're not. But you could have another go at carrying her off. If she loved you so much, I don't s'pose things are that rosy between them.'

'Charlie, I keep telling you, she's a woman of very strong principles.'

'Mate, they can't be that strong. Otherwise she wouldn't have let you into her knickers in the first place. Go on. It's worth a try.'

'I couldn't,' said Blue, 'I promised I wouldn't. And she'll be all settling down again now, it would only rock the boat.'

'Blue,' said Charlie. 'That's what they're there for, boats. Rocking.'

Debbie and Richard always had a row on Christmas Eve; Debbie said it was part of their Christmas tradition. It seemed funny afterwards, too; at the time, with emotions running high anyway, due to the stress of Christmas, it seemed more serious.

This year was no different. She went into the study to get some more Sellotape – why didn't she ever buy enough Sellotape, knowing that in every other year she ran out – and found Richard looking morose, staring out of the window.

'What's the matter with you?' she said briskly.

'Oh, nothing you'd sympathise with.'

'OK. Let me be unsympathetic. Just tell me.'

There was a silence, then he said, 'I'm worried about Mother. If you really want to know.'

'Richard, I'm sure she's fine.'

'No, Debbie, she's not. She's been very upset by our not going down—'

'I don't think she was that upset.'

'Of course she was. She loved last Christmas and so did the children. As did I.'

'We all did,' said Debbie carefully. 'I just thought this year it would be nice to be on our own as a family. We did invite her here, you know.'

'I know that.'

'And she refused.'

'Yes, I know that too.'

'So—'

'Debbie, we've been through this. She has the animals and so on to look after. And she likes to do Christmas her way, dress up the house, follow her own traditions . . .'

'Well that's very unusual isn't it? So do I!'

'We don't have traditions in the same way, you know we don't.'

'Yes, because we always have to follow hers.'

He ignored this. 'And the children love it there, you know they do. It just doesn't seem much to ask really, to make her happy.'

'It seems a lot to me. Doing everything her way. Packing everything up, trailing down there in a huge traffic jam, missing things here; the children might like Midnight Mass at Oxwich, but they also like going to our church for the crib service and seeing all their friends. And I like seeing all our friends. I'm looking forward to going to Jan's tonight and Sarah's on Boxing Day, instead of trailing round all those big houses, trying to make conversation with people I don't know and don't want to know.'

'Well, I can't help worrying about her,' he said. 'You make very light of her disappointment, but it really was considerable. She's been very brave, telling us about all the parties and so on she's going to, but the fact remains she'll wake up alone on Christmas morning and go to bed alone on Christmas night. And have her friends wondering why she isn't at least coming up here to be with her grandchildren, if we can't go down there.'

'Richard, I just said she could have been up here. Oh, this is a ridiculous conversation. I haven't time for it, anyway. Have you got any more Sellotape? I have about a dozen parcels

194

still to wrap up and we've got to go to the church in an hour.'

There was a long silence, then he said, 'I would not have believed you could have become so hard, Debbie. So hard and so – so aggressive. It makes me very unhappy.' And he walked out of the room.

Soon after, he reappeared. 'Now the children are upset,' he said. 'You know how they hate us quarrelling at Christmas.'

'Richard, I'm sorry, but I seem to remember it was you who started this, you who slammed the door, when all I wanted was a bit of Sellotape. For God's sake, why don't you help instead of picking on me?'

'Oh, just shut up,' he said. 'I really have had—'

And then Emma appeared in the doorway, her eyes full of tears.

'Just stop it!' she said. 'It's horrible, you shouldn't be quarrelling at Christmas; it's a time for being happy, loving one another, doing what Jesus would want.' Emma's school was of what Richard called a 'God-Bothering' persuasion.

'Oh, darling,' said Debbie, remorse flooding her, 'darling, I'm sorry. It wasn't a real quarrel, just—'

'Yes, it was. I heard Daddy shouting at you, I heard you telling him to help, it's horrible of you and it's not fair—'

'It isn't,' said Debbie, 'I know.'

'So – make up friends. Now. Say you're sorry, go on, both of you, in turn, and then Daddy, give Mummy a kiss and then Mummy give Daddy one.'

Debbie looked at Richard, who was still glowering, and felt suddenly overwhelmed with mirth. It was a bit like the marriage service, she felt, being told what to say each in turn by a third party; and then being told that the groom might now kiss the bride.

She managed not to laugh – just; and then said dutifully, 'I'm sorry, Richard.'

'Good. Now Daddy . . .'

Richard was clearly finding it less amusing; he remained silent.

'Daddy. Go on.'

'Go on, Richard,' said Debbie. 'I did.'

'I'm sorry,' he said very quickly.

'Right. Now Daddy, kiss Mummy. Go on . . .'

Finally satisfied, Emma left the room; Debbie started to laugh. Richard stared at her, then reluctantly smiled too.

'Come on now,' she said, 'do it again. I wasn't very impressed with that kiss. I didn't feel you meant it.'

'Of course I did.'

'No, you didn't. Come here, Richard. *This* is a kiss. In case you don't remember. Bit of a while . . .' She started to kiss him; and as so often, her emotions heightened by the row, she began to feel sexy. And felt him, with great unwillingness, start to respond.

'Lock the door,' she said.

'Debs! No, the kids are all over the house.'

'They can manage without us for a few minutes. I heard Emma telling the others we were making up friends. I really think we should, don't you?'

'Debbie—'

But she had already started pulling up her skirt, slithering out of her pants; she pushed him against the desk, started unzipping his fly – and suddenly, with a rather awkward grin, he reached for her.

It was over in minutes; excited, joyous, half-guilty sex. Afterwards, flushed, breathing hard, pulling her clothes into order, feeling absurdly happy, she smiled at him and said, 'You can still do it, Mr Fielding, still show me a good time. Right, what's next? Oh, yes, the Nativity Service. How appropriate. Poor old Mary didn't know what she was missing.'

'Debbie!' said Richard, his voice shocked. But he smiled back at her just the same.

'I'm off to the shower,' she said. 'Oh, and I tell you what, how about we all go down to Wales for New Year?'

This was a considerable sacrifice as her new friends at Know How were having a party, and it would have been fantastic, lots of media and publishing people.

'I think that would be very nice,' he said. 'Thank you. And for the early Christmas present. Much better than the CDs I found hidden in your drawer.'

'Richard! That's not very nice, poking around in my drawers.'

196

'But I thought that was what you wanted,' he said, 'to have me poking around in your drawers.'

It was quite a long time since he had made her laugh, she thought; or made her come, for that matter. She suddenly felt very happy.

'Happy Christmas, Richard,' she said.

Lucinda had offered to go into the office on Christmas Eve. She had nothing better to do, she certainly didn't want to get to her parents' any sooner than she had to, and working was the only thing that soothed the dreadful aching misery that seemed to be getting worse rather than better.

She had sent a note to Nigel, wishing him Happy Christmas and saying once again how desperately sorry she was for having made him so unhappy; and the night before, in a last and fairly hopeless attempt at making some kind of constructive contact, she had phoned him at the house. There was no answer, so she tried the farm in Norfolk; the housekeeper said she would fetch him and then came back, saying that he was very busy and couldn't come to the phone.

Lucinda had put her head in her arms, on the card table that served her as a dining table, and wept for a long time.

Blue was trying to enjoy the customary Christmas Eve piss-up at McArthur's, held on the trading floor after the market had closed at midday. Apart from anything else, he thought that a few glasses – just a few – would help to cure his hangover. They did, briefly, but then he started feeling drunk again: drunk and absolutely miserable. He left the group and went and sat by his desk, staring at the empty screen; if someone had offered him a gun, he thought, he would have held it to his head and fired it.

'Blue!' It was Stella, one of the receptionists; the girls didn't usually venture onto the trading floors as the welcome they got, although enthusiastic, was not exactly subtle or gentlemanly. 'Blue, you OK?'

'No, not really, Stella love, I'm not,' said Blue. He reached out an arm, put it round her without looking at her; the screen blurred. She stood there, and then suddenly bent down and kissed the top of his head.

'What is it? You didn't just get fired, did you?'

'No, I didn't get fired.'

'Bonus OK?'

'Bonus fine, thanks.'

'So – girl trouble?'

'Girl trouble, Stella. Got it in one.'

'Oh, I'm sorry. Well, all I can say is she must need her head examined. No one in her right mind would turn you down, Blue. I certainly wouldn't.'

'You wouldn't?'

'Course not.'

He turned his head and looked up at her, past her considerable breasts, to her concerned face. She had very large blue eyes: a bit like Lucinda's, he thought. They were regarding him with an almost maternal sympathy.

'You should try again,' she said.

'What – even if the situation was totally hopeless?'

'Course. Always worth another try. She might just be playing hard to get,' she added helpfully.

'I don't think so.'

Stella bent down and kissed him again; her breasts, richly perfumed, moved into view. Christ. He'd almost forgotten what breasts could do to you. Apart from anything else, he was bloody sick of being celibate.

'Look,' she said, 'what you got to lose? It's Christmas.'

Blue couldn't quite see what that had to do with it, but a surge of recklessness suddenly rose up from somewhere. From between Stella's breasts, probably.

'All right,' he said. 'I will. Right now.'

'Well done,' she said, straightening up, patting him on the head like an approving parent. 'You do that and I'll go and get you another glass of bubbly. All right?'

'All right,' said Blue.

He picked up the phone and dialled Lucinda's office number. She probably wouldn't be there, but he certainly couldn't ring her at home.

It was nearly lunchtime; the office was dead. There was no point staying any longer. She was the only person there, apart from the doorman. She might as well go and do a bit of last-minute shopping. She still hadn't got anything for her sister. And then she could join the car park that would be the M4 on a Christmas Eve evening.

She stood up; her head ached. Well, she would walk to Oxford Street, that would clear it. She'd taken too many pills recently. She put on her coat, picked up her bag and walked out of her office. As she pulled the door after her, the phone started to ring. Damn. Well, whoever it was could wait until after Christmas. It couldn't be urgent. It would stop in a minute; she really couldn't face being wished Merry Christmas by one more author or agent, or journalist.

She walked down the corridor, pressed the button to call the rackety old lift. God, her head hurt. The sooner she got out in the fresh air, the better.

She pressed Ground; the lift began on its very slow, lurchy journey. It made her feel sick. She was always feeling sick these days. Sick and headachey. Was life ever going to get any better?

No answer. He'd hung on for ages. She'd obviously left. Well, he'd tried. He almost felt better; quite pleased with himself, in fact. He could tell Stella he'd tried and failed and then get on with wallowing in his misery.

He could see her coming back now with the glass of champagne. He'd drink that, and then he might even ask her out. She was sweet. And those breasts; you could drown in them. That's what he needed: a bit of breast engulfment . . .

'She wasn't there,' he said, 'before you ask.'

Lucinda reached the ground floor and looked out at the street; it was teeming with people, noisy, laughing, happy people. She really couldn't go out there and join them, not with this headache. She might have to give in and take a couple of aspirin . . .

'She might have gone to the toilet,' said Stella helpfully. 'You can't just give up that easily, Blue. She got her own office, has she?'

'Yes.'

'Well then. Try again. Just once more, go on.'

'Will you hold my hand?'

'My pleasure,' she said brightly.

Lucinda went back up to the office, unlocked the door, sat down at her desk, opened a drawer. She certainly had some painkillers in there. Quite strong ones that Blue had given her after one of their more spectacular lunches.

'Buck-up pills these are, Lucy. Take two and think of me.'

Don't think about Blue, Lucinda, don't. It won't help. It won't do any good at all. She pulled out the packet, got up again to fetch a glass of water. The phone rang.

'Go away,' she said to it. 'Just go away.'

And then thought that it might perhaps be Nigel. You never knew. He might just want to make peace: given that it was Christmas. She picked it up, hoping.

'Hello?' she said.

It wasn't Nigel.

'Lucy? It's me, Blue. I – er – I just phoned to say Happy Christmas. Hope that's all right.'

'Oh – yes, of course. Of course it's all right. Yes, Happy Christmas to you.' How could she sound like that, so calm and – and ordinary.

'Everything all right, is it?'

'Yes, thank you. Yes, it's fine. You?'

'Absolutely fan-bloody-tastic. Yes.' He sounded very cheerful.

'Oh – good,' she said. Obviously he'd recovered much faster than she had.

'Yeah, great.'

'Good. I'm so glad.'

'And – how's Nigel?'

'He's fine. Yes.'

'That's good. Very good news indeed. Well, Happy Christmas, Lucinda. Glad you're OK.'

And then she couldn't stand it any longer.

'Oh Blue,' she said. 'Oh Blue, please . . .' And burst into tears.

'Stay there,' he said. 'I'm coming over.'

He arrived within twenty minutes; she didn't have the strength to move, to run away, to tell the doorman not to let him in, any of the sensible, right things. She just sat at her desk, staring at the phone, still holding it, where she had placed it back on the receiver, contact with him of a sort at last. She would just see him and chat to him for a bit and convince him somehow that everything was all right and then—

'Hello, Lucinda.'

He was standing in the doorway.

Lucinda felt faint; faint with shock, with love, with grief.

'Oh,' she said, as if she was surprised he was there. 'Oh Blue, hello.'

He didn't move: nor did she.

'You all right?'

'Yes, I'm perfectly all right, thank you.'

'Because you were crying.'

'Yes, I know. Silly. Couldn't help it. Sorry.'

'Why were you crying, Lucinda? Is something wrong?'

'No,' she said. 'No, of course not. Well, obviously I'm a bit – emotional. At hearing from you, and – and but no, everything's fine. Yes, I'm just off to the country, you know.'

He looked exactly the same: a bit thinner, but quite normal. Obviously everything really was all right for him. Well, she was glad. Very glad.

'You spending Christmas with Mummy and Daddy?'

'Um – yes.'

'Very nice.'

'Yes, it will be.'

'And Nigel, I presume?'

'Well – well, yes. You? Where are you spending it?'

'With my parents, down in Chelmsford.'

'Good. That should be nice too.'

'Yes,' he said. 'Should be.'

There was a long silence; then he said, 'Lucy, I—'

He was going to tell her that he had someone else, that he owed it to her to tell her. She could guess, from the awkward expression on his face, from the rather flat note in his voice. She braced herself; and then it was all too much and she started crying again. And reached out to the box of tissues at the back of her desk and her sleeve slipped up her arm . . . and he saw.

'Lucy,' he said, his eyes fixed on it.

'Yes, Blue?' she said, blowing her nose, unaware of what had happened, what she had done, what miracle she had worked. 'Yes, Blue, what?'

He moved round the desk then, tipped up her head, made her look at him.

'If everything's so absolutely all right, perhaps you'd like to tell me why you're wearing that fucking watch.'

Chapter 13

January, 1990

Simon had expected all sorts of things from the meeting with the solicitors, but not this. One minute he and George Meyer and three other would-be major players in the drama had been sitting in the meeting room at Evans Dixon Campbell, and his only thought had been a distinct nervousness at the step they might be taking, mixed with a sense of excitement that at last things could be moving forward. And the next there she was, walking into the room, a clutch of files under her arm, a cool smile on her face.

Ms (God help them if they called her Miss or Mrs, he thought) Broadhurst. Ms Fiona Broadhurst. Age probably mid-thirties, he would have said: tall, and very slim, with light-brown hair caught back in a ponytail, and brilliant probing blue eyes in a pale and rather emotionless face. She wore a black suit and a white shirt, and black shoes, and she had extremely good legs. Her voice was quick and clipped, as if she didn't want to waste any more time than was necessary on speaking – and she had (Simon inevitably noticed such things), very pretty hands and nails. Unpainted, of course. She was, in a rather self-contained, cool way, extremely sexy. Which would make meetings more pleasant, he thought, smiling at her; she didn't smile back. So – maybe not.

She was a partner in Evans Dixon Campbell, a medium-sized set-up near Charterhouse Square; they were in the boardroom, which was as plainly decorated as Fiona herself, at half-past ten in the morning. An extremely nervous-looking girl brought in a tray of coffee and biscuits; Fiona refused a cup and poured herself out a large glass of water.

'Good morning,' she said, shaking hands with each of them

in turn. 'Very nice to meet you all. I'm Fiona Broadhurst, this is my assistant Clare Lomax. Mr Meyer, perhaps you could go first.'

They went round the table; Simon, who had got to know the other two during the first abortive attempt to find a solicitor, wondered how many would stay the undoubtedly tough course. There was a rather thuggish Northerner, called Terence Cunningham, and a clearly formidable lady, Anne Rudyard. And of course Flora Fielding, who was, as she put it, fighting fit and raring to go.

'Right,' said Fiona, smiling briefly at them all, 'let's get down to business, shall we? Perhaps you'd like me to summarise the case as I see it.'

There was clearly no alternative to this; she took a sip from her glass and started to speak. 'As I understand it, your case rests on whether the inducement to you to become Names was reckless or not; whether it was fraudulent or not. If it was fraudulent, then that would remove all liability from you. Of course, fraud is the highest burden of proof, it's almost criminal, up in the ninety per cent league. It's beyond reckless; reckless is not caring, fraud is *mens rea*. I presume you all know what that means?'

Simon was brave enough to say he did not; Fiona Broadhurst gave him a patient look and said, 'It's literally criminal intent, the knowledge of wrongdoing; it's what distinguishes murder, for example, from manslaughter. In this case, what you are seeking to prove is that Lloyd's, or to be more precise your Members' Agents Jackson and Bond and/or your main syndicate group Westfield Bradley acted fraudulently, rather than negligently. That they knew this very large swathe of claims was coming their way, mostly for asbestosis or pollution, that they didn't have the funds to meet them and were seeking further investment from people without examining the latter's resources sufficiently carefully, and without warning them of the possible consequences. Would you say that states your case clearly?'

The group looked at one another and nodded; George Meyer said it did.

'So what you are saying, as I understand it, is that you have been fraudulently induced into becoming Names, that you want your money back, plus some costs, you want interest on the money you have disgorged, and you don't want to pay any more.'

'Yes,' said Meyer, 'that's about the size of it.'

'Well, that's pretty straightforward.'

'Is it?' said Simon hopefully. 'Do you really think so?'

'Mr Beaumont, when I say straightforward,' said Fiona Broadhurst severely, 'I mean your aims are pretty straightforward, I don't mean a settlement will be. And of course in this country you won't get anything for pain, aggravation and suffering, all that sort of thing. The Americans are very keen on that, but it won't happen here, so I hope you're not expecting it.'

'No, of course not,' said Simon, anxious to distance himself from such self-indulgent nonsense.

'But as I say, your case is complex. And I can't say yet if I can take it on. At this stage, I need a great deal from you first, and I need to do a lot of work of my own. That said, litigation is teamwork and we will need to work together from start to finish.'

'What sort of work and what would you need from us?' said Cunningham. His voice was aggressive. 'I must say, I'd always thought lawyers took whatever they could get. I've never heard of this sort of auditioning business.'

Fiona Broadhurst took a sip from her glass and looked at him very coolly.

'Then clearly you've never been involved in a case of this kind,' she said. 'I, and the other partners here, assess cases very carefully, before committing prospective clients to heavy expense and high risk. As to the second part of your question, or rather the first, if we are to be pedantic, I would require each of you to come to me and say, "This is the situation, this is my contract, this is what induced me, these representations in this brochure, this is what I've paid already, this is what my balance is." I need to know what you're upset about, apart from the obvious which is that you don't feel you should have to pay. I need to know where you feel you've been misled. If you feel there has been a cover-up, if you feel the people in Jackson and Bond, or Westfield Bradley knew, if the market knew, if those who were dealing with Lloyd's knew, if those who had a vested interest in Lloyd's knew, and didn't properly disclose it. I need to know all these things; I need to have as much information as you can give me. I would like each of you to drop me a line, giving me a statement of what you owe, whether it's increased, whether you agreed at any stage to write more business and why. I shall then look at that and give you my decision, as to whether I think you have a case. And I should tell you, of course, at this stage, that going to law is a massive decision; it's terribly expensive and you must know there are no guarantees that you will win.'

'Could you give us some idea of costs?' said Meyer. 'Just a ball park figure perhaps?'

'Not really, no, not at this stage, because I don't have any real idea of how long it will take, but I do anticipate it would be very expensive. We would get a top QC, a top junior, our fees here are between two hundred and fifty and three hundred pounds an hour, less of course for assistants. But you're certainly looking at several hundred thousand pounds. A comparatively simple case, lasting six or seven days, can cost in the order of a hundred thousand, and a case like this, with this type of complexity, you could be looking at a lot more. We'd need experts of every kind, experts on the state of the market, experts on asbestosis, and I do know it would be very expensive. And we would want money on account, paid in advance, something like fifty thousand pounds. So I would advise you to think about it all very carefully before you come to see me again. More coffee, anyone?'

Nobody wanted any more coffee.

'Now Bel darling, what do you think you're going to be doing tomorrow?'

'Oh, can't imagine,' said Annabel. 'I mean, not shampooing, or gowning up, or sweeping up, or even blow-drying Carol's hair if I'm really lucky. Nothing like that, obviously.'

'Darling! So bitter. Let me cheer you up. I'm doing a session for *Seventh Day*, that's the magazine for the *Sunday News*, and guess who's going to come with me as my assistant?'

'Me?' said Annabel. Her voice came out sounding slightly squeaky.

'The very one. I was taking Merle, but she's got a stomach

bug, poor darling, and I thought, Well, why not? You've been a very good girl lately and—'

'Oh Florian! Oh, thank you so, so much!' They were in the staff room; Annabel hurled herself into Florian's arms, kissed him rapturously.

'Sweetie! If I'd known it would have this effect on you I'd have done it sooner. Move down the old bod a bit, tickle the fancy down there, and I might take you to the Maldives with *Vogue* next month. Only kidding,' he said hastily as Annabel pulled back to see if he meant it, 'but no, tomorrow's a definite. Saville Studios, that's in Whitechapel, at eight. Eight as in AM.'

'I'll be there,' she said.

She was actually there at seven-thirty, so frightened was she of being late, complete with a vast bagful of rollers, dryers, brushes, pins and tongs; at five to eight a girl arrived, pulled out a great bunch of keys from her pocket. She was so tall and thin that Annabel thought she must be the model, but, 'Hi. I'm Elise, studio dogsbody. Come on in, you look frozen.'

'Thanks. I am a bit.'

'I'll get you a coffee. You Florian's assistant? We love working with him, he's such fun and so brilliant. But God, this is going to be a long day. Six shots. Probably still be at it at midnight.'

At eight-thirty Florian arrived; he gave Elise a hug, nodded rather briefly at Annabel, as if underlining their professional relationship. She was mildly amused.

'This is going to be one hell of a day,' he said, throwing his coat over a leather sofa, taking the mug of coffee. 'The combination of Effie and our Sandra – God help us.'

'I like Sandra, Florian,' said Elise. 'I think she's really nice, terribly professional.'

'Yes, but darling, all the more reason for her to get cross with Effie. You know how otherworldly she is, never knows what way she's up . . . I blame the dope myself.'

'You're a fine one to talk,' said Elise briskly.

'Now that is so unfair,' said Florian. 'I never smoke on the job. Well, not this sort of job anyway. Do I Bel, sweetie?'

'Um – no, of course not,' said Bel.

Florian did a lot of drugs, it was one of the things that

worried her about him and indeed their relationship. Not only did he smoke dope constantly (although not at work, that at least was true), he took Ecstasy which she could just about accept, after all everybody did, but also cocaine. He had tried to encourage her to try it; so far she had resisted (apart from the occasional spliff obviously), but Florian's powers of persuasion were scarily strong. If anything was going to end their rather odd relationship, it would be that.

And it was odd; Annabel knew she should be strong and end it, but she seemed to lack the will. She would have said she was fairly determined, and absolutely not the kind of person to be mucked about; but here she was, going out with Florian, sleeping with Florian, proclaimed by Florian as his number one favourite girl in the whole wide world, while accepting that from time to time he slept with other girls, Well, she didn't actually accept it, she made a huge fuss whenever it happened, told Florian they were finished, that she never wanted to have anything to do with him ever again: and then found herself a week later back in his bed. And hating herself for it; and thinking that this was not the kind of behaviour she would have encouraged, or even accepted, in any of her friends. It was as if he had bewitched her, with his wit and his charm and his beauty; she knew she had to break the spell, but she needed something to help her. Like falling in love with someone else: that would do it. Only who could compare with Florian? Nobody that she had ever met . . .

They were going to be a good team, Simon thought: a bunch of really solid people, and he'd even liked Terence Cunningham, the Northern industrialist, belligerent bugger as he promised to be. Well, you didn't need too many gentlemen in this game; gentlemanly behaviour was one of the things Lloyd's had clearly been relying on. He wondered idly, while suppressing the thought as fast as he could, if Fiona Broadhurst was a gentleman in those terms, and decided she probably wasn't.

They'd gone for a drink after the meeting. Cunningham, like Meyer, had seen his wife walk away with a new man. 'She started out all sweetness and light, swore she'd stand by me, but after a bit she couldn't cope with the reality. Losing the

208

golf-club membership, seeing her friends in new frocks while she had to wear the old ones, it was all too much.' He glared into his beer. 'Frailty, thy name is woman, my dad used to say. Too bloody right.'

Simon was silent; he thought of Elizabeth, 101 per cent behind him, resolutely keeping their ship afloat, and thought too of Neil Lawrence, who felt unable still even to tell his wife; and thought then how he'd betrayed Elizabeth, and felt desperately remorseful. Lawrence had called him the day before in an appalling state; he sounded very drunk and it was only mid-morning.

'I just can't cope with this,' he said, 'I really can't. I just don't know what to do. I had lunch with my Members' Agent yesterday and I sat up all night literally just staring at the wall, thinking, What have I done? How did I get into this?'

'How much this time?' said Simon.

'Over three hundred thousand at least. Simon, both my houses together aren't going to meet that. I just feel violently sick, all the time. Christ, whoever said money isn't everything obviously had plenty. It's fucking everything, when you're losing it, I can tell you. I can't think about anything else. Can't work, can't sleep, it's literally hell. I know how people feel now, when they say they wish they were dead. I view that as a very attractive option.'

'No, you don't,' said Simon. 'Er . . . what does your wife say?'

'I still haven't told her,' said Neil Lawrence.

'Want to come in on this legal action?'

'Simon, I wouldn't dare.'

They had all been excited by the meeting, they agreed, in spite of Ms Broadhurst's rather daunting prognostication, and indeed daunting presence. 'I thought she was marvellous,' said Flora Fielding, 'didn't you, Simon?'

Simon nodded casually. 'She seemed very capable, yes,' he said, and then saw Flora looking at him with a certain humour in her dark eyes. Clearly she had observed his reaction to Fiona Broadhurst; no point trying to deceive *her* about anything.

'She'll do, I reckon,' said Cunningham. 'Let's hope she thinks we will. We certainly need someone on our side. Oh,

God. How could we have all been so stupid, getting into this mess?'

'Well, it sounded so bloody good, didn't it?' said Simon. 'I still remember someone ringing up, chap I'd been at school with, good man I thought, hadn't seen him much since, but he invited me to lunch, said had I thought about going into Lloyd's. He made it sound pretty enticing, but to be fair to him, I didn't rush it, talked to a few other Names after that; they were all pleased as Punch, so I went ahead. Bloody idiot I was.'

'What I can't understand,' said Anne Rudyard, 'is why we hadn't heard rumours. Things must have been getting pretty rocky years ago.'

'I did, to be honest, about three years ago,' said Simon, 'but I ignored them. Thought it must be isolated cases, couldn't possibly apply to me. And my Members' Agent told me not to worry.'

'Mine too,' said Meyer. 'Bastards. They must have known, mustn't they? Surely to God—'

'Well, we've got to prove it,' said Cunningham, 'as Ms Broadhurst says.'

'Not going to be easy, is it?' said Simon. 'Buggers,' he added.

'Absolute buggers,' said Meyer. He raised his glass. 'Here's to the formidable Ms Broadhurst. Let's hope she takes us on.'

'Ms Broadhurst,' said the group.

He did not fancy her, Simon thought, he most certainly did not. He had a wife in a million and he'd hurt her quite enough. Even though she clearly didn't love him any more.

Elise had been right; it was proving a long day. Annabel felt quite sick with tiredness: they had only done four of the six shots, and it was already half-past five.

Effie the model had arrived at nine-thirty; Annabel was quite disappointed when she walked in. She was so famous, had appeared on practically every magazine cover in the world, was only doing what was for her quite a pedestrian job because Sandra Keswick had given her her first-ever booking, and here she was, pale as death, her mousey hair lank, dressed in what looked like a tramp's overcoat over a pair of leggings and a misshapen sweater.

'Hi,' she said, sinking onto the sofa, pulling out a packet of

cigarette papers. 'Elise, could I have a cup of coffee and –
Florian, what are you doing?'

'Doing you a big favour, darling,' said Florian, putting the
papers and a tobacco pouch that she had placed on the table
back into her bag. 'You've got to work today, and extremely
hard; you can't start by being stoned. Maybe this evening,
when it's over. Now, here's your coffee, drink it up, there's a
good girl, and then we'll get started on the hair.'

'Fuck you,' said Effie, but she sounded surprisingly good-
natured about it.

'This is Bel,' said Florian, 'she's helping me today. Bel, we
need the big rollers plugged in, and honestly, Effie,' he held up
a long strand of her hair and looked at it disdainfully, 'this
needs a good cut. Who's not looking after it for you?'

'Nobody much,' said Effie vaguely. 'I tend to wait for
sessions. If you want to trim it, Florian, that'd be great.'

'We'll see how the time goes,' said Florian, starting to brush
through her hair. 'Maybe after lunch, if we're doing all right.
Elise, who's doing the make-up? And where's Paolo?'

'He'll be here in ten minutes, he's been with his printer,
sorting something out. Jonty's doing the make-up.'

'Oh, fantastic. I do like a day with Jonty. And she's so quick.
What time is she arriving?'

'Ten, I think. And Sandra's assistant's bringing the clothes.
She should be here by now.'

'OK, Paolo had better have a look at them, I suppose, before
we decide on the hair. But I'm thinking big. Always works
better for the papers.'

'Great,' said Elise.

There was a loud roar of a motorbike outside; Paolo Laurence
the photographer walked in dressed in leathers, carrying a
helmet, and trailed by a very thin, pallid boy wearing a pale-
blue tracksuit. Paolo was short, swarthy, with a thick Brooklyn
accent.

'Hi, guys.' He waved into the dressing room, and embraced
everyone, including Bel. 'You all know Ted, don't you? My new
assistant. Where are the clothes?'

'They're not here yet,' said Elise. 'Sandra's assistant's got
them. She'll be here by ten.'

'And want us through by eleven. I can't work like this. Get me some coffee, Elise darling, and some cigarettes, if you'd be so kind. Effie, can you lend me one for now?'

'Sure,' said Effie, holding out two cigarettes in a skinny hand.

'Thanks, babe. You look gorgeous. Love the boots. Where did you get them?'

'Milan.'

'Very, very nice. Ah – here's the lovely Sandra now. Sandra, my darling, greetings. You look fan-bloody-tastic.'

Sandra Keswick was really nice; a breath of sanity, Annabel thought, in this weird day, and then felt shocked at herself for thinking it. Was she getting old or something?

Sandra was blonde and quite glamorous, but apart from some impossibly high-heeled shoes, not really very fashionably dressed, in a bright pink Nancy Reagan-ish suit over a lime-green camisole, and a multi-stranded pearl choker. Her assistant Megan followed after her, almost invisible behind a mountain of clothes. Elise and Ted took them from her and began hanging them up on the rail in the dressing room.

'Hi, Effie darling,' Sandra said. 'How are you? Is Jonty here?'

'No, she got held up in traffic,' said Elise, 'but she'll be here in ten minutes.'

'She shouldn't get held up in traffic,' said Sandra severely, 'or rather, she should allow for it. Florian, have a look at the clothes, see what you think. The story's happy colours: yellows, pinks, blues. So I don't want anything strange, OK?'

'Sandra, darling, you know I don't do strange,' said Florian indignantly.

'Those ones in *Harpers* were pretty strange. Still, that's *Harpers*. Ah, Jonty, here you are. Get moving, there's a good girl, we haven't got any time to waste. Nice and upbeat, this is not about grunge.'

Jonty made all the others look quite normal, Annabel thought; she was wearing a man's collarless shirt over black footless leggings, with legwarmers and something a bit like a tutu. Her red hair was in dreadlocks and her lipstick, the only make-up she had on, was deep dark plum. If they wanted a fairly ordinary look, which was what Sandra had implied, why get her to do the make-up?

She was wrong; within half an hour, Effie's almost grey skin was porcelain pale with sparkling pink blusher, her eyes smoky pools, fringed with impossibly long black lashes, her lips outlined and glossed in deep dark pink. She looked radiant and sassy, certainly not grungey.

Florian started pulling out the rollers, terribly fast; Annabel fielded them, put them back on the rods, terrified of dropping some and looking inexperienced and foolish in front of all these amazing people. She thought she was doing all right, but Florian was edgy as he never was in the salon, snapping his fingers for things, irritable when she couldn't find the waterspray, furious when she dropped the pins. He'd never bring her again, she thought miserably, grubbing about on the floor, trying to pick them up quickly; to her amazement, Sandra Keswick bent down and helped.

'I have the butteriest fingers in Britain,' she said, smiling at Annabel, 'can't hold anything. Here you are, my love, best rinse them if Florian's going to use them.'

Annabel smiled back at her gratefully; she would never have thought of that.

Sandra and Florian were having a mild tiff over the hair for the next shot, a dazzling summer ballgown in cobalt blue, when a man walked into the studio. A distinctly attractive man, Annabel thought, studying him: bit old, probably over thirty, but still ... He was quite tall, with close-cropped hair and brilliant dark eyes, and he was wearing a dinner-jacket; she wondered if he was another model.

But 'Joel, oh my God, how frightful. Is it really that sort of time?' said Sandra. 'I'm not nearly ready.'

'Don't worry, you've got at least another hour. I had an appointment at the NatWest Tower, thought I'd come up here and collect you, rather than go back to the office. Find out what really happens at a photographic session. Looks like fun to me.'

'An hour won't be enough,' said Sandra. 'Come on, guys, for God's sake! This is Joel Strickland, everyone, our City Editor; we've got an awards thing this evening – we're both up for a gong – and we've been summoned to cocktails with the proprietor first, so we absolutely have to leave at six-thirty—'

'Darling, don't fret,' said Paolo. 'If we haven't finished by then, we'll just see it all through. You just tell us what you want, and you'll get it.'

'Well, OK. Joel, there are lots of magazines over there, and probably some wine.'

'No, no, I'll just have coffee, thanks,' said Joel Strickland. 'It's going to be a long night, better not start too early.'

'I'll make you some coffee,' said Annabel, jumping up from the sofa. She had had nothing to do for the past hour, and was feeling distinctly spare; Jonty seemed to have taken over her role as Florian's assistant.

'That's very kind of you,' said Joel. He smiled at her. He had a very nice smile. 'And who are you?'

'I'm Annabel, I mean Bel.'

'Aren't you sure?'

She smiled back. 'Well, my real name is Annabel. They call me Bel in the hairdressing salon where I work. I'm assisting him,' she gestured at Florian, who was backcombing a section of Effie's hair furiously while Jonty held the rest up. 'But I think Jonty's doing a better job.'

'Well, I know who I'd rather have as my assistant,' he said, smiling at her again. 'Come and sit with me and entertain me. I don't really fancy reading *Elle* or *Vogue*. How long have you been mixed up with all these terrible people?'

'Only since this morning,' she said, and then, realising what she had said: 'only they're not terrible, they're all very nice. But I've been training as a hairdresser for about – goodness, eight months now.'

'And – do you like it?'

'Yes, I absolutely love it.'

'Good. That's what I like to hear, people enjoying what they do. More important than anything, really.'

'Do you enjoy what you do?'

'I certainly do. Best job in the world, journalism. You get to go anywhere you want, meet anyone you fancy – I mean, how else would I be sitting here, talking to you?'

'And are you a reporter?' she said, ignoring this, and then, 'Oh no, sorry, silly me, you're the City Editor.'

'The title's grander than the job on a paper like the *News*.'

'And you're up for an award. How exciting.'

'Well, only up for one. I won't get it, though. Much too much competition. Still, it'll be a fun evening.'

'Bit like the Oscars?'

'Not terribly,' he said. She liked his voice; it was a bit raw and gravelly. 'A lot more drunken.'

'What was your story about?'

'Fraud,' he said. 'Juicy little number, but not strong enough to win. Guy from *The Times* will probably win, he wrote about Afghanistan and the drug kings. More of a proper story.'

'And— sorry, do you mind answering all these questions?'

She was genuinely interested. And he really was rather sexy.

'Of course not. God, what are they doing in there?'

'I think,' said Annabel, 'they're making the hair a bit bigger.'

'My word. That does sound serious. Go on.'

'I was going to ask if journalists worked on one story at a time, or lots.'

'Well, it depends. Reporters usually work on one at a time, but sometimes more than one in a day. On the City pages, it's different. There's lots of short, everyday stuff and then there might be one big story which can go on for weeks. Or even months. And you need to be very patient, piecing bits and pieces together. It's fun. Now, do you think we could share a glass of that nice wine Sandra mentioned. I think I want to get into the party mood, after all.'

'Well, I'd better not. But I'll get you one.' She looked over at the dressing room: Jonty was still holding up the hair, Florian was putting rollers in it, and they were having what was clearly a very engrossing conversation. They certainly didn't seem to be missing her.

'This really is very nice,' said Joel, setting down his glass. 'You're missing quite a treat. Now you mustn't let me bore you rigid. Tell me about you.'

'Oh, I'm not very interesting,' she said. 'Left school last year. Doing this now.'

'And are you a girl about Town? Smart flat, lots of designer clothes, all that sort of thing?'

'I wish. I don't earn enough for that. Still live at home with my parents.'

'Do you mind that?'

'Not really. It's quite a big house. And my parents are very good, really. They mostly leave me alone. Don't interfere. They're not too keen on me doing hairdressing, but—'

'Why not?'

'Oh, snobbery mostly. And they're kind of disappointed I didn't go to university. It's practically a religion for my father. He went to Oxford, and he was longing for me to go. But my brother will, I'm sure, and my little sister.'

'Well, I went and it didn't do me an awful lot of good. I'd probably be doing exactly the same thing if I hadn't gone. My brother didn't and he's got a very successful little building company, makes about three times as much money as me . . . You could tell your father that. What does he do?'

'He works in the City. He's on the board of a bank.'

'Yes? Which one?'

'Graburn and French.'

'Very good outfit. I sat next to the Chairman at some PR dinner just before Christmas. Nice man. The bank's doing rather well – not easy in this financial climate.'

'Is it? That's good. Poor old Dad needs some luck at the moment. He's been having quite a hard time.'

'Why?'

'Well – oh dear, I probably shouldn't be telling you this.'

'Of course you should. This is all strictly off the record. Promise.'

'Oh, OK. Well, he's just lost an awful lot of money at Lloyd's.'

'Has he really?' said Joel Strickland.

'So,' said Elizabeth, 'how was your meeting?'

'Oh, pretty interesting. Yes.'

'Was the solicitor hopeful? What was he like?'

'She, not he.'

'Oh yes. What was she like then?'

'Oh, you know.' She knew that note in his voice: carefully vague, wary.

'No, I don't.' Her eyes were sharper suddenly. 'I don't know at all. Tough, I suppose?'

'Very tough.'

'Middle-aged? Young?'

'Young is relative. But – younger than us, yes.'

'Very young, then,' and she managed to smile. 'And – attractive?'

'Yes, I suppose so. In a fierce sort of way.'

'Now what do you mean by that?'

'I mean she wasn't soft and simpering with blond curls.'

'What, like Lucinda Cowper?'

'Who?'

'Simon, don't pretend you don't know who Lucinda Cowper is. The Sloane at the meeting. The one you were drooling over.'

'I was not – oh, for fuck's sake, Elizabeth, can we stop this? Am I never, for the rest of my life, to be allowed to mention a woman and the fact that she is possibly quite attractive, without your moving into Othello mode?'

'Probably not,' she said, 'and I wonder whose fault that is.'

'God give me strength,' he said, and turned and left the room.

She heard him running up the stairs to his study and slamming the door – why, why shut the door? Who was he phoning? – *Elizabeth, stop it, stop it, he's right, this isn't helping*. She went into the kitchen, pulled a bottle of wine out of the fridge and poured herself a large glass, sat at the table staring at it.

She knew she was drinking too much at the moment; it was the only thing that seemed to help, to soothe the jagged depression and guilt. She and Simon seemed to be back where they had been over a year ago: hostile, not communicating, emotionally estranged. And he was right, she had to be more constructive, try to put it behind her. But, 'Oh God,' she said aloud and started to cry quietly: more at her own disastrous insecurity than anything.

It was just that she had been so – so absolutely hurt. And worse even than hurt, demoralised, her confidence shaken as she would not have believed it could be. She, Elizabeth Beaumont, coolly brilliant, absolutely sure of herself and what she wanted, had found herself replaced in her husband's affections by somebody else. Not just an affair, he had loved someone else: really loved her. That was the real blow, the below-the-belt blow, that she felt she could never, ever get over. Of course she had: in one way. She had believed him when he swore it was over. But the world was full of women: sexy, pretty, predatory women. And Simon was so dangerously attractive. Women just loved him; he was that rare thing, a male honeypot.

Of course they had had good times, happy times. But she was still dreadfully disturbed. And the worst thing of all was sex: how were they ever to be easy in bed again? What had this woman he had loved done to please Simon? Was she more compliant, more inventive, more responsive? She lay there in the bed with them, a drifting, dangerous ghost, and on the rare occasions when they did make love it was awkward, almost stilted, as Elizabeth struggled to forget, to let her body lead her back into pleasure – and found herself watching it, watching him, wondering if he was comparing this with what he had done with *her*.

And so, she was still very unhappy. Sometimes more than at others. And almost ill with jealousy and suspicion. And she just didn't know what to do about it.

In her pretty cottage in Hampshire, Gillian Thompson drank a cup of tea, very hot and strong, the way she liked it, and then picked up her beloved tabby cat, Mustapha, put him in his carrying basket and took him to her friend, May Williams, who lived just down the road in Moor Lane. May was also very fond of Mustapha, and had once or twice looked after him when Gillian had gone on holiday.

'I'm sorry it's such short notice, May, but I've been called away. Would you mind looking after him for a while? I so hate to think of him in that cattery.'

'Of course,' said May, scooping Mustapha out of his basket and stroking him fondly. 'I always love to have him, you know that. He'll never lack for a home while I'm around.'

'Good,' said Gillian Thompson. 'That's very comforting, May, thank you. I'm not quite sure when I'll be back, is that all right?'

'Of course. Would you like a cup of tea?'

'No, thank you, I've just had one and I ought to be getting along. I'll— well, thank you, May. Goodbye then.'

And then she was gone, her small feet in their nicely polished shoes tap-tapping down the brick path.

May watched her for a bit and then shut the door and went back inside to pour Mustapha a saucer of cream.

Gillian Thompson went back to her cottage, carefully closed all the windows and put a rolled-up blanket along the bottom of the living-room door; she took a couple of aspirin and switched on her gas fire. Then she lay down as close to it as she could and started to inhale very deeply and slowly.

219

Chapter 14

Spring, 1990

He looked awfully fierce. His eyes had that sort of hard, shiny look to them that she didn't like, making them unreadable. And his mouth was a different shape completely: narrower, tighter – he was obviously very cross. Oh God. Now what was she going to do?

'I'm sorry,' she said again. 'Really sorry.'

'Yes, all right,' he said.

'I know I should have told you before.'

'Probably you should. Well—' And then he smiled suddenly, his face appearing to crack almost in two, his widest, most glorious grin. 'Say it again. Go on. I want to hear it again.'

'I'm going to have a baby,' she said. Breathing more easily, feeling less frightened.

He shook his head quickly several times as if he thought his hearing might be affected. 'You're not having me on?'

'Well, no. I'm sorry if it's a shock, but—'

'It is a bit,' he said. 'Pretty shocking. I'm not sure why that should be. We've been doing all the right things. God in heaven, Lucinda, a baby. You and me. Yours and mine. Jesus. Are you quite, quite sure?'

'I'm terribly sure, yes,' she said. 'I've missed my period – well, nearly two now . . .'

'You know, I did wonder,' he said, 'then I thought, no, I never could count. Go on—'

'And I've had a test done. At the doctor – I don't trust those things you buy.'

'God,' he said again. 'This really is quite monumentally good news. Wouldn't you say?'

'Well, I think so, yes. So – you're not cross?'

'Cross? No, Lucy, I'm not cross. Why should I be cross, for pity's sake? Whatever made you think that?'

'Well – I don't know really. We didn't exactly plan it. And it's my fault, entirely.'

'How do you work that one out?' he said.

'I got behind with my pills. I left it too late to get another prescription, and then I – well, I thought supposing I was pregnant, I didn't want to take the pill if I was, it might harm the baby in some way, you know, so I thought I'd better wait till the next time, and—'

'You haven't got much commonsense, have you, Lucinda?' he said.

'I suppose not,' she said humbly. 'Not a lot.'

'Well, thank God for it,' he said. 'I don't know when I was so pleased about anything. Except when I saw that fucking watch on your wrist. A baby. My God. Here, come and give your old man a kiss.'

'You know what we've got to do next, don't you?' said Blue.

'Um – tell our mothers?'

They were lying in bed, Blue drinking champagne and Lucinda a mug of hot milk – 'You know, I was wondering why you was off the booze,' he said, 'but then you don't drink much, and I thought it must be a diet or something. Telling our mothers wasn't quite what I meant, but anyway, we must, yes. Mine'll be over the moon. What about yours?'

'Not quite the moon. But we can hope, I suppose.'

'Maybe it'll make her warm to me a bit. Get the top of the glacier melting at least. No, probably not. It'll force a few unpleasant facts further home. Like you and me are obviously having sex, like the relationship's just possibly going to last for a while. Reckon your dad might horsewhip me? Well, never mind, it'll be worth it.'

'You're so good about them, Blue.'

'Lucinda, I could forgive your parents anything. Anything at all.'

'Why?'

'They made you,' he said, kissing her tenderly. 'I'd call that a pretty good thing for them to have done for me.'

221

Lucinda, already emotional, started to cry.

What they really had to do, must do, he told her, cradling her in his arms, was get the divorce going.

'I'm not having my son born out of wedlock,' he said, 'and that's that.'

'Oh, now Blue, that's just silly.'

'Why?'

'Well, in the first place, we'll never get it all over and done with and us married by November.'

'Is that when it is?' he said, sounding startled. 'Blimey. You sure?'

'November, yes. It usually takes nine months, I believe. And in the second place, it might be a girl.'

There was a long silence, then: 'No,' he said, 'not possible. Out of the question.'

'OK. Well, anyway, I can try with Nigel. Try again. But I don't hold out a lot of hope. He just acts as if I don't exist.'

'Well, he can't act as if our baby doesn't exist.'

'Poor Nigel,' said Lucinda.

'Poor sod,' said Blue.

It had been a very exciting four months, she thought, lying awake staring happily into the darkness while Blue slept. Starting with Christmas, with telling her parents she couldn't come after all, that she had met a friend who needed her to be with her. They'd been predictably sniffy; her mother said it would mess up all sorts of arrangements, and that they'd been looking forward to having everyone there together. 'Can't you tell this friend to manage, just until after Christmas?'

'No, it's absolutely out of the question,' said Lucinda firmly. 'She's really in a terrible state. I couldn't possibly leave her.'

She was lying in Blue's bed as she spoke, and he was tenderly removing her knickers.

'Well, I think it's too bad,' said her mother, and then in a clear burst of Christmas spirit, 'perhaps you'd like to bring her to join us?'

'I – don't think that would be a very good idea,' said Lucinda; she heard a strange noise escape her, the result of Blue's tongue applying itself to one of her nipples.

'Oh, very well. But I do think it's most— Lucinda, are you all right? What on earth are you doing?'

'Just – just trying to comfort my friend,' she said.

Blue had taken her to meet his family on New Year's Day. 'Now they are a bit much,' he said, 'I warn you. Not too much like your folks, I'd say.'

'That's good news,' she said.

She had fallen in love with them, the whole noisy, cheerful, over-the-top lot of them; she could see they found her very strange, and Blue's choice of her even stranger. It had been very hard at first, she had been trying to play down her background, and had been feeling very tense and shy, trying not to say anything that could be remotely interpreted as snooty; the day was made even odder by the fact that Blue was Gary at home; it was oddly disconcerting. She was beginning to feel slightly desperate, when Blue's nine-year-old nephew, a bullet-headed replica of his uncle, had fixed her with beady dark eyes and said, 'Gary says you're well posh. We never met anyone posh before – what's it like then? You met the Queen and that?'

'Jason,' said Margo, Blue's mother, 'that's no way to talk to Lucinda.'

'Of course it is,' said Lucinda, relaxing suddenly, 'and actually I'm really not very posh as you call it, Jason, not at all.'

'Oh no, I don't think so, not actually,' whispered Holly, his ten-year-old sister, in a parody of Lucinda's accent.

Her father gave her a smart clip round the ear. 'I don't want any of your cheek, Holly. You be polite to the lady. I'm sorry, Lucinda.'

'Honestly, please, please don't be polite,' she said, 'I'd much rather they weren't. But anyway, Jason, no, I haven't met the Queen. But I have been to Buckingham Palace.'

'And was Princess Diana there?' said Holly, curiosity getting the better of her.

'Very sadly, no. I was with my father, he was getting a – a sort of medal. I think Diana was in her own palace. She's beautiful, don't you think?'

'Yes. You look a bit like her,' said Holly consideringly. 'Not as pretty, but a bit the same.'

'Well, thank you,' said Lucinda. 'I call that a huge compliment.'

'And what a good mother, isn't she?' said Margo. 'Lovely they are, those boys. I think she's wonderful, I really do. I don't reckon Prince Charles appreciates her properly, you know.'

'No, I think that's probably right,' said Lucinda.

'And her clothes. Really lovely. She makes the rest of them look pretty frumpy, doesn't she?'

'She certainly does. I like her hair a bit longer too.'

After that, things got easier very quickly.

For Blue, meeting Lucinda's parents, things were more difficult. Her mother was so patently horrified by him, it was almost funny. Lucinda had tried to warn them, to spell out what Blue was like, but he could have been an alien, landing on Earth from another planet for the violence of their reaction to him. They stared at him, transfixed, their smiles chilly, their faces frozen, through the longest lunch Lucinda could ever remember; her father only addressed him directly to ask him if he would like some more wine; her mother, clearly at a complete loss to understand the relationship, struggled to be more friendly, asking Blue about his work, about where he lived, about his own family, but it was painfully awkward. Quite apart from anything else, they had trouble with his name, ended up calling him Mr Horton. As soon as coffee was half-drunk, she stood up and said they must go.

'I'm so sorry, Blue,' she said, almost in tears as they drove away. 'They're just – just rather stupid.'

'It's OK.'

'It's not OK at all. They were rude – rude and insulting. And what for?'

'Well, I s'pose we've broken the number one rule: stick to your own tribe.'

'Your family don't mind me.'

'They do a bit. I mean, they like you and that, but they think it's well odd. Oh, except for my dad. He thinks you're wonderful. Calls you the princess. I didn't tell you that, did I?'

'No,' she said, 'you didn't. Blue, I do apologise.'

Blue pulled into the side of the road. 'Lucy,' he said, 'it's you I love. Not them. In fact, I love you more than ever.'

'Why?' she said curiously.

'Well, to have managed to have turned out so extremely well. I'd say it was a considerable achievement, myself. Now give me a kiss and let's stop worrying about them, OK? If I can live with them, then you can.'

'Not literally, please God,' she said, and shuddered.

Her friends she told gradually; a lot of them took Nigel's part, clearly considering her very much the villainness of the piece, and stopped seeing her. She was hurt; she hadn't expected that, had thought that the friendships would survive, that people would stay friendly with both of them. It seemed terrible that a rift in a marriage should have to gape so widely and so relentlessly. Some people did take her side though; she was grateful, and then introduced them to Blue rather nervously. On the whole it was the men who took to him more.

'Bloody clever,' said Katy's fiancé Hugh, 'fantastic what he does every day. Millions of pounds go through his fingers. Don't know how he does it without having a heart-attack.'

Others said much the same thing. Lucinda felt a bit silly; she had always thought what Blue did must be clever, but she had never really understood it, and certainly hadn't realised how extremely difficult it must be. She looked at him almost awed, newly and deeply impressed by him. He was very amused.

'You see, Lucinda, it's possible to be quite clever, do fairly well even, without ever having been to one of those schools of yours.'

They were living in his little house in Limehouse; she was still working at Harrisons. Graham Parker twinkled at her when she told him what was happening to her.

'I'm glad it's all worked out so nicely,' he said. 'I was a bit – concerned.'

'Thank you,' she said, and then, staring at him: 'What do you mean, it's worked out?'

'Lucinda,' he said, 'you must think I am very stupid. It's quite hard not to notice when someone actually working for you is having an affair. All those long lunch-hours? And what a lot of dental appointments you had.'

'Oh,' she said, blushing furiously. 'Oh no, I mean yes, I mean – well, thank you for putting up with it.'

'That's all right. I was more impressed than anything. Bit of excitement in my middle-aged life.'

But she continued to worry about Nigel until Katy told her he was surviving quite well.

'Honestly, Lucinda, you don't have to worry about him. All his friends have scooped him up, they're looking after him beautifully. I saw him at two dinner parties last week alone.'

She felt a stab of hurt; then of relief. But he still wouldn't reply to any of her phone calls or her letters.

'Well, he'll have to now,' said Blue. 'We got to get this thing sorted. Including the money.'

'Yes, I know – but how, without it all going to Lloyd's?'

'God knows,' said Blue. 'You need to ask a lawyer. They have the answer to everything. They'd better anyway.'

'Simon? George Meyer. I've been thinking about that smoking gun of Fiona Broadhurst's . . . and I've got an idea. It might not work, but it'd be worth a try.'

'Fine,' said Simon. 'What do you want me to do?'

'Set up a lunch.'

'Now that's something I am extremely good at,' said Simon, laughing.

Now what had she done, Debbie thought. Without consultation too. God, she'd be in trouble. Terrible, awful trouble. Scale 10 rows, there'd be. Maybe she should backtrack, say she must think about it. But why should she? Why on earth should she? It was entirely good, what she was doing. Contributing hugely, financially – and anyway, she was much better-tempered, much happier altogether, really. Certainly felt less – mad. And no one was suffering, and—

Her door opened again. It was Anna.

'Sorry. Should have asked you. How soon can you start?'

'Well . . .' The Easter holidays were about to begin. She didn't think she could possibly spring this on Richard, tell him he was committed to another whole day of childminding a week until they were all back at school. 'In about four weeks? That soon enough?'

'It'll have to be. If you could shave a week off . . .'

'Leave it with me, Anna, I'll try. But I can't promise.' In the six months since her arrival, Know How had won four new accounts and lost none of them: they really did need her.

'Fine,' said Anna.

'Easter in Wales with Granny then?' she said to the children, three days later. 'That be fun? She just invited us.'

And, 'Yes!' they all yelled; she would have been irritated, if it hadn't been part of her plan. For Flora had not exactly invited them. Well, she had, but only in response to a hint heavy enough to stun.

'Can we have an Easter-egg hunt in Granny's meadow?' asked Alex.

'Will there be lots of lambs?' said Rachel.

'Will I be able to ride?' said Emma.

She said yes to all of them, smiling her traitorous smile, and went to find Richard with the same exciting news. She could see he was not entirely without suspicion, but too pleased at the same time to pursue it.

'Right,' said Fiona Broadhurst. 'I've had a look at everything you've given me, and the implications. And I think you have a case.'

There was a complete silence; nobody spoke, not a muscle of anybody's face moved.

'If you're right about what you've said here, and if we can find any evidence of a cover-up, of knowledge of what was going on, while they continued to promote Membership – and I appreciate you're not the first to have made this claim – then I think there is a reasonable prima facie case and we can go on, if you still wish. I have to say, however, that what you've given me here is almost certainly not enough. I think we need to find the smoking gun.'

'What does that mean exactly?' said Meyer.

'It means we need something much closer to proof,' she said, looking at him slightly disdainfully. 'We need to find someone who has said something, or done something, that can be seen as at least fairly conclusive. I think we all need to do more work on the extent of your knowledge. I can't just make two and two add up to four and then stick it on a fraud case. There's still a very long way to go. Now, you'll probably want to discuss this again between you, and indeed I would urge you to, because apart from anything else, and as I said last time we met, you should be aware that this is a very big and expensive decision. I think you should discuss what you can afford, and I would urge you to put a limit on the cost, because that helps me as well in planning the case. And I would like to say at this point that if you do run out of money and can't afford to go on, then please don't think you can come crying to me because I've got bills to pay.'

Still nobody spoke. There was a long silence while she looked at them; then Simon said, 'Well, thank you for your time, Ms Broadhurst. And for considering the case so carefully. We will indeed discuss it again, but speaking for myself, I feel I would definitely like to go on.'

'Good.' For the first time she smiled at them properly: a warm, friendly smile, quite unlike the cool distant curves of her mouth they had seen before, 'I hope your colleagues will feel the same way.'

God, she was sexy, thought Simon.

'And if we do, if we're all in agreement, what would be the next step?' said Meyer.

'The next step would be that we would go to Counsel. Who, I hope, would say I'm right—'

'Oh really? So he has to agree with you as well? Before you advise going ahead?'

'It would be preferable if he did.' Another smile. 'Although so far, I have rarely had Counsel disagree with me on a case.'

You bet your sweet life you haven't, thought Simon. It would take a brave man to do that.

'But let us say that yes, he agrees there is a case or might be a case, then I would invite you to meet him. I really don't like this mystique that Counsel is some creature up in the clouds with the letters QC after his name. I feel you're paying for the show, and you should hear what he has to say. I would like you to have a dialogue. And I also want him – or her, that is a possibility – to share your passion about it, to know how you feel. He will want to know everything, as I did – exactly what your grievance is, apart from losing a lot of money. It won't necessarily be an easy conversation, but I would hope then that he would say yes, and then I would expect him to say what work we all have to do. And I have to say I don't want a lot of other disaffected Names brought in with similar stories; we don't want this to sound like some kind of self-indulgent dialogue about everyone's misfortune. I want precise information, the people who told you what a great club this was, and exactly how they told it, the language used, and when. We'll need chapter and verse; hearsay is no good to me. Litigation is teamwork – clients, solicitor, barrister, we've all got to do our share. I hope that's clear.'

'It is clear,' said Meyer, 'and I have to say to you I like it. I like this idea of our having such close involvement, some kind of control.'

'Good,' said Fiona. 'We do find it a far more pragmatic and indeed useful way to proceed. Now I would suggest that you go away and discuss the matter and then come back to me with your decision. In writing, obviously. Is that all right?'

She stood up, walked over to the door, making it clear she had no more use for them. 'Clare will see you out. I look forward to hearing from you. Good morning.'

They stood on the pavement outside, hardly looking at one another, Meyer and Cunningham slightly sheepishly lighting cigarettes.

'Not sure that'd be allowed,' said Simon. 'By Teacher, I mean.'

'What I need is a drink,' said Meyer. 'Shall we go and get one and see what we think?'

But they actually knew what they thought; and half an hour later, Simon agreed to draft a letter officially instructing Fiona Broadhurst to take their case.

It was as well the family were coming this year, Flora thought. The next year's results had arrived and next year there might be no house to come to. Correction. *Would* be no house to come to.

It had actually been a physical shock, reading the results; she felt faint, breathless, had to close her eyes, grip the arms of the wooden seat in the yard which seemed to be shifting slightly beneath her. And then she opened her eyes and forced them onto the piece of paper again.

£275,000, it informed her she owed. A sum she most assuredly had not got, would not have even if she sold everything she possessed. An unimaginable amount of money: the lack of which would expose her to an unimaginable future. How – why – had this happened to her? How had this shocking, ruthless thing broken into her life, consuming it, how had an existence as normal and ordered, as careful indeed as the one she and William had shared, turned into this ugly chaos? And as she only occasionally did these days, she longed for him to be there to talk to, to reassure her, to say he would take care of it all. He would not have been able to, of course; but they would have been together in the battles. Most of the time now, she was quite happy to be alone – indeed, she enjoyed it in many ways, liked her freedom and her independence; but very occasionally she looked down the years ahead, and found the view empty and frightening.

She gazed around her in a kind of desperation, seeking an answer, and seeing instead what she must lose to feed the monster: the house, the beloved house, of course; she had almost faced that, knowing only a miracle could save her from it, but suddenly she saw the other things that she had not properly considered, that must go with it. The stables, and thus the horses: the long days gone, of riding over the moors in the hot sun, in the company of the wild ponies and the hawks, surrounded with skylark song, and she would lose Tilly too, and Boy would have to go, and all these lovely easy holidays with the children. She would lose her meadow and the rest of her land, lose the particular views of Gower they offered, would lose the sweet summer darkness filled with owls hooting and foxes screeching, and the lovely dawns, drenched in birdsong; would lose the wild winter landscape, the towering black cliffs above the raging seas, the sound of the wind hurtling round her house. It would all go, greedily grabbed in order to pay some trifling part of some obscene reckoning, a reckoning that was in no way her responsibility.

It was wicked, it was monstrous, it was absolutely and totally unjust, the result of a small, foolish act of generosity on the part of her husband.

And there was absolutely nothing she could do about it.

'You buggers!' she shouted aloud, standing in the yard, holding the letter, waving her fist at the stormy sky. 'You absolute bastards!'

Boy, Tilly's pony, and her own beloved Prince Hal looked at her in surprise.

She was enjoying having Boy immensely, and enjoying her relationship with Tilly too. She was a sweet child, perfectly mannered, young for her age and a hugely talented rider. She and Boy could have made a pretty impressive mark on the eventing circuit, had the money been still there. But it wasn't . . .

They had come down after Christmas as promised, she and her father; they had stayed in the B&B for a couple of days and then, when Richard and the family arrived for New Year, perfect chaperones for Tilly, it had seemed very silly for her not to move in with them: and for Simon to leave. Emma adored Tilly, followed her about everywhere, mucking out the stables, sweeping up the icy yard uncomplainingly while Tilly encouraged her, gave her lessons, patiently answered her endless questions and not even Debbie could dislike her. Why was her daughter-in-law so awkward? Flora often wondered. It would be so nice if she could be sweet and pliable, like – well, like Tilly. She did find it hard to understand quite what her son's marriage was based on; she supposed it was the attraction of opposites. She and William had struggled with the same thing in the early years of their marriage. Of course, Richard had his faults, and she was far from blind to them; and as the years went by he seemed to her to become increasingly like his father.

On the other hand, Flora thought, she wasn't too much like Debbie. And crushed the rider to that thought that she hoped not . . .

'Is that Simon Beaumont?'

'Yes, speaking. Who—'

'Mr Beaumont, I do apologise for springing this on you out of the blue, but my name's Joel Strickland, I'm a financial journalist, work on the *Daily News*—'

'Oh yes?'

'I believe you're a Name at Lloyd's.'

'Correct,' said Simon shortly.

'Mr Beaumont, I'm investigating some of the – the events – at Lloyd's. For a piece I'm writing.'

'Right,' said Simon slowly. 'What sort of piece?'

'Oh, pretty broadly based – history, financial analysis, all that sort of thing. I personally think there's rather more going on than meets the eye.'

'Oh, really?'

'Yes, I do. Plus, you know, there is the human element, the stories behind the facts.'

'Well, I certainly don't want to be part of some bleeding-hearts story, sorry. How did you get my name anyway?'

'It wouldn't be bleeding hearts, as you put it. I can guarantee that. And I met your daughter at a photographic session. She was doing the hair, it was a fashion picture for the paper. Oh, she was very discreet, don't worry. But she thought you might like to talk about it.'

'No, I don't think so. Certainly not at the moment. So I'm sorry if she's wasted your time.'

'She hasn't. It's fine. Following up leads is part of the job. But if anything changes your mind – ring me. Here are my numbers . . .'

Simon put the phone down feeling irritable. He'd have to speak to Annabel; he couldn't have her talking about the family affairs to complete strangers. Especially if the strangers were journalists. Even so, interesting what the guy had said . . . very interesting. He could even be useful.

Joel Strickland was very good at dealing with rejection; it could be said it was his speciality. Which probably explained why he was so good a journalist. Rejection was a given, day by day. The trick was getting round it.

It had begun very early in his life with his father who, according to his mother, had taken one look at her new baby and left home. It never seemed to occur to her that Joel would find this a difficult piece of information; she hated Alan Strickland and she wanted to make sure Joel would too.

Joel had spent the first four years of his life living fairly happily with his mother, his brother and his grandparents; then the day after his fourth birthday, his mother had moved in with a rich car salesman who didn't like children.

'Well, he doesn't like them very much,' she said, cuddling Joel and John (she had been going through a bit of a religious phase when they were born), 'but I know he'll come round. Time being, you can spend the weekends with us, and then when Don gets used to you, I know you can join us. He's got a lovely big house and garden, be fun for you both.'

Don hadn't got used to them, not even after what seemed quite a long time; in fact they stopped even going to his house at the weekends. Their mother came to see them three nights a week instead. This slowly dwindled to two and then to one, and finally stopped altogether when she and Don moved rather suddenly up to Manchester, although she promised they could go up and stay when they were 'settled'.

They never saw their mother again; she was involved in a car crash six weeks later on the M6 and died instantly. She was driving a Jaguar S-type from one of Don's salesrooms much too fast, and Joel found out years later that she'd been extremely drunk. They all went to the funeral and his nan had gone up to Don at the sort of party afterwards and thrown a glass of red wine in his face. It had all been pretty horrible; but Don, clearly feeling a degree of guilt, had made over some money for him and John and it meant the four of them could move into a terrace house in Peckham rather than the council flat, and even Grandad stopped grumbling quite so much.

There was a grammar school in the area and Joel passed his eleven-plus; his nan was intensely proud, but Grandad said the whole thing, particularly the uniform, was a total waste of money, and going to the secondary modern had been good enough for him. Nan said in that case why had they been living in council flats all their lives, and that she'd go out cleaning to earn the money for the uniform if Don wouldn't help. Don sent a cheque for £250 and said he didn't want to hear that the money had been wasted.

John had failed his eleven-plus; he said truthfully that he didn't care, and that studying and him didn't really go together. He went to the secondary modern and dreamed of being a property developer.

Joel actually enjoyed the grammar school; he was a clever boy and he didn't mind working hard. He went on to do A-levels, and won a place at Hull University to read English. His nan was extremely proud and even his grandad said he hadn't done too badly. Don refused to help with the expenses, when they wrote and told him, but Joel got a full grant, and worked in bars in the evenings to keep his overdraft down.

While he was in his final year, his grandad got pneumonia and died: 'Well, he was getting on a bit, silly old fool,' Nan said, tears streaming down her face. She was completely lost without him and managed to follow him three months later.

Which meant that the only people there for Joel at his graduation were his brother John, now employed by one of the big building firms, and Joel's girlfriend, a pretty second-year called Joanne. Joel celebrated getting his upper-second and a place on one of the regional newspaper training schemes by proposing to Joanne. She accepted and wore her tiny diamond ring with great pride, but then told him six months later that she was in love with someone else. Not only in love, but three months' pregnant. Joel knew it wasn't his since Joanne had told him she was a virgin, and wanted to go to the altar that way; he wept that day, for the first and last time since his nan had died.

When he was twenty-seven he got a job as an agency reporter and two years later moved onto the staff of the *Daily News*; five years after that he was very happily on the City Desk. He'd bought a flat in Clapham with the proceeds of the Peckham house; he offered to go halves with John, but John was already earning mega-bucks, as he put it, putting in loft extensions. So far, the economic downturn hadn't affected him, rather the reverse: 'They can't move, you see, so they just expand what they got.' His house was large and flashy and he had a large and flashy girlfriend called Shireen who he said he'd marry when he had the time, or when she got in the family way, whichever came first.

Joel wasn't married, but he was living with one of the other reporters, a sexy, sharp-eyed little thing called Sadie, who was determined to be the first woman newspaper editor. She was so determined that she started sleeping with the Features Editor of the *Daily Sketch*; in the time-honoured way of these things, Joel was the last to know. And so at the age of thirty-four he was a successful and good-looking young man about town, with a very nice flat in Clapham, a Golf GTI, a lot of nice clothes, and an absolute horror of commitment. His view of women was fairly chauvinist and emotionally detached; they were there to enjoy, to have fun with, but he fought shy of anything more. He was also fiercely anti-establishment and a socialist at least in theory; he had sufficiently vivid memories of the harshness of his grandmother's life to find anything akin to the old-boy public-school ethos deeply suspect. Which, given that there was a great deal of that still in the Square Mile, lent his work an additional edge.

He did have a girlfriend, a pretty girl called Maggie who was an executive in one of the financial PR firms, and who was very keen indeed to move in with him. Joel was as keen that she should not. He was very fond of her, he enjoyed her company, and they had a very nice time in bed, but he lacked the emotional interest to develop the relationship any further. As soon as he had loved anyone, she seemed to be removed from his life; much better, therefore, not to risk it in the first place. It was perfectly simple, really.

'Wow. Get him. Totally gorgeous. Shirt-soaking time, Bel. My turn.'

Annabel looked; an Adonis had just walked into the salon. Young, but not too young, probably about twenty-three, she decided, blond, tall, wearing a light camelhair coat over jeans and very nice brown cowboy boots. He was a cross between a younger Robert Redford and Ryan O'Neal in *Love Story*. Totally, totally gorgeous, as Carol said. But Carol wasn't going to have him.

She pushed her mane of hair back and walked purposefully towards him, thanking God she wasn't wearing her old leggings, the ones that bagged a bit round her knees, as she had been the day before, but her new Miss Selfridge black and white striped short skirt and black tights. Her mother was right: you really shouldn't ever look anything but your best, you never knew . . .

She had actually made eye-contact with him, was congratulating herself that he'd clearly noticed her, when, 'Carol, take Mr Cartwright's coat, would you?' Susan the receptionist said, with a tart smile. 'And then tell David his client is here. Bel, I think the floor could do with a little sweep, dear.'

'Bitch!' hissed Annabel into Carol's ear. Carol flashed her her sweetest smile as she walked towards Mr Cartwright and held out her arm for his coat.

'Good morning,' she said, redirecting the smile. 'I'm Carol, your junior. Would you like to follow me over to the dressing-table. David will be with you in just a moment.'

'Temper temper,' said Florian as Annabel swept round his feet just a little too vigorously. 'Honestly, darling, he's not for you, much too much of a baby, it's men of the world you need.'

Annabel checked that Susan wasn't looking and stuck her tongue out at Florian; and then seeing that Mr Cartwright was momentarily not being taken care of, pushed her broom purposefully over to his dressing-table. Or rather work station as Miki now liked them to be called.

'Er – can I get you a coffee or something? While you're waiting?' she said.

Mr Cartwright directed a pair of rather intense blue eyes at her and smiled.

'That's very kind of you,' he said, in an accent that Annabel recognised as Old Money American, 'but I think the other young lady is bringing me some.'

'There we are.' The other young lady set down a tray of coffee on the table with a slight, Playboy Bunny-style bob. 'Can I get you some magazines? Bel, I think Florian's looking for you.'

Annabel gave up.

She was walking wearily past the Carlton Towers Hotel that evening, looking longingly at the cab rank, when she heard a voice. An American Old Money voice.

'Hello. Isn't it Cinders?'

She spun round; he was emerging from the hotel. Miraculously alone.

'Well, yes. Yes, it is.' He really was very, very handsome. 'I'm just looking for my pumpkin coach.' He grinned. Showing the inevitably perfect American white teeth.

'Haven't seen one. Do you have to do a lot of sweeping in that place?'

'Quite a lot.'

'Doesn't look a whole heap of fun.'

'It isn't.'

'You look tired.'

'Thanks.'

'Oh, I'm sorry,' he said, his face contrite. He had a dusting of freckles on his nose, she noticed (even more like Robert Redford – only this guy was far more handsome). 'My mother always told me never to say that to a lady.'

'Your mother was right.'

'Well – look. I don't have a coach or anything, but I'm taking a cab down to the Fulham Road. Could I make amends, offer you a lift? Or is that totally the wrong direction?'

Annabel would have said it was the right direction if he had been going to Birmingham, but, 'It is totally the right one,' she said, 'thank you.'

'That's OK.' He ushered her into a cab, very gentlemanly; then held out his hand to her. 'James Cartwright. Usually known as Jamie.'

'Hi, Jamie. I'm Annabel. Annabel Beaumont.'

'And you work in that place full-time, Annabel?'

'Oh yes. I like it,' she added firmly. She could feel the usual puzzlement coming. 'Except the sweeping. It's fun.'

'I felt a bit of an idiot in there,' he said, 'with all those women, but my mother said I absolutely had to get a haircut and the hotel recommended your place.'

'Lots of men do come in,' she said, 'there just weren't that many today.'

'Oh, right. Anyway, they did it very nicely.'

It was almost seven; the traffic was bad.

'This is terrible,' he said, 'I'm going to be so late.'

'For?'

'Oh, drinks with friends of my parents. My mother's already there. She will be so annoyed.'

'Well, you could call her. Do you have a number?'

'I do, yes. We could try a callbox, I guess.'

They tried three; they were all out of order.

'Look,' said Annabel, 'in about five minutes we'll be at my house. You can come in, use our phone if you like.'

'That's extremely kind of you. Are you sure you don't mind?'

'Of course not. Anyway, my dad pays the bill.'

'Great. Well, thank you. So – how come you work there?' he said, visibly more relaxed. 'You just don't seem quite – quite ...' He stopped, obviously afraid of committing another conversational gaffe.

'The sort of girl you find in a hairdressing salon?'

'Well, yes. Sorry, does that sound rude? Or terribly personal?'

'Not rude. A bit personal. Anyway, whether I am or whether I'm not that sort of girl, I'm to be found there, and I really, really like it. Honestly. I know it looks like shit and it is, a lot of the time, but it's also fun and it's what I want to do, and when I'm a stylist, which I will be in another year, life'll be a lot better. And even if I didn't like it,' she added with a grin, 'I could never admit it to my parents, so I'm stuck with it anyway.'

'Are your parents not too keen on the idea?'

'Not too keen. But they're coming round to it. And at least I'm earning something. However pathetic.'

'OK,' he said. 'Well, that's great.'

They pulled into Bolton Place. 'That one, down at the bottom,' said Annabel.

'Is this where you live?' he said, looking up at the house.

'This is where I live.' She saw more puzzlement. 'Come along in,' she said, rummaging in her bag. 'I don't seem to have my key, but Josie will let us in.'

'Josie?'

'Our housekeeper.'

'Oh OK. Would you wait right here?' he said to the cab driver.

Annabel listened, half-amused, as he made his phone call; he was clearly terrified of his mother.

'Yes, Mother, I know, I know, and I'm sorry. But the traffic was just— what? Well, I know I should have, but – yes, anyway. I'll be about ... Just a minute.' He put his hand over the receiver and turned to Annabel. 'How long from here, do you think?'

'Oh, the way things are going, about fifteen minutes max.'

'Fifteen minutes max,' he said. 'Is Dad there? Oh, he isn't. Well, he's obviously in the same traffic. Anyway, do say sorry to Deirdre for me. Yes, OK, I will. Yes, sure. Bye, Mother.

'Phew,' he said, putting the phone down. 'She wasn't very pleased with me. I'd best go. May I buy you a drink or something tomorrow, to say thank you? Maybe lunchtime?'

'Lunchtime?' she said, grinning at him. 'What's lunchtime?'

'Well, OK, evening then. Around six-thirty? Come to the hotel, why don't you?'

'OK. Six-thirty it is.' She'd get away somehow, even if it meant bribing Carol to stand in for her. 'Um – why don't you buy your mother's friend some flowers? There's a lovely flower shop on the Fulham Road, near the cinema; the driver'll know it.'

'That is a fantastic idea,' he said. 'Thank you so, so much. Well, I'll see you tomorrow.'

'Tomorrow. Have a good evening.'

She waved the taxi off, went back inside and shut the door, smiling. Prince Charming had finally happened along, it seemed. It was all a bit too good to be true.

He was nice – and charming – as well as gorgeous. And she was so sick of Florian, who had been messing her about – again. She was getting very tired of his lifestyle, the endless drugs, the obsession with style and appearance, the all-night clubbing – one more early Sunday morning in the wastes of Camden while they tried to find a cab, and she really would give him the push. Except – well, she did like him. And he made her laugh. And the sex was something else. She wondered what it would be like with Jamie ... probably not quite in the same league, too much of a gentleman. Still— Annabel, for heaven's sake! You only just met the guy!

Alan Richards, was extremely upset when he heard about Miss Thompson. Her death made a small paragraph in most of the papers; apparently she'd once been a modestly successful concert pianist and had given piano lessons to local children, in the Hampshire village where she lived, completely free for those whose parents couldn't afford to pay.

Musical philanthropist found dead in cottage, it said, continuing that the whole village mourned her passing; he'd spotted it in the *Sketch* as he travelled to work one morning. She had been such a pathetic old bird, all alone in the world, obviously terribly upset and frightened – and what had they done to help her? Nothing, nothing at all. His boss had refused even to write to her. He kept thinking about her, about how desperate she had been; a neighbour had found her apparently – another old lady, who'd been looking after Miss Thompson's cat. What must that have been like for her as well, the poor old soul? It had been a few days after Gillian Thompson had died, because she'd been laid up with the flu herself. Which would have made it even worse, since the body would have started to . . . Alan switched his mind away from the body with difficulty. There was to be an inquest; there had been no suicide note left in the cottage, but the neighbour had said that in her view, Miss Thompson had definitely killed herself.

'She'd been very depressed recently and she had money worries, I think, quite serious ones.'

Alan was so upset that he told Heather he couldn't go to the pictures that night as they'd planned; she said why didn't they just go for a drink, and he could tell her about it, it might help. Alan agreed that it might.

He spent the rest of the day reading and rereading the item in the paper, and wondering what, if anything, he could have done.

'I feel guilty, you know?' he said to Heather. 'She was so upset, and all I did for her was get her a cup of coffee and offer to call her a taxi, which was pretty thoughtless of me.'

'Why?' said Heather. 'I think that was kind of you, Alan. I think you obviously did a lot for her.'

'Rubbish!' said Alan. 'A cup of coffee and offering to get a taxi she couldn't afford? I feel awful, Heather, I really do.'

'Did you tell anyone about it there?'

'I spoke to Mr Clarke. He just said it was none of my business and that Miss Thompson had been looking for risk-free investment like everyone else. But she was in a rotten syndicate, one she'd no business to be in, that really exposed her to terrible risks.'

'Was she? Does that happen a lot do you think?'

'Well, I don't know. You know Barry? Barry Grove, the one who came with us to the races on Boxing Day?'

Heather said she certainly did, and wasn't likely to forget

him either, seeing as he'd been sick out of the door of her Mini as they drove out of Sandown Park.

'Yes, and I'm sorry, Heather. Very sorry, I told you before. Anyway, Barry agrees with me that things aren't quite as they should be.'

'Sounds like it. Still, there's nothing you can do now, Alan. Come on, let's have another drink and then I'd better be getting back.'

Alan went off to buy the drinks. While he was standing in the queue, he suddenly remembered Joel Strickland and his conversation with him in the George and Vulture. Maybe he'd get in touch now; he felt somehow that he owed it to Miss Thompson. And bugger Norman Clarke.

He looked in his wallet; yes, Joel's card was still there. He hadn't quite decided, but he'd talk to Heather about it, and maybe make the call in the morning. Not from the office though; that would be very silly.

Chapter 15

People were so complex, Debbie thought. You just never knew. Which she could see was hardly a philosophical breakthrough, and it would not have won her many points all those years ago with the college Debating Society, but in this instance anyway, it was a huge and pleasing surprise.

Here she was, ready to fight for her professional life, proclaiming her rights both as an individual and a woman, and ready to argue that Richard should be recognising that, rather than crushing her into submission – she'd been rehearsing the arguments for days – and instead he was smiling at her, telling her it would be fine if she worked another day, that he was quite enjoying being with the children more and that he was very proud of her success.

'I've told you, being at work suits you. You seem happier. It's working out very nicely, I think. And the house certainly looks tidier.'

This was undeniable; Debbie always said she had only to walk into a room to mess it up.

'Oh,' she said, the wind removed so far from her sails she seemed to be travelling backwards. 'Oh I see. Well – that's great. Fantastic. Thank you, Richard. So much.'

'No need to thank me,' he said. 'I was wrong the first time, and I don't mind admitting it. Although I do think three days is enough. I wouldn't be happy with any more. And maybe a little bit of the extra money could go towards a cleaner. Just once a week, say?'

Debbie said of course it could, and kissed him and thanked him again, and then thought that there had been no need to arrange Easter in Wales after all. And then thought what a truly awful person she was, told Richard she'd like to go to bed early – thereby inducing the sheepish smile she'd once thought so sweet and now found so irritating – and set about tidying up the kitchen.

Anyway, it had been fine so far. Flora was throwing herself into her grandmothering with her usual enthusiasm – it really was a bit over the top, Debbie thought, as if she was playing the part in some film – but it meant that she and Richard could actually have some time to themselves, go for walks, read, and even have some uninterrupted discussions.

She helped him with his CV – 'Don't mind me wanting to, I see so many coming into the office, and of course while that's a completely different world, you're still trying to grab people's attention,' acted as sous-chef as he prepared an Easter cake as a surprise for Flora, and generally felt rather surprisingly content. Although she could have done without the arrival from London on the Saturday of the Beaumonts, the ultra-smooth albeit charming Simon and the daughter, Tilly. The girl was all right, Debbie had warmed to her, but still quite annoying, with all that hair-tossing and that boarding-school voice, but the conversation would be so boring, all about horses and saddles and girths and feed and absolutely non-stop, right through most meals, with Emma listening shiny-eyed.

They arrived at about lunchtime; Tilly tumbling out of the Range Rover and across the yard, taking Boy's head in her hands and kissing his nose rapturously, Flora hurrying out to welcome them, giving Simon a quick kiss – surely they couldn't be . . . God, how disgusting, no surely not, stop it, Debbie – and then hugging Tilly. Simon was staying for twenty-four hours and then leaving Tilly until the end of the week; even though he'd lost weight, Debbie thought he still looked like a Ralph Lauren ad, what with the inevitable polo pony on his sweater and the new-looking tweed jacket.

They had lunch in the kitchen and then Flora suggested that she and Tilly went riding. 'You can go off on your own with Boy, darling, if you like, but I'd love to come with you.'

Tilly said nothing could be nicer, and that when they got back, she'd give Emma a lesson; Emma went red in the face with excitement.

'How long are you down for?' Simon said; and, 'Just till Tuesday,' Debbie said.

'That's a shame,' said Tilly. 'I'm here for a whole week and I could have given Emma lots of lessons.'

'Well, she could stay,' said Flora, 'even if you've got to go back. And is there any rush?'

'Yes, there is, I'm afraid,' said Debbie. 'I've got to go back to work.'

'Oh yes, of course. Well, just leave Emma, then – it's fine by me.'

'Oh Mummy, please say yes, please . . .'

'We could bring her back,' Simon said. 'I'm coming down to get Tilly on Sunday, I could easily drop Emma off with you. No problem.'

'Well, Richard, what do you think?'

Richard had clearly taken against Simon Beaumont; Debbie had watched, half-amused, half-sympathetic as Simon joked and chatted and flattered Flora, and teased the children, holding the table with his easy charm in exactly the way she knew Richard would have loved to do himself. Although he would die rather than admit it.

'Well, I don't know,' he said, 'isn't it a bit much for you, Mother?'

'Of course not. Don't talk like that, Richard, you make me feel like an old lady.'

'What absolute rubbish,' Simon said. 'I've never known anybody with quite such energy as you, Flora. Anyway, of course you must decide, Richard, she's your child. But the offer's there, it'd be no trouble. And I might not have to listen to all that ghastly music that Tilly likes so much on the way back, if Emma is with us. Although I suppose it'll be replaced by girth fittings or bit styles.'

'Daddy, you are so silly!' said Tilly, smiling at him. 'Please, Mr Fielding, I'd love Emma to stay. We'll take great care of her, won't we, Flora?'

In the end, Richard gave in.

◦

244

'Alan, I really think you should ring that journalist,' said Heather. 'What harm can it do? It might in fact do some good, not for that poor lady, all right, but maybe some of the others. Go on, give him a call. You could make it anonymous, if you liked. If you're worried.'

'Yeah,' said Alan. 'Yeah, I hadn't thought of that.'

'And from a public call box. Then there'd be no trace.'

'Blimey, Heather,' said Alan admiringly, 'you ought to work for MI6.'

The phone rang: on and on. There didn't seem to be anyone there. Maybe he'd left, gone to work somewhere else. That could be the best thing in a way. At least then Alan could tell himself he'd tried, that he'd done his best; he'd just give it four more rings and then . . .

'Joel Strickland.'

'Oh – Mr Strickland. Yes, hello.' Alan took a deep breath. This was it. Too late now. Although he could just put the phone down. No. No, he wouldn't do that. He owed it to Miss Thompson not to do that.

'What can I do for you?'

'Ah well, the thing is, you see . . .'

'Yes?' The voice was measured, patient.

'Mr Strickland, I'd like to – that is . . .'

'Do you have a story for me?'

'I – well, not – not exactly.'

'So – what then?' Still very patient. 'Part of a story perhaps?'

'Yes. Yes, maybe.'

'Well, good. Let's hear it.'

'I – don't quite know where to start.'

'How about the beginning?'

'I'm not sure what that is,' said Alan, rather desperately. 'It's just – well, that is . . .'

'Take your time,' said Strickland, 'no rush. Or would you like to meet?'

'No,' said Alan sharply. 'No need for that.'

'OK then. What's it about? Let's start with that.'

'It's about Lloyd's,' said Alan, courage suddenly rushing at him, taking him by surprise. 'I – well, I wanted to tell you something. Nothing very much. But something . . . well, it might be important, I don't know.'

'OK,' said Joel Strickland again. 'It might be. Might not. Why don't you tell me.'

So Alan started to tell him.

Nigel read Lucinda's letter twice before the full meaning of it sank in; then he put his head in his hands and started to weep. He would never have believed anything could hurt so much. Gentle creature that he was, if he had been able to get hold of this man, he knew he would have beaten him to a pulp: not just for stealing his wife, but in some strange way his family too. Lucinda was having a baby: the baby he had wanted to give her. It was all terribly unfair.

And so, the letter had ended, *as I am sure you will understand, I do now want a divorce, fairly quickly. I will obviously do everything I can to make it as painless as possible for you. Perhaps you could talk to your solicitor and let me know what you would like me to do.*

He'd like her to come back to him, that's what he'd like her to do. Not as she was now, of course, but as she had been, sweet, pretty, loving Lucinda, who had made him so happy and looked after him so well. Why had she gone, for God's sake, why?

He had tried so hard to be a good husband; he had been loving, generous, appreciative, he had encouraged her in whatever she wanted to do, had entertained her silly friends – it was at those dinner parties that he had realised how she really was another generation, all that giggling and stupid joke-telling, the men too. Although they'd been jolly kind to him since she'd gone, many of them had clearly felt that Lucinda was totally in the wrong. Which of course she was. And which she acknowledged, in every letter, every message.

'I have no excuse whatsoever,' she had said, that dreadful night when he had found out. 'You've been a perfect husband, Nigel, and I don't deserve you.'

Should he perhaps have tried harder then, to make it work? Let her stay, have forgiven her? But he knew it was impossible. Nigel was 101 per cent honest; he couldn't love someone who had deceived him as dreadfully and as relentlessly as she had.

He couldn't imagine now how he had got through those first

few awful months: had he been asked beforehand if he could endure such a thing, he would have said it was impossible. But somehow he had: he had gone to bed at night and got up in the morning, had his bath – he had never taken to showers – dressed, eaten his breakfast – so important, a good breakfast – and gone to work. Work had become a sort of drug, had immunised him against the pain and the humiliation. While he was there he felt safe; worked doggedly, for long hours, and told no one that Lucinda had left him. The only person he confided in was his secretary, Lydia Newhouse. Lydia had worked for Nigel for almost ten years, and absolutely adored him. She was completely at a loss as to how Lucinda could have done such a dreadful thing: or such a stupid one. Here was a man, as close to perfect as men came – a lot closer than her own husband, that was for sure – and this silly flighty girl had just thrown him away. Her outrage was immensely soothing to Nigel; he imbibed it with every cup of coffee she made him, every perfectly typed folder of letters she laid in front of him, every gentle enquiry as to whether she could get him anything else before leaving for the night.

But by that spring he was feeling a little better: was growing accustomed to his solitary state, almost from time to time enjoyed it; there were no strange meals set before him at night, no pasta dishes or elaborate salads, just a lot of sturdy pies and roasts, prepared by the part-time housekeeper he had employed, a Mrs Headingly, and left with clear step-by-step instructions for him to finish off. In fact, he was reverting, slowly if not pleasurably, to bachelorhood, and while he was often lonely, while his heart seemed permanently to ache, while the sense of absolute foolishness that Lucinda's adultery had bestowed upon him still woke him up in the smallest of the small hours and kept him sleepless, he could begin to contemplate at least a time when he might enjoy himself once more.

Until now: when he felt he had reached a new level of raw pain.

And by a most cruel piece of juxtapositioning on the part of Fate, the day before the arrival of Lucinda's letter, the next year's results had arrived. With horrifying implications.

Lucinda had been instructed by his solicitor to transfer all the assets into a holding account, where they were frozen while

247

he worked out what to do: clearly she could not continue to hold them. But the fact remained that her defection had inflicted another, terrible blow: his assets were no longer safe from the predators of Lloyd's, if Lucinda actually returned them to him. The dreadful irony of the situation was not lost on his lawyers; the errant wife holding the key to his financial salvation, or indeed the reverse.

It was Lydia who found him weeping at his desk, over Lucinda's letter – she had been instructed to write to him at work, rather than at home – and over a cup of very sweet coffee and a plate of the chocolate shortbread that was one of his staple comforts, she asked him if there was anything she could do. Emotionally weakened by being caught in such disarray, Nigel found himself telling her the latest sad chapter in his saga. 'I can't see her, Lydia, it would be more than flesh and blood could stand.'

Lydia thought for a while and then said she thought it was essential he agreed to the divorce.

'You can't go on like this, Mr Cowper. Things must be properly resolved. For financial reasons as much as anything else. And I think if you could bring yourself to meet her, face to face, it would all be so much simpler.'

Nigel nodded, blew his nose, took another mouthful of the coffee. 'I know you're right, Lydia, of course. Very well, you'd better set up a meeting with my solicitor. I have no idea what – what the procedure might be. I'll start with them and then maybe it won't be necessary for us to meet. Here is Lucinda's telephone number and address; perhaps you could write to her and tell her I'm seeing my solicitor, and that I'll be in touch. I don't think I could bear to speak to her until it is absolutely necessary. Just the same – the sooner the better, if you please.'

Before the baby starts to show, he means, Lydia thought, her heart constricting with sympathy. Heavens, she'd like to give that girl a piece of her mind.

Richard had gone for a walk in Richmond Park when Simon arrived with Emma and Tilly; Debbie had a feeling he'd gone there on purpose, in order not to see him. Which really was a bit pathetic.

Emma bore Tilly up to her bedroom to show her her collection of Julip horses, and Debbie invited Simon into the kitchen, wishing she'd thought to tidy it up first. His house would doubtless be a model of neatness.

He wandered round it, admiring all the things she liked best herself – her collection of old jugs, the jumble of photographs, the children's paintings she had had framed, then sat down and drank the mug of tea she had given him.

'Sorry, I don't have any wonderful home-made cakes like Flora's.'

'I'm not allowed cakes, wonderful or otherwise; my tailor's forbidden it.'

'Oh, OK.' That was so much the sort of remark that annoyed her; yet somehow, coming from him it didn't.

'So – how are things with you, Debbie? I think you'd got a new job, last time we met.'

'Yes,' she said, smiling at him, pleased and surprised he should remember. 'Fairly new.'

'And – what is it? PR?'

'Yes. Clever of you to remember.'

'Not at all. Do you enjoy it?'

'Yes, I love it. Too much, really.'

'You can't love anything – or indeed, anyone – too much,' he said, 'and anyway, why shouldn't you love it?'

'Well, I feel a bit guilty, you know, leaving the children and so on.'

'Oh, now that is ridiculous,' he said. 'Tough little things, children, and anyway, as I used to say to Elizabeth, when she said the same, they're all incredibly over-privileged anyway. It's not as if you'd sent them out to live on the streets.'

'No, of course not. Um – did she really say the same, Elizabeth?'

'She really did. But I encouraged her to work anyway, she'd have been miserable at home. Most of you girls would these days; it's all very well, this ideal of Mum being at home, baking cakes and making finger puppets. It's a different world now, and people like you and Elizabeth aren't bred for domesticity. You don't fit the mould, and it's unfair to try and force you into it.'

'I suppose so. It's nice to hear that from a man anyway. And Richard's been great, filled in for me after school and everything.'

'Good for him. I like to think I did my bit too.'

'Did you? I'd have thought you'd have had nannies and so on.'

'We did. But nannies get ill and are unreliable, and aren't much good at watching nativity plays or going to parents' evenings. So if Elizabeth had something on that she couldn't duck out of, I did it. It was fun, I liked it.'

Tilly and Emma appeared in the doorway. 'Tilly says I must go down to Wales next time she's there,' Emma said, beaming at her idol.

'Well, that's very kind,' said Debbie, 'but I'm sure Tilly would like a bit of peace and quiet with her horse.'

'Tilly? Peace and quiet!' said Simon. 'She wouldn't know peace and quiet if it came up and hit her. Would you, darling?'

'Daddy, that's so silly. How could peace and quiet come and hit you?'

'OK, sneaked up on you then. Anyway, we should go home, poppet, and see Mummy. She's missed you.'

'Well, thank you so much for bringing Emma home,' said Debbie, 'and for playing with her all week, Tilly. It was very kind indeed.'

'Mummy! We weren't playing. Horses are hard work.'

'They certainly are,' said Simon.

'Daddy! You don't know. All you ever do is look at them.'

'True. And I've had some very happy days doing that. Now Debbie, any time you want Emma driven down or brought back, just ring me. Here's my card.'

She looked at it. *Simon Beaumont*, it said. *Director, Private Clients Division. Graburn & French.*

'Thank you,' she said, pinning it up onto the board. 'I really appreciate it.'

He walked out into the hall, bent and kissed Emma, and then, clearly on an impulse, leaned down and kissed Debbie too.

'I've enjoyed our chat,' he said. 'Bye, Debbie.'

'Bye, Simon. So have I.'

When Richard got back, she saw him peering at Simon's card. 'What on earth is that doing there?' he said.

'Simon gave it to me. In case we wanted him to drive Emma down again. Or bring her back.'

'I see.'

'Wasn't that kind of him?' she said, well aware of what she was doing and unable to resist the temptation.

'Not particularly, I wouldn't have said. If he's driving down anyway . . .'

'Oh Richard, don't be such an old misery. Anyway, I like Simon. He's – he's really easy to talk to. Chatty.'

'I'm afraid I don't find him so,' Richard said. 'Bit too smooth for my liking. And yours, I would have thought.'

'Oh, for goodness sake. Well, you don't have to talk to him. I'm perfectly happy to do it.'

'I can see that,' he said.

He was clearly jealous; it was rather nice, Debbie thought; she couldn't remember when she'd last been able to do that.

It was all too good to be true, really: Annabel simply couldn't believe it. All this time, all these rotters, and now here he was, Prince Charming, seemingly as keen on her as she was on him. The first date had been perfect: he'd bought her champagne cocktails at the Carlton Towers and then said would she like to have dinner, that his parents were off doing something 'with a couple of other crumblies' and was there anywhere she'd like specially to go; she'd suggested Rumours in Covent Garden, because she'd thought he'd find it fun, and it wouldn't be too expensive if she had to pay for herself: although she didn't think she would, he was too much of a gentleman and clearly very well off. Or at any rate, his parents were.

They were over on a fortnight's trip; his father had business in London, he said, and his mother liked to shop, and he'd had some vacation owed to him, so he'd come along too. He was a lawyer, 'just a trainee, actually', pretty fresh out of Harvard; his father was also a lawyer, and had his own firm in Boston, where they lived, and which Jamie had recently joined. He loved the law; he said it fascinated him, creating order out of chaos, making people's lives better. He spoke about it rather as if it was something very noble, and didn't mention the considerable rewards it clearly brought the family.

They seemed to be very rich. They lived just off Beacon Hill, which was the very best area in Boston, her father said. He'd met Jamie on their second date when he came to call for her and had been very taken by him; she could see that he was struggling not to make it too apparent. He knew that would be guaranteed to put her off. Jamie was the youngest in the Cartwright family; there was an elder brother called Bartholomew (known as Bif) and a sister called Kathleen; they were both married. Bif was also a lawyer with the family firm. 'He's just so great,' Jamie had said, 'such a perfect big brother. All my life he's looked out for me, still does; don't know what I'd do without him.'

'That must be nice,' said Annabel, slightly doubtfully. Jamie's family and the stranglehold it had on him was the one thing that was worrying her. Already.

'Yeah, it is. And his wife, Dana, she's very, very beautiful. She works in real estate, makes a lot of money. And Kathleen works in an art gallery. She's an agent for the artists.'

'Do either of them have children?'

'Not yet. My mother worries that they're both leaving it too late.'

'How long have they been married?'

'Oh, Dana and Bif three years, Kathleen almost two.'

'But that's nothing,' said Annabel, adding, 'Is it?' not wishing to sound rude or in any way possessed of the sort of opinions Kathleen – or more possibly, her mother – might consider unsympathetic.

'Well, I don't know. I think Kathleen feels a little torn. She loves her job, and she is just so good at it, but I guess for a girl the whole point of getting married is to make a family.'

'I think it's much more to be with the person you love,' said Annabel, 'and to enjoy life together. You're a mother for a long time. That's what my mother says anyway.'

'Your mother sounds amazing,' said Jamie, 'doing that job and raising a family at the same time.'

'Yes, she is, although my dad did a lot. I think he was unusual for then. I don't mean he changed nappies and stuff, we had nannies, but if my mum couldn't get to a school thing, for instance, then he would come along.'

'He seems a pretty special guy altogether,' said Jamie. 'I really liked him.'

'I like him too,' said Annabel. 'He's fun. Anyway, that's enough of our families. What did you do today?'

'Well, I went up to Camden Lock, as you suggested. It was great. And then I took that train over to the new area all around where the docks used to be, Canary Wharf and so on. Fantastic. I just wished you could have been with me, that's all. Anyway, I've got you now. And this is another great place to be. What are you going to eat?'

He was actually a bit like her father, Annabel thought: charming, easy to be with. She felt happy with him, really happy.

When he took her home that night in a cab (having paid for dinner), he kissed her nearly all the way. It was extremely nice.

'You are really, really special,' he said to her, as she finally and reluctantly got out of the cab, driven by the cabbie's rather determined throat-clearing and coughing, 'and I can't wait to see you again. Tomorrow?'

'Tomorrow – yes, please.'

There was still over a week to go. It was absolutely brilliant.

'Hello! Isn't it Mrs Cowper?'

Of course it was: looking more beautiful than ever, and dressed a lot more sexily, in an above-the-knee skirt – more of those incredible legs on display, that was good – and quite a sharp little jacket in brilliant pink. Her tits seemed to have got bigger too. What had happened to her? Whatever it was, it suited her.

She looked puzzled for a moment.

'We met at the Lloyd's do, that legal-ish meeting.'

'Oh – of course. Yes.' She smiled at him, that wonderful half-shy, half-flirtatious smile. 'And you're Mr Beaumont.'

'We sound like something out of Jane Austen. Simon, please. How are you?'

'I'm fine. And I'm Lucinda.'

Lucinda. He remembered now. What an absurdly perfect name for her. 'It's lovely to see you. Whatever are you doing in this part of town?'

'It's nice to see you too. I was – um – well, having lunch with someone.'

'Right. Good lunch?'

'Yes, it was lovely, thank you. I'm haring back to work now, bit late.'

'I've been trying to get hold of your husband. To discuss something.'

'Oh – right.'

'But he hasn't returned my calls. I wonder if you could jog him? It's quite important – to do with Lloyd's, actually.'

'Well . . . well, the thing is . . .'

'Yes?'

'The thing is, we're – we're not together any more. So . . .'

'Oh. Oh, I'm sorry. How sad.'

'Yes. Yes, it is.'

Not for her, obviously; it explained a good deal. And not too surprising, really.

'But I will be seeing him, quite soon, so I'll try and get him to call you. But – but he might not. I . . . well, I don't have much influence over him any more, I'm afraid.'

'No, of course not. But that would be very kind. Tell me, where's work?'

'Oh, Bloomsbury way. I work for a publishers, Peter Harrison.'

'Oh really? Didn't you publish that biography of Soros?'

'Yes. It got marvellous reviews.'

'I know. I've been wanting to read it. I've put it on my birthday list. Look – let me give you my card. I did give it to your husband, but he might have lost it. Would that be all right?'

'Yes, of course. Well, it was really nice to see you again. Bye now.'

And she was gone, with another dazzling smile. He stood looking after her, smiling foolishly, drinking her in as she disappeared into the throng of people.

Catherine Morgan, who had been hurrying out of the Graburn & French building herself, it being the end of her working day, saw him chatting to Lucinda and felt a pang of jealousy. Only a very mild one; and obviously she couldn't possibly compete with Lucinda's starry glamour, but after four months of working for Simon Beaumont, she was definitely slightly in love with him. Not enough in love to make her unhappy, or to cause him a moment's unease; just enough to make going to work every day pleasantly exciting; enough to make her take more trouble with her appearance than she had for a long time; enough to make the most tedious documents or pages of figures a pleasure to type. She didn't see him every day; but when she did, he always smiled at her, asked her how she was, and if there was time, like before a meeting where she was taking the minutes, or in the lift, how the children were, how they were getting on, particularly Freddie; and when he smiled at her, that extraordinarily easy, charming smile, and said it was lovely to see her, she felt like skipping, or singing. She knew it was silly, that it was a grown-up version of a schoolgirl crush, but it still made life more fun. And her life had been pretty short on fun over the last few years.

In fact, everything seemed better; Freddie was terribly pleased to be back at Lynton House, and Caroline seemed not to mind in the very least that she was still at St Joseph's Fulham. They left after she did every morning so that she could, as promised, get into work early; she worried about this at first, about the fifteen minutes they were on their own before Freddie escorted Caroline to school, after locking up carefully, and then went on to Lynton House.

She managed to meet Caroline only occasionally a little late, and they usually got to Lynton House just before the boys all came out; apart from the mercifully rare nightmare days when one or other of them was ill it worked brilliantly. And for the holidays, she had found a very nice woman, Mrs Lennox, who lived a few doors away and who was happy to look after them.

Her life, Catherine thought as she walked through Leadenhall Market, really had improved dramatically. And it was all down to Simon, to charming, handsome, kind Simon Beaumont, who was, she saw, gazing at Lucinda as she got into a taxi, patently wishing he was going off in it with her. Oh well. If he'd been gazing at her, Catherine thought, she would only have tripped on the cobblestones and ripped her tights . . .

The more Joel Strickland heard from the players in this Lloyd's drama, the more he thought it would make a brilliant article. But God, it was hard getting it together.

That phone call from that poor terrified bloke – what did he think was going to happen to him, for God's sake, that he'd be put in the Tower? – had put quite a bit more of the jigsaw in place. And although he was very sorry for the old lady, a death always brought a story alive. Gave it a heart. His editor had been very lukewarm about the whole thing so far: had said what everyone said, that nobody was going to care very much about a whole lot of rich spoiled people crying because they were going to be a bit less rich. Initially Joel had agreed with him; he hated the braying complacent lot that Names seemed mostly formed from. But a little homework had revealed something rather different.

Gillian Thompson, for instance, hadn't been rich or spoiled; she'd been modestly well-off, or so it seemed, no more than that. And from what the bloke had said, a fairly recent recruit to Lloyd's. Poor old soul. Who had done that to her? Who had suggested she became a Name? And how had it been allowed to happen, when the minimum capital requirement was £75,000, and that was supposed to exclude your main residence? Well, maybe she had actually been much richer than it appeared. A lot of very rich people, particularly eccentric old ladies, chose to do that, to make a positive effort to conceal their wealth, left millions to cats' homes or whatever. Perhaps Gillian Thompson had been one of them. But then – she wouldn't have had to kill herself. So it really didn't add up. And anyway, according to that young man, she'd been put in the wrong sort of high-risk syndicate, along with a lot of other people.

Joel felt increasingly convinced that Miss Thompson's story was crucial to his own. He decided to go and visit May Williams, the unfortunate woman who had discovered her body.

Chapter 16

April, 1990

'Darling, whatever is it? Look, you know we don't allow tears here. Far too self-indulgent. You know the works motto, wear your heart tucked into your knickers. And look at you, mascara running everywhere, not a good look, you'll turn that blond solution brown if you're not careful and then all the clients will sue. Come on, sweetie, nothing's that bad. How about I take you out for a really glamorous cup of cocoa after work, no expense spared . . . here, wipe your eyes on this – no, not that, you silly bitch, not my foils . . .'

In spite of herself, Annabel half-smiled, rubbed her fist across her eyes. 'Sorry.'

'I should just think so, and you should see yourself now – you look like something out of the Black and White Minstrels . . .'

'Well, thanks!'

'That's all right. Oh God, here comes the Virgin Queen. Miki, darling, just leave us for two minutes, that's all I ask, just a tiny little upset here, and then I'm all yours – if you'll only have me.'

'Florian,' said Miki, 'in two minutes, Mrs Alexander will have left the salon for good. She's furious. Get upstairs and start calming her down *right now*. And Bel, if you have to cry, please do it in your own time. You've got two clients waiting to be shampooed; perhaps you'd be good enough to go and make a start on at least one of them. I'll speak to you later. I will not have this sort of nonsense in the salon, it is so absolutely unprofessional. Now wash your face and get back to work at once, please.'

*

Annabel really hadn't expected to feel this bad. She'd only known Jamie for two weeks for heaven's sake, and here she was acting like they'd been together for years. Maybe that proved how important it was. And at least she'd passed the biggest test of all: meeting his parents.

They'd had a totally perfect weekend, a lovely afternoon and evening in London – lots of cocktails at the Criterion in Piccadilly (fun), then dinner at Daphne's (divine), and then – then champagne and endless wonderful snogging in Jamie's room at the Carlton Towers. His parents were away for the night, he'd said, so he felt very relaxed. She couldn't quite get over a man of twenty-four feeling inhibited by his parents' presence several rooms along the corridor in a hotel, but still . . .

He told her he didn't want to have sex yet; he said it was too soon. She was half-disappointed, half-pleased by this; having grown up in a culture where sex had moved so far up the dating agenda that it was regarded by many as the norm on the second date at the latest, such modest behaviour seemed rather odd. But it was also rather touching; it made her feel quite special. She wondered if it was shyness on his part, or even fear, but as they lay on his bed, watching the dawn come up, he said he had had two quite serious relationships before, and that he simply thought that you should be very sure of yourself and your feelings before you asked someone to go to bed with you.

'It's a very full commitment, as far as I'm concerned. I don't think it should be like – well, like just kissing.'

She fell asleep contentedly in his arms, still half-dressed; she was sure the waiter who brought them breakfast in bed would never have believed the innocence of the night they had spent.

And then, on the way back from Bath, from another perfect day together, driving through the endless golden midsummer evening, he suddenly said, 'Stop the car, I want to tell you something.'

Half-frightened, she had pulled onto the hard shoulder and sat, heart thumping, waiting for some kind of harsh judgement, or final farewell.

'I want you to know I'm in love with you,' he said. 'I know it's all been very quick, but I'm quite sure. And I need to know how you feel about me.'

258

'I feel the same,' she said, 'darling Jamie. Just the same. So that's really good, isn't it?'

'Really good. And so I thought, we could go back to the hotel and – well, prove it to one another. Now that we're both sure.'

They drove the rest of the way with his hand tucked companionably between her thighs; by the time they got back to the hotel, Annabel was in such a state of acute sexual excitement she could hardly sit still, and her pants were uncomfortably damp: so damp indeed that she feared her fine voile skirt might reveal the fact.

And then, as they hurried into the foyer, hand-in-hand, giggling like guilty children, and went over to the desk to get his room key, they heard a voice. A low, drawling, slightly hard-edged voice: 'Jamie, darling, there you are. We wondered. Good weekend? Are you going to join us for dinner?'

It was his mother.

She was all right, Annabel supposed, standing shaking Mrs Cartwright's hand, keeping her back to the reception counter, smiling dutifully, wishing she'd at least had time to comb her hair, still extremely ruffled by some heavy-duty snogging in a cornfield just outside Bath, and for all she knew, containing lots of ears of corn. She was polite and gracious if a little chilly; she was certainly beautiful, in a blonde Grace Kelly sort of way, perfectly dressed and pressed and coiffed, and although she obviously wasn't very pleased to find her son in the company of a strange girl, and one moreover he was clearly very taken with, she made a good attempt at disguising it, urging Annabel to join them for dinner. Which of course she accepted; she could hardly claim a prior engagement when she and Jamie had been so unmistakably going up to his room together and as good as neon signs on their heads saying *Orgasms Imminent*.

And it had been agony in a way, trying to calm down, pretending everything was really cool, not being able to get him to tell her over and over again that he loved her, not being able to tell him the same thing, not being able to have sex, for God's sake. But precisely because she did love him so much and she

259

wanted to please him, and for his parents to like her, she managed it, listened politely to details of a night in Stratford, and a visit to the Birthplace and inevitably (they being Americans) to criticism of their hotel and comparisons with ones they had stayed at in the States, like the Bel Air in Los Angeles – OK, but no Shakespeare there, she managed not to say.

When Mr Cartwright joined them, it was better, he was just an older version of Jamie, and she had a lot of fun comparing them; he was also quite flirtatious in a very upper-class way, and she liked that. And when finally the endless evening was over, she knew that was it; she would have to go home, on her own, and there would be no sex that night, or even for many, many nights, as the Cartwrights were leaving the next evening.

But it was all worth it, because Jamie suddenly appeared in the salon at lunchtime next day, and she somehow persuaded Marcia to let her out just for ten minutes; and there, standing out in the street, he told her he loved her, and that he would see her soon; somehow, he'd be back, and if not she had to come over and stay with them in Boston, 'Because my parents both simply loved you, my mother particularly. She said you were absolutely delightful, and I don't remember her ever saying that before about any of my girlfriends.'

And then he gave her a kiss, a quick, light, lingering kiss and he was gone. Leaving Annabel not sure whether to laugh or cry. Within the space of the next twenty-four hours, she had done a great deal of both.

'Well, it's perfectly straightforward really.' Douglas Wilson smiled his wintry smile at Nigel. He ran the Divorce Department at Andrews & Sloane, the Cowper family solicitor for four generations. He seemed much sharper and less likable than his colleagues. 'If, as you say, she is willing to give you a divorce, and wants to make it as simple as possible, then I don't see any great difficulty.'

'Really?' said Nigel. He was finding the conversation deeply painful; Wilson talking about the divorce as if it was a business negotiation, something that could be dealt with quickly and efficiently. It hurt even more than he had expected.

'Well, no. There are only two grounds here, adultery or

260

unreasonable behaviour. Either would suit the circumstances perfectly well, but since she is pregnant by this other man, then adultery would seem obvious. I presume there could be no question the child is yours?'

'No,' said Nigel. His throat constricted suddenly and painfully; he looked down at his hands.

'Right,' said Wilson. 'Sorry, had to ask.'

'Of course. I understand.' He blew his nose.

'But you may prefer, for whatever reason, to petition on the other grounds, that of unreasonable behaviour.'

Somehow that sounded better: less hurtful, he would feel less of a fool.

'Possibly. Would – that is, does what she's done constitute unreasonable behaviour?'

'My dear chap, I should think so. But no, I take your point. Just the same, we could construct the case, find examples. She would have to be advised that was what you had decided. Perhaps you could discuss it with her? That always makes things simpler.'

'I – I don't know,' said Nigel. 'I don't know what to think. It's all so – so wretched.'

'I understand. Horrible business, always. But – has to be done. Better when it's over and everything is neat and tidy – can't get any further out of hand.'

'How might it get out of hand,' asked Nigel, 'as it's so straightforward?'

'Well, you'd be surprised how many cases I've seen that start like yours, everyone wanting to be friendly and generous, and end up with them fighting furiously over money. Would there be any problem there? Does she have money worries?'

'I don't think so, no.'

'But you're not sure. You see, she may have a very sharp solicitor of her own, who might feel she was entitled to various monies.'

'But – the other man is – is very well off,' said Nigel. Every word hurt; it was like biting on an abscessed tooth. He didn't think he could stand it much longer.

'Maybe. But have you ever met anyone who couldn't do with a little more money? No such person has ever sat in this office, I can assure you.'

261

Well, Lucinda would, Nigel thought; and felt his throat constrict again.

'So . . .' said Wilson, 'which ground should we go for? And for that matter, who will petition whom? Since it's uncontested, I imagine you will petition her, but—'

'Well, she can hardly petition me, can she?'

'She could, if she was being awkward. She could petition you for unreasonable behaviour, as a matter of fact.'

'But I never was. Unreasonable, I mean.'

Wilson looked at him: there was cynicism in that look, and doubt, and even a shadow of amusement. God, he disliked him . . .

'And anyway,' Nigel said, 'she doesn't want to be awkward. She keeps telling me that. She wants to be helpful.'

'In that case, I would say adultery would be the better grounds.'

'Yes, all right.' But he was suddenly haunted by the thought of the divorce case; of being branded a cuckold, unable to keep his wife. He'd look so stupid. Of course it was different these days, and divorces were heard in private; nobody would actually know, but even so . . .

He could imagine people talking, his friends discussing it – her friends discussing it. Saying maybe it was the age difference, maybe she'd been bored, maybe . . . Nigel's mind veered away from the other maybe.

'Perhaps the other, the unreasonable behaviour might be better though. Oh, I don't know. I really don't know.'

Douglas Wilson's jaw tightened. His colleagues, and particularly his assistant, would have recognised it as a sign that he was running out of patience.

'I really would advise you to discuss it with Mrs Cowper. And as soon as possible, then I can proceed. If she is being as cooperative as you say, then it shouldn't be too painful at all. Or even prolonged. Can we leave it that you'll do that and then contact me again?'

'Yes, all right,' said Nigel. He felt like hitting Douglas Wilson.

He went straight to the Reform from Andrews & Sloane and ordered a double gin and tonic. Even though it was only half-past five.

May Williams had refused to see Joel Strickland at first; she mistrusted the press and had had a bit of a bad time when she had first discovered poor Gillian Thompson's body. They'd been down like vultures, she told her sister, 'Asking me the most awful questions, like whether she'd had any male friends, or how her health had been, things like that.'

But he had managed to reassure her – 'I really am not that sort of reporter, I'm a financial journalist' – telling her he thought that Miss Thompson might have been badly served by the people demanding money from her. He had explained that the article wasn't about Miss Thompson herself, but about what he felt might turn out to be a big financial injustice.

She finally agreed, 'But I don't want to be asked anything personal,' she said firmly.

Joel said he wouldn't dream of it, and she didn't have to answer any questions that she was unhappy about. 'And the *News* is quite a respectable paper, it's not like the *Sun*.'

May Williams said, well yes, that was something in his favour and actually she liked the *News*, it had been her father's paper, and that if he came on Saturday morning, that would be best.

'I do some voluntary work on Thursday and Friday mornings,' she said, as if the remaining weekdays were completely out of the question. Joel said that would be fine and then had to spend at least half an hour trying to explain to Maggie that it was more important that he saw May Williams than that he took her to Brighton for her birthday. She was not impressed, and not even the booking of a table at Bibendum for the Friday night did a great deal to help.

He drove down to the village on the edge of the New Forest, where May Williams lived, parked near the church and had a look round before walking to May's house. It was a medium-sized village, not especially pretty, with a large sprawling bungalow element; but it had a large green in front of the church, which was clearly the heart of the place, providing grazing for the wild ponies. The church was obviously an active one, with lots of notices on its gate about jumble sales and quiz evenings in the hall. He wondered idly if Gillian Thompson had been a churchgoer; single ladies often were, and of course her free piano lessons would have made her popular; she was unlikely to actually have been the tragical solitary figure the tabloids had presented. Moor Lane, which was where Miss Williams lived, was just about a lane still, a cul de sac in fact, leading at its far end onto a park with swings and seesaws, and a tennis court and thence onto open countryside.

Miss Williams's cottage was very pretty, painted white with a slate roof and a large front garden, beautifully kept. A huge tabby cat sat keeping guard over her path. Joel presumed this to be Mustapha, of whom the tabloids had made much; he looked extremely contented. Fickle things, cats; a dog would still have been grieving. Joel was a dog person.

He knocked on the door; it was on a chain and he was asked to identify himself before May Williams opened it.

'We have to be so careful,' she said, ushering him in. 'There've been so many burglaries recently, and of course living alone, you are doubly at risk.'

Joel said indeed you were and smiled at her, presenting her with a cyclamen in a pot he had bought the day before; he had discovered that such gifts were very helpful; they induced a feeling of disproportionate gratitude in the recipient which in turn became a kind of pressure encouraging them to talk.

He could see that May Williams was certainly not going to prove an exception to his rule. Her pale thin face flushed with pleasure and she clutched it to her cardiganed bosom and said how very kind he was, and that she did hope his journey from London wasn't going to prove fruitless.

'I really can't tell you very much,' she said, 'but if anyone didn't deserve unhappiness and worry it was Gillian – Miss Thompson. She was such a good friend, and so generous, and worked so hard for the village; she did the flowers for the church almost every week, and as I expect you know, she gave her piano lessons completely free to the children who needed that. She was very popular – everybody is still terribly upset. Especially Mustapha,' she added, nodding in the direction of the extremely contented-looking cat which had followed Joel in. 'And I miss Gillian terribly. We used to listen to concerts together on the wireless and even went to performances in Bournemouth sometimes. It seems so dreadful, that she was driven to doing this awful thing.'

'Well, absolutely,' said Joel, taking the cup of coffee she had made; it was disgusting, both weak and bitter (how did people do that, he wondered), but he drank it with great relish and accepted a piece of very heavy fruit cake which she said she had made, pronouncing it delicious, 'and it must have been a terrible shock for you, finding your friend like that.'

'It was,' said May Williams. 'Absolutely dreadful. I had to get some tablets from the doctor, help me sleep at first.'

'I'm not surprised.'

'And I miss her so much,' she said again, tearfully. 'We really were good friends.'

'I can tell. Is that her cottage, up for sale?'

'Yes. That's sad too, seeing it empty and the garden neglected. Although she was talking about selling it anyway.'

'Oh, was she?'

'Well, yes. She said she might have to, to settle her debts. Although where she would have lived, I really don't know. She was so depressed, Mr Strickland, those last few weeks; she looked awful, I kept telling her nothing was that bad, but she said, and I shall never forget her words, "May, this is worse than bad, this is dreadful. I can't see any way out." If only I could have helped. I did say she could always stay with me for a time, but she said she couldn't possibly impose on me. Oh dear . . .' Her pale eyes filled with tears; she wiped them away, blew her nose. 'I'm sorry, Mr Strickland.'

'It's all right,' said Joel gently. He looked away tactfully, while she composed herself.

'That was her,' she said, handing him a photograph in a frame of a lady not unlike herself, holding a large bouquet of flowers and standing on a platform. She was smiling radiantly; even Joel, toughened by life as well as his job, found it sad to look at her, and think of her horrifically lonely end. 'It was taken a few years ago now, at her pupils' concert in the church hall. It's very good, don't you think?'

'Very good. Now tell me, Miss Williams, do you know when Miss Thompson first began to be so worried?'

'Well, not really. This is what I was concerned about, that I wouldn't be able to help you very much. She was a very private person, didn't ever give me any details about her affairs. She just began to mention being worried about her investments, and she did begin to call a halt to our outings to Bournemouth, I suppose that was – let me see – about eighteen months, maybe two years ago. But she never showed any really serious anxiety, until the last few weeks.'

'And . . . did she mention being a Name at Lloyd's?'

'At Lloyd's? You mean the bank?'

'No, no,' said Joel patiently, 'the insurance company.'

'Insurance? No, I don't think she had any problems with that.'

Joel moved onto a different tack. 'I think I read that her father left her quite a lot of money. Would that be right?'

'Yes, he was quite a rich man. He worked in the City, ran some sort of company. Gillian was his only child, and she inherited everything. Well, most of it – he left a fair amount to charity. I do know that made the newspapers at the time. Gillian was rather embarrassed about it.'

'Why?'

'Well, it was a rather odd charity, not something like Cancer Research or the RSPCA. I think Gillian would have preferred that. Not that she minded, of course, she was very pleased indeed with what he did leave her.'

'Oh, and what was the charity?' asked Joel. 'I seem to remember it was something to do with birds . . .'

'Yes, that's right, it was a bird sanctuary. Apparently, when Gillian's father was a boy, he had loved it. It was – oh, now where was it, somewhere on the East Coast, and it was gradually going under with lack of funds. He left them many thousands of pounds, and that was what got into the papers at the time.'

'I see. And where did he live, her father – round here?'

'No, no – in London, somewhere quite smart, I believe. He really was very successful and always beautifully dressed, even though he was well into his eighties.'

'Oh, you met him?'

'Yes, indeed, he came to visit Gillian from time to time. A charming man, she was terribly fond of him. "I don't quite live up to him, I'm afraid, May," she used to say. "He'd like me to be a bit more glamorous, like my mother." I told her that was nonsense. Now do you know, I've just thought of someone you should talk to, much more helpful than me.'

Joel looked expectantly at May Williams. 'Who is that?'

'Once or twice, after Mr Thompson's death, a young man

came to visit Gillian. Well, I suppose he wasn't all that young, but you know how it is, as you get older everyone starts to look younger. I mean, you seem like a boy to me—'

'Thank you,' said Joel.

'Anyway, this young man went to Mr Thompson's funeral and then came down here once or twice again, as I said. I used to tease Gillian, say he was her admirer. She would laugh and say she didn't think that was very likely. She said he was helping her with some investments and she was grateful. She liked him, said he had been a neighbour of her father's, and she knew she could trust him. I mean, he might know where things went wrong. And, in fact, when she talked about her worries, I said, "What about your admirer?" and she said, quite bitterly, that she thought he was the last person who'd be able to help her now.'

'Right,' said Joel, 'he does sound interesting, yes. So – do you remember his name?'

'I do, yes,' said May Williams. 'I never would normally, I'm hopeless at names, but I always managed his, because it was the same as the flour.'

'Flour?'

'Yes. It was Allinson. "I'm going to make an Allinson cake for Mr Allinson, May," she said and afterwards we always shared the second half.'

'So – how many visits did he make?'

'Oh, not many. I think she was a little sad when they stopped; he was a great music lover, you see, and they used to discuss the concerts and operas they had seen, and once he did actually take her to a Promenade concert – at the Albert Hall, you know.'

'Indeed?' said Joel politely.

'But, well, he lived in London and obviously had a lot of friends, and he only came once after that. And of course he was a busy man. Something in the City, I believe. But anyway, you should talk to him, I really think he might be able to help.'

'I will. And thank you so much. Er – do you know where he lived?'

'In the same London square as Gillian's father, I would imagine, if he was a neighbour, but I don't know which one that was. Perhaps it would be mentioned in some of the newspaper stories.'

'Perhaps,' said Joel. 'And his Christian name – do you recall that?'

'I'm afraid not,' said May Williams. 'Oh, I am so sorry, I really haven't helped much at all. I do hope your journey hasn't been wasted.'

'Absolutely not, I've enjoyed meeting you very much. And thank you for the lead.'

'The what?'

'Your idea about Mr Allinson. It really might help.'

He drove back to London as fast as his BMW could take him, hoping Maggie wouldn't be too cross. At least he'd got her a nice present, a Tiffany silver bracelet; although he had a nasty feeling that when she saw the Tiffany box, she might think it contained something smaller and more meaningful. Well, she'd find out when she opened it.

It was quite interesting about the mysterious Mr Allinson. He probably had nothing to do with Lloyd's, but it was worth finding out. Joel knew that some syndicates at Lloyd's did employ – well, not exactly employ, but give a commission to people who went about finding new Names for them. Trading on exactly the backgrounds and contacts that Joel so disapproved of. And if Mr Allinson really had been responsible for urging the sweet-faced, smiling Miss Thompson into the dangerous fold, then he would make bloody sure that all his readers knew about it.

Chapter 17

May, 1990

Lucinda hadn't been sick at all during her pregnancy until the day she and Nigel were to meet to discuss the divorce. She woke up feeling absolutely dreadful, having slept badly, haunted by dark dreams of Nigel hating her, shouting at her, abusing her, of the solicitor attacking her physically, of Blue and Nigel having a fight, and finally and most dreadfully, losing the baby. She woke up sobbing, her nightdress drenched with sweat, to find Blue shaking her; she clung to him, refusing to speak and then, suddenly overcome with nausea, had to rush to the bathroom where she threw up repeatedly.

'Sweet, what is it? For God's sake, you got to tell me. Get back to bed, I'll call the doctor.' He had come in after her, was standing looking down on her as she knelt by the lavatory, a ghastly colour himself. She blew her nose, managed to stand up, even to smile at him.

'It's OK, I'm OK, I've only been sick, for heaven's sake, there's nothing wrong.'

'Course there is. Look at the state of you – you're shaking all over. Go on, back to bed.'

'Yes, all right, but don't call the doctor. I'm fine, I just had some bad dreams, and you know it's today, with Nigel and—'

'Course I know it's today. I didn't expect you to be in this sort of state though. I think I'd better come with you.'

'No,' said Lucinda wearily, 'no, Blue, you are not coming with me. It's going to be bad enough for Nigel without you being there.'

'Well, thanks for that. I don't like it, Lucy, not one bit. I just don't like you going off on your own, facing him and all, and now if you're ill . . .'

269

He had been totally horrified by the suggestion when it came from Nigel; it had taken days to persuade him.

'I'm not having it and that's that,' he kept saying. 'You're not seeing him, not without me.'

Lucinda had been rather shocked by this; in fact, it led to one of their rare but colourful rows.

'It's not a question of you having or not having anything,' she had said, 'it's my decision, and I've made it. And I'm going. There's nothing more to discuss.'

'Lucinda, I know what's best for you, and it's *not* meeting Nigel.'

'I don't think you know what's best for me at all. Not in this instance. So please stop talking to me as if I belonged to you.'

'Well, don't you?'

'Of course not.'

'If that's how you see our relationship, I must have got it very wrong,' he said.

'Yes, I think you have. Very wrong. I didn't feel I belonged, as you put it, to Nigel – and I was actually married to him.'

'Well, you're going to be married to me.'

'That's totally irrelevant, and you're not listening to me.'

'I have been listening. And I don't like what I've heard,' he said and walked out, slamming the door.

In the end, he had agreed; but with extreme reluctance.

'I just don't like it,' he said now. 'I think it's wrong. He might do anything to you.'

'Blue, of course he won't do anything to me, that's not the point. I just feel awful about it all. You must see that.'

'You're too soft-hearted by half, you know that, don't you?' he said.

'Blue! For the hundredth time, just think what I've done to Nigel. Caused him so much unhappiness, humiliation, loneliness. And what did he do to me? Nothing. Just – just not be you. Yes, all right, I'm coming' – as he steered her back to bed, pulled the covers over her tenderly. 'The baby's fine, I'm sure. I don't have any pain or anything. I just feel terribly sick. At myself, you know.'

'You have to get rid of some of this guilt, Lucy,' said Blue, 'otherwise you're going to drive yourself mad. There's a long tough road ahead of you—'

'I don't see why it has to be long *or* tough. I'm not going to argue about anything. I want to do everything for him that I can.'

'You know,' said Blue, sitting down on the bed beside her, 'this is not the way to approach divorce, Lucinda. His solicitor's going to take you to the cleaners if you're not careful. I keep telling you.'

'But – he's welcome to. He can take me to all the cleaners he can find. I don't want anything from Nigel, anything at all. I want to help him. Anyway, I've got nothing to give him, that's half the trouble, why I feel so bad.' She started to cry again.

'I really think I'd better come with you,' Blue said. 'I can't have you going off in this state. And don't be too sure he won't be trying his damnedest to get something of mine.'

'You're *not* coming,' Lucinda said again, 'and that's ridiculous. How could he get any of your money? Why should he?'

'Because he needs every fucking penny he can get. And I've got a few. And you done him wrong. As he sees it.'

'And as any reasonable person would see it. Look – nothing like that's going to happen. I know it isn't.'

'Lucinda, you ever had any dealings with lawyers?'

'No. Except when we bought our flat. Oh, and when Nigel made over all that money to me; we had to go and sign some stuff about the more complicated things.'

'Thought not. They make you think black is white and then when they done that, they tell you it's black again. Blood out of a stone? No problem. They could get out a gallon before breakfast and then drink it. They're fucking villains. Every minute you spend with them, that's money in their pockets. So the more minutes the better. You can see them watching the clock, adding it up. So just you be careful. And I wish you'd let me find you someone, someone shit hot, not this dickhead who looks after your dad.'

'He's not a dickhead,' said Lucinda, 'and don't talk like that. I keep telling you— Oh God, I think I'm going to be sick again.'

It was truly shocking news. Elizabeth phoned after an early meeting, her voice sober: Neil Lawrence had taken an overdose, was in intensive care. Simon stood in the hall, feeling shaky and oddly frightened, as this awful creeping evil horror extended its tentacles, wound ever more tightly round him, dragging him further away from escape.

'Is there anything we should do?' he said.

'I don't know, Simon. His wife's with him. It's touch and go, apparently.'

'Poor sod.'

'Indeed. I wondered whether we should send a message, or . . .'

'Let's leave it a day or two, see if he pulls through. God, this thing is a nightmare. Poor bloody man. Do you know the wife?'

'No, never met her. She found him, poor girl. Someone called the agency, he was coming in later today.'

'Oh, Christ. Look, I'll speak to you later. Keep me posted.'

He walked back into the kitchen, still feeling sick, sat down at the table. Annabel was there, drinking orange juice.

'You look awfully pale, Daddy.' She put her arm round his shoulders. 'What's wrong?'

'Oh, nothing really. Nothing that need trouble you.'

How could he tell her, tell this beloved child, or indeed the other beloved children, that a man faced with the same problems as his own, the prospective loss of everything he had, had attempted suicide, had taken an overdose, had been so deranged with terror and shame that he had not even properly considered the effect of that on his wife and children . . .

Later, when she had gone, he called George Meyer.

'A friend – no, not really a friend even, an acquaintance – tried to kill himself last night. Took an overdose—'

'Oh God,' said Meyer, 'how bloody awful.'

'I know. He's up to his neck, half a million's worth of debt, no hope of paying it, had kept it from his wife, obviously finally cracked. Nice chap, I really liked him.'

There was a silence, then Meyer said, 'It's the solitude of it all, isn't it? Even when you've got people to share it with. What it must be like when you're keeping it from everyone . . .'

'I know, I know. And it's so unfair. I mean, he was a decent, god-fearing person, struggling to do his best for his family; four bloody kids he's got, it's not as if he'd committed some crime—'

'Could you ever imagine doing that?' said Meyer abruptly.

'No, not in a million years. You've let them win then, haven't you? Christ, it's awful. I keep thinking, could I have done something for him, helped in some way . . . When's it going to end, George?'

'God knows,' said Meyer, 'and I actually doubt if He's very interested.'

'You know something?' Simon said suddenly. 'I'm going to talk to that journalist I told you about. I said no at first, didn't want to get involved with the press, but people need to know just how bad this fucking business really is.'

Tim Allinson had decided: it was time to get out and move to the South of France. He'd almost decided that before, but he'd thought one more summer season, and then he'd sell up. There was plenty to sell; the flat in Pelham Crescent certainly worth a bit, and there were a few paintings, and some very nice furniture, and he certainly had Lloyd's, or to be precise the Westfield Bradley Group of Syndicates, to thank for all that. He'd always loved Nice: or perhaps Antibes, that was so beautiful, fish restaurants to die for and there was the Hotel du Cap, best Bellinis in the world, in his opinion. And he could afford to retire, pretty well. He had some investments, and you never knew, there were lots of rich widows down there. But – it was getting dodgy in England now. He hadn't liked being told, very nicely of course, to stop working a house-party, as his host had put it, the weekend before.

He'd been invited to Wiltshire; the Saturday was to be spent trout fishing. Tim loved fishing; his favourite was salmon fishing in Scotland, but as he got a little older, he found a warm sunny day spent sitting by some beautiful lake, in good company and with a fine picnic, the fish biting obligingly frequently, increasingly pleasant. It was a good party too; his host was an old school-friend, there were some very pretty women as well as some congenial men, and if the Friday night had been anything to go by, both the food and the wine cellar were of the highest standard.

He hadn't expected to be able to do any work, as he thought of it, but there was one guest who seemed to offer a possibility at least. Quite what he was doing there Tim wasn't sure; he was what his mother would have called a rough diamond, a thick-accented Geordie by the name of Mick Bridgeman, aged about fifty, tall, overweight but very pleasant, with a fine line in filthy stories and a young wife who might have been overawed by the occasion and clearly wasn't; she was a confident creature, very pretty indeed, with blond hair and huge blue eyes and very impressive breasts. She called herself Thandie – what a name – and said she was a model; she had chattered away happily at dinner, very well aware that most of the men's eyes were on her, giggling at their feeble jokes and fulsome compliments, and rather sweetly unaware of the chilly attitude of the other wives. Ill at ease she wasn't; just not quite properly a part of them all. And didn't care in the least. Presumably she was not Bridgeman's first wife; Tim, who was of necessity a great social observer, would have put her as probably the third.

He sought her out after dinner, when they rejoined the women – amazing how these conventions survived in the country – and found that he was right:

'Yes, we got married just before Christmas, had our honeymoon in the Bahamas – Mick's got a villa there. Oh, it was beautiful – have you ever been?'

Tim said that he hadn't, but he would like it very much; after another half-hour's chatting, she was summoned away by Bridgeman. 'Big day tomorrow, Thandie, got to get a bit of shut-eye,' but not before making a promise to invite Tim out to the Bahamas 'next time we go'.

Tim thought he might move in, very gently, on Bridgeman over the picnic and then perhaps make a carefully vague reference to Lloyd's tonight . . .

But, 'All very well, old chap,' his host had said, 'singing the praises of Lloyd's, but it just isn't the safe bet it was. I wouldn't touch it these days – few nasty stories coming out.'

Tim had said, only very mildly indignant, that Lloyd's was as safe as the Bank of England and he'd only been talking about it to Mick Bridgeman, not trying to suggest he joined – which of course he wouldn't have done, he always made the formal approach on his own patch, but just the same it had shaken him. He didn't want to get caught with his very expensive trousers down. Best cut his losses – or rather his gains – and find something else to do. Like wooing widows.

Michael Booker, one of the Members' Agents at Jackson & Bond, was delighted to accept a lunch invitation from Simon Beaumont.

'Just wanted to talk a few things through with you,' Simon said, 'given the time of year and the approach of the results. And you've bought me enough meals in the past.'

'True enough. Jolly good. Look forward to it.'

'Excellent. And I've asked George Meyer along.'

'Fine. Splendid.'

Simon had booked a table at Simpsons in the Strand. He was well-known there, they'd get good service and at worst a very good lunch; he and George were there before Booker, drinking neat tonic water with ice and lemon.

'We need very clear heads,' Simon had said.

Booker walked in; he was tall and dark, just slightly overweight and dressed in a superbly cut suit that almost but not quite concealed the fact. He came over to the table, smiling, hand held out.

'Jolly nice to see you both.'

God, these people are incredible, Simon thought. Skins like four-ply rhino-hide.

'And you, Michael. We're on gin and tonic – suit you?'

Booker said it would suit very well.

Conversation was easy; asked what he had been doing with himself over the past couple of months, Booker outlined a programme of hunting and shooting, interspersed with some very good golf in the Algarve where he had a house.

'And a bit of work, of course. Have to pay for it all somehow.'

'Indeed,' said Meyer.

Booker ate heartily – oysters, beef and ale pie, and a wonderfully Bunter-ish trifle. He talked on unabated, glimpses of his meal constantly on show as he chomped. Finally as he waved away the cheese trolley – 'Supposed to be watching my weight' – he said, 'And what about you chaps – everything all right with you? Any particular issues you wanted to discuss?'

Simon, who had resisted more than one glass of a very fine Merlot with great difficulty, said there were a few. 'And when do we get next year's results?'

'Ah,' said Booker, 'yes. Thought you might be asking me that. Well, good old Lloyd's –' *God, thought Simon, maybe he's going to tell us it's better, maybe we can all begin to breathe a bit more easily* '– punctual as usual. Around the beginning of April.'

'And – what news might you have for us?'

'For you? Well, not entirely good, I'm afraid. No. No, indeed.' His face, already flushed with the Merlot, had become rather sweaty; it was not an attractive sight.

'Not good?'

'No. Not entirely. 'Fraid Westfield Bradley in particular have taken a bit of a pasting. This year.'

'Not like last year,' said Simon drily.

'What? Oh, yes. Yes, quite true. Bit of a bad patch altogether. Yes.'

'Michael,' said George, 'this is more than a bad patch. It's gone on and on.'

'Indeed. But – well, that's why I was glad to come today, have a chat. I didn't want you rushing off to sell your houses, do anything hasty.'

'Unfortunately you're a little late to prevent that,' said Simon. 'We've both done some house-selling. I still have my main residence—'

'Oh, good man. Want to hold onto that.'

'Yes,' said Simon, 'I do actually. But it looks a bit more difficult. I am actually wondering what to do.'

'Well, you know, you can always speak to me. My door's always open, in a manner of speaking.'

'That's very good to know, of course,' said Simon, 'but to be perfectly honest, I don't feel we can talk frankly without there being a risk of your coming up against a clash of interest or divided loyalties.'

'There is no way that can happen, Simon. I don't quite follow.'

'Well, just for example, in a letter to me last November you showed how support for the Westfield Bradley Syndicate over the period 1986–7 dropped by about seventy per cent – more than £300 million. But you only reduced my participation by about ten per cent. Why didn't you take me right out of them?'

'Simon,' said Booker, a note of near-indignation in his voice, 'we were seriously concerned that if everyone pulled out, the syndicates would go down the pan. It's absolutely crucial that syndicates remain operative. For all our sakes.'

They sat staring at him in silence for about twenty seconds; then Simon spoke.

'Michael, I am speechless. I think you've just made my point.'

Booker left quite shortly; when he had gone, Simon ordered another bottle of Merlot.

'Well, what do you think?' he said. 'Was that gun smoking or not?'

'I'm not sure,' said Meyer, pulling a notebook out of his pocket. 'I take his point about keeping the syndicates going. But let's write down every bloody word and pass it into Ms Broadhurst's tender keeping.'

They had agreed to meet in the lounge of Selfridges Hotel at teatime. It was ideal for their purpose, Lucinda said, having proposed it; it was very quiet, it was about halfway between both their offices, and it was very unlikely that they'd see anyone they knew there.

'Because that would be terribly awful, wouldn't it?' she said.

Nigel agreed it would. 'Terribly awful' had been one of her catchphrases. It had always rather amused him. It didn't now.

He was as wretched at the prospect of meeting Lucinda as she was; he could hardly face even thinking about it, and at least twice during the morning he picked up the phone to cancel the whole thing. It seemed so impossible an ordeal he couldn't imagine ever getting through it. But four o'clock saw them both walking up the stairs at the same time: recognising one another, smiling faintly and saying hello, and then being led to one of the low chintz-covered sofas and ordering tea.

'And scones,' said Lucinda, smiling at the waiter, 'scones, oh and Little Scarlet strawberry jam if you've got it. He loves scones, don't you, Nigel?'

He managed to nod gloomily.

The whole experience was far, far worse than he had expected; the pain was so awful he thought he might pass out from it. Sitting there, looking at her, so lovely, her fair hair scooped back in a ponytail, her large blue eyes fixed tenderly – if rather nervously – on him; it was like a form of particularly awful torture. She was wearing a blue jumper over a white shirt, and then quite a full skirt, just the sort of thing she'd always worn; she looked altogether exactly the same – had he really expected her to have changed? – and certainly nothing showed, thank goodness; she was thinner, if anything. That helped – a bit. The alternative would have been unbearable.

'You look – well,' he said. Simply speaking was an effort.

'Thank you. So do you.'

'Yes, well. I've been to Norfolk a lot at the weekends. Country air, you know.'

'Of course. How is the farm doing?'

'Oh – pretty well. Thanks.'

'Good, I'm glad. Oh, and before I forget, I don't suppose you'll want to, but Simon Beaumont, you know that nice man from the Lloyd's meeting, he wants you to ring him about something.'

'Why have you been talking to Simon Beaumont?'

'Oh, I bumped into him last week. In the City.'

And he knew why she had been in the City: meeting Him. He winced.

'Well, I don't want to talk to him,' he said. 'I know what it's about, that lawsuit against Lloyd's, it's the last thing I can be doing with at the moment.'

'Of course, I understand. I'll – I'll call and tell him. Don't give it another thought.'

She smiled at him: her sweet perfect smile. This was agony; he should never have agreed to it. He must get it over: the sooner the better. Otherwise . . .

'Lucinda, we have to talk.'

'Yes, Nigel, I know. You're not eating your scone.'

'I don't want the bloody scone,' he said, and his voice sounded quite violent even to him. That was better: if he could get angry with her, he could cope.

'Sorry,' she said. 'Sorry, Nigel.'

'It's OK. Let's just get on, shall we, with deciding what we're going to do. How we're going to play it.'

'Play it?'

'You know what I mean, perfectly well.'

'Yes. Sorry.'

'The thing is,' he said, 'my solicitor says that we have to decide who's going to petition whom.'

'That means who's going to divorce who. Is that right?'

'Yes, that's right . . . I presume you've talked to someone about it.'

'No, I haven't actually. Except – well, except my – my family.' She meant Him: the person he couldn't bear to think about.

'Right. So – no one legal.'

'Well, no. I thought you should tell me what you want first, and then I'll just go along with it. I want to be helpful, Nigel, that's the very least I can do for you.'

'Indeed,' he said coldly. He kept looking away from her; it was so awful, she was leaning towards him, her huge eyes all earnest and sympathetic.

'I'm so sorry,' she said. 'So sorry. You do know that, don't you?'

'So you keep saying.'

'I know it's awful. Awful for you.'

'Oh, I don't know.'

'Well – good. Maybe not quite so awful then.'

'It's been totally fucking awful,' he choked out, 'more awful than you could possibly imagine. Why did you do it, Lucinda? How could you do it? Why didn't you stop, right at the beginning, before – before anything— Oh shit!'

The tears had begun: he could feel one running down his nose, and the shame of that was intense. He was sitting here, supposedly cool and in control, sorting out the details of their divorce, and he was blubbing like a baby. He fumbled in his pocket for his handkerchief, blew his nose, wiped his eyes.

'Sorry,' he said. 'So sorry.'

'Oh Nigel,' she said, and he looked up at her then, at the break in her own voice, and saw that she was crying too, tears spilling out of her eyes, trickling down her cheeks. 'Nigel, don't say you're sorry. I feel so ashamed, so dreadfully ashamed, making you so unhappy, oh dear, dear Nigel,' and she moved nearer to him, put her arms round him, and he clung to her, useless as he knew it was, feeling just for a moment the briefest sensation of happiness as he felt her warmth again, smelled her, loved her still, so, so much.

'I'm sorry,' he said again, pulling back quickly, wiping his eyes again. 'No, really, I'm fine. I – I wonder if you can get a drink here, this time of day.'

'Of course you can, of course, it's a hotel, for heaven's sake.' She waved at the waiter. 'Could we have – what do you want, Nigel? Whisky?'

279

'No, I'll have a brandy,' he said. 'Make it a double, would you? What about you?'

'No, I won't. I'm not – I don't want one, thank you,' and he thought she was going to say, 'I'm not allowed to,' and he wrenched his mind with such effort from the reason that he felt quite dizzy.

'I – just excuse me a moment, would you?' he said, and got up and walked rather unsteadily to the Gents.

Lucinda sat wondering if it was possible to hate yourself more than she did at that moment; she felt faint, ill with it, she even took a sip of his brandy when it came to steady herself. So extreme was her remorse that she thought she might, even then, have gone back to him, had it not been for the baby; made it work, managed somehow. But – she couldn't.

And when he came back he was looking calmer.

'Sorry about that. Look, we'd better get down to business.'

'I – Nigel, before we start talking about the divorce, what about the money? What about Lloyd's? It's been worrying me so much, now that it's back in your court, so to speak . . .'

'Me too,' he said, taking an enormous slug of the brandy. And you know, what I discovered, I really think my solicitor should have told me: had I gone bankrupt two years after I made over that money to you, and I would, you know – or I will – the transfer would have been null and void anyway. So it wasn't so clever.'

'Oh, that's terrible. God, they're awful, those people, aren't they? So awful. Did you ever go to any more of those meetings? Maybe they could suggest something else.'

'I didn't,' he said. 'In fact, I rather lost faith after discovering that. This lawsuit idea, it's just fairyland, isn't it. Who'd win against them?'

'True. What we ought to do is something really clever, trounce them once and for all. I mean, here's an idea. Suppose I claimed all the money, and then gave it back to you. How would that be?'

'Don't be silly,' he said, 'they'd work that out in a trice. Anyway, I don't want to be offensive, Lucinda,' and for the first time that day he managed a real smile, 'but I really don't think you would be able to. You are the guilty party, after all.'

'Yes, of course. I do know. Just joking. Well . . .' She was silent for a moment, thinking of Blue, of his words that morning, about lawyers convincing you black was white, getting a gallon of blood out of a stone. 'There might be something. Lawyers are very, very clever, you know. They can do all sorts of things the rest of us might never think of.'

'Mine isn't,' said Nigel gloomily. 'What about yours?'

'Like I said, I don't have one yet. I was going to use Daddy's, but maybe I can find a really clever person and see if there isn't a way round it all.'

'Lucinda, there can't be. I've made a frightful hash of it all, and now I've just got to pay up. If I end up bankrupt, which I very well could, I'll have to put up with it. Get a job in a shop or something. Go and live in a council flat.'

'You wouldn't lose the house, would you?'

'I could, apparently. They say they don't want you to sell your home, but if people haven't got anything else, and they've used their houses as security, it just has to happen. I could lose everything. Down to the last cufflink, that's what they say to you at Lloyd's when you become a Name. So – even Grandpa Cowper's gold and diamond ones would go.'

'No, they won't.' She stared at him, stricken afresh. Those cufflinks epitomised Nigel in a funny way: they were his heritage, the symbol of his family, his roots. She had put them on for him so many times before they went out; he loved them, was intensely proud of them. 'You are not losing those cufflinks, Nigel,' she said, suddenly fierce, 'nor the house, nor the farm. We'll work something out, I promise you. I have no idea how, but . . .'

She went straight home after their meeting; she was tired. Blue was waiting for her there, drinking whisky, white-faced.

'You all right?' he said. 'Feeling OK, no more throwing up, how was he, what did he say, he'd better not have been difficult—'

'Oh Blue, do shut up,' said Lucinda wearily, 'and – look, I was wrong this morning. I think I'd like to talk to a shit-hot lawyer. As soon as possible. Will you help me find one, please?'

281

Chapter 18

May, 1990

Richard had announced that he was going off on a teaching conference for three days. 'It sounds very interesting, and I think it's the sort of thing that would make my CV look a bit better. As you pointed out, it's not great in some ways. Of course I realise it's half-term and it will make things difficult for you, but I'm sure other working mothers manage. They can't all have teacher husbands.'

He had smiled at her but there was an edge to his voice. There was no way she was going to ask him not to go, Debbie thought, no way he could claim her job put obstacles in his path.

'Of course. No, it's fine. There's lots of people I can ask. I might even get one of our babysitters to do it.'

'I don't think I like that idea,' he said. 'They're a lot to look after, especially Rachel. I can't think some half-baked schoolgirl could possibly cope with them full-time, it's a bit different from an evening, Debbie.'

'Richard, I was thinking of one of the sixth-formers, they're not exactly half-baked. Anyway, don't worry about it.'

'I'll try not to,' he said, and turned to walk out of the room. She noticed that his shirt was very creased at the back, and wondered if all the teachers at school had noticed it too and gossiped about what a rotten wife he had. It wasn't ordinary creased, it was unironed creased: which was not too surprising because she never did iron the backs; it saved her a lot of time over a week of seventeen shirts, if you counted school ones as well. Which obviously she did.

But they were still happy; the extra day didn't seem to be causing any problems and she'd even found a cleaner. She wasn't much good, but it seemed to be the principle that counted. Maybe she could put her onto the ironing instead.

And to prove she was really grateful for his help and support, she had agreed to put their names down for an allotment, a long-time ambition of Richard's.

'If that's not love,' she said to Jan, 'I don't know what is. Honestly, it'll be more boring than sex. Well, most of the sex,' she added hastily.

'Well,' said Jan, 'I shall never pass the allotments again without thinking of you and Richard working at it. If you get my drift.'

'I do, yes thank you,' said Debbie, 'and you are never, ever to talk about it in front of him.'

'The allotment? Or the sex?'

'Oh, shut up. Luckily, there's a really long waiting list.'

'Bit like the sex then,' said Jan.

Flora offered to have the children for half-term. 'It must be so hard,' she said, 'managing while you're working, and of course with Richard doing this course . . .'

'Well – yes.' Was there anything he didn't tell his mother? God, it was annoying.

'And what about the summer holidays?' Flora went on. 'While we're on the subject. Even if you do go camping in France for some of the time—'

'I didn't know we were going camping in France,' said Debbie briskly.

'Oh darling, I'm sorry. Richard just said it was a possibility – perhaps he wants to surprise you . . . Oh, how stupid of me.'

'No, Flora, it's fine. We may well do that, I'm afraid I haven't given much thought to the summer. But yes, half-term would be wonderful. Thank you. One of us will bring them down.'

'Splendid. And hopefully stay a day or two. Tilly will be here too, and Emma adores her, doesn't she, so we shall have a full house. Which will be very nice for me. Goodbye, Debbie. Let me know when they'll be coming.'

Debbie put the phone down, and instead of feeling relieved and happy, she felt cross and miserable. Courses, summer holidays – what else did he talk to his mother about? Their finances? Their sex-life?

Nothing would surprise her.

'Goodness.' Lucinda had been looking for the address of a literary agent; a manuscript had come in, completely hopeless, like so many of them, and it had to be sent back with one of the charming and regretful notes that were her speciality. Other people sent printed cards; Lucinda, with her tender heart, felt that rejection of what represented at the very least a great deal of hard work, should be softened. Only she couldn't find the address. She couldn't find a lot of things these days; her brain seemed to be shrinking as her uterus grew. She forgot conversations, appointments (she had learned to check her diary at least three times a day), people's names even. But it didn't seem to matter; she had never been so happy. Every time she thought about caring for their baby, hers and Blue's – and Blue as well, of course – she felt as if she was looking at some wonderful, warm sunlit meadow.

The only darkness cast over the meadow was Nigel; Nigel and his dreadful, patent misery. And it was quite a big darkness, for it was her fault. Blue told her repeatedly – and quite kindly – that she was being ridiculous, that Nigel was an adult, he could look after himself, that his life by any standards was pretty bloody all right.

'Blue, how can you say such things,' she said reproachfully, the first time they had this conversation. 'Was that how you felt when we were apart, that life was pretty bloody all right? I don't think so.'

'Course I didn't,' he said, kissing her, 'but that was different, that was you and me.'

'Yes, and this is Nigel and me. Oh dear. What can we do to help him? What?'

Whereupon Blue had said he really couldn't quite see how he could be expected to want to help Nigel, or even that Nigel needed any help, but that he was fixing for her to see a solicitor mate of his: 'Not quite your idea of one, Lucy, went to the same shit-awful—'

'Blue, don't use that language, you've got to start thinking of the baby.'

'Sorry. Same bloody awful comp as I did, dragged hisself up from there, but my God, he's got a brain and a half. Three-quarters, actually. OK?'

'Yes, OK. But bloody isn't much better than shit.'

She was off to see him that afternoon, actually, which was probably why her brain was so feeble; she was very nervous.

She finally found the agent's address; not in the Roladex where it belonged, but tucked into a pile of reviews, waiting for filing. Along with Simon Beaumont's card.

'Goodness,' she said again now, talking to herself, for Graham was out at lunch, 'I promised to call him, completely forgot.' It had been important too, Simon had said; how stupid of her. She'd better make amends – do it at once.

He was very pleasant, of course, said it didn't matter in the least – 'But sweet of you to ring at all.'

'Yes, well, I think it's so awful not to do what you say. And I've not done about a hundred things today, I shall get fired if I'm not careful. I tell you what,' she said suddenly, looking at the row of books on her shelf, 'I can ship over a copy of that Soros book you were talking about, if you haven't got it yet. It's the least I can do, after forgetting to ring you.'

'Don't be silly, it's only been a few days and I told you it didn't matter. I wouldn't dream of accepting the book.'

'Well, you should dream of it. I've got at least a dozen here. Take it off your birthday list. When is it?'

'Next week, actually. May the twenty-seventh.'

'I'm coming into the City that very day to – well, to see someone – so I could drop it into your office. I'm looking at your card now, you're in Threadneedle Street, aren't you, and I'm meeting my friend in Cornhill.'

'That's astonishingly kind. You wouldn't like to have lunch with me, I suppose, instead? Really make my birthday?'

'No, sorry,' she said, and giggled. 'I don't think he'd find that very amusing. But I'll leave the book in Reception for you, shall I?'

'Absolutely not. I'll come down and get it. Or give you an after-lunch coffee, how about that?'

She hesitated, then said almost regretfully, 'No, I'll be dashing back to work. Sorry again.'

'Never mind. Bye, Lucinda.'

She sat smiling at the phone rather foolishly. He was rather dishy. Then she shook herself. Honestly, Lucinda, whatever would Blue say?

Debbie had agreed to take the children down to Wales on the Saturday; this had caused major ructions from Emma. 'But Mummy, there's a horse show on Saturday, Granny says, and she and Tilly are going – can't we go on Friday? Oh, please please, we'll be finished at school by three and—'

'No,' said Debbie, 'we can't. Not possibly. I'm working on Friday, and Daddy's off on his course . . .' It seemed a bit odd that, a course starting over a weekend, but she didn't press him on it, she knew it would be interpreted as awkwardness.

'So? We could get there late. Granny always likes that, and—'

'Emma, no.'

Emma jumped up, rushed out of the room, slammed the door. 'I hate you!' she shouted, from the top of the stairs.

Richard's eyes met Debbie's. 'She's starting early,' he said, and grinned. She grinned back. He seemed much happier suddenly. Maybe he'd just begun to accept that things had changed.

A compromise was finally reached; the cross-country event was being held at Margam Country Park, which was near Swansea. Debbie and the children would meet Flora and the Beaumonts there.

'It'll be so much fun,' said Emma, her eyes shining. 'There's a course with lots of jumps, and Tilly and Boy have a really good chance of doing well, Granny says. We can follow them round—'

'What, over the jumps?' said Alex. 'I can just see you doing that, Emma, making that stupid trotting noise—'

'Oh, shut up,' said Emma. 'You don't know anything, you're stupid. Tilly says—'

'You shut up yourself. I'm sick of Tilly anyway and horses.'

'Nobody could be sick of horses.'

'Well, I am.'

'Well, bad luck, because we're going to be riding all half-term, Granny says.'

'Well, bad luck to you because she says we're going to be doing lots of surfing.'

'Oh, be quiet,' said Debbie, 'otherwise we won't go at all.'

They continued to squabble; they knew an empty threat when they heard one.

'Well, this is fun.' Debbie stood in the sunshine, smiling at Flora, surprised to find she meant it. Very surprised. Here she was, surrounded by people in wellingtons with labradors and shooting sticks, yelling at one another in what seemed pretty well a foreign language, and yet she was really enjoying herself. 'Isn't it? When the weather's good, a day of horse trials is unbeatable. Even if you don't like horses, Debbie, which I know you don't.'

'It's not the horses I don't like, it's the—' and then she stopped, horrified at what she had nearly said.

'Horsey people,' Flora finished for her. 'Don't look so upset, nor do I – well, not some of them. Dreadful insensitive lot, they can be. But they can be fun, and there is one quality they nearly all share, which is courage. They're mostly very brave – Like the horses they ride. Which is a nice quality, I think,' she added. 'Right, come on, everybody, time to move on.'

She had seemed a little subdued when Debbie had first arrived; they both had, she and Simon – nerves, probably, for Tilly, but they were entirely caught up now with the drama of the day, and with Tilly's part in it.

They had spent about ten minutes at the jump; watched three horses take it, seen one rider come off, one horse stumble and then recover and one soar over it. Debbie was beginning to get the hang of the whole thing, or at least of being a spectator; you moved from one jump to the next, stood patiently at the back as the first horse approached, unable to see much, then shuffled forward for the second, pushing the children in front, and then got a front-row seat – or rather stand – for the third. A few people even carried small stepladders round, which they stood on. She would never have believed she would find it fun, or even remotely interesting, but here she was, clapping and shouting, 'Oohh!' and 'Ahh!' and 'Hurray!' in the prescribed manner.

'When will it be Tilly?' asked Emma. 'Please say she's soon, I can't wait much longer.'

'I think she's next but one,' said Flora, 'we'll hear her announced on the loudspeaker. I honestly don't think she'll do

287

very well,' she said under her voice to Debbie, 'not her fault, she and Boy just haven't had the time to practise, but she's very talented, she might come in moderately well. Ah, here's Simon, did you find her?'

'Yes. She's a mass of nerves, poor child. We shouldn't have let her do it, Flora, she was sick last night you know, and I—'

'Oh, nonsense,' said Flora. 'She'll have a marvellous day's riding, meet some of the other young people from round here, and at worst, it's a wonderful experience. I mean, just being here taking part is a privilege. Look at it, all of you.'

Debbie looked: at the graceful parkland of Margam, the ruined abbey below them, the blue sky above studded with seagulls, and all around them, the golden gorse of early summer on the endless rolling green of the hills. And at the horses, beautiful, gleaming, perfectly schooled, so brave as Flora had said as they took the sometimes impossible-seeming jumps, their riders so absolutely at one with them that they hardly appeared separate beings; she closed her eyes for a moment and listened instead, to the thudding of the hooves, the shrieking of the seagulls, dogs barking, people clapping and shouting, heard her children all laughing, and she felt briefly and absurdly happy and wished that Richard was there with her.

And then they heard, 'Number Seventeen, Miss Ottilie Beaumont, on Golden Boy,' and everything was blotted out and they stayed where they were, afraid that if they moved they might miss her. The jump was a horror, two almost at once, set in a zigzag. Flora whispered what a pity it was they were at this one and not one of the easier ones, for if Tilly came off there it would be far more dreadful for everybody than if it happened at some remote spot the other side of the course.

Debbie found herself suddenly nervous, digging her nails into her palms as they saw the bright blur that was Boy and Tilly a few hundred yards away, soaring over the first two jumps, heard the applause, watched them go out of sight for a while, and then reappear, clearing the water jump that preceded the zig-zag, saw them coming towards it now, stood totally silent, all of them equally terrified, as she drew near enough for them to see her face, white and absolutely set in its concentration, her eyes fixed on her own personal horizon, and then she was there, upon them, taking the jump; Debbie felt first one hand grabbed suddenly, by Emma, and then another, by Simon. Amused and touched, she glanced up at him; he was pale, his eyes fixed on his daughter as if he could take her over by sheer willpower. Tilly cleared the first fence, turned Boy neatly and dug her heels hard into his side; he seemed to hesitate for what felt like minutes and, 'Oh, no, no,' whispered Emma, and, 'Go on, go on,' groaned Simon, and then, then it was all right, and Boy seemed to take heart, jumped again, a little late it seemed to Debbie; he cleared it, but then clipped it with his hooves, stumbled slightly, and then recovered. Tilly pulled him up, and they were off again on their way, disappearing into a thicket.

'Water next. She'll be fine there,' said Flora. 'God, she did well. They both did. Oh, I'm so proud of her.'

'Me too,' said Simon, and he released Debbie's hand suddenly, as if he had only just realised he had been holding it. He grinned at her. 'Sorry,' he said, laughing, 'got a bit carried away.'

'I don't mind,' she said, laughing back at him. 'Goodness, that was wonderful. How do you think she's doing, Flora?'

'We won't know for a bit. She's not going very fast, so she'll lose on time—'

'Granny!' said Emma. 'She was going like the wind.'

'I know, darling, but some of the others were going faster than the wind. And she'll lose marks for clipping that fence. But she should get round now. This is definitely the worst jump and she was looking very comfortable . . .'

Comfortable was the last word Debbie would have chosen: how odd they were, these horsey people, she thought.

In the end, Tilly did pretty well, came in at seventh place, and they all went back to Broken Bay for a triumphant supper, Emma as flushed with triumph as if it was she who had ridden Boy to glory, not Tilly. Halfway through the meal the phone rang; it was Richard, to make sure they were all right and had arrived safely, and Emma spent about twenty minutes talking him round the entire cross-country course – 'and then it was the water jump and she cleared that easily and then she did

289

really well at the brush' – until, mindful of Richard's hotel phone bill, Debbie interrupted her and spoke to him briefly herself. He sounded very happy and almost excited. 'I might have a bit of good news by the time I get home,' he said, refusing to say more; Debbie had had quite a lot of Flora's wine and said she couldn't wait for him to get home and that she'd wished he'd been at the trials.

'Did you ever ride in anything like that?' she asked.

'Good Lord, no,' he said, 'no good at all,' and she asked Flora later if that had been true.

'Well, he wasn't much good, no. Bit of a wimp when it came to horses,' Flora said slightly dismissively; and, remembering her words about horsey people possessing courage, Debbie saw for the very first time that Richard was not entirely perfect in his mother's eyes, and felt oddly soothed by it.

After supper they started to play Scrabble, but Simon, who was rather drunk, started doing unsuitably rude words and Debbie took the opportunity to get the children off to bed. Tilly was dropping with exhaustion, and by the time Debbie came back to the kitchen, Flora had disappeared too.

'She said to say goodnight to you,' Simon said. 'She's very tired.'

'Oh, right. She doesn't often admit to that. Well, I might follow her myself.'

But: 'Debbie, don't go,' he said. 'Stay and chat to me. I'll find some more wine.'

'Well . . .' Suddenly it seemed a rather nice idea. 'Just for a bit.'

'Good. Thank you.' He disappeared down the cellar steps, came back grinning. 'Here we are. That was a fun day, wasn't it?'

'Great fun, yes.'

'It was lovely for Tilly. After all her heartbreak. And she did pretty well too.'

'She did. And she's so kind to Emma, I really do appreciate it.'

'As long as horses are involved, Tilly will do anything. She'd scrub out a stable quite willingly. Ask her to unload a dishwasher and you get a rather different reaction. Anyway, jolly little thing, your Emma. Good fun.' He topped up her glass.

'Don't give me too much, I don't want a hangover.'

'Well, I intend to have one. So we might as well share one. We can sit at Flora's breakfast-table in dark glasses with ice-packs on our heads.'

'I don't think she'd find that very amusing,' said Debbie.

'Oh, nonsense. She's a very broad-minded woman. You seem to be getting on better with her,' he added unexpectedly.

'Yes, I think I am.'

'Good. And how are things with you then?'

'Um – fine,' she said. 'Thank you.'

'Good. Hubby still being wonderful?'

'Yes,' she said, slightly defensively.

'So, where is he? I wasn't really listening.'

'Oh, he's on a course. And it's half-term, so Flora's having the children.'

'Isn't she wonderful?' He rubbed his hand across his eyes. 'Christ, I'm tired.' He poured himself another glass of wine, waved the bottle at her. 'More? Go on, Debbie, just a little one. Do you good. So – what sort of course?'

'Oh, a teaching one.'

'Has he got a new job yet?'

'No, no yet.'

'I'm sure he will soon,' he said easily, 'and what about your job? How's that going?'

'You don't want to hear about my job,' she said, and, 'Yes, I do,' he said. 'I want to know all about you, as a matter of fact. I find you very interesting, Debbie. Go on, tell me about your job.'

So she did, trying to make it sound entertaining, while at the same time not exaggerating what she did. He listened intently, asking the occasional, totally relevant question; she found it oddly refreshing. There wasn't anyone she could talk to about her job; not Richard, not Flora, not her parents, they all disapproved; nor most of her old friends, for apart from Jan, they were jealous and clearly felt she had set them and the life they had all shared aside, in order to pursue something more interesting.

'So – is PR your forte, do you think? Or do you feel you might like to do something different one day?'

'I think most of all I'd like to be a journalist,' she said. 'I love what I see of their jobs. Of course it's tough, and terribly hard work, but . . .'

'Well, you clearly don't mind that,' he said. 'No one who works and has small children ever stops. What do you think drives you, Debbie?'

'I'm not sure,' she said. 'I just think you ought to do everything you can while you can. Pack everything in, really tightly, you know? But it's hard on the children, I do realise that.'

'Oh, they're tough little things, children,' he said. 'They survive suprisingly well. Tyrants, children are, bit like husbands.'

'You don't mean that.'

'Of course I do.'

'I'm sure you're not a tyrant,' she said.

'Oh, but I am, in my own way. You'd be surprised.'

'Yes, I would. You told me you were very proud of Elizabeth last time we talked.'

'And so I am. For most of our lives, I've been bloody proud of her, and she wouldn't have been the person I loved otherwise. I could see that.'

Debbie was silent; wondering if Richard ever said he was proud of her. She somehow imagined not.

'But if Elizabeth could hear me talking now,' he said, his mood suddenly changing, 'uttering all these fine words, she'd kick me in the balls and with good reason. I've behaved very badly, Debbie, very badly indeed.'

'I'm sure you haven't.'

'I'm afraid I have. All my fine words sound pretty hollow, even to me. And look at what else I've done, landing my family in the most appalling financial mess . . .'

'Now that *is* nonsense,' she said. 'If you mean Lloyd's, as far as I can make out, no one could possibly have known what was going to happen. I went to that meeting, don't forget; I'm sure all of you were acting for the very best.'

'I'm afraid that's rather arguable.' He drained his glass again. 'Give me some more, there's a good girl.'

She filled his glass again, knowing that she really shouldn't, that he was getting very drunk, and at the same time not wanting the conversation to end. She felt hugely flattered that he was talking to her, baring his soul; and at the same time, along with the flattery, she was feeling something else, a sliver of sexual awareness. She would never have believed such a thing possible, not for him, who was everything she disapproved of. He was still that, of course, but the sliver was undoubtedly there and it was really quite pleasant. She'd forgotten quite how pleasant, actually.

He looked at her over the wine and tried to smile. 'I've done some pretty terrible things, you know, really pretty terrible. And Elizabeth is terribly angry with me and hurt and – oh God.'

He dashed his hand across his eyes; when he looked up at her again, she saw there were tears in them. 'I'm a Grade A shit, Debbie, that's what. A Grade A, five-star shit. I deserve everything that's coming to me.'

Debbie looked at him, and felt a wave of such sympathy she could hardly bear it. She put her hand out across the table, took his.

'Simon,' she said, 'Simon, you mustn't say that. It's simply not true. You do your absolute best for everyone, I'm sure you do.'

'No,' he said, shaking his head. He put his hand over one of hers, held it against him. 'No, Debbie, that's not true. I've failed her horribly, and I'm failing them all horribly and – oh God.' Tears were actually falling now, and his face was working; he looked not only wretched but desperate, unrecognisable as the confident, charming man she had thought she knew. 'What am I going to do, Debbie, what in the name of heaven am I going to do?'

Debbie reached out, stroked his cheek, wiped away some of the tears.

'It'll be all right,' she said, as if he was one of the children. 'It'll be fine, I'm sure.'

'No,' he said. 'No, it won't be all right, it can't be, it can't possibly be. You know what I heard only the other day? A chap I know, in this like the rest of us, nice chap, you know what he did, took an overdose, couldn't cope any more. He's actually all right, they managed to save him. I bet he wishes they hadn't. And you know, I was thinking, I can see why he did it . . .'

'Simon, don't. Please, please don't talk like that.'

'I can see it very clearly, he'd be safe now, away from it all, the shame and the misery, and you know that really is the only sure way ... I'm frightened, Debbie, do you know that? Absolutely shit terrified.'

She got up and went over to him; he turned on his chair and she drew his head towards her, onto her breast, stood there, stroking his hair and his arms went round her then, and she felt strange – strange and disorientated – as if she hardly knew who she was, or what she was doing.

And, 'Simon, dear Simon, don't ...' she said. And then, quite suddenly, the door opened and Flora came in.

Chapter 19

May to June, 1990

'Right, then, Lucinda.' Steve Durham smiled at her. 'You don't mind if I call you Lucinda, I hope?'

'No, of – of course not.'

'Good. And you call me Steve. So – let's have a little chat about this marriage of yours, Lucinda, shall we? And see what we're going to do about it.'

'Well, all right, yes.' She didn't like Steve Durham one bit. Blue had told her she wouldn't. 'But he's what you – *we* – need, Lucinda. I'm afraid he's not really your sort of person. Which is fine – you don't have to ask him to a dinner party or anything.'

Lucinda didn't say that she never asked anyone to dinner parties any more. It was one of the things she missed. There was nothing to stop her of course, Blue was very hospitable, was always suggesting she invited people round, anyone she liked; it was just that she couldn't imagine it working. Not with her old friends, anyway. And his friends – well, they weren't dinner-party people, not really. Go and get smashed, go to the races, go away for flashy weekends, yes, sit round a table chatting, probably not. Although she and Blue chatted endlessly, so perhaps she was being silly. After the baby, she'd get all that sort of thing organised . . .

'He comes highly recommended, and not just by the odd mate. Fantastic reputation across the profession – always wins. Which is what we want, isn't it?'

'Well – yes. Of course.'

She felt uneasy in Durham's rather flashy office, all black leather and chrome; and not in the gentlemanly precincts of

Lincoln's Inn either, but in a building just off Regent Street. Durham was flashy too and also dressed in black leather, or at least his upper half was; he wore a very fine black leather jacket over a bright blue shirt and white silk tie. Lucinda had the rather wild thought that her mother would not have had him in the house and then mentally shook herself. Nor would Mrs Worthington have had Blue in the house, were there any choice in the matter. As for their own family lawyer, 'sharp as the corner of a round table' as Blue had put it, he was certainly not going to be able to help her help Nigel.

'Now, I don't want you to be nervous about any of this,' Durham said.

'I don't feel in the least nervous,' said Lucinda rather stiffly.

'Good. So let's get down to business. Your husband's name is Nigel. Nigel Cowper. Quite a name that, spelled that way – does he come from some terribly ancient English family?'

'Well, quite ancient, yes. I think they go back several hundred years.'

'Very nice. I can only trace my family over a few hundred months. Then it gets very muddy. OK. So you were married – how long?'

'Four years.'

'I see. And – no children?'

'No,' she said quickly.

'Right. And you lived – where?'

'In our house, in Cadogan Square.'

'Very nice. And Nigel lives there still, does he?'

'Oh, yes.'

'And have you remained on good terms with Nigel?'

'Yes. Very,' she said firmly.

He sighed and shook his head.

A girl in a very short skirt, made inevitably of black leather, and an over-tight white shirt, came in with the coffee.

'Thank you, Shirley. Milk, Lucinda?'

'Oh, yes, please. And no sugar.'

'Fine. There we are.' Shirley poured her the coffee, passed it to her, gave a cup to Steve.

'Thanks,' he said. 'No calls now, please.'

'Right. Um, what shall I do if Mr Harcourt—'

'Shirley, I said no calls.' His voice was harder suddenly.

Lucinda didn't like that voice any more than the rest of him. It wasn't the Cockney accent, or whatever you were meant to call that now, Estuary English – Blue's accent indeed, she loved that – it was the harsh, slightly nasal tone to it. She felt it could become bullying very easily.

'And would you say the marriage was happy? Until you met Mr Horton, of course.'

'Yes. Very happy.'

'And . . . Mr Cowper treated you well?'

'Terribly well. He was very – very kind and generous.'

'So until you did meet Mr Horton, you had no complaints?'

'No. I still don't. None at all.'

'Right. Now Lucinda, forgive me, but I'm not sure we have much of a case here. Or that you need someone like me.'

'Why is that?' she said.

'Well, there you were, happily married to a kind and generous man, against whom you had no complaints. You aren't going to find many judges to take your side.' She was silent. 'I mean, it looks quite bad – on your part. You run away and leave him, for no reason whatsoever, set up home with Mr Horton, and now you're pregnant with Mr Horton's baby. I'm afraid that makes you very much the guilty party.'

'Yes, I suppose it does.'

'A short marriage, with no children – that doesn't earn you a huge amount of assets that weren't yours in the first place. Mr Cowper is pretty well off, I gather?'

'Well, yes. But that's—'

He interrupted her. 'Is that mostly in liquid assets?'

'I'm not sure what you mean.'

'Well, is it cash sitting in the bank, or in stocks and shares, or tied up in property, or what?'

'Oh, I see. Well, he does have some stocks and shares, and quite a lot of cash. At least, he did. But most of his real wealth is in land. He's got about two thousand acres in Norfolk, for instance.'

'And property?'

'Well, there's a farmhouse there, and some cottages. It's a working farm, you see.'

'Ye-es. And in London?'

'There's the house in Cadogan Square.'

'Right.'

'Oh, and then I suppose you could count the income from the family business. It's a manufacturing company, still privately owned. It's quite small, but Nigel's the Chairman and he owns the majority share. But Mr Durham—'

'Steve, please.'

'Steve. There's something I want to explain—'

'We'll come to that in a minute. I'd rather get the facts sorted first. Were any of these things acquired after he met you?'

'Oh, goodness no.'

'So, he'd built up or inherited everything prior to your marriage? There's nothing you've contributed to, financially?'

'Well, no.'

He was silent, then he said, 'Of course. Now – there was no baby for you and Nigel?'

'No.'

'Was that – forgive me for asking this, Lucinda – was that agreed between you?'

'Oh, yes.' She wasn't going to get into discussing that; not with him.

'So you did want to have a baby together?'

'Well, we did one day, yes. But – there was plenty of time, we felt.'

'And yet you and Mr Horton are having a baby pretty soon after you began cohabiting.'

'Well, yes.'

'So you must have been pretty keen on the idea?'

'Oh, I was. Yes.'

'So – it was Nigel who didn't want children?'

'I didn't say that.'

'OK, we'll leave that for now. Now I understand there has been a trust fund set up for you.'

'Yes, that's right.'

'In a very generous settlement, by Mr Cowper.'

'Yes.'

'Which of course will now probably be redistributed at the discretion of the courts.'

'Yes, I suppose so.'

'Look,' he said, 'I don't often say this, but I'm not sure there's a lot I can do for you.'

'What do you mean?'

'Well, to be honest, you have a pretty weak case. This is a short marriage, you made little or no contribution to it, and you're now living with another wealthy man and having his child.'

'I know, I know. But – but can I explain now?'

'Yeah, OK. Go ahead.'

He sat back, looking at her with what she could only describe as disdain. Lucinda suddenly felt rather cross, was even tempted to leave his office. But the thought of Grandfather Cowper's cufflinks kept her going.

'There's something I don't think you realise,' she said. 'I thought Blue had told you.'

'He didn't tell me anything,' said Steve Durham. 'Mind if I smoke?'

'Yes,' said Lucinda firmly, 'I'm sorry, but I do. Now please, let me finish. Nigel's about to lose almost everything he's got to Lloyd's.'

'Oh yes? Well, that settles it. He certainly won't have anything over for you in that case.'

'I know,' said Lucinda. 'That's the whole point.'

'Sorry? I don't get it.'

'Mr – Steve, if you'd just listen to me for a bit, you will get it. I have had an idea, and I think it's quite a good one. But I'm really going to need all your – your experience – to even remotely bring it off. Can I go on?'

'Go ahead.' He was looking slightly more interested.

'Well, you see . . .'

It didn't take long; and when she had finished, he stood up and walked over to the window looking down at Regent Street. Then he turned round and grinned at her.

'It's going to be tough,' he said, 'but I like it. I like a challenge. I reckon we can do it somehow. Somehow or other.' He turned back to Regent Street for a moment or two and then said, 'I must admit, Lucinda, you're a lot cleverer than I thought you were. Very impressed I am. Very impressed.'

'Oh, good,' she said. 'I'm so pleased.'

*

She thought – and please, please God, let it not be wishful thinking – they had got away with it. That Flora actually hadn't seen them, not *in flagrante* as it were. Not that it was *in flagrante*, of course, but who could have blamed Flora for thinking it was, rather than an innocent – well, nearly innocent – comforting embrace.

Simon had reacted with incredible speed, pulling away from her, reaching for the wine bottle and making a great thing of pouring yet more; and she had gone equally fast over to the sink and made a great thing of washing glasses.

'You've caught us at it, Flora, I'm afraid,' Simon had said, and she had turned then in horror, but he was grinning up at Flora ruefully – and Debbie had never known quite what rueful was until that moment – 'getting drunk together. I've been boring the pants off poor Debbie, and she's been really gallant, letting me run on and on.'

'I see,' said Flora briskly, and Debbie felt her stomach heave with fear; but then, 'Well, I just wanted a cup of tea. Can I interest either of you in something so wholesome?'

'Absolutely,' Simon said, 'do us both good. Here, Debbie, could you rinse these cups out as well?'

And keeping her back still carefully turned to Flora, she said, praying her voice would sound normal, 'Yes, course,' and then when it did sound fairly all right, risked going on. 'Sorry, Flora, did we wake you up?'

'No, no, I couldn't sleep. Often happens these days.'

'It's a symptom of our common disease,' Simon said to Debbie, smiling. 'Lloydsitis, very nasty. Others include nausea, headaches, nightmares. Oh, and loss of appetite.'

How did he do that, she wondered. How could he switch from wretched to light-hearted at the click of a switch – or rather the turn of a door-handle? It was a great gift.

'You've missed out tremor of the hand,' said Flora, and this time she smiled at them both and then turned her attention to the teapot and Debbie dried the mugs suffering, she noticed, from considerable tremor of the hands, and then Flora poured out the tea and they all went off to bed.

Where Debbie lay awake for hours, staring into the darkness, suffering from intermittent tremor just about all over, wondering what on earth Flora might have thought: and

300

indeed what she might do, had she thought it. Like tell Richard. Richard with his incredibly strict, old-fashioned morals, who got jealous if she danced with other people at parties. What would he say? How would he react?

Would she? Could she?

Well, she could, and she would.

It was truly hideous: here she was, Flora's daughter-in-law, married to her only son, and apparently behaving like a trollop in her house. But then, Debbie thought, the waves of panic receding, Flora had seemed fine, not really suspicious; although obviously a bit surprised. And anyway, what exactly would she want to tell Richard? Well, and here the waves began to rise again, well, that Simon had had his arms round Debbie and she had been bending over him, clearly about to kiss him; and Flora didn't like her, never had, and would be delighted to blacken her in Richard's eyes . . .

At six, having slept about two hours, woken by the sound of horse's hooves, she went downstairs and sat at the kitchen table, the same kitchen table, trying to work out exactly what Flora could have seen, and then when that failed, she went out into the garden, bathed in mist; and saw Simon sitting on a low wall.

'Hi,' he said. 'You all right?'

'Not really,' she said, 'bit – you know – worried.'

'About last night? No need. She's fine. I was just chatting to her – she's gone out riding. I kind of dug a bit and she couldn't have been easier or more relaxed. I'm sure she doesn't suspect a thing. Not that there was a thing to suspect.'

'Simon, there was. And I'm married to her son. Don't be ridiculous, please.'

'Darling—'

'And don't call me darling. I don't like it.'

'Sorry. But you really are worrying about nothing. Promise. You'll see.'

And indeed when Flora got back she seemed very happy and they all had breakfast in the kitchen and Flora proposed a picnic and was actually very warm towards Debbie. So, perhaps Simon was right. But she continued to worry, just a little, on and on; and also to remember the sliver of attraction

301

and wonder what exactly might have happened, had Flora not come down.

Lucinda swallowed hard. It was important to keep calm. Important and difficult. With Blue looking so cross.

'I just don't understand,' he said, 'why you won't talk about it. It's ridiculous!'

'Because – well, because I need to think about it.'

'Think about what? Whether you're going to go ahead with it? Because I'm telling you, Lucinda, any doubts at all and I'm out of here. I've been very patient for a long time, listening to you fretting over that over-aged schoolboy of a husband of yours, saying how sorry you are for him, how worried about it all, and I've had enough. You get rid of him, and fast; I want to get married, before the boy's born—'

'Blue, that really won't be possible.'

He stared at her. 'Why not?'

'Because divorce can't just be done in – in five months.'

'That's bollocks,' he said, 'complete bollocks. I know that for a fact. It's uncontested, for God's sake. You're supplying the grounds, no one's arguing about it, it could be done in no time, no time at all.'

'That's not what Steve Durham said.'

'In which case, we won't be using him. We'll find someone else. He's going to cost me enough, I'm not listening to that sort of crap.'

'Blue, please. Look, we have to be very – careful about all this.'

'Careful? What have we to be careful about, for God's sake? It's an open and shut case: you left Nigel, you're up the duff by me—'

'Blue, please don't use those horrible expressions.'

'I'll use what expressions I like,' he said. 'What's the matter with you, Lucinda? This bloke seems to have affected you very badly.'

'He didn't. He just made me – think. That's all.'

'Think about what? Us? Because I'll have his balls off if that's the case.'

'Blue, stop it! You just don't understand. I—'

'You're too right I don't,' he said. 'I'm going out. And when

302

I get back, I'd like a bit more of an explanation, all right? So you'd better be ready with it.'

He stood up, picked up the keys he had thrown on the table when he first came in and stalked out of the door, slamming it hard. She looked after him, near to tears, wondering if she was in fact brave enough to go through with what would, at best, be terribly, terribly difficult. And then she thought of Nigel, dear, dear Nigel, living in a council house and forced to sell his diamond cufflinks, and she knew she had to be.

'. . . And this is Flora Fielding. Flora, Colin Peterson. Flora has one of the most beautiful houses on Gower, Colin. You'd give your eye teeth for it, I'm sure.'

'Oh really? Are you looking for a house on Gower?' said Flora, as politely as she could. She didn't feel very polite. She felt irritable and wondered for the hundredth time why she hadn't simply said no when Philippa Webber had invited her to this wretched dinner party. She would have much preferred to be at home, where a very self-important Tilly was acting as babysitter, with Mrs Connor in the cottage 500 yards down the lane on call and Mr Connor popping in regularly throughout the evening.

But Philippa invited her to dinner at least once a month, determinedly kindly, and Flora kept saying no; most people would have got the message that she didn't actually ever want to dine at Sea View – Sea View, for God's sake, how could anybody still be calling their house Sea View? – but Philippa was message-deaf.

It was impossible not to like the Webbers; they had moved to the area ten years earlier, and William in particular had tried and failed to dislike them, and the Fieldings had entertained them occasionally and Flora became deeply ashamed of herself after William died and they phoned, once or twice a week, to ask if she'd like to go for a walk with them, or if they could do any shopping when they went into Swansea; they brought her flowers, and in the early days, Philippa had delivered her some soup from time to time, or a quiche that she had made, saying, 'I know how easy it is not to bother,' and just very quietly and sweetly kept an eye on her.

And so it was that, from time to time, Flora gritted her teeth and drove along the South Gower Road with dread in her heart for an evening of admittedly very good food (Philippa was an excellent, if rather over-fussy cook) and to meet the Webbers' friends who were rather alien to her, living as they did in large modern houses in Swansea, or even Cardiff, and who drove flashy cars and went on holiday to places like Gran Canaria and Florida. Her daughter-in-law's view that Flora was an appalling snob was absolutely correct.

It transpired that Colin Peterson, a widower, Philippa rather archly announced as she guided them into the dining room, was not looking for a house on Gower, or not personally at any rate; he was a property developer and responsible for several of the flashier developments on the outskirts of Swansea. Since property developers would have been prominent among those compulsorily ejected from this world by Flora and into the bowels of hell, she was fairly appalled to find herself placed next to him; he had other vices too, in her book, he wore a Ralph Lauren shirt, complete with polo emblem, a matching Christian Dior tie and silk handkerchief, and nails that looked to her suspiciously manicured.

On the other hand, he was, she swiftly discovered, rather good company. And disarming. He told her he would no more touch Gower with a single new brick than throw himself off the Worm's Head, and that although he made his crust putting up modern houses, he was in fact a member of various Victorian societies and spent a lot of time getting up petitions to save terraces and other antique structures. His passion in life was actually sacred music. Flora was suspicious of this claim, until a few discreet remarks about Bach and William Byrd revealed him to be telling the truth, and she left the Webbers' dinner party a great deal later than she had planned, feeling warmed and almost happy. Not least by Colin Peterson's suggestion that they might perhaps attend a forthcoming concert in Cardiff Catherdral.

And after all, wearing clothes covered with those dreadful Trade-marks – or logos as you were supposed to call them, Tilly had told her – wasn't exactly a capital crime. She had managed to overlook Simon's, after all.

Annabel really, really couldn't believe it. Half of her at least – more than half probably – had expected never to hear from him again. It had only been just over a week, after all, and OK, he had said he loved her, but that often happened with holiday romances, which is what it was in a way, and America was a long, long way away, and he had a whole life there, and he was young and gorgeous and . . . and . . .

'And he's asked me to go over and stay with them,' she said.

'Who, darling?'

'Dad! You haven't been listening.'

'Sorry. I was, with one ear.'

'Not even half, I'd say. This is important, Daddy. This is my life you're not paying attention to.'

'Darling, I said I was sorry. I've got a lot on my mind.'

'Yes, OK. So have I. Jamie, you know that gorgeous American boy, I told you about him.'

'Oh, yes. And you really like him?'

'I really like him, Dad. And he's asked me to go over to Boston and stay with him and his family. For a few days.'

'Well, that sounds great. I'm delighted for you.'

'He must be quite keen, don't you think? To suggest that?'

'Very keen. And – do you think you'll go?'

'Well, of course I'll go. Don't be silly.'

'Didn't you meet his parents?'

'Yes, I did.'

'And?'

'And they were great. Well, his dad was great. His mother was a bit terrifying. Jamie seemed to find her quite terrifying too.'

'My darling, never have anything to do with a man who's frightened of his mother. Not a good scene.'

'You're joking, aren't you?'

'Only partly. Anyway, when does he want you to go?'

'Some time in July. God, I hope I can get the time off. Oh, it's so exciting, Daddy, isn't it? I must ring him right now – or would it be better to write, do you think? Cooler?'

'Definitely cooler. He wrote to you, after all.'

'Yes, I know, but— yes, you're right. I'll write today, when I've asked for the time off. They'd better give it to me. I work my tail off for that bloody place, haven't had a single day's holiday so far. Oh, wow, I really can't believe it! It is just so wonderful – wait till I tell Carol . . .'

Carol was very impressed. 'He must really like you. And he is so gorgeous.'

'Totally, totally gorgeous,' said Annabel.

'And rich,' said Carol. 'Blimey. Some people have all the luck. You'll have to get some new clothes.'

'Yeah, I thought of that. And – will you put some more highlights in my hair?'

'Course. We could even cut it, like you've been talking about for the past six months, year or whatever.'

'No, I don't want it cut,' said Annabel, 'he likes it long. He likes skinny girls with small tits and long hair, he told me so.'

'Lucky, that,' said Carol, 'about the tits, I mean. Most men like a good handful; he must be very unusual.'

'Don't be crude,' said Annabel.

'OK, OK. So, what's he like at the business then?'

'Carol!' said Annabel. She felt herself blushing.

'Oh, come on. Or isn't there a lot to tell?'

'I – don't want to talk about it,' said Annabel.

'Oh yeah? I know what that means. Either he wasn't any great shakes, or you haven't done it yet. Which?'

'I said I didn't want to talk about it. Carol, please. Haven't you heard of respecting people's privacy?'

'I've heard of it,' said Carol cheerfully, 'but I don't really believe in it. I think,' she said, looking at Annabel rather intently, 'you haven't done it. Have you? Come on, you can tell your Auntie Carol.'

Annabel was silent.

'Blimey,' said Carol, 'I hope he's not a virgin. Oh look, there's Marcia now, go and ask her for the time off. She should give it to you all right, long as you make it late July. It's really quiet here then.'

Joel Strickland was just filing a rather mediocre story on negative equity – the new buzz word in the property business – and wondering if he could cut and run after lunch (well, it was Friday, and the City would be dead) when his phone rang. It was Simon Beaumont.

'Look,' he said, 'if you're still interested in talking to me, I could spare you half an hour next week. I don't know how much use it would be, I imagine my story's pretty much like everyone else's, but you're welcome to it.'

Joel said he would be very interested in talking to him and that he'd be very grateful.

'Right then. Suppose we say Thursday, around seven? Royal Garden Hotel suit you?'

'That's great,' said Joel. 'I'll be there. Thank you. Er . . . anything in particular change your mind?'

'Yes, as a matter of fact. Friend of mine, another victim, tried to kill himself recently. I think this is a story that needs to be told.'

'Well, I agree with you,' said Joel, 'and thanks very much.'

Simon was actually still only half-convinced this was a good idea. He had an inbuilt suspicion of journalists. And Neil Lawrence's story, while shocking, wasn't his to tell. It wouldn't help his family, dragging the whole thing onto the front pages. But then he wasn't going to name any names. It was *his* story he was telling, not Lawrence's; that had simply been the catalyst. And this man was a City editor, for God's sake, not a tabloid reporter. He'd have a basic understanding of the whole bloody thing; was rather more likely than most to tell it how it was. And it did need telling.

He sat staring at the phone, feeling nervous and almost excited, as if he had done something rather momentous, without being sure why. He was easing up the lid of Pandora's Box, and God knew what demons would be released. Well, someone had to do it.

'Freddie, where's your lunchbox?' said Catherine.

'Um, don't know. Must have left it at school.'

Freddie's normally pale face had become slightly rosy and his big brown eyes were firmly fixed on the cereal packet he was reading.

'Darling, you are hopeless. That's two this term already. You must be more careful, Freddie, lunchboxes cost a lot of money.'

'Sorry.'

'And now what am I going to put your lunch in?'

'He can have mine,' said Caroline helpfully.

'What? That pink thing – My Little Ponies all over it?' said Freddie. 'No thanks. I'll just take a plastic bag, Mummy, it'll be fine.'

'Well, it's not really allowed. But we don't have much option, do we? Now I must go. See you this afternoon. Have good days. Love you.'

'Love you,' they said in unison. She left them, worrying as she always did, praying silently that they'd be all right, and hurried down the street towards the tube station. It wasn't ideal, but it did mean Freddie was happier. So much happier. And doing well. So it really was worth it. And there probably wasn't anything to worry about really.

'Right,' said Freddie, ten minutes later after they had cleared away their breakfast things, and picked up their school bags. 'Let's go. Get it over with.'

'Freddie,' said Caroline.

'What?'

'Don't you think we ought to tell Mummy?'

'No. Why do you have to ask me that, every day? We can't tell her, she's got enough to worry about. I'll be all right.' He looked at the clock. 'If we leave now, we can go the long way round. Come on.'

Caroline looked at him rather sorrowfully. 'You really are ever so brave,' she said.

Debbie could never remember being so frightened. Or so shocked. She sat staring at Richard, as if willing the words back into his mouth, safely unsaid; she wondered if she looked as distressed as she felt, how obedient her facial muscles actually were.

'So, that's what she said.' Richard was beaming.

'Yes. Yes, I see.'

'And what do you have to say about it?'

'Well, I . . . well, obviously it's amazing. Absolutely amazing. Yes.'

'Isn't it? And if I hadn't gone on that course, I'd never have found out about it. To think I nearly didn't go. Of course, it's not settled yet . . .'

'Oh, it's not?' Don't sound too hopeful, Debbie, just don't.

'No. There has to be an interview, but it's purely a matter of form, Miss Dunbar – Morag – assured me. She had to get the approval of the Board of Governors, and so on. But she'd want me there in Scotland for the autumn term, and she's already advertised it, I can't think how I missed it, and actually done some interviews, so she can tell the Governors that she's not just giving it to the first person who's come along.'

'No. No, I see. But – it's only deputy head? Isn't that a bit of a backward step?'

'Oh Debbie, no, not in this case. It's a very famous school – I'd certainly have applied if I'd seen the job advertised. And Morag Dunbar has told me, confidentially, that she's up for the top job at the senior school, and – well, she didn't exactly promise anything, but she made it pretty clear that I'd be head designate.'

'Oh, right. Well, that is fantastic, Richard. Congratulations. I'm so proud of you.'

'Thanks.' He looked suddenly ten years younger, his eyes shining. 'I'm pretty proud of me too. And of course, it being a boarding school, we'll be incredibly involved with the boys. We get a house in the grounds—'

'A house in the grounds?'

'One of the best. Not ours, of course, it goes with the job, but a very pretty one, and quite big. I can show you a photograph.'

'You mean we won't have our own house?'

'Well, no. Of course we can buy one anyway, either up there or nearby, as an investment, or we can keep this one and let it, but they'd want me on the spot. It's very much part of the job. And you'd be very much part of the team, of course. It's something we can do together, Debbie – you know how much I've always wanted that.'

'Me!'

'Well, yes. Deputy headmaster's wife – pretty important, you know. Not just helping me with running the school, but right in there with the boys and their lives. Don't look so scared, darling, you'd be brilliant.'

Don't mention your job, Debbie, just don't. Don't even think about it. It's important not to panic. It could all come to nothing; this is just conference chit chat. Keep calm.

'And what about the children?' she asked. 'They'd have to move schools, would they?'

'Well, obviously, yes. But Alex can go there, of course, to

Saint Andrews. It'd be the most marvellous opportunity for him, it's such a brilliant place. And the girls – well, there's a very good girls' prep very nearby, apparently. Almost a sister school. The girls can both go there.'

The outrage was beginning to surface.

'You seem to have made an awful lot of decisions without me,' she said. 'I might not think it was right for them.'

Just for a moment he looked taken aback: very slightly.

'Well, of course you must go and see it,' he said. 'Obviously, you've got to be happy about it. All of it. But you will be, I know. Morag Dunbar has invited us all up to stay for the weekend in a couple of weeks' time. I know you'll like her, Debbie, she's very – very warm. She's so looking forward to meeting you. She does see you as a very important part of the package, of course. I can see you're a bit worried about it. But I know you'll be marvellous, take to it all like a duck to water. Come here, darling, and give me a hug. I know I'm always saying this, but I mean it: I could never have done this without you, your support.'

She resisted the hug; she had to keep her distance on this, she had to.

'You know, Richard, I'm really not sure about it,' she said. 'I mean, I've never done anything like that in my life.'

'Darling Debbie, you'll be wonderful. Children always love you. And you're so organised—'

'Richard, I am not organised.'

'Yes, you are. Look how well you've managed with your job and everything.'

'I know, but—'

'Of course, that would have to come to an end, but – well, this is so much better for everyone, isn't it?'

She couldn't help it then. It came out, in spite of herself, in spite of willing it back so hard it hurt physically, escaped, out of her head, out of her outraged heart, made its way into words and thence into the hitherto sweet evening air.

'Everyone but me,' she said.

It was a very big mistake.

Flora hadn't intended to come to London; she liked it less and less. But she had a few remaining stocks and shares she had been hanging onto and felt that a personal conversation with her stockbroker was essential; and there was a very good lunchtime concert at St Martin in the Fields that day which she could go to first. Flora, like Debbie, preferred her days crammed full. And then she found another concert at the Wigmore Hall in the evening, and decided to go to that too, and to stay with Richard and Debbie instead of going back to Wales as she had planned. And then, Simon just mentioned casually on the phone, while thanking her for having Tilly, that Friday was his birthday and she felt that she could cram in a visit there as well. She changed the appointment with the stockbroker to half an hour later – do him good to work late – and arrived at Graburn & French just after three, with a copy of the new P.D. James book. He'd never read P.D. James; Flora had told him quite severely he should.

'She combines superb plots with superb writing. Quite rare, in my opinion.'

She was sitting in the marble-floored atrium of Graburn & French, waiting for his secretary to come down and collect her, as the gentleman at the desk had instructed her to do, when a dazzlingly pretty girl walked up to the reception desk, holding a package. She looked vaguely familiar to Flora; but she couldn't think why. 'Hello,' she said, 'I've got something here for Mr Beaumont. Mr Simon Beaumont.'

'Fine. If you'd like to just leave it with me, I'll see he gets it.'

'Well, that'd be terribly kind, but he did say to tell you he wanted to come down and get it himself.'

'Oh, all right. I'll give him a call. What name is it?'

'Cowper, Lucinda Cowper. Thank you.' She looked round the hall, saw Flora and smiled at her. 'Hello! We've met, haven't we? At that Lloyd's meeting, wasn't it? I remember your lovely blue jacket.'

'Oh, of course!' said Flora, standing up, holding out her hand. 'Flora Fielding.'

'He'll be right down,' said the man. 'Popular today, Mr Beaumont – two beautiful ladies waiting to see him.'

'Oh really?' Lucinda smiled at Flora again. 'You too? Well, lucky him.'

The lift doors opened, and Catherine Morgan emerged; she came across to Flora.

311

'Mrs Fielding? He says he's on his way down, and— Oh, hello,' she said to Lucinda. 'How lovely to see you.'

'Lovely to see you too,' said Lucinda. 'Catherine, isn't it? How are you? And you're working for Simon, how nice.'

'Yes, but I'm only in the outer circle, so to speak,' said Catherine. 'He's been terribly kind, gave me a job here.'

'Not just kind, I'm sure,' said Lucinda. 'And how are your children?'

'Fine. Yes. How clever of you to remember.'

'Well, I do remember some things,' said Lucinda. 'The others seem to drop through the rather wide mesh that my brain's turned into.' She patted the small but unmistakable bump of her stomach. 'This is what I blame. Anyway, I've come to see Simon too. I've brought him a book for his birthday. I work for a publisher,' she added, rather inconsequentially.

'I too,' said Flora, 'have brought him a book. Not the same one, I trust. Mine is— Oh Simon, hello. Happy Birthday.'

'And from me,' said Lucinda.

'Lucinda! How lovely to see you. How lovely to see both of you. I'm having a wonderful day. And Catherine's children have made me cards. I am very spoiled.'

'I so believe in spoiling,' said Lucinda. 'Well, on birthdays anyway.'

'I'm glad you do. Well well well, what a pulchritudinous gathering. A birthday party, you might almost say. Why don't you all come up to my office?'

'No, I must fly,' said Lucinda, 'I'm so late already. But I hope you like the book.'

'I'm sure I will. Flora, some tea? Come on, just a quick one. Bye, Lucinda, thank you again.'

And he ushered Flora into the lift, followed by Catherine.

'Such a sweetie,' said Lucinda absently, to nobody in particular.

Chapter 20

June, 1990

Debbie had thought things couldn't get any worse. Not since she had made what she had mentally labelled The Killer Remark. But they *had* just got worse. And in front of Richard's mother.

Richard had hardly spoken to her, apart from essential conversations about arrangements, since ... She could still hear herself saying it, still found it hard to believe she had been so stupid. And so cruel. He was obviously incredibly hurt, and rightly so; she knew it had been horrible of her. It had just – just come out. He had told her that all the pleasure and excitement of the job had been destroyed for him.

'I don't even want to go now,' he said, glaring at her, white-faced, across the room that evening. 'Can't see the point.'

'Richard, of course there's a point. Don't be silly, I didn't mean—'

'What you meant was it would be crucifixion for you. Well, I'm not going to be the one to hammer the nails in, Debbie, and be blamed for it for the rest of our lives. I suppose I could go on my own, that's an option.'

'Of course it's not. And of course I'll come. I was just – just a bit taken aback, that's all. Surely you can see—'

'What I can see, Debbie, is that *your* life, *your* job, come first and mine an inconvenient second. Well, that's not what I call a marriage.'

Debbie said, rather boldly, since things surely couldn't be any worse, that a marriage was something where the two people involved tried to compromise and move along together.

'I totally agree. And for the last few months, there's been precious little of that. It's been all about you, your job, your

313

childcare arrangements, your future. Mine didn't seem to be getting much of a look-in. Well, isn't that true?'

'Richard—'

'Certainly not from where I'm sitting. I'm here, providing a very useful resource for you, and the fact that I'm doing a crappy soul-destroying job that doesn't even supply me with adequate funds to do what I want for my family is neither here nor there to you. Well, you'd better do some very hard thinking, Debbie, because something's got to give.'

She had tried, desperately, to apologise, to explain, to try to show him that it had been simply a shock, that she would get used to the idea, that she was very, very proud of him; but she might as well have talked to the spare-room door that he finally slammed in her face when he went up to bed. There was no chance of any allotment therapy, as she had come to think of it, that night. Or the next or the next.

He had gone down to Wales alone to get the children; he had said it would be nice to spend some time with them on his own. She had mooched about the house, hoping that when he returned, he might feel better. He didn't.

And now Flora was here.

Only for the night; she had said she must move off early the next day, that she had to see to the horses. She had come in quite late, full of talk about the concerts and some impromptu birthday party Simon Beaumont had held in his office.

And then it happened.

They were having breakfast; Debbie had dutifully cooked mushrooms and scrambled eggs because that was what Flora liked best; the children had said how lovely to have a yummy breakfast, usually they just had rotten muesli, which didn't do much for her motherhood-cred; she had thought Richard might be pleased too, but he chomped gloomily through his meal, not speaking unless he had to.

And then Flora said, 'Now, Richard, what was this exciting news you told us about, when you phoned from Scotland.'

'Oh, it was nothing.'

'Really?'

'It was,' Debbie said. 'Richard's been offered a new job, up in Scotland, as Deputy Head of a really good prep school.'

'Really?' Flora said. 'How exciting! Why on earth didn't you tell me?'

There was a brief silence, then, 'Because I'm not going to take it,' Richard said, standing up, gulping down what was left of his orange juice.

'Not going to take it? Why ever not?' Flora said, and he replied, with a look at Debbie of such intense dislike that she winced, 'because Debbie and I have discussed it, and we don't feel it would be in the family's best interests.'

'What?' said Flora. 'But—' and then stopped, because Debbie's eyes filled with tears and she stood up, her chair scraping on the floor and said, 'Excuse me, please,' and rushed out of the room. Flora looked at Richard rather hard and then said, 'Well, that sounds like a pity. But I'm sure you know best. Now I must go. Richard, would you drive me to the station, please?'

And Debbie had come down and kissed Flora goodbye and tried to pretend everything was all right and that she wasn't crying at all, and waved them off, and eventually Richard came back and said he was going into school as he had a lot to do and needed some peace and quiet. And came home that afternoon clearly still hating her. And so it had gone on.

Later, she had tried again.

'Can we please, please talk about this? Properly, without all the emotional garbage. I really can't say I'm sorry again—'

'You don't have to. In any case, I don't want you saying things that aren't true.'

'It is true, for fuck's sake!' She was shouting now, desperate with frustration and anger.

'Don't swear.'

'I'll swear if I want to. Look, Richard—'

'Debbie, you said you didn't want to go to Scotland, and as far as I'm concerned, that is that. Unfortunately.'

'I didn't say that, it's so unfair. I simply said it wasn't ideal for me. I regret that very bitterly, I shouldn't have said it. But I've said I'll go, said I'll give up my job. What more do you want – blood?'

'I want a wife who's behind me,' he said, 'properly, not grudgingly.'

'I am *not* grudging. Oh, this is hopeless. What have you

315

done about the job anyway? I really think I have a right to know.'

'I've turned it down,' he said. 'I've told Miss Dunbar that we can't come, that you don't want to, that it's wrong for the family.'

She felt ice cold and then violently sick; her head swam, she felt she might faint.

'You've actually done that? Formally? Without discussing it any further?'

'Yes, I've actually done it. I wrote to her yesterday.'

'Richard,' said Debbie, 'you had absolutely no right to do that. You're mad.'

'Well, that's great. I do what you want and then you tell me I'm mad.'

'It is not what I want,' she said, her voice very low now, shaking with emotion, 'and you know that perfectly well, underneath all your wretched pride and self-importance. You've done it to hurt me, God knows why.'

'Perhaps you should look at your own behaviour,' he said, standing up, walking over to the door. 'I really don't think there's any future in this discussion, Debbie. I'm going to go and do some work.'

He shut the door very carefully and quietly after him; she sat staring at the chair where he had been sitting. Feeling really very frightened.

'So, that's about it, really,' said Lucinda. 'That's what we're going to do. Isn't it clever? Aren't you pleased?'

Nigel looked at her, sitting there on the big sofa – they had agreed to meet at the Selfridges Hotel again, it seemed ideal in every way – looking so lovely, so sweet and earnest, smiling at him gently, her blue eyes shining, and felt a slight sense of unreality. It didn't quite seem possible. Was she really saying all these things, making these suggestions, without any great difficulty, with apparent relish even? This was not the Lucinda, surely, that he had fallen in love with and married; she had changed, changed a lot, and it must be that man, brutalising her, distorting her sense of honour, of what was right and wrong. And trying, as far as he could see, to distort his.

'Of course, you'll have to back it all up,' she said, 'the story. Which is true, obviously.'

'Well . . .' He hesitated. 'Well, Lucinda, is it?'

'What do you mean? Nigel, we're not going to get very far with this if you're going to be difficult. It's all for your benefit, you've got to remember that.'

'Yes, yes, I know.'

'So – what isn't true?'

'Well – well, I don't really remember that stuff about the gallery.'

'Don't you? Well, that just goes to show how very unselfish I was about it. Not making a fuss. I mean, surely you remember that I was working for the gallery when you met me?'

'Yes, of course.'

'But you don't remember anything about them asking me to go to New York?'

'Not really, no, I can't say I do.'

'Oh dear. Well, I'll have to remind you. Maybe I hardly mentioned it. I was so excited about getting married, becoming Mrs Cowper . . .'

'Yes, you were,' said Nigel sadly.

'I know.' She put her hand on his, looked at him very tenderly. He snatched his hand away as if she had hurt it physically; he couldn't bear her to touch him.

'But – well, Nigel, we have to move on. It's happened, and I'm a beast, and I did this awful thing to you and now I'm going to make it up to you as best as I possibly can. So that Grandfather Cowper's cufflinks stay safe.'

He was silent.

'But you've got to do your bit. You've got to help. Otherwise . . . Nigel, look at me. Please! Do you want this to work or not?'

'I suppose so.'

'Of course you do. So – try, please try to do your bit.'

'And remember things that didn't happen?' He sounded bitter, even to himself.

Lucinda sighed. 'Nigel, they *did* happen – I promise you. I'm going to talk to Virgil Barrymore myself, and I'm sure he'll be able to convince you. Honestly. They asked me to go to New York and I didn't. It's terribly simple.'

'And what about the other stuff? Leaving you with the money in the trust fund because I'm worried about you?'

'Well, aren't you?'

'Of course I am.'

'Well then.'

'And how do you think your Mr Horton will feel about that? And – and the other thing you said.'

'Oh, he won't mind,' said Lucinda, and she sounded very confident. 'He'll be fine. Now, about the house and how we're going to deal with that . . .'

Nigel gave up and tried to concentrate on what she was saying. She was clearly much sharper than he had ever suspected. Maybe that was one of the ways he had gone wrong. He shouldn't have been quite so trusting. The plan was very clever. Very clever indeed. And it would certainly be an answer – of sorts.

But one thing he was quite sure of, however confident and sharp Lucinda might be. Horton wouldn't like it; he wouldn't like it one bit.

Catherine had reached such an extreme of worry now about the money that it had, in a strange way, become unreal. She knew she could do nothing about it; therefore it seemed the only thing to do was to take no notice of it. It was like some extremely severe pain that somehow she had got used to living with; she took painkillers in the form of her work and her children and her very few friends, and they allowed her to get on with her life to a large extent. It was only at night, when the painkillers wore off, that she had to face it all: the letters – increasingly pressing – from her Members' Agent, the gnawing indecision over whether she should sell the flat, the horror of having once more to remove Freddie from his school, where he was clearly now so happy, and the absolute terror of what might happen to a lone and penniless mother with huge debts she was completely unable to pay – the children taken into care, her begging in doorways? And she would pace the flat, her stomach churning, her head throbbing, feeling she was in danger of becoming completely out of control. She found it difficult to eat, which was probably just as well, she thought, it saved her money after all, and woke most mornings with sore eyes and a throbbing head. She had managed to persuade the doctor to prescribe her some sleeping pills, and they helped, but gradually they were becoming less effective, and she needed two a night now rather than one to grant her the blessed oblivion.

But in the office and at the school gates she seemed cheerful, competent, brave and to a certain effect felt all those things; she surprised herself. Perhaps, she thought, she should have been an actress. She would surely have won an Oscar.

She looked up one afternoon from her word processor to see Simon smiling down at her.

'Hello, Catherine. I want to ask you a favour.'

'Of course.'

She had expected him to give her some extra work to do, or perhaps to stay late one day; what he actually wanted was for her to join the Graburn & French box at Ascot, 'To help look after some of our lady guests.' She had been getting something out of a drawer at the time; she was so shocked she slammed the drawer shut and her finger in with it. It hurt quite a lot, but she hardly noticed the pain. She said it sounded wonderful, but she couldn't possibly; that she had nothing to wear, that she was bound to drop and spill a great many things, that she would have nothing to say, that he was being much, much too kind, that— and he had interrupted this torrent of self-denigration to say that, on the contrary, he was not being much too kind, rather the reverse; he was planning to make her work very hard. She would be of inestimable value to him, 'just looking after people, quietly and nicely'.

'I need someone keeping an eye on things in the box, making sure glasses are topped up, that everyone's had enough to eat, that people know where the loos are, especially the wives, that nobody's being left out, all that sort of thing. You've no idea how easily it can go wrong; some quiet little person isn't properly introduced, gets left in a corner while Hubby goes flashing his money around at the Tote. You'd be ideal. It's the week after next – Wednesday, if that's all right. And if you're worried about clothes, go and get yourself an outfit on expenses. I'll sign the chit. Oh, and if you're worrying about them,' he said, indicating the photograph on her desk, 'we can easily cover any expense there.'

'No,' she said, 'that really would be too much. I've got this nice woman, Mrs Lennox, who helps in the holidays. I'm sure she'd take care of them.'

She asked Mrs Lennox, who said that she would be happy to look after the children; she'd collect them from their schools, bring them back to their own home and keep them until Catherine returned; she would give them a good tea, supervise their homework, and bathtime and bedtime too, if Catherine was going to be back late. It would be a pleasure.

Catherine, relieved and excited, and, feeling increasingly like Cinderella suddenly granted an invitation to the ball, went shopping.

She bought her outfit at Fenwicks: Simon had given her a budget of £200 which seemed like a queen's ransom to her, but he said rubbish, they'd spend more than that on tips to the waitresses. She'd got a dress and jacket similar to one of the outfits Princess Diana had worn the year before, which made it absolutely safe, style-wise, she decided. It was very simple, in brilliant pink silk, the jacket lapels trimmed in black; and then she bought a very plain black straw hat and fairly low-heeled black court shoes. She would be on her feet all day long, Simon kept telling her, and she wanted to be comfortable.

When she tried it all on for the children, they both told her she looked like a princess herself.

They seemed perfectly content at the idea of Mrs Lennox looking after them: well, Caroline was. Freddie didn't seem quite himself altogether; he was rather pale and tired-looking, but whenever she asked him if he was all right he told her not to fuss.

'I'm fine,' he said, 'honestly. Don't worry about me.'

She asked Caroline if she knew whether Freddie had any problems. Caroline said she was absolutely certain he didn't.

Elizabeth had planned to leave the agency early; she knew Simon wanted to talk to her about the lawsuit, and she had been particularly distracted herself. She had suggested they went out for a quick meal at one of the local restaurants together and spent as long as it might take on his worries.

Just after lunch the Client Services Director came into her office and said there was a problem with a presentation the next day to a hugely important new business pitch. It was going to take a lot of sorting out. She called Simon. 'Sorry. I'll do my best to be back by nine. That won't be too late, will it?'

'I suppose not,' he said. He sounded tired and deflated.

'Sorry, Simon. But it's really important.'

'Of course.'

And how many times had they played out this drama, with her trying to prioritise; usually, she had to admit, putting her work first, because after all it couldn't wait and Simon could . . .

'See you at nine, then.'

It was half-past ten when she got home.

Simon was sitting up in bed reading; he looked at her, his face expressionless.

'Good of you to come home.'

'Simon! I was working.'

'Of course. As always. Important client, no doubt.'

'Important would be client. Presentation tomorrow, last-minute hitch. God, I'm tired.' She kicked off her shoes, rubbed her neck.

'Really? I'm so sorry.' He was silent for a moment, then said, 'Well, I'm just the unimportant husband, of course. It's one law for the rich in this house, isn't it, another for the poor. Me being the poor. Obviously.'

'Simon—'

'It's true. You can stay out all hours, go to dinners, cancel evenings with me, that's all fine. God help me if I step out of line.'

She was silent for a moment while the words hit her consciousness; and then she felt flooded with anger.

'How dare you,' she said, slightly breathless with her rage. 'How dare you compare your behaviour with mine! Let me remind you, Simon, I have not been having an affair, I have not announced that I am in love with someone else, I have not threatened to leave. I just get on with my job. Trying to keep things together, you know. Before we go bankrupt.'

'Oh, for fuck's sake, shut up about it all!' he said. 'I have had it up to here with my bad behaviour. How much longer do I have to drag myself round in sackcloth and ashes. It's nearly two fucking years ago now, Elizabeth. For Christ's sake, give me a break.'

She stared at him, physically shocked. 'Simon, I—'

'What do you think it's like for me, living in this nightmare?' he said. 'This Lloyd's nightmare? I'm doing my best, just as I'm doing my best for you and the family. And everything I try to do, to make things better, I get pilloried for – selling Chadwick, selling all our pictures . . . Christ Almighty, I decided tonight I really have got to sell the *Lizzie*. It's bloody terrifying, Elizabeth, and I know it's my own fault, but I need you with me, supporting me, not dragging me constantly through the mire, reminding me of my shortcomings . . .'

He stopped, and she saw with a sense of shock that there were tears in his eyes; he dashed his hand across them. 'Oh, just fuck off, why don't you?' he said bitterly. 'Get some sleep, ready for another important day tomorrow.'

A long, long silence; then she sat down suddenly, put her hand on his arm.

'Simon, I'm sorry. So, so sorry. I – I didn't think. Didn't realise how badly you felt, how worried you were. I should have done.'

'Yes, you bloody well should. I've never felt so alone.'

That was it, she realised, staring at him, that was what had gone wrong; they both felt alone. Were alone. They were separated by a vast abyss of recrimination and rejection, and how were they ever to cross it now? How would they ever be close again, close and tender, not cold and harsh? Would she – could she – ever know that tenderness again, when so much held them apart; and much of it of her making, too, she acknowledged that. For she had not been generous, she had not been forgiving; she had clung to her pride, her refusal to admit quite how much she was hurt, because if he knew that, he would have won.

And she felt absolutely terrified suddenly that it was gone for ever, that she had thrown too much of what was left away.

'I think I'd better go,' he said.

'Go where?'

'I don't know. Just – leave here. This house – you. I'm clearly no use to any of you. I mean it, you'll be better off without me. I'll get out, Elizabeth. We've lost one another, there's no way back.'

She stared at him.

'Don't you feel that?' he said. 'Honestly? Don't you think it's time to give in? Because I do. We've fought this for a long, long time and we're not winning, are we?' He stared back at her, his face heavy with despair. 'God, I used to love you so much,' he said, 'so very, very much. And you loved me. But it's gone. I really think that it's gone. I've tried, Christ knows I've tried, to get back, to get *you* back, but I can't. We've gone too far.'

Elizabeth sat on the bed, knowing only she could save them now, that he had indeed done all he could; and knew she must – somehow – try to explain. Which would require a brand of courage she wasn't sure she was capable of; the courage to let down her guard, to be no longer cool and self-sufficient, but frail and weak and dependent.

And for a moment she thought she couldn't; and then she knew she must – and it was the most difficult thing she had ever asked of herself.

'It's not you,' she said, dragging the words out slowly and painfully. 'It's me. I feel so – despairing.'

'Well, I'm not surprised.'

'No, you don't understand. Despairing of myself. Being unable to – to manage it.'

'Manage what?'

'Manage living with it. It's so . . . so hard.' She felt her eyes fill with tears, bit her lip, tried to smile. 'I just feel I'm not what you want any more. That I can't be.'

'Of course you can. You were always what I wanted.'

'But I wasn't, was I? You did want me; but you wanted her too. And now . . . well, all the time, all the time we're together, whenever we get close, whenever we make love, I think of her. Or rather of you and her. What did she do? To please you? Was it different from me? Did she know how to arouse you, did she do things I never discovered you like . . .'

'Elizabeth—'

'No, listen to me. It's so important. You've got to understand. It's why I'm so jealous. So afraid. I – I watch myself in bed with you, and I can't . . . can't . . .' Tears began to fall on the bedclothes; she brushed them angrily away. 'How hard do you think it is, admitting this?'

'Why should it be hard?'

'Simon, please. I'm telling you how I feel. That I feel

323

inadequate, when I'm with you. Of course it's hard. It's horrible. I – I'm in despair. Despair about myself.'

Simon looked at her, and then reached out and touched her face, very gently.

'Well, now you know how *I* feel. All the time. In despair about myself. My darling Elizabeth, you have got it so, so wrong. Let me tell you a few things; they may hurt a little, but you have to understand too. I have never wanted anyone as I want you. Ever. After all these years, I still want you, desperately. What happened was a kind of – of lashing back. Of course, there was more to it than that, I don't pretend that was the only reason.' He smiled at her. 'I'm not a fine example of the husband breed, I know. But you seemed to put me last, always. No, that's not right. You just dumped me emotionally while you got on with your important life. I was too demanding, took too much time from you. That's hard to live with. And someone else put me first for a while and that was very pleasant. But – God, it wasn't enough. It was you I really wanted. If you only knew how much I want you. Still. And, yes, how much I love you.'

'Do you?'

'Of course I do. And I can see how you can wonder how, when I betrayed you so completely. But actually, it wasn't so complete. It was only because I couldn't have you. In the way I wanted, the way I did have once. Now I know that's a feeble excuse, and it isn't even meant to be one, and Christ we've been over this so many times, and I'm so ashamed of myself, and shocked at the way I behaved, but just this one last time, let me tell you it's you that I wanted and loved and needed, and you that didn't seem to want or love or need me. You may tell me that is not right, but it's what I felt, Elizabeth. And I still feel that. I really do. That you've removed yourself, from my life. You've been marvellous and taken me back and carried on being the wonderful wife everyone so admires, but I've lost the essential you. The you that was really close to me.'

'But you haven't, you see, that's what I'm trying to say. The essential me is still here. But I hid her. It was the only way I could cope, by pretending, staying cool, saying, "Look, everybody, look at me, still smiling, still succeeding, still in control. It didn't really matter, Simon's little fling, it's fine, I'm not the sort of woman who can't deal with a little infidelity".'

'Well, you did a pretty good job,' he said. 'That's certainly the impression you gave me as well. And of course, then I began to think, If she can deal with it this well, maybe she didn't care that much – and what does that say about her and me and our relationship?'

She sat there, staring at him, shocked and frightened.

'Oh dear,' he said, 'what dangerous territory we stray into, in our efforts to exalt ourselves. I stray into infidelity, you into rejection of a different kind altogether. One emotion following another. But at least I understand now, understand your behaviour, and I can – just possibly – draw you back to me. I know how hard it must have been for you to tell me that, and I know it means you do indeed still love me. And do you know what that makes me want to do?'

'No,' she said, almost irritably, and she looked at him, and saw he was smiling his most infectious, glorious smile.

'It makes me want to shout out of the window, take space in newspapers, hire a plane with a banner behind it saying *Elizabeth Beaumont loves me, and that makes me the luckiest man in the world*. And if you'll come and sit a bit nearer to me – yes, that's right, and take those silly shoes off, and maybe the jacket . . . I'm going to try and persuade you I mean it.'

It was very good sex: quick, urgent, violent. It was the first time she had wanted it, really wanted it since . . . well, since then. And the first time she had felt confident enough to release herself, and that there hadn't been some dark anger and misery hanging over their bed. She felt loved, truly loved and totally engaged by him, she had almost forgotten that, in her long grief and anger, forgotten how sex could consume everything but itself, time and place and other concerns lost in its intense rituals and delights. She came, more than once, crying out, her body arched with pleasure, willing it to go on and on. And afterwards, lying on the bed, still half-dressed, almost surprised at the depth of her desire, her body eased, stilled, her mind released of tension, she said, 'I've missed that so much, Simon. So much.'

'Me too. But it seems we can still do it. We just have to practise a lot.'

'I'd like that.'

'I have never loved anyone as I love you, you know. In every way. Try to believe it. Try to go on believing it.'

'I will.'

'Tell me,' he said, very quietly and tenderly, kissing her, 'did you never think of retaliating, finding someone else, restoring your self-esteem that way?'

'No,' she said, 'of course not, Simon. I wouldn't and I couldn't. Ever. It wouldn't have done any good. And I just don't fancy other men, you know that.'

'Never?' he said curiously.

'Never. Well, not really.'

'It's just as well,' he said, 'because anyone who got a taste of that would never let you go again. You're what I want, my darling, darling Elizabeth. I swear to you. Nobody else – not even . . .'

'Not even?' she said, hardly daring to ask.

'Not even the redoubtable Flora Fielding.' He grinned at her. 'I know you're jealous of her in a funny way. And she is very beautiful, and rather fascinating, and I do like her very much, but she's exactly not my type. I like them sleek and sassy – ideally only half-dressed in expensive designer wear, including some ripped Janet Reger knickers.'

'Are they ripped?' she said, looking down at them, half-surprised. 'Well, never mind. It was worth it.'

'Now that is an accolade. I might add that to my messages in the media. *And she values me more than her Janet Reger knickers.*'

She laughed and realised she felt quite different. Stronger. And very much happier. She was a realist, she knew she would return to the jealousy and the rage every so often, but she also felt, for the first time since it had happened, that she might be able to survive it.

'I love you,' she said suddenly. She hadn't said it for a long time; it was very sweet and very good to be able to do so.

'I love you too,' he said.

Chapter 21

June, 1990

'And perhaps I could buy you a drink after the meeting?' Was she really saying this?

'That would be very nice.'

She was going to buy a man – not a particularly attractive man, but a very nice one and quite important – a drink. On expenses. On *her* expenses.

'The Royal Garden would be quite near. Would that suit you?'

'It would, yes, thank you.' Derek Earnshaw smiled at her; he clearly found the idea almost as exciting as she did.

She would be in the bar of a smart hotel. At teatime. Well, high-teatime. Fish-fingertime. Only it wouldn't be fish fingers for her, it would be olives and those extra-thin crisps. Washed down by some extremely cold Chardonnay.

'Right. Well, I'll see you at about three, Debbie.'

'Fine.'

She had given up on Richard: there simply seemed no point. Life was altogether horrible. Until today.

Somehow she had turned her back on all of it; had gone back to work and summoned up the other Debbie, the cool, efficient, clever Debbie, who was a success at her job and who everyone seemed to approve of. And the contrast was so great that she felt even more the other Debbie; she felt sexy, larky, a bit of a witch. It clearly wasn't going to last; like Cinderella she would have to go back to her kitchen, back to her corner, but today, today at least, was hers.

This was her first proper account: one she was handling all on her own. A small publishing company producing personalised books for children: where the hero – or heroine – could bear the name of the child who was to receive it.

'I think you should handle this one,' Anna had said. 'You've got kids – you'll have lots of ideas.'

She had: several. The one she was proudest of was that every child receiving the book could enter a competition to write a short story of their own: the winning entry would then be properly printed and presented to its new author.

'It'd be easy on a Mac, wouldn't cost much. And the panel of judges could include a well-known children's author. Maybe the child could even meet him or her.'

'I like that,' Derek Earnshaw said, 'it's very clever. As you say, it wouldn't cost much to do; flyers tucked into the book, and we can do it on the computer. Yes. Well done.'

He had liked her other ideas too; walking into the bar at the Royal Garden Hotel with him, Debbie felt absurdly excited and pleased with herself; rather as if she was walking into a theatre on the red carpet, or—

'Debbie! Hello. How lovely to see you.'

It was Simon Beaumont. She had only ever seen him in country mode; here he was in a dark-grey suit looking extremely smooth and handsome. And somehow younger. He stood up and gave her a kiss; she felt starrier still.

'Lovely to see you too, Simon,' she said. 'This is Derek Earnshaw, a client of mine. Derek, this is Simon Beaumont.'

'Who would dearly love to be a client of hers,' said Simon, smiling, holding out his hand. 'Lucky man. Well, I won't keep you. Enjoy your drink. Nice to have met you,' he added to Earnshaw.

If she had written the script herself, Debbie couldn't have done it better.

As they settled at a table at the far end of the bar, she saw Simon had been joined by a man. A young, rather tasty man, with dark, slightly spiky hair and a very sharp suit. Not Savile Row, like Simon's, just . . . sharp. Pity he hadn't been there a few minutes earlier . . . Debbie, concentrate. You're a professional woman, not a bimbo. You have a client to look after.

'Nice chap,' said Derek Earnshaw. 'What does he do?'

'Oh, he runs a bank,' said Debbie airily.

Simon liked Joel Strickland: very much. He hadn't exactly been expecting a hack in a beer-stained jacket, but a bright and personable young man with a clear grasp of his subject seemed too much to hope for. Nevertheless, that was what he had got.

'Now what can I tell you,' said Simon. 'I haven't got too long, I'm taking some clients out to the White City, to the dogs. You ever do that?'

'Yeah, I've been with the boys at the Sports Desk once or twice. Good fun.' He grinned at Simon. 'Can I say first of all that I'm so grateful to you for seeing me. And I simply want your story, everything you can tell me about the Lloyd's experience. As it affected you, obviously.'

'Well, not a lot, as yet. This could be one of your more disappointing interviews.'

'I doubt it,' said Strickland. 'You're looking at a man who travelled up to Scotland to interview the CEO of the Royal Bank of Glasgow, only to be told he never talked to journalists. And meant it. Then there was the Italian heiress who spoke no English and the conman who had found God.'

'Well, that sounds a bit more promising.'

'Not really. God had told him to join a religious order on some remote island somewhere and that was all he was prepared to talk about. As he'd not yet been there, it wasn't very interesting.'

Simon laughed. He could see why Annabel had wanted to help Strickland. He was a bit too sure of himself, but then that was inevitable, doing what he did.

'OK then. Ask me some questions.'

The interview ran along fairly predictable lines; when had he first considered becoming a Name, who had introduced him, how much business had he written; had he been encouraged to increase his underwriting; had he had any say in which syndicates he went into.

'Sadly not. Although how could I have known anyway, that Westfield Bradley was one of the less – what shall I say – less scrupulous groups. And yes, I'd been advised that I'd always make money on Marine and Motor. I said I'd like to be in those. They said fine. Which I was. But a few other things as well. Like Non-Marine. Only much later did I learn that was a hold-all which included asbestosis.'

He had felt absolutely no suspicion, he said. Lloyd's record was impeccable, a lot of his friends did very nicely out of them. 'I thought I was pretty lucky to have been invited in.'

'You didn't think of doing any real homework?'

'To my endless regret, no.'

'And – good years followed?'

'Very good. Ten of them. Can't deny it. But then – then it began to turn a bit nasty. The rumours began towards the end of eighty-seven, I'd say. The storm and the crash hadn't made anyone feel any more secure, either, given that we were underwriting risk. I remember sitting at a lunch and someone saying he thought there'd be enormous calls on Names soon and that Lloyd's was in debt to the tune of a billion or whatever. And we said, almost cheerfully, you know how one does, "Well, nothing we can do about it." We were all confident our particular syndicates would be all right, that our Members' Agents would look after us – and it's always the other fellow, isn't it, who gets caught.'

'And – you can't get out, of course, can you?'

'Not really, no. You can resign in theory, but that only lets you off the hook with any new business they write. For everything you've signed up to, it's the grave and beyond. The whole thing is an absolute scandal. They can come after your executors if they think it will do them any good. So to an extent it was head-in-the-sand time. Until I got what you might call the first minus accounting. In eighty-eight. And even though it wasn't a complete bolt from the blue, I'd kept on telling myself it couldn't happen to me.'

'And how did you feel?'

'Absolutely sick. Terrified. I was shitting myself. Almost literally.' It was quite therapeutic, talking to Strickland; or like being in the confessional – recounting the rising debts, the sale of Chadwick, the pictures, the shares, feeling his own financial success trickling away like sand through his fingers.

'And this year, worse still. I may have to sell the London house. But I'm going to law, planning to sue them . . .'

'Really?'

'Yes. Lot of us, all with the same Members' Agency. We'll be sueing *them*, incidentally, not Lloyd's as a whole. That really wouldn't wash.'

330

'And who's masterminding it, so to speak?'

'Oh, a chap who might well talk to you, very nice indeed, same sort of story as mine, used to have it all, big house, kids at public school, only difference is his wife's left him. I've been lucky there. Very lucky. Anyway, we've decided it's the only thing to do. We're just not prepared to lie down and tell them to take it. And one of the reasons I decided to talk to you was that a friend of mine recently tried to kill himself. Nice chap, in total despair, hadn't even told his wife. Took an overdose. They saved him, but I'm not sure he was very grateful for it. It doesn't bear thinking about. And he's not the only one, of course.'

'I know it,' said Strickland soberly. 'I interviewed the neighbour of some old lady who did exactly that. Ghastly. Tell me, does the name Allinson mean anything to you?'

'Don't think so. Why?'

'Oh, got a bit of a lead from someone. You don't think your friend would talk to me, do you?'

'I'm not sure. I can certainly ask him. He'd be very happy to see the whole of Lloyd's cast into the fiery furnace.'

'Thanks, I'd appreciate it. Very brave of you to sue them. How's it going?'

'Oh, slowly. There's a long way to go. We haven't even got a barrister yet, but we've got a very impressive solicitor. We're enrolling as many as we can, to help bolster the fighting fund. I think we'll probably get quite a lot. I'd be pleased with a hundred or so; some of these cases have thousands of protagonists. Anyway, I think that's about it. I'll speak to both these chaps, see how they feel about talking to you.'

'Well,' said Joel with a grin, 'it certainly wasn't a disappointing interview. Tell me, can you remember which year they suggested you increased your underwriting?'

'Oh, eighty-three, eighty-four, I think.'

'Well,' said Strickland, 'as far as I can make out, claims were being made as far back as the 1970s by persons suffering from asbestos-related diseases. Presumably that's the basis of your case against them – that they must have known.'

'Broadly speaking, yes. But I don't think we should discuss that now. Probably against the rules. I'll check with the solicitor.'

'Fine. I'd be very grateful.'

'To be honest, I've enjoyed it,' said Simon, 'and now – ah, Debbie. You leaving?'

'Yes, 'fraid so. Mr Earnshaw has a train to catch.'

'I see. Can't tempt you to join us then? I hope she's looked after you nicely Mr Earnshaw.'

'She has. Very nicely, thank you. Bye now.'

'Who was that?' said Joel when the two of them had disappeared; he was staring after them. It was fairly obvious his interest wasn't in Earnshaw.

'Oh, young friend of mine.'

'She's very attractive.'

'Yes, she is. Bit troublesome though.'

'Sounds interesting. In what way?'

'Oh, hard to say. I always remember Roald Dahl saying that sharing a house with his daughters was like living with a lot of unsettled heifers. Debbie is a very unsettled heifer.'

'She seemed to like you.'

'Only in a daughterly way,' said Simon. 'She sees me as slightly older than God.'

They were standing waiting for the lift when Debbie realised she had left her scarf behind.

'I'm sorry,' she said to Earnshaw. 'Stupid of me. Oh, here's the lift. Keep it for me. Or,' she added as he looked at his watch, 'you just go. It's fine.'

'Sure? I really am running a bit late.'

'Perfectly sure.'

'Thank you again. I feel very excited about the whole project.'

'Good. Me too.'

She supposed a psychiatrist would have said she left the scarf deliberately. So she would have to go back into the bar. And pass Simon Beaumont and his tasty, sharp-suited companion. And be drawn into further conversation with them. If so, she would deny it; or at least claim that it had been entirely unconscious. It wasn't the sort of thing she did. She wasn't dappy, not in that way anyway, and she might not be speaking to her husband at the moment, or rather he might not be speaking to her, but there was no way she'd be going to such lengths to meet some complete stranger just because she liked his haircut. Those days were long gone. Sadly.

She walked back into the bar, trying to look relaxed. 'Hi,' she said as they both looked up at her. 'I left my scarf behind. Stupid of me.'

'Well, your loss is our gain. Want a quick drink with us?'

'Oh, no. Thank you. It's very kind but I've got to get home.'

'Oh, come on,' said Simon. 'Another half-hour won't make much difference. Hubby looking after the children?'

'No, actually, he's not. A – a friend is.'

'Well, what are friends for? Go on, spoil yourself. You could even call it work. Joel here is a journalist, could be an important contact for you.'

'Well . . .' The tempation was almost overwhelming. A drink with two attractive men, in a rather stylish bar, overlooking one of London's nicest parks. It would be the end of a perfect day really. And she just felt so – so soothed by it all. After days of Richard not speaking to her, treating her like a piece of dog poo that had found its way onto his shoe, here she was being flattered and sought after, it was – well it was irresistible really . . .

'I'll have to go and ring my friend,' she said.

Jan was very excited on her behalf. 'Of course you must stay,' she said. 'They're all fine here. Watching a video of *Knight Rider*.'

'And Richard hasn't been round, asking where I am or anything?'

'Not yet. If he does, I'll tell him you're getting drunk with your lover. OK?'

'I wish.'

'Good for you. Have one for me.'

'I will. And I won't be more than half an hour later than I said.'

'Debbie! Don't waste an opportunity. And get a move on, they'll give up on you in a minute.'

But they hadn't; and Simon had bought a bottle of champagne for the three of them. She sat down next to him and opposite Joel, and watched him watching her, admiring her and smiling

333

at her as she chattered and joked and teased Simon about Flora. 'She's my mother-in-law, totally beautiful and wonderful in every way,' she said to Joel.

'Except that she annoys Debbie to death.'

'No, she doesn't. Well, not to death. Anyway, Simon is rather taken with her—'

'I am not. But I am very fond of her and I do admire her. She might be someone you could talk to,' he said to Joel. 'She's in this thing too – that's how we all met.'

'She sounds like quite a mother-in-law,' said Joel.

'She is. Hard to live up to. Do you have a mother-in-law?' God, why had she said that? How awful, how embarrassing, how crass . . .

'No, thank God.' He looked amused, recognising her confusion. 'I've been spared that so far.'

'Let me top you up, Debbie,' said Simon, 'and then I must go.'

'No, no, don't give me any more—'

'Why not? It suits you. The last time we were together, Debbie and I,' he said to Joel, 'we'd both had rather too much, hadn't we, darling? And talked a bit too much.'

If she hadn't been so drunk and so excited, she would have hated the 'darling'. As it was, it simply added to her sense of euphoria.

'Just a bit.'

'That was in Flora's kitchen, in case you get any funny ideas, Joel. Oh Lord, look at the time. I must go. You two finish the bottle, I'll take care of the bill—'

'No, no,' said Joel, 'that's ridiculous, the *News* will pay. Please, Simon, I insist.'

'OK. Well, nice talking to you. I'll get back to you about those people. And the lawsuit.'

'So, are you doing a piece about Lloyd's?' said Debbie when he had gone.

'Trying to. Most of them won't talk, but Simon's opening a few doors.'

'Good. You're the City editor of the *News*, did Simon say?'

'Deputy. He promoted me. Now tell me, what's a nice girl like you doing in PR?' He was joking; but the dark brown eyes were thoughtful as he looked at her.

'I like it,' she said defensively. She was always surprised by journalists' hostility to PR; she had observed in her short spell in the business that at least some of the time they were quite grateful for the information they were given.

'Really?'

'Yes, really. It's fun. And it means you can meet journalists,' she added. She smiled at him, but her voice was just slightly barbed.

'Well, obviously that's a very important bonus.' He grinned back at her.

God, he was *so* sexy. Dark eyes just were – more brilliant, more unreadable. And he did that thing of looking at her mouth.

'And what does your old man do?'

'He's a teacher. He's a headmaster of a school in Ealing.'

'And – he enjoys that?'

'No, not much. He's frustrated. He's been offered a new job,' she added, 'up in Scotland.'

'So, you'll be moving up there, will you?'

'I'm – I'm not sure,' she said carefully. 'We're thinking about it.'

'Well, it's a long way away,' he said. 'Big move. Away from all your friends and so on.'

'Yes. But it's important for him . . .'

'Well, I've certainly got you wrong,' he said, smiling at her again, a rather rueful smile. 'Thought you were a go-getting girl about town. And what do I find? A dutiful wife.'

'And what's wrong with that?' said Debbie, although it was nice he'd thought she was go-getting.

'Nothing at all. It's very impressive. Very impressive indeed. I would say you're a dying breed.' He raised his glass to her. 'To wifehood.'

'Don't say that,' said Debbie. 'Now you've made me feel dull and dreary.'

'Oh no,' he said, and his expression was quite serious now. 'You could never seem dull and dreary. Quite impossible.'

She felt herself blush, sat staring at him, unable to think of anything to say.

He did it for her. 'I must go,' he said.

'Me too.'

'It's been really nice meeting you.'

'Thank you. I've enjoyed it too. Very much.' She looked at her watch. 'God, it's late. Goodbye, Joel.'

'Goodbye, Debbie. And if you're ever in the *News* offices, come and say hello.'

She arrived at Jan's still high; high on champagne, on her day, her success – and meeting Joel Strickland. 'You lucky cow,' said Jan cheerfully.

'I think we should move,' said Blue.

'Move!'

'That's what I said.'

'But why?'

'Well, this is hardly a family home, is it? No room for a nursery, no proper garden, terrible pollution. The country's the place for children to grow up.'

'The country!'

'Yeah.'

'Oh.'

'I thought you'd like the idea, Lucinda. Thought you was a country girl at heart.'

'Yes, I am, but . . .'

'You said yourself, you wanted ponies and that for our kids.'

'Yes, I do.'

'Not much room for ponies in Limehouse.'

'No, that's true. So where were you thinking we might go?'

'Chislehurst,' said Blue, without a moment's hesitation.

'Chislehurst! Where's that?'

'Kent.'

'Oh. Oh, I see. But I don't know anybody in Kent.'

'Lucinda,' said Blue patiently, 'you're one of the friendliest people I know. You'll make friends, no time at all.'

'Yes, but—'

'But what?'

'I think I'd rather go where I did have a few friends already. Old ones. Like – like Gloucestershire, for instance.'

Blue thought for a moment, then he said, 'No, don't think so. No offence, Lucy, but your parents have tended to put me off Gloucestershire. Doesn't feel like my kind of place. No,

Chislehurst's the job. Beautiful properties, easy run into London Bridge for me. And anyway, Luft lives out there and so does Harry; you'll find yourself with loads of friends ready made.'

'Well, maybe we could have a look,' said Lucinda. 'Can I have some more coffee, Blue, please.'

'Course you can. God, it suits you, being pregnant. You look absolutely gorgeous this morning.'

'Thank you. I feel quite gorgeous. Actually.'

'Well, seeing as it's Sunday, maybe we should pop back into bed. Just for a little while.'

'Yes, let's,' she said, smiling at him. It was funny, but being pregnant made her feel even more sexy, she thought, as she took his hand and let him lead her into the bedroom. She'd have thought it would be the reverse, but . . .

'Oh Blue,' she said, squirming happily as he started removing her robe, kissing her (just very slightly) rounding stomach, his tongue moving down thoughtfully, carefully, beginning to probe her pubic hair. 'Oh Blue, I do feel so terribly, terribly lucky.'

'You feel all sorts of things to me,' he said, beginning very tenderly to part her legs.

Afterwards, when she was settling into herself again, no longer fractured with the violent piercing pleasure, languorously, warmly peaceful, Blue curled up behind her, rather absent-mindedly playing with her breasts – her wonderfully full breasts, the sort she had always dreamed of having – she said, 'Blue, I would love to move to the country, of course. But maybe not yet. Not till I've had the baby, and I can give it my full attention. It's a lot of work, moving.'

'Yeah, all right,' he said, already half-asleep. 'Whatever you want.'

It was the first time, she realised, quite shocked at her own ability to do so, that she had been anything other than entirely honest with him. But it really would have spoiled the lovely Sunday to have to go any further into why she didn't want to move yet.

Chapter 22

June, 1990

The great sporting occasions in the English calendar are only in part about sport. If all they offered was horse racing, rowing, tennis, rugby, albeit of an extremely high standard, there would be far less interest in them; reports would be confined to the sports pages and programmes, stands and stadiums would be of more modest proportions, car parks a great deal smaller, and the amounts of money changing hands considerably less. What gives them their magic, draws in both players and spectators from all over the world, is the disparate elements they gather about them: of sporting prowess and titillating gossip, of high-level gambling and high-class fashion, of a passionate regard for tradition and a breathtaking display of innovation, of huge commercial interest and a blatant exhibition of the English caste-system: and more recently, the cult of the celebrity. And nowhere does this apply more powerfully than at Royal Ascot.

There really was still something special about Ascot, Elizabeth thought, looking down from the agency box on the sixth floor, in spite of the vulgarity, the drunkenness, the overt commercialism. It was, if the sun shone, a wonderful spectacle – the blue sky, the green ribbon of the course, the pastel shades of the hats and the vivid colours of the jockeys' silks, moving in a kaleidoscopic pattern; the beautiful gleaming animals, so clearly out to enjoy themselves, to show off; and an almost tangible sense of enjoyment settling over the whole thing, to create a glorious tapestry. And the sun *was* shining today.

She was very pleased with what she was wearing: a cream silk suit, very simple, and a wide-brimmed black straw, with a cream ribbon. And very high-heeled shoes with fine ankle straps which she'd regret, she knew, by the end of the day. But they were lovely – what Annabel called Fuck Me shoes. She'd been very shocked when her daughter had first said that; Annabel had simply giggled and said, 'Mu-u-um! (turning the word into three syllables in the way she had).

She turned her mind to the real business of the day. Of all the corporate entertaining the agency did, she still enjoyed Ascot most. It was such fun, a kind of charming carnival that took a miserable spirit to resist. And it still had a huge cachet; clients seldom refused an invitation to Ascot.

Her agency took a box for one day, usually Ladies' Day; Simon's bank for two; sometimes they overlapped. This year was one of them. They had never managed to actually go together and for pleasure; they certainly never would now, Elizabeth thought. The extravagance was unthinkable.

They arrived that day, in the same hire car, kissed, parted, made their way to their respective boxes (half an hour before their earliest guests), agreeing to try and meet in the paddock, but otherwise at home very much later, all their attention and loyalty now turned to their clients; and what an illusion they presented, she thought, glossy, good-looking, monied, and giving absolutely no hint of the financial nightmare that stalked them.

Lucinda had always enjoyed Ascot, loved the dressing-up, the way you could be really excessive without it seeming vulgar. She had had some lovely hats over the years; and this year was one of the best. She had chosen it with great care, a wide-brimmed, beribboned thing from Harvey Nichols; she had actually considered some smaller, chic-er styles, but they didn't really suit her changing shape; the traditional sort balanced it better, somehow. She was quite pleased with her dress as well, pale-blue silk, like the hat, gently high-waisted with narrow sleeves. At least one bit of her could look slim.

She hoped she would enjoy it this year; it was certainly going to be different. McArthur's were taking a large party, but she couldn't help feeling that Ascot in a pair of corporate boxes on one of those top floors wouldn't be quite the same as being in the Royal Enclosure with lots of lifelong chums, and she had so loved the picnics and then meeting everyone in the evening in a great mob in Kensington. She wondered just slightly anxiously if Nigel would be there; that would be difficult. But then, he certainly wouldn't be up on the fifth floor or wherever the box was.

She'd been to the Derby with Blue – he liked to do the big ones, as he put it – and that had been huge fun; she did love his friends, they all made such a fuss of her, treated her as if she was royalty, even though they did tease her a lot as well, and she supposed a couple of the girls were a bit less friendly. But it hadn't mattered and she'd actually drunk a bit, two whole glasses of champagne and then a glass of wine, rather too much considering she was pregnant. Blue had been quite cross with her. She'd ended up feeling very odd indeed and having to lie down on the back seat of the pale-blue Rolls that he had hired for the day.

He'd put some enormous sum of money on a horse, and lost it; he'd just laughed and said he could take a hiding as well as the next man. His generosity was one of the things she loved most about him.

Everything seemed to be all right again; she had managed to explain a bit about the divorce, about what Steve Durham had said they might be able to do. Of course she hadn't gone into the details, because Steve was still fine-tuning them, as he put it, and one or two of them might be a bit upsetting for Blue, she could see, until he really understood, but he seemed perfectly happy about everything so far. And Nigel had seemed fairly happy with what Steve had suggested. As indeed he should be; it really was all rather clever.

She slithered into her dress and went to ask Blue to do it up at the back. 'You're putting on weight, Lucinda,' he said, kissing her between her shoulder-blades. 'This is quite tight. Wonder what's causing it . . .'

Catherine was still very nervous about her role; but she did think she might be able to enjoy her day just the same. And it would be nice, just for once, not to be haring back to Fulham, praying the tube wouldn't be delayed, arriving breathless at Caroline's school gates . . . and then rushing her along to Lynton House to meet Freddie and then tea and homework and trying to have fun and then . . . well, and then back to the nightmare. Until the next day.

Freddie was still being odd, almost distant, her beloved, loving little boy, refusing the last few nights even to kiss her good night. And even Caroline had seemed worried: while insisting she wasn't.

'Everything's fine, Mummy,' she kept saying, whenever Catherine tried to press her. 'Honestly, we're both fine.'

And they had both seemed quite cheerful about Mary Lennox looking after them.

'You just enjoy it, Mrs Morgan,' she said. 'Be lovely for you, with the Royal Family and everything. Do let me know all about Princess Diana, won't you?' She clearly saw Catherine as practically taking part in the procession down the racecourse.

Simon had briefed her very carefully on the clients, which wives she most needed to keep an eye on, and instructed her to tell him at once if something was worrying her. Catherine, however, was more worried about spilling drinks than anything.

Nigel was trying not to think about Ascot. They had always gone every year on Ladies' Day, Lucinda looking prettier every time, and they'd had such fun. Met all their friends and pooled picnics and had a bit of a flutter, and then he always loved the sing-song at the end, it was so unlikely somehow, and then the slightly dodgy drive back to Kensington, hoping they wouldn't get stopped by the police and that Lucinda was as sober as she said she was. He'd been trying not to even think about it this year, but Lydia Newhouse always went with her girlfriends, it was understood that she had the day off, and every time he looked at her empty desk, he seemed to see Lucinda in some fluffy hat, smiling at him over the picnic-table, and he could hardly bear it.

Joel Strickland was going to Ascot; it wasn't exactly within his brief as City Editor, but several press tickets had arrived, and he loved the races. He actually found flat racing slightly boring, he preferred the jumps and the sporting highlight of his year was Cheltenham, but Ascot was always fun, and he had a few hot tips from the Sports Desk. A load of *News* writers were going together in a mini-bus: Sandra Keswick and a photographer to cover the fashion, Suzy Jameson to do the gossip, as well as the sports guys. They'd have a laugh.

He was also working-class boy enough to find it quite amusing to be there, mingling with the toffs, dressed up to the nines; none of it impressed him exactly, but Nan would have been speechless with excitement, he thought, buttoning his morning coat, admiring himself in the mirror; and Grandad would have been disgusted. Funny old business, class; so important, and not just in England, he'd discovered, attending economic press jollies in Europe and the States. There was no one snobbier than the East Coast Americans: unless perhaps the French.

Anyway, it would all be good fun, and he always enjoyed being with Suzy, who was pretty and sassy with extremely good legs; she was also brilliant at her job. She was cunning in her pursuit of gossip; manicurists, florists and chambermaids were her favourite sources of information: she knew they were far more likely to spill spicy beans than the friends and relations of her prey. Her finest hour had been when she managed to prise out of a laundry-deliveryman details of a well-known socialite (married) who suddenly started sending twice the number of sheets for laundering every week. 'And to pay me with cash; that seemed a bit funny,' he said to Suzy, over a third whisky and soda. 'I mean, always suspicious, cash, wouldn't you say?' Suzy agreed.

Suzy was one of the reasons Joel wasn't taking Maggie with him; he and Suzy tended to work together to a degree on such occasions, but she was overtly flirtatious and Maggie was intensely jealous. She was jealous not only of the other women in Joel's life, even the working colleagues, but the job itself, the way it took him to parties and smart hotels and on the odd overseas binge. Working in the City herself, she knew how it ran on social contact, and she knew how much Joel enjoyed it; she pretended not to care, but she always grilled him after a dinner, or a conference. When he was in a good mood it amused him and he would tease her about it, tell her he'd sat next to an amazing female fund manager at dinner or helped some bimbo of a PR over her fear of flying; but when he was tired or stressed it irritated him and he would clam up, tell her he didn't want to talk about it. It was hard to say which response annoyed Maggie more.

He was going to have to do something about her soon; it

simply wasn't working. He was terribly fond of her, but he didn't want to spend the rest of his life with her: which was patently what she wanted. He hadn't met anyone he wanted to spend the rest of his life with, and most of the time he couldn't imagine that he ever would. Joel wanted to enjoy life: and that included women. Being with them, talking to them, having sex with them. That's what they were for: making life better, sweeter, more interesting. Not setting up house with, or – God forbid – having babies with. Time for that, far into some unimaginable future . . .

Meanwhile, the immediate future was today at Ascot. With Suzy. Without Maggie. And there would be lots of pretty girls to appreciate.

And his presence there was not entirely self-indulgent. You could always pick up a good financial story – or at any rate, some good financial gossip – at Ascot, crawling as it was with the great and the good, or rather, the great and the wealthy. He had once spotted a fairly well-known millionaire practically in tears, staring at his tote tickets: he had lost twenty pounds. He'd given that one to Suzy; but another occasion had provided him with the first straws in the wind of a big money-laundering operation: nowhere better to quietly hide a few grand than at a race meeting. And maybe today, he'd get something for his Lloyd's story.

Which was very slow in coming together; he was even considering spiking it. What was it about that thing, that everybody shut up like a clam every time you tried to make them talk? Simon Beaumont was very unusual. And his Editor certainly wasn't keen, said who was going to care about a lot of rich greedy people getting their just desserts. He'd been much more interested in a story about Gordon Brown and John Smith agreeing to support the ERM.

Annabel watched the royal procession on television in the staff room at Miki's. It would never normally have been allowed, but Florian said they needed to study their handiwork, and brought his little portable set in. And there was no hair left to do, for an hour or two; the salon was deserted, thank God. They were all completely exhausted.

Ascot Week was a nightmare in the salon, they had warned

her. From 8 a.m. onwards, on each of the three days, clients were coming in to have their hair styled, put up, plaited, their hats put on, turned round, adjusted; all in a hurry, all watching the stylists and the other women like hawks, lest they were getting put back in the queue, or had the same hat as someone else. The more Annabel saw of these women, the more she admired her mother and felt she wanted to be like her. How could they exist like this, fretting and fussing endlessly over absolutely nothing, as far as Annabel could see, apart from their clothes and their hair and their aerobic classes and how they were going to manage to go ski-ing before Easter or cruising before Christmas, or without the nanny during her weekend off.

'If I went to hell,' she said to Florian, after the last Ascot head had wafted out of the salon, 'I think it would be a life like that, I really do.'

Florian told her she had been in hell for the last two days, and suggested a little bit of heaven with him that night to make up for it. 'And it will be heaven – you know I can guarantee it.'

'In your dreams,' said Annabel briskly.

'I'm so sorry.'

'No, no, it was my fault. I wasn't looking where I was going. The sun's so dazzling coming out of that tunnel – Simon! Hello!' He was looking pretty dazzling too, Lucinda thought; he really was amazingly good-looking. Well worth bumping into.

'It certainly is,' he said. 'Wonderful day, isn't it? And you look gorgeous, if I may say so. That's a lovely hat.'

'You certainly may. Thank you. Isn't it beautiful here today?'

'It is. Can't beat it when the sun shines.' He stood back, smiling at her. 'So, where's your – your . . .'

'My fiancé? He's in a box with lots of his cronies. None of them were very interested in the horses, which seemed a bit of a shame, so I came down. It's my favourite part of Ascot, visiting the paddock.'

'Mine too. I had a similar experience with my guests. If you like, we could take a turn together.'

'That would be nice.'

They walked in silence, easily companionable, watching the

horses beginning to form into a line for the next race, dancing and skitting about, eyeing one another up, like so many models backstage, preparing to walk down the catwalk.

'So, are you up with the corporate lot then?' he said.

'Yes. It's a new experience actually. Quite interesting. Blue – that is, my – my fiancé – he works for one of the big banks.'

'Yes, I think you told me. I've forgotten which one?'

'McArthur's.'

'And what does he do there?'

'He's a market maker.'

'I see. Amazing creatures, aren't they?' he said, breaking off, studying the horses. 'Those beauties, I mean, not market makers. Much smaller than you'd expect, somehow.'

'Yes, I always think that. Do you like horses?'

'Oh, they're all right. My younger daughter would like to be one. Or marry one.'

Lucinda laughed. 'How old is she?'

'Thirteen.'

'And she has a pony?'

'She does. Rather expensive little toy. We can't house him any more, thanks to Lloyd's; he lives further away than Tilly would like now, but at least she still has him. He's down in Wales with Flora Fielding – can't remember if you met her or not – another Lloyd's victim.'

'Yes, I did. She was rather lovely, I thought. So, are you up there with the corporates as well?'

'I am indeed. Another bank – merchant variety. I should be getting back to them really. But if you want to look in at my box later, it's number five hundred and two, and bring your fiancé, we'd love to see you both. Catherine is here.'

'Catherine! How nice. In your box?'

'Yes, and she's working rather hard up there. So she'd particularly love to see you – have an excuse to stop for a moment.'

'Then we'll most definitely come. And I'm sure Blue would love to meet you. Thank you.'

Flora Fielding had only been to Ascot once, and had sworn she would never go again. It had been, she said, one of the silliest experiences of her life. William had been invited along by some cousin of his, she had had to get all dressed up in the sort of

345

clothes she most hated, and spend the day with a lot of people pretending they were interested in horses, most of them with apparently no very clear idea even of how many legs they possessed. So when Simon Beaumont had invited her to join his party – 'lend it a bit of class' – she had looked at him with total horror.

'It's sweet of you,' she said, 'but wild horses wouldn't drag me there.' And when Simon said there were no wild horses at Ascot: 'It might be better if there were,' she said.

Just the same, with the insane notion that perhaps she might catch sight of Simon or Elizabeth, or even Catherine – now that *had* been a nice idea of his, to take Catherine, he really was a very sweet man – she spent half an hour or so watching it on television, rather half-heartedly since she was shelling peas and shredding beans for the freezer at the same time. She didn't see Simon or Catherine, of course, but she did see, with a certain sense of shock, an old friend of William's, walking into the Royal Enclosure with a very pretty woman on his arm on one side and a minor Royal male on the other. It was the very same old friend who had encouraged – no, persuaded him – to become a Name, who was a Working Name himself; indeed, who had assured him – or rather her – that it was as safe as houses, and the Westfield Bradley Group particularly so; that it was one of his major syndicates and if it went down, which was, of course, unthinkable, they would go down together. Well, Eddie Smythe – Edward Trafford Smythe, to give him his full name – didn't look remotely as if *he* was about to go down.

How extremely irritating, Flora thought, putting down her knife and the bean she was shredding, peering at the rather small screen to make quite sure she hadn't been mistaken. And then the camera moved on.

Well, appearances could be deceptive, of course; nobody would think Simon was on the brink of bankruptcy either. All the same – it was interesting. She just might look him up, find out how he was faring. It was his fault, after all.

'Come on,' said Suzy to Joel. 'I'm going down to the paddock, do a bit of trawling, you can help. I need a man on my arm. And you don't seem to be fully employed.'

'I'm very busy,' he said indignantly. 'I've got horses to back. Surefire one for the last race.'

'Oh yeah? Why am I not tempted to join you in that one? Sandra, you coming?'

'Yeah, why not. Although if I see one more red Dallas outfit I think I might scream. Come on, Joel, you can carry our notebooks.'

'You go ahead, I'll catch you up.'

He arrived ten minutes after them. Sandra was with her photographer, interviewing a very pretty, very young girl dressed entirely in black and white. 'I can see the headline now, can't you?' said Joel to Suzy. 'Something about My Fair Baby?'

'Bitch,' she said, 'but yes, maybe. Oh goodness, there's our Joan, doesn't she look fantastic! And look, there's the divine Linda Evangelista.'

'Ah, isn't she the one who said she wouldn't get out of bed for less than ten thousand dollars?'

'Absolutely. Clever boy.'

'Well, I wrote a little piece about models' earnings. Now who's *that*?' He indicated a ravishing blonde, with the unmistakable rangey walk of the model. 'Know her?'

'No.'

'She looks familiar. Now who . . . Oh, I know, yes. Excuse me, Suze.'

Suzy watched him, smiling almost indulgently, as he moved in on the girl, said something that made her laugh, and then got very firmly elbowed aside by a swarthy, rather handsome man, who hurried her away. 'What was that about?' she asked.

'Oh, I met her at a photographic session a while ago.'

'Joel! When did you start hanging around photo shoots? You must be getting desperate.'

'I went to pick up Sandra for that do – when I didn't get an award. She's called Effie. Almost didn't recognise her. She wasn't so blonde then. Anyway, I reckon I was in with a chance until that chap came up.'

'Yes, well, he's a very famous owner. His dad's a sheikh. So I think she'll do just slightly better to stick with him.'

'Not necessarily. Money isn't everything.'

'Oh, really? Joel, you are dreadful. What about poor Maggie?'

347

'Poor Maggie knows exactly where she stands,' he said, his face harder suddenly.

'Does she?'

'Yes, of course she does. What is it with you girls? You seem to belong to this trade union that bands you all together. Against us.'

'With blokes like you around, we need to,' said Suzy, 'and don't look so cross, I was only teasing you.'

'I'm not sure you were,' said Joel, 'but let's not squabble about it.' He grinned at her. 'You go ahead. I'm going over to the bookies, see if I can lose some money.'

'Fine. See you later.'

He was on his way back to the press tent, when he saw Simon Beaumont waving at him. He wouldn't have been surprised if he failed to recognise him, or simply nodded and walked on. But Simon was clearly in an extremely cheerful state of mind, and had undoubtedly had more than one glass of champagne.

'Just won three hundred quid. Won't solve all my problems, of course, but – how's the story going?'

'Oh, slowly. But thanks a lot for all your help. And your friend Neil Lawrence called me, said he'd be happy to talk.'

'Good. And did you have a nice chat with Debbie after I'd gone?'

'Oh – yes, thanks,' said Joel. 'Yes, she's – great fun.'

He had actually felt Debbie was more than great fun; he had been what he called 'bothered' by her for several days; she had stuck in his head, and he wasn't sure why. She wasn't particularly pretty – although she had those amazing brown eyes, and actually, yes, a completely sexy mouth – and her figure wasn't exactly sensational, she was small and rather skinny. But she was very attractive, no doubt about that, and amusing in a rather quirky way; had she not been married he would probably have asked her out.

'Anyway,' said Simon, 'come up for a drink a bit later, why don't you? Girl in my box, works for me, horribly affected by it all, she'd probably like to talk to you. And my wife'll be there by then, she wanted to meet you too, not sure why. Or was that my daughter? Can't remember.'

'Is your daughter here?' asked Joel, half-hopefully. He still remembered Annabel in all her engaging beauty: much too young for him, of course, but . . .

'No, no, she's working. Big day for hairdressers, I'm told. Anyway, you come up around four-thirty or five, when things are winding down a bit, box number five oh two, have a drink, meet Catherine.'

'Is Catherine your wife?'

'No, she's the one you should talk to. See you later.'

'Who was that?' said Suzy, tucking her hand into his arm again.

'Oh, just someone I know.'

'Now he's what I call really attractive. I mean really.'

'Bit old for you, Suze, surely?'

'Well, that's where you're wrong, you see. I like an older man, when they're in good nick. And he is in very good nick. You should have introduced me.'

'Sorry, sweetheart. Next time. I'm going up to his box at teatime.'

'Can I come?'

'No, you can't. It's strictly invitation only. Sorry.'

'I bet you did a lot of brown-nosing to get it too,' said Suzy cheerfully.

'Suzy! As if I would!'

It was all right, Catherine thought; she hadn't spilled anything yet and she had, in fact, as Simon had prophesied, found herself quite busy. One wife in particular didn't seem to be having a specially good time, and appeared to prefer chatting to Catherine to anyone else. And she had met Martin Dudley, the Chairman, for the first time, and although she didn't exactly like him – he was a bit of a bull-in-a-china-shop sort of person – he had been very nice to her and kept thanking her for what she was doing.

His large-bosomed wife, who was dressed in bright pink, kept rounding up the other wives like a deep-voiced sheepdog and ushering them to the Tote, the Ladies, the balcony of the box, or the paddock, when it seemed very clear to Catherine that they would much rather have been left to their own devices. Still, she supposed she must know what she was doing; Catherine's late husband, Frederick, had always said chairmen's wives were actually frustrated chairmen. And the day was passing really fast; she had hardly had time to think about the children. She looked at her watch; yes, they'd be at home having tea by now with dear Mrs Lennox. She hoped Freddie was feeling a bit more cheerful.

'Simon, hello. This is my fiancé, Blue Horton. Is this really all right, Simon?'

'Absolutely! How do you do, Blue, very nice to meet you.' So this was the Adonis who had persuaded Lucinda away from her dull husband: interesting. It wasn't his looks, that was for sure. He looked a bit of a thug: heavily built, with close-cropped hair and a rather thick neck. A working-class thug, moreover. Extraordinary.

Blue held out a hand to Simon. 'Pleased to meet you at last. Lucinda never stops talking about you.'

'Oh really? I find that a little hard to believe. Glass of champagne?'

'Won't say no, although Lucinda tells me I've had quite enough. I personally don't think you can ever have enough champagne, but there you go. Had a good day?'

'Pretty good, yes. Won a bit.'

'Lucky you. I've lost a lot.' He smiled at Simon; and suddenly Simon could see it. What this man had was charm: in lorryloads. He was easy, and at the same time possessed of huge energy; he almost crackled, standing there, his dark eyes roaming the box, following Lucinda as she embraced Catherine, smiling fondly at her, then coming back to Simon. 'Your wife here?'

'Oh no. She's entertaining on her own account.'

'Oh yeah?' He looked genuinely interested, wasn't merely being polite. 'She got her own business, has she?'

'Well, almost. She's MD of an advertising agency.'

'Blimey. I've heard of these Superwomen. Never met one in the flesh, though.'

'Well, you can,' said Simon, 'if you hang on a bit. She's promised to come up at about five.'

'Well, we could do that, yeah. Thanks very much.'

'Blue, this is Catherine,' said Lucinda, leading a rather weary-looking girl over. 'I told you about her, remember?'

350

'Lucinda, if I remembered everything you told me, my head would burst,' said Blue Horton.

Catherine was beginning to feel very tired. It had been a long day, and a huge strain. She hadn't been able to eat anything; whenever her hand stretched out, to take a smoked-salmon sandwich or mini-quiche, someone would put a glass of champagne or a plate of petit fours into it, to take to somebody else. She looked longingly down at the course; she would have given anything just to have been able to take in the scene properly for five minutes, to actually see a race. She could have been anywhere at all, she thought wearily; it was a bit like being an air hostess, and she'd completely missed the royal procession. Simon had said very thoughtfully that she must go and have a look at it, but she was quite small, and it was impossible to see anything at all past the thick wall of broad morning-suited backs and bobbing, feathery hats.

The mood in the box was jovial; everyone seemed to have won something, or were eager to relate what a lot they had lost; indeed, that seemed to be almost more enjoyable.

'Yes, damn near a grand altogether,' said a red-faced man, and: 'You're doing well,' said another. 'I did the fatal thing, you know, got the winner in the first race and then spent most of the day losing it twice over. Not a word to the wife, though.'

And had they any idea at all how lucky they were, Catherine thought, to be able to regard the loss of what would have paid Freddie's school fees for more than a term with such absurd equanimity?

'Here, why don't I hold that plate for you for a minute so you can eat some of it yourself. I've been watching you – you look very hungry.'

Catherine turned and saw a young, rather dashing-looking man, with very dark hair and eyes, grinning at her. 'Joel Strickland,' he added, holding out his hand for the plate.

'How very kind,' said Catherine gratefully, seizing a couple of fondants and (she was afraid) literally shovelling them into her mouth. 'It is very nice to meet you, Joel. And how do you know Simon?'

'I'm a journalist. I interviewed him not so long ago.'

'What paper are you on?'

351

'The *News*. I'm the City Editor.'

'Gosh. I don't think I've ever met a journalist. Not a real one. I did some work experience once for the local paper, but I wasn't much good at it,' she added.

'I can't believe that. So what's your role here?'

'Oh, general dogsbody, really. Making sure everyone had enough to eat and wasn't being neglected, that sort of thing.'

'I can see you've been pretty effective. Nobody is close to starving – apart from you, that is. Why don't you sit down for a bit, enjoy that food.'

'Oh no, I couldn't possibly,' said Catherine. 'I'm not here to sit down. Let me get you a drink.' She signalled to the waitress.

'OK. Well, tell me – how have you found Ascot?'

'Oh, wonderful,' she said brightly – and then meeting his sharp, amused eyes – blushed and said, 'It wasn't quite how I expected.'

'Really?'

'Yes. I thought it would be much more about the racing – the horses, you know.'

' 'Fraid not,' he said. 'Of course, it is a great meeting, but most of the people who come for the racing aren't up here. This lot just want to drink a lot, show off their hats, and tell everyone how much they've lost. And—'

'Catherine, how lovely to see you.' It was Lucinda. 'Simon said you'd be here.'

At which point, someone jogged Catherine's arm, and the glass of champagne she was taking from the tray went all over Joel's shirt and tie.

'Oh dear, let me—'

'It's all right. Please don't worry. Occupational hazard, I'd say.'

'Catherine, stop fussing,' said Lucinda, 'He's right, you expect to get showered with champagne here, don't you?' she added to Joel. 'Can I find you some tissues or something? Or replace that drink?'

Simon, who had been watching this scene out of the corner of his eye while apparently holding a very serious discussion about the exchange rate with his Chairman's brother, thought what a treasure Lucinda was, and hoped her charming fiancé realised it.

*

Simon was pleased with the day. People had appreciated it, seemed happy, a great many male egos had been stroked, and female ones flattered, the atmosphere was easily relaxed; the sun had been warm, the champagne cold, the food delicious and the view of the course – for those who had wished to admire it – breathtaking. And many business relationships had been strengthened by the sharing of the day's pleasures – which was, after all, the whole idea . . .

'Simon! Hello, darling. I've come for a quick visit, as promised. How's everything?' It was Elizabeth: looking stunning. God, he was proud of her. He kissed her.

'I'm fine. Except I'm even poorer.'

'Me too. Lost lots.'

'Mrs Beaumont? Blue Horton. You're the Superwoman, I understand.'

'On a good day, perhaps.'

'Well, I wish our Managing Director looked like you. Can I ask you a question about your business?'

'Of course.'

'What I can never understand, some of those ads, those really good ones – take the Cinzano one for instance, with Joan Collins and that Rossiter chap – everyone knows the ads, says how bl— how marvellous they are, then you ask them what the product is and they say Martini. Or Campari, or something like that. So what's the point? Seems like that's a bit of a wank—'

Lucinda had come over, tucked her arm through his.

'Blue,' she said warningly.

'Sorry, bit of self-indulgence anyway on the part of your industry. I mean, the whole point of an ad surely is to sell the product?'

'Well, yes. You're right. And it's very clever of you to make that point.'

'Bet I'm not the first,' he said, grinning at her.

'No, you're not. But you know, the real trick is to register the brand and what it has to offer in a distinctive and memorable way. And—'

And the argument might have gone on for some time, had not Catherine slowly and very gracefully slithered to the floor of the box in a dead faint.

'She looks to me as if she doesn't have enough to eat,' said Elizabeth severely to Simon, as if it was his fault. Various people helped Catherine to a chair, fetched water, pushed her head between her knees.

'Quite possibly,' he said. 'I worry about her a lot.'

'Look, I'll take her home,' said Lucinda. 'I'm actually very tired – no, really Simon, I am, ask Blue. Didn't I just say I was tired, Blue?'

'Yes, you did.'

'And Blue's got to stay and take his clients out to dinner,' said Lucinda. 'But I was never going to do that anyway, being . . . well, you know.'

'She's in the family way,' said Blue, and the infinite pride with which he spoke was hugely touching; Elizabeth felt like hugging him. Simon, she noticed, looked slightly shocked at this; she'd been watching him drooling over the delicious Lucinda. Obviously he hadn't realised. God, men were stupid.

'Yes, and I'm not supposed to get too tired. So why don't I take the car and drop Catherine off? Blue, you can go up to Town with someone else, can't you?'

'Oh no,' said Catherine, who was so embarrassed at having let Simon down as she saw it, she felt she might faint again. 'There's no need, honestly.'

'It's quite all right,' said Lucinda, 'it's a big car. You can lie down in the back, if you like. Blue, darling, I'll see you later. Try not to get too drunk. Come on, Catherine. Now, are you sure you're all right to walk to the car park?'

'I think I'll come with you,' said Blue. 'Make sure you're OK. Everything's breaking up now, anyway, and—'

'I can't let you change your arrangements just for me,' said Catherine feebly.

'You won't be. We're having dinner in the West End, at Langan's. I'll meet up with everyone there.'

'Well, if you're really sure, it's terribly kind.'

'We're really sure,' said Lucinda.

'Lovely, isn't she?' said Blue to the room in general, watching Lucinda as she helped Catherine into her jacket. 'Heart of gold too. Can't believe she's mine.'

Even from a man with at least two bottles of champagne inside him, it was a very touching tribute.

The box emptied quite quickly after that. Joel, realising with a certain amount of selfish irritation that he had missed his chance to talk to Catherine Morgan, went first, and the others followed. It had been, they all agreed, a wonderfully successful day.

But when Catherine, Lucinda and Blue reached Fulham, they found Mrs Lennox and Caroline both white-faced and fighting down hysteria. Freddie had disappeared.

355

Chapter 23

June, 1990

It was when the policeman asked Catherine whether Freddie was a trusting sort of child that she became visibly frightened. Until then, she had forced back the tears and remained calm, for Caroline's sake as much as anything: Caroline, who had sat wide-eyed and white-faced, utterly silent while Mary Lennox choked out her story; while her mother questioned her as to what they had been doing, where they had been last time she had seen Freddie; while the school was rung, neighbours contacted; while Blue knocked on door after door in the area, asking if anyone had seen him, if they could look around their gardens, their garages, their houses, in the absolutely unlikely event of Freddie hiding there; Caroline, who shook with terror when the police arrived, who clung to her mother's hand as if it was a lifeline as they asked her when she had last seen her brother; Caroline, who started to weep when Catherine produced a picture of him for the police.

But at that question, with all its sinister, scarcely-hidden agenda, Catherine cracked and began to sob, quite loudly, cradling Caroline in her arms, and the sturdily kind police-woman who had been standing until then, simply observing the scene, signalled a pause in the questioning and ordered the young Constable, who looked hardly old enough to have left school himself, to go and make a nice big pot of tea.

'It's all right,' said Catherine, wiping her eyes. 'I'm sorry, of course you must go on. It doesn't matter about me, what matters is finding Freddie.'

They had been fantastic, the police, from the moment Blue had rung them. 'We're just wasting valuable time now,' he had said. 'Let's get the professionals in.'

The officers had arrived in ten minutes, four of them, calm and capable. Two were dispatched to do a proper, systematic search of all the houses in the area, while the questioning went on and on. How long had Catherine known Mary Lennox, who else did she know in the area . . . It was all very nicely done, very straightforward with no hint of reproach, but it inevitably made her feel irresponsible. They asked for a photograph; she gave them the one she carried with her in her bag, a school photograph of a smiling, pretty little boy; both Mary and Caroline confirmed that he had been wearing his school uniform when they had last seen him, that he hadn't changed into his jeans when he got home. That was when the police asked if he was trusting.

'Perhaps we could talk to you again, Mrs Lennox,' the officer in charge said. 'Will you tell us once more exactly what happened this afternoon, after you fetched Freddie from school.'

And she went through it again: how they had come into the flat, how she had given the children some milk and biscuits, and how, after they had done their homework, she had settled them down in front of the TV while she went to cook their tea. When it was ready, she had gone to fetch them and Caroline had been sitting there on her own, and had looked faintly surprised when Mary asked her where Freddie was.

'He went to the toilet and then he said he was going to find you.'

She had been too engrossed in *Home and Away* to help Mary look for Freddie; it was only when Mary went back again, 'And I was getting worried by then,' that Caroline said he was probably hiding in the garden next door, and ran round it several times calling him.

Mrs Lennox had then telephoned Lynton House, while knowing it was very unlikely that Freddie would have gone back there, and a friend of Catherine's whose number she had been given to use in 'a real emergency'. 'And then, I was just wondering if I should call the police, when Mrs Morgan arrived home with her friends here.'

Blue and Lucinda were now sitting drinking tea, determined not to leave until they felt that the situation had somehow been resolved.

Catherine was questioned repeatedly. Was Freddie happy at home, and at school? Did he have much freedom? Did he, for instance, go about on his own or was he always supervised? What did he like doing – what were his hobbies? Might he suddenly decide to go to the cinema? At this point Catherine cracked again. She shouted at the Sergeant that of course he wouldn't suddenly go to the cinema – what child would – and the officer said, very gently, that she'd be surprised what children did get up to on the spur of the moment, having gained a bit of freedom, and that it was his duty to uncover every possibility.

'Yes,' said Catherine, 'yes, of course, I'm sorry. But no, I don't think so. We never go to the cinema, he's not a cinema sort of child . . .'

'And – would he have had any money on him?'

'Well, I did give him a bit for today, just in case something happened, as an emergency, you know. Just a couple of pounds.'

'But he hadn't spent it? As far as you know, at any rate, Mrs Lennox, seeing as you picked him up from school.'

'No, no, he had no reason to, no opportunity,' said Mary Lennox. She seemed to have aged twenty years.

'That could be important,' said the policeman. 'If he's got a couple of quid, he could go on a bus or something,' and then everyone looked at Caroline as a sound escaped her that was a mixture of a whisper and a squeak.

'What, darling?' Catherine said sharply. 'What is it?' but she shook her head, scarlet in the face now, and looked at her mother out of eyes that were wide and terrified.

'What, Caroline? You have to tell us, come along, please, darling, it could be important.'

She was finally persuaded to leave the room and talk to her mother outside.

'Some boys took it,' she said. 'They took his money.'

'What boys?'

'From school.'

'I don't understand – do you mean his old school? Your school?'

Reluctantly, Caroline nodded.

'But when? How?'

It turned out that 'some horrible big boys', met Freddie every morning.

'They turn out his pockets and his school bag, take what they want. They say they'll beat him up if he tells.'

'Oh no!' Catherine thought of all the occasions when she had rebuked Freddie for losing things. 'Why didn't you tell me, Caroline, if he felt he couldn't?'

'They said they'd beat me up as well.'

'Oh, God.' She clutched Caroline to her, wondering how she would ever be able to let her out of her sight again, wondering how children could be capable of such things.

'Well, it's one good thing,' said the Police Sergeant, when she told him this. 'It means he didn't have any money after all, so he can't have gone far. Not under his own steam anyway.'

'No news yet,' said Lucinda the next morning, putting the phone down. 'Poor, poor Catherine. How on earth do you think she got through the night? And is there anything we can do for her?'

'Nothing,' Blue said. 'The police are doing what they can. Bloody impressive they are, I asked them on the QT what about perverts and that, and the Sergeant said they were already doing a search, any known ones in the area . . .'

'Blue, that's so horrible.'

'Yes, I know, but it's got to be faced.'

'I wonder if I should go over there or something –'

'No, don't,' he said. 'We're not family, we're not even close friends. We just happened to be there.'

'Yes, and it was so kind of you to stay, be so late for your dinner. She's lovely, Catherine, isn't she?'

'Yeah, she's OK. Poor cow. Just think about it – no husband, no money, hardly any friends, far as I can make out, those fuckers after her . . .'

'Blue . . .'

'Well, they are. I'm sorry. And now her kid's gone missing. Bloody awful. I hope those coppers question the other kids.'

'Yes, she said they were going to the school today.'

'Little buggers. God, children are evil. Poor little sod, being bullied on top of everything else.'

359

'Yes, I know. But at least he's back at his nice little school now; he must be all right there.'

'Lucinda,' said Blue, 'I despair of you sometimes. Do you really think nobody gets bullied at "nice little schools" as you call them? Children are savages, all of them, and being pushed into some poncey uniform and taught to speak nicely don't make no difference at all. Believe me. Luft went to one of those schools, got bullied so badly, and by his housemaster an' all, he says he'll never get over it.'

'Yes, I see,' said Lucinda meekly.

Alan Blake, the headmaster of St Joseph's Fulham, was just walking back into his office after taking Assembly when the police arrived. He said he would instigate an immediate enquiry: 'But I must say I think it's a bit unlikely. This is a church school, we have a very strong anti-bullying code here. And for boys to attack an ex-pupil – well, that's almost unthinkable.'

'Oh yes?' said Sergeant Lockyer. 'Well, that's very good to know. We'd still like to talk to the school. If you please.'

'Of course.'

'What was this boy like then, Freddie Morgan?'

'He was a nice enough lad. Very well-spoken. You'd have to talk to his form teacher, of course. I'll get her in.'

'His sister's still here, I understand.'

'Yes, she is. But too frightened herself to identify anyone. Ah, Mrs Shelton, this is Sergeant Lockyer. Terrible thing, Freddie Morgan – you remember him – he's disappeared.'

'Oh no!'

'Yes. Yesterday teatime. Anyway, the Sergeant wants to know a bit more about Freddie, how he got on here . . .'

'Well, all right, I suppose. Caroline settled much better than he did. He never really fitted in.'

'In what way?' Sergeant Lockyer asked.

'You could tell he'd been somewhere rather different. It wasn't just his accent – we have a lot of middle-class kids here – it was his attitude. He worked so hard, it was all he cared about. Never wanted to go out to play—'

'All bullied children dread playtime, Mrs Shelton.'

'Bullies? Oh, I don't think so, not here. We have a very strong anti-bullying policy—'

'Yes, so Mr Blake here was telling me. Just the same, a group of boys set about Freddie every morning, even after he'd left, took stuff out of his school bag. And while he was here he often came home a bit scuffed up and upset, apparently.'

'Well, that's not so unusual,' said Mrs Shelton. 'Boys will be boys, bit of rough and tumble's inevitable. Did he say that, though – about the boys taking his stuff?'

'No, he never spoke about it to anyone. His little sister told us. It was the first time his mother had heard of it.'

'Well, I'm very surprised,' said Mrs Shelton. 'Of course, taking him away when he was just beginning to settle in wasn't wise. I told his mother, but she seemed determined.'

'Right. Well, wise or not, she did it. Now, how shall we play this? Should I speak to the school, or will you?'

'I think it would be better if you did,' said Mr Blake.

'So do I. Good. As we'll be asking them to grass on their mates, basically.'

By the end of the morning, five boys had been grassed on, and were in Mr Blake's study.

Simon felt, absurdly he knew, guilty about Freddie. Catherine called him first thing to say she wouldn't be in and why. His motives in taking her to Ascot had not been entirely professional; there were several women in his department who could have filled the brief he had set her and would possibly have done it better, given Catherine's clumsiness. But they lacked her gentle charm, and besides, he rather liked his role as benefactor; enjoyed Catherine's gratitude, slight hero-worship. These days, when he spent much of his time feeling foolishly incompetent, it was all rather agreeable. And now that rather lofty gesture had gone horribly wrong. Her little boy was missing and all he could do was tell her to take all the time she needed, that if there was anything he could do, anything at all . . .

God, poor woman. What a nightmare. In fact, what a nightmare her whole life was. He phoned Elizabeth to tell her about Freddie; she was very upset.

'Simon, how dreadful. I'm so sorry. Poor, poor Catherine. I can't think of anything worse. I still dread it daily, you know – something happening to one of the children. So much more terrible than it being us.'

361

'It rather puts everything into perspective, doesn't it? Which reminds me – I'm asking a couple of agents to come and have a look at the house. Value it, you know. Hope that's all right.'

'Yes, of course,' said Elizabeth.

'Good. Thanks. I know – well, I know how much you mind.'

'Oh, I know you do. And it's all right.' She was so much happier suddenly, so astonished by the way they seemed to have moved together again, that nothing seemed quite so serious. And certainly, compared to the loss of a small boy, the sale of a house, however beloved, could not seem remotely important.

'Now, I just got a call from the solicitor.'

'Oh yes?'

'She wants to have a meeting this Friday afternoon with the barrister. Flora will be coming. All right if I ask her to stay the night with us?'

'Of course,' Elizabeth said. 'It would be nice to spend a bit of time with her.'

'Good. Thank you.'

'No need to thank me. Oh, and Simon—'

'Yes?'

'Simon, lots of love.'

'And to you,' he said.

Catherine couldn't imagine wanting to live any longer, unless Freddie were found. Somehow, she felt oddly hopeless. There was something about this whole thing that forbade positive thinking. It was the way Freddie appeared to have vanished from the face of the earth, the way no one had even seen him walking along the road. Of course, all parents said their children would never go off with a stranger, would never go off on their own; but Freddie really wouldn't. Not the Freddie she knew, anyway. He was too responsible, too sweetly concerned for her, too understanding about their situation, to want to impose any further anxiety on her. He had once taken a two-pence piece from her purse without asking, when she sent him to the newsagent, to buy himself some liquorice shoelaces, and came back in an agony of guilt, promising to give his next week's pocket money to Childline. So sweet he should have thought of that charity, it wasn't as if – Catherine suddenly felt her brain jerk into violent, feverish action. Childline. Had Freddie ever . . .

She called Caroline, who was watching television in a sort of stupor, clutching the collection of rather grubby My Little Ponies that Catherine had found for her at the charity shop.

'Caroline, darling. This is very, very important. You've got to tell me, just like you told me about those boys: did Freddie ever – ever phone Childline?'

'Um – is Joel Strickland in today?' Debbie tried to sound casual. Really, really casual. As you would if you were in a newspaper office, doing your job, and had a friend who worked there.

'Not sure.' Nicky Holt, Assistant Fashion and Beauty Editor of the *News*, looked at her coolly. Debbie had come in to tell her about the new body range with built-in deodorant that one of their clients was launching, and Nicky had clearly been underwhelmed by it. 'He a friend of yours?'

'Sort of – yes.'

'Well, want to go along to his office? He might be there. Keeps funny hours, our Joel.'

'Oh, OK.' She was beginning to regret ever mentioning him. He probably wouldn't remember her properly if he was there, and then she'd look really stupid. He and Nicky could have a giggle about it and he'd say, 'Yeah, she's a bit of a loser as far as I can make out – typical PR.'

Debbie had been wondering if she should try to see him for the past three days, ever since she'd made the appointment with Nicky, and changed her mind hourly. And had finally thought, what had she got to lose – although she wasn't even sure why she was doing what must surely qualify as chasing him. She was married, for heaven's sake; she had three children; she wasn't exactly fancy-free, the girl about town he'd imagined. Only she'd managed to persuade herself that it wasn't chasing him, it was just being friendly. After all, he had said to come and say hello if she was in the office, and as Simon had said, he might be a very good contact one day. And if she hadn't tried to see him, and he'd seen her walking out, maybe even past his office, he might have thought that was odd and unfriendly of her.

'Know where his office is?' Nicky asked, and feeling even more stupid, she said no, she didn't.

Nicky gave her a funny look and said, 'Straight down through the News Room, turn left, first office on the right.'

'OK, thanks.'

She managed to find the office without asking anyone else, and peeped in; he wasn't there. It was an interesting office for a newspaper, quite different from the chaos of the Fashion and Beauty Department, with its heaped-up sweaters and shoes and rails of clothes and mountains of bags, and even from the din of the News Room, where everyone seemed to be shouting at everyone else, and phones rang endlessly. Joel's office was very neat, with a computer screen showing City prices, and stacks of files and framed copies of various successful stories he'd done on the wall, including one that simply said WIPE OUT, in enormous red letters on the front page from the Monday after the crash and the great storm of 87. She waited a moment or two in case he was with someone else and came back, but he didn't.

She left then, feeling this was a clear sign from Fate that she was never destined to meet him again. And really, what would be the point if she did?

Flora was quite upset when Simon told her about Freddie. She remembered Catherine and liked her.

'How ghastly. Has she told the police?'

'Oh God, yes. They've been fantastic, apparently; they're doing a search with dogs in the area even as we speak. They've just issued a press release and a photograph of the poor little bugger to all the papers. And they're preparing posters as well. Poor Catherine. It doesn't look good. I've never met him, and I hate to say this, but it sounds as if he's a natural for abduction – not very streetwise, pretty little chap from the photographs I've seen. God, Flora, as Elizabeth said, it does put things in perspective rather, doesn't it?'

'It does,' said Flora soberly. 'I'm so sorry. Please let me know if there's any news.'

'I will. Now the real reason I'm calling is that Fiona Broadhurst just phoned, says she's got a barrister for us. Wants us to meet him this Friday. I know it's short notice, but could you manage it?'

'Think so. I'll see if I can stay the night with Richard and Debbie.'

'Come to us, why don't you? Elizabeth would love to see you.'

'How kind. If you're sure. It will be quieter than their house.'

'Not necessarily, if Annabel's playing what goes for music. That's settled, then.'

Flora put the phone down and then decided she couldn't postpone any longer returning Colin Peterson's call. He had invited her to a concert in Cardiff Cathedral the following week. She would have loved to have gone, it was a glorious programme, but it really wasn't a good idea. He plainly admired her and he was too nice, too kind, to be given any kind of encouragement.

'Right then,' said Sergeant Lockyer, looking at the five boys: big, all of them, tough and aggressive, two of them quite spotty, grown out of their junior school and its gentle ways. 'Which of you shall I talk to first?'

It was the usual story: they hadn't meant any harm, Freddie should have been able to take a bit of teasing, they hadn't realised they were upsetting him. They displayed a degree of bravado at first, then crumbled when Lockyer said he was going to get their parents in.

That was when one of them, the biggest and spottiest, said, 'If you really want to know who else was upsetting him, you might try the other lot. Those poshoes up the road, the ones Freddie went running back to.'

The person Catherine spoke to at Childline was extremely nice. Extremely nice and extremely unhelpful.

There was no way, she said, she would ever divulge whether or not a child had phoned, or his possible whereabouts. The whole point about Childline was that it guaranteed the children confidentiality.

'They trust us totally, you see. We would never betray that trust.'

'Yes, but I'm his mother. And he's missing. And I know he's been phoning you. Surely you could make an exception.'

'I'm so sorry,' said the sympathetic, regretful voice. 'We really can't. And anyway, children very often give false names,

365

false addresses, false ages even. So the Freddie that you describe could well be absolutely unrecognisable to us.'

'But couldn't you just look at your records? Try? He might not have done that, probably wouldn't, in fact; he's not very – very worldly.'

'I can't, no. I'm sorry.'

'But—'

'And there is another thing, you see. I'm sure you are genuinely Freddie's mother and your motives are extremely good, but parents do also give false information, in order to gain access to their children.'

'I do assure you I am *not* giving you false information,' said Catherine. 'I'm simply asking for your help. The police . . .' she heard her voice tremble '. . . the police are looking for my little boy. Doesn't that make a difference? And— would you tell them?'

'No, I'm sorry, we wouldn't even do that. Unless they subpoenaed us, which to my knowledge has never happened. I can't stress enough how important confidentiality is to the children. If the police are looking for your little boy, then I'm sure they're doing everything possible. I'm so sorry.'

Catherine put the phone down and screamed aloud.

Chapter 24

The Lloyd's débâcle had many and far-reaching financial consequences. There was a very large number of bankruptcies. Financial instititions had to write off bad debts. The way part of the City at least operated, on the Old Boy network, was changed forever.

The guarantees which had been issued so freely by the clearing banks to Lloyd's were being called in. A great deal of money made its way into the Channel Islands and into numbered accounts in Switzerland. The smaller merchant banks saw a downturn in profits. A great many expensive and beautiful houses came onto the market. There was a considerable increase in work for lawyers specialising in finance.

But for a handful of people in those few days in June, the only thing of any importance to do with it at all – and there could be no doubt that it had a great deal to do with it – was the disappearance of one small boy, made so unhappy by the consequences of that débâcle that he had run away and was, quite possibly, in terrible danger.

Catherine wasn't sure what would be the worst of the things that might have happened to Freddie: she forced herself to face them one by one, feeling that since he might be enduring them, then so must she. Abduction, abuse, murder – each one worse than the last. She kept thinking of her son as she had last seen him, before she left for Ascot; he had been smiling, so cheerful – and so brave, as she now knew, having learned of the bullying. How could her beautiful, clever, courageous little boy have suffered this awful thing. How could the life she had made for him so carefully, filled with the things that she felt mattered, with books, with music, with friends, with fun – and they had managed to have fun, in spite of everything, the three of them – how could that life have turned so ugly, so treacherous?

And why had she not seen the dangers? Why had she not suspected them? How could she have not known he was so desperate that he had been driven to calling Childline? How blind, how insensitive, how incredibly selfish she must be! She should never have taken that job with Simon: never. It was too demanding, it had distracted her from her children and their concerns, beguiling her as it did with its interest, its glamour, with its proximity to . . . She should have stayed with the local estate agent, so that all her energy could still be invested in the proper place.

She worried too about Caroline, who had retreated into herself and was silent most of the time, clinging to her and crying if she tried to go out, begging to be allowed to sleep with her, refusing food except for the normally forbidden sweets and crisps. Of course she should have them, Catherine thought. What harm could they do? Far less harm indeed than the wholesome life she had tried to create for them.

She longed passionately for some family of her own to be with her, for a sister or even an aunt; she had very few friends in any case, had lost touch with the old ones, and the more recent ones were either still out in Hong Kong or ex-Hong Kong, and there was no one she felt sufficiently close to who might begin to understand how she felt. Her parents-in-law phoned once a day, and offered to come and see her, but she simply thanked them and told them, as politely as she could, to stay away. They were too far from being friends, from feeling like family; they would simply provide extra strain.

The police had been wonderful. There was someone called a Family Liaison Officer, a nice girl called Sheila who spent a lot of time sitting quietly in the house, reading or trying to talk to or play with Caroline, fielding phone calls, advising Catherine on what she said to the press, who were beginning to gather over the story.

'You might want to give the story to someone, but I wouldn't recommend it, not at this stage.'

'Give it to someone? Talk about Freddie being missing, you mean? Of course I wouldn't do that – why should I?'

'Good,' was all Sheila said.

As they moved into the third day, as the second ghastly night finally ended, Catherine began to lose hope. And running through her fear was an ongoing seething rage at Lloyd's. Whose fault she felt the whole thing undeniably was.

Sergeant Lockyer didn't like Donald Archer, the Head of Lynton House, where Freddie had been a pupil twice. If Alan Blake had been inclined to self-deception about his school, Donald Archer was rampantly complacent.

'I don't know where you got this story from, but it can't be correct. We simply don't tolerate bullying here,' he said, peering over his half-moon glasses at Lockyer. 'It just doesn't happen. It's one of the reasons for our success, why parents choose Lynton House above most of the other private schools in the neighbourhood. And our academic record, of course.'

Sergeant Lockyer said that he could appreciate that, but the story was undoubtedly true.

'We got it from a child at St Joseph's who has a brother here. It was confirmed by Freddie Morgan's younger sister. And I might add that the boy had been driven to calling Childline about it.'

Donald Archer looked very shocked. 'I don't know what to say,' he said finally.

'What I'd like you to say, and to Freddie's class initially, is that he has disappeared, possibly run away, that you have been informed of bullying by members of the school which could have been a factor, and it is essential that we are able to talk to those responsible.'

'I don't know that I could agree to that. I don't get the connection, to be frank with you.'

'Really? The bottom line of the connection, you might say, is that your boys would be treated as suspects.'

'What – in Freddie Morgan's disappearance? But that's absurd!'

'It might seem absurd to you, Mr Archer, but that is how we have to proceed with cases like this. So could you call them together as soon as possible. Oh, and please stress that covering up for friends and so on is not an option. This is a matter of life and death. Or,' he added, 'we could say it for you.'

As Alan Blake had done, Donald Archer said he thought that might be better.

Nigel was doing some fairly ugly calculations when Lucinda phoned. It was becoming perfectly clear that he was going to have to sell the farm – or most of it. And having done that, he would remain in desperate trouble. If he still owned it, he would have had to sell the house in Cadogan Square as well, just to have some money to live on: but that was in trust for Lucinda. For the time being. And anyway, what would he be able to buy? God, it was a mess. He felt as if he was being sucked down into a whirlpool of panic and fear, and slowly drowning.

How had this happened? How had his neatly structured life gone so dreadfully awry? All the rules he had grown up with, living within your means, paying your debts, treating people decently – none of them had any relevance to this hideous new world he had found himself in. He struggled to stay calm, but it was very difficult. Of course he took a salary from the family firm, but it was a pretty modest one really, and at the moment the firm was making no money whatsoever: indeed, he had an uneasy feeling it was running at something approaching a loss. He had a meeting with his accountant the following week . . . he was dreading it.

'Nigel, hello. It's me.'

'Oh – yes. Hello, Lucinda.' He wasn't sure he could bear to talk to her at the moment.

'How are you?'

'Bit worried, actually.'

'I'm sorry. What about?'

'Oh, nothing much. Just a few hundred thousand pounds to find, you know the sort of thing.' His voice sounded bitter even to himself.

'Well, that's exactly what I'm ringing about. My solicitor has written a brilliant letter and he's sending it to yours, OK?'

'Ye-es.'

'Stating what I – we – need.'

'Oh yes?'

'And you've got to stick to the plan, Nigel. No weakening. All right?'

370

He was silent. Then: 'Have – have you told your Mr Horton about this?'

'Of course I have. There is simply not a problem, he's perfectly happy with it.'

'Really? All of it? Even the . . . well, you know, the difficult part?'

'Well – yes. I mean, he's agreed in principle and honestly, the rest is just small print, isn't it?'

Nigel agreed it might be called that; while thinking that Horton was exactly the sort of person to read small print very carefully. And not be entirely pleased with what it said.

'So, just sit tight, all right? Everything's going to be absolutely fine.'

'Yes, all right,' he said. He was hating this whole thing, so deeply did it go against his instincts. Not that his instincts were doing him much good at the moment. Or would do, when he was living in a bedsit in Paddington or whatever . . .

'Good. Now Nigel, such awful news.'

'What?'

'Do you remember Catherine, Catherine Morgan? She was at that Lloyd's meeting, the first one that we went to, pretty girl. She spoke – she was the widow, with two young children. Had lived in Hong Kong.'

'Um – yes. Yes, I think so. What's happened to her?'

'It's not her, it's her little boy, Freddie. He's disappeared.'

'Disappeared? How terrible. Where?'

'Well, from his home in Fulham. He was with their babysitter, nice lady, I've met her. Anyway, it was the day before yesterday, after Ascot. He's just vanished. The police are involved and everything, but there's been no sign of him at all yet. I feel so desperately sorry for her and I just wish there was something I could do.'

'What a ghastly thing,' said Nigel.

'Isn't it? It's in some of the papers, and they've put out an appeal on the box as well. They keep saying foul play is not suspected, but you just think of these awful creatures about, and beautiful little boys like Freddie and . . . God, it's horrible.'

'It is,' said Nigel, 'totally horrible. I'm so sorry. If you're in touch with her, do please give her my – my sympathy, will you?'

'Yes, of course. I'd suggest you rang, but I suppose every

time the phone rings she thinks it might be news, so best not to really.'

'Yes. Probably. Anyway, I don't really know her at all and it's a very private situation, I'd have thought. Oh dear. What a rotten world.'

'Totally rotten,' said Lucinda.

Nigel had never known the joys and anguishes of parenthood, but suddenly even losing his farm didn't seem quite so important.

In a scene which Blue Horton would have delighted in playing before Lucinda, three boys from Lynton House had been brought to the Headmaster's study. ('Appalling,' Donald Archer said afterwards. 'Some of my brightest boys – scholarship to Winchester, one of them.')

One, the smallest, had owned up of his own volition, and then his best friend had sneaked (as he put it) on the other two.

'It was only teasing,' said the oldest boy defensively, 'that's all. We thought he could take it.'

'Evidently not. And what form did this teasing take, exactly?'

'Well . . .' The small one blushed violently. 'Well, it was mostly about – about money, actually.'

'Money?'

'Yes. Well, sort of. He had to leave Lynton, you know, because his mother couldn't pay the fees any more, and he went to the state school down the road.'

'And you teased him about that? Doesn't sound very amusing to me,' said Lockyer.

'No, no, of course not. We were jolly sorry for him, anyone would be. But then when he came back he was a bit – different. Sort of – boastful. Said his mother was working for a big banker chap in the City, that everything was all right now.'

'Oh yes?' God, children were complex creatures. 'So . . .' Lockyer turned to the biggest boy. 'Perhaps you could take up the story. What happened next?'

'Well, it was all a bit odd really. I mean, there obviously wasn't any money, he was still living in the same grotty little place and he didn't have much of the proper kit for anything and he couldn't come on the trip to France we were all going on.'

372

'So you teased him about that?'

'Well, we didn't exactly tease him.'

'Were you nice to him then?'

'Yes. Sort of.'

'You were nice to him. Funny he should have run away then. There must be a bit more to it than that.'

'There isn't. Honestly.'

'I fear we might have to involve your parents in this, if you can't cooperate a bit more. This is very, very important you know, it isn't some game.'

Silence.

Lockyer turned to Donald Archer. 'Perhaps you could call the boys' parents.'

'No, don't do that.' It was the third boy, the one who hadn't spoken yet. 'OK, we did rag him a bit, but it was his fault. We wouldn't have if he hadn't been so full of himself.'

'You ragged him, as you put it, about not having what the rest of you had got. I see. Anything else?'

'No, not really. Well, he was a bit of a goody-goody. Toadied up to the masters, that sort of thing. So – yes, there was that. And then he was always arriving at school without his packed lunch and stuff like that. He really was pretty hopeless.'

'Right.' Lockyer looked at Donald Archer then back at the boys. 'It didn't occur to you, obviously, that he'd been trying to tough it out, that he was ashamed of not having the proper kit as you call it, of having to leave for financial reasons?'

Silence.

'I'd have thought it would be better to try to help someone who was having problems, who was "pretty hopeless" as you put it, not . . . er . . . *rag* them. I'm sure your headmaster would agree with me.'

'Er, yes,' said Archer. 'Yes, absolutely. Those are the values we do encourage here. Naturally.'

'Well, that's good. I'm pleased to hear it. Anything else?'

'Not really. Except recently, he started saying he'd liked it at the state school, that the boys had been quite good eggs, that we were a load of snobs, sort of thing, so we said, "Bug off back there then".'

'I see,' said Lockyer.

They were silent.

'Did you know he was so desperate he was calling Childline?'

'Childline!'

'Yes, that's right.'

'Well, no,' said the biggest boy. 'Of course we didn't.'

'Well, I suppose that's something.' Another long silence, then, 'So do any of you have any idea at all where he might have gone? Know anyone he knew, either inside or outside school, that we should talk to?'

They all shook their heads; they looked very uncomfortable.

'This could be life or death, you know,' said Lockyer, repeating his threat of earlier.

'Honestly, sir,' said the biggest boy. 'Honestly, if we knew, we'd tell you.'

Reluctantly, Lockyer was forced to believe them.

Chapter 25

June, 1990

Simon sat staring at this person who quite literally held his fate in his hands and hoped Fiona Broadhurst knew what she was doing. He had not expected this tall, blond patrician, with that odd mixture of clipped and drawling accent that characterises the Old Etonian. He had somehow expected Fiona to produce something rather different, a bit of an oddball even, after all her protestations of wanting them all to work as a team and not regard the barrister as the member of some superior race. Lindsay-Cowan QC did not seem to him a team player at all, and if no one else was going to regard him as the member of a superior race, then that was how he regarded himself.

He smiled at them all, rather graciously, indicated to them to sit down on the shabby leather sofas that lined his chamber walls and asked them if they would like China or Indian tea. That settled, he spoke. And Simon immediately felt better.

'Right,' he said, 'now the first thing I want to say is that we may get these bastards and we may not, but if we don't I shall certainly enjoy trying. Although I can see it may be rather less enjoyable for you. Especially if we don't win. But if we do win, of course, we shall be making history. There are literally hundreds of these cases being prepared even as we speak. Or rather as *I* speak. I'm sure you are aware that seventy per cent of losses have fallen on thirty per cent of Names. I think those figures speak for themselves. They cannot be attributed to coincidence.'

He paused, looked round the room, pressed the fingertips of both hands together. He ought to be in an Ealing comedy, Simon thought; they'd never have needed an actor to play barristers or solicitors with him around.

'Now one of three things will happen. We will win outright.

Unlikely. We will lose. Very possibly. We shall get settlement. Moderately likely. Although not as likely as that we shall lose.'

'So what the hell are we here for?' said Meyer.

'We are here because we have a chance. Albeit a modest one. And we will at least tweak the tiger's tail. That will be very pleasant. They are not enjoying this, you know, the tigers. They have not experienced a total deficit as they are doing now, for twenty-one years. They have their backs to the wall. Unfortunately, they hold many of the cards. Strictly speaking, and within the letter of the law, they have right on their side. You underwrote the losses which they have sustained. You signed documents, you neglected to research the situation thoroughly, you were not, so far as I can see, very pro-active in taking out reinsurance. Not that it would have done you a great deal of good in certain cases. I understand Stop Loss policies are extremely costly and with a very large excess. And, of course, you took their money during the good years. Many people would say you have very little to complain about, that you are crying over some rather sour spilled milk.'

The group was silent. It was a bit like getting a wigging from the Headmaster, Simon thought. He looked rather nervously at Fiona Broadhurst; she was sitting, her hands folded demurely in her lap, carefully studying her shoes. Which were rather more racy than usual, he noticed distractedly. Higher of heel, and bright red. He liked them; they went rather well with her black suit. She was wearing a silk shirt of almost exactly the same colour. He felt intrigued by this rush into colour; hitherto she had been seen only in black, white and beige. Maybe she fancied Mr Lindsay-Cowan.

He saw Lindsay-Cowan looking at him, a slightly amused expression on his face, and wondered if his inattention had been noted, or interpreted as a fierce concentration on the matter in hand. He rather feared the former.

'Now, as I understand it, the main thrust of your quarrel with Members' Agents Jackson and Bond, or the Westfield Bradley Syndicates or possibly both – is that they were continuing to press people into Membership, people they well knew could not afford the massive risk they were being exposed to, and in the full knowledge of that exposure. That would be a strong case indeed if it could be proved, but I fear that would be extremely difficult. You would need witnesses from within the organisation, prepared to admit that this was the case, copies of incriminating documents, notes, and written accounts of conversations. All highly unlikely, I fear, although not impossible. I know that you also feel the undoubted existence of the so-called Baby Syndicates – these syndicates within syndicates – could be incriminating, if proven. Very tricky. You would need to produce a Members' Agent who would admit to it in court, or certainly in a sworn statement. Even more unlikely.'

'What about a tape-recorded statement?' said Simon.

'If they knew you were recording them, then yes. If not, then – no. But if you can persuade someone into talking, discussing their situation, it would be very valuable. A lot of the work, as Ms Broadhurst will have told you, is down to you. This is not a situation where you can wander off into the sunset and expect me to come up with the answers. I need help, suggestions, leads, witnesses. Ms Broadhurst will give you further guidance on the sort of thing I'm talking about, but basically your most useful function will be to get witness statements. Talk to everyone you can, in your syndicate, not just those of you involved in this case. Supposing a Name increased his Premium Income Limit at the year-end from £150,000 to £180,000, ask exactly why he did so, who he talked to, who encouraged him, ask for any relevant documents. We have a right to disclosure of all documents that touch and concern the case, and that touch and concern all the issues in the case. Both of our claim and whatever defence they put forward.'

Simon looked round the room. Everyone, even Flora, was staring at Lindsay-Cowan transfixed. Like a lot of frightened rabbits, we are, he thought, caught in his headlights; and found he didn't quite like it. They were the clients, they were paying the piper, and in this instance, it seemed, it was the piper calling the tune. Or was it? Was it simply Lindsay-Cowan's manner that was making him feel that?

He was grateful when Fiona Broadhurst asked if there were any questions and if not, she knew Mr Lindsay-Cowan had another appointment.

'I have a question,' said George Meyer. 'How accessible will you both be? Because I can see many occasions where one of us will want clarification on whether a line of enquiry we're pursuing might be relevant and indeed, the sort of thing Simon asked, whether tape-recorded conversations are admissible evidence. So how often and how easily can we contact you? I think that's very important.'

Fiona Broadhurst gave him one of her coolest looks, uncrossed her legs and then crossed them again – God, they were good legs, Simon thought, while trying not to think it – and said, 'I can't speak for Mr Lindsay-Cowan, but you may call me as often as you like. I would only remind you that any time spent on the case will cost money. It goes without saying that talking to my assistant will be more economical.'

'I have a very important question. What happens next?' asked Flora. 'I'm interested in timespan here. Are we talking about months, years, centuries . . .'

'Many months, certainly,' said Lindsay-Cowan. 'Let me outline the probable sequence of events. We issue and serve our writ and serve our Statement of Claim. We receive their Defence and if necessary, seek further clarification of the Defence by serving a Request for Further Particulars. We then have a pre-trial review at Court and receive a timetable. We prepare our list of documents and they do the same, and we then exchange Lists and call for copies of relevant documents, review these and prepare our witness statements. Experts will be instructed to review all this. My junior will be available to review everything and we will work together with Miss Broadhurst. That will take several months. After that, providing it is all satisfactory, we exchange with the other side: we get their witnesses, their documents, their experts' reports. They get ours.

'More time will pass. Finally, we'll decide to get on with it. We then have a pre-trial review, to fix a date for trial. Which will include the length of time we think we will need in court, depending upon the number of witnesses and documents. We agree some dates with the Court – what's called a window – for the trial, anything from three months to a year hence, and then we write to all the witnesses, find out which dates suit them best, which suit you, suit me. And we need a judge, of course; the dates need to take that into consideration. And then we'll be told we can have our trial in, let us say, nine months from then. So I would say, we're looking, at the very least, at two years from now.'

'Two years!' said George Meyer.

'Yes. Two years minimum.'

They looked at one another. It sounded a desperately long time. How could they all survive it?

'If you don't mind,' Lucinda said to Blue on the phone, 'I think I might go and visit Catherine this evening. I know she's not a close friend, but I can't bear to think what she's going through, and just having someone to talk to might help. It's three days now . . . Well, this is the third night. Although I'm sure she knows that.'

Catherine's ravaged face greeted her at the front door of the flat in Fulham.

'Hello, Lucinda,' she said, and her voice was heavy and lifeless.

'Hello. Can I come in?'

'Of course. Caroline's asleep, thank God. Being brave for her sake is the hardest thing of all.'

'Oh Catherine.' Lucinda put a tender arm round her shoulders. 'I'm so, so sorry.'

Catherine managed a half-smile. 'It just gets worse, you know? Every hour. I look back to when I first heard and it didn't seem quite so terrible then. I mean, it was terrible, of course, an awful shock, but there seemed . . . hope. Now that's gone. It's just completely – over.'

'You mustn't say that. It's not over.'

'It feels over. He feels over. I can't believe I ever had him with me, warm and alive and breathing, instead of – instead of . . .'

'Catherine, he's not dead. I'm sure he's not.'

'You're not sure,' Catherine started to shout. 'You're not sure about anything of the sort, so don't be so bloody stupid. If he was alive, someone would know; and if someone knows and hasn't said, it's because they're . . . they're . . . Oh my God, when I think of what might be happening to him, what might be being done to him, all these awful perverts about, hurting him, frightening him . . . oh God, Lucinda, I can't stand it, I

379

just can't stand it any longer. If it wasn't for Caroline I'd kill myself, I really would, it would be a relief.'

She dropped her head into her hands; she was shaking violently. Lucinda sat there, holding her, crying herself now, wondering what she could possibly say or do that might help.

'I'm sorry,' said Catherine, looking at her through watery eyes. 'Sorry, Lucinda. I shouldn't have shouted at you.'

'Don't be silly. If it helps, shout some more.'

'It doesn't. Nothing helps. It's literally unbearable, every minute worse than the last. Oh God, Lucinda, why did he do it? Why did he go? What did I do?'

'I'm sure you didn't do anything,' said Lucinda, stroking her hair, 'nothing at all.'

'I did, of course I did. I must have done, hurt him, or frightened him, or just . . . just . . . Oh Lucinda, when you have that little baby,' she nodded in the direction of Lucinda's stomach, 'just never let it out of your sight, never ever.'

It was absurd, this, Simon thought; here he was, acting like some sentimental girl, as if she was a person, a person with feelings, rather than a boat. It was just that, well, they were as one on the water, he and the *Lizzie*, taking on the sea and the wind, everything else wiped out in the glorious and absolute concentration of sailing. He could set out feeling wretched, anxious or tired, as he felt today after the gruelling interview with Lindsay-Cowan, and come back restored, exhilarated. Or he could set out feeling joyful, triumphant, or sweetly happy and return even more so. The *Lizzie* had no negative associations for him; even danger, even fear, became things to laugh at, to boast of when they had overcome them together; she was absolutely intrinsic to his happiness. And now she had to go. This was their last day together, he had found a buyer for her, she was to be taken off, away from him, she was about to become a memory. And even the famous Beaumont ability to be upbeat, positive about it, was being severely challenged.

It had been a very good evening with Flora; Elizabeth had made a huge effort with the food, having acquired some Welsh lamb, and although they ate in the kitchen, she had dressed up the table with candles and flowers. Simon had been very touched.

Flora had admired the house and sympathised with the prospect of having to part with it – 'Don't tell me about selling lovely houses; sometimes I wonder if I can bear it; sometimes I know I can't' – and they had sat up late, the three of them discussing the lawsuit.

Elizabeth had been clearly anxious, for Lindsay-Cowan QC, they warned her, had been far from positive; indeed, had implied at times that it would be little more than a display of legal gamesmanship that he was personally relishing. Only Flora, intrepid Flora, had been truly enthusiastic; Simon had a feeling this was partly down to her approval of Lindsay-Cowan's approach. He was exactly the sort of person Flora liked, Simon realised: upper-class, hugely articulate, tough-talking. He thought how much Debbie would loathe him for the very same reasons, or most of them: and in this case, inclined to Debbie's view.

'So, you're persuaded to go ahead, are you?' Elizabeth had said; and 'Not if you're unhappy about it,' Simon had replied, half-hoping she would say she was.

'No, no, I'm not really. It's obviously a big risk, but if you think we're in with a fighting chance . . .'

'Oh, no doubt about that, I'd say,' said Flora. 'And besides, as Meyer said at the first meeting, it could be argued this is a far better use for the money than filling Westfield Bradley's insatiable coffers. If we've got to go bust,' she added, holding out her glass to be refilled, 'let's do it in style.'

In a reckless surge of courage, Simon said, 'All right, he's got my vote. If that's really all right with you, darling,' and fetched a bottle of champagne to toast their success.

The talk turned to other things: to Tilly, to Boy, to Annabel, who arrived home, to poor Catherine and the missing Freddie; and then Flora said, 'If you'll excuse me, I shall go to bed. I've got to leave at about six, very busy day tomorrow. It's been wonderful, such a happy evening, thank you both so much.'

'Is this really all right?' Simon said to Elizabeth, and, 'Yes,' she said, 'I wouldn't stop you for the world. And perhaps you should tell Joel Strickland about it; it might add to his story.'

'Good thought. But I think I'd better ask the Headmistress's permission first. It might be against legal rules.'

'I can't wait to meet this person,' said Elizabeth. 'She sounds terrifying.'

'She is.'

Simon left London at the same time as Flora; the day was too lovely to lose and he wanted as long as possible with the *Lizzie*. As he walked down to the *Lizzie*'s moorings, looking up at the blue, mist-streaked sky, he heard his name.

'Simon! Hi. You going to France?'

It was a woman's voice. He turned.

'Felicity! Hello. Lovely to see you. That's my plan.'

'Me too. To Saint Valery. Let's meet there for lunch.'

'Great idea. Whoever's first, order the wine. See you there.'

Felicity Parker Jones. He had known her a long time, had sailed with her, raced with her even. She was the one person he might have wanted to be with that day: cool, unsentimental, brave herself. There would be no tedious questions, no sympathetic comments. But she would understand, she would know how he felt, and then see no need to express it. She was also extremely attractive: about Elizabeth's age, tall, slim, blonde, and very funny. That would help too.

He waved to her and jumped down into the *Lizzie*, feeling suddenly better.

Sergeant Lockyer was just putting the first spoonful of his wife's very good leek and potato soup into his mouth that lunchtime when the phone rang.

Mrs Lockyer answered it, then called him. 'John, quickly. It's about the little boy.'

He gulped down the soup, burning his tongue, and ran to the phone. 'Yes?'

'Sorry to bother you on your day off, Sergeant. Had a chap on the phone, wants to talk to you about the boy. Can you call him? Right away?'

'Yes, sure.' It was unlikely to be a paedophile; they didn't usually give their phone numbers. But nothing was certain in this business; indeed, that was the only certainty. Get on with it, Lockyer, stop philosophising.

'What'd he sound like?'

'Oh, you know, bit upmarket. Quite – anxious, I'd say.'

'Right. Could mean anything. Well, I'll give him a call.'

Catherine was trying to force herself out of the chair where she sat hour after hour, and get some kind of lunch organised for Caroline when the phone rang. She had long ceased to think any call could be good news; the best she could hope for was a kindly enquiry as to whether there was any news and that was almost unbearable.

'Hello,' she said dully, thinking, Please God don't let it be Mary Lennox; for the fourth time that day.

'Mrs Morgan? It's Sergeant Lockyer.'

Not Mary Lennox; not a kindly enquiry.

'Yes?' She could hear her own voice, torn with fear.

And then there seemed to be an interminable silence, while she waited for the news she knew had to come; that Freddie was dead.

And then: 'It's all right, Mrs Morgan. I've got Freddie here. He's alive and well.'

Never underestimate a child, thought Sergeant Lockyer, never. They are so much cleverer, and more capable, than adults give them credit for. He looked at the pair of them, one slightly wearier and scruffier than the other, both half-defiant, half-sheepishly relieved that they had been caught.

'Well well well,' he said. 'What a lot of trouble you've caused.'

Such a brilliant hiding-place: a poolhouse. Providing shelter, tap water, a toilet – most of the necessities of life, apart from food. And where, as long as the owners of the poolhouse and indeed the house, were not likely to be present for a few days, a small boy with a willing accomplice could be perfectly safe, and even comfortable. It explained quite a lot: explained how the small boy in question had managed to vanish into thin air for three days, how he hadn't been spotted anywhere, looking scruffy, buying food . . .

Indeed, had the weekend not arrived, and had the weather not been so beautiful, and the pool looked so inviting, he might well have remained undiscovered for a great deal longer.

*

'What you did was extremely stupid,' Lockyer said severely to the pair of them, to Freddie and his best friend from school, Dominic Mays, as they sat in the kitchen of the house in Chelsea, one of the very few in the area with its own poolhouse, waiting for Catherine to arrive. 'Extremely stupid. You've caused a great deal of anxiety, and a great deal of work; you've cost and arguably wasted a lot of police time, Freddie's mum has been off her head with worry— Ah, here she is now. Just saying how worried you've been, haven't you, Mrs Morgan?'

Catherine, gaunt and white-faced, accompanied by a wide-eyed Caroline, nodded feebly and sat down. Freddie stared at her across the room, smiling rather uncertainly. She stared back, unable even to smile, so violent were her emotions; it was all she could do simply to look at him, as she had not thought to do again, drinking him in, alive, safe, unmolested.

'Sorry,' he said. 'I'm very sorry. I thought—'

'You thought what, Freddie?'

'Oh, doesn't matter.' He still sounded odd, almost detached. Well, it wasn't so surprising.

'So what do you have to say for yourselves?' Paul Mays, Dominic's father, and in charge of him – together with the au pair – for a few days, while his ex-wife Denise went to Paris with her new boyfriend, looked only a little better than Catherine. Guilty conscience, thought Lockyer, and good reason; should have picked something up, surely. And then thought probably not, and went back to contemplating the cleverness of children. And the comparative foolishness of adults.

'We are very sorry,' said Dominic, 'but it seemed such a good idea to us. And Freddie was so miserable, weren't you, Fred? I just wanted to help.'

Freddie nodded silently.

'Dominic,' said Paul Mays, 'didn't you think for one moment that if it had been you, I would have been worried. Worried to death?'

'No,' said Dominic, with all the devastating honesty of childhood. 'I'd have thought you'd be glad to be able to stay at work a bit longer.' Denise Mays' expression at this point was an interesting mixture of amusement and contempt.

'And why didn't you come forward when the police asked?'

'They said Freddie had been badly teased and they wanted

384

to talk to anyone who might have been involved. I was being nice to him and I knew he was perfectly safe.'

Dominic was also at Lynton House; like Freddie he was unhappy there, but for different reasons. He was fat; he was being teased mercilessly, in fact, which was what had drawn him and Freddie together. He had begged to leave, but his parents, guiltily aware that he was eating himself out of his misery at the divorce, had told him that he should ignore the teasing, that his tormentors would get tired of it and find another victim. All the usual platitudes, in fact; the usual, easy platitudes.

He and Freddie had become close friends.

'He was really unhappy,' said Dominic, 'just like I was. And then one day he was crying, said he had to run away, it was the only thing to do, but he didn't know where he could go; had I got any ideas? I said he could stay in the poolhouse for a bit, at my dad's new house; no one would know, and he'd be really safe. Which he was. Anyway, how did you find out?'

'One of your classmates rang up this morning. Or rather, his father did. He'd had an idea Dominic might have been in cahoots with you, and he was right. Bit more sense than you two.'

'Well, words fail me,' said Denise Mays. It was clear they did nothing of the sort. 'I cannot believe, Paul, you could have been so unaware of what was going on, right under your nose. I shall think very hard about leaving Dominic in your care, in future. What on earth were you doing? Were you out? Did you go away? I mean, how could this have possibly happened?'

'I was working,' said Paul Mays, looking at her with intense dislike. 'Working late. Leaving early. This is what I do. As you may remember.'

'Unfortunately, yes. As for you, Dominic, how could you be so selfish, so absolutely stupid—'

'He's not,' said Freddie. 'He's a really, really good friend. And clever. It wasn't his idea, we worked it out together. Please don't be cross with him, it's not fair.'

'So, how did you get here? From home?' said Catherine. It was the first time she had spoken. 'It's quite a long way.'

'No, it isn't. I walked.'

'You walked!'

385

'Yes, I gave him a map,' said Dominic. 'It only took him about half an hour. And it was just lucky everything worked out, him being looked after by that lady, and Mum being away that week, and me being there with Dad.'

'Very lucky,' said Lockyer.

'It was all right at first, quite fun, specially before Dad came home; if the au pair was snogging her boyfriend we could even swim, or play table tennis and there was masses of food.'

'Oh Dominic,' said Paul Mays, and he buried his face in his hands.

'And how long did you think Freddie could stay there?' said Lockyer.

'Well, we weren't sure. It was going to be more difficult at the weekend, especially if Dad didn't work on Saturday.'

'Do you often work on Saturdays, Mr Mays?'

'Quite often, yes.'

'He's a workaholic,' said Denise Mays witheringly.

'And then Mrs Patton—'

'Who's Mrs Patton?'

'The housekeeper. She said she'd booked someone to clean out the poolhouse next week, ready for the summer holidays. So we weren't quite sure what to do next.'

'I see,' said Lockyer. 'Well, you know now. You, Dominic, you must never do anything like this again. And you, Freddie, you say sorry to your mum. You should both be very ashamed of yourselves. Very.'

They said they were. Very.

And eventually, Catherine and Caroline and Freddie were driven home again. The nightmare over.

For a while, at least.

Chapter 26

'I think,' the voice was even cooler than usual, 'you probably know the answer to that question.'

'No,' said Simon, 'I don't think I do.' He'd suddenly panicked about talking to Joel Strickland, thought he'd better check that it wasn't against the rules legally, before it was too late.

There was a silence; then she said, 'Clearly it would be much safer not to talk to the press at all. I have to warn you also that if you say too much, then you could compromise a settlement.'

'Yes, I see.'

'We could discuss the skilful use of publicity, if you like. But an out-and-out campaign on what might be called a shit or bust basis can sometimes be seen as desperation.'

Had she really said that? How extraordinary. How revealing. 'Yes, I see.'

There was a pause; then, her voice almost amused, she said, 'Of course, I could claim I had tried to hold you back, but had failed. Or we could say, in a without-prejudice meeting, that I feared you were about to go to the press.'

'Yes, I see,' he said again. He didn't really.

'In other words, I'd say carefully used publicity could be helpful. Recklessly used, less so. It's a fine line.'

God, they talked gobbledygook, these people. And got paid millions for it.

'But if you were playing with a completely straight bat, you would leave them out of it. The press, I mean.'

'I never was much good at cricket,' said Simon.

*

387

None of it had been quite how Catherine would have imagined, had she been brave enough to imagine it. There was no joyful, hugging, kissing reunion; no ebullient little boy hurling himself into her arms with cries of 'Mummy'.

Rather, a subdued small stranger, awkwardly polite, kissing her briefly, saying he was fine and sorry to have worried her and then – nothing. She didn't press him, thinking he had, after all, been under considerable strain, and that time would do its work. But when they had reached home and he had had some lunch – he was extremely hungry – and she had suggested a walk and he had refused it, and they had watched TV for a while and then she had suggested a game of Monopoly, his favourite, and he had refused that, she began to feel worried.

'How about going to the Pizza Express?' she said. 'For supper?'

An unimaginable treat. He shrugged. 'OK.'

'Yes, *please*,' said Caroline.

They ate their pizzas in a strained silence; in spite of herself, by the time they reached home again, a certain rage was building up. Surely he was old enough to realise what agony he had put her through, how much she must have worried, how terrifying it had been. An explanation would have done; but none was offered. When she tried to question him, he just shrugged and said nothing.

'He's being weird,' said Caroline, restored to complete normality with the blinding resilience of children. 'Can I go and play with Katy, Mummy?'

Catherine had managed to stay calm, to get him to have a bath; he was surprisingly dirty, considering he had spent four days virtually in a swimming pool. She offered to read to him – he still liked that even now, big boy that he was, liked the attention – to take them both to the zoo next day. But Freddie remained silent, uncommunicative, and had taken himself to bed early. When she looked in, terrified he would have run away again – would she ever get over that? – he was sucking his thumb as she had not seen him do for years, and fast asleep.

And by Monday, he was still not saying anything.

*

'Look, Nigel . . .' Douglas Wilson's voice was quite indignant.

'Yes?' Nigel braced himself, signalled to Lydia Newhouse to make some coffee. 'Strong,' he mouthed. He was going to need it. This was going to be a difficult conversation.

'I've had a letter from your wife's solicitor about the divorce. And I must say it's really rather extraordinary, what's being suggested by way of a settlement.'

'Oh, really?' Just keep calm, Nigel, try not to sound emotional.

'Well, yes. But he says that you and your wife have agreed to it, in broad terms. Is that right?'

'It is, yes.'

'I can see why she's agreed to it, but are you really happy with all of this? It's extraordinarily generous. You were only married for four years or so, she made virtually no financial contribution and you have no children.'

'I know all that, and yes, I'm perfectly happy. I . . .' He took a large mouthful of the coffee; it was wonderfully strong. He felt it steadying him. 'I want her to be well provided for.'

'The – the boyfriend chap – he's pretty well off, you know,' Wilson went on. 'I mean, those boys are rolling in it, the ones that survived the crash anyway. I see he lives in Limehouse . . .'

'Yes, that's right. Well, that's not an expensive area, is it?'

'Nigel, those particular houses are very expensive. Very expensive indeed. Nasty little boxes, but— look, my dear chap, she left you. With no provocation whatsoever, as far as I can make out. I mean, you were a most generous husband. I presume you weren't knocking her about—'

'Of course not!' said Nigel indignantly.

'Sorry, I have to ask. Or, forgive me, playing away.'

'Playing away?'

'Well yes. I mean, there was no question of – of any adultery on your part?'

'Absolutely not.'

'And as far as you were concerned, the marriage was perfectly happy.'

'Yes,' said Nigel, and his voice was very sad. 'As far as I was concerned, it was.'

'Then why this absurdly generous offer? I don't understand. You really don't have to do this.' Douglas Wilson sounded almost impatient. 'You don't have to give her anything like this. Certainly not the money in that trust fund and most certainly not the house. It's ridiculous.'

'It's not ridiculous. I want her to be well provided for.'

'But she *is* well provided for. Extremely so. And what's all this about the gallery in New York – is that right?'

'Oh yes. Absolutely right. Yes. She was very – very cut up about it. I'd like to make it up to her.'

'What – to the tune of a hundred thousand quid? It's sheer madness!'

'I – suppose you could say that, yes. But she might be a rich woman now in her own right, if it hadn't been for me – look at it that way.'

'Well, obviously you've thought about it all,' said Wilson, 'and it's your money. But I'm still not happy about it. I'm going to write to her solicitor as a matter of principle – with your agreement, that is – pointing out, as I said, that it was a short marriage, and she is now living with and is pregnant by, a wealthy lover. And I don't think she has any claim on the house at the very least. Certainly not its full value. And the cash settlement over the New York gallery is simply absurd.'

Nigel was silent.

'Look,' said Wilson, 'he's obviously a sharp little tyke, this solicitor – suggested by the boyfriend, I expect. He's probably told Lucinda he can get her anything she wants. And she's told him you're a soft touch. I don't think we should just lie down and take it.'

'But—'

'Trust me, please. I do know what I'm doing. A good divorce settlement is a compromise. I don't see much evidence of that on their side. In fact, none at all. So let's at least make a bit of an effort.'

'Yes, all right. If you think we should.'

'I do.'

Nigel put the phone down; he still didn't like this, one bit. It went against everything he saw as right. And he couldn't really believe they were going to get away with it. But – all the alternative routes seemed closed. And if it only saved Grandfather Cowper's cufflinks it would be better than nothing.

*

Catherine shrank back in horror. She felt physically sick. How could she have done that? When only two days earlier she had been praying as she had never prayed in her life before, for the safe return of her little boy. Offering God every kind of bargain. It wasn't easy, as she had very little to give up or away, but she managed a bit: she'd never work again, she'd never see Simon again, never even speak to him if he phoned, she'd give all her remaining clothes to charity, she'd spend all her spare time working with the homeless, she'd . . . anyway, God would have got the idea.

And now she had pulled this precious little creature up from the sofa where he was sitting silently staring into space, shrugging when she asked him if he'd like her to get him some of his favourite cereal, the frosted sort that she so totally disapproved of, and taken him by his shoulders and shaken him violently, screaming at him at the same time.

He had been terribly shocked; his huge blue eyes had got even wider, tears had filled them and he had gone first red and then a ghastly greenish-white; and then as she released him, saying, 'Freddie, Freddie, I'm so, so sorry, I love you so much, I'm sorry, I'm sorry, forgive me,' he had simply turned away from her and run into his bedroom. She heard something heavy, his bedside table perhaps, being dragged across the room and pushed against the door – there was no key in the lock – and then . . . silence. Total silence. No answer to her pleas to open the door, to her apologies, to her own sobs. Catherine ran into the bathroom and was violently sick.

Freddie stayed in his room all day; he emerged in the early evening, asked politely for a sandwich and said he was going to the lavatory and then went back in, pushing the bedside table against the door once more.

She didn't go to bed that night; she had slept in the chair, her torture chair in the sitting room, so that if Freddie did come out of his room, she would know.

As the early July dawn broke, she couldn't take it any longer. She knew he was awake, she'd heard him moving around. She knocked very gently on the door.

'Freddie! Darling, it's Mummy, please let me in.'

Silence.

'Freddie. Please. I so want to talk to you.'

Silence.

'And I'm so, so sorry about shaking you yesterday. I shall never forgive myself. Please let me in. Tell me what's wrong, I need to know, so I can try to put it right.'

Another shorter silence, then very reluctantly, 'OK.'

He opened the door and let her in; he was very pale and there were deep shadows under his eyes.

He looked at her very solemnly, didn't smile, didn't speak.

'Sweetie. Please.'

'What?'

'First of all, will you forgive me for yesterday.? I was – upset. I was very tired, from worrying about you and everything. It's no excuse, but I wanted so much to find out what was wrong, and to know how you were feeling. I love you so much, Freddie, you've got to believe me.'

He shrugged.

'Freddie! Don't you believe me? Surely you do. I love you and Caroline more than anything in the world. Well, I don't love anyone else, anyway, not since Daddy died.'

'Why do you want to get rid of us then?' he said, and with each word his voice got louder, until he was screaming, high spots of colour on his face, the eyes still huge and strained.

'What do you mean? Of course I don't want to get rid of you.'

'You do. You wish we weren't here. You said it yourself, I heard you. That's why I went – I thought it was what you wanted. I thought it would make things easier.'

'I don't understand,' said Catherine slowly, 'I really don't. Of course I didn't say that. I would never have said it. You and Caroline are the only things that make my life worthwhile. Honestly.'

'Well, I heard you. I heard you myself with my own ears. On the phone to someone.'

'Freddie, please tell me exactly what I said. I need to know.'

'I can't see the point,' he said sulkily. He was fiddling with his pyjama cord, pulling it apart at the end.

'Of course there's a point. I need to know what you heard. What I said.'

'You said, and I don't know who it was to, but I can remember the exact words, you said, "If it wasn't for the children, especially Freddie, I wouldn't mind. Without them, I could cope with it easily." Don't tell me that doesn't mean you wish we weren't here. I'm not that stupid.'

'Oh my darling,' said Catherine, and she was crying herself now. She picked up her son's hand and he pulled it away. 'I do remember now, I was talking to some old friend of Daddy's. I remember exactly. Of course I do. We were talking about, you know, this awful business that's taken all our money away—'

'Lloyd's?'

'Yes, Lloyd's. And – I did say that, and what I meant was that all I cared about was you two having to go through such a horrible time. I don't mind one bit. It's you who get the worst of it, having to keep changing schools and getting bullied and teased. I wish you'd told me about those boys, darling, the big ones on your way to school. Anyway, it's you two who can't go on school trips and who have the wrong games kit. I do have to worry about it all, of course, and I don't like living in this funny little flat, although I think we've been quite happy here at times. But it doesn't matter to me one bit. What matters to me is you being unhappy and not having all the things you should have, and having to look after Caroline for me if I'm late. Don't you see? Oh Freddie, you silly old thing. Is that why you went? Because you thought it was what I wanted?'

He nodded; his eyes fixed on her face as if he would never look away from it again.

'Oh darling. That's terribly, terribly sad. I'm so sorry you thought that. Because if it wasn't for you and Caroline, I would just ... well, I really wouldn't be able to bear it. Including being without Daddy. You're all I care about; and if you'd listened a bit longer to that conversation you'd have heard me say that too. Do you believe me?'

He sat still staring at her, and then gradually, very slowly, the stony little face softened; and he smiled, a small, quavery smile, and then he moved nearer her, and let her put her arm round him, and then suddenly, in a huge rush, he hurled himself at her, threw his arms round her neck, so tightly she could hardly breathe and said, his voice muffled against her, 'I love you, Mummy. I'm sorry you were worried. So sorry. I thought – I thought I was being helpful.'

He started to cry then; she felt his skinny little body heaving, felt his tears trickling down her neck, felt his breath warm as he sobbed, on and on, and she sat there stroking his hair, kissing his head, and thought of all the times she had thought she would never know any of this again, that she would never be able to hold him again, never comfort him again, never laugh with him again – and she felt so weak with the relief of having him close to her, safe and sweetly loving, that she began to cry again as well.

'Oh dear,' she said, after a bit, wiping her eyes on her sleeve, her nose on the back of her hand, 'what a silly old pair we are. Both crying when we're both happy.'

He pulled back from her then, looked at her, his face swollen and blotchy, his nose running and his hair all ruffled, and said with a gulp and an attempt at a smile, 'You look hideous, Mum.'

'Well, thanks a bunch. So do you. What about we go and make ourselves some porridge? And eat it in peace before Caroline wakes up and starts making a fuss about her lunchbox. Those horrid boys from Saint Joseph's didn't take your lunch, did they?'

'Sometimes. Threw it in the road.'

'Oh darling. If only you'd told me. You must have got very hungry.'

'Well, Dominic gave me some of his. Usually.'

'I think he could spare a bit of food,' said Catherine, laughing, 'but he seems a dear little boy. Why didn't you ever bring him home?'

'Well . . .' Freddie hesitated. 'There's not much to do here, is there? No garden, no toys. Sorry, Mummy, but it's true. You should see his bedroom – it's like a toyshop. Huge Scalextric, he's got his own telly, and his own computer, he can play games on it. And in the garden, he's got this massive climbing frame and treehouse and swing thing, and a sort of lookout up in the trees.'

'Oh dear,' Catherine sighed. 'I can see that's difficult. But he's not very happy, is he? Even with all that. His mum and dad getting divorced and everything.'

'Yes, I know. But I still feel . . . embarrassed.'

The adult word took her by surprise; she felt very shaken. 'I'm sure you do and I understand.'

'Do you?'

'I think so. But we can do things with Dominic – we can go to the park and the adventure playground, and we can play games with him, all of us, like Cluedo and Monopoly, I bet you he'd like that.'

He looked doubtful.

'You ask him. See what he says.'

'Well, I might.' He looked at her again, and then said simply, 'Sorry, Mum. Lots of sorries.'

'It's all right. I owe you lots of sorries too, I think. Now let's go and make that porridge.'

Annabel was so excited she could hardly breathe. In just three days' time she would be on the flight to Boston; Jamie was going to meet her at Logan Airport and take her into Boston by the water shuttle: 'It's the scenic route, really the best way into Boston for the first time.'

They were all so pleased she was coming, he said, and it sounded so wonderful, what had been arranged for her. Every day there was something special: a tour of Boston, a party so she could meet all Jamie's friends, a concert by the Boston Pops – 'they're amazing' – a shopping trip with his mother and sister – 'we have the equivalent of your Bond Street here'; and then for the second week, a trip down to Cape Cod to the family house there: 'It's by the ocean, you'll just love it'. She simply couldn't believe it was all happening and had feverish dreams every night about her flight being cancelled, arriving at Boston to find Jamie had gone away leaving only his mother to look after her, and losing all her luggage on the way to the airport and only having a pair of knickers and – rather strangely – a pair of wellington boots to see her through the entire fortnight.

Carol had done her hair beautifully, highlighted it and cut it just a bit, into really long layers; and Annabel had treated herself to a manicure and pedicure and a sunbed session. James was about to see the whole of her, and she didn't want his ardour dimmed by a lot of pallid skin.

She could hardly remember what he looked like now; she knew he had wonderful blue eyes and floppy blond hair and a really, really good mouth and that he was tall and quite athletic-looking – but not too much, no bulging muscles, thank God – but she couldn't quite remember how he smiled and what his eyes went like when he was gazing into hers, and all that sort of thing. She had bought a new camera, so that she could take thousands of photographs of him – she hadn't got a single one, it was pathetic – and a new Walkman. Her old one was really clapped out and a bit big; this one was much smaller and all silver, really stylish-looking. She didn't want Jamie thinking she was some kind of nerd.

Florian had been really sweet, teasing her a bit inevitably, singing 'The Battle Hymn of the Republic' very loudly whenever she came into the staff room; but also advising on the exact right length for her hair, and on her last day he gave her a present – an absolutely beautiful tortoiseshell and silver comb for her hair. 'Well, darling, we want you looking classy. I can't have you letting the salon down, and those scrunchy things you've taken to wearing are just too suburban for words.'

She was so touched, tears filled her eyes, but when she reached up to kiss him, he shied away like a nervous pony.

'Darling, don't, I'm trying to forget how extremely exciting you are. And no sex on the first night, remember.'

'Why on earth not?' she said, laughing.

'Oh, over-enthusiasm is just so common. His mother won't like it.'

'His mother won't know.'

'Don't bet on it. I know her type. She'll be listening, you mark my words, and examining the sheets in the morning.'

'Florian!' said Annabel. 'You are just so awful.' But she had been wondering about precisely what sleeping arrangements the daunting Mrs Cartwright might have made, and how easy it might be to breach them if they were unfriendly.

'Sweetie, it's true. She'll be less foxy after that. So – you just lie there, thinking of me, OK?'

'OK,' said Annabel.

Simon had called Joel Strickland and fixed to meet him for a drink in order to tell him about the lawsuit and why he thought it was important to go ahead. He found himself talking a lot about it, suddenly. He had kept fairly quiet about it before, fearing people would be embarrassed, bored, wouldn't know what to say. Now it seemed to him that everyone should know. Why he was doing this. What he was trying to put right. Why it was important. He talked to people in the office and over lunch, and he talked to his tennis and squash partners, and he talked to neighbours and friends, and he told Elizabeth to talk about it too. He would have told Annabel to talk about it if he had thought she would. He felt oddly exhilarated and liberated suddenly; it was an exciting prospect, revealing not only a great injustice but what he was going to help to do about it.

And on the very day he was going to meet Joel, it happened.

'Quick word, Simon,' the Chairman had said to him in the lift, as he came back from lunch – a ridiculously expensive lunch – and, 'Of course,' he had said, 'I'll be right up, give me five minutes,' and five minutes later exactly he had walked into the large, wood-panelled cliché of an office with its leather chairs and sofas and portraits of William Graburn and Theodore French; he was slightly surprised to see two of his fellow board members in the room, but presumably they were going to discuss some important deal. He smiled at them, said, 'Hi,' and they half-smiled back and said nothing. It was – slightly odd.

'Drink, Simon?' Dudley said, and he shook his head, saying, 'Got work to do' – and God, what he wouldn't have given for one just a very short while later, only it was too late then, far too late – and sat down comfortably in one of the leather chairs, smiling expectantly at the three of them, thinking that when Dudley had said whatever he wanted to say, then he must talk to them about Lloyd's too ... And Dudley did actually say, 'Tell me about this Lloyd's business,' and he had begun to tell him, said, yes, it wasn't very funny – in fact, it was perfectly awful, but he was pretty confident that he could survive at least another year, and he was going to law and—

'Yes, but what are your debts? That's what I'd like to know.'

'Oh, about ... about half a million,' Simon said, feeling just slightly less sure of himself.

'Half a million? You have personal debts of half a million?'

'Well, yes, give or take a few thousand.' He felt almost resentful at the over-serious tone Dudley was taking; the bank loaned millions every day, for God's sake, what was five hundred thousand here or there?

'And – do you have half a million pounds? That you can put your hands on?'

The other two seemed to be finding the carpet particularly interesting.

'Well, not precisely, no.' Why were his guts lurching in this unpleasant way? 'In fact, very reluctantly, I'm putting our house on the market. Although I've actually decided to take Lloyd's to court. With a few other like-minded people.'

'You're taking Lloyd's to court? Yes, I thought that was what you said.'

'I am, yes. Our solicitor thinks we have a case.'

'And – does this mean you won't be paying your debt to them?'

'Well, I suppose it does, yes. If we regard them as debts. Which actually we don't. We think they've acted fraudulently, and—'

'You consider Lloyd's have acted fraudulently?'

'Yes, we do. As a matter of fact.' He looked at Dudley; and at the others. They were all now fixed on him, he had their full attention.

Dudley sighed, then said, 'I see. I find that extraordinarily hard to believe.'

'I'm sure you do,' said Simon, trying to keep his voice light. 'We all did at first. But if you look at the facts – I could take you through them if you like . . .'

'I think not. Certainly not at present. You say others are taking this route?'

'Oh yes. There are scores of lawsuits being prepared. We're a small group, but growing in number as people gain confidence in what we feel certain is a case. And—'

'Simon.' Dudley was now studying the leather-bound blotter book in which his secretary presented letters for signature each day. 'Simon, I'm extremely sorry, but I simply cannot contemplate having one of our main board directors involved in litigation against Lloyd's. It's out of the question.'

There was a complete silence in the room. A pin dropping

would have been an appalling intrusion. Simon eased his collar slightly, discovered his forehead was inexplicably wet, pulled out his handerchief, and wiped it.

'Lloyd's is one of the prime institutions in the City of London. Many of our clients have connections with them; some are Managing Agents there.' He paused, then said, 'Tell me, if you met your debt this year, by selling your house, would you then be in the clear?'

'Well, of course not,' said Simon. It seemed incredible to him that Dudley should ask such a question, that he didn't understand. 'The whole point about the Lloyd's liability is that it's unlimited. It's there until death, quite literally, if you get involved with a long-tailed syndicate – that's one where claims may arise long after the period of cover has expired – and they can be coming after you for fifty years. It's hideous.'

'Nevertheless, you signed up to this arrangement, I imagine?'

'Well, of course I did. Yes. We all did.'

'Without a great deal of thought, it seems.'

'Perhaps not enough,' said Simon reluctantly.

'And there were good years, I believe. That lovely house of yours in Sussex, I seem to remember your telling me, had to go to Lloyd's.'

'Indeed. But—'

'So, let's just go over this again. You owe them half a million at the present time.'

'Yes. That's correct.'

'What about next year? What will you do then?'

'Well, as I say, I would hope we'd have won our lawsuit.'

One of the others cleared his throat then said, 'Leaving that aside for the moment, it does seem to us, Simon, that there's a possibility of serious financial embarrassment here.'

Looking back afterwards, he could define that as the moment when he stopped hoping. He knew what they were doing now; acting as a team.

'Really?' was all he said.

'Right,' said Dudley. 'Now, I've been looking – and I hope you'll forgive me – at your contract. There are some very clear references in that, as I'm sure you're aware, to your being subject to a bankruptcy order. Which seems to me a possibility.

Or that you are unable to compound with your creditors. Equally so. Or indeed that you are acting in a way that brings discredit to the bank. Any of those would necessarily result in your offering your resignation.'

Simon felt as if he was going to vomit. 'Surely nothing we've been discussing this afternoon would justify such a thing,' he said, struggling to keep his voice level and composed.

'But Simon, I'm afraid it would. Certainly taking legal action against Lloyd's would qualify. Your financial embarrassment likewise. And I'm sure you are aware of Clause Twelve, Point Three in the contract.'

'Not precisely, no.'

'Then I think I should read it to you.' He opened a drawer and pulled out a document. It had clearly been placed there for the purpose, for this moment. The whole thing was like a bad play. Or an episode in a soap. Dudley was reading aloud. ' "Nothing in these terms and conditions of employment shall prevent the Bank from terminating your employment without notice, or salary in lieu of notice in the event of gross misconduct" – well, of course, no one is suggesting that, Simon,' he gave him a sweaty smile, ' "or if you are subject to a bankruptcy order . . ." '

'But I'm not.'

'Well, I think we are agreed you are in grave danger of it. If I might continue: "or have a receiving order made against you." And then of course there is Clause Twelve, Point Seven, which states that the same conditions apply "if you conduct yourself in a manner prejudicial to the Bank".'

Simon was silent.

'Perhaps you have financial reserves?' said Dudley.

'No,' said Simon, 'of course I don't. Lloyd's have taken them all.'

'I see. Well, look, Simon, I'm sure we can work something out here. Dropping your lawsuit would be a start. I would like to suggest that the bank makes you some kind of loan—'

A lurch, of a more pleasant type. A hopeful lurch.

'But I'm afraid it would be absolutely out of the question. Completely against company rules. Perhaps you have sources who could do that for you personally?'

'I don't,' said Simon simply.

'Right. Pity.' Dudley paused, returned to the pen tray. 'Well – look. Give it some thought. I would hate to lose you, Simon. You've been a marvellous asset to the bank – and over many years.'

So marvellous, thought Simon, that you're going to drop me in the shit without more than a moment's consideration.

'But I'm sure you must see I can't fly in the face of bank regulations. It would simply be unfair to the other directors. Most unfair. Now look, I'm sorry, but it's getting late and I've actually got to see someone at four. Have to prepare for it. Thank you for your honesty, Simon, much appreciated. I'm sure we can work something out. Perhaps you could come back to me in, what shall we say – ten days? That seem fair to you?'

'Oh yes,' said Simon, 'after twenty-five years' service and bringing countless millions into your wretched coffers. Perfectly fair. I mean, if that's what the contract says, you must abide by it. Of course. Certainly not try to find a way of working round it. You bastard – you miserable, mean, cowardly bastard.'

Then he turned and walked out of the room, shutting the door very carefully after him.

Everything seemed very quiet; except for a heavy thudding noise. It took a while for him to realise it was his heart. He leaned against the wall for a moment and closed his eyes, then walked towards his office. He had been fired. Fired without warning, as if he was the meanest office boy. One of the most successful operators in the business, with millions entrusted to his care every day, he had been booted out, ignominiously, told he was no longer of any use, his nose rubbed in the dirt as he went. In response to a non-crime, a trumped-up felony. He felt at once outraged and completely vulnerable, and if he had been asked to say his name, or where he lived, he would have been hard-pressed to do so.

Until that moment, he realised, it had all been a bit unreal. Yes, the debts were frightful, yes, the family silver was going fast, yes, he felt in turn scared and stupid and remorseful; but somehow, for some reason, it hadn't properly hit him. There had been a screen of some kind, like those things they used at Covent Garden, a sort of mesh behind which you could see things taking place but which lacked clarity and reality. And he had been on one side of it, still in charge, smiling and talking and charming and reassuring other people; and the reality, the real ugliness had been on the other, unable to touch him. But now it had changed. The screen had lifted, everything was absolutely in focus; and he opened the window of his office, his office on the sixth floor, looking down at the street far below him, and seriously considered jumping out of it.

Chapter 27

June to July, 1990

Elizabeth went home unusually early. Simon had suggested they ate out – 'just supper at the Italian place, OK with you?' – and Annabel was waiting for her with what she called her trousseau, for her trip to Boston and Cape Cod.

'I want your approval, Mum. Tell me if it's right or not.' Which as compliments went from a sometimes stroppy teenager, was pretty fulsome.

'I do feel a bit as if I'm being checked over, like one of Tilly's horses, but it's still very exciting. And Jamie tells me in every letter he loves me, and can't wait to see me. Oh Mummy, I'm so happy!'

'And I'm so happy for you,' said Elizabeth, giving her a kiss. Annabel was a little young for what seemed like a pretty full-on commitment, but then she'd only been twenty herself, for God's sake, when she married Simon. And – well, that had worked out all right. On the whole.

'Want to come out to supper with Dad and me?' she said. 'Just down the road? He's promised to be early.'

'Oh – might be nice. Thanks.'

At eight o'clock, Elizabeth poured herself and Annabel a glass of wine. 'I thought we could have it with Daddy, but it's getting so late.'

At eight-thirty, Annabel said if her mother didn't mind, she'd make herself an omelette. 'I'm knackered and I've got an early start tomorrow. Sorry, Mum.'

At nine, seriously annoyed, Elizabeth heard a taxi pull up outside; heard Simon walking rather heavily up the steps and fumbling with the door key. He only fumbled when he was drunk. Elizabeth went out to the hall.

'You made it then?'

'What? What do you mean?' He was so drunk his words were slurring; that was very unlike him.

'I mean you invited me to have supper with you. Early, you said. It's a little late for an early supper, but maybe we could still go.'

'Oh God. God, I'm sorry, Elizabeth. I – well, I forgot.'

'Obviously. Annabel was going to join us, but she's given up now.'

'Well, we could go still. Only I'm a bit – bit tired. Could you wait while I have a quick shower?'

'Oh, all right. But make it quick. I'm very hungry. Could I ask where you've been?'

'Not now, Elizabeth. Give me five minutes.'

But after ten she went up and he was lying on the bed, half-asleep; wearing only his shirt and underpants. She shook him hard.

'Simon! For God's sake, what's the matter with you? Where have you been?'

'Oh, with Joel Strickland. Drinking.'

'I can see that. What on earth were you with him for? What's going on?'

There was a long silence, then: 'Talking to him.'

'About what?'

He sat up and swallowed hard, seemed to be trying to dredge up some courage from somewhere. Then he said, and his voice was odd, cracked, 'Well, I'd better tell you. Yes. Get it over with.'

'Get what over with?'

He sighed heavily. Then: 'I've been fired, Elizabeth. Fired from the bank. Sorry.'

And as she stood there, staring at him, he began to weep.

'I'm so, so sorry,' he kept saying, as she stood there, cradling his head against her breast, and 'No, no, don't even say it. You have nothing to be sorry for. It'll be all right, Simon – *we'll* be all right. I know we will.'

'No. I don't think we will. How can we be, when—'

'Simon, we'll be all right, I promise. The bastards, the filthy, sneaky bastards – How could they do that? It's unjust, immoral – you must sue them.'

'I can't do that,' he said. 'It's in my contract, clear as could be. They have a perfect right to sack me without notice. Under the circumstances.'

'After twenty-five years of service? Of loyal, brilliant service? Without a word of warning?'

'Oh yes. I've actually checked with the solicitors. Nothing I can do.'

'The shits,' she said. 'The filthy, fucking shits.'

She didn't often swear; he grinned at her suddenly.

'That's better,' she said.

He lay there, holding her, berating himself, going over and over the old ground: how could he have been so stupid, so blind, how could he have put them all at risk – 'and not just Lloyd's, that hotel business too. I deserve to be shot, Elizabeth. The bank's right to get rid of me – I couldn't run a market stall.'

'No, you probably couldn't,' she said, briefly amused by the concept, 'but I'll tell you what, Simon Beaumont, you'd have a jolly good stab at it, you wouldn't just give up. And you're not going to now, either. You must go ahead with this lawsuit—'

'No, no,' he said, 'I can't risk any more of our money.'

'Yes, you can,' said Elizabeth. 'I want you to. In fact, I insist you do. Mind you, I'm not sure what money you're risking, but . . .'

'Oh Elizabeth,' he said, reaching out, stroking her face, 'what would I do without you? And what did I do to deserve you?'

He left her after a while to go back to his study: 'I'm all right, you won't find me slumped over an empty bottle of paracetamol. But I've got work to do. And you need your beauty sleep.'

When she got up at six, to get her hair done before an appointment, she found him asleep in his dressing room; she left a note telling him to ring her when he woke, wishing desperately that she could stay. But she knew she couldn't; she was more use to him in the office.

Catherine was trying to get back to some semblance of normality – the flat was a complete mess – when the phone rang. She jumped, conditioned by the trauma of the previous few days to regard it still as an instrument of torture.

405

'Hello?' she said slightly doubtfully.

'Oh – is that Catherine Morgan?'

'Yes. Yes, it is.'

'Mrs Morgan, you probably won't even remember me, but my name is Nigel Cowper. We met at one of those dreadful Lloyd's meetings.'

'Of course I remember you.'

'Oh, you do? Well, I just rang to say how delighted I was that your little boy had been found. I'd heard about it from Lucinda, and I felt so sorry for you.'

'How very, very kind,' said Catherine. She felt deeply touched. She did indeed remember Nigel, but primarily because he had been with Lucinda. Her only clear recollection of him was of considerable height and a very sweet smile.

'I was tempted to phone before, but I thought every call would be a nightmare, and Lucinda kept me posted. And she rang me this morning to give me the good news. You must be so relieved.'

'I am, yes. Everyone's been so kind, I feel really touched. Thank you so much for ringing, Mr Cowper.'

'Oh, not at all. And do call me Nigel.'

'All right, but you must call me Catherine. Thank you, Nigel. And for ringing. It was terribly kind of you. I really appreciate it.'

'My pleasure. Well, goodbye, Catherine.'

'Goodbye.'

She sat staring at the phone for a moment, smiling and thinking again what a sweet man he was. She couldn't, if she was honest, see how Lucinda could possibly have left him for Blue. Of course, it was none of her business, but Nigel was clearly such a gentleman, so kind and courteous, and Blue was . . . well, very kind, but . . .

Joel had been very shaken by his evening with Simon. He sat in his office the next day, thinking about it, feeling depressed and impotent. He had seldom seen anyone in such patent distress. It was dreadful; Simon had sat there, emotionally naked, stripped of his confidence, his humour, his charm, talking intermittently and drinking endless brandy and sodas until Joel finally suggested it was time to leave, and poured him into a cab in the courtyard of the Savoy.

At first, he hadn't told him anything; he had come in looking ghastly, white and drawn, but clearly struggling to appear normal. Joel wondered what had happened – whether Elizabeth had left him, or Lloyd's had made a final, crucifying demand. Finally, Simon blurted it out, and in rather strange obtuse terms, of being given his cards and joining the dole queue, clearly unable to actually say it, what had happened, so that in the end Joel had to say it for him, simply to release him from embarrassment at least. 'Fired, do you mean?' he said. 'Simon, surely not. I'm so sorry.'

'Yup, that's about the size of it,' Simon said, 'for doing absolutely fucking nothing. What do you make of that, Strickland, eh? I didn't abscond with the company's money, I didn't upset any clients, I didn't give away any secrets, I didn't even fiddle my expenses. I just wanted a bit of justice for us all, you know. Tell a few home truths about those fuckers. It's not right, is it, not fair.' He lapsed into silence again, looked round, said, 'Christ, it's hot in here. I'm going to take my jacket off. Don't care if it is against the rules. All right with you, old chap?'

'Perfectly all right,' said Joel.

'Now, I want you to write about this, Joel. About this injustice. People ought to know. People *have* to know.'

'Sure. Of course.'

'It's just not fucking fair. Is it?'

'No, it isn't.'

'It's not right. This is not justice as we all know it.'

'No, it isn't.'

And then he looked at Joel and said, 'Christ, Joel, what am I going to do all day? Can you tell me that? Eh? Because no one else'll give me a job now.'

And that, Joel thought, as the cab pulled out of Savoy Court, was perhaps the worst thing for him of all.

He wondered if Debbie knew, whether she would want to know, and having decided she would, whether he should ring her and tell her. They seemed to be quite good friends, she and Simon, and it would be one call Simon wouldn't have to make. Unless he'd made it already. And – well, and it gave him an excuse to ring her.

There was clearly no theoretical point in that – she was married, she had children, he could hardly ask her out – but he couldn't quite put her out of his head. There was something about her that intrigued him. And, who was to say she was happily married; that she wasn't on the brink of divorce – no, that was ridiculous, Simon would have told him that – but certainly who was to say she wouldn't be up for a quick fling. She'd tried to see him the other day, Nicky Holt had told him, so the interest was obviously reciprocated. He might ask her out for a drink, at least; get to know her a bit better. No harm in that. And— 'Oh fuck it,' Joel said, and dialled her number.

She was very upset indeed to hear about Simon. 'That's dreadful, Joel. Awful. How could they do that? I mean, he's on the board and everything.'

'I'm afraid it's rather horribly easy for them. These contracts are very carefully worded. Apparently, their big worry was this lawsuit he's involved in. They say it could bring the bank into disrepute.'

'Into disrepute? That's complete rubbish. Oh, poor Simon. I'm so sorry. I just can't imagine him without that job. It's as much a part of him as the colour of his eyes. Or those perfect suits of his. D'you know what I mean?'

'Of course. Very well expressed. Well, I thought you'd want to know.'

'Yes. Thank you, Joel, for telling me. I might try and call him. I wonder if Flora's heard?'

'Is that your exotic mother-in-law? Debbie, do you think she'd talk to me, about this Lloyd's piece? Simon was going to ask her, but I can't really bother him now. He's already lined up some other poor sod to talk to me. And I feel more than ever now that I want to write it.'

'Well, she might. Do you want me to ask her?'

'It would be great if you could.'

'OK. I'll ask her and call you back.'

'So – that's the whole story,' said Flora. 'You can see why I'm feeling depressed.'

She was sitting in a restaurant in Cardiff with Colin Peterson, having agreed, very much against her better judgement, to go to the concert, and then to have dinner with him afterwards. And was surprised to find herself not only enjoying the experience, but telling him her troubles. Her financial troubles.

'I can indeed,' he said. 'I'm so sorry. And you say you have to give them this next sum of money pretty soon?'

'Yes, in theory. I believe they'll stretch it a bit, if you plead hardship. They're very gentlemanly, in their conduct.'

'I'm sure. I believe being gentlemanly has done them a great service.'

'Indeed. I remember William being very impressed by it, by the fact that they were such decent chaps, as he put it. Including his own cousin, who actually got him in. It's hard to believe, isn't it?'

'How did you feel about it, at the time?' asked Colin Peterson.

'Oh, I didn't feel anything much. William was an accountant, quite a successful one, I had complete faith in him. I would never have questioned that sort of decision anyway. It wasn't in my domain.' She laughed suddenly. 'That sounds terribly old-fashioned, doesn't it? But we had a very old-fashioned marriage. He had an extremely clear idea of what my boundaries were and I really didn't question it. He gave me an allowance for the housekeeping, and a second one for clothes, and that was that. I didn't have any money of my own, well, very little from my photography, and in an odd way very little status. But I didn't question that either.'

'But that's how it was then, wasn't it? My wife and I had very much that sort of marriage. I saw to the financial side of things, to earning the money, to sorting out things, major things, when we needed a new roof or a new car. She was concerned with the children, the housework and the cooking, schools, holidays. Arguably much more important, of course. It made life very simple, in retrospect. There was no overlap of tasks. Of course we discussed things, but we each knew where our priorities lay.'

'When – when did she die?' asked Flora.

'Oh, quite a long time ago now. Five years. I'm getting quite good at living on my own. Still don't like it, mind.'

'I do, you know,' said Flora, 'in a way. Of course I miss William dreadfully, every single day, but he was a bit of a –

fusspot. I have to admit I like being able to make decisions, act on them, and I'm pretty good at being on my own. I always was. I'm an only child.'

'But you were – happy? Oh, forgive me, I shouldn't have asked.'

'Not at all. Yes, we were perfectly happy. When he died, part of me did too. But I don't approve of people who give in. I'm a fighter. And I still have a great deal. My family, my work, living in that glorious place. Only . . .' and she heard her voice shake, suddenly, '. . . only I won't. Much longer.'

'No?'

'No. I'll have to sell it. And pretty soon. I don't know how I'm going to give them this next lot of money—'

'Could I be extremely ungentlemanly,' he said, 'and ask how much it is.'

'Two hundred and seventy-five thousand pounds,' she said, so quietly she could hardly hear it herself.

'I'm sorry? For an awful moment, I thought you said two hundred and seventy-five thousand.'

'I did. Yes. It's quite a lot, isn't it?'

He stared at her, clearly shocked. 'Quite a lot, yes.'

'And unless I sell the house, I can't pay it. Can't pay it if I do sell the house, but it'll help.'

'Have you tried discussing it with them?'

'Of course. And they're always very kind, very polite. Very gentlemanly. As I said. But they always finish by pointing out that I do owe it to them, that I signed the contract with them, that I have to pay that debt, just as I shared in the money in the good years. Oh God.' Horrified, she felt her eyes fill with tears; impatiently she brushed them away. 'Sorry.'

'Don't be silly. It's completely understandable. Er, forgive me, but do you really have no other assets?'

'Not now. Well, unless you count William's vintage Roller. Which is worth very little really. I've sold all my shares, a couple of paintings—'

'What about mortgaging the house?'

'Well, I had thought about that, but I can't service the loan. I have very little income left, now the shares have gone, just a bit of capital.'

'Sell some land?'

'Colin, land on Gower isn't worth much. It really isn't. I've only got about ten acres – that's not going to save me. And besides, if I still own the house, they can come after it. They say you don't have to sell your main residence, but obviously they can see if it's much too big for you. You can't say "Right, I've given you all I can" when you patently haven't. And every year the debt goes on, even though I've obviously resigned my Membership. You're never safe, you know. It's unlimited liability, that's the whole point.'

'Ghastly. It sounds quite criminal. But you know . . .' he hesitated, 'your land would be worth quite a lot, to someone like me.'

'No, it wouldn't. This is mostly greenbelt, not available for building on. The planners are incredibly strict – and thank God for it. I wouldn't see executive homes covering Gower, not for anything. Oh, I'm sorry, that must sound very rude. I know that's what you do . . .'

'Now I did tell you,' he said, 'at our first meeting, that I wouldn't want to build on Gower. I think it would be a crime. But if you have to sell your beautiful house anyway . . .'

'Yes, I know, I know. But at least if I can leave it intact, leave the land intact, I could look myself in the face.'

'And where would you live? If you had to sell?'

'Oh, I don't know,' she said wretchedly. 'This is where I come back to, day after day, night after night, the same place on the roundabout. I know that they'd probably take the proceeds of the house in settlement, if I really didn't have anything else, and leave me enough for some wretched little hole somewhere. They don't like seeing old ladies tipped destitute onto the street, it's bad for their image.'

'Is their image really of any concern to them?' he asked.

'Oh yes, I think so. It all comes back to being gentlemen, you see. It's very bad for business.'

'Obscene. And this wretched little hole you see yourself living in, would that be here? Would you stay in the area?'

'It would be very hard, to see the house lived in by someone else, my land belonging to someone else. But I can't see myself anywhere else. I don't really like anywhere else. I love the sea, I love the moors and the cliffs and the Gower skies, it's all a part of me. But you know, something's happened just these last few days that's changed the way I see things. Made even losing my house seem less important.'

She told him about Freddie; he seemed quite upset.

'How dreadful. And you know this girl?'

'Yes, I've met her. She's very sweet, but another victim – that's how it happened. She had to take the little boy away from his prep school, then he was being bullied . . .'

'Oh dear, how sad. I'm so sorry. But at least he's been found.'

'Yes. God knows what she's been through.'

'Indeed. Now . . .' He hesitated. 'Flora, will you allow me to put my mind to this for you? I'm quite financially ingenious, you know. I've had to be, doing what I do. I probably can't come up with anything, but – well, two heads are notoriously better than one. Now what about another glass of wine, or even a brandy? I imagine you as a brandy girl.'

'What about your driver? Won't he be getting tired?'

'I pay him to be tired, and he's a very patient fellow.'

She agreed to the brandy. He reached out an arm, beckoned to the waiter then asked her to excuse him while he went to see his driver. She studied him as he walked away; he really was not her sort of person. Everything about him was too perfect, his suit, his shoes, his haircut, even his almost-covered-up North Country accent. William would have been highly critical of him, they would have laughed at him together, agreed that he was not quite right, over-polished, over-careful, trying to be the country gentleman he so patently wasn't. And that would have been very mean of them, very unpleasant even, she thought, reflecting on his kindness that evening, his concern for her situation, his offer to help. And what was so marvellous about gentlemen after all? Hadn't they just agreed that Lloyd's was full of them?

Debbie was watching *Playschool* with Rachel, who had a stomach bug, when the phone rang. She ignored it; the answering machine could pick it up. Rachel was drowsy; if she dropped off now, it would do her so much good. And it was very unlikely to be important; Anna had called from the office only half an hour earlier to check on a few things and to tell her it was really quiet and that she should take the next day off, if Rachel still wasn't well. And anything else could certainly wait.

Rachel did go to sleep; Debbie eased her onto the sofa, fetched a pillow and a duvet and went to make herself a cup of coffee and to check the answering machine, to see who had called.

The voice was pleasant, with a Scottish burr, and asked for Richard. 'This is Morag Dunbar,' it said. 'I wonder if Mr Fielding could give me a call. Nothing very important, just to get a date in the diary for the next visit, and to say that the house is ready for inspection, if Mrs Fielding would like to come up with him. I think she'll be quite pleased with it.'

Chapter 28

July, 1990

She stood there, staring at the answering machine, feeling an odd mixture of hope and fear. Surely, surely it was impossible. Nothing could save them now, her or the house. But – she pressed the button, listened again.

'Flora, this is Colin Peterson. Look, I wonder if I might come and see you. I've done some thinking, as I promised, and I have had a bit of an idea. Give me a ring. Here's my home number.'

How sweet he was, she thought, and how rotten she had been, looking down – well not looking down exactly but – yes, Flora, looking down. Shame on you.

She picked up the phone and dialled the number: his answering machine cut in. Well, he'd be at work, of course. She left a message, thanking him for his kindness and asking him to ring her: 'Perhaps you'd like to come for kitchen supper one night next week. It all sounds very intriguing. I'll look forward to hearing from you.'

He rang her within the hour; they fixed a date for the following Monday.

'I won't say any more now, except that I think I just might be onto something,' he said.

'Joel, it's Debbie. Debbie Fielding.'

'Oh – hi. How are you?'

'Fine. Now, I haven't been able to get hold of Simon, but I did ring my mother-in-law for you. She's happy to talk. She didn't know about Simon, she was very upset.'

'I'm sure she was. Thanks, Debbie. That's really great.'

'Here's the number. She said to tell you evenings were best.'

'OK. Thanks very much. So – it's Mrs Flora Fielding, is that right?'

'That's right.' The mother of my husband, Debbie thought. My appallingly badly behaved, mean-spirited, devious husband. Who still doesn't know I know how devious he is.

Joel hesitated. Then he said, 'Debbie, I don't suppose you'd like to come for a drink one night?'

There was a very long silence; he could hear her considering his invitation, hear her being tempted by it – and then deciding against it.

'I'm sorry, Joel, it'd be great, but I really can't. Thanks just the same.'

An observer watching them put their phones down would have found it difficult to say who was the more regretful.

Richard had taken to eating his supper in complete silence. It would have been better, Debbie thought, if he'd looked at the paper or read a book, but he just sat there, refusing to meet her eyes, chewing – she really hadn't noticed before how thoroughly he chewed everything, since they had always talked a lot over meals; Flora, she supposed, would have insisted on it, saying it would help his digestion – and then saying, 'Thanks,' before taking his plate over to the dishwasher and rinsing it carefully, putting it in, and then walking out of the kitchen.

Every meal it annoyed her more; at first she had put up with it, thinking it wouldn't last, but this was the fourth day at least. Every day as she prepared the supper, she decided on a different tactic: she had tried reading, scribbling on a press release she was working on – that had really annoyed him, she could tell – had even tried to talk to him, eliciting only monosyllables in reply, and it went on, the silence, like some cold, impenetrable fog. Tonight she had decided not even to bother to cook; there was no point really. She gave the children their tea, ate some of it herself – fish fingers, she had forgotten how delicious they were with lots of tomato sauce – and when he came out of his study at half-past seven, their usual suppertime, she just looked at him disinterestedly and then back at the television. *EastEnders* was on; it had been one of her favourites, but Richard particularly hated it so she had given it up. Along with a lot of other minor pleasures.

'Are we not eating tonight?' he said, his voice very cold.

'I'm not,' she said, and smiled at him, knowing that would annoy him more, 'but you do go ahead.'

'Is it ready?'

'No, it's not. Sorry. I'm sure there's something in the freezer though. Have a look.'

She returned to Albert Square; she heard him moving swiftly across the room, didn't realise what he was doing until the television was switched off. She looked at him, quite shocked; he stared back at her, his face white with rage.

'How dare you behave like this?'

'Behave like what? I've been trying very hard, actually. Cooking your supper, ironing your shirts, all that crap. And checking you could cope with the kids the days I was working. I'm sick of sitting opposite you every night while you concentrate on not communicating with me. Oh, and chewing your food really carefully. I'm sure your mother would be proud of that.'

He waited, then he said, and he sounded very tired, 'We can't go on like this, it's ridiculous. I'm beginning to wonder if there isn't someone else in your life.'

She stared at him, her heart thudding violently. Had Flora – might Flora . . . no. Surely not. He would have reacted before this. Wouldn't he?'

'What an extraordinary thing to say.'

'It may be extraordinary but it's what I feel.'

'Well, you're mad. Completely mad. Of course there isn't.'

'Well, I have to take your word for it, I suppose.' He was silent, glaring at her; she gazed steadily back at him, feeling nonetheless a flush mounting.

'Anyway,' he said finally, 'we can't go on like this.'

'I quite agree.'

'So – what are you going to do about it?'

'I really think that's up to you, Richard – up to you to do something.'

'And I think rather differently. I didn't start all this – this miserable business,' he said. 'It's been you that's caused all the trouble.'

A small explosion took place somewhere; it manifested itself in a bright light flashing between Debbie's eyes, and a loud cracking sound in her ears. She contemplated – and it seemed quite a slow process, she could feel herself carefully considering each option – slapping his face, boxing his ears, kicking him in the crutch, even spitting at him. None of them seemed quite appropriate to the situation, offensive enough, hurtful enough. And then inspiration came.

'I do hope,' she said, and even managed to smile, a cool, polite smile, 'I do hope you've been in touch with Morag Dunbar. About the house, about our visit up there. It must be nearly a week since she called. It really does seem a bit rude to ignore her.'

She knew he'd got the message; she'd heard him checking it, listening to the machine when he got in.

There was a cliché of some sort about people freezing; she couldn't quite remember it. But she saw it then; saw Richard apparently cease even to breathe, saw his eyes fix on hers, every facial muscle motionless, saw one of his hands pause on its way to push back his hair the way he did when he was nervous or upset, one foot slightly behind the other. He looked like a shop-window dummy; absolutely absurd. She wanted to giggle.

A long, long time later he released a breath; then said, 'How do you know that?'

'Richard, I heard the message.'

'You mean she spoke to you?'

'Of course not. It was on the answering machine.'

'And you didn't tell me.'

'No, I didn't tell you. But I knew you'd got the message, I heard you listening to it.'

'And you still didn't say anything.'

'No, I didn't say anything. I can't think what I would have said. Actually.'

Another silence, then, 'That was a filthy thing to do. Keeping that to yourself. Filthy and devious.'

'Oh, really? Not as filthy and devious as telling me you'd turned the job down when you hadn't. Making me feel as bad as you knew how. I call *that* really filthy. Actually. So – have you been in touch with her, Richard, or have you not? I really would rather like to know. For obvious reasons. Arrangements and all that sort of thing.'

417

'Any arrangements I might make,' he said, 'certainly won't include you. Be quite sure of that, Debbie.'

Joel switched off his tape recorder feeling rather depressed. He knew he shouldn't feel like that, that his Lloyd's feature was shaping up at last, but Neil Lawrence's story had been truly dreadful. He'd lost everything, his house – well, two houses actually – his car, his job, and now his wife. Not surprising the poor sod had tried to kill himself.

That had been before the wife had gone – but she had, taking the children with her. Lawrence said it really seemed the only thing to do. 'Whatever way I turned, I came to the same dead end.'

That was a rather good phrase: he might even call the piece that. And what was it Simon had said? Oh yes, that it was 'an absolute scandal', the whole thing. He liked that too.

And then, Neil Lawrence said that he hadn't wanted to be rescued, that coming round had been one of the worst moments of his life. 'This was not a cry for help. It was an escape bid. OK, a cowardly one, but . . .'

His wife had called him a coward, apparently: that was one of her reasons for leaving him. Poor bugger. He was living in a bedsit in Camden Town now, on benefits of some kind or another.

'How did you get into it?' Joel said, calling the barman over to buy Lawrence another beer. He was downing them as if they were water and he was dying of thirst.

'It was a bloke I met playing tennis. At Queens, you know. God, I can't believe I could ever afford such nonsense. Nice chap, we played a few times, and then he asked if I'd ever considered becoming a Name. It was in the early eighties, money still growing on trees, we were all getting a bit reckless; you bought shares, they doubled in value overnight; you bought a house, it had put on twenty grand before the ink dried on your signature. It sounded like another good idea, and I was rather flattered, to tell you the truth. It was a bit like being asked to join the Reform, or Wentworth Golf Club.'

'And what was his name?'

'Allinson,' said Lawrence. 'Tim Allinson.'

'My God!' said Joel. 'Do you know, you are the second

person I've interviewed who's been led to the slaughter by that bugger.'

'I'm not surprised. It was a sort of job for him, as far as I can make out. I'd nail the bastard to a tree if I could get hold of him.'

'And have you tried? To get hold of him, not nail him to a tree?'

'I have, yes. I used to see him, in the early days. Since things went belly up, he appeared to move. Certainly changed his phone number. Funny, that.'

'Yeah. And didn't go to Queens any more?'

'He did not.'

'God, I'd like to track him down,' said Joel. 'Well, thanks so much, Neil. You've been terrifically helpful. And you don't mind my using all this?'

'God, no,' said Lawrence. 'What have I got to lose?'

That was what had depressed Joel. It was so patently true. He bought Lawrence another beer and left.

There he was. Standing leaning on the rail in Arrivals; then when he saw her, holding out his arms, and she left her trolley and just ran into them. And oh God, he was so gorgeous. So totally, unbelievably, wonderfully gorgeous. And so nice, such a gentleman. You forgot about gentlemen when you worked somewhere like Miki's.

'Hi,' he said, smiling at her, standing just slightly back, studying her.

'Hi, Jamie.' She smiled back, thinking how much she had missed him, how odd it was that he had become, so quickly, the most important person in her life.

'You look lovely,' he said.

'Thank you.'

He gave her a quick kiss. 'I can't believe you're here.'

'You can't? Neither can I!'

He retrieved the trolley, pushed it along with one hand, his other arm round her. 'We're not going on the water shuttle after all. It's a bit of a scrum when you get to the other side. You can see all that tomorrow. Dad's driver's here, he'll take us home.'

Annabel wouldn't really have minded if he'd said they had to walk. She was here. He was here. She wouldn't have minded anything.

Two hours later, she was beginning to mind just a bit. Everything was lovely, of course, but rather formal. The car was huge and the driver equally so, huge and very black; he took her luggage which looked almost non-existent in the vast boot – or rather trunk as he called it – of the car, and then settled into his seat and said, 'Straight home, Mr James?' His rearview mirror was vast too, and every time Annabel looked into it, he seemed to be watching her, so there wasn't the opportunity she had hoped for, for a good, ice-breaking snog. As it was, Jamie sat rather carefully away from her, although he did reach out after a bit to hold her hand. She saw the driver, whose name turned out to be Tony, watching this too.

The drive from the airport, which turned out to be on an island, wasn't exactly long, but it was very slow; the traffic was awful, 'Rush hour, I'm sorry,' said Jamie, adding that it was mostly awful all day long anyway. They hit the city at about five; Annabel was beginning to feel terribly tired – well, it was already around ten, London time by her calculation – and to her horror as she heard Jamie say, 'Here we are,' she realised she'd been asleep.

God, supposing she'd snored. Or dribbled.

'Sorry,' she said to Jamie, who just smiled and said, 'That's OK, you must be exhausted,' but he was so polite, he'd never have told her if she'd been doing anything disgusting. Or even unladylike.

The Cartwright house, which she stood blinking up at, hazy with sleep, was not in the least how she had expected. It was on a square that could easily have been in London, tall, perfectly proportioned, bow-fronted; it was beautiful. She said as much to Jamie; he smiled and said, 'We like it.' And his voice was filled with pride. 'And here's Mother. Mother, hello. She's arrived, safe and sound.'

'Annabel, my dear.' Mrs Cartwright was wearing immaculate white trousers and a blue and white striped shirt. She kissed Annabel – or rather, sent a kiss winging into the air somewhere past Annabel's head – and then stood back smiling at her. She had a particularly strange smile; Annabel had noticed it before in London. It was situated entirely in her mouth, revealing a row of perfect and very neat teeth, and made no connection with her eyes whatsoever. 'How wonderful to have you here. How was your flight?'

'Oh, fine, thank you. Yes. I'm a bit tired, but—'

'Of course you are. Come along in, let me show you straight up to your room. I expect you'd like a rest before dinner.'

Annabel followed her, feeling suddenly nervous.

Inside, the house was also strangely familiar: tall, graceful windows, elaborate fireplaces, flowers in huge vases on polished tables, wooden floors, beautiful oriental rugs. It was odd. For a wild moment Annabel wondered if she'd managed to leave England at all.

Her bedroom was charming: the wallpaper blue and white, with a pretty white fireplace and a white iron bedstead; the carpet was pale blue, the curtains white muslin, the quilt pale blue. A bookshelf was filled with children's classics, *Little Women*, *What Katy Did*, *Anne of Green Gables*, *Alice in Wonderland*. A posy of blue and white flowers stood on the bedside table and two embroidered samplers hung on the wall on either side of the fireplace. It sent a very clear message. This is a young girl's room: no sharing.

'I do hope you'll be comfortable. Regard the bathroom next door as your own; towels in there for you. Is there anything you would like now, Annabel? A cold drink – I'm afraid it's awfully hot here – iced tea, or home-made lemonade?'

'Lemonade sounds lovely.'

'I'll send some up.' She made it sound as if the lemonade might ascend the stairs of its own volition. 'Now, do take your time, have a bath if you like, no hurry at all, drinks downstairs at six-thirty in the drawing room. All right?'

'Wonderful.'

'And just family supper, no need to dress up. Kathleen and Joe will be joining us and Bif and his wife Dana. They're all longing to meet you.'

'I'm longing to meet them too.'

Where was Jamie? Why wasn't he with her? Who had she come to visit? Something resembling ice-cold water seemed to be creeping slowly down her spine.

He was waiting for her in the hall when she came down; not sure what to wear for what Mrs Cartwright (who had now instructed her to call her Frances) called family supper, she had put on a flowered crêpe dress, mid-calf length, cut on the bias, with cap sleeves; it was what she called her tea-dance dress.

'You look lovely,' he said, and gave her a kiss – on the cheek.

She grabbed his hand. 'I want to be alone with you,' she hissed.

Jamie looked almost shocked. 'Not now. Maybe later. Now come into the drawing room . . . Annabel, this is Kathleen and her husband Joe.'

'Hello, Annabel,' Kathleen said. 'How wonderful to meet you.'

She was very pretty, with impeccably-styled blond hair exactly like her mother's and Jamie's blue eyes; she was wearing a red silk suit with wide shoulders and elbow-length sleeves, very high heels, and a heavy gilt link necklace, which seemed to Annabel much too old for her; but her smile was warm and friendly and she seemed very nice.

'Lovely to meet you too.'

'Hi, Annabel,' said Joe. He shook her hand; his was sweaty. She wasn't so sure about him. He looked just slightly sleazy. He was wearing a dark suit buttoned over a burgeoning stomach, and his dark hair was already receding. 'Welcome to Boston. You ever been before?'

'No. It seems lovely.'

'Glad you like it.'

'Duck Tour tomorrow,' said Jamie. 'First thing.'

'Oh no! Poor Annabel.'

A maid dressed in black with a white apron appeared with a tray of champagne glasses. This was ridiculous, Annabel thought. What family supper?

'Annabel, how lovely you look.' It was Frances Cartwright, dressed in a suit almost identical to Kathleen's, in brilliant peacock blue, the lacquered helmet of fair hair clearly re-glued for the occasion.

'Thank you.'

'I love that natural English style. Tell me, is that Laura Ashley?'

'No!' said Annabel, unable even to try to sound polite. 'Miss Selfridge.' Laura Ashley! As if she'd be seen dead in the stuff. Whatever would Florian have said?

'Now have you had some champagne?'

'Yes, thank you.' She had; half a glass already. It was cold and fizzily perfect and exactly what she needed. She had felt her spirits lift.

'Bif! I didn't hear you come in!'

'Sorry, Mother. Now you must be the delectable Annabel.'

She smiled at him. 'Hope so.'

He was exactly like Jamie, same colouring, same lovely smile, just slightly more heavily built. And more sensibly dressed certainly than Joe, in a linen suit and open-necked silk shirt.

'This is Dana, my wife.'

Dana was a Kathleen clone, only dark-haired; she too was wearing The Suit, in black, with a huge pearl choker.

'It's lovely to meet you,' she said, her smile much warmer than Frances's. 'I hope the flight was all right.'

'It was fine. Thank you.' She allowed the maid to refill her glass. She noticed that everyone else's was still full. Well, what the hell. She needed it.

'Daddy's going to be a little late,' said Frances Cartwright to Jamie, 'so we'll give him half an hour and then go in. Big deal going through, apparently. I'm so sorry, Annabel.'

'That's perfectly all right. Of course.'

'Don't ever get involved with a lawyer, Annabel,' said Bif. 'You'll never see him.'

If anyone else had said that, it would have been irritating, since she was here precisely because she was involved with a lawyer, but from him it seemed rather amusing.

'Fine, I never will,' she said. She smiled bravely round the room; she could see that Frances was not amused.

The maid brought a plate of canapés round; Annabel shook her head and drained her second glass, smiling hopefully at Jamie; he was looking at his mother, not her. The icy trickle started again. Why was she here? Why had she come?

By the time they sat down to dinner – without Mr Cartwright – the combination of an empty stomach, an eighteen-hour day and three glasses of champagne had made Annabel rather drunk. She had a little trouble even walking from the drawing room into the wood-panelled dining room, and sat down rather quickly on her chair. She was next to Jamie: that in itself seemed rather amazing, and Joe on her other side. She put her hand under the table and groped for Jamie's; it didn't come to meet hers. What was the matter with him?

'So, what do you do, Annabel?' asked Dana. 'Jamie said it was something rather glamorous.'

'I'm a hairdresser,' she said.

'A hairdresser!' said Frances Cartwright. Her tone outdid Lady Bracknell.

'Oh.' The silence was frozen: just for a moment. Then Dana rallied. 'What fun.'

'Yes, it is. And it's terribly hard work. And actually very creative. And what I want more than anything is to have my own salon.'

'Your own salon?' said Kathleen.

'Yes. It's the only way to get to the top. Which I certainly intend to.' There. That would show them. God, she felt drunk; eat some bread quickly, Annabel, for God's sake.

'And – where do you live?'

'Well, with my parents at the moment. In London.'

'Oh yes. And your father is a banker, I think Mother said.'

'Yes, he is.' No way was she going to tell them what had happened to him. 'And my mother is Managing Director of an advertising agency.' It seemed important she got that in quickly; she wanted them to know her mother was a person in her own right. It would tell them a lot about her family, a lot that she wanted them to kow.

'Oh really?' said Dana, her dark eyes thoughtful. She glanced quickly at Bif.

'How wonderful. She must be extremely clever.'

'Yes, she is. She's totally brilliant at it. And she worked so hard to get there.'

'And – how many of you are there?' asked Kathleen. 'Do you have brothers and sisters?'

'One of each. Both younger than me. Toby's fifteen and Tilly's thirteen.'

'Quite a young family, then. So, when did your mother return to work? Quite recently, I imagine.'

'She never stopped,' said Annabel firmly. 'We all grew up accepting that she worked. We liked it. It was just – how things were.'

'Good gracious, how impressive,' said Frances, making it clear that she found this totally unacceptable. 'I can never understand how women manage to work and care for their families. I certainly couldn't have done it. Jamie, dear, give Annabel some water. And some wine, of course.'

But water first, more important: she'd noticed. Oh God. Oh God. She wanted to go home. Or to bed. With Jamie.

The evening got worse. She managed to sober up a bit, but the meal was endless, four courses, and she felt very dazed. And it seemed terribly hot. She found it harder and harder to sound interesting or even remotely intelligent; glancing at her watch which was on English time, she saw that she'd been up nearly twenty-four hours. They must realise. How could they do this to her? How could they?

Mr Cartwright arrived home at ten, clearly in a bad temper; he came into the dining room, managed to smile at her and welcome her, and then told his wife to have dinner served in his study.

'I have to send some faxes, make some phone calls. Bif, you might come with me for a moment, just want to check a couple of details with you.'

Bif rose from the table at once, followed his father out of the room. Dana smiled at her mother-in-law.

'This one's been a brute, hasn't it?'

'A complete brute,' said Frances Cartwright. 'I'm so sorry, Annabel. This must seem rather rude.'

'No, no, not at all. But—'

'Now what plans do you have for tomorrow, Jamie?'

'Well, we're doing the Duck Tour in the morning, as I said.'

'The Duck Tour! Jamie, you can't take Annabel on that. It's appalling.' She said to Annabel, 'A trip round the town on some sort of old military tank and then it takes to the water. Terribly touristy and really rather vulgar – the guides are all out-of-work actors.'

'I think they're rather fun,' said Dana.

'It sounds like that to me,' said Annabel staunchly. She smiled at Jamie. He was looking at Frances.

'I really think she'll like it, Mother but if you—'

'Jamie, I want to go,' said Annabel firmly.

'Well, you'd better go then,' said Frances. She sounded almost cross. 'But don't say I didn't warn you.'

'I promise I won't,' said Annabel. At least she'd get Jamie to herself for a bit.

'And we'll want to be settled at the Hatch with our picnic by five,' said Kathleen. 'Don't you dare be late for that!'

'Of course not. It's the Fourth of July celebrations,' said Jamie to Annabel. 'I told you about it, it's absolutely wonderful – a concert by the Boston Pops and a huge firework display over the Charles River. We're all going – we take a picnic, sit on the grass and listen to the music. You'll love it.'

'I'm sure I will,' said Annabel. She felt like crying. All of them going. All of these awful people.

'Do have a truffle,' said Kathleen.

'Thank you.' It might help, the sugar, keep her awake. She ate two in swift succession. And then realised, to her horror, she was feeling increasingly nauseated. Really, really nauseated. And swimmy and sweaty and ... 'I'm sorry,' she said, pushing her chair back, standing up. 'Could you show me where the bathroom is, please, Jamie. I feel – I think—'

She rushed from the room, followed by Jamie; just reached the cloakroom in time, didn't even have time to shut the door . . .

Later, lying on her bed, being offered cold water by Jamie, feeling more wretched in every way than she could ever remember, some words of Florian's swam into her head.

'I hate being sick,' he'd said. 'It's so common.'

Common indeed; as was getting drunk, getting drunk in your new boyfriend's parents' house. How could she have done that? It was just that she'd felt so miserable and disappointed and nervous and— no excuse, Annabel, no excuse at all. What her mother would have thought, if she knew, she couldn't bear to imagine: although her father might have found it amongst other things mildly amusing, she decided, the Cartwrights

426

being exactly the sort of people he most disliked – and took just a little comfort from it.

'I'm so sorry, Jamie,' she said, pushing the water away, 'so terribly sorry. Whatever will they think of me?'

'I'm sure they'll simply feel very sympathetic,' he said. 'It was obviously something you ate on the plane.'

'Jamie, it wasn't. It was champagne and truffles, too much of both. Oh God, I'm so ashamed, I feel sick again just thinking about it.'

'Nonsense. Now I think you should try to get some sleep now; you'll feel much better in the morning.'

'I won't,' she said, realising things could hardly get worse, 'not unless we get to spend some time together, just the two of us. That's what I've come for, Jamie, to see you. Your family are lovely, but I kind of thought we'd be alone together this evening.' She patted the bed beside her. 'Come and lie down with me, Jamie, please.'

'Annabel, not here, not now.' He looked shocked and embarrassed in equal proportions. 'We can't – Mother's waiting to hear how you are; she's so worried about you.'

I bet she is, Annabel thought. 'Yes, all right, but please come back later.'

'Annabel, you don't understand. Their room is right along the corridor.'

What had Florian said? And why did she keep thinking of Florian, for goodness sake! *She'll be listening out for it. Inspecting the sheets.*

'Jamie,' she said, 'I don't get all this. What are we supposed to be, a pair of virgins, or something?'

'Well, no, of course not,' he said. He looked wretched. 'But you're a guest in their house; we have to observe their rules.'

A wave of rage swept over Annabel: rage and strength. She sat up suddenly. 'Well, I'm sorry,' she said, 'but if this is being a guest in their house, I really don't buy it. I didn't come all this way to be with your mother.'

'Annabel—'

She ignored him. 'Either we spend some time together, on our own, or I'm on the first plane back to London tomorrow, OK? Now if this room is along the corridor from your parents, where's yours?'

'On the next floor,' he said, still looking wretched.

'Right. Tell me exactly and I'll be up later. OK? I mean it, Jamie, this is horrible. I love you, I've missed you, please, please try to understand.'

'Well, I've missed you too,' he said, 'but—'

'But nothing. Look, all right. I'll stay here tonight' ('wait till the second night' – Florian again) 'I still feel a bit rough. But tomorrow – just you and me, all right? Except for this pop concert in the evening, maybe?'

'It's not a pop concert,' he said wearily.

'Well, whatever sort of concert. I want to go on this quack tour thing and I want to see the city and I want to be alone with you, preferably in a bed. God, Jamie, we're talking about loving each other, and we've never had sex; it's ridiculous. I mean don't you fancy me or something?'

'Yes, of course I do. But—'

'No buts. That's the deal. Gosh, I feel better already. Tell you what I'd love, do you have any Diet Coke?'

'I'm not sure,' he said.

'Well, go and check it out. Then I'll leave you in peace. Until tomorrow.'

He stood up, looking down at her.

'Go on. It's not a lot to ask.'

'I know. Sorry.' He looked more like a frightened little boy than a lover; Annabel felt violently impatient with him.

'It's all right. And you'd better bring me a bowl as well. I do feel better, but . . . it might happen again.'

When Jamie came back, bearing the bowl, but no Diet Coke, just a jug of iced water, she was fast asleep. He breathed a sigh of immense relief and tiptoed out, shutting the door behind him, smiling nervously at his mother who was hovering in the corridor.

'She's asleep,' he said. 'Good night, Mother.'

'Good night, Jamie. Sleep well. I do hope she'll be all right. Something she ate on the plane, no doubt.'

'No doubt.'

He was aware of her watching him as he walked towards the staircase and turned up it, out of sight; for the first time in his life it irritated him.

Chapter 29

It was very odd, Simon was discovering, not to be in the office every day. His life had revolved around it for almost thirty years; it had become, like all the best work situations, a second family, with its own customs and traditions, its own language and in-jokes, working its own inexorable timetable through the days and months and years. His staff had become his children – only rather more tolerant and polite – his office as personally designed and furnished as his own drawing room, and from it, from his career and its success, had sprung much of himself, his charm, his confidence, his capacity for hard work without appearing to be doing very much at all and his ongoing, unquestioning ambition. He had had dreams of becoming Chairman one day; at very least Managing Director, but he had awoken now to the harsh reality of, at very best, some non-executive directorships, and at worst the half-life of early retirement and some meaningless consultancies.

His career, he realised as he sat in his study at home those first few days, the study that had seemed so pleasant an alternative to the office and now appeared a solitary cell, was actually over. He would never again be at the heart of City life, never again have his advice seriously considered, or his opinion sought, never be quoted in the *Financial Times* or the Business sections, never be asked to chair this committee or that, to speak at dinners, to represent his firm at conferences.

The perks of his job – the first-class travel, the car, the driver, the easy acquisition of tables at fashionable restaurants, the best seats at theatres, the best view at sporting events, he could live without – although it would not be an easy adjustment. It was the other, much more important things, that his job gave him, that he would miss: the things that made it challenging, difficult, that pumped out the adrenalin and speeded up the clock, that created the sense of being not personally but professionally important: those were the things that he knew he would look back on and long for. For a few weeks, a couple of months at the most, people would make an effort, buy him lunch, talk vaguely of consultancies, and then they would, for the most part, fade into embarrassed invisibility. And he would be reduced to one of what he had labelled the 'when men', who sat in bars, looking increasingly shabby and out of place, talking to anyone who would listen, of when they had been important figures, movers and shakers, when they had worked for this bank or that institution, when they had sat on boards, when they had influenced the progress of companies, when they had made their clients rich.

Only – he wouldn't. He swore, that first day, that he wouldn't. He would walk away from it all, do something quite different, make his own, new way. It had been done before; other men had become bankrupt and gone on to make new fortunes, carve out new careers, and he could too. He could and he would. Only then, a few hours later, reality kicked in and he thought that those other men had not been pursued by a host of demons for money; he owed Lloyd's and would for the rest of his life. God, it was unfair, so dreadfully desperately unfair. All his life he had worked and fought and schemed and manoeuvred and been rewarded for it; and now nothing could ever see him rewarded, see him safe. And all he had done, to find himself in this helpless, hapless situation, was make one piece of fatally bad judgement, in the very best of faith. Other mistakes could be rectified, but not that one; and at the end of that first, awful day, he could see that the Simon Beaumont he had been, that he had wanted to be, might as well have died for all that his future could possibly offer.

'I've decided to bite the bullet,' said Catherine. 'In fact, I don't feel I have any choice any more.'

Blue and Lucinda had invited her and the children to tea; she had revealed that it was her birthday. Lucinda had gone to enormous trouble, ordered a cake from Fortnum's, made piles of smoked-salmon sandwiches and given her a pink cashmere sweater; and Blue, ordered to make the day nice for her, had decorated the front of the house with balloons and a banner that said *Happy Birthday Catherine* and bought musical candles for the cake. They all sang 'Happy Birthday' and Catherine was so touched she cried. Blue had then taken the children to see what would be the Marina, and Lucinda and Catherine were sitting in the kitchen, pretending not to be eating any more cake, while actually picking at it constantly.

'What bullet?' said Lucinda.

'I'm going to ask for help. From Frederick's parents.'

'I'm sorry to be dense,' said Lucinda. 'Who's Frederick?'

'My husband. Oh dear, I thought I'd told you his name. That's why Freddie's called Freddie.'

'But I thought they were vile. I thought you said you'd rather die than go to them?'

'I would, if it was just me. But I just feel I've reached the end of the line and even if I'd rather die, the children wouldn't. I'll almost certainly lose my job. Simon's secretary, who's never liked me, called on Friday and said he'd gone, and that Personnel or HR as we have to call them now—'

'What on earth does HR stand for? Sounds a bit royal.'

'Sadly not. Human Resources. Which is what we all are. Not employees, not people, but human resources. Anyway, they want to see me. Which means they're going to tell me to leave. I knew it would happen. I was very much in Simon's personal gift, so to speak. God, how can they be so stupid as to sack him? I feel like marching in and giving them a piece of my mind.'

'I'll come with you if you do,' said Lucinda. 'It's just the beastliest thing. And he was so brave, when I talked to him, saying what a good thing it was, that he needed a change before he got too old . . .'

'I know. All right, we'll go together. Anyway, I can't manage any more. I can't earn enough to pay Freddie's school fees, and I'm not having him going back to that terrible place, it's too cruel.'

'No, I can see that.'

'The worst aspect of this whole thing is that none of us have done anything wrong,' said Catherine. 'We're being punished just for trying to do the right thing for our families. We haven't stolen anything, or embezzled any funds, or – well, or done anything really. I was saying that only yesterday morning to Nigel.'

'To Nigel!'

'Yes. Oh gosh.' Catherine blushed suddenly, looked at Lucinda. 'I hope it's all right, talking about him and to him, and so on. I hope you don't mind.'

'Catherine, of course it's all right. Why ever shouldn't it be?'

'Well, I don't know. He was your husband and I know you're still friends . . .'

'Friends, yes. And he *was* my husband, but he's about not to be any more. Don't be silly. Where did you see him?'

'Well, we were in Peter Jones – you know, I've still got an account there, and I never use it and our bath towels are just threadbare, and I thought, Golly, why not. I can pay it off at five pounds a month for the next twenty years, so in we went and bought them, huge great fluffy things, so lovely, and then the children wanted to ride on the escalator and we were going up and he was coming down and – well, we all had coffee together. I was jolly surprised he remembered me actually, as we only met once.'

'Of course he would have remembered you,' said Lucinda.

'Well, anyway, I waved at him and – and well anyway like I said, we all had elevenses together. And a super chat. He was rather good with the children, kept asking them silly riddles and things. They thought he was wonderful.'

'He would so have loved children,' said Lucinda, rather sadly. 'But – well, I'm sure it's not too late.'

'I hope not. Anyway, that's what we were talking about, how blameless we'd all been and how this great thing had come along and knocked us right off our perches . . .'

'Exactly. Oh, I'm glad you had coffee with him, it would have cheered him up; he's awfully lonely, poor lamb.'

'Yes, it was fun. Anyway, back to my in-laws. I'm throwing myself on their mercy. And I can tell you, merciful is the opposite of what they are. They're really horrible, although they were very supportive and concerned, I must say, when Freddie was missing; kept ringing me and asking if there was anything they could do.'

'Well, they are his grandparents.'

'Yes, I know. But not exactly interested ones. Mind you,

432

they've only met the children twice, once before we went to Hong Kong when Caroline was just a baby, and once when we came home. Oh, and they flew out for Frederick's funeral, of course. Which must have been absolutely terrible for them, they were jolly brave then. But he's a bully and she's just totally mean-spirited. How they produced Frederick, I'll never know. But they have got lots of money and even if they'd see me starve – which they would, quite happily – they won't let that happen to the children.'

'But – what could they do for you?'

'Oh, they've told me before, when I first came home. They've got a huge house. Well, it seems huge to me. It's not specially nice, it's a sort of two-storeyed bungalow, a bit like South Fork in Dallas, you know?'

'Golly,' said Lucinda. 'Where is it?'

'In the depths of Somerset. Miles from anywhere. Anyway, they've offered to put me and the children up there until we get ourselves sorted out, goodness knows how I'm supposed to do that. I know it sounds kind, but I can tell you it will be dreadful. I'll be made to feel like Jane Eyre or something, completely the poor relation, and Mrs Morgan actually said I could claim benefits and give it to her in return for board and lodging.'

'What?'

'Yes, it's true. I tell you, they are not very nice. But Freddie and Caroline will both be secure, not latchkey kids living in a poky flat. Lots of fresh air, room to run about and play – so good for them, don't you think?' She smiled bravely at Lucinda.

'Well, yes, of course. But won't Freddie have to move schools again?' asked Lucinda. 'I thought—'

'Lucinda, I can't keep him at Lynton House. And he'll go somewhere similar. They'll be so much better off. And in due course, maybe I can get a job down there and even a place of our own again.'

'You're very brave, you know,' said Lucinda.

'Honestly, I'll be fine. I'm just dreading the crawling back to them, having to admit I couldn't manage after all. They'll be so horrible, and told you so-ish.'

'Of course, they wouldn't do something really helpful if they've got all that money and pay your debts? Or buy you a little house?'

'No, of course not,' said Catherine, and she looked genuinely shocked. 'They see it as absolutely my fault, signing all the money over to Lloyd's, and they really don't like me. They think their son should never have married me.'

'Then – sorry, but why do they want to have you living there?'

'Oh well, I think they enjoy the Lord and Lady Bountiful number. Their friends, who seem mostly as awful as they are, will think they're wonderful, and I probably won't even have to have meals with them, except at weekends. I'll eat in the kitchen with the children at teatime if I can.'

'It sounds absolutely dreadful,' said Lucinda. 'I'm so, so sorry. If we had our new house in Chislehurst or wherever it is we end up, you could come and be Jane Eyre there. Only of course you wouldn't be and anyway, we haven't. Oh Catherine, it's so unfair. All of it. You, Simon, Nigel, lovely Flora, all your lives just fractured into pieces and none of it even remotely your fault.'

'Well, it is a bit,' said Catherine. 'I shouldn't have been so gullible.'

'Catherine, for goodness sake. Stop being so totally ridiculous. Oh hello, Blue darling. Nice walk?'

'Yes, thanks. Your Freddie's very bright, Catherine, asking me about what I did – said it sounded like a game of poker. How does he know about poker?'

'Freddie!' said Catherine. 'That wasn't very polite.'

'Sorry. Daddy used to play sometimes, out in Hong Kong. He explained it to me a few times.'

'Perfectly polite,' said Blue. 'I'm impressed. It is exactly like poker, what I do. Well, almost exactly. He can come to me for a job any time.'

'You don't employ minors, I suppose?' said Catherine.

It was very clever, Colin's plan, Flora thought. And she could see it was just about feasible. It wouldn't exactly save the house for her – and certainly not her meadow – but it would leave her far from destitute, with Lloyd's neatly done down. She sat and smiled at him after he had finished.

'Thank you so much. I really do appreciate your devoting so much thought to my problems. I'm deeply touched. And I do see that it could work . . .'

'Almost undoubtedly it could,' he said. 'But – I sense a "but"?'

She nodded. 'Bit of a one. I hate to sound ungrateful, obviously. And I'd like to give your plan some careful consideration. It's just that it's not – not really me.'

'Flora! Nor would be sitting in a debtor's prison which was one of the other possibilities you mentioned.'

'No, I know. You're right. Or living in a small terrace house in Swansea. Look, let me have a think about it, would you? And then we can proceed to the next stage.'

'Of course.'

'And meanwhile, will you have some more cottage pie?'

'I certainly will. It's absolutely delicious. Is it made from saltmarsh lamb?'

'Is there any other sort?' said Flora, and smiled at him. 'Now – some more wine to go with it? I presume your driver's coming for you?'

'He is indeed. So – yes, please. And maybe we should change the subject. There's another lovely concert in Cardiff Cathedral in two weeks' time. Would you like to go?'

'I'd love to,' she said.

After he had gone, she went outside and sat on the stone garden bench with another cup of coffee. It was a beautiful night and the moonlight on the calm sea was almost daytime-brilliant. Owls hooted above her meadow and she heard the raucous cry of foxes in the fields. She put her cup down, walked to the gate of the meadow and, after hesitating for a moment, opened it and set off down the path to the sea, shining her big torch in front of her. A heavy scuffling fifty yards ahead of her startled her for a moment; then she smiled. She knew what it was. Mr Badger as William had called him – or to be precise Mr Badger's great-grandson's great-great-grandson – setting off across his run. He followed exactly the same route on his hunting expeditions, as all badgers do, and always used the same place, just above the ditch to relieve himself; his run was as clearly marked across the meadow as any manmade footpath. He froze briefly in the beam, then scuttled firmly across, his big, heavy body moving the grass on either side of him. She switched her torch off; the moonlight, brighter without it, shone down on what looked like scores of rabbits: good pickings for the foxes and their young families.

Some of the grasses and the cow parsley were almost waist-high at the moment; scenting the sweet darkness. If there was a heaven, she thought, it must be very like this. And if it wasn't, she didn't want to go there.

There was nowhere she could imagine loving like this: not even the wilds of the Scottish Highlands, or the rocky coast of the Algarve, both of which Colin had suggested as possible new homes for her. And – if she adopted his plan, would she not be betraying it, this place and its beauty? But then she would have to leave it anyway, and who knew what the new owner might do? And if she was far away, at least she wouldn't have to see it.

She stood for a while, looking at the sea, then turned and walked back up the meadow towards the house. The lovely grey stone house that had housed her husband's family for more than two centuries. Briskly unsentimental in most matters, Flora felt an almost human passion for the house. It was part of her, part of her bones, guardian of her memories, her griefs and her happinesses, witness to almost three-quarters of her life. Everything she cared about was held in those walls; leaving it would be like dying, having her heart removed from her. How was she going to bear it?

As she had borne other griefs and hurts, she supposed: William's death, the endless miscarriages she had suffered; because she was her, because she was strong. It was just that, faced with the loss of so much that she cared about, she didn't feel very strong at all. She was beginning, in fact, to feel rather feeble. Defeated, even ....

'Oh for heaven's sake, Flora Fielding,' she said aloud. 'Pull yourself together.'

And she went in and began to clear the kitchen table, while concentrating on what a surprisingly good – if unlikely – friend Colin Peterson was proving to be.

'Hello, Debbie.'

'Simon, hello. How lovely to hear from you.'

It was; it always was. She had grown so fond of him, and she'd been worrying about him, wanted to tell him she was thinking of him, not known how to contact him. Ringing him at home was clearly not an option. Elizabeth would certainly not have been pleased; and his mobile phone had been switched off, on the two occasions she had tried it.

'How's things?' he asked.

'Oh, you know. Much the same. How are they with you?'

'Oh, fine,' he said, and she could hear the effort in his voice. 'It's wonderful, not being chained to the office and the diary.'

'Yes, it must be. You've actually left, have you?'

'I certainly have. I never went back. I wasn't going to make extremely unequal bargains with them, just for the privilege of sitting at my desk for another couple of weeks. They've given me a bit of a handshake, nothing like I should get, but it'll help.'

'So what are you doing?'

'Oh, I'm very busy. At the moment. Truly. Loads of loose ends to tie up. House to sell, all that sort of thing.'

'Yes, I see. Well, is there anything I can do for you? Because—'

'No, no, not really. Just wanted to bring you up to date, see how you were, give you my home phone number – that is, not the family one, but my personal one. You never know – you might want to talk to me again.'

'Simon! I'll always want to talk to you, don't be silly. Look – can I buy you a drink? It's my turn. Then we can chat a bit more. And I promise I won't even mention my husband.'

'How sweet of you. I . . .' He hesitated. Then: 'Well, that would be very nice. Yes, thank you. Where would you like to meet? Your end of Town?'

'It would be easier. What about the Royal Garden again? I really liked it there and it suits me.'

'Fine. So – when and what time? Your call. I have all the time in the world.'

'How about Wednesday evening? That'd be good. Richard's taking the children to some film, as an end-of-term treat. They won't be home till eight at the earliest.'

'You're on. Wednesday, six-ish. Bless you, Debbie. I'll look forward to it. Bye, my love.'

It seemed ages since anyone had used a term of endearment to her; absurdly she felt her eyes filling with tears. Get a grip, Debbie, for God's sake!

The Fourth of July concert had actually been rather wonderful. Annabel had even managed to enjoy it in the presence of the Cartwright family in force. They were so proud of their city, so proud of the show it had put on, so genuinely anxious that she should enjoy it that she had felt almost ashamed of herself for her feelings about them twenty-four hours earlier. It had been a sort of cross between Glyndebourne and the Last Night of the Proms; they had sat on the grass by this thing called the Hatch Memorial Shell, which was a vast (and, she had secretly thought, rather vulgar) red and gold shell-shaped concert platform, and drunk champagne, being very careful of her consumption, and Frances Cartwright had produced a suitably grand picnic, and Dana and Bif had laughingly provided a silver candelabra, and they listened to the Boston Pops playing all sorts of familiar classics, including a Broadway medley, as they called it, from the big shows like *Les Misérables* and *Phantom of the Opera*, and a lot of rather rousing marches. The finale was the 1812 Overture; and then there was a spectacular and very long firework display, set off over the Charles River, lighting up the sky and the water. Annabel had always loved fireworks, they affected her emotionally, tended to make her cry; the whole family teased her about it. She sat there, on the grass, gazing at them, her head still filled with the music, and tears began to roll down her cheeks; it wasn't Jamie but Bif who noticed and nudged his younger brother as the last waterfall of stars fell slowly to earth.

'Annabel's crying – what have you done to her?'

'Nothing,' said Jamie indignantly, and put his arm round her shoulders. 'What is it? What's the matter?'

'Nothing,' she said. 'I always cry at fireworks, they make me feel so happy, and these are just so wonderful.'

Nothing could have endeared her to the Cartwrights more; they all laughed and made a great fuss of her and suddenly it was all right for Jamie to have his arm round her, she didn't feel they were at all disapproving, rather the reverse, and when they finally reached home, walking through the warm smiling crowds, greeted constantly by friends, she realised he had been holding her hand all the way.

*

438

Later, much, much later, as the household fell silent, she left her pretty, virginal room and crept up the stairs to his. 'This is as much a little boy's room as mine is a little girl's,' she hissed at him, and indeed it was; she had seen it earlier, a big rectangular room, with dark green curtains and cream walls, and bookshelves filled with things like *Huckleberry Finn* and *The Man in the Iron Mask*, and a fantastic display of lead soldiers on a large table, and an incredible train layout, with endless tunnels and signals and points – Toby would have loved it – and to bring it into the twentieth century, a computer, a fantastic music system, a television and a very sleek-looking video-player. But it was very much a bedroom with accessories, not a bedsitting room, as she had at home – there was no sofa, no coffee-table; clearly no question of him having any privacy. His life was lived with the family; it was as simple as that.

But they had privacy now; she abandoned her bathrobe onto the floor and slithered into bed beside him. She was naked, but he was wearing pyjamas.

'Jamie,' she said, 'take them off. At once. Let me help you.' She tugged at his trousers, giggling; and felt his erection. With a slug of pleasure and, if she was honest, a stab of relief. She had begun to wonder . . .

'And I don't want to hear even a syllable of any words like "mother" or "parents",' she said. 'Their light is out, and your dad's snoring, if that makes you feel any better. Oh Jamie, I do love you. I really, really do. And that was such a wonderful evening.'

He began to kiss her, sweetly and slowly; his hands moved on her, over her, a little hesitant, but then with more confidence. She felt the first real shoots of desire, began to squirm, to breathe more quickly; he stopped suddenly, moved away from her and said, 'Should I . . . that is, do you want me to . . .'

Briefly puzzled, then amused, she said, 'Jamie, I'm on the pill, don't worry. All I want is for you not to stop.'

'I won't,' he said. 'I can't.' And then he moved onto her, and into her, and began to move and she with him, and her memories of the evening, the music, the fireworks, the happiness all merged together with her body and his, and it wasn't just sex, it was absolute happiness and pleasure as she closed round him, and melted and sank and rose and climbed into the brightness, and finally came gloriously and triumph-antly, the pleasure as vivid, as violent, as piercing as the fireworks she had watched and wept at with him, what seemed like another lifetime ago, and, 'I love you,' he whispered as he came too and they lay there together as the pleasure slowly eased and ebbed away, and for the first time since she had arrived she felt properly happy.

If Frances Cartwright had heard them, or indeed inspected the sheets, as Florian had predicted, she gave no sign of it. She greeted Annabel at the breakfast table quite warmly, offered her hash browns and mushrooms and orange juice, and said she hoped she had slept well.

'Very well, thank you,' said Annabel. 'That was a wonderful, wonderful evening. Thank you so much. I shall never forget it.'

'Good. I'm so glad.' The smile came, the awful, chilling smile; how did she do that?

'And today we're going to just wander about,' said Jamie, who had come in, sitting down beside Annabel, 'take it easy. I thought this evening, Annabel and I would go out for supper on our own, if that's all right. We could go to Legal, the one down by the Aquarium.'

'Legal?' said Annabel.

'Yes, short for Legal Seafoods, probably the most famous seafood restaurant in the world.'

Not more than Wheelers, that's for sure, thought Annabel, but she smiled and said, 'How lovely.'

'What a good idea,' said Frances, 'and you know, Bif and Dana love it there, maybe they might join you,' and just as Annabel's heart was doing a combination of sinking and raging, Mr Cartwright – who had now instructed Annabel to call him Philip – said, 'Frances, leave them be. They want to be alone, for God's sake,' and she restrained herself with great difficulty from going over to him and kissing him.

The wandering about was actually much nicer than the Duck Tour, which wasn't ideal for someone with jet-lag and a still-delicate stomach. Of course, it had been quite fun chugging through the streets and seeing the big sights like the State House where the Declaration of Independence had first been

440

read (and on which the Capitol Building in Washington had been modelled, Jamie told her proudly), and hearing all the Boston folklore like Paul Revere's Ride and the Tea Party and the Red Sox, about its prominent citizens, like Harriet Beecher Stowe and Louisa May Alcott and Malcom X, and the Kennedys, of course – they had actually owned a building at the top of Beacon Hill, it seemed – and then lurching down into the water, and seeing the waterfront (which was less pretty than she had expected), and at least she had felt able to hold Jamie's hand at last, and even kiss him from time to time.

But she had actually agreed with Frances that the commentary was fairly tedious, and pretty corny and unfunny. And it had been terribly hot. But as they left the house next day, walking through the cobbled streets with all the pretty little shops and cafés that marked out Beacon Hill, and down across the Common into the town, she felt she was seeing the real Boston, stylish and charming, and she loved it. They went into the Trinity Church with its massive gilded dome and windows by Burne Jones and William Morris, and to the Boston Public Library with *Free For All* carved over the door in huge letters. They walked down Newbury Street, where the posh shops were, Chanel and Gucci and Ralph Lauren: 'Mother and the girls are planning on bringing you here tomorrow,' Jamie said, and he showed her a jewellery shop on Boylston Street called Shreve Crump & Low where, it seemed, all the very best diamond rings for the very best people's engagements were to be bought. 'Dad bought Mother's ring here, and Bif bought Dana's and Joe Kathleen's,' said Jamie. She wondered why he was showing her; but she admired it and said it reminded her of Tiffany's.

'You know New York, do you?' said Jamie and seemed surprised; she felt mildly irritated that he might see her as a sort of naive traveller, dazzled by being in the States at all.

'Jamie, of course I've been to New York, several times,' she said, 'and LA and San Francisco. And Disneyland when I was little,' she added. 'Where you must have been lots of times,' and was shocked when he said he never had. 'Mother didn't think it was somewhere she wanted to go,' he said without a hint of resentment.

They lunched in a pavement café on Charles Street: 'I'd like to show you more, but whatever we don't do, we're going to Harvard this afternoon,' he said. 'We'll drive down, in my car. I want you to see it, it's so beautiful. We all went there, Dad, Bif, me, all my uncles, and my grandfather and great-grandfather.'

She did like Harvard very much. They parked and walked through the cobbled streets. Jamie seemed incredibly proud of it; it was almost as if he and his family were personally responsible for it.

'It was founded in 1636,' he said, and she was clearly meant to be totally impressed by this; she supposed America didn't yield many such ancient buildings. They walked through the great iron gates and into Old Harvard Yard, a haven of big redbrick houses and bricked pavements, tall trees and huge lawns; a statue of John Harvard, the founder, stood in front of one of the buildings. 'Touch his foot for good luck,' Jamie said. She did, as countless thousands clearly had done before her; the foot was very shiny.

'This is where you spend your first year, as a fresher, living in one of these houses,' Jamie said, pointing at one of the redbricks. 'I lived there, in that one. I was never so happy in my life.'

'Never?' said Annabel, reaching up to kiss him, and: 'Well, until now,' he said quickly.

'And where did you spend the other years?'

'Oh, in buildings in the town. That was fun too, of course, but that first year was magic.'

She was silent; she felt she was learning more about him in this one day than in the whole of the admittedly short time she had known him.

They left the yard, strolled up to Havard Square. 'See there, those stone tables? They're chessboards; people earn money by playing with other people, giving them lessons.'

'Goodness, how lovely.' And it did look so, sitting in the shade of the big trees, an eternal picture of student life, with all the time in the world to waste. But it summed up exactly why university hadn't appealed to her – what seemed like comparatively aimless, undirected days; she was like her mother, she looked for purpose.

*

442

She fell asleep driving back and woke with a headache; it was very hot and the garden, with its big trees, looked inviting. But Frances Cartwright was there, and so was Kathleen: Kathleen looking flushed and rather agitated.

'May I tell them?'

'Yes, of course.'

'Kathleen has some wonderful news. She's going to have a baby. She's just had it confirmed by her doctor. Isn't it exciting?'

'Kathy, that's just great news,' said Jamie. He went over to her and gave her a hug. 'Congratulations.'

'Thank you, Jamie.'

'How lovely,' said Annabel. 'Congratulations, Kathleen.'

'Thank you. I didn't want to say anything before, not until the test results were in. But there's no doubt about it, it seems.' She looked down at her stomach and smiled rather foolishly. 'I can't quite believe it.'

'She's feeling fine, apparently,' said Frances. 'No sickness, not tired – you're very lucky, Kathleen.'

'Yes, my doctor said that.'

'Well, we must drink a toast. Only I suppose we should do it in something non-alcoholic. I'll go and organise some fruit punch. My goodness, a grandmother at last! I thought it would never happen. I must tell Daddy. He'll be very excited.'

'I'll come and help with the drinks,' said Jamie.

Frances walked briskly into the house, Jamie following her; Annabel smiled at Kathleen.

'Joe must be thrilled.'

'Yes, he is. He's coming over later. Mother's already organising something special for dinner, asking Dana and Bif over. I know you were going out, but I hope you'll stay. It would be nice to have you and Jamie here.'

'Yes, of course we will,' said Annabel. 'I feel very honoured to be part of it.' And she did; she really liked Kathleen. And things were easier now; she and Jamie could go out another night.

Jamie reappeared with a tray of drinks. 'Here we are. Mother is already on the bush telegraph. Dad's coming right home, Kathleen, and Caroline and Jerome are coming over too.'

'Caroline and Jerome?'

'Yes, well, Mother felt they must be part of the evening. She is your godmother, after all.'

'Yes. Yes, I suppose so.'

'Only thing is,' Jamie said, lowering his voice, 'this is going to make things a little difficult for Dana.'

'I know it. I thought of that. It will increase the pressure on her a lot.'

Annabel didn't like to ask why; and then she remembered Jamie saying: 'Mother worries they're both leaving it a little late.' She had thought then it was nothing to do with his mother; she thought so still.

Frances had reappeared, she was smiling radiantly. 'Caroline and Jerome are on their way. They're so thrilled. I knew you'd want them here, Kathleen.'

'Yes, of course.'

'And I've sent a fax to Grandma Cartwright. She'll be over the moon; she's always said it was her one remaining ambition, to be a great-grandmother. My goodness, I feel quite overcome with the whole thing. Such a lot to plan and to think about, isn't there?'

Anyone would think, Annabel reflected, sipping her fruit punch, that it was Frances's baby, and not a lot to do with Kathleen at all.

It had been a very nice evening; Richard felt suddenly more cheerful. They had gone, he and the children, to see *Teenage Mutant Ninja Turtles*, and then, as a really special treat, to tea at McDonald's in Kensington High Street. Richard knew he shouldn't really approve of McDonald's, he felt the food was rubbish, and he didn't like the way they seemed to be springing up all over the place; but the children loved it, loved the novelty of eating with their fingers and the little cardboard containers of chips and the sickly sweetness of the milk shakes. When they had all finished, he said, 'Right, home. The tube's just over the road. One stop to the Central Line.'

They were waiting to cross the road, when an open-topped tourist bus pulled up by them. Rachel gazed at it, transfixed.

'Can we go on that?' she said. 'Oh please, please Daddy, please! Up on the top, *please!*'

'It's going the wrong way, Rachel.'

'Doesn't matter, does it?' said Emma, who was something of an expert on London transport, the result of endless smart birthday outings given by her classmates. 'We could go back to Piccadilly or something, and then get the tube. Doesn't matter if we're late, it's the holidays. Oh please, Daddy, it would be fun.'

Richard hesitated. The children sensed a weakening and ploughed in.

'Go on, Daddy,' said Alex.

'Please!' said Emma.

'I don't suppose they'll let us on,' said Richard, but luck was not on his side: it was one of the stops on the circuit where people could get on and off.

'Coming to join us?' said the conductor and, 'Yes!' shouted all the children at once.

They got on.

The traffic was heavy; it was going to be a long slow journey, he thought, sitting back resignedly. But a pleasant one; the evening sun was very warm and the plane trees practically brushed their heads as they drove along. And there was Kensington Gardens, on their left and— 'Look, there's Mummy!' shouted Emma suddenly. 'Look, there, at the top of that slope, in front of that hotel. Look, there, with that man, see? Mummy, Mum, Mum! Oh and look, it's Simon, it's Tilly's dad. Mum, look up here, on the bus!'

And they all started shouting, shouting and waving; but Debbie neither heard them, through the thick noise of the traffic, nor saw them, for she was reaching up to kiss Simon Beaumont, and as they all watched and waved, they saw him put both his arms round her and give her a hug; and then they began to walk slowly down the ramp, his arm round her shoulders, hers round his waist.

The children, faintly anxious by now, looked at their father, who was very white, his hands clenched tightly together. Emma moved closer to him, slipped her hand through his arm.

'They've probably been doing some work together,' she said, some deep precocious instinct telling her that such comfort was necessary.

Chapter 30

July, 1990

Thank God for the *Daily Mail*, Joel thought. Just suppose he'd missed that. That small miracle, worked for him by Nigel Dempster with an item headed *Trouble in Paradise?*

The paradise referred to was Paradise Island, just off Nassau, and the trouble upon it was the failure of a building company to complete the renovation work on one of the private homes on the island, owned by one Mick Bridgeman. *Multi-millionaire British industrialist Bridgeman is furious at being forced to entertain a party of guests at the Ocean Hill Hotel, rather than at his home. Bridgeman's lawyers have been instructed to sue if the house is not finished within the next two weeks. The persistent frolicking of Bridgeman's stunning young wife Thandie, with another guest, rock musician Nelson Crewe, has not improved Bridgeman's mood. Other guests include Italian supermodel Bibi, the fashion designer Giles Courtney, and his friend Dick 'Tracy' Lord, and Irish charmer Tim Allinson, walker to the stars. Watch this space for further fireworks.*

'Got him!' Joel shouted, and punched the air, and then rushed out of the office, almost knocking over Suzy Jameson.

'Hey, Joel, watch where you're going.'

'Sorry, darling. You weren't exactly strolling yourself.'

'I know, I know. I've got a very important story to chase.'

'Well, me too.'

'Not as important as mine. Couldn't possibly be. Di's driving down to collect poor old Charley-boy from hospital, get him home in time for her birthday. I want to get there before she does.'

'Aah, how sweet. Little birds keep telling me she wants to spend it with someone different.'

'God, you're a cynic. The poor guy's broken his arm so badly, the bone was sticking through his flesh – or so I read in the papers so it must be true – and you accuse his wife of adultery. How unfair.'

Hugh Renwick, the *News* Editor, was extremely unimpressed.

'Course you can't go swanning off to the Bahamas. It's a wild-goose chase. I just don't buy this story anyway. It's a non-starter, lot of rich spoiled people who can't take their medicine when they clearly have to.'

'But it isn't like that,' said Joel, thinking of Catherine, of Gillian Thompson, of Neil Lawrence, of Simon Beaumont. 'You've got it wrong. There's much more to this story, I swear to you. People are in complete despair, actually topping themselves—'

'Well, there you are,' said Renwick. 'They can't take their medicine. Suicide is only another way out.'

'For fuck's sake, Hugh, you're not listening. These people are complete crooks. They've been taking money from people who can ill afford it, just ordinary middle-class folk, not rich at all, in the full knowledge that all these terrible claims were just out there, waiting. It's a conspiracy.'

'And none of these "ordinary middle-class folk" have had any money out of Lloyd's, I suppose? Over the past ten years?'

'Well – yes. Some.'

'See? They're just a load of greedy tossers.'

'They are *not* tossers, for Christ's sake. I've got a lot of stuff now, from people who've talked to me, stories that would really touch the readers' hearts.'

'Well, none of it touches mine. Sorry, Joel. Just drop it, would you. I need you for good solid stories, not this fancy crap. Like that piece on educational trusts I asked you for. How's that going?'

'Oh, I've got a few leads,' said Joel impatiently. He thought of Tim Allinson, sitting out there, juicily ripe for plucking; in a few days he could be gone and so would any chance of getting his story. He could hardly bear it.

'Well, follow them, would you? Get on with it. Otherwise

you're going to find yourself in Shit Street, rather than Fleet Street, I warn you.'

'Yes, OK,' said Joel, 'but you could be sorry.'

'We saw you, we saw you!' The children came into the kitchen where Debbie was sitting, checking the post. She had got home five minutes before them.

'Saw me where? What are you talking about? How was the film?'

'Great,' said Alex.

'Lovely,' said Rachel. Emma was rather quiet, looked at her mother awkwardly as she poured herself a glass of squash.

'Where did you see me?'

'Coming out of the Royal Garden Hotel,' said Richard. His voice was very cold. 'With Simon Beaumont.'

'Oh – did you?' She felt herself flush; and cursed it. As if she had any reason to. 'Yes, we were having a drink. He's been fired, you know, from the bank and I—'

'I don't think we should talk about it now,' said Richard.

'Richard, there's nothing *to* talk about.'

'Good. Well, come on, children. You did promise straight upstairs. And then I want to ring Granny, see if you can go down to stay with her a bit sooner.'

'Ye-es! Could we?'

'I'm not sure I want them to,' said Debbie. 'I've got things arranged for the end of the week.'

He looked at her: with such withering dislike she felt sick.

'Really?' he said, and walked out of the room, shutting the door behind him.

'Well, at least I know the real reason why you don't want to go to Scotland,' he said. It was much later; Debbie was in the sitting room, ironing and watching Wimbledon highlights on *Match of the Day*.

She stared at him. 'What did you say?'

He switched the television off. 'I said I know now why you don't want to go to Scotland. It would put an end to your relationship with Simon Beaumont.'

Her stomach lurched. Had Flora . . .? No, no, surely not.

'Richard!' she said, struggling to sound calm. 'You're going

448

mad. Of course I'm not having a relationship with Simon Beaumont.'

'Is that so? Is that why you were coming out of a hotel with him, kissing him, carrying on . . .'

'Please don't be so ridiculous. I was *not* carrying on. We'd had a drink, he's been fired, I wanted to cheer him up.'

'Oh, I'm sure you did. Lucky man. It's a long time since you wanted to cheer *me* up.'

'That is so untrue,' she said in a low voice.

'It is not untrue. I can't remember when we last had sex.'

'Richard! Please!'

'Anyway, let's not argue about that. We have to decide what to do.'

'What on earth do you mean?'

'I mean about our marriage'

'Our marriage? I don't understand you – what is all this about? I am *not* having an affair with Simon Beaumont, nothing could be less likely, he's just been rather kind to me and—'

'Very kind, obviously. Debbie, I'm not stupid. I've observed you with him.'

'With him? I'm never *with him.*'

'You're with him at Mother's. Going off for little walks, kissing him goodbye . . .'

'Oh, for God's sake. Richard, you're completely crazy. And if I was carrying on with Simon, do you think I'd do it in your mother's house, under your nose?'

'Quite possibly. You're obviously obsessed with him. Tell me something, truthfully please: was that the first time you've met him in London?'

'Well, no.' It seemed better to tell the truth; lying was dangerous.

'I see. More drinks in other hotels?'

'You've got this so wrong, I can't begin to tell you. Simon is just not the sort of person I – I like. Well, I do like him very much, but that's all. He's old enough to be my father, nearly, and you know how I hate all those public-school sorts of people.'

'You just said you liked him.'

'Yes, I do like him. But I don't fancy him. Get that into your skull, would you? *I do not fancy Simon Beaumont.*'

449

'I'm sorry, but I find that very hard to believe. Given the evidence of my own eyes earlier this evening.'

'Well, try a bit harder.'

'Oh, shut up,' he said wearily. 'Anyway, I'm going to take the children down to Mother's tomorrow. Whether it suits you or not. I don't want them upset by all this, and we really do have to get things sorted out. Not just our marriage, but what I'm going to say to Morag Dunbar, and—'

'Yes, I wondered when we were going to get round to her. What did you think of saying to her? "My wife was kissing a man on the steps of a hotel in broad daylight and I'm going to divorce her." She'll think you're insane. You *are* insane.'

'You're entitled to your opinion,' he said, 'but I'd like the children's things packed, please. I've spoken to Mother and she's happy to have them tomorrow. She's expecting us around teatime.'

There was clearly nothing she could do about it; he seemed absolutely determined. She nodded and said quietly, 'Yes, all right.'

But as she started piling up clean clothes and rummaging in the bottom of the ironing basket for Emma's jodhpurs and dragging the holdalls out of the hall cupboard, she felt increasingly sick. What if Richard asked Flora if she thought there was anything between her and Simon? What might she say? What in God's name might she say?

'Letter for you, Lucinda. From the States. Got a new boyfriend?' Graham winked at her.

'Don't be silly,' said Lucinda. She felt herself blush. She took the letter and put it to one side; she couldn't have Graham thinking it was in any way important. She looked up and saw him still smiling at her.

'Now that is quite suspicious.'

'What is?'

'Not opening your letter.'

'Why?' she said, playing for time.

'Well, it's hardly normal behaviour. It just looks as if you feel guilty about it, and aren't going to open it till you're on your own.'

'Well, what's wrong with that?'

'What, feeling guilty? Depends what about.'

'Oh, stop it,' said Lucinda, and threw a rubber at him. He fielded it neatly and threw it back at her.

'Stop it, Graham. You shouldn't throw things at pregnant women.'

'Pregnant women shouldn't have beaux in America.'

'I have not got a beau in America. In fact, it's from my boss. The one I had before you.'

'Oh really? The gallery owner?'

'That's right.'

'But why is he writing to you here? Why not to your home address? Oh dear, I might have to mention this to Blue. Unless you get the reports on those historical novels to me by tomorrow morning.'

Lucinda giggled. 'You'll have them.'

Later, slightly nervously, when Graham had gone to a meeting, she opened the letter.

Darling Lucinda,

How wonderful to hear from you. My life has not been the same without you. In fact, I can't imagine how I've survived. I'm intrigued by your request. I'm happy to help if I can, but I think I'd like to know a little more. I'm coming to London en route to France, to see a couple of painters in the last week of July. I'll be with Greg, my partner – you'll love him, Lucinda, and he'll love you. Let's meet then and you can tell me all about it. Longing to make the new man's acquaintance.

All love, Virgil

'Damn,' said Lucinda. 'Damn damn damn.' It was getting tougher; she was tempted to give up on this one. And Blue was pressing her harder and harder about moving; she just didn't know how much longer she could hang on.

But if she didn't – well, that would be Nigel done for. He'd lose everything, including the cufflinks. Maybe, if she told Blue the exact plan . . . but that would mean he'd have to hear about the difficult bit, and he just might not like it. In fact, he certainly wouldn't like it. Of course, he had to know in the end, but the longer she could put it off, the better. She really

451

needed to talk to someone about this. Someone with lots of commonsense. But they'd need to know Blue as well as Nigel. Like – well, maybe like Simon. Yes, she'd talk to him about it. Take him out to lunch. See what he thought.

She reached for the phone and dialled his number.

'Debbie, dear, it's Flora.'

God, what was she going to say? That she'd told Richard she'd found her and Simon snogging in her kitchen? That she had offered to give a testimony to his solicitor— Debbie, stop it. They won't even be there yet.

'Hello, Flora,' she said carefully. She was sitting in her office at Know How Promotions.

'I haven't heard from that young man yet, the journalist. If he wants to talk to me, it had better be today. Once the children are here, it will be very difficult to find the time.'

'Oh, OK. I'll call him. Sorry, Flora.'

She rang Joel, too weary and miserable to feel even remotely awkward; told him what Flora had said.

'Oh sorry. Yes, I was going to call her. But – well, to be honest, Debbie, I don't think I can do this story after all.'

She was shocked out of her lethargy. 'Not do it? Joel, that's a terrible shame, when you've got so much good stuff. Why?'

'Oh, the Editor's more or less told me to spike it. I can't make him see how good it is. How important.'

'Oh, I see. Well, I suppose in that case—'

'Yeah. But I will ring your mother-in-law. It would seem rude not to. And you never know, I suppose. Thanks, Debbie.'

Flora was a fantastic interviewee; she didn't waffle on, didn't get emotional, just gave him the facts – which were pretty dramatic, losing first her husband and then everything she had as a result – in a well-ordered, carefully thought out way. She could have been a lawyer, he thought; and thanked her and then sat thinking for a while, replaying bits of the recording. And in a rush of reckless courage, decided to go away, finance the trip himself. Some stories were too good to be missed. And then he rang Debbie back.

'Just to let you know, I've spoken to your mother-in-law. She was just ace. Thanks so much.'

'Don't be silly. I didn't do much.'

'You led me to her.'

'Well, not very difficult really. You sound more cheerful.'

'I feel it. Much more. I've been thinking: I know this is a good story. I'm going to take a flyer on it.'

'What do you mean?'

'I'm going to do it anyway. I've got this incredible lead, bloke out in the Bahamas—'

'The Bahamas? You going there? Doesn't sound as if your Editor's spiking it.'

'He still might. And he's not paying my fare – I am. That's what I mean about a flyer.'

'Gosh. That is quite a gamble.'

'I know. But I think it'll pay off.'

'Great.'

She was taking this call in her office, feeling totally wretched. The children had hardly said goodbye to her, they were so excited about their extended visit to Gower. Richard had said he would be staying down there himself until Saturday; and every time she thought of him talking to Flora about her and Simon – surely, surely he couldn't be that mad? – every time she thought about it, she felt she was going to throw up.

She had cried a lot, too, although not until they left that morning, she'd been too shocked and angry; but then she'd gone back into the house and put her head onto her arms and sobbed. What had happened to her marriage, to her happy, child-friendly marriage? What had happened to the girl who had adored her children and loved her husband – and all right, been bored quite a lot and felt tired quite a lot and not wanted sex quite often. That was like most marriages where there were young children and every second of the day was filled and it was a struggle just to keep afloat in the great tidal wave of feeding and washing and tidying and nappy-changing. Where real life interfered with at least the outward signs of love, where getting the children to the dentist or collected from school or into the bath had to take precedence over reassurance and appreciation and opinion sharing, and where discussions about money and mortgages and whose turn it was to go to the supermarket became so much more pressing than

453

conversations about music and books and politics. But that passed, usually, and the marriage survived it; hers looked as if it might not. So – when had it all gone wrong and how could she have handled it so badly?

There was no neat answer to that question; it had just been a long, slow slither into resentment and reproaches and misunderstandings and an apparent unwillingness to try and make things better. Only ... she felt sure there had been a turning-point when it all went wrong; and travelling back in her head, slowly and painfully, she realised it had been that first evening, when Flora had told Richard she couldn't pay the school fees any longer and he had said that he would, and – well, that had been the point of no return.

And now Richard was on his way to Wales, to stay with his mother and no doubt discuss Debbie's perfidy and possibly, quite possibly, hear what Flora had to say about the matter. And she thought back to that evening, when Flora had walked into the kitchen and she saw the scene through Flora's eyes, saw her son's wife holding another man in her arms, his head on her breast, and her stroking his hair and clearly about to kiss him. If she had seen it, of course. Which she surely must have done. And even if she hadn't exactly seen it, there had been a pretty charged atmosphere in the room. What reasonable person could feel no trace of suspicion, confronted by that?

Joel was still talking. 'Flora was telling me about the immorality of her situation, and how she'll almost certainly be losing the house her husband's family had owned for many generations. That's terrible, Debbie.'

'Yes, it is terrible,' said Debbie. She could hear her own voice sounding very flat, struggled to lighten it. 'And it is a beautiful house, just on the cliffs, you know. The children love it.'

'I'm sure. Anyway, she even said she might have someone else for me in a day or two, or certainly a bit more of the story. She really was fantastic, Debbie. I'd love to meet her.'

'I'm sure you can. So – Bahamas next stop?'

'It's certainly looking that way. Thanks again.'

She was horrified to feel a sob rise in her throat. She swallowed hard. 'Well, have fun. I must go. Bye, Joel.' She slammed the phone down, threw her head back and fought down the tears. This was ridiculous!

The phone rang again.

'Debbie? It's me. Are you all right?'

She was *not* going to tell him about her troubles. She just wasn't. She was not about to come over like some saddo, with marital problems. Not cool, not clever, and very dangerous.

'Yes. Yes, I'm absolutely fine. Thanks.'

'Oh, good. I thought you sounded a bit—'

'A bit what?' she said irritably.

'A bit down.'

'No, no, not at all. Couldn't be higher actually,' she said. Only on the word 'actually' her voice wobbled.

'You're not, are you?' he said. 'What is it, what's the matter?'

'Oh, nothing. Nothing serious anyway.'

'Good. Well, I'll call Simon now, and get a bit more of a lowdown on his situation.'

'Great. Well—' And then she thought of how extremely unlikely it was that she would speak to Simon, ever again, and that made her feel terribly sad too, and this time the tears did start, and there was no stopping them, and no stopping Joel hearing them either.

'Hey,' he said, 'there is something wrong. I'm sorry.' And then there was a pause and he said, 'Want to tell me about it? I owe you, that's for sure. I'm free after work. Or do you have to get home?'

'No,' she said, sniffing loudly, misery making her horribly truthful. 'I don't have to get home. There's nobody there.'

'Great,' he said. 'Criterion suit you? At about six-thirty?'

'I really shouldn't,' she said.

'Nor should I. So let's. Bye, Debbie. See you later.'

Now why in God's name had he done that? Very, very silly. Getting involved with a married woman. A not entirely happily married woman, if Simon was to be believed. Not that Joel was getting involved; he was just having a drink with her. Better make sure it was only one. Maybe he should cancel it; it would be much wiser. He had enough complications in his life already. Maggie would go crazy when she heard he was going to the Bahamas, would want to come, he'd have to deal with all that ... God, why did he get in such messes with women? It

455

was stupid. It was all part of what Suzy had once told him was his emotional immaturity. He'd hated her for that, but thinking about it later, he could see she had a point. He might be thirty-four, but he'd never managed to grow up emotionally; in some ways, he was still about eighteen. Well, it wasn't his fault, it was all these bloody women being wrong for him, treating him badly and then forcing him to treat them badly in return. How was he supposed to become mature and well-adjusted when there was no one to show him how? No one who loved him, warts and all, who would take him for the shit he was, and make him want to be less of one. Well, Debbie Fielding certainly wasn't going to do that for him; he'd call her in half an hour or so, say he'd got to go out on a story. She might be a bit upset, but . . .

But half an hour later, he was writing a rushed piece the Editor had demanded on the growing dangers of a recession; and by the time he had finished it, it was a quarter to six and really much too late to cancel. Joel had, buried in the depths of his less noble instincts, a genuinely kind heart, and Debbie had managed to touch it.

Debbie was equally uneasy; she shouldn't have done that, shouldn't have agreed to see him. It was crazy, when she was so upset. Totally crazy. She spent most of the afternoon picking up the phone to cancel the arrangement, and then putting it down again.

Chapter 31

July, 1990

'Right,' said Jamie, 'I want to ask you something.'

They were sitting on the beach in front of the Cartwright house on Cape Cod. Annabel loved Cape Cod, loved everything about it, its great stretches of white beaches, and long-grassed dunes, the woods, the cranberry swamps, the fishing villages, and the wild salty wind that filled the air. After the oppressive heat of Boston, she felt she had gone to heaven; at her first glimpse of the house, built in whitewashed brick and silvery clapboard, set just behind the beach, she literally shouted for joy.

Jamie looked at her and grinned. 'That's all we ask from our visitors. Rapture. Good girl.'

'It's heavenly. Absolutely heavenly. Oh Jamie, I love it. Is this really yours?'

'Well – my parents'. Was my grandfather's. It's the family treasure.'

'It's much better than diamonds, that's all I can say. Oh, it's so exactly the sort of house I'd love to have.'

The house was charming, all sanded floors, white walls and brick fireplaces and French windows everywhere, opening onto the lovely air. It was 'furnished comfy' as Jamie put it, lots of wicker chairs and low tables and carefully-casual painted furniture; a verandah ran round three sides of it, there was a deck at the front, right on the beach, and a lush garden, with hammocks slung between the trees.

'If I die and go to heaven, I shall expect it to be just like this,' Annabel told Frances, wandering round, her eyes shining; Frances smiled at her graciously and said she was glad she liked it.

'Of course, the area's not what it was, so touristy now, and the marshlands are constantly under threat; my husband gives a lot of money every year to the grass-planting programme.'

'This is where the Pilgrim Fathers first settled, you know,' said Jamie. 'Well, not exactly here, of course, up there on the northernmost tip, near Truro. We can go there tomorrow if you like.'

'I would like,' said Annabel.

It was a different world down here; the Cartwrights all became easier, less watchful of one another. Even Frances's hair seemed to relax a little. Kathleen, who was beginning to feel less well, spent long hours lying in a hammock, smiling blissfully at anyone who came near her, and Dana and Bif set off every morning to sail the Sound, as they put it.

The days slipped by in an easy, sunlit chain, each one as happy as the one before. Hugely and happily energised, Annabel demanded Jamie took her everywhere; they rode the cycle trails, wandered the villages, walked through the dunes and the salt marshes, went on a whale-watching cruise, and crewed for Dana and Bif for two wonderful days. 'This is the nearest to flying you'll get on this earth,' Bif shouted at her, as they leaned backwards over the side of the boat, hanging onto the sail sheets, and indeed it was exactly like that, she thought, looking up at the tall sails and the blue sky and the clouds scudding beyond them. She suddenly thought of her father selling the *Lizzie* and realised how dreadful a loss it was.

She insisted they visit Martha's Vineyard: 'I don't care how corny it is, I want to go and I might see Carly Simon, you never know.' They didn't, but she still liked it. They made a pilgrimage to Hyannis Port, a disappointment since the famous house and its famous inhabitants playing the famous games of touch football were miles from view; you had to take a cruise to be shown so much as a chimney-stack, Jamie said: although they did go to the John F. Kennedy Museum, with its films of the family at play.

By the end of the week, she had eaten so much seafood in the endless fish restaurants and bars that she said she would turn into a fish; 'A mermaid would be nicer,' Jamie said.

That was at lunchtime though – even here there were strict

Cartwright rules. Philip Cartwright cooked every night on the barbecue; there was no question of going to a restaurant except on the last night. She didn't mind that so much; it was very different from the formality of the dining room in Boston; they sat at a long table on the verandah, or the beachside patio, and felt the warm wind grow colder and then went inside and played games – Scrabble and backgammon, before being allowed up to bed. Even that was easier here; Frances seemed to have accepted their relationship: their rooms were side by side, with only a bathroom dividing them.

And besides, she had grown used to the family by now. Being with them was like belonging to a club, and you knew you had to keep to its rather archaic traditions and customs, otherwise there was no point joining. And it was actually a nice club, close and rather protective; members were watchful for one another, wary of strangers, generous to those they had accepted.

And she had been accepted, in spite of the terrible first night; they had allowed her entry, albeit probationary, and she felt almost one of them by that last evening, as they sat at a long table in one of the endless local seafood restaurants, laughing, teasing one another, tired out by the fresh air and the sun; she was between Bif and Jamie, and Philip twinkled across the table at her.

'We shall miss you, Annabel. Shame you can't stay.'

'I wish I could,' she said, and meant it from the bottom of her heart.

She had to leave at midday, to catch her flight from Boston in the evening; the last night with Jamie was sweetly sad. They made love rather quietly and gently, their bodies now easily familiar, and then lay in one another's arms, and the last thing she heard him say as she drifted off to sleep was, 'How am I going to get through the rest of the summer without you?'

She remembered thinking it would be easier for him, with the cool white beaches and brilliant skies to console him, than for her in a manically hot hairdressing salon, but was too sleepy to say so; she slept dreamlessly and woke up to find him sitting up looking at her.

'You're so beautiful,' he said, 'so lovely. I shall miss you so much. Look at the colour of you, pale honey,' and he picked up a tress of her long sun-streaked hair and kissed it, kissed her hands, her breasts, her flat brown stomach. She felt the sadness then; no – more than sadness, something close to grief. Jamie had become part of her, part of herself; she felt completely happy with him, unquestioningly, joyfully happy. They had created a world within the world that week especially, where they were absolutely together, cocooned from everything else. They ventured out of it, of course, they talked to other people, laughed with other people, did things with other people, but from time to time throughout each day they returned to it; it was their place, their country, fashioned by them and for them, a joyful, easy loving place; and now she had to leave it, and for a long time, God knew how long, to be alone again.

'Oh Jamie,' she said, 'I can't bear it, I can't be without you, it's horrible even to think about. We've been so happy and now we're going to be so unhappy.' And she looked at days, at weeks, at months without him, without him holding her hand and kissing her and making love to her and talking to her and laughing with her, looked at being alone and lonely and it was impossible to see any point in any of it.

'Let's go for a walk,' he said, and they got dressed and walked down the garden and onto the beach. It was very early – 'Only six o'clock,' she said, surprised, and the water and the sky were only just turning blue. She gazed into the distance across the water, the distance that was another place in every sense, where she had to go, where she would be so very alone, and she started to cry.

That was when Jamie said he wanted to ask her something.

He had even bought a ring, a diamond ring, from Shreve Crump & Low, he told her, and indeed gave her the box; she sat staring at it, on her finger, on the proper finger, laughing and crying at the same time.

'I can't believe it,' she said. 'I can't believe I'm engaged to you, that you know you want to marry me.'

And, 'Why ever not?' he said. 'You're so lovely and you make me so perfectly happy, why should I even think about looking for anyone else?'

'Oh dear,' said Annabel, 'I'm sure this isn't the right thing to do when you've just got engaged,' and she cried harder than ever.

'Of course we have to wait a while,' he said. 'You're very young, your parents don't even know me, I'm only just qualified. It will be at least a year, probably two, but I wanted to get it settled. I wanted to know I had you, that you were really, really mine.'

'I'm really, really yours,' she said, smiling, kissing him. 'Make no mistake about that.'

And then thoughts began to come into her head. 'Jamie,' she said, and she felt oddly frightened suddenly, 'have you told your parents?'

'Not yet,' he said. 'I wanted to make sure you wanted it first. But they'll be so pleased, they love you, they all love you, and—'

'Could you not tell them? Could it be our secret – just for now? I want to go away from here today, with only us knowing. It will help me, help me not mind so much. I don't want fuss and celebrations today; it would be too much, too difficult. This is our day, our very own; and it's not so sad now, it's a special, special day. Let's keep it that way, can we?'

He was clearly disappointed. 'I wanted us to tell them together,' he said.

'But – are you sure they'll be pleased? Won't they think we're too young and all that?'

'No, no,' he said, 'we have a tradition in our family for marrying young. Bif was only twenty-two when he and Dana got engaged, and Kathleen only twenty. And Father was only twenty-two when he married Mother. Who was only twenty. So they'll think it's completely in order. I'm not in the least worried about that.'

'Oh I see.' She digested this for a moment, this dutiful following in the Cartwright family tradition, and her being an appropriate part of that, and then said, 'Maybe we can tell them together, but another time, another day. Please, Jamie. It's about us, isn't it? Just us?'

'Well, not really,' he said. 'It's about our families too. Surely.'

'Yes. But it's us who love each other, us who are going to get married. My God. I can't believe that. You and me, getting married. How very grown up.'

461

'Quite grown up, yes,' he said, and laughed. 'My lovely Annabel. You are just so perfect. The perfect Mrs James Cartwright.'

Just for a second then, the sliver of a second, she felt – what? Alarm. No, not alarm, but nerviness. Not at the thought of being Annabel Cartwright, but Mrs James Cartwright. And of having to be a perfect Mrs Cartwright, like Frances, like Dana, like any of them. A perfect member of this perfect clan. Because that is what she'd have to be. And it might be . . . difficult.

And then it passed, as swiftly as it had come.

Flora and Richard were just finishing supper when the phone rang.

'Do you mind, darling, if I take it? I think I know who it is.'

'Of course not.'

'Ah,' he heard her say, 'Edward. Yes, thank you, how nice of you to call. Well, as I said, anything you could do . . . Oh. Oh, I see. Well, even advice would be helpful. Yes, very. I mean, do I have to sell the house, for instance, or . . . look, I'm busy at the moment, got someone here, but I'm coming up to Town again next week, probably on Wednesday. Maybe we could meet then. I could even buy you a return lunch, to show my gratitude . . . what? Oh well, that's very kind. Look, I'll call you after the weekend, when my plans have firmed up a little. Yes. Fine. Thank you, Edward.'

'So – was it who you thought?' said Richard.

'It was indeed. Nasty little rat, responsible for all my troubles.'

'You weren't talking to him as if he was a nasty little rat.'

'No, I know. I'm being a bit devious. Think I might be able to get some information out of him, which might help Simon Beaumont in this lawsuit he's mounting.'

'Oh yes?'

'He was William's cousin. If he was a relative of mine, I'd disown him. Dreadful man. Oily, self-satisfied little creep.'

Richard had avoided so much as mentioning Simon, his suspicions, his unhappiness indeed; had simply told his mother that Debbie was working all week and it would be immensely helpful if the children could come down two days early. But now . . .

'You seem to know Beaumont rather well,' he said.

'Quite well. I'm very fond of him. He's been a tower of strength through this whole thing, and not just to me. Nothing gets him down, it seems; although he's been fired now from Graburn and French – the bank he works for. Very harsh, that. Poor Simon. Something to do with his contract and bringing the bank into disrepute.'

'Shame,' said Richard. He sounded singularly unsympathetic, even to himself.

Flora looked at him. 'He's not really your sort of person, I know. Nor mine, I would have thought. Your father wouldn't have liked him very much. Bit flashy, he'd have said. But as I say, I have grown fond of him. And he's helped many people. Given that poor girl Catherine Morgan a job at his bank, advised another man who'd tried to kill himself, can you imagine. And of course he's Tilly's father, so I would feel fondly towards him. And he is very charming, very good company.'

Richard felt suddenly rather desperate; this was more than he could bear, having to listen to praise being heaped on Simon Beaumont's head.

'I'll just – just go and see the kids,' he said, 'make sure they're OK. If you don't mind.'

'Of course, darling.'

'And then I'll come and help you clear up.'

'No need. You look tired. Have an early night, why don't you?'

He did feel tired. He wasn't sleeping, and a terrible paralysis seemed to have overtaken him. He had to phone Morag Dunbar, say something; if only that he wasn't coming. Or that he would be coming up alone. Or . . .

'No. No, I'll come down again in a minute.'

He did; she had made him some of the hot chocolate he loved.

'There you are. Lots of sugar in it. Like your father didn't allow. I do lots of things he didn't allow, these days. It helps.'

'Do you still miss him so much?' he asked.

'Yes, of course.'

'Oh Mother.' He looked at her, his grey eyes so exactly like

463

his father's, very concerned. 'You shouldn't be so – so brave. It makes us forget. Well, no not forget, but forget to worry about you.'

'Richard, I'm fine. You know I am.'

'You're not really though, are you?' he said. 'You've got this awful thing to cope with, all on your own. It's not right, we should help you more.'

'Oh, rubbish,' she said. 'I'm much better coping on my own. If you kept coming to see me, fussing over me, I'd get very bad-tempered. I'm a tough old bird.'

'Yes, I know. But partly because you have to be. I'm so sorry. I wish I could be with you more.'

'Oh Richard, don't be ridiculous. You have your own life. And I'm very happy, really I am. Apart from all this wretched business, of course. Now look, would it be OK with you, and Debbie of course, if I get Mrs Connor to look after the children just for one day next week? If I make it clear they're not to leave the house or the garden? She's very firm with them, I promise, and she knows them all. And Tilly will be here, she's very sensible, and extremely grown up. It really is important to me, this meeting.'

'Yes, of course,' he said. 'Of course it is. Do you really think you'll have to sell the house?'

'Oh, without doubt, I'm afraid. I'm so sorry, I had hoped it would be yours one day. And I love it so much, as you know. But – needs must and all that, while the devil drives. And the devil is certainly driving.'

'He does seem to be.'

Richard was in something of a state, Flora thought: both edgy and down. And he'd lost weight. A row with Debbie, perhaps? She'd wondered why he'd wanted to bring the children down on his own. Well, it was none of her business. She would only make it worse if she tried to interfere. And it was very nice to have him to herself. He might open up a bit as the evening went on.

'Richard, darling, would you like some more wine? I can easily—' The phone rang again. It was Simon.

'Sorry, Richard, won't be long. How are you, Simon?'

'Oh, you know. Not great. Discovering what boredom's

464

about. And loneliness – that's been hard, not being surrounded by people all day.'

'Of course,' said Flora, 'but it will be all right. You'll make it so. Now I mustn't be long, sorry, got Richard here, we're chatting. I've spoken to William's cousin, and he's still a Working Name. Yes. And do you know, he had the gall to tell me to trade through – said it was like the races, run of bad luck.'

'And what was his explanation for your troubles?'

'Oh, he said he couldn't understand it. I asked him if he'd put me in the same syndicates as himself, as William had requested, and he said yes, of course. I asked him if he was still in the same ones, and he became a bit shifty, said he'd had to move some of the money around, but generally speaking, yes, he was. Simon, I know there's something going on. There must be. He's living in Chelsea, he's got a couple of racehorses, and a villa in some dreadful place in Spain. If he really was in the same syndicates as me, he wouldn't have any of that.'

'Baby Syndicates,' said Simon, 'must be. Buggers.'

'D'you think?'

'Absolutely. Must be the explanation. Has to be. What's his name?'

'He claims it's Edward Trafford Smythe.'

'What do you mean, "claims"?' said Simon, laughing. 'God, you're like a tonic, Flora. I feel better already.'

'What I mean is, I'd bet anything he's called just plain Smythe and some uncle or other was called Trafford. So common, that sort of thing. Anyway, I've arranged to have lunch with him next week. On Wednesday, at the Savoy. Are you free?'

'Free every day, unfortunately. Something for me to look forward to.'

'So – what do you want me to do?' asked Flora.

'I want you to keep totally stumm, act like you're really impressed by him. I'll be there, apparently lunching with someone, and you can introduce us. Very casually. Ask me to join you. I'll take over after that, see if we can trick him into saying something damning. It's worth a try, anyway.'

'Fine. How exciting. I shall feel like Miss Moneypenny.'

'Well, I don't feel too much like Bond, I'm afraid.'

'You will. How's Tilly? I'm so looking forward to seeing you both. The children have just arrived, Emma can't wait for her to get here . . . And how's Elizabeth? Give her my love.'

'I will. So who's there with you – Debbie?'

'No, no, Debbie's not here, she's in London. Working. But Richard's here. Going back on Sunday, I think.'

Great, thought Richard. She was only telling Debbie's lover her husband was away and for how long. Although surely he'd have known. It was probably a clever ruse on Beaumont's part, to appear totally innocent in front of Flora. Debbie might even be with him now, egging him on, the pair of them laughing at him. A sudden lump rose in Richard's throat; he felt rather sick and very, very sad. He got up, turned away, started loading up the dishwasher. He was dangerously near tears.

'Sorry, Richard.' Flora put the phone down. 'But we're hatching a plot. Our solicitor says we have to find a smoking gun if we're to have a hope of bringing these people to justice, and Simon and I think we might be able to, with the help of Trafford Smythe. Oh, and a tape recorder.'

'A tape recorder!'

'Yes. We think he's running some of these Baby Syndicates and we're going to try and trick him into saying so.'

Richard was distracted from his misery. 'What on earth are Baby Syndicates?'

'Usually they're little self-contained cells, inside the main syndicate, created for the underwriter's friends and relations. So they're nominally still in the Bloggs Group, or in our case, Westfield Bradley, but when a particularly attractive bit of business comes along, they write it into the Baby Syndicate. It's absolute skulduggery. Richard, are you all right?'

'Yes, yes, I'm fine.'

'Good. Yes, poor old Simon, he's taken a terrible pasting. It's so hard, having held a prominent position as he did . . .'

'Could we just stop talking about bloody Simon Beaumont?' Richard said, and he was almost shouting at her. 'I don't want to – to –' he stopped.

Flora stared at him. 'Yes, of course,' she said calmly, 'if you like. Sorry.' A few seconds went by, then she said, very gently, 'Is there some problem between you and Simon?'

'I – don't know,' he said, and then the tears came, filled his eyes, a huge wave of sorrow sweeping over him. It was terribly embarrassing; he sat at his mother's kitchen table and buried his head in his hands. 'I really don't know. I'm sorry.'

'Don't apologise,' said Flora. 'Don't be silly. Do you want to talk about it?'

'No. Well – yes. Maybe. I . . .' and then a rush of desperate courage came over him and he said, staring at his hands, not meeting her eyes, 'Mother, you know him pretty well, it seems. I expect this sounds crazy, but – well, have you ever thought – had reason to think – there was something going on between him and Debbie?'

There was a silence that seemed rather long to him, then; 'Let's have a drink, shall we?' she said.

Lucinda sat waiting for Simon in Fortnum's Soda Fountain. It had been her suggestion that they should go there; 'I'll buy you tea. Lots of crumpets and things. In return for your advice.'

'Nothing I like better than lots of crumpet. I'll be there.'

She saw him coming in; got up, went over to him and hugged him.

'Darling Simon. So sweet of you to come. How are you?'

'Oh, you know. Not too bad considering. A lot better for seeing you.'

'I can't believe that. I'm beginning to feel a bit portly.'

'Well, you certainly don't look portly. Never was an adjective less suitable. Let's order, shall we, and then I can concentrate.'

'I don't quite know where to begin,' she said. 'Milk in your tea?'

'A bit, please. What about the beginning? Alice had a point there, I always thought.'

'Well, the beginning is me leaving Nigel. No, it's not, it's Lloyd's. Or maybe . . . well, anyway. As you know, Simon, he's going to be horribly badly hit, poor angel.'

'Indeed.'

'Steve Durham and I have put our heads together and come up with something quite clever.'

'Who's Steve Durham?'

'My solicitor.'

'Right. Go on.'

467

'Well, we thought – Simon, you won't talk to anyone about this, will you? It's a bit . . . delicate.'

'Of course I won't.'

'Anyway, what we thought was that I should get as much from Nigel by way of a settlement as I possibly could.'

'Hmm. Difficult, I've have thought. You're not exactly the innocent party, my darling, are you?'

'No, of course not. But Steve has managed to make things look a bit more as if I am.'

'Really? He must be a genius.'

'Well, I think he is. I mean, for a start, he thinks I can get the house.'

'The one in Cadogan Square?'

'Yes. Because Nigel made it over to me anyway, and he's said he wants me still to have it.'

'Nigel! Is he involved in this deception?'

'Oh yes, very much so. He has to be. He's finding it all very difficult, of course, because he's so terribly upright, but I've managed to persuade him. Anyway, he's saying things like he's worried the relationship might not last, that he feels I'm in a very vulnerable position, being pregnant and not married and he wants me to be financially secure. And that he wants me to have the house at least. And then he put a lot of money in trust for me and Steve is arguing that it would be unreasonable to take it back at this stage. When I could be relying on it.'

'I see. He's going to come over as a bit of a patsy, isn't he?'

'Maybe, but it'll be worth it. And then there was another angle Steve thought of – that maybe I'd given things up when I married Nigel – a job, for instance. And of course I did.'

'You did?'

'Yes. I was working for an artist, as his sort of PA. Sweet man, called Virgil Barrymore. Anyway, he did ask me to go with him when he moved to New York and I didn't because I was marrying Nigel.'

'Ye-es.'

'And the thing is that Virgil's paintings sell for squillions now, and I could have been working on a percentage, earning ten per cent of a squillion. And been financially independent. Virgil's coming over to London next month, and he's going to – well, I hope he's going to – agree to say that.'

'Lucinda,' said Simon, 'this is rather incredible. You're a very clever girl.'

'No, I'm not at all. And Steve thought of most of it. I'm just – well, maybe a bit ingenious.'

'Very ingenious. So let's say you win, and you get all this money, and the house – then what?'

'Well, then, first of all, we set up some kind of educational trust. A charity that benefits poor deprived children. Probably overseas somewhere. And some of the income will come from property which the trust owns. Including the house in Cadogan Square. I'll borrow against it and put all the money into that. And Nigel will be able to get at it, you see; he'll be one of the major trustees . . . It will have to be quite a complex process, but Steve is sure it can be done and Lloyd's won't be able to touch it. And Nigel will have lost everything – on paper. To me.'

'Christ,' said Simon, 'that is really very, very clever. I wish this man Durham was my lawyer.'

'I'm sure he would be if you asked him. But yes, it is clever, isn't it? I mean, even if I don't get everything, which Steve says I won't, he really thinks I'll get a lot. Which means Nigel will get a lot.' She looked smug and started on the pile of smoked-salmon sandwiches.

'Hmm.' Simon studied her. 'There's only one thing that I don't get about it all.'

'What's that?'

'Your part in this. I mean, it's all very well Nigel saying he's worried the relationship won't last, but here you are, bursting with happiness—'

'Literally,' said Lucinda.

'Exactly. So why should any divorce judge believe all this guff about Nigel being afraid the relationship won't last.'

'Well . . . oh dear, this is the difficult part, Simon. I've got to say I'm a bit worried about it too. About the relationship. Say I do feel insecure. I've got to put that in a letter. And also I certainly can't be living in some mansion that Blue's bought, because Nigel's also going to say that the little house where we are is most unsuitable for a baby. So we'll have to stay there until the thing's gone through. It has to look really good on paper, you see. Steve's explained that if it's not presented properly, and convincingly, no divorce judge will approve it. I'm sure Blue won't mind, not really, that he'll go along with it if I explain properly. Well, I thought so at first. Now I'm not quite so sure.'

'So he doesn't know anything about all this?'

'Well, no, he doesn't. None of it. I'm beginning to wish I'd told him about it in the first place, so he could get used to the idea slowly. But it's a bit late for that now. So – I wondered what you thought about it, exactly how I should play it, so to speak.'

'I think,' said Simon carefully, 'you have to tell him just the minute you can. Be completely honest. And I also think you have to be prepared for him minding quite a lot.'

'Oh dear, do you?'

Simon thought of Blue, his pride in and love for Lucinda, his driving, pugnacious energy, his old-fashioned, working-class proprietorial attitude and tried to imagine his reacting sympathetically to Lucinda's plan. It wasn't very easy.

'I do, my darling, yes. I should get it over just as soon as you can, if I were you. Really soon. Before it's too late.'

'Oh,' said Lucinda. 'Oh, goodness. Well – all right, Simon. If that's what you really think.'

'It's what I really think,' said Simon.

Chapter 32

'Oh God,' said Debbie. 'Oh God, oh God, oh God.'

She felt – what did she feel? Scared. Very scared. Shocked at herself, at what she had done. Disbelieving of what she had done. Excited, of course. Emotionally and sexually.

And happy. Brilliantly, feverishly, shakily happy.

She was at her desk; the same desk she had been at, twenty-four hours earlier, in the same office, and that in itself was hard to believe, that she was still sitting there, working, or supposedly working; that the world had not dropped from its axis, time had not speeded up nor stood still; that all around her, people were working and chatting and laughing and fretting, doing the same sort of things in the same sort of way, as she was presumed to be doing. And she looked the same – she kept checking that, for reassurance, getting the mirror from her drawer, looking at her face, scared of what it might show. Things like recklessness and betrayal and greed; but none of them were there. It was the same face, pale, rather thin, with the same eyes, large and admittedly rather dark-ringed, and the same mouth – thinking of what that mouth had been doing and saying only twelve hours earlier, Debbie flinched, wondered how it could possibly not show.

And she sounded the same; she kept hearing herself saying things like, 'I'm fine, thanks,' and, 'I'll get that release off today,' and, 'I could send a bike with the samples,' and, 'Yes, of course I can run off that presentation document.'

And yet, everything had changed. Nothing was the same, nor ever would be again, whatever she did now, and however much she might wish it.

She was no longer nice – or quite nice – respectable Debbie

Fielding, married happily – or quite happily – to Richard, mother of three children, struggling to keep her family and her job and her husband all going in the same direction, with just about the same degree of success, her main concern being when she could get to Sainsbury's and whether she had over-spent on the credit card that month. Indeed, she wondered how any of those things could possibly have ever concerned her for more than a moment or two. She was Debbie Fielding, adulteress; she had a lover, a man who was not her husband, who she had been to bed with, and she couldn't wait to do so again, and she felt really bad and really wonderful in equal proportions and at the same time.

She couldn't quite believe she had behaved so badly; that they hadn't just had a drink the night before, maybe even dinner, done a bit of flirting, maybe even kissed and – well, kissed. But – bed. Sex. On the first date. As you might say. It was awful. Dreadful. Shocking. A nice girl like her . . .

He had been waiting for her at the Criterion. Careful not to appear wretched, desperate, silly, she had made an effort, done her best with her hair, put on lots of make-up, rushed out and bought herself a new shirt at Next (that being the only store that could remotely pretend to be cool anywhere near the office), rather than the shabby T-shirt she'd pulled over her tear-stained face, been ready with a light-hearted version of her story. He'd asked her what she wanted to drink: 'White wine spritzer, please,' she said (it took a lot of those to make her drunk), and after ordering it and a beer for himself, Joel had just sat looking at her for a minute and then said, 'You look great.'

'I don't think so.'

'No, you do. I mean it. So – want to talk about it? Whatever's upsetting you so badly?'

'Not – not really.'

'In that case,' he said, grinning, 'you've got me here under false pretences, Mrs Fielding—'

'Don't call me that. Mrs Fielding is my mother-in-law.'

'Sorry. But it's what you are. I thought. OK, Debbie then, you've got me here under false pretences. What shall we talk about instead?'

472

'Um – not sure.' This was awful; her mind was a blank, she couldn't think of a word to say; she stared into her glass, feeling hot and cold and thoroughly miserable. She should never have come, it had been a terrible idea, she'd just drink the spritzer and then go, and—

'Mind out what you're bloody doing.'

It was Fate: taking over her life, making the events of the next three hours absolutely inevitable; Fate in the form of a man, slightly the worse for the hour or so he had already spent in the bar, pushing past them, knocking Joel's arm, and thus the contents of Joel's bottle of beer over Debbie. Over quite a lot of her, but most markedly, her chest.

'Oh God, I'm so sorry,' said the man. 'God. Here, let me get a cloth from the bar, wait there . . .' He disappeared.

Joel sat looking at Debbie rather ruefully, and then pulled a handkerchief out of his pocket and started dabbing at her jacket. 'I'm sorry. How awful.'

'Oh, doesn't matter. Honestly. It's an old shirt.' About three hours old; nicely ruined. And now she'd smell like a brewery for the rest of the evening. Good thing it was nearly over.

The other man reappeared, with two clean tea-towels, and started dabbing at Debbie's jacket as well. It was quite funny really, she tried to tell herself, and then began to feel irritable instead.

'Give those to me,' she said, and made for the Ladies, where she applied lots of cold water, but the stain was quite bad. And the smell. And she couldn't take the shirt off as she wasn't wearing anything underneath except her bra. Well, best thing was to make her excuses and leave. She went back to the bar, to where Joel was sitting, looking rather depressed.

'Look, I think I'd better just go home. I can't sit here, smelling of Budweiser or whatever it was for the rest of the evening.'

'Oh, OK.' He was clearly embarrassed, miserable about the way the evening was turning out. He drained his glass. 'I'll escort you to the tube.'

'Yeah, all right, thanks.'

They walked out into the evening sunshine; or rather the petrol-induced haze that was Piccadilly Circus at the end of a hot day. Tourists sat around, wearing only shorts. 'Maybe I should follow their example,' said Debbie, trying to sound light-hearted. 'Just take the shirt off.'

'Fine by me,' Joel said.

A bunch of girls walked past, giggling and chattering, carrying Miss Selfridge bags; Joel looked after them. Debbie felt irritated and still more depressed; they were all young, pretty, clearly unencumbered by husbands or babies.

'Nothing like a bit of retail therapy,' Joel said.

'Well, no,' said Debbie.

'You know, I don't mind shopping. Maggie – she's my girlfriend – says it's one of my few virtues.'

OK, he had a girlfriend. Well. Of course he would have done. Men like Joel always had girlfriends, with great figures and designer clothes, not small and skinny and chainstore-dressed. But why had he told her then? To let her know he had one, perhaps that this was a strictly platonic meeting: or to make himself appear more fanciable, or— Stop it, Debbie, concentrate, there's no way it matters to you whether he's got a girlfriend or not.

'But I mean – what bloke wouldn't like it?' he said. 'Hanging around with crowds of women, preferably near the changing room. Great.'

'I don't think my husband sees it quite like that,' said Debbie. And thought how wholesome the conversation had become, him talking about his girlfriend, her talking about her husband.

'In fact,' Joel was looking at her now and smiling, 'I just got an idea. It's Thursday, isn't it? Late-night shopping. Let me buy you a new shirt.'

'Oh Joel, no.'

'Oh Debbie, yes. Come on, it'll make me feel better, less guilty. I'd like to. What's your favourite shop?'

'No. I can't let you do that.'

'Why can't you?' He grinned at her. 'I'll enjoy helping you choose. And hanging round the changing room.'

Suddenly she felt more cheerful. It would be fun. *He* was fun. And as an alternative to going home to an empty house and feeling a total failure and waiting for Richard to ring, it was pretty attractive.

'All right,' she said, 'you're on. But you're not paying for it.'
'I am. But we can argue about that later.'

They went to Miss Selfridge, the big one inside Selfridges itself. It was full of lovely sexy tops, strappy T-shirts, denim shirts, boned corselettes; none of which remotely replaced the shirt. It was also full of girls, young girls, with their bosoms breaking out of their tops and their long legs bare. Joel began to feel slightly dizzy.

'That's nice,' he said, pointing at a strapless, clingy dress, very, very short.

'It is,' she said, 'it's totally gorgeous, but I don't see it in the office.'

'I don't know. Might get the clients pouring in even faster. It would look bloody good on you, I tell you that.'

'Joel, I don't think so.'

'Try it on. Go on.'

Slightly to his surprise, she did, came out of the changing room smiling. She had an amazing smile, it was that big mouth of hers and those perfect white teeth. She was a bit like Julia Roberts . . . Joel! Come on!

She was wearing the dress; it looked incredible on her. She was very skinny, and it only came about a quarter of the way down her thighs, so that he was able to see more of her legs. Her really rather amazing legs.

'You should get it,' he said.

'You think?'

'Sure. Turn round. Give us a twirl.'

She twirled, laughing, and then it happened: the dress, which really required more of a bosom than she possessed, slipped, and for a moment, maybe five moments, Joel found himself staring at her breasts. Which were small, OK, but absolutely perfect: firm, dark-nippled . . . Joel had never liked big breasts. Well, not as much as he liked small ones. He swallowed, felt a response, a very strong response, it threatened to become embarrassing, and tried to tear his eyes away. And then she hitched up the dress, and her eyes met his, half-startled, half-amused, and – something else? what? something slightly carnal – and disappeared into the changing room. And Joel turned away and tried to distract himself by staring at some jewellery, and then she reappeared, wearing a white cotton shirt, slightly over-sized, the sort Princess Diana had worn and made famous the year before, photographed with the princes.

'I think this is a bit more suitable,' she said.

'Well, it's great,' Joel said, 'but I still think you should buy the dress.'

'Well, I don't,' she said firmly. 'That is no dress for a – a mother.'

'But Debbie, you don't look like a mother.'

'I'm not sure if that's a compliment or not. I mean, I *am* a mother. I'm not ashamed of it.'

'I know you're not. But mothers look mumsy. You look – well, like a very sexy girl. Who should be wearing that dress. Preferably not all of it. Go on, get it.'

'Joel, I'm not buying it.'

'OK. Let's get the shirt. I'll pay.'

'You won't.'

'I will. I really do want to. Now are you going to leave it on?'

'Yes, I am. Get rid of the smell of bitter or whatever it was.'

'It was not bitter,' he said, 'and it was not Budweiser. I have my pride. It was Michelob.'

'Is that a trendy beer?'

'Very trendy. Ask your husband.'

'He wouldn't know a trendy beer if – if it was chucked all over him,' she said, and then, 'I didn't say that.'

'Yes, you did. Sorry.'

She was happy and easy now, an intimacy forged by the shopping experience; her mood had changed. He didn't feel sorry for her now. He just wanted to spend some more time with her.

'Where shall we go next?' he said.

'I really ought to go home' Debbie said.

'No, you shouldn't. What for? And I haven't just spent ten quid on you for nothing. Come on, tell you what, let's buy ourselves a picnic and go up to the park.'

He watched her struggling with this, knowing that he shouldn't have asked her, and half-hoping she'd say no.

She didn't: she grinned at him. 'OK,' she said.

So they went back into Selfridges and bought some French bread and some pâté and some strawberries and a bottle of white wine – 'won't show on your new shirt' – and got a cab up to Regent's Park. Where they settled on the grass, near one of the ponds, and Joel opened the wine and the sun was warm, slanting through the trees, and they set out their picnic, chatting easily about work and colleagues and films they had seen and their ambitions and even those of their partners, and he thought how lovely she was and what fun – interspersed with thoughts of how lovely her breasts were, and how good her legs, and how much he would like to see the bit in between, only clearly he wasn't going to. And thought that really the evening should end like this, happy, flirty, quite safe.

And then she lay back on the grass, clearly just slightly drunk, flung her arms out to the sides, and said, 'Oh, this is such fun.'

And he suddenly wanted to know a bit more about her.

That was when things got really dangerous; looking back, she had seen she should never have done that, should have remained sitting primly upright; because he leaned over her, smiling down at her, and said, 'S-o-o . . . what *was* the matter? This afternoon?'

She shouldn't have told him that either; she shouldn't have become so relaxed, so happily reckless.

'Oh, it's all totally silly,' she said. 'Just a – a domestic, you know.'

'I do.'

And he did; Maggie and he had lots of domestics, over stupid things like leaving the milk out of the fridge and him playing music he knew she didn't like, or should have known she didn't like. And more serious things too, like him not phoning her enough, or forgetting some footling anniversary, like it was six months since the first time they had sex, and he hated them, they seemed so unnecessary, a waste of emotional energy; rows, he felt, should be about real things, important things. His nan, who should have known, he thought, having been happily married to his grandad for over fifty years, despite her frequent assertions that he was a silly old fool, always said that you should only have a row if it was impossible

477

not to; and to Joel that made perfect sense. If you could shut up about whatever it was, bite it back, then a nice day or a good evening wouldn't be ruined, cut off in its prime. He was very good at shutting up and biting it back; it was all part of his rather intense personality.

'Oh Joel, it's so complicated,' Debbie was saying now. 'I can't go into it all. But – we fell out weeks ago, over his new job – he got one in Scotland.'

'And let me guess, you didn't want to go to Scotland.'

'Well, not terribly. And unfortunately, I sort of said that.'

'Right.'

'And then the other day he saw me leaving a hotel with Simon—'

'With Simon?'

'Yes.'

'What hotel?'

'The Royal Garden. And – and he decided we must be having an affair. It's just ridiculous!'

'Is it?'

'Well, of course.'

'I'll tell you something,' he said, 'if I saw you leaving the Royal Garden Hotel with Simon Beaumont, I'd probably think you were having an affair as well.'

'You wouldn't! But why?'

'You can't be that dumb,' he said.

'But he's miles older than me, and he likes things like horses and drives a Range Rover and—'

'Dear God,' said Joel, and he started to laugh. 'If that was your defence, I really am beginning to feel very sorry for your husband.'

'But why?'

'Debbie, Simon Beaumont is extremely charming and incredibly good-looking, added to which he's a smooth bastard and—'

'No, he's not,' said Debbie heatedly.

'He must seem so, to your husband. And he's successful—'

'Not any more.'

'No, OK, not any more. Nice set of knives to twist in a husbandly wound though.'

'But it was broad daylight, and we'd only had a drink.'

478

'Did you know that fifty per cent of adulteries are committed at lunchtime? In hotels. When it's usually broad daylight, it must be said. Dear oh dear. Poor old Richard.'

'Oh shut up,' she said irritably, and she began to tidy up the picnic and to pull her jacket on.

'Well, you are being rather naive.'

'I am not.'

'Yes, you are. I'm surprised at you.'

'Well, I'm sorry for that,' she said. 'Now I think I'd better get back.'

'Oh, for God's sake,' he said, 'stop being so touchy. I've paid you a compliment, why do you have to take it the wrong way?'

'Doesn't sound like much of a compliment to me.'

'Well, it should. I'm saying there you are, so lovely and sexy and funny and fun, and of course the poor chap's jealous. Of any man who comes near you. You must see that. I mean, there you were coming out of a hotel with a particularly fine example of one. Man, I mean, not hotel. Give the poor guy a break.'

She felt rather odd suddenly. Odd and very disturbed. But more than anything, cross. What was he doing, telling her how she should behave, that she should understand how Richard must feel? It was arrogant in the extreme.

'Joel, I'm afraid you don't understand at all,' she said, trying to sound cool. 'And it's not really anything to do with you. As far as I can see. Look, we'd better go, it's getting very late and—'

'It is something to do with me,' he said.

'It is not. Why should it be?' Her temper was rising. She stood up, glaring down at him.

'Because you did, at some stage, agree to tell me about it. Because you were crying this afternoon, so you're obviously upset. And I like you enough to mind about that. Because I think you've been quite foolish. Actually.'

'Just shut up, will you. I don't want to listen to a lecture from you, I have quite enough of those already. Everyone does it—'

'Well, I'm not surprised,' he said, 'actually. When you're so – so dense.'

'I am not dense!'

'Yes, you are. Irresistibly, sexily, gloriously dense.'

Debbie scowled at him; he looked at her, his dark eyes snapping with amusement. 'You are so . . . so . . .' she said.

'What? So what?'

She struggled to find some cutting phrase, then finally 'Rude' she said, 'Really, really rude. I don't know what I'm doing here. Why I came out with you at all.'

Joel began to laugh; he sat there, on the grass, looking up at her. Then he reached up and caught her hand and pulled her down onto the grass beside him.

She tried to pull her hand free. 'Don't.'

He hung onto it, still laughing: then said, suddenly more serious, 'I'll tell you what you're doing here, and why you came out with me. Because you bloody well wanted to. I know you did. I'm not a complete idiot. You wanted to be with me, like I want to be with you.'

'Don't flatter yourself,' she said, and then was so appalled that she should have said anything so crass, that she stopped and just sat there staring at him.

'I'm not,' he said. 'I'm not flattering myself one bit. You may not have wanted it quite as much as I did, but I think you knew exactly what you were doing – shit, Debbie, stop glaring at me like that.'

'What do you expect me to do?' she said furiously. 'Smile dotingly at you?'

'You could try,' he said, and then he leaned forward and kissed her. On the mouth. Quite hard.

And she sat there and wanted to push him away, to slap him, to stalk off to the road and into a cab – but she couldn't. Because his mouth, working on hers, his tongue, seeking out hers, was having an extraordinary effect on her. She felt it, that mouth, felt it in her whole head, which was throbbing suddenly, and thoughts were moving around in it – no, not thoughts, nothing so orderly, just scarily strong responses. And in her breasts now – how could a kiss, a kiss on the lips, reach your breasts – but it had, it was making them desperate for touching, for caressing, for kissing too, and it was all she could do not to reach for one of his hands and place it there. And then the sensation moved on, lower, lower, somewhere in the region of her stomach, or even, oh God, yes, even there, and she felt herself grow sweetly soft and liquid and still the darts of pleasure moved on, travelling as if on fine threads, fine piercing threads, broadening now, making their way through her, pushing, reaching, parting her on their way, until she was entirely consumed by them and all she could think of was how quickly she might be able to answer them, to respond, and when Joel said, 'Shall we go back to my place then?' any other answer but, 'Yes,' was unthinkable. Absolutely, gloriously, emphatically unthinkable.

Her phone rang as she sat there, thinking about him, about herself, how wicked she was.

'Hello, Debbie.'

'Oh. Hi, Joel.' God, she sounded ordinary. So ordinary.

'How are you?'

'I'm fine.'

'You are indeed. Very fine. I can't stop thinking about how fine you are.'

'Well – good.' She'd forgotten how to handle these sorts of conversation.

'Yes. I just called to say, I'm off to the Bahamas first thing. I'm financing it myself – just praying the Editor will buy it.'

'I'm sure he will. It sounds tough.'

'Oh, it will be. But – I wondered if I could see you again tonight. If Hubby is still away.'

'Well . . .' If she said no, if she never, ever saw him again, she could be excused, on grounds of temporary insanity, temptation beyond endurance, momentary weakness; it wouldn't have been an affair, just a bit of very bad behaviour, but not life-threatening, marriage-wrecking; no one need know, she could just bury it deep within her and her hence-forth totally blameless, wifely life; she could give up work, insist she wanted to go to Scotland, learn to make cakes, take a pride in her housework, and even if she did get found out, surely to God everyone was allowed one mistake, one piece of folly, so she'd just say no and . . .

'Yes, of course,' she said. 'That would be very nice.'

'And anyway,' she said to him later, draining her rather large glass of Chardonnay, finding it impossible not to smile, 'since my husband is convinced I'm having an affair with someone else . . .'

'It's clearly fine for you to be with me. I'm your alibi. The more time you spend with me, the better.'

'Well, I suppose so.'

'OK then. Your place or mine?'

'Joel! What do you think?'

'Oh, and I've got a present for you,' he said, when they got back to his flat, handing her a parcel. 'Open it quickly And put it on. And then take it off again. Straight away.'

It was a strapless, clingy stretch dress. Very, very short. Debbie burst into tears.

Chapter 33

July to August, 1990

She really hadn't wanted to tell anyone yet; she wanted to keep it safe, safe from everybody's eyes and opinions; she didn't want it discussed and pronounced upon, she didn't want to be warned about it, told it was too soon or too much, didn't even want to be congratulated. It was nothing to do with anybody else, when the next step was so far into the future; it was her treasure, to be locked safely away for her eyes only, a source of happiness to be drawn on when she needed it.

She didn't say anything to her parents; simply that she had had a lovely time, that Jamie had been totally wonderful, that his family was great (although his mother could be difficult), that she had loved Boston and adored Cape Cod, and that she couldn't believe it was actually over.

Both Simon, who had met her at the airport, and Elizabeth, who had sat on her bed and chatted with her before she went to sleep, had felt there was more to be said, without knowing whether it was good or bad. She was too reserved, too anxious to discuss detail – the houses, the beaches, Frances's hair – too wary of talking about it.

'You don't think it's over?' Elizabeth said to Simon later.

'No,' he said, 'she's too happy for that. Maybe the family weren't particularly welcoming.'

'Don't think so,' said Elizabeth. 'She had so much good to say of them, especially Jamie's brother. What's his name? I keep forgetting.'

'Bif.'

'Extraordinary name.'

'Americans are very strong on nicknames,' said Simon. 'They're all about class. If you're called Bunny or Binky or –

483

yes, Bif – you're posh; but not Butch. Same for girls. You'd be probably called Bootsy.'

'But why?'

'It's a diminutive for Elizabeth.'

She shuddered. 'Thank God I'm English. Anyway, she obviously loved Bif. And Mr Cartwright. And she seems very happy. Let's try not to worry about it. Any news on the house?'

'The Hong Kong lot loved it, but they made a very low offer.'

'Oh dear.'

'No, no. The longer we manage to keep it, the better. Not just sentiment, the value's creeping up all the time.'

Two days later, Annabel couldn't bear it any longer. She'd had a phone call from Jamie.

'Please, please let me tell the family. They haven't stopped talking about you since you left, how much they loved you, how right for me you were.'

She hesitated, then: 'All right, but not till I've told mine. I'll fax you when I've done it.'

Her parents were having a drink together in the garden; Annabel went out to them. She had her ring on, her hands in her pockets.

'Hi. Mind if I join you?'

'Of course not. Don't be silly.'

She sat down, took a glass of wine. 'Thanks. How's it going, Dad?'

'Oh, you know. Fine. Lot of people inviting me to lunch.'

'Good. You'll be back in work in no time then.'

'Could be.' He grinned at her; his usual confident grin. She was comforted. In spite of her total faith in him, she had been worrying.

'And then we won't have to sell the house?'

'Possibly not.'

'Great. Um . . . I want to tell you something.'

'Ye-es?'

She took her left hand out of her pocket, held it out to them. 'Do you like that?'

They looked at it in silence; then, 'It's lovely, darling,' her father said, 'absolutely lovely. Er . . . any significance in the finger?'

'Just a bit,' she said. 'Jamie's asked me to marry him.'

There was another silence; then her mother went over to her, hugged her.

'Darling,' she said, 'how absolutely lovely for you. I'm thrilled. Congratulations.'

And her father said, 'Sweetheart, that's wonderful news. Lovely. I'll get some champagne. Pity the others aren't here.'

That was all they said about it, either of them; they just sat there in the lovely warm evening drinking champagne, and let her talk endlessly about Jamie and how much she loved him and how happy she was.

'I know you'll think we're too young, but we're not. I just know it's right. He's so – so sweet, oh that sounds corny but it's how he is, totally sweet to me and gentle, and he's funny and we laugh lots, and never stop talking, which is like you guys really, and enjoy masses of the same things and— well, he's perfect and it's perfect. I do hope you're happy about it.'

'Darling, of course we are,' her father said, kissing her.

'It's lovely to see you so happy,' her mother said. 'Now tell us more about the family, they obviously made a big impression on you.'

Days later, when Jamie phoned to say how thrilled his parents had been, how his mother wanted to know when Annabel could come over for an engagement party, that they assumed it would be quite a long engagement, 'at least two years, Mother thought, and I guess that's about right', that they loved the thought of having her living in Boston with them, that of course she must bring her parents with her when she came over for the party, and her brother and sister too, and when might the party in London be, what London papers were they announcing it in, they thought they'd put it in the *Boston Globe* and maybe the *Washington Post*, and that his mother was writing to Elizabeth 'right now' . . . . all through that phone call, almost against her will, she kept contrasting the two reactions of their two sets of parents and thinking how lucky, how very lucky she was.

Catherine had been quite shocked by how upset Simon was when she told him she'd been sacked. He went rather pale and his hand shook as he picked up his mug.

She'd asked him round for tea, rather diffidently, thinking he might be busy, but he had accepted with great enthusiasm.

'I'd love it,' he said, 'a wonderful oasis in my rather barren diary.' But: 'Christ,' he said now, 'I'm so sorry. The bastards. Catherine, my love, I am so, so sorry. I never dreamed they'd get rid of you.'

'Oh, I did,' she said almost cheerfully, 'I thought it straight away. It was fairly irregular, our arrangement, you know, and the other girls didn't really like it. They did give me two weeks' money in lieu of notice.'

'How astonishingly generous of them,' said Simon. 'Well, I suppose it'll help. Oh, darling! What are you going to do?'

'Not sure,' she said. She didn't want to tell him she had been driven to throwing herself on the mercy of her parents-in-law; it would make him feel worse. 'Get another job, I suppose. Maybe go back to the one I had before. They were quite sorry I left.'

'Yes, but that won't cover the school fees, will it?'

'Um, no. Probably not.'

'So – oh God, I feel so terrible.'

'Simon, don't. It really isn't your fault. Or even your problem.'

'Of course it's my problem. I'm very fond of you, Catherine. I loved having you in the office. And it was so nice to think of Freddie being happily back at his old school.'

'Well . . . quite happily,' said Catherine, 'there were still problems, as you know. But, well, I've got various ideas. Please don't worry about us, Simon. We'll be fine. You know what we all felt when Freddie went missing. Nothing really mattered except getting him back safely. Which we did. So . . .'

She was shocked to see there were tears in his eyes. She went over to him, put her arms round his shoulders.

'Dear, dear Simon, don't. You're so sweet to worry about us, but . . .'

'Sorry,' he said. 'Guess I'm feeling a bit emotional altogether. My eldest, Annabel, you know, she's got herself engaged to some Yank . . .'

'Engaged! But she's only eighteen or something, isn't she? Mind you, I was only nineteen.'

'I know, but it's different these days. They don't marry so

young. And yes, she's eighteen. God knows what will come of it; her mother and I both think – hope – it'll never happen. We've hardly met him. But if it does, then she'll go and live in Boston, she says. Not ideal. Still, it's her life, not ours. Her we have to think about.'

'Of course. But from what you've told me, she's pretty feisty. I doubt it'll last. With him being all that way away.'

'Maybe not.' Freddie had appeared in the doorway, smiled at him rather uncertainly. 'Hello, Freddie, I presume. Very nice to meet you. Your mother says you're all going to the adventure playground. I won't keep her much longer.'

'That's perfectly all right,' said Freddie graciously. 'Perhaps you'd like to come with us?'

'Well, that's very kind, but I do have to get back. I've got lots to do. You enjoying the holidays?'

'Very much, thank you. Going on lots of picnics and things. With my friend Dominic.'

'And where does Dominic live – near here?'

'Quite near.'

'I tell you a very good place for a picnic, the Isabella Plantation in Richmond Park. Very good for hide and seek, and wonderfully greedy ducks. They'll eat anything you don't.'

'That's a very good suggestion,' said Freddie, 'perhaps you'd like to come with us when we go there?'

'I might just do that. Thank you for the invitation. Meanwhile, look after your mother, won't you?'

'Of course.' He looked up at Simon consideringly. 'I wish you were our grandpa,' he said, 'instead of the one we've got.'

'Freddie!' said Catherine.

'Now that *has* done wonders for my ego,' said Simon, laughing.

He told Elizabeth about it, that night in bed.

'Do you think I'd make a good grandpa?'

'I do actually,' she said seriously. 'Like you're a wonderful father.'

'Thanks for that. Do you mean it?'

'Yes, I do. But I hope Annabel isn't going to rush you into it.'

'Into grandfatherhood? God, what a thought. Oh Mrs Beaumont, what is to become of us? Give me a kiss. Hey . . .'

487

His hand, moving thoughtfully over her breasts, stopped. 'What are these? You seem to be turning into Samantha Fox.'

'I know,' she said. 'Odd, isn't it? They've suddenly got bigger.'

'You're not—'

'I'm not. Most emphatically. That would be one problem too many. But I did talk to my gynaecologist, actually. Earlier in the week.'

'And?'

'She says it happens sometimes. Especially in ladies of my age. So she's changing my pill. To a lower dose one.'

'Oh, OK. They tender, those luscious page three breasts?'

'Bit.'

'They're very exciting. If I'm very careful of them, could I – could we . . .?'

'You – we – could.'

They did.

Afterwards, he held her and told her he loved her, and she thought with a kind of astonishment how everything was changing. She felt confident again, confident and happy and at the same time, gentler, more compliant. They were rediscovering each other physically, slowly and sweetly, and each time she felt safer, the ghost gone from their bed. It was very lovely. He was very thoughtful and patient and careful with her, and she always came: often as she had in the early days, not once, but many times, riding it on and on, each more exquisitely violent than the last. Life, for all their troubles, had become very good again.

He turned away from her now, eased by the sex into a deep sleep. He had been sleeping badly, ever since he had been fired. He had been wounded, humiliated, in a way he couldn't admit to anyone, even her, although of course she knew. It was worst at night, as with all troubles, and many, many times she would wake at two or three and find him gone, and see the light under his study door. But – he was, as always, being brave, positive, uncomplaining. She had never admired him more.

The air was soupy with warmth: that was Joel's first impression of Nassau; it was like a warm cosh as you got off the plane. The second, as he travelled through it in a cab on his way to

Paradise Island was of a kind of charming Toytown, with its packed streets and sudden squares, its wonderful colonial-style buildings and its policemen dressed in gold-braided white uniforms with white pith helmets and white gloves, constantly and rather ineffectually blowing whistles and shouting at traffic; and endless horse-drawn carriages painted in a rainbow of different colours, driving tourists round the city. The noise was astonishing: car horns set on permanent 'go', roaring motorbikes, shouting children, and an incredible mishmash of music – reggae, rock and the native soca – coming not only from the cars but from the stereo systems carried on the shoulders of teenage boys, the grinning, cheerful teenage boys.

The women were gorgeous, beautifully dressed in brilliant silks and satins, wearing flowered and beribboned hats, smiling, swaying their way through the traffic, beautifully dressed all of them, but it was the men who really fascinated Joel; coxily confident in their three-piece suits, open-necked silk shirts and snakeskin shoes.

His taxi driver, beaming, friendly, proud of his city, offered to take him on a swift tour. Joel accepted, writing off the inevitable rip-off against background information for any early conversations he might have with Allinson and others in the party at the Ocean Hill. He saw, against a slightly jet-lagged blur, the port, the major buildings – the Senate Chamber, the Supreme Court and the Government Publication Office, all of them grand in concept and perfect examples of colonial architecture. 'And what's that there?' he said, pointing to a lovely three-storey structure, with encircling verandahs, apparently empty.

'That's the Royal Victoria Hotel. Queen Victoria she stayed here, and Winston Churchill – and you heard of Rhett Butler?'

Joel said he had. 'The man he was supposed to be based on, he used the hotel, ran the blockades. The government owns it now, don't know what to do with it. You want to see the port?'

'Is it worth seeing?'

'Not really. Tell you what, we'll go to Government House, it's very beautiful. That's where the Governor General lived.'

It was rather gorgeous, Joel thought, neo-Classical, set at the top of a long flight of steps, painted pink and white.

'Your Queen stayed here, did you know that?'

'I didn't, no. I know her uncle was here in the war.'

'Oh, yes. The one who gave up the throne for love, yeah?'

'Well, yes.'

'Blake Higgs, you heard of him?'

'Er, I think so,' said Joel politely.

'Yeah, he wrote a song about the two of them. The Duke and Duchess.' He launched into song; 'It Was Love, Love Alone.'

'Very good,' said Joel.

'Lot of your royalty came here. Lot of princes and princesses. Prince Charles came – his wife is very beautiful, yeah?'

'Very beautiful.'

'I wish she'd come,' he said, and laughed. 'There, that's Graycliff, used to be where the West Indian Garrison lived – they guarded the city. Now it's a very, very good restaurant; you should go there. You plan to see anything of the Goombay?'

'I don't know,' said Joel carefully. 'What is it?'

'The Goombay Festival. Lasts for four months. Street parades, fashion shows, cook-outs – it's fun, man.'

'Then I'll try to catch something.'

'You do that.'

The tour continued to Potter's Quay, with its fruit and straw and shell markets: 'And there you are, the Paradise Island Bridge. You want to see any more now, or shall we go to your hotel?'

'Let's go to my hotel.'

He had tried and failed to book into the Ocean Hill Hotel on Paradise Island where the Bridgeman party were staying; having discovered the cost for even two nights, he was quite relieved. All the hotels on the island had been fully booked; he had had to settle for the Palace, in Nassau itself. It was hardly slumming it; its style had been clearly influenced by Government House, being also pink and white and colonial in concept, although its 170 rooms (as against the Ocean Hill's mere 70) spoke for its lower caste. But it would provide him with a base, from which to inveigle himself into the Ocean Hill; and if he failed to collar Allinson, he would have the very slight consolation of knowing he had saved several hundred pounds.

490

Even so, the investment in the trip had been considerable; he had bought some extremely expensive clothes – a linen suit from Armani, some lawn shirts from Harrods, some shoes from JP Tod, all befitting a guest at one of the most expensive hotels in the world, and some horrendously expensive leather luggage from Mulberry. It had better be worth it.

That was before he had discovered he couldn't get into the Ocean Hill. Bit of a waste, he supposed: but it would last him a lifetime. And in his pocket a new leather wallet, also from Mulberry – a present from Debbie.

'That's to make sure you think of me at least every time you spend any money. Which I daresay will be quite often.'

'I'll think of you all the time,' he said, kissing her. 'I don't need a wallet to make me do that.'

He checked in, established that the hotel ran a limo service – he could hardly arrive at the Ocean Hill in one of Nassau's rackety taxis – booked one for the evening and another for the following day, and went down to the palm-lined pool for a swim. He longed to go to bed, but he had to survive until the cocktail hour at the very least. He'd decided that would be the easiest way to collar Allinson. He was still there; Joel had phoned and checked before even leaving London.

'God, you must have fun doing your job,' said Debbie enviously. 'It's like a James Bond movie.'

'Oh, it is. Especially when I'm in bed with very beautiful girls, which I am all the time, of course.'

He was worried about Debbie; he knew he had walked into a quicksand. He kept hearing Simon Beaumont's voice saying, 'bit troublesome', and he could see she could be. Not just because she was married, and clearly not particularly happily, more because of how she was. Difficult and wilful. Why, in the name of God, had he got into this situation? He simply hadn't been able to resist it, that was why. It or her. She was quite – unusual. She seemed to employ the opposite of feminine wiles. Here I am, she said, take me or leave me. And he had been quite unable to leave her. Then.

But it had to be stopped: now. Before he got in any deeper. He'd call her when he got back, and they could part, friends still, loving, sexy friends after a sweet but very short adventure. He was good at those sorts of partings: always had been, seemed to have the knack of keeping emotions at bay. Probably because he'd been doing exactly that all his life.

It had been sweet though, and the sex had been amazing. Funny thing, sex; you could go to bed with women, sexy, independent, sophisticated women who had seemed to promise everything, and be disappointed. Then you had sex with a mother of three, from the suburbs, and found yourself completely swept away. She had been extraordinarily – driven. That was the only word for it. Fiercely determined to give – and to get – pleasure. And pleasure there had been, in abundance.

'You can't want any more,' he had said, laughing. 'You can't – I'm exhausted.'

'Yes, I do, I do, please,' she had said. 'It was so lovely, I want it again. If I can do it, you can.'

And somehow he had; encouraged by her hands and her tongue and her need and her greed. It had been astonishing. And very, very good.

It was five-thirty; fighting the almost overwhelming temptation to lie down on his bed and sleep, Joel put on his Armani suit, and one of his new silk shirts, and set out in his limo for the considerable challenges of his trip to Paradise Island.

Chapter 34

July to August, 1990

'I really liked that house,' said Blue. He was sitting at the table, drinking whisky; he smiled at her, patted the chair next to him. 'Come and join me. You never settle these days.'

This was the time to tell him: to explain why they couldn't move. And if he was really angry, well, that was her own fault. He'd get over it, he'd understand – in time. Of course he would. But . . .

'Which house?' she said, playing for time.

'The one in Weybridge. In Saint George's Hill – the one we saw this afternoon.'

'What, the one without a swimming pool?'

'That's the one. As opposed to the one with a swimming pool we saw last week some time.'

'But I thought you wanted a pool.'

'We can install a pool, Lucinda. It's not very difficult. Get a man with a digger along, show him where to dig, line it with tiles or whatever and fill it up with water. One swimming pool.'

'But is there room?'

'Of course there's bloody room. That garden is almost two acres. There's room for an Olympic pool. Now, I know I said Surrey wasn't ideal and it isn't, not for me, worse journey, but I liked the area and I think it'll be good for you and the boy.'

'Yes, I see.' Come on, Lucinda, say it. Get it over. He can't kill you.

'Very nice people around for you to make friends with, lot of scope for you in that house, do whatever you want to do. I think we should put in an offer straight away. Then we can move in, hopefully, in a couple of months. Three at the latest.'

'Blue, I'll be having the baby in three months. I really won't want to move then. I do wish you'd agree to let us wait. And Blue, there's something—'

'Lucinda, this is beginning to get on my nerves. I'm fairly patient but you are testing me rather.'

Now she'd missed her chance; he was irritable already. So – not just now. Wait for the next good mood.

'What on God's earth is the point in waiting? It's not as if the house is in a bad state, it seems fine to me. Just needs redecorating. It's even got a nursery.'

'With Peter Rabbit wallpaper,' said Lucinda witheringly.

'What the fuck's wrong with Peter Rabbit? Thought you liked all that sort of thing. And I just said redecorate, didn't I? Or did I not? Bloody change it before you do anything else.'

'Oh, stop swearing!' cried Lucinda. 'You know I hate it. And I hated that house and I don't want to move into it.'

'Lucy, you said you loved it. At the time. What's the matter with you?'

Lucinda hesitated. She had actually liked the house rather a lot. It was big and rambly, the very best of 1930s architecture, with huge sunny rooms, gorgeous parquet floors, a massive ranch-like kitchen with an Aga in it, and a wonderful garden, with an almost wild woodland area, furthest from the house. She could already see herself and a little two-year-old person, holding her hand, toddling through the long grass. It was perfectly lovely. But she couldn't have Blue buying it before the divorce went through. She really couldn't.

'I did like it,' she said, 'very much. But I don't want to move yet. I just don't.'

'OK. We'll buy it and move in after the boy's born. Have our first Christmas there. How would that be?'

It was hugely tempting: but it still wouldn't do. Steve Durham would be furious.

'No,' she said, 'no, I can't, Blue. I don't want to even think about moving until after I've had the baby. I wish you could get that into your head.'

'Oh for God's sake,' he said, 'I give up. I just bloody give up. I've never heard such fucking rubbish. I'm going out.'

And he was gone, slamming the front door behind him. Lucinda looked after it, quite frightened. She did seem to have made a mess of things. If Nigel knew how hard she was working on his behalf, how many lovely houses she'd refused, how difficult it had been – well, she'd tell him when it was all over. It would seem quite funny then. Hopefully.

'This is an amazing place,' said Joel.

'Isn't it? Never been here before then?'

'No.'

'Of course, it's even better in the winter. When it's less humid, slightly cooler. And – it must be said, a little chic-er. But, well, our host wanted to bring us here now. And who am I to complain?'

He grinned at Joel; Joel grinned back. He could see how Allinson had done so well; he was charming, easy to talk to, amusing, self-deprecating. He could hardly believe how simple it had been, making contact with him. He'd arrived at the hotel, just as the rich darkness was falling, made his way to the cocktail bar, ordered a Bellini and asked the barman if he knew a Mr Allinson. 'In Mr Bridgeman's party,' he added, handing the man some credentials, lest he think Joel was some kind of fraudster, trying to muscle in on the guests.

'Yes, sir, I do. Been here 'bout a week, I'd say. He usually comes down around now.'

'Good.'

He settled in a corner with his Bellini, enjoying the sunset, watching the flow of people into the bar. The drink made him sleepier; he swallowed a handful of nuts, desperately trying to pump up his energy levels. Half an hour, three-quarters went by, the Bellini long drunk; he asked for a Virgin Mary, afraid of what further alcohol might do to him. A waiter brought it over; then he noticed the barman saying something to someone, pointing him out.

And Allinson walked over to him, smiling; it was as simple as that.

'Sorry,' said Joel pleasantly holding out his hand, 'Joel Sherlock. You probably want some peace and quiet, after a long hard day here.'

'No, no it's fine. I'm sorry, I'm not sure . . .'

'I think you knew my uncle,' Joel said, 'Peter Sherlock. He's

495

a banker, with Chase, in New York. He said if I ran into you here, to say hi.' He thought of his real uncle, Mick Strickland, white-vanman and occasional wife-beater. What would Tim Allinson make of him?

Allinson frowned briefly, then said, 'Oh – possibly. Does ring a faint bell. How is he?'

'Pretty well, thanks. Yes.'

'Give him my best wishes, won't you?'

'Of course.' He obviously left no contact unturned, real or otherwise.

'I think we only met once. Anyway, no matter. Nice to meet you. You staying here?'

'Sadly not, couldn't get in. Staying at the Palace.'

'Oh, no! Not even on the island?'

'No, 'fraid not. But hey! Life's tough sometimes. Seriously, it's not too bad. And I'm only here for forty-eight hours.'

'Oh, really? You working?'

'You could say that. I'm in the export business; my company's got certain interests out here.'

'Oh, OK. Well, not a bad place to find yourself. Where do you live?'

'Oh, London – Kensington. And I've got a house in Berkshire.'

Body language is a powerful thing; its messages are subtle but instantly translatable. Allinson turned just imperceptibly towards Joel, and at the same time sat back in his chair. He clearly found him worth a little time and attention.

'So – working holiday?'

'Indeed. Monday I'm off to San Francisco. But I'm taking tomorrow off, exploring the place. That's why I came up here tonight, see if it was worth spending it here, or whether I should stay in downtown Nassau.'

'Oh, here, I'd say. Definitely. It really is marvellous. Not just the hotel, that is, but the whole island. You should go out to Paradise Beach, do a bit of para-sailing. It's a bit naff, but great fun. And—' A noisy group had come into the bar, two men of about fifty, and two extremely well-endowed and well-tanned blondes; they waved at Allinson. He waved back. 'Be over in a minute.' A pause, then: 'Mine hosts. Very nice, very nice indeed, but . . . well, you know. Quite exhausting.'

His eyes met Joel's in the flattery of conspiracy: 'we know, you and I, what's what', that look said; and Joel made a desperate attempt to return it.

'I'd ask you to join us,' Allinson said, 'but—'

'No, no, I'm having dinner with someone at my hotel. In fact, I must get back there now. Now that's what I call impressive,' Joel added. An extremely tall and beautiful girl had walked into the bar; she was tanned deep olive, not the slightly bright brown of the other two, and she was wearing a long, brilliant print silk dress, modestly cut at the front, outrageously low at the back and slit up the sides. A gleaming dark rope of hair hung over one shoulder in a plait; she was a class act if ever Joel had seen one. She waved at Tim and after glancing at the others, walked over to him.

'Hi, Tim.'

'Hello, my darling. Come and meet a new friend. Joel Sherlock. Joel Bibi, star of *Vogue*, *Harpers* and God knows what else. Joel's just visiting. Slumming it at the Palace.'

'That's a shame.' Bibi smiled at him. She had a low, slightly husky voice, with the obligatory American overtone to her Italian accent. She was gorgeous.

'Yes. Well, you know,' said Joel, 'one has to put up with these things. I'm thinking of spending tomorrow up here.'

'Oh, really? Well, it's pretty nice. Isn't it, Timmy?' Her eyes met Tim's. 'Although I'm a little tired tonight. I thought I might take tomorrow off, not go out on the yacht.'

'Do you know, my darling, I thought the same. A little of our young rocker friend goes a long way.'

'Although not as far as Thandie would like, I think. Anyway, I'd better go and join them. Nice to meet you, Mr Sherlock.'

If only she'd meant it, Joel thought.

'I'd better be off too,' he said. 'Maybe I'll see you tomorrow then? This is a great place for cocktails.'

'You might well. In fact, if you're at a loose end at lunchtime, come and find me. They do a marvellous poolside buffet.'

'Thanks. Very good of you. Nice to have met you anyway.' He shook Allinson's hand, waved at Bibi, and then went out to his limo. Fate seemed to be not only on his side, but to have picked him as her only teammate.

*

Debbie was hanging out the washing when Richard arrived home. She had spent the whole weekend in an orgy of house-keeping, had vacuumed and polished and dusted, washed paintwork, changed all the beds – and even done some weeding. She wasn't sure why, since she had no interest in pleasing Richard; she supposed it was so that he would have less to berate her with, when and if he came home. She had no idea what she was going to do; her life had become so confusing, so through-the-looking-glass-ish; no one would believe it if she told them about it: that she was having an affair with one man and her husband had accused her of having one with someone else.

It was a bit like being in a film; she kept looking at herself in various mirrors as she went around the house, and thought she looked much too ordinary to find herself in such a situation; she needed to look interesting, glamorous, mysterious, with a sun-tan and big hair ... now who would she cast as herself, she wondered, pulling some pillowcases out of the basket, rum-maging for pegs. Who could play someone so wonderfully intriguing, and obviously terribly sexy? Julia Roberts? That actress, Nicole Kidman, who was supposed to be getting engaged to Tom Cruise? Madonna? Yes, she'd be good: she'd be sexy enough. The idea made her giggle. She must tell Joel, he'd have some ideas. She kept thinking of things she must tell Joel.

'Hello.'

She jumped, dropped two of the pegs. It was Richard; he had come through the French windows that led from the kitchen. She looked at him and struggled to appear at least politely pleased to see him, while wishing desperately he was going to be away another five days. Or five weeks. Or five years. How could you live with a person who made you feel like that?

'Hi. Good journey?'

'Yes, it was OK, thanks. I was going against the traffic, of course. Terrible going the other way. Especially at the M5 turn-off.' He yawned.

'Were the children all right?'

'Yes. You know what they're like there, completely happy the minute they arrive.'

'Of course. Good.'

There was a silence; then he said, 'Let's go inside, shall we.'

'Must we? It's lovely out here.'

'Yes, we must. I want to talk to you.'

'We can talk out here.'

'Debbie, I want to go inside, all right?'

'All right.'

She followed him, wondering, half-hoping indeed, if this might be the beginning of the end.

'Richard has got it into his head that you and Debbie are having an affair,' said Flora.

They were sitting on the stone bench in the meadow; below them the sea was calm, brilliantly smooth and blue. Simon felt quite dizzy.

'He what?'

'Yes, I know it's ridiculous: of course it is. But he's very upset.'

'Christ,' he said, staring at her. 'Christ Almighty, how – how absurd.'

'It is a bit.'

'But – why? I don't understand.'

'Apparently he saw you and her coming out of a hotel last week. And she was kissing you and you were hugging her.'

'Flora, that's insane. I hug and kiss everybody – it's what I do. I've been known to hug and kiss you – would you like to suggest you're having an affair with me? Maybe that would distract him.'

'I know that. Of course. But Richard doesn't. He's a very, very jealous person, Simon. Like his father. And he was saying how much you obviously liked her, right from the start, how he noticed some sort of chemistry between you.'

'What!'

'Anyway, I did my best. Told him it was absurd. But I think he thought I was holding something back.'

'Flora! For Christ's sake. What was there to hold back?'

'Nothing, of course,' she said. She didn't meet his eyes.

'Bloody right there's nothing. Unless you are thinking of that moment in the kitchen a few months ago. In which case, let me tell you I was extremely upset and Debbie was . . . well, simply trying to make me feel better.'

'Which is precisely what I thought. I did see you, of course, I'm not completely senile, but I can recognise incipient sex when I see it.'

'Good phrase, Mrs Fielding.' Simon smiled for the first time. 'And the other night, she'd heard about my being fired, and offered to buy me a drink. That's all. So what did you actually say?'

'That I was sure nothing could be further from the truth and that I had never been given any cause to think it.'

'Well, thank you for that.'

'But I'm not sure he believed me. Altogether. The thing is, Simon, you and Debbie are quite close, there *is* some chemistry between you – he's right in that at least.'

'So what do you suggest?' he said. 'Any denial would be incriminating. He's obviously mad, I know he's your son, but—'

'I don't think he's mad,' said Flora, and her voice was cooler now. 'I think he's very unhappy, I think Debbie hasn't been as supportive as she might be, although I can see she's having a very difficult time.'

'What, over this Scottish business? Yes, she told me about that. Bit of a mess.'

'There you are, you see,' said Flora. 'You are close, you seem to know a lot about each other. I agree he's leaping to absurd conclusions but I do have to say, I can see – just about – how that has happened. Maybe that's what he's picked up.'

'Dear sweet Jesus,' he said, 'and I thought you were my friend.'

'I am your friend, Simon. I feel desperately sorry about the whole thing, and I wish I could help more.'

'So – where is Richard now?'

'On his way back to London. To see Debbie.'

'Oh God,' said Simon wearily. 'What a fucking mess.'

That he didn't apologise to Flora for his language showed her how extremely upset with her he was.

Joel slept till nine, then took the limo out to Paradise Island, spent the morning on Paradise Beach. He had never tried para-sailing; it was fantastic, rather like flying very slowly through the warm air. After that he went out on a Jet-Ski a couple of times, snorkelled for half an hour and then changed into shorts, polo shirt and deck shoes, put his wet swimming shorts into his rucksack and made his way up to the Ocean Hill.

It was still only half-past twelve, far too early to appear for lunch. The rich lunched late. He went into the bar, got himself a glass of iced water and wandered outside to explore the grounds. They were spectacular, terraced gardens, complete with statues, lush green lawns, brilliant flowers, a great swathe of tennis courts, a large lake and what looked like a chapel.

'Incredible, isn't it?' It was Bibi. 'Hi. I saw you wandering round the courts. Tim and I were contemplating a game, but the standard seemed a little high. McEnroe was the last person to play here. Oh, and Gerulaitis.'

'Sounds challenging,' said Joel, laughing.

'Just a little bit. What are you doing now? Timmy's gone to change.'

'Oh, just exploring.'

'Oh, OK. Well, I'll maybe see you by the pool. That'd be nice.'

'Indeed.'

She smiled at him; she was the same height as he was. Her eyes lingered, rather pointedly, on his mouth. Confusing. Very confusing.

'I'll see you later then,' she said. 'Oh look, there's Timmy coming now.' And she leaned towards him and kissed him briefly, but quite firmly, on the mouth.

'Tell me,' said Joel to Allinson when he had greeted him, 'what on earth is that place over there? That looks like a chapel.'

'A chapel, my boy. Genuine late twentieth century.'

Joel nodded. If nothing else came of this trip, it would make a fantastic travel piece. They walked across the drive to the chapel: it was purest kitsch, complete with stained-glass windows.

'Big favourite for Nassau Brides,' said Allinson. 'Can you wonder?'

They strolled back to the hotel, changed and then went down to the pool, which was set in the heart of the gardens. Waiters scuttled about ready to do their masters' bidding. Joel watched them, the way they practically genuflected when they delivered a glass of water, wondered if they would lick his bottom if he asked them and decided they probably would.

'Right. Buffet's over there, or you can order off the card. I usually have a club sandwich, they're excellent. And what about a beer?'

'Good idea,' said Joel. 'This is very kind of you.'

'Oh, not at all. Nice to have you to talk to.'

'Is Bibi around?'

'She's gone to have a nap. She doesn't eat.'

'Today I do.' Bibi flopped down on a lounger next to Joel, removed her bikini top and started to apply sun lotion to her breasts. They were incredible: full, but very firm. Joel tried not to stare at them, but she saw him trying and smiled, before closing her eyes and surrendering herself to the sun.

'So, what exactly does your company do?' said Allinson.

He was ready for this. 'We import glass and fine china. Which I'm sure you know have a huge sale here.'

'Oh right. Interesting. And where do you manufacture?'

'Mostly in the North of England, but we also have a factory in Limoges.' He was rather proud of that; a nice esoteric touch. He had just happened to read an article in one of the in-flight magazines about the pottery and porcelain of Limoges, and had added it to his story. 'And then we have another line, completely different – linen. We buy a lot from Russia, sell it to hotels, mostly American.'

'Uh-huh. Family company, is it?'

'Yup. My grandfather started it. I'm third generation. I enjoy it, but it's hard work.'

'Most ways of making money are. Mine host now, he works like the proverbial black. One mustn't say that any more, of course. But – eleven months of the year, pretty well eighteen hours a day, he's at his desk.'

'What does he do there?'

'He manufactures nuts, bolts and screws, and so on. Supplies firms like that new IKEA place.'

'I see.'

'And the voluptuous Thandie is the third wife. She's very sweet, but entre nous a little exhausting.'

'And – where do you live?'

'I'm in the throes of trying to decide that. I think I must be tired of life, because as Dr Johnson would have us believe, I'm suddenly tired of London. I'm contemplating Jersey or Guernsey, possibly New England. I don't have a family, I'm as free as air.'

He was obviously very rich then, Joel thought, if he could even contemplate the Channel Islands. Bastard. He'd been sinking beneath Allinson's charm; he remembered Gillian Thompson and Neil Lawrence and hauled himself briskly to the surface.

'And – what do you do? God, this sun is hot, must find some sun lotion. Excuse me a second...' He rummaged in his rucksack, found the Ambre Solaire and managed to switch on his tape recorder. It would be muffled, to say the least, but he should get something. He lay back again, smiled at Allinson. 'Sorry. You were saying?'

'I wasn't. But I think you'd asked me what I do.'

'Yup.'

'Oh, a bit of this, bit of that. My family owned a textile company, which I inherited and then sold a few years ago on the birth of man-made fibre. Best thing I ever did. Invested the money in stocks and shares, which have more or less stood the test of time. Although Black Friday didn't do me much good.'

'My uncle said he thought you worked for one of the banks.'

'No, not really.'

'Or was it Lloyd's? Lloyd's of London. Or was that wrong?'

'No, not entirely wrong. I wasn't a Working Name. I introduced people to Lloyd's, people I thought would benefit.'

'Sounds like *Blind Date*,' said Joel, laughing.

'Was, a bit. Only they got money instead of sex, or husbands or wives. Much more useful. I think I did a lot of good,' he added, settling back under the umbrella. 'Increased a lot of people's incomes for them.'

'But you weren't a Name yourself?'

'Oh, I was, yes. For a while.'

'I'd heard they were having a rough time.'

'Who, Lloyd's? A little, yes. Nothing serious.'

'I read something the other day about – what was it called? – asbestosis.'

'You don't want to believe everything you read in the newspapers, dear boy. I can show you a great many people who are still making a lot of money from being Members of Lloyd's.'

'I'm sure. God, this is nice. I'm in danger of drifting off. And I have to leave in about an hour. Might take a quick dip.'

'And I'm going to find some cigarettes. See you later.'

It was a risk; Allinson might find someone else to talk to. But he didn't want to appear as if he was interrogating him. He swam a couple of lengths, sharpening up his brain, deliberately breaking the warm easy spell he had been basking in, then paused, hanging onto the side at the deep end, breathing heavily. God, he was unfit. He was suddenly aware of a hand slithering into his trunks, caressing his buttocks.

'Hi,' said Bibi. 'Nice bum.'

'Well, thanks.'

She moved slightly, and moved her hand too, so that it was at the front of him, probing his pubic hair, seeking out his cock. His inevitably flaccid cock.

'Sorry,' he said. 'Cold water. Not a great aphrodisiac.'

'That's OK,' she said, and laughed. 'Do you normally need aphrodisiacs?'

'Absolutely not.'

'I didn't think so. It's very nice to see someone young here. A young man, anyway. They all seem to be a hundred. Except our friend the rocker, of course. How old are you, Joel?'

'Thirty-four.'

'Uh-huh. Good age.'

'I'm glad you think so. Er, here's Tim back again. I think we might get out.'

'He's not my keeper,' she said, and added, 'Or yours.'

'No, of course not. But—'

'Go on then,' she said. 'I'll see you later.' She set off towards the steps, pulling a sarong round her.

'That was great,' Joel said, settling down again beside Allinson. 'You going in?'

'No, too soon after lunch. Mind if I smoke?'

'Of course not.'

Allinson produced a pack of cigarillos, lit one, inhaled deeply.

'So – no truth in the rumours about Lloyd's then?' said Joel.

'None that troubled me,' said Allinson easily.

'Now come on . . .' Time was passing, he needed to bring this to some kind of conclusion. They couldn't chat about the joys of Lloyd's for the rest of the afternoon. 'Don't tell me you didn't know about it at all. I mean, why did you get out?'

'Well, there's no doubt it's going through something of a bad patch,' Allinson said. 'There have been a lot of claims and a few people have got their fingers burned. But like I said, you have to look at the big picture. Last bad patch was 1961. That's not a bad record.'

'But you still encouraged people in? As did Lloyd's.'

'Well, yes. It's a business, for God's sake. And it needed further investment. My job was to help them find that. Look, I don't know how you run your company, but I imagine you don't go round telling your customers about the mistakes you've made. That, let's say, several consignments of porcelain get smashed every year. You tell them you have a very small percentage of breakages.'

'Correct.'

'Well then. Lloyd's weren't about to tell a whole lot of prospective investors that they might get their fingers burned. That's not good business practice. They told them the truth – that the last time anyone lost a lot of money was twenty-five years ago.'

'Oh, OK,' said Joel slowly. 'Very good.'

'They took the view that any problems could be solved by substantial further investment, as I said. More Names, spread the risk. Which is where I came in.'

'Excellent,' said Joel. He grinned at Allinson. 'I really admire that. Good presentation, as you say. Tell me, is it true you have to be super-rich to be a Name?'

'It used to be. Lately they've lowered the bar considerably. Allowed much smaller people in. Who, of course, were delighted to join such a prestigious club . . .'

'Of course. Lot of snobbery there, I imagine. Which you could presumably cash in on.'

'Indeed.'

'Must have been fun.'

'It was, actually, you're right. There is no doubt I brightened a lot of people's lives, and their bank accounts.' He smiled at Joel.

'But – have they continued to be brightened?'

'I hope so. I really don't follow them all up, you know. They're not my concern. The Members' Agents do that.' He paused. 'You seem very interested in all this. Any particular reason?'

'Well – yes, to be honest. I had been considering joining myself, as a Name. So I am interested. Would you recommend it?'

There was a long silence; then Allinson said, 'Possibly not. Just at the moment. Give it a year or two, then talk to me. I'll give you my card.'

'Great. But I thought you weren't involved any more?'

'Not officially, no. But I can certainly put you in touch with the right people there.'

'Thank you. I'd really appreciate that. In the fullness of time. So – are you saying it's not true about the asbestosis?'

'My dear boy, I've told you. I don't worry about the detail.'

'Of course not. Do you think they suspect it?'

'Who, the Lloyd's people? Some of them may, I suppose.' He lay back, pulled his Panama hat over his eyes. 'It's quite a strong rumour.'

'But they need to keep the money coming in?'

'Absolutely. Only way to get by.'

'And is it working?'

'Oh, too early to say. I hope so.'

'And – you never find yourself lying awake at night, any of you?' Joel sat up now, moving in for the kill. Ready to run.

'Why should we? We've helped a lot of people make a lot of money.'

'But not the ones you've hauled in over the past – what – seven years? They must be losing it now.'

'I don't know that I like the phrase "hauling in",' said Allinson rather stiffly. He had pushed his hat back, was sitting up, looking at Joel.

'But that is what you've been doing, surely . . . And now it's all gone wrong and they're hopelessly in debt; people have actually killed themselves, you know. In despair. People who simply can't afford to meet the claims.'

'That's ridiculous!' said Allinson.

'It's not ridiculous. People whose lives have been ruined, completely ruined. Like – well, let's just take one person, shall we? Does the name Gillian Thompson mean anything to you?'

'It does not. And I think this conversation has gone on a little too long.'

'Gillian Thompson was a nice old lady, Mr Allinson, who gave piano lessons free and who baked you cakes when you went to see her about her investments. She killed herself, a year or so ago – lay down by her gas fire and died. Because there was nothing else for her to do. She was competely penniless, thanks to Lloyd's. She'd sold everything she had and it still wasn't nearly enough.'

'I told you, I've never heard of Gillian Thompson.'

'OK, so what about Neil Lawrence? Bankrupt, four children, attempted suicide. He was one of your imports too. Into the same syndicate, I understand. Obviously you have connections there. You don't remember his name?'

'Of course not.'

'Well, he remembers yours. Rather vividly. It's all right, I'm going. Immediately. But just before you drift off to sleep tonight, after another excellent dinner, spare a thought for those two, would you? And possibly the hundreds more you've duped.'

'I take great exception to your language. I'd like you to leave.'

'I'm going. It's all right, I like my air clean. Here's some money – I think it will more than cover my lunch. Goodbye, Mr Allinson. It's been very interesting talking to you. I can't say I've exactly enjoyed it, but I've certainly learned a lot.'

Safely in a taxi, he pulled out the tape recorder. It had worked surprisingly well. Some of the conversation had been lost, but it was nearly all there, albeit rather crackling and muffled, Tim Allinson's complacent public-school tones providing the heart of his article. A devastating article. It had been worth all that money.

He had half-expected Allinson to call him, but he didn't. Of course, he wouldn't have known his real name, nor that he was a City journalist, that there was anything to worry about. He'd

507

just think he was a bit of a prig, who'd abused his friendliness and kindness. Well, he could handle that.

He went back to the Palace, showered, had a drink, and then ordered dinner in his room. He heard the trolley coming along the corridor before he had dressed; he was still naked under his bathrobe. That had been quick.

There was a knock on the door; he opened it. It was, indeed, room service, a nicely laid trolley, with a bottle of claret as he had requested. But the person pushing it was not one of the friendly waiters.

It was Bibi.

'Hi,' she said, 'I see you're ready for me.' And she shut the door behind her and started pulling his robe off; she stood looking at him, smiling, studying his body. 'I see you weren't lying then,' she said, her hand reaching out for his cock which was already – well, already appreciating her. 'No aphrodisiacs necessary.'

Chapter 35

August, 1990

Debbie felt very confused. Richard was being really nice to her. Nice and considerate and appreciative: just when she wanted him to be beastly and selfish and cold. It wasn't fair. It really wasn't fair.

And it hadn't been anything like the end. Or even the beginning of the end. In fact, the first thing he'd said, after sitting her down and making her a cup of tea, and while she was bracing herself to hear that he wanted a divorce, was, 'I'm sorry.'

She was so surprised she knocked over her tea. Which at least provided her with an excuse to move about, stop looking at him, stop him looking at her; by the time she had mopped the table, made another mugful, she had composed herself, felt able to cope with whatever he might say next.

'Start again.'

'Yes, OK. I – I said I'm sorry. I think I overreacted. My mother helped me to see that. She said she was absolutely sure there was nothing going on between the two of you. She said she thought you and Simon were very fond of one another, but it was no more than that.'

'Right. I see. I did tell you that, Richard.'

'Yes, I know you did. And – I apologise. It was very – very wrong of me.'

'I see,' she said again. Thinking how wildly, absurdly ironic all this was. Because had he not accused her of the affair, had he not gone rushing down to Wales with the children, she would never have gone out with Joel that night. And their affair would never have begun. And she'd be drearily back to trying to fit the mould and going to live in Scotland. So, thank

509

God he had accused her. She couldn't really be blamed . . .

Debbie! Get a grip. You're having an affair with another man, you've been to bed with him, you've had wonderful, noisy, astonishing sex with him – you can most certainly be blamed, and for a great deal.

She sat silent, wondering what on earth she could say.

'I know I haven't behaved entirely well,' said Richard. 'It was very wrong of me, lying about the job in Scotland. I'm sorry.'

'It's all right,' she said, and then, because he was being so generous, felt she should be generous in return. 'I've never stopped feeling bad about how I behaved either. I didn't want to go, but I knew how important to you it was, and I would have come. I really would.'

'Really?'

'Yes.'

'Then perhaps there is a way forward.'

Panic hit her. 'How?'

'Well, maybe we could still go. I want it so much, and I'm sure you'd love it. I know we've started badly with it, but . . .'

'I'm aware how much you want it,' she said, and it was true; it was the thing he had dreamed of, worked for, for years – how could she possibly deprive him of it? 'But . . .'

'But what?'

'But – I'd just like a bit of time. You know.'

'What for?'

Could he mean that? Could he not realise how upset she'd been, how miserable. How he'd hit her below the belt again and again?

But then, what right did she have to talk to him like that? She, Debbie, the adulteress. Who had rushed into bed with another man the minute Richard's back – albeit a very ungracious and unattractive one – was turned. How hypocritical was it possible for her to be? She felt ashamed of herself suddenly. She had to do this, had to be brave.

'I—' she said, but at the same time he spoke, rescuing her from her better self.

'Sorry. Of course I can see that you need time. I can wait, Debbie, try and make it up to you. And I was thinking maybe you could get a job up in Scotland? So you don't have to devote all your time to the school and everything. I mean, that was a bit unrealistic of me. I can see that. I know how much it matters to you, your job. I really do.'

'Yes,' she said, feeling still worse. 'Yes, it does. Well, thank you. Um – another cup of tea?'

'Actually, I think I'd like something a bit stronger,' he said. That was quite unlike him too.

'Debbie, my darling, it's Simon. Are you all right?'

'I'm fine, yes, thank you. It's very nice to hear from you.'

'And can you talk?'

'Oh yes. Richard's gone for a jog.'

'Look, Flora told me about this absurd idea of your husband's – that we were having an affair. I can only say I wish. Obviously. But – I do feel responsible, just a bit. Are things any better?'

'Yes, I think they are,' she said after a pause. 'He seems to have decided he's wrong about it all. In fact, he's apologised to me. For accusing me.'

'Oh, really? Good.'

'Yes. Flora seems to have been fantastic, really fantastic. I can't quite work out how to thank her. I mean, she could have said . . . well, you know. Couldn't she?'

'She could. But she wouldn't have. Too sneaky. She's a class act, your mother-in-law.'

'Yes. I don't quite know what to do though. It seems a bit odd to ring her up and say, "Thank you for not telling my husband you found me and Simon snogging late one night". But I'd like to say something.'

'Darling! Not quite snogging. Although of course I wish we had been.'

'You know what I mean,' she said firmly.

'Yes, I do. And I think you should say absolutely nothing. Flora would consider it rather – what shall I say – rather suburban, making a big thing about it.'

'Suburban?'

'Suburban.'

'Oh God, she's such a snob,' said Debbie.

'She is. And something of a time warp. But you can't help admiring her for it. I think she's rather wonderful.'

511

'Yes, but she doesn't think you're common,' Debbie said emphatically, 'or suburban.'

'Well, I should certainly hope not. I'm sure she doesn't think you are, either. So, what happens next – in the Debbie Fielding soap opera?'

'Don't call it that,' she said sharply.

'Sorry. But – do you and Richard disappear into a Scottish sunset together?'

'I don't know,' she said, and her voice sounded very sad. And then, 'Simon, it's lovely of you to call, but I'm terribly busy, I'm sorry.'

That hurt; that hurt a lot. He'd been going to offer her lunch, a drink, hear how things were, advise her. But his role of confidant for her, which he'd rather enjoyed, seemed to be over. She was terribly busy; and he wasn't. Not at all.

'Of course,' he said. 'Well, just call me if you want to chat. About anything. I'll be very much around. As always. Maybe next week?'

'Yes, course, Simon. Thank you. I will.'

But he knew she wouldn't. He couldn't quite work out why; but something had changed. Everything seemed to have bloody changed.

You what!'

The roar was so loud the entire editorial floor heard it.

'You bloody arrogant little shit. Who the fuck do you think you are, taking it upon yourself to decide what stories you'll write! And against my explicit instructions. I told you, I don't want any bloody stories about Lloyd's. I told you several times.'

'Yeah, I know.'

'So you think you know better than me, do you?'

'In this instance, yes. Maybe.'

'Well, you don't. And you'd better try managing without me in future. I don't employ people lost high up their own arses.'

'Hugh—'

'You can get out, all right? Today. *Now.*'

'Yes, all right. But could you—'

'I could nothing.'

'Hugh – just read the first two hundred words, would you?'

'No, I will fucking not. Why should I read two hundred

512

words on a subject I know will send our readers straight to sleep?'

'Because it won't. Because it really is hot stuff. Trust me.'

'Why should I bloody trust you?'

'Because I'm telling you to. Go on. Two suicides and a conman. And a supermodel. In the Bahamas.'

That was pushing it, but it might persuade him. Joel could see curiosity shifting his outrage – just a bit.

'Well, you can give it to me. But don't think it's going to change my mind.'

'Of course not. Here you are.'

He held out a page of copy. Renwick snatched it from him, stalked out, slamming the door behind him.

'My God,' said Suzy, who had been on her way into Joel's office, and was practically knocked over by the blast, 'what's got into him? Or maybe he hasn't been getting into anything this weekend.'

'Me,' said Joel. 'I've got into him and he's fired me. He says.'

'Joel! You've been fired! Why?'

'I haven't really,' said Joel, 'or at least I don't think so. I'll let you know. God, I'm knackered. I only just got off a plane.'

'Joel, it's me. Debbie.'

'Oh – hi.'

'I just wondered how it had all gone. If you got your story.'

'Oh – yeah. Yeah, I did. It went really well. Got a lot on tape.'

'Great. Well done.'

'Thanks.'

He sounded extremely distant and cool; she felt sick. Could this really be the same Joel she had been in bed with, gloriously in bed, only – what? – forty-eight hours ago? No, more like seventy-two. But still. Ringing him had clearly been a bad idea. After about three hours of picking up the phone and putting it down again at various stages while halfway through dialling the number, she couldn't not do it. She had to speak to him. But now – bad idea. Best just finish the conversation as soon as possible.

'Good, I'm pleased. So, has the Editor bought it?'

'I don't know yet. The early signs are that he hasn't. If being fired is anything to go by.'

'Fired! You've been fired?'

'Yup. Supposed to be packing right now.'

'Oh Joel. I'm so sorry.'

'Thanks. Look – I don't want to sound rude, Debbie, but I have got rather a lot on my plate at the moment. Maybe later, yeah?'

'Yes, of course. Sorry.'

'That's OK. Bye for now.'

Debbie could never remember feeling so completely crushed. Or so stupid. Or so miserable. She put the phone down and, determined not to cry, addressed herself to a press release about a self-tanning lotion. It didn't prove much of a distraction.

'Simon! Whoever would have thought I'd see you here! How are you? This is Edward Trafford Smythe. Great friend of my late husband's. Edward – Simon Beaumont.'

'How do you do,' said Trafford Smythe. Simon didn't like the look of him at all. He was rather florid, and he was wearing a striped shirt with a white collar. Very naff, as Annabel would say.

'How do you do?' he said.

'Are you meeting someone, Simon?' asked Flora. 'I suppose you are.'

'No, I've met them and they've gone. Market makers,' he said to Trafford Smythe, 'busy afternoon ahead, playing with the Dow.'

'Ah yes.'

'Well, we've only just had our main course. Why don't you join us?' said Flora. 'You wouldn't mind, would you, Edward?'

'No, of course not.'

'Well, that's very kind. Let me at least pay my way, buy another bottle of wine. That one looks quite – tired. You look like a claret man to me,' he said to Trafford Smythe. 'Am I right?'

Trafford Smythe said he was.

Flora turned the conversation to horses for a while; it was very successful. Trafford Smythe was a great race-goer and he owned a couple of horses himself. By the time the second bottle of claret had disappeared – three-quarters of it into him

– he was relaxed, slurring his words, inviting Simon down to the yard where he kept his horses.

'I'd love that. Thanks.'

'And what do you do?'

'Me? Oh, I'm a banker. Yes. Work for Graburn and French.'

'Very nice. They surviving the recession?'

'More or less. It's not easy of course, but—'

'Edward and my husband William were great friends,' interrupted Flora. 'He used to take William racing, didn't you, Edward? And he got me into Lloyd's. Which I'm trying to forgive him for. No, seriously, I can't possibly blame you.'

'Oh really? You a Working Name?' said Simon.

'Absolutely. You had anything to do with them?'

'No, no. Bit too cautious.'

'Ah well, things aren't too good at the moment, of course. But they'll pick up again. I told Flora she should be trading through, not pulling out. Increasing her underwriting, if anything.'

'I've told him that's out of the question. Sadly. That I've got to sell the house. As I think I told you, Simon.'

'Yes, you did. Damn shame.'

'You know,' said Trafford Smythe, 'you shouldn't have to sell your house, Flora. Lloyd's don't want people out on the street, so to speak. Any more than they want them bankrupt.'

'Is that so?' said Simon, his voice oozing credulity. 'Well, Flora, maybe you'll be all right after all.'

'Indeed,' said Trafford Smythe. 'You'd do far better talking to the Hardship Committee. See what they can suggest.'

'I'll certainly try. And Edward is being very patient with me, Simon, explaining things about Lloyd's I still don't understand. You couldn't try again, could you, Edward? I was just asking him why my biggest syndicate, Westfield Bradley and, I believe, some of the others, has two Marine and two Non-Marine syndicates and not just one of each, like all the rest. What was it you called them, Edward?'

Right, thought Simon, here we go: please God. He reached into his breast pocket, pressed the record button on his tape recorder. He had been practising it for the last few days, and he did feel a bit like James Bond. Here it would come: how they had accomplished all this skulduggery and double-dealing, spelled out in this ghastly character's plummy tones; really, Flora was a genius, she'd handled it so well. And then he could give it to Fiona and get lots of brownie points for it. It had all been so easy. So pathetically easy. Really. For the price of a bottle of claret, he was going to bring down Lloyd's. Well, perhaps not Lloyd's but at least Westfield Bradley.

He waited while Trafford Smythe rolled the brandy he had bought him round in his glass, then smiled at the man encouragingly. Flora did the same.

'Ah . . .' Trafford Smythe said, leaning back in his chair. 'Baby Syndicates, I imagine you mean. Such an interesting idea. Well, it's very simple: they enable a successful underwriter to expand without diluting the profits of the main syndicate. By careful management of the best business.'

'Oh really? I'd understood they were a bit – suspect,' said Simon.

'No, not at all. They're not corrupt and they're not illegal. Otherwise I do assure you I wouldn't have anything to do with it.'

'So, how is it that you and I are in the same syndicate and you're a millionaire and I'm going bankrupt?' said Flora. 'That's what I still don't understand. I mean, how do you get to be in one of these profitable divisions?'

'Ah, now that comes down to where your Members' Agent put you in the first place. Generally he would spread your risk, of course. And in a large syndicate group there are many subdivisions, as you might say. I'm afraid you have found yourself in one or two of the weaker ones. That, I must admit, may not have been reinsured adequately. And of course I did urge William to take out Stop Loss. For some reason he didn't do that.'

'Well, I've obviously had it all wrong,' said Simon. 'I thought it was a case of the underwriters making sure their friends and relations were getting all the good business, sitting on a raft if you like, and everyone else sinking or swimming furiously about with the bad. Is that not right? Not ever the case?'

Go on, say 'Yes, that does happen sometimes, that does go on.' Give me a break, Mr Trafford Smythe, please, for the love of God, that claret cost £27 a bottle.

But, 'No,' said Trafford Smythe, meeting his eyes with a certain disdain. He seemed perfectly sober suddenly. 'No, that's a complete myth. Put about by all those people who can't handle their losses, who are arguing the toss, and who have no right to do so. I don't know who's been telling you all this, Mr Beaumont, but whoever it was, they were extremely wrong-headed. Or thinking very wishfully indeed. Now I must go. Thanks for the wine. Very good. And don't forget, I'd be delighted to show you my yard. Any time that suits you.'

They stared after him, in silence: then Flora said, 'I'm sorry, Simon.'

'Don't apologise,' he said. 'Don't be silly. It wasn't your fault. You were marvellous.'

'So were you. Damn. Dreadful little man. I really can't believe he was related to William. So common. Did you see he was wearing a tie pin? A tie pin! Really.'

'No,' said Simon, and started to laugh. 'Flora, you are the most terrible snob.'

'I prefer to think of it,' she said almost sternly, 'as having standards.'

'I see. All right. Let's have another drink, Flora. Here's to standards. It's not the end of the world. Serves us right for trying to be too clever. Bastards, aren't they? The reason they don't want people selling their houses is because it leads to bad publicity, and the reason they don't like people going bankrupt is that there's no more money for them. These hardship committees exist not to get you off the hook, as far as I can see, but to keep you on it, do deals with you to get regular payments from you out of future earnings. Oh God.'

They ordered some more coffee, sat chatting for a bit.

And then she said rather quickly, clearly hating having to say it at all, 'Simon, if – when – I sell the house, then I'm afraid that Boy will have to go. Hal as well, although a friend will probably take him on. I'm so sorry.'

'Oh, that's all right,' he said. 'And of course I've thought of it.' He hadn't, actually. The prospect of having to break that piece of news to Tilly was so awful that his eyes filled with tears. He blew his nose, forced a smile at Flora.

'We'll think of something,' he said, 'don't worry.'

'Yes, I'm sure you will,' she said, and then, looking at him curiously, 'Does anything ever get you down, Simon?'

'Not often. Which is just as well at the moment.'

They'd probably been as nice as they could be, Catherine thought, which wasn't very nice at all. But at least they were trying.

Lucinda had lent her her little Peugeot 204 to travel down in. 'I insist, I never use it, honestly, and if I do want a car there's Blue's Golf GTI; even I don't need two cars, although I shall soon, at the rate I'm growing.' It had been better than travelling by train, but it was a long drive to Somerset; the children were hot and fractious by the time they arrived. All they needed was to run around unfettered for a while; Phyllis Morgan clearly couldn't see this.

'Come in and sit down quietly, children,' she said, 'and you'd better have a drink. I've made some lemonade for you. Here you are. Catherine, will you have some?'

'Please!' said Catherine. But the lemonade wasn't properly cold and very bitter; she could see Caroline struggling with it, and shot her a sympathetic glance.

'Dudley will be in soon, he's coming back specially to see you. Although he's terribly busy.'

'That's very kind,' said Catherine.

'And I had a golf match which I cancelled.'

'Well, thank you,' said Catherine. She couldn't think what else to say.

'It's a pity you don't play,' Phyllis said. 'You'd make some friends that way.'

'Maybe I could learn.'

'Well, I doubt it. Golf lessons are very expensive.'

She was laying down markers already.

Lunch was not nice, fatty lamb chops, which the children could not force down, pushed to the sides of their plates. 'I do hope they're not fussy eaters,' Dudley said, noting this. 'I've no time for that sort of thing. When I was a child we had to sit at the table until everything was gone. Never did me any harm.'

He said this a great deal. Catherine wondered, as she had so often, how these people could have produced her beloved Frederick.

Over a trifle, which bore a strong resemblance to the ones served at motorway service stations, the move was discussed.

'It won't be easy,' Phyllis said, 'I'm not going to pretend it will. But we've discussed it and we feel that we have to offer you a home. It would be extremely uncharitable not to; you are our son's wife and these are our grandchildren. Our friends are all filled with admiration.'

'Yes, it's very, very kind of you,' said Catherine.

'Can we get down?' said Caroline hopefully.

'Not until I say so, dear. Now, we thought we could convert part of the top floor into a sort of flat for you. So that you can be self-contained. We don't want to be living in one another's pockets all the time.'

'That would be marvellous,' said Catherine. 'Would it have a kitchen?'

'Not as such,' said Dudley. 'The cost of that would be prohibitive. But we thought we'd put in a gas ring and a point where you could boil a kettle, make yourself a cup of tea, that sort of thing. We imagined you'd make the children's tea there, and so on, although of course you're welcome to use our kitchen. As long as you give Phyllis plenty of notice.'

'And of course you're welcome to eat with us if you want to,' said Phyllis, 'but we thought you'd rather cater for yourself most of the time. Perhaps Sunday lunch we could eat together as a family.'

'Yes, that would be nice.'

'The children may play in the garden, of course, but they must treat it with respect. No bikes, or footballs, young man.'

'Could we have a swing?' Caroline asked. Having her own swing was the peak of her ambitions.

'It might be possible, I suppose, if we could find somewhere where it was out of sight. I'll have a think about that.'

'Thank you.'

'I imagine you'll be doing your own shopping,' said Phyllis. 'I'll keep a section of one of the fridges clear for you. So that we don't get into a muddle. I presume you're getting some kind of National Assistance money.'

'A bit,' said Catherine.

'And I'm very pleased to see you've got a car. You'll be rather cut off here without it.'

'Oh, it's not mine, I'm afraid. A friend has lent it to me for a while.'

519

'He or she must be a very good friend,' said Dudley. He sounded disapproving, as if loaning her a car was somehow fraudulent.

'She is indeed,' said Catherine, thinking longingly of Lucinda, sweet generous Lucinda.

'Well, I don't know what you'll do down here without one. There is a bus, but only twice a day, morning and evening.'

'I – daresay you could give me a lift from time to time. Or maybe I could drive one of your cars occasionally.' There were three in the drive: a flashy new Jaguar, a Ford Escort, equally new, and a rather older, battered Polo.

'Well, I don't know. Possibly the Polo. We keep it for emergencies though; I wouldn't want it gone for long at a time.'

'What about things like the school run?' said Catherine, rather desperately. 'How will I do that?' This was worse than she had expected.

'Ah, yes. Schools. Now, as I said in my letter, we are prepared to take on the school fees. It's a great deal of money but – well, hopefully it will be worth it.'

'I hope so too. That's terribly generous of you. I really do appreciate it.'

'And then, as a quid pro quo, we would want complete control over their schooling. We would expect to choose the schools, to be very involved in their progress. We don't want any bad reports,' said Dudley, looking rather sternly at the children.

'Well, of course. But I'd like to have some say in the choice of school.'

Dudley looked at her. 'I suppose that's reasonable,' he said, after a moment's consideration. 'But Phyllis and I have discussed the whole thing and we feel that Freddie should go to boarding school.'

'Boarding school!' Catherine's voice rose in protest. Nothing could have prepared her for this horror. 'What – straight away?'

'In the autumn term, yes. There's an excellent prep school near Shaftesbury, only about thirty miles or so away. Gets boys into all the major public schools. I imagine he's very behind, all the upheavals he's been through, not to mention that stint in the state system. We went to see this place the other day and it we've got absolutely no money, and we've got to live somewhere. Oh dear.'

'Catherine, I'm so, so sorry.' Lucinda's voice was heavy with sympathy. 'I wish I could help, I really do. But our house is so tiny, and—'

'Yes, I thought you were going to move?'

'Oh, don't. So did Blue. So does everyone And we will, after – well, after the baby.'

'But why not now, when it's easier?'

'Oh, don't you start,' said Lucinda, and her voice wobbled. 'Sorry, bit of a row last night. Blue really wants to move.'

'And you don't?'

'Oh Catherine, it's terribly complicated. I can't explain.'

seemed excellent. They could take him, provided his present school gives him a good report.'

'But I don't want—' Catherine looked at Freddie, who was wide-eyed with misery. 'Er . . . Dudley, could the children go outside to play, please? It's been a long drive down here and they do need to work off a bit of steam.'

'Well, I suppose so. Mind the flowerbeds, both of you. And no climbing the trees.'

'I really don't want Freddie to go away to school,' she said, when the children were safely outside. 'He's not ready for it.'

'Nonsense. He's nine years old. I went away at seven, didn't do me any harm.'

'Well, I think it would harm Freddie,' said Catherine. 'He's just had this very bad bullying experience at school . . .'

'Yes, but that was at the state school, surely,' said Phyllis.

'It was, but his prep school in Fulham was just as bad, it seems.'

'Catherine, you can't wrap children in cotton wool,' said Dudley. 'He has to grow up, learn to cope.'

'I think he's coping very well,' said Catherine stoutly.

'Well, clearly not if you think he can't go away to school. If you come and look at it, I'm sure you'll agree with me. And for Caroline, there's a very nice girls' prep school about five miles away.'

'And that's another thing, they'll miss each other,' said Catherine. 'They're always together, terribly close. They'll be terribly unhappy, they'll—'

'Oh nonsense,' said Dudley. 'Half Freddie's problems, I'd say, not enough male influence in his life. Few friends of his own sex be the making of him. Trust me on this, I know what I'm talking about. Now I'm going to leave you girls to have a chat and get back to the office. Bye, Catherine. You can sort out exactly when you move in with Phyllis, but the conversion could take a couple of months.'

And he was gone, in a roar of exhaust and petrol fumes.

'It was ghastly,' she said to Lucinda on the phone, 'and I just don't know what to do. Golly, I wanted to thump Dudley. I won't have Freddie going away to school and he says he'd rather go back to St Joseph's than that; he's really upset. But

Chapter 36

August, 1990

'Joel,' Hugh Renwick walked very fast into his office. Fast was good; slow was bad.

'Yup?'

'Joel, this isn't bad. Not too bad anyway. Get it finished, let me have the rest. Not more than fifteen hundred words. Then I'll decide.'

'Yes, OK. Thanks. Shouldn't take too long.' He wasn't going to tell him he'd actually finished the piece.

'Better not. If I do decide to run it, it'll be Thursday's paper. Maybe Friday.'

'OK.'

'But I probably won't.'

'No.'

'And I want it pretty damn quick, as well. Don't start wanking over it.'

'No, OK.'

There was nothing Renwick hated more than writers overpolishing their copy, seeking the perfect phrase. With the possible exception of his two major columnists.

'People want stories to read,' he would say, 'not bloody essays. The stories are what matter.'

Joel took his story into evening conference, handed it to Renwick at the end. He read it in silence.

'OK, it'll do.'

'Yeah?'

'Yeah. We'll shoehorn it into tomorrow's paper.'

Tomorrow! That was better even than he'd hoped. It must be good.

523

'Have you called Allinson yet?'

'No, not yet.'

'Do it, soon as you can. And Lloyd's as well – they'd better be given the chance to respond.'

'Sure.'

Renwick picked up his phone, then put it down again, and said, 'So you paid your own expenses on this, did you?'

'Yup.'

'And what would you have done if I hadn't run it?'

'I thought someone else would,' said Joel.

'Arrogant little bugger, you are, Strickland. That would have cost you your job.'

'I know.'

'Anyway, you can put a chit in, if you like. Just the air-fare and the hotel – nothing else, mind.'

'Thanks.'

'And next time, you're out on your ear – understood?'

'Understood.'

The accent that had become familiar to him came down the phone.

'Ocean Hill.'

'Oh, good – good morning,' said Joel, looking at his watch, doing a quick calculation. 'Is Mr Allinson there, please? Mr Tim Allinson. He's in Mr Bridgeman's party.'

It was around lunchtime there; with luck, he'd catch the bugger by the pool. He hoped Allinson hadn't gone out on the yacht.

'Just one moment, sir, please.' A lot of clicking, a lot of silence, then: 'I'm sorry, sir. Mr Allinson isn't in his room.'

'Oh, OK. Well, maybe he's in the dining room. Could you have him paged? It's quite important.'

'Very good, sir. Will you hold on?'

'Of course.' It felt like forever. It actually was quite a long time, at least five minutes. Thank God the *News* was paying.

Finally: 'Hello, Timothy Allinson. Who is this?'

'Mr Allinson, sorry to disturb your day. Joel Strickland here, *Daily News*.'

'Oh yes? What can I do for you?'

'I just wondered if you'd like to comment on a story we're running in our paper, about Lloyd's of London.'

'What sort of story?'

'It's about the considerable hardship endured by people who were Names and really couldn't afford the risk.'

'How extraordinary. That certainly isn't a picture I recognise. Complete drivel, I assure you. I don't know where you got your facts from, but—'

'Well, the thing is, Mr Allinson, you have already contributed in some measure. You gave me some very interesting quotes yesterday. By the pool. About the way certain syndicates operated, how *you* operated on their behalf. Saying, for instance, that they had "lowered the bar" as you put it, deliberately inviting people with quite modest incomes to become Names because they needed to keep the money coming in; only way they could cope with the rising spiral of claims.'

'What on earth are you talking about? I really don't recall any of this. Who did you say you were?'

'Joel Strickland. Oh sorry, I think I introduced myself to you as Joel Sherlock. It's one of my pseudonyms. Confusing for you, I can see that. Anyway, I'm sorry you don't recall it. I have it all on tape. Would you like me to read it over to you? It really is rather interesting.'

'This is outrageous! And let me tell you, if any of that appears in your newspaper, I shall sue.'

'That's your prerogative, Mr Allinson. Meanwhile, would you like to comment further on what you said?'

'Certainly not. Except to say that it is clearly a complete fabrication. I have always behaved with the utmost integrity.'

'So you would deny saying that, despite knowing Lloyd's were "going through a bad patch", as you put it, you were still inviting people to become Names?'

'I have nothing more to say to you. Except to warn you once again that I shall sue if this story and its absurd claims gets into your paper.'

'Very well. Thank you, Mr Allinson.'

Joel put the phone down and smiled at it.

'That was for you, Miss Thompson,' he said.

Now he must ring Lloyd's. Give them the right to reply too. And then maybe, just maybe, he should ring Debbie.

He didn't actually ring her until the next day. When he was going to say that this week was difficult, but he'd hope to see her the one after. He'd worked out quite carefully what he ought to do: ease out of the relationship quite quickly, but not too quickly, or he'd break her vulnerable little heart; and then, when that was done, he must finish with Maggie as well. So that she could find the decent chap with the ring, before it was too late. And he should probably join a monastery, or be castrated – possibly both.

Only then, having begun to think about Debbie, he could see her rather vividly, that face with that mouth, and those large, rather haunted eyes, and that skinny body and those legs, and he remembered standing in Selfridges staring at those breasts, and suddenly he did want to see her rather a lot and quite soon. And thought it would be unkind not to, he had rather encouraged her, and it would be cruel to drop her again, just like that . . . And told himself she wasn't a baby, she was thirty-four, for God's sake, and not an innocent, she was a married woman with three children, she couldn't possibly be wanting anything more than a sexual adventure either; she was – or should be – far less needy than Maggie; in fact, she already had a lot of what Maggie wanted. Like a husband and children. And so, yes, he would see her and it would be fun, and they'd have more of that amazing sex, and he'd be very careful what he said, and then gradually, although not too gradually, he'd back off. That was the best.

And now he'd better ring Maggie, fix to see her that night and give her the perfume he'd bought her in Duty Free. He hadn't bought anything for Debbie in Duty Free; that really would send out the wrong messages.

'Hi. You OK?' He sounded more friendly now. Less cold, less distracted.

'Oh yes, fine. Thanks. What – what happened? About the story?'

'Oh, we're running it.'

'Fantastic. I'm so pleased. When? And you haven't been fired?'

'I haven't. Well, not yet. And tomorrow. Hubby back?'

'Yes. Yes, he is.'

'And—'

'Oh, it's fine. Well, you know. Fine as it could be.'

'Great.'

Go on, for God's sake say something, she thought. Say something that means something. That might help. He didn't.

'How was it, in the Bahamas? Is it lovely there?'

'Yeah, it's great. Really beautiful.'

Maybe now. Maybe he'd say, 'I wished you'd been there,' or, 'I'll take you there sometime.'

'Good. Well, I can't wait to hear about it.'

There was a pause then; she felt more frightened than she'd ever been in her life, more than when she was going to get her Finals results, more than when she'd gone into labour with Alex, more than when Flora had found her and Simon in the kitchen . . . just sheer, gut-tearing terror.

And then he said it. Said he'd missed her, said he wanted to see her. Asked when could that be.

She said she'd have to check a few things out and that she'd call him back. And then sat staring at the phone wondering what on earth she was going to do.

You silly bugger, Joel Strickland. Now what have you done? Why on earth did you have to sound like that, all keen and emotional? Shit. Shit . . .

'Lucinda, my darling, it's Simon. You busy?'

'Simon! No, of course not. I'm reading the most boring book ever. And then I've got to read several more.'

'Oh, OK. Sounds great.'

'How are things with you?'

'Oh, you know. Bit difficult, but I'm pretty hopeful. I wondered if you'd like to have lunch on Friday? Or indeed Thursday? I have lots of time.'

'Oh Simon, I'd adore it, but I just know I can't. Well, not Thursday. I'm so sorry. Maybe Friday – no, I've promised Blue I'd meet him. We had a bit of a barney the other night and I'm having to be very careful not to upset him.'

'So . . . you've told him, have you?'

'Well, um, no, not exactly . . .'

'Lucinda, that sounds like being a little bit pregnant to me. Either you've told him or you haven't.'

'Actually, I haven't. Haven't found the right moment. But I'm absolutely determined that I will, I promise. I can see you're right.'

'I can see I'm right too. Can't often, mind you, but this time . . .'

'Yes, I know. Um, Simon, you really are all right, are you?'

'Of course I am. I'm working terribly hard on this lawsuit, and seeing dozens of people about possible consultancies. Don't worry your extremely pretty little head about me.'

'I would never worry about you,' said Lucinda, and he could hear the smile in her voice. 'Never in a million years. I never knew anyone so totally, totally positive.'

'Quite right,' he said, and she could hear *him* smiling.

'Goodbye, darling Simon. Speak soon.'

'Sure. I'll try my luck again. Till next week, then. Call you Monday. Lot of love.'

Joel called Simon as he struggled unsuccessfully with the temptation to get a cab home.

'Could we meet? Six-ish, something like that?'

'Joel, you just made my day. Someone who wants to meet me.'

'Is it that bad?'

'No, of course not. Where?'

'Balls Brothers, Blomfield Street any good to you? Isn't that where all you City types hang out?'

'Indeed,' said Simon. 'See you there.'

Joel was looking very pleased with himself. 'I just wanted you to know I got a lot of good stuff from our friend Allinson.'

'Did you now? Well done you. Did he confess to anything?'

'Yes and no. Enough to make a story, and it's going in tomorrow's paper.'

'Great. Worth the trip, eh?'

'Very much so. God, it was tough – five-star hotels, fantastic food, beautiful women—'

'Wish I'd been with you,' said Simon, laughing.

'You'd have loved it. Anyway, you're very welcome to the

tape, or at any rate a copy of it. What I got might not be enough to help you, not for a court of law, but it's good background information at the very least. I really want to help you with your case, Simon. I owe you a lot.'

'OK. That's very good of you – I appreciate it. Especially as I've just drawn a spectacularly blank card myself. I was feeling a bit downhearted. You've actually got some stuff on this tape, have you?'

'You bet. Our slimy friend Allinson saying all sorts of stuff about huge losses on the horizon which Lloyd's knew about and how they'd felt the only way was to pull more people in, without actually being upfront about it. It's jolly good.'

'Joel, that sounds incredible. Fantastic. Thanks so much. God, maybe I've found the smoking gun.'

'The what?'

'What our very sexy lawyer calls the smoking gun: an admission by someone that something slightly dirty was going on. Very hard to come by.'

'I'm sure. Well, I should say this gun is definitely pretty smoky.'

'Good. Well – well, I can't tell you what you might have just done for me. Bless you. I'll buy you the most stupendous lunch sometime. Now tell me, where did you go exactly? I love the Bahamas. Once stayed at the Cotton Bay Club, on Eleuthera. Glorious. Wonderful sailing. Very romantic too. Elizabeth and I were on our second honeymoon – or was it our third? Can't remember.' He grinned at Joel. 'It might amuse you to know I've been accused of having an affair with Debbie Fielding. By her husband.'

'Yes, I heard,' said Joel. He spoke without thinking.

Simon stared at him. 'I didn't think anyone else knew. Who told you?'

'Er, can't remember.'

'Joel! Come on. Course you can remember. It's important – this is my reputation at stake.'

Joel was silent; Simon sat watching him, reading his body language, working things out in his head.

'It wasn't Debbie, was it?'

'It was, yes,' Joel said. Very reluctantly.

Simon sat digesting this piece of information. Then he said,

'You're not having a thing with Debbie yourself, are you?'

'No, of course not. Well, not actually a thing, no.'

'Look, it's nothing to do with me, Joel, but that girl is dynamite.'

'I know it,' said Joel, clearly trying to appear lighthearted, amused.

'No, seriously. She's quite .... dangerous, I'd say. Not in herself, but like I've told you, she's not very happily married. And she's very emotional. Reckless even.'

'I daresay she is,' said Joel. He pushed his hand through his hair. 'Honestly, Simon, can we just forget this conversation?'

'Well,' said Simon, 'I know you probably see me as older than God—'

'Of course I don't.'

'But – affairs with married women – not a good idea. In my experience.'

'Yeah?' said Joel. 'Sounds interesting.'

Simon ignored this. 'You get sucked in, involved with all kinds of – of stuff you don't really understand. That you can't understand. Personal, intensely private stuff. No one can understand what goes on inside a marriage. Except the two people concerned.'

'Look,' said Joel, 'sorry and all that, but I really would rather not talk about this. In fact, you're jumping the gun quite a bit. I haven't even said I'm having an affair with Debbie: you did. So let's leave it, shall we?'

Simon looked at him; then he sighed, a heavy, almost despairing sigh. 'All right, I'm sorry. But – just know that you're playing with fire. Sorry about the cliché.'

'I'll remember,' said Joel.

Simon left quite soon after that; having shaken Joel by the hand, thanked him for the offer of help. He felt very optimistic suddenly. At this rate, they might even win. They *would* win. Lloyd's would lose. He'd get his house back, get his job back, buy another boat, stable Boy . . .

He could hardly sleep that night for excitement, made a very tired Elizabeth listen while he told her about it.

'I really think this could be a bit of good luck at last. What do you think, darling?'

530

'I think,' said Elizabeth sleepily, giving him a kiss, 'that you should send Joel Strickland an enormous bottle of champagne.'

Blue felt uneasy. He wasn't sure why, but he did. There was something going on, he could sense it. He didn't for one moment think Lucinda was having so much as a flirtation with anyone else, he believed her when she told him how much she loved him – and anyway, she was almost seven months' pregnant and while he might think she'd never looked more beautiful, it wasn't something most men would agree with. But – she was up to something. He knew it. And it was keeping him awake at night.

He'd tried asking her, of course. Not what she was up to, but if there was anything bothering her, anything she wanted to talk about. Like was she worrying about having the baby. Frightened of the actual process.

'Because if you are, we'll just arrange for you to have it with a general anaesthetic. I'm sure it can be done.'

But: 'Blue,' she said, 'of course I'm not. I'm going to go to lovely Mrs Parsons, where all my friends go.'

'And who's lovely Mrs Parsons?'

'Oh, she prepares you for the birth. Teaches you relaxation exercises and special breathing and so on. She's wonderful, everyone says so.'

'Good. Glad to hear it. Anything else? Your mother hasn't been upsetting you, has she?'

'My mother! No, of course not. I speak to her about once a week and she's knitting lots of matinée jackets and stuff.'

'And Nigel, he's not getting at you?'

'Nigel – *getting* at me? Absolutely not. Blue, what is this? I'm totally, totally fine. Please stop fussing over me.'

Just the same, he knew there was something going on. And if he didn't find out what it was – and soon – he'd go stark staring bloody mad.

Early next day, Simon appeared on Catherine's doorstep with a large bunch of white roses.

'Simon! Come in! That's jolly naughty. Thank you so much. But—?'

'They're to say sorry,' he said, setting down in the kitchen while she put the kettle on.

'What on earth for?'

'For failing you. Getting you into such a hole. I feel dreadful.'

'Simon, you did *not* get me into a hole. You gave me six super months. Golly, without that I'd be in a bin by now, I should think. Please, please don't feel bad about it.'

'Well, I do. Can't help it.'

'Try to help it. You look very smart, where are you off to?'

'The Caprice. For lunch.'

'Sounds very glamorous.'

'Well, you know me,' he said with his broad grin. 'My life is one long glamorous event after another.'

'Well, it does seem that way a bit. Who are you lunching with?'

'Oh, rather frightening lady. Who I quite fancy actually. She has a certain dominatrix charm.'

'Crikey,' said Catherine.

'Now tell me about the in-laws. How was that?'

'Awful,' said Catherine, and then realised he would worry about her even more if he knew the truth, and managed somehow to make the story sound amusing.

'So there I'll be, up in the attic, like Mrs Rochester . . .'

'Sounds more like Jane Eyre herself to me. God. They seem to be terrible people.'

'Oh, they're OK. Hearts in the right place and all that.' She smiled at him determinedly. He smiled back.

'Don't you dare go off to Somerset,' he said, 'I'll miss you far too much. I must go.'

On the doorstep he bent, gave her a kiss. 'Look after yourself,' he said, 'and don't forget, you can always call me if things get really tough. Don't know what I can do, but I'm quite a good listener.'

'You certainly are.'

'I'll say one thing about this wretched business, it's given me a whole lot of awfully nice new friends.'

'It's done that for all of us,' said Catherine, 'and you're the most awfully nice of all.'

'Bless you,' he said, and kissed her again.

Fiona Broadhurst rarely accepted lunch invitations. She felt the time was far better spent working. But Simon Beaumont had been rather pressing on the phone, said he needed to talk something over with her. She wore her red shoes in honour of the occasion and a new black suit from Armani with a rather shorter skirt than usual.

'Here's to the case then,' she said, raising her glass, looking round her. The Caprice seemed to be filled with women in red suits. She felt rather pleased she was in black.

'Indeed. And thank you for all your help so far. Now, I've got what I think is some pretty good news. Although not quite as good as I'd hoped . . . big disappointment yesterday.' He told her about the lunch with Flora and Edward Trafford Smythe, how disastrous it had been, how he had admitted to nothing.

'He wouldn't. None of them would, not wittingly. Certainly not with a victim present. Have you not heard of closed ranks, Mr Beaumont?'

'Simon.'

'Have you not heard of closed ranks, Simon? I'm afraid they don't come much more closed than Lloyd's. I've been doing some investigations myself.'

'Really?'

'Yes, of course. Or rather had my assistant doing it.'

'Sorry we don't qualify for the full service,' said Simon lightly.

'Mr – Simon, I did explain at the beginning that my assistant's time costs much less than my own. I'll do it all myself, if you wish, but the fee will increase drastically.'

'Let's leave the status quo.'

'So – was the lunch good at least?'

'It was. Not as good as this one though. Company not nearly as attractive.'

She smiled at him; it was one of her cooler, more distant smiles.

'But,' he said, 'here comes the good news. Friend of mine, journalist on the *News*, he got something approaching a confession from one of the Lloyd's pimps.'

'Not an expression I'd advise you to use in court.'

'I'll try and remember. Anyway, it's all on tape, apparently and—'

'And how did he obtain this recording?'

'Oh, he was staying at the same hotel, they got chatting – apparently innocently – by the pool one afternoon.'

'So the Lloyd's representative knew he was being recorded, did he?'

'No,' said Simon, wondering if she could be quite as bright after all as she seemed. 'No, of course not. He wouldn't have talked if he had.'

'Yes, I see.' She looked at him carefully, then she said, 'I'm afraid that wouldn't be admissible in court.'

'Why?'

'Well, because of the danger of tampering. Think about it.'

He thought about it; she watched his buoyancy slowly collapse.

'So – not a lot of good then?'

'Not really.'

'Pity,' he said finally. 'I really thought I'd found our smoking gun.'

'I'm afraid,' said Fiona Broadhurst, 'it's got to be a lot bigger and smokier than that.'

'Oh. I see.' He looked stricken now, white-faced and infinitely sad. She felt very sorry for him.

'But,' she said quickly, 'it still might be of use. Even though it's inadmissible, a judge could still be interested in hearing it. It might just help sway his view of the case in our favour.'

'I think you're just trying to make me feel better,' he said.

'Simon, I'm not in the business of making people feel better. Except by actually winning their cases for them. What I just said was true. It might well help. And we need all the help we can get. This case is going to be extremely tough. As I hope I've made clear to you, at every stage.'

'You have indeed. Er – how tough? On a scale of one to ten?'

'About eleven and a half,' she said, and then because he was still looking rather unlike himself, 'but our senior partner says those are the best cases. The ones you know you can't win. All the better when you do.' She hoped this would make him smile; it didn't quite.

The maitre d' approached the table. 'Call for you, Miss Broadhurst. Behind the bar.'

'Oh – yes. Sorry, Simon, I have been waiting for some important information about a case. Please excuse me a moment.'

As she talked, she watched a woman stop by Simon's table,
stand there talking to him. She was very tall and blonde, and
she was wearing a cream and blue printed silk dress and jacket;
she stood out in the roomful of power suits. As Fiona got near
to the table, the woman bent down and kissed Simon quickly,
then moved away. No introductions then: interesting.

Simon smiled at her, half-stood up as she sat down. He had
amazingly good manners, she thought: a bit old-fashioned, but
very – very nice.

'Great suit, that. And I love the shoes.'

She'd noticed him loving them at the last meeting; she
didn't miss much.

He poured her another drink; they sat there for quite a long
time chatting. He was dangerously easy to talk to; despite it
being one of her sacred tenets never to reveal any personal
details about herself, by half-past three when they left the
restaurant, Simon Beaumont knew rather more about her
than she would actually have chosen to tell him. The blonde
was long gone, had smiled briefly as she passed them.

'It's been fun,' Simon said, 'I've really enjoyed it. Loved
talking to you. And I feel very sad for all those chaps out there.'

'Which chaps?' she said, smiling, eased by two glasses of
champagne and one of Sancerre – Simon Beaumont certainly
wasn't behaving like someone about to go bankrupt.

'The ones who aren't going to be your husband. Shame.'

She flushed. 'I've talked too much.'

'Not at all. I've enjoyed it. Very much.'

He kissed her on the cheek, smiled and handed her into her
taxi; she drove off feeling sleek and rather pleased with life.
She wondered if he had that effect on all women. And felt
rather sorry for his wife. Or possibly even jealous of her. She
couldn't decide which.

'Daddy! Hi. You look a bit tired. Shall I fix you a drink?'

'No, darling, I've had quite enough to drink for one day.'

'Well – nice sparkly water then? With ice and lemon? I want
to talk to you about something.'

535

'All right. I'll be in the garden.'

'Mummy said to tell you she'd be back around ten. And to call her if you want.'

'OK. I will.'

'Elizabeth? It's me.'

'Oh – hello, Simon. Good day?'

'Yes, pretty good. Tell you about it later.'

'Be quite a bit later, I'm afraid.'

'Annabel said ten-ish.'

'More like eleven-ish, worst luck. Did you get my message about the house?'

'No.'

'Oh. Well, those Americans came back with a better offer: two point two. Which would pay off Lloyd's, just about . . .'

'For this year.'

'Oh Simon. It's not going to go on, is it?'

'Elizabeth, you know it is.'

She sighed. And then he could hear her being positive and brave. 'Well, anyway, it would pay them off for this year, and buy us quite a nice house somewhere like Fulham.'

'Sure. Great. So—'

'And then there are some Arabs.'

'Ye-es?'

'They are offering a bit less, but the agent said he knew he could push them up. What do you think?'

'I don't know.' He suddenly felt exhausted. 'Let's talk about it when you get home.'

Annabel came out with a tray: ice, lemon, and a bottle of water. 'There you go. Full kit.'

'Thank you, darling. Just listen to that bird. I think it's a blackbird. Or is it a thrush?'

'Nightingale?' she said, humouring him. 'Yes, it's lovely. Anyway, I had a long chat with Jamie today.'

'Ah. Your fiancé.'

'That's the one. He wants to come and see you.'

'Really? Why?'

'He wants to ask you formally for my hand in marriage. Isn't that sweet? I mean, a bit old-fashioned but – sweet.'

'It's not really old-fashioned,' said Simon. 'I think it's simply good manners.'

'Yes, of course.' She smiled at him. 'That's what he says. He is old-fashioned, that's the whole point about Jamie. Or one of the points. And his family are too. Normally he wouldn't have asked me without speaking to you, but – well, things got a bit out of our control. Anyway, he's coming later in the month, just for a few days, so he can ask you, and maybe get a few things sorted out. I know you'll both love him, he's so adorable. And so nice.'

'I'm sure we will.'

'And – this is a bit difficult, a bit delicate even, but Daddy, do you think you will be selling this house?'

'I'm afraid so.'

'What – even when you've got a new job?'

'Yes. You see, I owe Lloyd's an awful lot of money.'

'It's such a shame. I can't even remember living anywhere else. I love it so much.'

'Me too. But we've just got to bite the bullet.'

'Yes, of course. Well – well anyway, Jamie said his mother had made a suggestion.'

'Oh yes?' Already he disliked Frances Cartwright. Quite a lot. He felt he was about to dislike her more.

'Now this is really up to you, I promise. Really, really. I wouldn't dream of doing it against your wishes, yours and Mummy's. But she – well, she suggests we might get married over there. You know? Not in Boston, but down at Cape Cod.'

'Get married over there! In America?'

'Well, yes. The house is just so gorgeous, and right on the sea, I really, really loved it. And the garden is huge and would take a ginormus marquee and . . . well, I wouldn't have even considered it if we were staying here, but as we'll be somewhere much smaller, I can't see it working. And you know I've alway wanted to be married at home, not in some horrible great hotel, and the weather is so reliably wonderful, whereas in England . . .'

'But Annabel, Cape Cod isn't home. This is your home, England is your home—' He stopped; he felt very upset. He had always loved the idea of bringing Annabel down the aisle, he had dreamed of it since she was a little tiny thing; it was the father's ultimate fantasy, he supposed, going down the aisle in Chelsea Old Church, where Annabel had been christened, where all three children had been christened, and then of having the reception at home, in The Boltons, in the great green garden, with its tall ivy-covered walls, and where there was also plenty of room for a marquee. Where so many parties had been held, where the ghosts of long lovely days, of warm flower-scented evenings would always remain. That was what all weddings should be, family parties, held in the family home. Only – only he was being robbed of it, of his dream, for they wouldn't be here, not by then; it would be home to strangers who would never have, or so he felt, any real right to it. The family house would be some rotten little place in Fulham. And his daughter, his beloved daughter, would be getting married in another country, in the home of a family of people he didn't even know.

'Daddy, I promise I won't do it if you don't like the idea,' she said. 'I promise! But – well, it is so lovely there, and I know you'd love it too, and—'

She was flushed now, anxious at his reaction; he made a Herculean effort to smile at her, to dissemble.

'I'm sure I would. And I'm very, very happy to consider it, if it's what you want. But hey, who knows where we'll be living then? In – what is it? Two years?'

'About that. Maybe a bit sooner. We did – well, wonder. You and Mummy can talk to Jamie about it when he comes. You're going to get on so well, Daddy, I know you are.'

'I'm sure.'

Don't go, he wanted to say, please don't go. Don't go and live in Boston, don't get married in Cape Cod; stay here with me, in England, where the blackbirds sing their hearts out for you, and the weather sends you what it will and the evening air is soft; stay in the place that made you, and where all your friends are, and everyone who loves you. But of course he didn't say any of it. He smiled and said, 'It sounds as if it could be huge fun. We'll have to hire a jumbo jet to transport everyone over there, but . . .'

She kissed him. 'Honestly, Daddy, I haven't decided, not at all. It's only an idea. Now, have another glass of water.'

'You know, I think I might actually have some wine,' he said.

＊

Elizabeth was much later than she had said; it was almost midnight when she got in. He was half-asleep by the time she slithered into bed beside him.

'Sorry,' she whispered.

'It's all right.' Silence, then: 'I love you, Elizabeth,' he said, 'very much.'

'I love you too.'

And then he made love to her, very sweetly and tenderly, and afterwards he said again, 'I love you,' and fell asleep, holding her in his arms.

And in the morning he was gone.

Chapter 37

'Daddy's gone sailing apparently,' said Elizabeth. 'He went early, left me a note. I'm glad, it'll do him good. He's missed it terribly, and it's been such an awful strain for him, all this.'

'Where's he gone?'

'Oh, to the club in Chichester. David Green's lending him his boat. He said they might even go over to France together, take a couple of days.'

'Did he say anything about the wedding last night when you came in?'

'The wedding? No,' said Elizabeth, smiling at the thought of the very short, sweet conversation she and Simon had had. 'No, he didn't. Why?'

'Oh, tell you another time. Got to go. I was late yesterday, Marcia was not pleased. You in tonight?'

'Think so.'

'Well, we can talk then. Bye, Mum.'

As she walked down the road, Annabel passed a newsagent: she bought the *Daily Mail* as she always did, and then noticed the *Daily News* next to it on the stand. With a line across the bottom of the front page: *An Absolute Scandal. Joel Strickland, City Editor, on the failures behind the successes of Lloyd's of London.*

'Gosh,' she said, and bought two copies. Something to read while she had her coffee break.

'Elizabeth, I'm planning a dinner party.' Peter Hargreaves put his head round her door. 'Early next month, hopefully the first Thursday. I'd like you and Simon to come. I'm inviting a couple of long-service clients and a handful of good, long-suffering friends.'

'Which am I?'

'You're both. Which is why I'm keen to know about Simon. Could you let me know ASAP?'

'Of course,' said Elizabeth. 'He's gone sailing, but he's bound to check in towards the end of the day, let me know when he'll be back. I'm afraid it's very unlikely that he won't be able to come. I don't mean that the way it sounds,' she added smiling. 'I mean, I'm afraid he won't have anything else on. His life's taken a bit of a dive.'

'Poor chap.' He hesitated, then said, 'But you seem rather happy.'

'I am happy, Peter. More than I've been for a long time. Whoever said money wasn't everything was right.'

Her phone rang.

'Mummy? Mummy, it's me! You must get a copy of the News. Joel's piece is in. Daddy's in it, and Mrs Fielding, and that poor girl whose little boy went missing, and— well, just about everyone really.'

'My secretary's got a copy – I think she always buys it – yes – oh, my goodness! I wonder if Daddy's seen it?'

Seen the reference to him: to Simon Beaumont: *successful City banker, who has lost almost everything, including his job. 'I was too trusting,' he says, 'some would say naive.' Beaumont is lucky, he still has his beautiful, high-earning wife and his happy family. Others have been less fortunate, their marriages broken by the strain of facing bankruptcy, of having to remove children from schools, leave much-loved family homes . . . . I have heard of several cases indeed of suicide . . . one elderly lady, who had handed over her father's entire fortune into Lloyd's tender keeping found herself unable to pay her debts, and was discovered by a neighbour, lying dead by her own gas fire.*

'Flora, you're in the papers!' Colin sounded quite excited on the phone. 'Have you seen it, the *Daily News*?'

'No, I have not,' said Flora crisply, more troubled by the thought that Colin expected her to be a *Daily News* reader rather than anything the article might say.

'Well, I'll read it to you. "Widowed Mrs Flora Fielding is one of many who face considerable hardship and may be forced to sacrifice her beautiful eighteenth-century house in order to meet debts. 'Lloyd's appeared to be run by gentlemen,' she said, 'and foolishly, I trusted them. As did many others, misled by the sense that we were fortunate to be joining a rather exclusive club . . .' "'

'Goodness,' she said. 'I must go out and buy a copy for myself.'

Catherine, alerted to the story by Lucinda, went out to buy a copy of the *News* and promptly spilled her coffee all over it as she read about the beautiful young widow (could that be her?), who had had to take her vulnerable little boy out of his school where he was so happy and doing well and put him in another, where he was bullied so badly that he ran away from home. For some reason she wondered if Nigel had seen it.

Nigel had; the article had been placed on his desk by the devoted Lydia, and while he was enjoying it very much, he did reflect with deep gratitude on the fact that he had not been asked to participate in any way. It just wasn't – wasn't very seemly somehow.

Lucinda was very excited. Blue had called her at the office and told her to go and buy a copy of the *News*, which of course she hadn't had to, since the PR Department got all the papers every day. She rang him back.

'Blue! So many of our friends, isn't it wonderful? And did you see they described Catherine as beautiful? So nice for her – and of course she is.'

Blue said there were two or three inaccuracies in the story as far as he could see, but that that was the most serious.

'You are just so beastly,' said Lucinda.

'No, I'm not. Just truthful.'

Debbie was reading the article for roughly the fifth time when Richard phoned her.

'There's an article about Lloyd's in the *Daily News*,' he said, 'with my mother in it.'

'Really?'

'Yes. By someone called . . . let's see, Joel Strickland. It's rather good. You don't know him, do you?'

'Um, I've met him once or twice, I think. Yes.'

'Very well-researched. So did you put him onto her?'

'No, of course not. How could I?'

'Must have been Beaumont then. Anyway, she seems quite chuffed about it.'

'Good, I'm pleased to hear it. I must – I must have a look at it.'

She did, for the sixth time and then the seventh; and then decided to ring him, and tell him how great she thought it was.

'Thank you. Yes, I'm quite pleased. Just waiting to hear from our friend in the Bahamas.'

'Oh, yes. Do you think you will?'

'His lawyers, more likely.'

'Will they be able to sue?'

'No, they won't. I've got him on tape. There's not a word there that he didn't actually utter.'

'Oh, right.' She was learning a lot about journalism, if nothing else. 'And what did Lloyd's say?'

'They had no comment to make, beyond that they'd always acted in good faith. Which, of course, is their motto. Anyway, glad you liked it. I must go, it's spawned rather a lot of work, I'm afraid. See you soon.'

'Yes, hope so.' Shouldn't have said that: might have sounded too keen. Pathetic? Clinging?

'Very soon,' he added. 'I'll call you. Promise.'

Not too keen then.

She rang off, put the article in her bag and tried to concentrate on her work.

Blue had cancelled lunch with Lucinda. 'Sorry, Lucy, got to do a bit of schmoozing. Another day.'

'Blue, it's fine. Honestly.'

She smiled at him; he grinned back, came over to where she lay in their bed and gave her a kiss.

'Love me?'

'Of course I do. You know I do. I was proving it like anything last night, remember?'

543

He put on a theatrical performance of being puzzled, frowning, banging his forehead with his fist.

'No. No, sorry, can't think of anything you did last night. You'll have to remind me . . . No, Lucinda, not now. See you later.'

She smiled at him, snuggled down again under the duvet. It was one of the best things about Blue's early starts; she could go back to sleep for a whole hour afterwards.

But – now maybe she should fix that lunch with Simon. He had seemed at a bit of a loose end, poor darling. It must be so awful for him, not having a job any more. She'd ring him when she got into the office – it was too early now – and suggest it.

It had been a particularly busy morning at Jenkins & Jenkins, insurance brokers, the phones ringing non-stop. Maurice Crane, one of the executives there, took off his spectacles as lunchtime approached, rubbed his eyes and thought that he really was getting too old for all this. He sent up a small prayer of gratitude that retirement was now only a few months away and made his way to the Gents before going out for his customary roast-beef sandwich.

As he pushed open the door, he felt suddenly rather dizzy and put out his hand to steady himself on the doorframe; felt a little better and stepped forward. And slipped on a patch of water on the tiled floor and fell heavily.

He was found only a few minutes later, and half an hour after that he was lying on a trolley in Casualty at St Thomas's Hosital. Shortly afterwards he was diagnosed with a fractured femur. His leg was put in plaster and he was sent home in an ambulance, and told he would need several weeks off work to recover.

Maurice Crane, looking out of the window at his sun-filled garden, felt that this was not an entirely cruel blow on the part of Fate.

Annabel was beginning to feel bad about the conversation with her father the night before. He'd obviously minded quite a bit, although he'd been terribly good about it and pretended he didn't. He really was the nicest man in the whole wide world. With the possible exception of Jamie, of course.

She was already going off the idea of getting married in America. Frances Cartwright would take over, for a start. And half her friends wouldn't be able to come. And there'd be all their friends there instead, people she'd never met. And the wedding didn't have to be in a hotel, for heaven's sake. You could hire all sorts of places these days for weddings, like Ham Polo Club or Syon Park. That would be all right. It wouldn't be as all right as the house, of course, but . . . Over a three o'clock lunch she talked to Florian about it. He had been very sweet about her engagement, had only teased her briefly and then kissed and congratulated her, and told her she'd broken his heart and that he was sure she'd be very happy.

'Where would you have a wedding reception, Florian? If you weren't going to have it at home?'

'Sweetie! Is this a proposal?'

'Er, no. I just want some advice. Thing is, we have to sell our house in Chelsea and I hate the idea of hotels.'

He sat looking at her curiously for a bit, then said, 'You mustn't put your hair up for the wedding, darling. Such a mistake, makes brides look so unlike themselves.'

'No, all right, Florian.'

'And don't have too many highlights put in either. That pale brown of yours is much prettier.'

'Yes, OK. But there's more to life than hair.'

'Is there? Who says?'

'Oh, please. Answer my question. Where could I have my reception?'

He considered this for a bit, then said, 'Here?'

'Here? Florian, what are you talking about?'

'I mean it. Downstairs is vast and so is the beauty salon on the first floor, then there's the garden at the back and the roof garden at the top. The salon won't do of course, too much stuff, but you could fill the basins with flowers. It's as near to home as anything could be, I'd say. And so convenient for a quick comb-out.'

'But Miki would never allow it.'

'Sweetie! He'd probably pay you to have it here. Think of the publicity. And he's very fond of you, and he'd know the guest-list wasn't going to be exactly C. I mean it, I think you should consider it. I dare you.'

She considered it in silence, then leaned forward and kissed him. 'It's a lovely idea. I'll talk to Daddy about it tonight.'

'You do that. And don't forget you heard it here first. I want full credit. And an invitation.'

'Florian! As if I'd get married without you there.'

'Pleased to hear it. I'll come on the honeymoon as well if you like, give the boy a bit of guidance.'

'Oh, do shut up,' said Annabel. She suddenly felt very happy: thought how horrified the Cartwrights would be and felt even happier . . .

As she walked back into the salon, she looked around and realised how much she loved working there, loved her independence. Her mother was right; doing work you loved really was one of the most important things in the world. If not the most important . . . Annabel! Really! That has to be your husband, for heaven's sake!

'Debbie, it's Joel. Sorry about earlier.'

'That's OK.' She'd just been deciding to finish whatever it was she had with him. It was too dangerous, it was foolish, he clearly didn't care about her in the least – and why should he? – it rendered her incapable of doing anything very much and – well, it was much better finished. She decided that roughly every thirty minutes. How appropriate, she thought, as she heard his voice, that she was deciding it just then. Fate was clearly taking a role in the drama. It was a perfect opportunity.

'How are you?'

'Oh, fine. Yes, thank you.' She was trying very hard not to think how sexy his voice was. Trying not to think how sexy *he* was. Trying to think what a rat he almost certainly was. Trying to force her own voice forward to say what it ought to be saying. Somehow it wouldn't.

'How are things at home?'

'Oh, you know. All right. Bit strained. He's trying really hard to be nice. Joel . . .'

'Sorry. Look, I don't know when we can meet. I – I'd like to though. Of course.'

'Yes, me too. But Joel . . .'

'So – when?'

'Well,' she said – now come on, Debbie, this is the moment,

just tell him, tell him there's no point seeing him. 'Well, Richard's going to go down to Wales again next week. So that's a possibility. Although Flora's got some agricultural show she wants us to go to. Exciting, huh?'

'You could make anything exciting, Debbie. So – next week's a possibility, yes?'

'Oh yes. Definitely a possibility. Or definitely hopefully as they say in Wales.'

He laughed. 'I like that. OK, well definitely hopefully next week then.'

And maybe by next week she'd feel clearer about what she wanted to do.

'You haven't heard from Simon today, have you?' he asked.

'No. Why?'

'Oh, I just wanted to get hold of him. There's no reply at home, I've tried several times. If he rings you, could you ask him to call me?'

'Yes, of course.'

'Bye, Debbie. Definitely hopefully next week then.'

'Definitely hopefully.'

Joel felt bad about Simon; he'd been less than courteous to him about Debbie; he owed him better than that. And he was sure Simon's advice had been good. It was just proving a bit hard to follow, that was all. Every time he decided he really mustn't see her again, he found himself arranging a meeting. Ridiculous. Absolutely ridiculous.

'Elizabeth?' It was Peter Hargreaves on the internal line. 'Any news from Simon yet?'

'No.' She frowned at her watch. 'He should have called by now. It's nearly five. I'll give him another thirty minutes and then ring the Yacht Club. He's probably propping up the bar, forgotten the time.'

The piece in the *News* had caused a lot of interest. Joel had already been on *PM*, been booked next day for the *Today* programme and GMTV, and given quotes to the *Mail* and the *Telegraph*.

He'd done it before, he was a natural: confident, articulate, opinionated. Debbie heard his slightly hoarse tones on *PM* as she drove home, and nearly rammed her car into the one in front. Not only did she have a lover, she thought, she had a lover who was a celebrity. It all contributed to her sense of unreality; and the feeling that she was in a film.

It was after six when Elizabeth finally got hold of David Green, who was working very hard at being his bluff and cheerful self. 'Sorry, Elizabeth, no news from the old bugger yet. No, he went out on his own in the end. I had too much to do here. I've been trying to radio him, but the bloody thing seems to be switched off. I'm sure he's completely tickety-boo, probably just going into harbour on the French coast now. He does love it over there. Expect he'll have a few glasses of the old vin rouge and then remember to call us. Yes, of course I'll ring you the minute I hear. What's that? No, no, he didn't take his mobile phone. Said it would sink the boat. Sorry? No, the weather's been OK. Well, bit of a squall mid-Channel this afternoon, but nothing Simon couldn't handle. Good God, he's been sailing all his life.'

That phrase haunted Elizabeth all that long, terrible night: until reports came in early next day of a sailing boat found drifting mid-Channel, its boom flapping and no sign of anyone on board.

Simon had indeed been sailing all his life. All his life, right up to the moment it ended.

Part Three

Part Three

Chapter 38

August, 1990

Elizabeth had always said that she would be able to bear anything except the loss of one of her children. She was discovering she was wrong. She couldn't bear the death of her husband either.

Her husband, who she had for the most part been happy with, whose company she enjoyed, and with whom she could share pleasure and fun: the husband she had been married to and loved for almost twenty years; a husband she could see she was fortunate to have and for whom she felt a great affection; a husband who was far from perfect and from whom she had become estranged, but who she had then returned to, and very happily.

But she had been terribly mistaken; she had, she discovered, loved Simon most intensely, to the point of not being able to contemplate life without him. Indeed, in those first searing days, had she not had the children, she thought, she would have followed him, waded out into the sea to join him, welcoming it as it closed over her head, sharing his death as she had shared his life. There seemed, apart from the children, no point whatsoever in continuing to live. No happiness, no comfort, no pleasure, no relief from the pain. It was so agonising that she quite often found herself fighting for breath, as if it was physical, boring into her body instead of her heart or her head or wherever the grief was precisely felt. She was faint, dizzy with it, viewing her life from some distant place, where there was no normality, no sense, no logic, just this awful dark chaotic misery. All the things that she had imagined important to her – her career, her house, her clothes, her jewellery – had become dross; she would have discarded them all without a moment's thought, a second's regret. Not even in exchange for Simon's life, that was too simplistic, too crass a thought even to tolerate, but simply discarded them, for what use did they have, of what importance could they possibly be, now?

And she thought of all the hours and days and weeks when those things had kept her from him, as she had worked, shopped, travelled, without him, hours and days and weeks when they could have been together; the nights when they had fought over his philandering, the days when she had allowed jealousy to get the better of her, and draw an icy veil between them, the times when they had fought instead of making love, and she could hardly even contemplate the wanton waste of it all.

She felt not herself at all in those first few dreadful days, but some alien being, a stranger to herself, who had possessed this treasure, this great love, and wilfully neglected it and thrown so much of it away.

The body – how could it have happened that her brilliant, handsome, charming husband had become a body – had been washed up on a beach near Gravelines, just north of Calais in the afternoon of 26 August. They knew it was Simon, because his passport was still in the pocket of his jeans; she was actually notified of the discovery by a very nice and gentle woman police officer, who came with a colleague to the house, a boy who looked little older than Toby, who sat silently through the brief conversation, clearly terrified that she might have hysterics or start asking him questions.

She had known at once what they had come about, of course; had asked them in and sat them down in the drawing room, had sat down herself, her eyes fixed on them. The woman had asked if there was anyone who could be with her, and she had said no, not wanting the children to hear any of what she felt sure were grisly details, that she would be all right. And had sat there, very quietly, while she was told that the body must remain in France while they did a post mortem there: 'Why, why must they do one?' 'To establish the cause of death and rule out foul play, Mrs Beaumont' – but that if she felt able to appoint an undertaker, she could apply to have the body brought back.

'And where – where would it – he – be taken?' she asked, afraid that they would say home, wanting to protect the children from that too, and he said to the mortuary at the Coroner's Court near the Brompton Road where the inquest would be held. 'And I'm afraid there will have to be an inquest, for the same reason as the post mortem.'

'Yes, I see,' said Elizabeth. 'And – when might that be?'

'The inquest?'

'No, the funeral. When could we get him back, hold the funeral?'

'As soon as the Coroner releases the body. After that, the date would be at the discretion of the undertakers, of course. And . . .' She hesitated, then said, 'I'm afraid that it is quite an expensive process, Mrs Beaumont, repatriation.'

'Oh, really?'

'Yes. It would cost – well, several thousand pounds.'

'Well, that's all right,' said Elizabeth, 'obviously.' And saw that the policewoman was wondering what she meant: that it was obvious she could afford it, or that it was all right to charge for such a thing – which actually she didn't think it was; it seemed the least they could do, bring Simon back to her quickly and easily.

Suddenly she wanted them out of there, wanted to be on her own. 'Well, I think that's everything, thank you so much for coming,' she said, and then as she stood up, the room swam and she had almost fainted. The policewoman had been so kind, had sat her down, made her some tea, while the boy stood in the room, silent and watchful.

When she had drunk the tea and was feeling better, the policewoman asked her if she would like to have someone with her; she had said her children were in the house, and she would be with them. 'Well, if you want any further help . . .'

'No, no, it's fine. Thank you.'

'I was going to say, you only have to ring the station.'

'Thank you,' she said again, wondering how you could thank someone for doing something so savage to you, for telling you that your husband was not only dead, but had been drowned, under circumstances that clearly required investigation; and they left.

She called the children to her; they were all in the garden

553

room, playing music. She sat them down beside her, the girls on either side, Toby on the chair opposite, and somehow she managed to tell them. She would never have believed how difficult it could be to formulate words and even sentences and then to turn them into speech; every one was more excruciatingly painful than the last. She looked at them all, her children, and thought how astonishing it was that only two days earlier, they had been normal, happy, unconcerned by anything more serious than exam results, ponies, wedding venues, and that now they had stepped over into horror, into ugly uncharted territory, its only landmarks pain and remorse.

They sat there for many hours, the four of them, until long after it was dark, unable to move, the children asking questions from time to time, she struggling to answer them in ways that might be less horrible, less frightening than others; and when finally they went to bed, assured by her that it was fine, that she needed anyway to sleep – as if such a thing was remotely possible – Toby and Tilly moved into Annabel's room and she heard them talking far into the night.

The next day, at the suggestion of the kindly policewoman, she phoned some undertakers, chosen purely for their proximity to the house, and – absurdly – because they always had nice flowers in their window; she asked them to contact the French police as she had been advised she should, and was surprised that they knew the procedure, had obviously done it before.

After three more days, endless, hideous days, Simon's body was taken to the mortuary in the Kensington and Fulham Hospital and she was asked to go and identify it formally. By now, friends had been notified, and she realised that entirely without any volition from her, they had formed a sort of rota, made sure that she had someone on call night and day. Peter Hargreaves and his surprisingly homely wife Anne were a huge support, as was David Green, who had moved temporarily into a cousin's house in Chiswick and had been to see Elizabeth several times. He was very upset himself, filled with remorse and guilt that he could have allowed Simon to go out on his own: 'But he was such a good sailor, and the forecast was good. God, how could I have been so stupid, so criminally stupid?'

Elizabeth found herself comforting him, telling him that of

course Simon had been a good sailor, that he had made the trip across the Channel dozens of times on his own, that there was no need for David to reproach himself for a moment. When actually she wanted to hit him and kick him and scream at him and tell him she hated him.

The night before the identification, she lay awake, horror-movie scenes playing themselves out in her mind; the courage required even to go to the mortuary was so great she felt almost lightheaded.

David Green went with her. When they arrived at the mortuary, they were shown into a waiting area. A man came in, holding out his hand to her.

'Robert Jeffries. I'm the Coroner's Officer. I'd like to pretend I was in charge, but I'm afraid I'm not.'

Elizabeth smiled at him obediently while marvelling that her facial muscles would do anything so extraordinary.

Robert Jeffries was kindly and patient; he explained that there was no need for her to actually look at the body, he would be satisfied if she identified Simon from some photographs. She felt she should be brave enough to look and said so, said she felt as well that she needed to, in order to believe what had happened; Robert Jeffries said very gently that it might be rather traumatic for her, that she should realise the body would not look as she might imagine; she said no, no, she realised that, she expected it to be bloated and unpleasant-looking and he said more gently still that perhaps she didn't realise that there was some decomposition.

She had to rush out of the room then, to the lavatory where she was very sick; after a while she came back and said that yes, she would prefer to look at the photographs if that was really sufficient.

Robert Jeffries went to fetch them, and she sat there, frozen with fear, David holding her hand, and when the photographs were brought, the effort required to lift her eyes and to look at them was so stupendous that for quite a while she simply couldn't do it. In the end, she managed by counting: when she got to ten she would look, she told herself; she got to ten and couldn't, so she went to twenty, and after thirty, she managed it. And then although it was totally horrible and nauseating and she wanted to be sick again, because of what the body was like, bloated and frigid, it wasn't actually quite so terrible, because it wasn't Simon lying there. It had been once, but it was no longer; all the clichés about empty shells and the lights being on but no one at home were absolutely true. This – this body in the photographs had Simon's hair and Simon's face – just – but it wasn't Simon. It had nothing to do with the warm, charming, loving man she had been married to, it had some ghastly echoes of him, and the watch and signet ring it had been wearing and which Mr Jeffries showed her were his, but it all had as little to do with Simon himself as a lump of ice has to do with running, sparkling, sunlit water . . . It really wasn't the worst thing: not by a long way.

The worst thing, she was realising, was not knowing. Not knowing if it had been deliberate. If he had chosen to kill himself, if he had been unable to face life any longer. Or if it had indeed been an accident, that he had been knocked overboard, possibly by the untethered boom, and had desperately tried to get back on board. That was a dreadful thought, of course: but not as dreadful as that he had deliberately turned his back on her, on all of them, found them wanting, unable to give him sufficient hope and courage to carry on.

And that hardly seemed possible. She kept telling herself that. Simon was so brave, so positive, so ready to fight. And he had left no note, no hint of the merest kind that his death had been planned. His will had not been taken from the drawer in his big desk where they were kept together, hers and his; it had clearly not been disturbed for years, for a small spider had made its way between the pages and become fossilised there; it would have been shaken out had the file been moved. No, she just didn't believe he could have done that to her, to their children, shown them such dreadful wilful cruelty.

When she felt a little better, Mr Jeffries said he would like to have a conversation with her, if she felt up to it. He took them to a café for some tea, which to her amazement she did seem to want, and said that he wondered if she realised that there would be an inquest.

'The purpose of which is to establish who the deceased is,

and when, where and how he came by his death. The how and when a person died, but not why. There is no question of apportioning any blame on any individual. It's important you understand that.'

She nodded feebly and said she did.

'Good. Now it's my job to investigate the death rather than the cause of death, which will be the post-mortem result, and then to present the evidence in court.'

'Yes, I see.'

'There has been a post-mortem performed in France. I can give you the details of that, if you would like.'

She said she would, while not exactly liking it; she just felt she had to know as much as she possibly could, however much it hurt.

There had been no evidence of anything suspicious going on, Mr Jeffries said, of a fight or anything like that; no injuries to the body, except a bruise and swelling to the back of the head, presumably caused by the swinging boom which had possibly knocked him into the water. He had been wearing a life-jacket but it was not inflated; but this would not have been for any sinister reason, Elizabeth explained. There were two types of lifejacket, one which inflated automatically on contact with the water, and one which required a tug of its cord to inflate it.

'The thing is, you see, the automatic sort are more cumbersome; a lot of people don't like them, there's been considerable debate about them.'

Mr Jeffries nodded and made further notes. 'And then toxicology has revealed the presence of some alcohol, not an inordinate amount, perhaps the equivalent of two or three glasses of wine, and also the presence of some analgesia. Again, nothing excessive, possibly a couple of paracetamol. But of course, those would interact with the alcohol.'

'Indeed.'

'He wasn't on any medication permanently? Was his health good?'

Very good, she said, and he wasn't on any medication; and began to formulate wild theories: perhaps Simon had been hit on the head quite early in the voyage, had taken the para-cetamol for the headache that had consequently developed.

But the alcohol – had he had it to give himself Dutch courage, so that it was easier to hurl himself into the cold foaming sea: or had he had it while the sun was still shining and sparkling on the water to increase his enjoyment of the lovely day, an escape from the rigours of his life.

How was she going to know?

And how was she going to bear not knowing?

What about his state of mind? Jeffries asked. Had he been depressed about anything? Useless to deny that, although she denied the depression, simply said that he had considerable financial worries, that he had lost a lot of money to Lloyd's, and his job as well, that he was very worried.

'But he was fighting back, you see, he was in the throes of taking out a lawsuit against Lloyd's; he was being very positive, he was like that.'

'I'm sure,' Jeffries said gently, and then asked what Simon had been doing the day before he went off. Had he seen anyone who might have heard him say something, or . . .

'He saw lots of people,' she said, 'as he did every day. He was very, very sociable.'

'Anyone in particular?' he asked, and she tried to remember what Simon had said, whom he had seen that day; said she would try to make a list of people he might have contacted.

'Thank you, Mrs Beaumont, that would be very helpful.' He hesitated. 'It's usual to talk to the GP, the bank manager, people like that, if you could add those names to the list.'

She got the impression he saw suicide as a very real possibility, which made her more inclined to think it too.

But – that was no good, no good at all; she had to believe in him, in his absolute determination to win, whatever life threw at him. That had characterised him all his life, ever since she had known him; she would not allow herself to think it had changed.

Mercifully the children took this view, at least at first; it didn't seem to occur to them that their father might have taken his own life, although Annabel was beside herself, afraid she had made his last hours unhappy.

'I went on and on about my stupid wedding, saying I wanted to have it in America, not in some hotel here, and I could see he was upset. Why couldn't I have kept my mouth shut, or waited till you got home! God, I'm such a stupid selfish idiot.'

She cried for hours while Elizabeth held her, tried to comfort her, to reassure her; where she got the strength from, she had no idea. Tilly, white and frozen with shock, said almost nothing; Toby was angry, noisy, berating David Green, the Sailing Club, his mother for not stopping him: 'There must have been some sort of bad weather warning. Why didn't you know? Why didn't they all know, intead of just waving him off, saying, "Have a nice day"?'

Useless to try and reassure him, to argue with him even; Elizabeth let him rage, enduring his hostility, telling herself it was good for him, better than Tilly's mute grief and Annabel's self-reproach.

At first, the official view seemed to be that it had been a dreadful accident; everything on the boat was in perfect working order, and although the radio was switched off, that was not so unusual. But when they knew more about his financial situation, the sky darkened further; the debt to Lloyd's, his having been fired, made suicide seem increasingly likely. They asked Elizabeth if she was quite sure there had been no note; at this she had finally lost her temper, screaming at them that of course she was sure, she had looked everywhere, and they were welcome to look too if they liked – why should she conceal such a thing from them? They took statements from his doctor, from colleagues, from friends, from Elizabeth herself; she supplied them with a list of everyone he had seen, or might have seen in those final few days.

'And before you dare to ask me about our marriage,' Elizabeth said, a rush of hostile emotion focusing against the extremely pleasant young man who was questioning her, 'let me tell you it was happier than it's ever been.'

But some frightened and remorseful part of her still felt that Simon might have decided that enough was finally more than enough. In which case, she surely must bear some of the blame.

Chapter 39

August, 1990

It was, everyone said afterwards, a very splendid funeral. Simon would have loved it, lots of them also said. Elizabeth felt vaguely comforted. It would have been dreadful, she thought, to have planned and executed an event that the main guest – which was how she had somehow thought of Simon through the day – had disliked or disapproved of.

Organising it had been less dreadful than she had expected; indeed, she would almost have said she enjoyed it. Somehow it removed her from the grief and anxiety of the rest of her life and gave her a focus. She was determined that it would be as colourful, and as musically diverse, as she could manage.

Simon had not been exactly religious, indeed he was a sworn agnostic – 'Can one be a sworn agnostic? I think not?' – but he had always rather liked churches, insisted on visiting any he came across on their holidays, pressing the children to accompany him until they were old enough to object and refuse. Tilly had still not reached that age. He was enchanted by them all, as much by the tiny village churches of the Cotswolds and of Sussex as the vast sky-brushing vaults of the cathedrals of England and France. He loved the small white-washed churches of the Greek Islands, the gilded mosques of India, and the gloriously ornate duomos of Italy: and perhaps most of all the small clapboard, tin-roofed churches of the Bahamas and Key West.

He loved music too, although, 'I'm a bit Radio Two,' he would say apologetically, liked the more popular operas (*Bohème* never failed to make him cry), and the more popular composers. 'I'll go up to Mozart soon,' he would say to Elizabeth. 'I'm going to do just one more year of Beethoven first.' And he loved singing, his easy baritone voice joyfully loud at carol concerts and weddings. And even other people's funerals. 'I think we owe it to them to do our best,' he had once said to Elizabeth before the funeral of an old schoolfriend who had died of cancer. 'He deserves a jolly good effort, send him on his way,' and sang 'To Be A Pilgrim' staunchly to the end, tears streaming down his face.

And he loved the music of words, loved the poets, loved Shakespeare and what he called 'the proper words' of the Bible, the King James version, had famously refused to read at a charity carol concert unless they would promise him that. So she had a lot to work on and a lot of friends to draw on for the eulogies. The children had all said they would like to read, even Toby who was still angry and withdrawn from her; and Tilly, who was the most musical, had helped her draw up a short-list.

The church was to be Chelsea Old Church which had been their local, where they had gone at Easter and Christmas and where they had both hoped Annabel would be married; a friend who was a florist had asked to be allowed to do the flowers.

'I don't want paying; I just want to see it properly done.'

Elizabeth said, half-laughing, half-indignant, that they were not on the street yet, and that she would get someone else if she wasn't allowed to pay; they agreed on a vastly reduced fee.

Absurdly, she gave a lot of thought to what she would wear; it seemed to matter that she would look right, that Simon would have liked it. Black felt wrong, at war with the mood of celebration and thankfulness she was trying to create, most other colours an assault on the solemnity of the occasion. Finally, she settled on red, her favourite, and the colour Simon had always loved her in: a dark red jacket over a black skirt and black camisole, and her favourite, high-heeled Manolos, and she had gone to Harvey Nichols for a new hat, quite grand, a wide-brimmed straw with black feathers wrapped around the crown. She tried it all on and wondered if it was too much, too showy; then thought Simon would have approved and that other people's feelings were of no importance at all.

She asked the children what they would like to wear; Annabel said could she wear the drifty chiffon she had bought for America: 'I don't want to look dreary for Daddy.' Tilly chose a simple cream linen shift and Toby shrugged, said whatever she liked, so she suggested a suit but then at the last minute he said he'd rather wear his Eton uniform.

'Dad was so proud of me being there,' he said. 'I think he'd have liked that.'

'I think so too.'

It might look a little odd, she thought, but what did it matter?

The night before the funeral, she fell asleep in the garden; it was a beautiful night, the country was still going through one of its rare heatwaves, the air heavy and scented. She felt restless and anxious, knew she wouldn't sleep; Annabel was out with Florian, who she said had been fantastic – 'He wants to come to the funeral, is that all right?' – and she had shared a rather silent supper with Toby and Tilly who were now struggling to distract themselves by watching a week's recording of *Neighbours*. They found it strangely comforting; Simon had often said that the programme wielded enormous force for the good. 'It's all that sitting down and discussing issues, as they call it. And they all wear cycling helmets. What more can you ask?'

As she looked in on them, neither moved; it was clearly extremely diverting. And so she sat down in the garden, under the chestnut tree and looked up at the stars and thought about Simon, and hoped that she would do well enough for him next day; and as much as she was able to do, sent up a small prayer to the Being beyond the stars, who she didn't really believe in, that all would go well; and woke up freezing at one o'clock to see Toby's face staring down at her.

'Darling! Hello.'

'Hello. Look – I'm not sure I can come tomorrow.'

'Not come? But Toby, why not?'

'I just don't know if I can face it. It's going to be so awful – you seem to have turned it into some sort of party, asking all those people when it ought to be just us—'

'Toby, mostly they asked if they could come. And it's not a party, it's a – a gathering of friends. Who cared about Dad, remembering him . . .'

'And that's another thing, lot of phony religion.'

'Darling, it won't be phony.'

'Yes, it will. He wasn't religious, it's hypocritical. That's why I'm reading what I am, if I come. It's not about God.' He was reading Canon Henry Scott-Holland's lovely piece 'Death Is Nothing At All'.

'Of course.'

Silence; he didn't look at her, stood kicking at the grass. Then, 'I just don't like it,' he said. 'It feels wrong.'

'Toby, please come. I'll need you there. And Daddy would have wanted it, he really would. I thought that was why you're wearing your uniform, to please him.'

'Well, I might,' he said finally. 'I'll think about it some more. But I'll sit at the back, so I can get out easily if I want to. I don't want to sit with you.'

The *you* was hostile, it hurt almost more than anything; but she managed simply to smile and say, 'Yes, of course, if that's what you want.'

'Right. Well – night.'

'Good night, darling.'

She went indoors; in spite of the warm night, she felt cold and chilled through.

In there is my husband, Elizabeth thought, looking at the coffin in church, lying silent and still, as he never was in life, lost to me now, locked away from me in there; and she thought too that there was no more forbidding object than a coffin. You could cover it with flowers, drape it in flags – as her soldier grandfather's had been – carry it with love, set it down with care, but it remained obdurate, unyielding, excluding.

There were two bouquets on Simon's coffin; one of red roses, one of white. The red was from her, and said simply *Simon, from Elizabeth with all my love* and the white from the children, saying more poignantly still, *Daddy, with our love*. She sat staring at it, trying to feel something and couldn't. It worried her, frightened her even; she should be sobbing, inconsolable, instead of sitting here, cool and calm with her children; and worried that people would be noticing, would be thinking she was unfeeling.

She had felt dreadful earlier, as she got ready, sipped cold water – all that she could face – comforted the girls and tried not to mind Toby's retreat from her; had felt wretched and lonely and exhausted, half-afraid she would do something awful, like faint, throw up, hurl herself on the coffin (hadn't Elizabeth Taylor done that once?), and when the car had come for them, and they had all got in, Toby as well to her great relief, it required a huge effort even to speak to dear Collins, lost to them for several weeks now, ever since Simon had been fired, but who had insisted on driving them that day. He had rung to tell her so and said that if the bank objected, they could take a running jump as far as he was concerned; he was going to do it and that was that.

'I'd rather lose my job than not be there with you all,' he'd said, and she honestly believed he meant it.

'Lovely to see you, Collins,' she said, working the first of many miracles that day and smiling, and he said that it was very good to see her again too, and helped them all into the car.

'Plenty of time,' he said, as he had been saying soothingly to them over the years even when they were terribly late, and moved off slowly in the direction of the Old Brompton Road.

'Tilly, are you all right, darling?'

'No,' said Tilly, her face green-white, and wrenched the door open just in time for her to be violently sick.

'Not to worry,' said Collins very calmly, pulling over to the side, and he produced from the bowels of the boot a basin, which he handed Tilly, and a large plastic water container and a kitchen roll, with which he proceeded to swab down the side of the car.

'You have to be prepared when you're driving a lot of City gentlemen about,' he said, getting back into the car. 'Far from the first time, I can tell you. Most of them less tidy with it too. You just say, Miss Tilly, when you feel you can go on.'

'I feel I can go on now, thank you,' said Tilly, managing to smile. 'I feel much better now.'

'That's the way,' said Collins. 'That's the way.' And he passed her a small bottle of water. 'Try that – just small sips now.'

They were three-quarters of an hour early. Which Elizabeth had wanted. She couldn't face the long walk through a packed church, everyone staring at them curiously, had thought the children would not be able to bear it. She had hoped that Toby might join them at the front once he was inside the church, but he didn't; he settled firmly in the back pew, his arms crossed, his face – increasingly like his father's – frozen. Elizabeth and the girls sat in the very front pew, Tilly a better colour now, still pale, but less green and waxy, with her small basin tucked under the pew for security; Elizabeth had asked Collins if he would like to sit with them, but he had been very shocked.

'I'll be at the back, ready for when you need me again.'

He was sitting just across the aisle from Toby, carefully not looking at him.

The church began to fill up; friends, relatives, business associates. There was a large contingent from Graburn & French, including Martin Dudley the Chairman; that was brave of him, Elizabeth thought, and then realised the true reason: Simon had been so popular, the outrage at his firing so great, that Dudley would have had a full-scale rebellion on his hands, had he not been there. Sarah, Simon's chilly and devoted secretary was there, very red-eyed, and so, very sweetly, she thought, was the commissionaire, who had settled beside Collins. Everyone had loved Simon, she thought, everyone; and smiled at Tilly, who was holding her hand and had clearly had the same thought.

Almost everyone from the Agency had come: she hoped rather irrelevantly that someone was answering the phones at least. Peter Hargreaves sat in the pew behind her, with his wife; had greeted her with a kiss and then to her great surprise, sank onto his knees in prayer. She would never have thought of him as religious; looking round, she realised that many other people were doing the same thing. She wished she could find the comfort in prayer and God and the vision of everlasting life that the vicar had so clearly imagined she would.

The new friends were all there, the Lloyd's friends as she thought of them, including a rather cool-looking girl with brown straight hair, wearing no make-up, sitting next to George Meyer. Could she be the sexy lawyer, who she had been worried about? Hardly Simon's type.

And there was Florian, dear Florian, looking rather stern, dressed in a dark suit – who would have thought he'd have such a thing – his wild curls neatly tamed, and a few other people from the salon, or so she supposed – young pretty people and a short stocky man in a dark suit. Miki, she suddenly realised. That was amazing, he must be very fond of Annabel.

Florian had been a tower of strength to Annabel, and who would have thought that either? More than anything this week, she had learned how unpredictable people were.

Neil Lawrence was there, glassy pale, and Flora, of course, looking even more wildly bohemian than usual, in a black flowing skirt and lace-up boots, but rather surprisingly a wonderful aqua-coloured embroidered silk jacket. She was sitting with her family, with Richard and Debbie, who was looking particularly dreadful, white and drawn, and their two older children. She was surprised at that, but touched, that they should think Simon sufficiently important in their lives to bring them.

There were two other children, she couldn't think who at first and then realised they were Catherine's. Catherine who looked terribly pale, her grey eyes huge, biting her lip.

And the lovely Lucinda, quite pregnant now, very sober and still, and beside her – what was his name? oh yes, Blue – looking very fierce, scowling into the aisle. And there was that nice, rather attractive journalist, Joel something or other and . . . who was that? That tall, thin man, walking rather nervously down the aisle, trying to find a seat in the now packed church? Lucinda clearly recognised him and half-rose to greet him, while looking nervously at Blue, but then she saw Catherine smile at him and move her children up and create an empty seat beside her. There were several people she hardly, or only just recognised, and this man was one; and she found that comforting too, that people she had never known, just on the fringe of Simon's life, loved him enough to want to be there.

And there was one person who had certainly loved him, and who might have wanted to come and indeed, Elizabeth had been half-afraid that she would; but surely, surely she would stay away?

The organ was playing, lovely, lovely Handel and Bach, and the sun was streaming in and it all seemed rather joyful and she wondered wildly, briefly, where she was and what she was doing there. And then she stiffened, for the church fell silent, and the rich voice of the vicar rang out into it, saying, 'I am the

Way, the Truth and the Life . . .' and he was walking down the aisle, leading the procession and there was the coffin, set down beside them and Annabel was sobbing quietly, looking at it, and huge tears were rolling down Tilly's face as the organ broke into her choice for her father, 'Lord of All Hopefulness'.

Annabel felt so terrible, she could only concentrate on getting through each minute. One at a time, just one at a time, and when the sobs threatened to engulf her, she held her breath and actually counted the seconds away. She couldn't let her mother down and she couldn't let her father down. She was going to manage somehow, she was going to be strong.

She half-wished now she had agreed to let Jamie come; he had written, the sweetest letter, saying how sorry he was, how sad he would never get to know the father she clearly loved so much, and saying he would do whatever she would most like, come to be with her or stay away and know he was thinking of her every moment of the day. At first she had wanted him to come and had talked to her mother; but then she thought he had never really known her father, never met the rest of the family; he would be a stranger in the tight loving circle they had formed, and she would be worried about him as well as everything else, and it didn't seem a good idea.

Frances Cartwright had written a rather gushing pair of letters, one to her, one to her mother, assuring them of her 'caring thoughts and loving prayers'. She clearly meant well but it made Annabel feel a bit sick. There was a much nicer letter from Kathleen, saying she couldn't imagine anything worse than losing her father, and a lovely one from Bif and Dana, saying how sorry for her they were and how they wished they could do anything, anything at all to help.

She felt nervous as well as terrible; she was reading first, the twenty-third Psalm, and she couldn't imagine how she could possibly get through one line of it, let alone twenty. She just wasn't brave; she was totally lily-livered, actually; she had said as much the night before to Florian, and he had said rubbish – anyone who could work at Miki's had to be tough as all get out, but of course this was different and she must just act brave. He'd been so great right through this, had made her laugh, made her think about other things, listened while she told him

567

it was all her fault: for the suggestion of suicide had now, because of the inquest, impinged upon them all, and that had been almost unbearable. Her mother had tried to reassure her again and again that he had been happy, strong, the very last time she had seen him; had been looking forward to his sailing and even to his lawsuit, she just didn't believe he would have even considered taking his own life.

Florian had said he didn't believe it either; he'd never known a guy less likely to do something so feeble and selfish, and he'd listened quietly while Annabel had told him how unhappy she'd made him about the wedding and then said, 'Darling, you need your bumps examined. That is not, repeat *not*, something that would have even turned his head in that direction. You're just a dumb blonde, obsessed with her wedding, do you really think he's going to take that seriously?'

'I'm not a dumb blonde,' she'd said crossly; and he'd laughed and said not literally perhaps, in either sense, but maybe it was something she could work on and he'd be happy to help; she wouldn't have believed she could have spent the night before her father's funeral giggling in a restaurant.

Only, it wasn't the night before, now, it was the day, and she had to read those dreadfully lovely words and – she just couldn't and – and she felt her mother nudge her gently, and whisper, 'Good luck, darling,' and she walked to the lectern and looked at them all and took a deep breath and began, heard her voice shake, stopped, thought she couldn't go on, and then saw Florian's face looking at her very thoughtfully, and as he realised she had seen him, he smiled very briefly and sweetly at her, and that got her through, even though her voice continued to shake at times and when she finally reached, 'And I will dwell in the house of the Lord for ever,' she heard someone begin to cry very quietly and realised it was her, and she went back to her mother's side, tears flooding now but no longer important, because she had done what she had to do for both her and for her father.

Catherine had continued to hold her children's hands throughout the service. She felt a great need for human contact, for warmth, for reality in this nightmare that made no sense at all. She recognised that she had – like so many women, she felt sure – been half in love with Simon, and it wasn't just because of his kindness to her, or even because of his charm and his gift for making her feel important. Indeed, she knew that much of the resentment that had come her way at the bank from other women working there, was that they had all been beguiled into thinking he cared about them in the same way. It still hadn't mattered, she had still felt special.

He had been that rare thing, a joy to know; he had made everything sweeter, funnier, warmer just by being there. He had been so kind, in a way that very successful people seldom are; he had done so much for her, and had continued to do so, hadn't just made the grand gesture and then left her to sink or swim, he had kept an eye on her and her situation, asked her if she had any problems. And she had never heard him saying anything unkind about anyone; the world for him had been a pleasant place, he saw the best of it, and it would be less pleasant now, without him.

She couldn't imagine what his poor wife must be going through, facing life without him; her view must be bleak indeed. Or his children; those poor children. She, more than anyone, knew what it meant to children to lose their father. These were older than hers, but still so vulnerable – especially, she felt, Toby . . . She heard footsteps in the aisle then, looked round and saw him, dressed in the absurdly idiosyncratic uniform of Eton College, walking down from the back, his face very set. Catherine watched as he too mounted the lectern and read with extraordinary maturity and confidence the very piece she had chosen for Frederick's funeral, and sat listening to this light, adolescent voice telling them all what his father would have wished them to think, had he had any choice in the matter: 'I have only slipped away into the next room . . . Call me by my old familiar name . . .'

'Oh dear,' she whispered under her breath, trying not to cry for she felt dreadfully and freshly alone: and then realised that Nigel was looking at her over the heads of her children, looking at her with great concern, and then he half-smiled at her, and she smiled back, and suddenly felt a little better.

Toby had finished reading; he felt very odd, not even sure where he was, although he knew, of course, that he was in the church, standing there, staring straight at the congregation, beyond his father's coffin, and suddenly he felt the need to say something else, and he took a deep breath and said, 'I expect many of you will be wondering why I'm wearing my school uniform right in the middle of the holidays.' He even at this point managed a smile. 'I thought I should explain. My father was incredibly proud that I got into Eton, and incredibly proud that I was there. I think today is about doing what he'd like, and I thought he'd like me to be wearing these ridiculous clothes.'

Everyone smiled; there was even a light wave of laughter. And then Toby couldn't face the long walk back, but needed to be with his mother, and he went to the front row where they all sat, and said, 'Budge up,' to Tilly, and sat down very quiet and still, his head bowed, and then, as the organ rose again, he reached across Tilly for his mother's hand and held it as if he would never let it go again. And when Tilly got up to read, he moved into her place, closer still to Elizabeth and he looked up at her and smiled and then, big boy that he was, put his head on her shoulder and stayed there, unmoving, for a long time.

Tilly read beautifully, her voice calm and confident, more so than her big sister's. 'This is a poem my father and I both loved, it's by Gerard Manley Hopkins and it's called "Heaven-Haven".'

Flora sat listening to her, thinking of her friendship with Simon, the friendship that had become so important to her, of the walks they had had together on the beach and the cliffs and the moors, and thought how empty life would be without it, that friendship, and thought too, that he had exactly arrived 'where no storms come . . . Where the green swell is in the havens dumb. And out of the swing of the sea', and in spite of her sadness, of the tears and sorrow in the church, the sad droop of Elizabeth's lovely head, of Annabel's fresh tears, she felt they were all briefly comforted.

Just the same she felt very much afraid he had decided he couldn't go on. In spite of his brave words, his refusal to accept defeat, she felt it was likely, that in the end it had all become unbearable. Everything he did, the way he had run his life, his behaviour towards other people, had been directed by his image of himself; he was kind and thoughtful and generous and genuinely courteous, to be sure, but he was, and he knew it, a golden boy, fortune-favoured, loved by the gods. And when fortune ceased to favour him and the gods turned away, and the gold turned to dross, then he was lost, and without direction. She would have died rather than admit it, voice her thoughts, but they remained stubbornly with her, and would not be shaken off.

The eulogies were over now; two people had spoken, John Lyons, one of Simon's oldest friends from Charterhouse, and Peter Hargreaves who had known him ever since he had married Elizabeth. Peter's words were comparatively few; he spoke of Simon's generosity of spirit, of his uncomplaining attitude when Elizabeth had to work late 'yet again', of his loyalty to Elizabeth and his pride in her, and of his charm and generosity as a host.

'Perhaps the best tribute any of us can pay Simon is to look at, indeed to study his family. His family who loved him so very much and who he loved so much, who he was so proud of, and who he so enjoyed. His children have all their parents' virtues; they are beautiful, bright, charming, they enjoy life, they are doers, achievers, they are generous, they have many, many friends. These things can only be taught by example, by saying "do as I do", not "do as I say" and Simon's example was superb. We shall miss him dreadfully; but there is much of him still here, in these children and in his beloved Elizabeth, for which we must thank God.'

Lucinda's baby had taken it upon itself to make its presence very much felt throughout the service, kicking, punching, writhing about. It did seem to her to be unarguably a boy, and in the image of its father, strong, restless, fairly forceful. She sat there, her hand on her abdomen as if that might calm it, thinking about it, about this new little life that had begun, a new Member, as Blue rather sweetly called it, watching the family in the front row, how close they were and how they comforted one another, and she made a vow to her writhing baby that she would create for it, and its brothers and sisters, of whom she hoped there would be several, a family as warm, as strong, as loving as Simon's. That was the best you could do for your children; it was more important than anything,

anything at all, and however sad the day, she felt she had learned an important and lovely lesson from it.

They all stood now to sing the last hymn: 'Jerusalem', 'Simon's favourite,' the rector had said, and as the organ drenched the church in wonderful, inspirational sound, Debbie felt she would be crying forever. She could see that her wretchedness must seem rather excessive; particularly to her husband. But she couldn't help it and she didn't care, and anyway, her sorrow was partly for her husband and their life together. It wasn't just Simon she had lost, her friend and guide through nearly two years now, it was the previous years, the innocent happy-family years, that had ended as she had met him. Whatever happened now, they would never return, those years; she was in a new life, on new territory, and she must learn to navigate it as best she could. Just now she felt absolutely lost and afraid; with no idea what might happen to her. She felt that life had her in its grasp, was toying with her, trying to decide what it might do to her. She would have hoped to find inspiration in that lovely service, a clear indication of what she might do; she had watched Simon's wife and Simon's children who had clearly all loved him so much, and she yearned to find the same strength of emotion in herself: and found it wanting. That was what made her really afraid.

They had knelt for prayers, for the final blessing; and then, as the choir sang 'God be in my head,' the coffin was borne from the church, followed by the family and closest friends, bound for the crematorium and the fearsome, final goodbye; they all sat there is silence as the sun streamed into the church, remembering Simon, not wanting to leave. They had been told they were all welcome at the house, but not liking to be the first to go, the congregation had broken into groups, family, colleagues, friends, united by only one thing, and uncertain now whether to smile, to move, to greet one another.

Joel, surprised at his misery, had been sitting at the back of the church, carefully far from Debbie and her family, carefully not looking at her, not looking at anyone indeed, waiting for it to be all right to leave. And then, as if it was the most natural thing in the world, the organ stopped playing Bach, paused for about thirty seconds, and then, as promised in the order of service, only no one had quite taken it in *After the service, Simon's favourite song* – the organist moved into 'Your Song' by Elton John. Joel would have expected it to sound inappropriate, cheap even, but somehow it didn't; it was played a little slowly, to be sure, but quite beautifully, and seemed to suit that moment of that day to an extraordinary degree. Of course, it happened a lot these days; he had been to an aunt's funeral recently and they had all left the church to 'My Way' (that had indeed been awful), and the vicar had told him it was what a lot of people wanted, a release from the formality and the strain, and lots of people had jazz bands. Certainly this had an extraordinary effect; people were eased into smiling, moving, greeting one another, saying how lovely it had all been, the Simon they had all known brought in some odd way back into their midst.

His desire to escape quite gone, Joel sat there, listening, not thinking very much at all; and then he stood up, turned to his left – and found himself staring straight into Debbie's large brown eyes. He was struck by two things: the obvious depth of her grief and some kind of panic in those eyes, smudges of tiredness and sorrow as they were, the lashes wet with tears. And then he was struck by something else, very, very strongly; indeed, it shocked him with its violence: a great blow of emotion, emotion for her. He wasn't quite sure what it was even, but love, tenderness, concern, they were all there, and he wanted to tell her, to show her, to make sure she knew.

And Debbie, staring back at him, felt it too, and acknowledged it; it was startling and unexpected and absolutely new, and although the service and the music and losing Simon and the family's grief had heightened everyone's emotions, made them raw and even a little dangerous, she knew quite clearly, they both did, she and Joel, that this was a new and important thing between them, only just beginning, and it had only a little to do with what had happened before.

The party, for such it became – and to which Debbie went, but Joel did not – was surprisingly splendid, held in the garden of the house. There was champagne, there was sunshine, there was a jazz band, people talked and laughed and regaled one another with stories about Simon, and the children felt briefly better, released from the formality of the morning and the horror of seeing their father's coffin slide through the curtains in the crematorium chapel.

'Why do they have to do that?' Elizabeth whispered to Peter Hargreaves, who had gone with them, and, 'God knows,' he said, adding (and making her smile) that God had little to do with it.

Tilly tirelessly played horses with Emma; Florian and Annabel sat behind one of the big trees, drinking champagne and sharing joints; Toby asked if he might take over for a stint on the drums and was granted ten minutes of 'Chatanooga Choochoo' and 'Summertime'. Flora sat in the shade drinking a great deal too much and chatting most happily to Peter Hargreaves; Lucinda cheered all the men up by giggling at their increasingly foolish jokes; Caroline and Freddie charmed everyone by taking round plates of food; and Catherine, who thought perhaps she should help too, but knew better than to pass round or hold anything, sat and talked to Nigel, who had been pressed into attending the party by Flora Fielding, who had always rather liked him because he reminded her of William.

Only Elizabeth remained absolutely unhappy through it all; and even she, as the shadows crept into the garden and lengthened, felt at the very least a satisfaction that she had done her best and that Simon would have been pleased.

Chapter 40

August, 1990

Morag Dunbar smiled at Debbie. She was a pretty woman, blonde and blue-eyed – in her mid-forties, Debbie thought, dressed exactly as she would have expected in a pale-blue twinset, tweed skirt and navy leather loafers.

'I can't tell you,' she said, 'how thrilled I am that you and your husband are going to join us. And your delightful family, of course. I think we can offer you all a very good life up here. Alexander seems to like what he's seen of the school – such a pity you couldn't have come up earlier when the children were still here – and I can tell you the school will certainly like him. A cricketer! We're rather short of them. Now for the girls, I'd suggest Saint Margaret's, in Calderigg; it's only about ten miles away, a delightful school, quite academic although not too much so, and very caring. I know the Head very well and—'

Debbie couldn't stand it any longer; she shot a beseeching glance at Richard. To her immense relief, he responded. He really was trying; she had to give him that.

'Well, the thing is, Morag, we still have to have a conversation about the logistics of all this, Debbie and I. She has her job in London, and needs to give them proper notice, and then we don't want to rush the decision about the girls' school.'

'Oh dear.' Morag's face was sterner suddenly. 'I thought you had made your minds up. That is certainly what you led me to believe.'

'I've made *my* mind up,' said Richard, smiling at her slightly nervously, 'and indeed we will be coming, but Debbie and the children possibly not until next term. I can do a term here solo, as it were, and then—'

'That won't be nearly as satisfactory,' said Morag. 'I need a

575

wife who can provide the pastoral care the children need: that would be very much your role, Mrs Fielding—'

'Debbie,' said Debbie politely.

'Debbie. Very much your role. I can see you'd do it extremely well, I have only to look at your own children to see your talents in that direction. And you like the house, I hope?'

'Yes, it's lovely,' said Debbie, and indeed it was, a grey stone villa set among trees, on the edge of the grounds. It was the only thing about this whole miserable adventure that she had liked.

'And I'm sure your employers would understand that you need to be here for the beginning of term. That is just over four weeks away now, so they would have a little time to replace you. What is it you do, Debbie? I'm sorry, your husband did tell me, but I've forgotten.'

'I'm in public relations,' said Debbie.

'Really? My goodness, we can put you to work on the school's behalf; we desperately need our profile raised – is that the right expression?'

'Yes, it is.'

'Good. And I'm sure you'll like the girls' school, Saint Margaret's, that is. It's such a happy place, but there are others and I'd be very happy to show them to you.'

'Yes, but you see . . .' Don't get excited, Debbie, don't get aggressive. Just stay calm.

'I'm sorry, Morag,' said Richard. 'I'm afraid that we do have to ask for this term's grace for my wife. It's been a bit of a bombshell for her, and she needs time to adjust, sort things out her end; she's hoping to continue working for her firm on certain projects, you see, much easier now with this wonderful new email – I don't know if you have it here . . .?'

'Not yet, no,' said Morag, 'but I have looked into the possibility, naturally.'

'And then we have to sell our house, which won't be easy, long-distance, with the property market in disarray.'

'Yes, I can understand that. Well, it's rather disappointing, I must say. I had hoped . . .'

'I know, and I'm very sorry,' Richard smiled at her, 'very sorry indeed. It's my fault really for not – not planning it all properly, not talking it over sufficiently with Debbie. But there

576

is one other thing: my mother is going through a very difficult time, she's lost all her money at Lloyd's and she's got to sell the family home, and I think one of us should be near her while she's going through that.'

'Of course,' said Morag. This seemed to be a far more reasonable excuse for Debbie's delayed arrival. 'How dreadful. I've got friends in her situation – I think we all have. Well, perhaps she could come up here and live with you. The house is quite big, after all, and I'm sure she's very good at helping out with your children.'

'I hadn't thought of that,' Richard said, looking rather nervously at Debbie. 'She's fiercely independent, I'm afraid.'

'My dear, they all are,' said Morag. She clearly saw Flora as a decrepit old lady, 'but think about that at least. Where does she live now?'

'South Wales.'

'Ah, yes. Well, that would be quite a move. Debbie, more tea?'

'No, thank you. Perhaps I should go and check on the children—'

'They're fine. Our school cook is giving them scones and milk and they've had a wonderful time running about in the grounds. I don't think they've got any doubts about moving up here.'

God, she was like Flora, Debbie thought, knowing what was best for everyone.

'Anyway,' Richard said, 'that's what we've agreed, Debbie and I. That she and the children will come up at Christmas. I do hope that will be acceptable to you. Otherwise . . .'

Morag Dunbar sighed, picked some imaginary flecks off her skirt. Then she said, 'Well, it's far from ideal. It might have been helpful if you'd said all this in the first place. But – I've made my decision that you are our ideal candidate, and the Governors are in agreement. We'll just have to muddle along for the first term. We have a new matron starting, I might have to take on a temporary assistant for her.'

'Well, that's wonderful.' Richard was flushed with relief and happiness. He grinned at Debbie and he suddenly looked young again, young and happy, the person she had fallen in love with. And then out of love . . . No, Debbie, don't. He's been marvellous, he's backed you all the way on this; don't even start looking down that road. She smiled back at him.

'Yes, it is. Thank you, Morag, so much. I'm sorry about it, but I really will—'

The door opened and Emma burst in.

'Mummy, Daddy, it's so great up here and there are stables – that would mean I could have a horse, my own horse! We can come, can't we? I love it, really love it!'

'Emma, we're still talking to Miss Dunbar,' said Debbie.

'Oh, sorry.'

'That's perfectly all right, Emma. You like riding, do you? Yes, we have stables and you can have riding lessons if you want.'

'And keep a pony?'

'Well,' she looked at Richard and laughed, 'that costs a lot of money. You'll have to clear that with your parents.'

'But I could if they said yes?'

'You could,' said Morag, smiling at her and then glancing across at Debbie with a look that said, 'I told you so'. 'Now run along back to the kitchen, Emma, there's a good girl. I won't keep your mummy and daddy much longer.'

Not now, perhaps, Debbie thought: but you will, Morag, you will.

She was trying very hard indeed not to think about Joel. It wasn't easy. She seemed to think about him all the time. But – she supposed that was inevitable. He had had a profound effect on her life, albeit briefly. She had broken her wedding vows for him; she had behaved in a way she would never have believed possible, that she was deeply ashamed of, not only going to bed with him, but going to bed with him so – so wantonly. Not a lot of wooing had gone on. She had wanted him and she had taken him; if Richard ever found out, it would be the end of their marriage, it was as simple as that. He wouldn't just be jealous, he'd be shocked and disgusted, and with very good reason. And he didn't deserve it. She had realised that, in the dreadfully sad, difficult days after the funeral. He might be boring and fussy and demanding, and he might have done some fairly mean things recently, but he was basically kind and good, and he loved her. And she loved him. Of course she did.

And – he hadn't found out, and he was unlikely to, so long as she didn't ever see Joel, or have anything to do with him ever again, and she could keep it as a secret, in all its shockingness, for the rest of her life.

She would be a good wife and mother, and plan her life around Richard and the children, which was quite easy a lot of the time, especially as Richard was being so extremely nice still – just what had Flora said to him? – and to make amends for her one, all right two, lapses into adultery.

It helped, of course, that Joel clearly didn't regard it as any more than a fling – he had hardly come back from the Bahamas begging her to run away with him; but she was quite sure it wouldn't have made any difference. It had been great: and it was over. And she was lucky to have got away with it. They both were.

And besides, she wasn't some glossy, free-living, sexually motivated creature, to be found in the pages of *Cosmopolitan*, she was Debbie Fielding who had enough trouble staying in control of her life as it was: where, in the chaotic disorder she inhabited, every second encroached upon by a child, or a husband, or a dog, or a job, was she supposed to find space for a lover? However much she might want that. Which she absolutely didn't.

'So – any more thoughts?'

Colin refilled Flora's glass. She jumped; she had been fretting over Boy and how she was going to tell Tilly she couldn't keep him much longer, while the little girl was still in shock and grieving over the death of her father.

'Oh sorry, Colin. I'm a bit distracted.'

'I'm not surprised. Anything I can help with?'

'Don't think so. It's all to do with Simon's family – you know, my friend who died last month. Who was drowned.'

'Oh yes. You were very fond of him, weren't you?'

'I was, yes. Very fond. Don't look at me like that, Colin, he was only a friend. A good friend.'

'I always wonder why people say "only a friend",' he said. 'Friendship seems to me to be the loveliest relationship. Don't you think?'

'I do. Much less selfish than love.'

There was a silence, then he said, 'Well, as I was saying, any more thoughts – about the house?'

'Oh yes, a few. I'm not quite ready to talk about it, I'm sorry.'

'That's all right. But I imagine you have to make your mind up soon.'

'I do, yes. And can I say yet again, how grateful I am for your help. Really.'

'I don't want you to be grateful,' he said, 'I want you to feel happy about it.'

That was the trouble, of course; she couldn't feel happy about it. She was very unhappy about it, in fact. Not because it was illegal – or was it immoral? Probably it was both. Desperate times called for desperate measures – and besides, Lloyd's didn't inspire ethical behaviour. But it felt wrong for her. Uncomfortable. A notion that didn't fit, like a hat that was too tight.

And yet – it was very clever. It had a lot to commend it. Not least that she would be far from destitute. In fact, in the fullness of time she'd be rather well off. And Lloyd's would be rather satisfyingly done down. Not totally of course; they'd get the proceeds of the house, and that would draw the line. It would have to, because there wasn't any more. Her last cufflink – in their terms – would be gone. She'd sold everything else of value that she had; pictures, the odd good carpet and rug, the Chippendale table that had been in her family for generations, the set of ten Regency dining chairs, a couple of Lalique vases. None of them had raised very much. It was extraordinary, she thought. You could own these treasures; people said things like, 'God, is that really Chippendale?' or, 'Lalique! What, real Lalique?' and had to be practically helped to a chair, and then you sold the lot for less than the price of a small family car.

She wondered if that ought to go, her old Fiesta; it would make a few hundred, no more. And if it went, then she'd be left with the twenty-year-old Land Rover. Maybe that had antique value – maybe she could sell that. And what about her jewellery? That would have to go if they knew about it; well, they weren't going to. Her engagement ring, not spectacular, but a very nice row of diamonds – slipped onto her finger by William as they stood watching the moon on the water in Rhossili Bay – and her mother's pearl necklace: she'd planned to leave them both to Debbie. And she *would* leave them both to Debbie, even if she had to bury them in the garden, as people had buried things in France during the war.

And then there was her grandfather's gold watch-chain, that was meant for Richard, and her grandmother's gold and drop-pearl tiara that she had worn on her wedding day: for some reason, she had thought lately that she would like to give that to Tilly. She hoped that wouldn't upset Debbie, but she could see it settled rather nicely in Tilly's long blond hair, on her wedding day. But maybe when she knew about Boy, Tilly wouldn't want to know her any more. She'd be desperately upset. And come to that, Flora thought, trying to drag her attention back to Colin, she herself was going to be pretty upset if she was forced to sell Prince Hal. Sell him: how could she sell him? She would honestly rather have him put down. God, it was a mess. But if she didn't do something soon, she was going to be destitute.

But – Colin's way, she wouldn't be destitute. She'd be sitting in a nice house in the Algarve or the Scottish Highlands, with a bit of money over, to live on. Quite a bit of money. She'd have to start off modestly, Colin had said, a flat or something – a flat, her in a flat! – so that if they asked, she could show them. And then in a year or two – well, then she could buy something rather more substantial. And buy another horse. Or even put Hal in livery somewhere for those two years and then have him back. God, it was tempting. So tempting.

'I do think,' she said, smiling at Colin, draining her glass, holding it out to be refilled, 'I do think I'm probably going to say yes. And I daresay I've had too much wine already, but I really would rather like some more . . .'

There was a short paragraph in the *Telegraph* about the funeral and about Simon, describing him as a successful and popular City figure. Maurice Crane's wife Daphne brought the paper out to him as he sat in the sun, drinking his coffee.

'You knew him, didn't you, Maurice?'

'Who?'

'Simon Beaumont.'

'Yes, I do. He does all his personal insurance through us. Why, what's happened to him?'

'He's dead,' said Daphne. 'Drowned in a sailing accident.'

Maurice was very shocked; he took the paper from her and read the report three times.

'What a terrible thing,' he said. 'What a really terrible thing.' And wondered if he ought to get in touch with Mrs Beaumont, whom he had spoken to once or twice, to say how sorry he was; and decided after all that it might be better not to.

Jamie had arrived three weeks after the funeral – 'just for a few days, is that all right, Mummy? I'd so love to see him, it would help, and I don't want to go over there.'

Elizabeth had said of course it was all right, she was longing to meet him, and anyway, it would do them all good to have to make an effort for someone, talk about other things; but she had dreaded it for herself nevertheless, an intrusion into their intense, supportive little unit.

He really was very sweet, Elizabeth thought; she liked him a lot. Extremely good-looking too, and with the most perfect manners. And he adored Annabel, and was endlessly considerate of her, even if she was being a bit difficult. Which she was quite frequently these days. Well, it was understandable. Apart from the grief which was still awful, they were all on edge. The inquest had still not even been scheduled; it would be months ahead apparently, because of the French police and their enquiries, and it was going to be hideous. Whatever the outcome.

Toby was particularly haunted by the whole thing, not only that his father might have killed himself, but that everyone was about to be told that his father had killed himself. He had been very sweet to Elizabeth since the funeral, but now he was in a moody, truculent state.

'I mean, Dad had lots of reasons to do it, didn't he? Losing his job, losing all the money.'

'He did, darling, yes, I'm afraid.'

'But it's such an awful thing to do. So cowardly. So – so kind of giving in. And so awful for us. He must have thought of that!'

'Of course he would have done.'

'I mean, we didn't care about any of it. Did we? I'd have left Eton if that would've helped, and gone and lived in some crappy place. Wouldn't have mattered. He was still Dad.'

'Yes, he was. And I'm sure he knew all that.'

'So – why? If he did it? It was so – so cruel. I just don't get it.'

'I don't know, Toby darling. And actually I don't think he did

582

do it. I think it was an accident, a terrible accident, I don't believe he would have hurt us like that. He would just have stuck it out.'

'Yes, but he was such a good sailor. And it was only the Channel . . .'

'The Channel can be pretty nasty, Toby.'

'Not that nasty. Not for Dad. Well, if he did do it, it was a filthy thing to do. To all of us, specially you. I just feel so – so angry with him! More than miserable, even.'

'Toby, I know you do. And I'm sorry.'

Tilly was outraged at the very suggestion, said she knew he wouldn't have done such a thing, that he was too brave, too positive, 'Just too happy. He stayed happy through it all. Everyone said so.'

Just the same, the whole process of the inquest haunted her; she was tired, not sleeping well. And she had the ordeal of going away to a new school. Elizabeth worried about that too, how she would cope, away from home, away from her. And Annabel was quietly, sadly thoughtful, old enough to absorb all of it, all the arguments, the reasons for and the reasons against it, and finding sorrow either way.

Elizabeth was planning to go back to the agency in another week; she desperately needed to be forced to think about other things, to put her mind back to work. She asked the children if they'd think it very bad of her, that she might seem uncaring, and they'd all stared at her as if she'd suggested leaving the country or joining a nunnery.

'Of course we wouldn't mind,' said Tilly finally. 'Why should we? You need your work, Mummy, and it needs you. It'll help you lots, I'm sure.'

And then she asked if, for the same reason, she might go and stay with Flora for a few days, see lots of Boy, before she went off to school. A little anxious, for the question of Boy's future had occurred to Elizabeth as it didn't seem to have occurred to Tilly, she had said yes.

'I'll drive you down, maybe this weekend – Bank Holiday, isn't it – it'll be fun. I'd like to see Flora, anyway. She's been a good friend to this family.'

And she'd like to say so to Flora's face, Elizabeth thought; she knew she had been less than friendly to her, less grateful than she should have been.

'Work seems to cheer Annabel up,' Jamie said to Elizabeth; they were having lunch together, in the kitchen. 'She really seems to love it.'

He sounded slightly surprised; Elizabeth smiled at him.

'I know you probably think it's a funny job for a clever girl like her, who could have gone to university, all that stuff. We did too, at first. But she's very good at it and you know, Jamie, being good at your job and enjoying it is the most wonderful thing. Having fun with it – that's really lucky.'

'Yes, I suppose so,' he said.

'Do you enjoy your work?'

'Well – yeah, I guess I do. But law's pretty dry and dusty, and because Dad runs the firm and tells us all what to do, I don't feel like that too much.'

'Yes, I see,' said Elizabeth, thinking briefly not so much of Jamie, who was after all fairly fresh out of law school, but of his brother Bif, and his brother-in-law Joe and wondered how much they were all told what to do by Mr Cartwright.

'But I mean I'm really pleased Annabel has got her job, if it makes her feel better. Um – did you feel like that when you were young?'

'I did indeed, and I still do. I started work really young – I was only nineteen. I decided, rather like Annabel, not to go to university. I'd done a secretarial course, and I had this chance to go to an agency as a PA, and I just knew I could work my way up. You could then, you can't now – you need degrees and so on. I'd always been fascinated by advertising, used to study the ads in my mother's magazines, particularly the American ones. American advertising was so clever, so ahead of ours then.'

'Yeah?'

'Oh, yes. Two especially I remember – one was for cigarettes, for a brand called Virginia Slims, directed at women and it had this great copy line, "You've come a long way, baby" – the implication being that if you weren't smoking Virginia Slims you were a funny old-fashioned thing: and another for a hair colour by Clairol which showed a gorgeous blonde, and the line was, "Only her hairdresser knows for sure". Mind you, we had "Which twin had the Toni?"'

'What was that?' Jamie was clearly fascinated by her passion, rather than the subject-matter.

'The ad was for a home perm called Toni, and they had a photograph of identical twins: one had a home perm, and the other a three-guinea salon perm – I still remember that, the three guineas. No one could tell the difference – or that was the story. It was great.'

'And – when did you have Annabel?' said Jamie.

'Oh, I was twenty-one. I was married by then, to Simon, and though it wasn't exactly what we'd planned, there she was, the most beautiful, well-behaved baby in the world.'

'But you went on working?'

'I did indeed. It was that important to me. And it was very hard sometimes and I'm sure for her as well, and the others when they came along. But I was me, and Simon was Simon, and for both of us that was how we liked – well, me to be. Working, passionate about something. And good at it, which is where we came in.'

'Yes, I see.' He clearly didn't.

'Your mother didn't work, I know.'

'No, she didn't. She was kind of out of a different mould.'

'And what about your sister? She's having a baby, I believe?'

'Oh – yes. Well, she'll give up work, pretty soon now. She'll be like my mother. Dana, she's my sister-in-law, she's more like you, having a little struggle with herself, Bif says.'

'In what way?'

'Well, she just loves her job. She's a lawyer and she's very successful. But the – the what-do-you-call-it, the clock . . .'

'The biological clock?'

'Yeah, that's it, it's ticking away. And Kathleen being pregnant makes the pressure on her harder. And she knows that Bif wouldn't want her to work, if she had a baby, so they're kind of trying to work things out. Mother says she knows she'll come round in the end,' he said, clearly unaware of the irony of what he was saying.

'Right. Well, it's a difficult one. And there isn't a right answer. You just have to find your own way.'

585

'I guess so. Um . . . Annabel seems pretty keen on that Florian guy.'

'Yes, she is. He's been a very good friend to her, over all this. But he is just a friend, Jamie, you don't have to worry about him.'

'No, I didn't think so,' he said, sounding only half-convinced. 'Er – Mrs Beaumont, my mother is still keen for us to have an engagement party – over in Boston – so that all our friends can meet Annabel. Not yet, of course, but maybe in the New Year, when everyone feels a little better. And of course she'd want you and Tilly and Toby to come. She's so looking forward to meeting you all.'

'And I'm looking forward to it too. Well, it's a very nice idea, but a little hard to think about just yet.'

'Of course. Now – I was going to speak to Mr Beaumont about all this, of course.' More unconscious irony.

'Of course.'

'But I . . . well, I take it you're happy about our engagement. And I'm very sorry I didn't ask him – and you, of course – before. I got a little carried away. I do love Annabel very, very much. I promise you I'll do everything in my power to make her happy.'

'I know that, Jamie. I'm sure you will, and of course we're . . . that is, I . . .' how long was it going to be before she ceased to think of herself as herself and Simon, 'am very happy about it. But I do have to say, I think she is very young. I imagine you won't think of getting married too soon?'

'No, no of course not. But she'll soon be nineteen and then – well then she'll be twenty –'

'Indeed.'

'Mother was only twenty when she married Father. She thinks that would be OK for us. I don't know what you'd think,' he added quickly.

'How can I argue? I was only twenty-one when I got married. But things were a little different then. And what about Annabel, what does she think? She's the important one, surely.'

'Yes, of course. I think she agrees that would be about right.'

'Good.'

'Anyway, we won't be taking her away from you just yet, I promise.'

586

Now why did that strike such a chill around her heart, Elizabeth wondered. And then knew. It wasn't that Annabel would be moving to Boston – she was prepared for that. It was the 'we'. She really didn't like that 'we'.

Sitting on the verandah of her father's beachside house in Barbados, Felicity Parker Jones sat reading a clipping she had been sent from *The Times*, about the tragic death of the prominent City banker, Simon Beaumont.

She felt quite upset; she had liked him enormously, and he'd been a terrific sailing companion. She was surprised he'd been drowned at sea; he'd been such a brilliant sailor, had dealt with conditions far more difficult than a mid-Channel squall. But then: those squalls could be very nasty. Most people thought of the Channel as the generally calm water they crossed on a ferry from Dover to Calais; not the raging treacherous fury it could suddenly become.

'Damn shame,' she said aloud; and when her father came out to join her for breakfast she showed it to him.

'Good God,' he said, 'poor chap. How dreadful. You'll miss him, Flick, won't you? In more ways than one. Have to make a few adjustments.'

'I will indeed,' she said.

587

Chapter 41

August to September, 1990

'Joel, go away. Just go away. Please.'

'Why? Why should I?'

'Because I don't want to see you any more. That's why.'

'Now that's not true,' he said.

'Yes, it is.'

'Debbie, it isn't. You can tell me you won't see me any more if you like, but you can't tell me you don't want to.'

'I can. I just did.'

'I know, and it was a lie. You're very bad at lying, Debbie, you know that?'

She was silent; staring at him. He had arrived at her office, just as she was leaving; it was the second time he had done that. And today he was bearing a large bunch of roses. Which was hugely romantic, of course, and rather glamorous, like something out of a Jilly Cooper novel, and OK, quite – no very – exciting, but wasn't helping her in her resolve.

'Please go away,' she said feebly again.

He had called her in the office, the day after they got back from Scotland.

'I'd like to see you, Debbie,' he said. 'I think we've got things to talk about.'

'What sort of things?'

'Us.'

'Joel,' she said, fixing her eyes firmly on the picture on her desk of Richard and the children, 'there isn't an us.'

'I think there is. Can I come and see you?'

'No, of course you can't. Don't be silly. I'm trying to work.'

'So am I. But I can't concentrate.'

'Well, I'm sorry to hear that.' God, she was being so cool. Two weeks ago, she'd have given anything to hear him say that. Anything. Well, that was two weeks ago. This was now.

'Debbie! I need to see you.'

'No. Please don't do this, Joel. Please. Look, it was very . . . very nice, but—'

'Nice! Is that how you'd label it? Not very flattering.'

'You know what I mean. Of course it was much more than nice. But – it's over.'

'Tell me why? Apart from a few minor obstacles, like your husband and children.'

'It was . . . Well, it was . . .'

'What was it? Describe to me what it was.'

'Well . . .'

Her office door opened; it was Anna. Who hissed she was sorry to disturb her, but could she do the copy on the new diet book by lunchtime.

'Of course,' she said, her voice quite loud, 'I've nearly finished it.'

'Great. Thanks, Debbie, you're a wonder.' She went out and closed the door again.

'I heard that,' Joel said. 'I think you're a wonder too. So when can I see you again?'

'You can't.' And she put the phone down.

That was the first time he came to her office; was waiting outside when she left for the day, blinding her with the sweet shock of it, making her knees weak, her stomach turn over and over.

'Joel!'

'That's me. Where can we go?'

'Nowhere. I mean, I'm going home. I'm late already and—' And then she looked at him, looked properly at him, and absolutely unable to resist him, said, 'Well, maybe just a coffee or something. But only so I can explain.'

She really had tried, so hard. She told him how she felt deeply ashamed of herself, of what she had done. 'It was awful, terrible.'

'Hold on!' Joel said. 'I seem to remember it being not entirely awful.'

'Well – yes, of course. Of course it wasn't. But you know what I mean. It was awful and terrible of me; and I shouldn't have done it.'

'I'm glad you did.'

She sighed and tried to explain how loyal and supportive Richard was being about going up to Scotland, how he had risked losing the job altogether, to give her some time. 'I really can't go on seeing you, Joel.'

'Don't you want to?' She hesitated; he pounced on it. 'There you are, you do want to.'

'Joel please stop it. I – I might want to, but I can't. It was just a – a fling, and OK, it was great, but—'

'That's exactly what I thought,' he said, 'that it was just a fling. To be honest. But it wasn't. Not for me. It was a shock, that – I'm rather good at flings, I've had lots of them, and don't think I'm proud of that either. But when I got back from the Bahamas, I realised you'd meant a bit more than that. A lot more. And I tried to hang onto it being a fling, but I couldn't. I – I seem really to care about you, Debbie. I almost wish I didn't, it would make life much simpler, but I do.'

And Debbie sat there, looking at him, looking into his dark eyes, the expression in them surprisingly and unexpectedly tender, and she could hardly bear it, she wanted him and what he was offering her so much; and then she took a deep breath and tried once again to explain.

Which was obviously not very effective, since here he was again, two days later.

Catherine couldn't ever remember being so unhappy. Well, of course she could – when Freddie had run away, and when her husband had died, but even those dreadful events hadn't wiped out her existence as a fully operating human being. She had been able to decide for herself where to go, what to do, how to care for the children. Now she seemed to have been completely taken over by the Morgans, and she had no option but to do what they said. Even down to when they would all eat, what times they could leave the house, where the children went to school. It was horrible; she felt like some kind of programmed automaton.

She tried very hard to remain cheerful for the children's

sake, to pretend she was looking forward to going to live in the country, to enthuse about their new schools, to say how kind Grandma and Grandpa were being to them all, how lucky they were. And could see she wasn't exactly deceiving them: although they were both trying to be brave too, having been told that really there was no option.

She had won one battle and that was over Freddie's school; she had said that he was not to go away to school, that Frederick had been terribly against it, had hated his own prep school, had been bullied dreadfully.

'Nonsense,' Dudley said. 'Happy as Larry he was, never heard a word of complaint.'

'No, Dudley,' she said, emboldened by the strength of her feelings. 'That's not true.'

'How do you know?' he said, glaring at her through his horn-rimmed spectacles.

'Because he told me. He always felt he couldn't tell you, he was too ashamed.'

'Ashamed! What do you mean, ashamed?'

'Well, he said he felt he should have been able to make a go of it, be popular and do well, not get bullied and beaten, and have to come running to you.'

'He wasn't beaten,' said Phyllis firmly. 'I do know that, the school didn't believe in corporal punishment.'

'Phyllis, I'm sorry, but you don't know. He *was* beaten, by the bigger boys.'

'Oh, bit of toughening up, you mean,' said Dudley; he had been looking very uncomfortable, and now visibly relaxed. 'That's not beating, Catherine, never did anyone any harm, that sort of thing.'

'It did Frederick harm,' said Catherine staunchly, 'and I'm not going to subject Freddie to it. I'm sorry, and I know it's wonderfully generous of you to want to send him to that school, and to take us in, but I can't have him sent away. Not yet.'

The Morgans seized on that 'not yet'; a compromise was reached of weekly boarding 'next year'. But they were deeply dismissive of Catherine's revelations about the bullying, clearly felt she was being naive; it gave force to her argument, she felt, that Frederick had felt unable to tell them about it.

Caroline's school seemed all right; it was full of rather over-confident little girls who all seemed to have ponies, but who were very friendly at the welcome tea party, at the beginning of September, two weeks before term proper began.

'So good of them to take her at such short notice,' Phyllis said. 'I wrote the Headmistress a very appreciative letter. I understand that Caroline was behind in most subjects when she did her test. Of course, I did tell them she'd been at a state school and they said that would explain it and they were prepared to make allowances.'

'I didn't think she was behind,' said Catherine, genuinely surprised, because Caroline had said the test she'd had to do was 'peezy'. She felt a pang of loyalty for St Joseph's.

'Oh yes, very. Still, if she works hard and possibly has some coaching, she should catch up, it seems.'

Catherine was silent.

They were due to move down on 10 September; term for both of them started a week later. Catherine had accompanied Phyllis to the second-hand uniform sale and watched her buying everything in a size too big for Caroline: 'Then it will last longer – it's so expensive, you probably don't realise.'

The conversion to their 'flat' had been done; it consisted of putting a gas ring and a sink into what had been a very small bathroom. 'We'll leave the bath, as we may want to convert it back again,' Phyllis said. 'Dudley suggests fitting some kind of casing over it, to make a useful surface for you – such a good idea, don't you think?' And had installed a minute shower into the lavatory. 'It saves expense with the plumbing, you see,' Dudley had said. The children had small individual bedrooms, made by partitioning one big one, and Catherine's bedroom was even smaller, with a single bed; while she was sure there wasn't the slightest possibility of her ever needing a double again, she still felt rather written off, as she said to Lucinda.

'You're dreading it, aren't you? Poor Catherine.'

'No, no, not dreading it,' said Catherine firmly, for once she started to talk about her misery, she knew she would never stop, and the children might overhear her. 'A little apprehensive, of course. But – well, you know, it will be nice

592

not to be so desperately worried about money and to know the children are at good schools. And I'm sure I'll make lots of friends in no time . . .'

She could hear the hollow ring in her voice now, thinking of the mothers at Caroline's school, all briskly sporty, wearing Puffas and dirndl skirts, shouting at one another in accents that made Lucinda sound common, about pony club camps and point-to-points, and how marvellous it was that the girls were starting lax the next term. Where among them would she find one friend, let alone lots?

'Well, you must come up for the day as often as you can and see me,' said Lucinda. 'Oh dear, I shall miss you.'

'I'll miss you too. I was thinking about Simon . . . Lucinda, do you think he did it deliberately?' Catherine's face was very distressed.

'I don't know,' said Lucinda. 'It seems at least quite possible, I'm afraid. I mean, think about it – it wasn't just the money, he'd lost his job – it was all very – black.'

'Yes, but he was the opposite of black. Right to – to the end. So brave and cheerful. Oh God, I do hope he didn't. It's such a terrible way to go.'

Annabel was lying in Jamie's arms; it was the night before he was going back to Boston. She was crying.

'Darling, darling Annabel, don't cry. I know how unhappy you are at the moment about your dad . . .'

'It's not just my dad,' said Annabel, sniffing, and then started crying harder. 'Oh dear, that sounds dreadful, as if I didn't care. What could be worse than that?'

'It doesn't sound dreadful at all.'

'Yes, it does. But I'm so dreading you going away again, I miss you so much, I get so lonely for you. And I feel so specially lonely at the moment. Toby's being such a brat, I mean I know why, of course, he misses Dad almost the most, they did all kinds of things together, but he's so angry all the time. Well, you've seen it.'

'Yes, I have.'

'And Tilly – I just don't know what to do about her. She keeps asking me if I think Daddy – if he . . . well, you know, did it on purpose. And I'm so confused about it, Jamie, I just don't know. It's so horrible, either way. And I find it so hard to lie to her, but she so wants it to have been an accident.'

'And – what do you think?'

'Well, I'd like it to have been. But I'm truly not convinced. I mean, as fast as I decide one way, I begin to think about the other. What – what do you think, Jamie?'

'Darling, I didn't know your dad, so it's impossible for me to say. But if he was really as – as upbeat as everyone says, and if he loved you all as much as he obviously did, then I can't believe he'd have done it. Especially to your mother.'

'Yes, I know.' Annabel was silent. 'Yes, I think he really did love Mummy a lot. And specially recently, they seemed to be happier than I could ever remember.'

'I would say he absolutely adored her.'

She looked at him. 'Why do you say that?'

'Oh, she was talking about him the other day. About the early days of their marriage, about how he wanted her to work because, as she put it, he wanted her to stay the way she was, the way he – what was it – oh yes, the way he liked her to be.'

'Yes, that's true, she told me that. Oh dear, she must feel so terribly unhappy. I wish I could help her.'

'I think you are helping her. A lot. Just by being around. You obviously have fun together.'

'Yes, we do. Every so often we forget, start giggling about something and then it's always the same, she suddenly stops giggling, starts to cry. And then I feel so guilty.'

'Don't,' said Jamie, 'it'll get better, take her longer to start to cry. I bet you.'

She looked at him and smiled. 'You're quite wise, aren't you?'

'Not very. Dad says I'm a numbskull.'

'Jamie, that's horrid of him.'

'Oh, he doesn't mean it,' said Jamie hurriedly. 'Mother says he doesn't mean it.'

'Well, obviously she knows how clever you are.'

'Kind of. She always says Bif got the Cartwright brains, the real brains as she calls them. She says Kathleen and I have to make do with her family intellect. Of course she's joking, or she couldn't say that about her own family. But there's something in it.'

Annabel was silent.

'You won't forget about – about the engagement party, will you?' Jamie said, rather tentatively. 'She really wants to start planning it.'

'Jamie . . .' Annabel stopped. She'd been about to say that she really couldn't agree to having a party, just to enable Frances to start planning it; but she knew it would upset Jamie terribly.

'Of course I won't,' she said, 'but you must give us time. Mummy has a lot to get over yet, with the inquest and everything. And then there's all the financial worry. She's got a meeting with the solicitors tomorrow, actually. Then we'll know how things really are. I mean, we'll still have to sell this house, no doubt about it, but how much there'll be left for another house, we don't know.'

'And – any more thoughts about the wedding?' said Jamie. 'I mean, whether you might consider having it in Cape Cod?'

Annabel felt a stab of irritation. Was this insensitive or was it insensitive?

'No, Jamie. Well actually, yes, Jamie. I really don't think I do want that. I want to be in England, to be at home.'

He went very quiet. After a long time he said, 'Oh yes, I see. Well, I can understand that. But if you only have a small house . . .'

'If we only have a small house,' said Annabel, 'there are places we can hire. Like the Polo Club at Ham, for instance, it's lovely there. Or . . .' She giggled suddenly, remembering Florian's suggestion. 'What about the salon? There's loads of space and a roof garden, and—'

'Get married in a hairdressing salon? Annabel, are you mad?'

'Probably,' she said rather sadly. She could see she'd upset him; a bad idea when he was going home, a waste of their last night, in fact. She propped herself up on her elbow and smiled down at him. 'Sorry. Silly idea. I've got a much better one.'

'Yes?' He turned his head, started kissing her breasts, teasing her nipples with his tongue, his hand moving round to her buttocks, moulding them, working on them. He was beginning to be confident with her body, with what made it want him most.

'Wouldn't have been this, by any chance, would it?'

'It absolutely would,' said Annabel.

Elizabeth spent a long, harrowing afternoon at the solicitors. Nothing could have prepared her for how it would make her recognise the finality of Simon's death. She could remember them both making their wills, laughing about how rich one of them would become on the other's death, finding it all rather entertaining, deciding which of the children should have what.

This had been the opposite of entertaining. The facts were stark. Terrifying even. She had thought that because Simon had resigned from Lloyd's, when the first problems arose, his liability would shortly have ceased. 'I'm afraid not, Elizabeth,' John Fraser, their solicitor said gently. 'A resignation merely releases you from underwriting new business. You can still be liable for any business you've underwritten in the past.'

She had stared at him, stricken. 'You mean that, as long as there are claims against a syndicate, even though you've pulled out, you're liable?'

'I'm afraid so. In some cases, at any rate. Which would seem to include yours.'

'Do you know, I really didn't realise that. How frightful.'

'It is fairly frightful, I agree,' Fraser sighed, 'but those are the facts, I'm afraid.'

'So we – I – sell the house, give Lloyd's that money and anything else they can get their hands on, and it could still be going on, them taking money from me, in ten years' time.'

'I'm afraid so, yes. It's a great pity that Simon had taken out a bank's guarantee on your house, of course. Lloyd's don't generally insist on the sale of the main residence.'

'Indeed it was. But he made a foolish investment, in an overseas property business.'

'Yes, I know. And I imagine the bank is out to get its pound of flesh.'

'It is. God . . .' She paused. 'So – whatever I do or make, they can go on taking for as long as they like?'

'Well, no. The debts don't pass to you personally, but because Simon's estate unfortunately does, they can take everything that's in it.'

She suddenly felt dreadfully sick; the floor swayed

underneath her. She closed her eyes, clutched the arms of the chair.

'Are you all right, my dear?'

'Yes, yes, I'm fine. Thank you. Sorry.'

'Don't apologise. Have some water.'

He poured her a glass; she sipped it and the feeling began to pass.

'Go on,' she said. 'I'm all right now.'

'Sure? Good. Now, there is quite a lot of good news.'

She managed to smile. 'The Lloyd's directors are all about to be put in a plane with faulty engines?'

'I'm sure you're not alone in wishing that. But your earlier statement was incorrect; whatever you earn, and I am aware it is a lot, is yours. Lloyd's can make no claim on it.'

'Great. Well, it's lucky I love my job so much, and that I'm reasonably good at it. And reasonably well rewarded.'

'It is indeed. That's not all, though. There are two substantial sums that Lloyd's cannot get their hands on.'

'Really? Like what?'

'Well, you have a widow's pension from the bank.'

'From Graburn and French?'

'Yes.'

'But – but John, they fired him. Without notice and without salary in lieu of notice – that's what they said. And repeated it in a letter. Those words are engraved on my heart.'

'Fact remains, Elizabeth, they are required by law to pay you the pension.'

'Goodness.' She was silent for a moment, digesting this. Then, 'And – and how much would that be?'

'I've made preliminary enquiries. In the region of thirty thousand pounds a year.'

'Thirty – thirty thousand?'

'Yes. And so they should.'

'Are you sure? Are you quite sure?'

'Absolutely. The other sum due to you is very considerable.'

'Tell me,' she said. She was beginning to feel quite sick again.

'It's Simon's personal life cover. Which is written in trust for you.'

'God. How – how much is that, John?'

'Two hundred and fifty thousand pounds.'

'Oh. Oh, I see.' This was incredible.

'And that is tax free. So – I hope that will help a little. Relieve some of those middle-of-the-night fears. Grief is bad enough without gnawing financial anxiety as well.'

She arrived home feeling very confused. She went straight upstairs to their bedroom, took her jacket off, lay down on the bed.

It was a huge relief, obviously, that they wouldn't be destitute, on the street. That, in fact, they would still be quite comfortably off. The house had to go, of course, but they didn't need such a big house now, after all. Something much more modest would do. It was just that she loved it so much. Well, she had loved Simon so much, and she was – somehow – managing without him. It would be the same with the house.

On the other hand, and this was difficult to face, it did mean that Simon was indeed worth a great deal more dead than alive. And that meant that he had perhaps, just possibly . . . No, come on, Elizabeth, face it, face this hideous, ugly fact: it meant that suicide was much more likely. It was his last gift to her; financial security, when he had – as he saw it – deprived her of it absolutely.

'Oh Simon,' she said aloud, looking at the photograph of him, her favourite, standing on the deck of the *Lizzie*, his hair whipped by the wind, smiling his most gloriously infectious smile. 'Oh Simon, you shouldn't have done it. You really shouldn't.'

Chapter 42

'My darling, you look wonderful. Positively blooming. *Love* the hair.'

'Thank you. You look pretty good yourself.'

'I feel it. Now, come and sit down, let me get you something. Er . . . are you allowed—'

'I am. And if I'm not, I'm having it anyway. But this is on me. So champagne?'

'Champagne it is. A little Bolly would go down a treat. And I won't argue, although I should as an English gentleman . . .'

'Virgil, you've been away too long. Lots of English gentlemen allow ladies to pay these days. Lots of English ladies are quite rich in their own right. Queens of the boardroom and all that.'

'Mmm. I like boardroom queen. I might start claiming that title myself.'

Lucinda giggled.

'And are *you* a boardroom queen, Lucinda?'

'Me? Absolutely not.'

'Good. I don't want you getting all tough on me. I want you as I remember, giggly and a bit hopeless.'

'Virgil! I was not hopeless.'

'You were, just a little.'

The Bollinger had arrived, duly ice-bucketed. 'You can't beat the Ritz, can you?' said Virgil. 'I always forget how wonderful it is. We have the Plaza, of course, very similar in a way, but not quite the class . . .'

'Is it similar?'

'Very. Complete with palms – and wonderful pastries. But I prefer the Pierre myself. More discreet. Or even the Carlyle –

599

that was Kennedy's favourite, you know. Very stylish indeed.'

'Oh, I'd so love to go to New York,' said Lucinda wistfully. She felt her life rather lacked style at the moment; she looked at Virgil in his pale-blue linen shirt, his black linen suit, his perfectly cropped black hair, and thought he epitomised it.

'My darling, come. You'd adore it. And it would adore you.'

'Well, maybe not just now.' Lucinda patted her stomach and smiled at him.

'No, and many congratulations on that. Is – that is, does Nigel . . .'

'Nigel doesn't,' said Lucinda firmly. 'I have a new – oh dear, what should I call him?'

'Beau?'

'More than a beau. A fiancé.'

'How sweet. How old-fashioned. Although the relationship is clearly not terribly old-fashioned. So – what happened?'

'I – I just met him,' Lucinda said, 'and fell in love.'

'Well, darling, that's very lovely. And is he another good old English toff?'

'No, he isn't. He's – well, he's not a toff at all actually, he comes from – from Essex. Originally.'

'Essex! Lucinda, how exciting. You've got yourself a bit of rough. Well, I would never have thought it of you, of all people.'

'I don't know why not,' said Lucinda, slightly irritably.

'Because you are the archetypal posh English rose. When you first came to work at the gallery, I really thought you were too good to be true. Charming cliché after charming cliché. And when you married Nigel – well . . . How is the old fruit? Heartbroken? Or does he have Another?'

'Not yet, I'm afraid,' said Lucinda, 'but I keep hoping.'

'So, you ran off, did you? With this rough diamond?'

'In a word – yes. That sums it up pretty well. I'm not proud of it, Virgil, I can tell you.'

'Well, darling, we all do things we're not proud of,' said Virgil, allowing the waiter to refill his glass, 'in the name of love, I mean, I stole Greg from the most gorgeous boy from Harlem. I felt very ashamed, for about two minutes. But you're happy?'

'Oh, so happy.'

'Well, that's what matters. Nigel will get over it, sweetie. He's got lots of money, after all; some other English rose will bloom for him.'

'That's the problem,' said Lucinda, 'he *hasn't* got lots of money any more. He's about to be very poor, unless I can help him. Poor as well as lonely.'

'Something tells me,' said Virgil, looking at her thoughtfully, 'that this might be where I come in.'

'Hopefully, yes.'

'And what do I come in doing?'

'Just – just saying something, that's all.'

'Saying something. Hmm. In writing?'

'Well – yes.'

'What sort of something? Go on – I like seeing you squirm, Lucinda. Spit it out, as my old dad used to say. I can only say no.'

'All right. It goes something like this . . .'

She told him what she wanted; he sat staring at her, then burst into peals of mirth.

'Darling Lucinda. What a glorious notion. As if you were worth that!'

'I might have been.'

'Sweetheart, you weren't. Not a quarter of it.'

'Oh,' she said, and felt her heart literally drop, somewhere deep into her bump. 'Oh, don't you think so?'

'I don't. Frankly.'

'Right. Well . . . well, I'll have to think of something else then.'

'Here. Have some more Bolly. And don't look so dejected. Nobody knows you weren't worth it, except me. So – tell me what I have to do exactly. And I'll do it.'

'Oh, Virgil!' She hurled herself at him, kissed him on both cheeks. 'Thank you so, so much, it's so good of you.'

'It is quite,' he said. 'It could be classed as perjury, if anyone was looking. I'm only doing it because it amuses me. And I want to hear *exactly* what is it about dear old chinless Nige that you want to do this for him. I long to know, darling. It sounds terribly intriguing.'

'Not really,' said Lucinda, 'but I will explain as best I can. You see, the thing is . . .'

'Mummy . . .'

'Yes, darling?' Elizabeth looked up. Tilly was standing in the doorway, very white and big-eyed.

'Mummy, I'm terribly sorry, but I just don't think I can go.'

'Go where?'

'To – to my new school. To Saint Anne's. I just can't go away at the moment. I can't face it, not leaving you and Annabel and home and—' She started crying, rather loudly, like a small child. Elizabeth got up, went over and put her arms round her.

'Oh Tilly. Darling, you should have said before. Of course you don't have to go. I've been dreading it too. And worrying about you. I thought you were looking forward to it, getting away, change of scenery and all that.'

'Oh Mummy, no. Dreading it more every day. I'm sorry, I should have said, but I didn't want to worry you.'

'It doesn't matter a bit,' said Elizabeth, thinking that actually it did; it would mean endless fractured arrangements, endless new ones. Term began in two days; even a week's notice would have helped, and . . . 'Now come on, darling,' she said, taking a deep breath, berating herself for her selfishness, 'let's discuss it properly. See what we can sort out. The first thing to do is ring Mrs Priest at Saint Anne's. I'll do it now, while you get us a cup of tea.'

She'd turn into a cup of tea soon, she thought wearily. God knows how many cups she'd drunk since Simon had died. Cups that she hadn't really wanted, that people had urged her to drink, the making of which had been something to do . . .

Mrs Priest was surprisingly accommodating.

'Of course I understand. She needs more time. A new school is quite an ordeal anyway, and with what Tilly's had to endure . . . It's a pity she didn't say sooner, but honestly, Mrs Beaumont, let her take her time. A couple more weeks won't make much difference, and she's a bright girl, she'll catch up.'

'There.' Elizabeth smiled at Tilly as she came back into the room with the tray. 'No problem at all. They say you can take your time, start when you're ready. Isn't that good?'

'Well, sort of,' said Tilly, 'but the thing is, Mummy, I don't want to go away at all. Not ever, I won't ever be ready. I've just

602

realised it over the past few days. I want to be home with you, looking after you.'

'Now Tilly,' said Elizabeth firmly, 'I can't have you, any of you, thinking you have to stay at home with me. I'm going to be fine. I'm going back to work next week, you know I am, and I want everyone to do what they want, not what they think they ought to do.'

'It's not what I think I ought to do,' said Tilly, starting to cry again, 'it's what I want to do. I'm scared, Mummy, so scared.'

'What of, sweetheart?'

'Of – of what might happen next. It's all so awful, starting with Chadwick going, and Boy, and then all the other things, and Daddy losing his job and Josie gone, and now us selling the house, and Daddy being – well, Daddy gone; it's like some monster is swallowing us up, bit by bit. I can't go away, I just can't. I want to be here, holding on to what we've got left. I feel safer here – at least I can see what's happening . . .'

'Tilly, darling, come here. I'm so sorry, so very sorry. But everything is going to be all right, you know. I saw the solicitor the other day, and we will have some money now, apparently.'

'Like what?'

'Well, like . . .' This was hard, the words in themselves – widow, pension, life assurance – were so final, so frightening, she didn't want Tilly to hear them, to draw the same conclusion that she had. 'Like money that was in trust for us, things like that.'

'What, that Daddy had arranged?'

'Yes. That have been arranged for many years.'

'Like what?'

'Like . . . well, it sounds so silly, doesn't it, but apparently the bank have to pay me a – a –'

'Pension?'

'Well, yes. That's right.'

'A widow's pension?' Tilly sounded angry suddenly. 'That's what you mean, isn't it? You're a widow and that horrible bank, they have to give you some money because Daddy died. Although they wouldn't give him any more when he was alive. Well, I'm glad, I suppose.' She paused, then said, 'But that is so, so scary.'

'What is, darling?'

603

'Well,' to think that you – we – have more money because he's – he's – I mean, doesn't that make you think he might have done it on purpose? To help us?'

'No, Tilly, I don't,' said Elizabeth. 'I am absolutely one hundred per cent certain that he wouldn't. I keep telling you this. He wouldn't have done it to us, he knew – he knew how . . . Oh Tilly, darling . . .' And then she was crying too, as hard as Tilly, and they sat there for a long time, holding one another. And she promised Tilly she would find her a day school.

'But darling, I'll have to work – you know that, don't you? I won't be around at the end of the school day. You'll be,' she managed to smile a crooked, watery smile, 'you'll be a latchkey kid.'

'Don't mind,' said Tilly staunchly. 'Don't mind a bit.'

Later, when Tilly had gone to meet Annabel at the salon, and to walk home with her, Elizabeth pulled out the *Good School Guide* and started leafing through it. A good day school, over-subscribed four times as all London schools were, that would take a child at two days' notice, how on earth was she going to find that? Or the energy to do it? It would be lovely to have Tilly at home, of course, but . . . God, she felt so tired. So deathly, deathly tired. It really wasn't helping. Not one bit.

Catherine was packing rather lethargically when the phone rang.

'Is that Catherine?'

'Yes, it is.'

'Catherine, it's Nigel. Nigel Cowper. I heard you were moving to Somerset.'

'Who told you that?' said Catherine.

'Lucinda.'

'Oh, I see.' She tried not to sound surprised. They really did seem on awfully good terms, she'd even seen them chatting together and Lucinda giggling after Simon's funeral.

'Anyway, I wanted to say goodbye. Well, a bit more than that,' he said. 'I wondered if you'd let me take you all out to tea before you went. I so enjoyed our coffee that morning at Peter Jones, I thought we could do it again. Your children are a great credit to you, you know.'

'That would be lovely,' said Catherine. 'The children aren't exactly proving a credit to me at the moment, they're fighting very loudly over who's going to watch what on the TV.'

'I'm sure that's quite normal,' said Nigel kindly. 'So – so would that be all right? It's also to say thank you for – for taking me in at the church that day. I was feeling pretty much of a sore thumb, not knowing anybody really. I was so grateful to you, for spotting me.'

'Oh Nigel, honestly,' said Catherine, thinking that it would be hard not to spot Nigel, all six foot three of him, clutching the inevitable umbrella, even though England had been going through a heatwave, and the papers had been calling it 'Tinderbox Britain'. And then she suddenly looked at her new life, her awful, friendless, sterile future life, to be lived in that hideous house with the hideous Morgans, cooking on her gas ring, with no doubt every phone call monitored and charged, and wondered how she was going to bear it. 'It was a pleasure to have you with us,' and heard her voice shake slightly.

'Catherine, are you all right?' The unmistakable Etonian accent, the light, clipped drawl (could a drawl be clipped?) was very concerned.

'Yes, I'm fine,' she said, taking a deep breath, steadying herself. 'Honestly.'

'So, what about tea? What day could you do?'

'Well, Lucinda and Blue are driving us down on Sunday. Very sweetly. So – it would have to be Saturday, I'm afraid. Hobson's Choice. Is that any good to you? Of course I'll understand if it's not. You're probably terribly busy.'

'What – on a Saturday afternoon? Of course not. So, where would you like to go? Where would *they* like to go?'

Catherine suddenly felt rather reckless. After all, this was the Last Chance Saloon; it was most unlikely she'd have a man asking her where she'd like to go, even for tea with her children, for a very long time.

'How brave are you feeling?'

'Oh, pretty brave. I mean, I believe children like McDonald's – you know, that hamburger place . . .'

'I do know, yes,' said Catherine, 'but if you're feeling very brave, we could go one better. It would do a lot for their street cred.'

'Their what?' asked Nigel. He sounded rather baffled.

'You know, it would be kudos for them, something rather cool they'd done.' Although, she reflected rather sadly, the children's new schoolmates would probably be more impressed by a point-to-point than what she was about to suggest.

'Oh well, I'm all for that.'

'It's a place called Planet Hollywood. It's in Leicester Square. It does serve burgers, but really good ones, and apparently they have the actual costumes worn by Judy Garland in *The Wizard of Oz* and Superman's cloak, hung up around the place. It's owned by Arnold Schwarzenegger and Sylvester Stallone, you know?'

'Er, no, I don't think so,' said Nigel. 'Will they be there?'

'Very unlikely,' said Catherine. 'So – what do you think?'

'I think it sounds very exciting. For me as well as them. It's certainly a long way from the Derry and Toms roof garden, where I used to be taken if I'd been good.'

'How grand. I was taken to Lyon's Corner House,' said Catherine, and then found herself wondering what she would wear. Which was obviously ridiculous, for Nigel was hardly going to take any notice of her, it was the children's treat. But she didn't want to look frumpy. In her Last Chance Saloon.

Debbie was helping Richard to sort out his papers. He was leaving in a week and there was, he kept saying, a lot to do.

They had had a surprisingly happy family time in those last few days; lots of picnics, a day at the Safari Park at Longleat, another at Battersea funfair. The photographs showed an endless succession of idyllic scenes, everyone smiling, laughing, hugging, waving at the camera. Debbie supposed that the usual facts of family life must have been going on, that people must have had tummy-ache or blisters or felt sick from the roundabouts, or wanted to go on the roundabout again, that there must have been whining and complaining and fighting; but in her memory and in those photographs, there was only happiness, freeze-framed for ever.

Richard was half-excited about his new life, half-sad at leaving the old one behind. 'But it's only for a term,' he said, determinedly cheerful, 'and then we'll all be together again. Won't we?'

And Debbie smiled and said of course they would, crushing the panic she still felt when she contemplated her own part in that life, but aware that there was nothing whatsoever she could do about it. She had promised herself that she would keep her share of the bargain: be a good, a very good, wife and mother, in return for Richard respecting her wishes and her ambitions for herself. She was infinitely grateful to him for that, for risking Morag's disapproval, and thus losing his golden opportunity, and he had done it with a good grace and a generous heart. And that must be repaid.

Chapter 43

September to October, 1990

There she was in all the papers, crying. Because her little boy
had gone away to school. Sitting in the car, driving away, her
husband very cheerful-looking beside her.

Well, if it was all right for Diana to cry, Catherine thought,
then she would too. Of course, Prince William was going to
boarding school – a fact which Dudley had made much of:
'same age as Freddie, Catherine, if it's good enough for
William, it should be good enough for Freddie' – and Freddie
would be coming home again that evening – quite late, he had
to stay at school for prep – but he was still terrified, white-
faced and shaking with nerves in his too-big uniform. Phyllis
had insisted on going with them, which hadn't helped, telling
him to pull himself together and saying that he was a big boy
now, as he sat in the back, twice asking Catherine to stop so he
could be sick.

This was terrible, she thought, holding his head, trying to
comfort him afterwards.

He had gone in quiet and resigned, and without a backward
glance, ushered by his form master, and in the company of a
bigger boy. 'Such a good system, isn't it?' Phyllis had said.
'They allot seniors to take care of the little ones, as of course
they would if he was boarding. Now, we've got a long drive
home, Catherine. I hope you realise you're going to have to do
this every day.' Catherine said she did.

But at least she would be driving; she actually had a car, and
it promised to transform her life. Lucinda had said, when she
came to collect them all, that she had been thinking and that
really, for the time being, she would like Catherine to have her
Peugeot.

'I've got the GTI, after all, and I can't drive them both at the same time. I don't know why I didn't think of it before. Parking's a nightmare out there, and Blue thinks it's a really good idea.' She didn't add that Blue had said that clearly the car would have been driven into several walls within the space of a week, and that he hoped Lucinda was ready to say goodbye to it. 'So you take this, and—'

'Lucinda, I can't.'

'Of course you can. It'll help, and make me less worried about you, down there on your own with those dreadful people.'

'I think I may have exaggerated how dreadful they are.'

'Well, I hope so, for your sake. But . . . your own family charging you board and lodging – it's outrageous! No, you take the car, and I shan't worry about you quite so much. And besides, you'll be able to come up and see me more easily, think of it that way. You'll be doing me a favour. And I'm going to come with you tomorrow, follow you in the GTI. Don't argue, I want to. Blue's going to some stupid car-racing thing, and I'll be on my own otherwise.'

Phyllis had been rather put out by the whole thing, by two cars arriving in her drive, one of them clearly quite expensive, and at the news that Catherine would have a car after all.

'I don't know where we're going to put it,' she said. 'The drive will look like a car park. Dudley won't be pleased at all.'

She also clearly disapproved of Lucinda; she was icily polite to her and asked her to park the GTI in the lane: 'It's rather blocking the entrance where it is.'

'I will, when we've taken Catherine's things out,' said Lucinda. 'It's one of the reasons I came down – we couldn't get everything into one car.'

'There does seem to be rather a lot. I hadn't expected furniture, Catherine. I don't know where you're going to put it.'

The 'furniture' consisted of lamps, books, a couple of mirrors and pictures, a music system and a TV and a small child's desk. Lucinda smiled at her with rather exaggerated sweetness.

'Well, she is moving here to live,' she said.

'I realise that. But – three suitcases as well! You must have a lot of clothes.'

She showed them upstairs, carrying two small carrier bags, and then said she had to see to tea.

'I do hope you'll join us,' she said to Lucinda. 'I can always make another round of sandwiches.'

'Well? Did I exaggerate?' Catherine said when they were sitting on her rather small bed.

'No, Catherine,' said Lucinda. 'You didn't.'

The three of them walked down the lane to wave her off; Catherine felt very tearful.

'I shall miss her,' said Freddie.

'Me too,' said Caroline. 'So much.'

'Well, we must go and see her lots,' said Catherine determinedly, swallowing her tears. 'Now let's go and sort our new home out, shall we?'

And they had; and it didn't look too bad, with the pictures up and the mirrors, and she had put on a tape of Elton John, who they all rather liked, and were leaning out of the window, watching the evening sunshine on the lovely sloping hills and meadows of Somerset, and each of them put an arm round her waist. She smiled down at them and said, 'You know what? I think we can be happy here.'

'Course we can,' said Freddie stoutly.

It seemed a very long day, waiting to collect him; all she could think of was his white face, and her terror that he might cry and be labelled a sissy, or be sick again, with no one to help him.

It was such a terrible ordeal for a little boy, and especially one who had been through what he had. Three new schools in a year, if you counted going back to Lynton House; and two of those experiences terribly unhappy. He must see school as some kind of torture chamber.

He would be so lost and frightened, and then he wasn't very big; it was always the littlest ones who got bullied, he'd be marked down straight away. And he wasn't much good at games, although he tried very hard, partly because of the stint at St Joseph's, where they hadn't done much. And if he was behind in the work as well, how would he cope? The whole thing suddenly seemed to her too much to ask of him; they should have stayed in London, found a way to survive . . . Stop it, Catherine, you couldn't, you'd have starved to death.

She looked at her watch as they pulled into the drive; still only 9.45. However was she going to get through the day until six: how would Freddie get through it? Caroline was still at home, so they had gone for a walk together – there wasn't a lot else to do – and accepted Phyllis's invitation to join her for lunch in the garden. And then she kept thinking of Freddie at lunchtime, supposed it was horrible food, fatty gristly meat: would he be forced to eat it, would he sit there wretched, all alone, trying to cope? Every time the phone rang, she jumped, sure it was the school asking her to come, that Freddie was too upset to stay.

She and Caroline spent the afternoon marking her new school uniform; it was rather nice, brown kilts, blue blouses and oatmeal sweaters, and dark brown hats and coats.

'I'm sorry it's so big, sweetie,' she said, as Caroline tried it all on, stood there rather awkwardly, her kilt and coat hanging round her calves. 'I don't think I can shorten the kilt, because of the pleats, but I can probably do the coat. Only . . .'

'It's OK,' said Caroline bravely. 'Honestly, I'm growing so fast, that's one thing Grandma's right about, it'll probably fit me by half-term.'

Catherine hugged her, trying not to cry again; and thinking how brave her children were and how she didn't deserve them.

She was so terrified of being late, she was back at the school by twenty to six. The area slowly filled up with Range Rovers and Volvo Estates, with mothers shouting at each other and ignoring her.

What on earth am I going to do, Catherine thought, if he doesn't like it, if he's unhappy here? We really have burned our boats – how could we possibly move again? And she felt so sick with apprehension she thought she might follow Freddie's example and throw up in the hedge. Caroline picked up on her mood and stood, huge-eyed, biting her lip.

Endless small boys appeared, all looking exactly alike in their uniforms, but there was no sign of Freddie; after ten minutes she was frantic, about to storm the school, which you were most emphatically not allowed to do, but she didn't care, he might be inside crying, or hiding from her, afraid that she would see he was upset . . . or had he got a detention already? Or had he – oh God – had he run away again? Then three small boys came out like rockets, cannoning into her.

'Hi, Mum, this is Groom and this is Hutchings, we're all new and guess what, Mum, I'm doing soccer trials tomorrow and we can choose out of art or IT and there's a choir, I'm trying for that as well . . .'

She stood there, smiling at Freddie, trying not to cry at the same time, and at Groom and Hutchings too.

'No problems here then,' said one of their mothers, and, 'Super, absolutely super, isn't it?' said the other.

However lonely she was, Catherine thought, however dreadful her in-laws, it simply didn't matter. If the children were happy, then she could stand anything else. Anything.

They drove home, Freddie talking non-stop: the other boys were really cool, his form master was great, he was in Nelson House ('there are four, all named after famous soldiers and sailors, but Nelson is the best, everyone says so'), the work was fine, he was ahead in Maths even.

Phyllis met them on the doorstep, received a truncated account of the successful day, gave Catherine an 'I told you so' look and then said, 'There was a phone call for you. A man.' Her tone carried a distinct note of disapproval; clearly she felt Catherine had no business to be cohorting with men, even over the phone.

'Oh,' said Catherine, her mind raking wildly over any men who might have rung her. 'Did he give a name?'

'Yes, Mr Cowper, he said. He asked if you could ring him back. I said it would be better if he rang you, as it was long distance.'

'Yes, of course,' said Catherine, wondering how on earth Nigel had got her number. Lucinda, she supposed. 'Thank you. When did he – that is, what time . . .'

'About six,' said Phyllis. 'Now I must go, I'm off to a drinks party. I'll see you tomorrow. Glad the day was a success, Freddie. What did I tell you? And if you were boarding, you'd still be there – just think of that.'

'Wish I was,' said Freddie.

'He loved it,' said Catherine, smiling into the phone when Nigel rang later in the evening. 'Truly loved it. Of course, it's early days, but it really seems to suit him. And guess what, he said he wanted to board.'

'Take no notice,' said Nigel briskly. 'I wanted to board at his age, and then spent the next year crying myself to sleep. But I'm so glad it went well.'

'It's sweet of you to ring,' said Catherine. 'Thank you.'

'Not at all. Nothing so terrifying as a first day at a new school. Couldn't stop thinking about him. Well – tell him well done from me.'

'I will. Goodbye, Nigel.'

'Goodbye, Catherine. Enjoy country life.'

Well, that was clearly that, she thought, putting the phone down. Goodness, he was a nice man. Lucinda must be completely mad. And he was clearly still hopelessly in love with her.

Debbie was actually quite enjoying her new life. Without Richard. Well, of course she missed him, missed him a lot, she was used to having him around all the time, he was her husband, for heaven's sake; but it made a fantastic difference to how much she got done, having her evenings to herself, deciding how to spend them, being able to work if she wanted to, or watch any old crap on the telly, or have an hour-long bath and read. The children liked it too; they liked having her undivided attention. Rachel and to an extent Emma, would burst into noisy tears if anything went wrong, or she was cross with them, and say they missed Daddy, but she could see they didn't too much. Well, obviously they did, they looked forward to the alternate weekends, kept a little calendar of them, ticking off the days, but day to day, or rather evening to evening, she had never known them so biddable, so calm.

She'd found a nice lady called Jenny to look after them after school but she had said firmly several times that she couldn't ever stay later than six-thirty and that was the very limit, six was more like it. Which was fine; Debbie was almost always home by then.

She ate supper with them most nights, which they liked; it meant two things, they could talk to her properly, 'sitting-down talking' as Emma put it, and there was an undeniable improvement in their diet. Fish fingers, pizzas, toasted sandwiches were replaced by pasta, filled jacket potatoes, fresh tuna steaks, sometimes even proper steaks. Debbie felt guilty as they proclaimed their pleasure in this; had she been short-changing them all these years, giving them stuff that was quick and easy, telling herself it was what they liked, when they actually preferred proper food? They had to wait a bit longer for it, but Jenny gave them what she called fruit plates when they got in from school, and then let them watch *Neighbours* and *Home and Away*, instead of nagging them to finish their homework. It didn't seem to be doing them any harm; indeed, they got on with it more readily afterwards, having imbibed the happily homely doctrines of Pippa and her fostered brood and the camaraderie of Ramsay Street.

Richard rang three nights a week full of enthusiasm: 'It's so wonderfully peaceful up here, Debbie. I feel quite different, unstressed, you know, and with much more energy, and the school's the most marvellous place – the children are all so bright and confident and really want to work and learn, and as for the games . . .' He said he couldn't believe he was actually in charge of it all, was terrified of making mistakes, spoiling it. 'It's like being given some superb car to drive and being terribly worried about crashing the gears, or scraping it. But I seem to be managing. Morag's been absolutely fantastic, so patient with me, so encouraging . . .'

And Debbie kept saying good, great, that's marvellous, how wonderful, and how they were fine, but they missed him and were counting the days till half-term when they were all going up there, while counting the days herself, only backwards rather than forwards, thinking, Only two whole months left, or, Only ten weeks, and wondering how she was going to bear the ending of it. Because, of course, she just didn't want to go.

The house was on the market, but only a few people had

been to look round. She lived in terror of hearing from the agent that one of them had liked it, wanted to buy it, expressing great disappointment at being told nobody had.

'It might help to drop the price a bit, Mrs Fielding,' the agent said. 'It really is a buyer's market, you know,' and, 'No, no,' she said, crossing her fingers. 'No, I think it's too soon to do that. Let's keep on trying a little longer.'

Joel hadn't rung her again; he seemed finally to have accepted what she said. The only thing that worried her was that he knew that Richard was about to go up to Scotland; and he knew this because she had told him. It had been a terrible mistake, that; she had hardly been able to believe that she had done it, had sat staring at him, feeling herself blushing helplessly.

The last thing she wanted was Joel to know that she was living on her own for three months. It had just – well, just slipped out. Things did, sometimes, when you were feeling stressed. And she had been feeling very stressed; sitting there in the café drinking horrible coffee, staring at the flowers he had brought her, wishing he hadn't. Of course she couldn't take them home; she took them in to poor old Mrs Turner three doors down, who hadn't been well and was very depressed. First taking one out, and pressing it in the huge *Dictionary of Quotations* that Flora had given her for Christmas. Well, it wasn't often someone brought her flowers these days, it would be nice to have a memento. It wasn't one of the roses, because it was so hard to press roses, they were too fat, it was a spray of the white gypsophila that was in the bouquet with them.

Anyway, she couldn't un-tell him. He knew now. But he wasn't going to do anything as a result: obviously. She'd told him to leave her alone, and she was sure he'd respect her wishes. He was that sort of person.

The children had all finally gone to bed that evening, and she was settling down happily to her new favourite programme, *Capital City*, which Richard would have poured great scorn on, all about the yuppies and their dealings in the City, when there was a ring at the bell. Probably Jan, wanting to borrow something; it was another bonus of Richard's absence that she saw more of her now. He had been jealous of Jan and their closeness, suspecting they told each other rather more than he would have liked; in fact, Debbie had at one time kept a small box of groceries in the hall cupboard which she would get out if Richard arrived home unexpectedly and plonk it in Jan's arms, explaining that she'd done a bit of shopping for Jan, or the other way round . . .

She left the TV on and went to the front door smiling as she opened it. 'Hi, Jan,' she said.

Only it wasn't Jan, it was Joel.

'I had to see you,' he said. 'I couldn't bear it any longer. I'm sorry.'

'Joel,' she said in a low voice, 'you should be terribly sorry. You can't do this – you can't come and see me at my house; the children are all upstairs, probably still awake.'

'Well, I am sorry,' he said, 'but I was getting desperate.'

'You'll just have to put up with it.' She was flushed, angry with him, finding it surprisingly easy to be firm.

'Why?'

'Joel, you know why. I'm not going to spell it out again, and I'm not going to let you in. Just go away and—'

'Mum! I'm thirsty.' Alexander appeared at the top of the stairs, peered down at Joel. 'Who's that?'

'It's a man come to see the house,' she said.

'He can't come now, we're all in bed.'

'I know, Alexander, that's what I've just told him. I'll be up with some water in a minute.'

'If you don't agree to see me now,' said Joel, 'I'll come to your office tomorrow.'

'I'm not in the office tomorrow.'

'OK. On Thursday in the office. I'm not going to force my way in now, because if I did, everyone really will be in bed. Including you with me.'

'Joel, why are you doing this? Why can't you respect what I want to do?'

'Because it's not what you want to do. That's why. And I won't let you think it. And I know you're married and I know you've got three children, but I also know you're not very happy—'

'Yes, I am,' she said, and thinking of that last week, that

enchanted last week, found that it was true. 'We're perfectly happy together, thank you.'

'Bollocks,' he said. 'Absolute bollocks. Anyway, you're much too lovely to be locked into a miserable situation and to have to spend the rest of your life in some Scottish convent—'

'It's not a convent.'

'It might as well be.'

'Oh, Joel . . .' But the truth of what he had said, or the kernel of the truth had reached her heart; she felt tears stinging at the back of her eyes.

'So – which is it to be? Now, or the day after tomorrow?'

A long silence, while she fought against it. It won.

'The day after tomorrow,' she said, very quietly. And knew how extremely stupid that had been: and how almost impossible not to say it.

'All right,' Flora said. 'Colin, I've made up my mind. Let's do it. Anything rather than let them have this house.'

'Fantastic,' he said, 'I'm so pleased. Look, we'd better not discuss it on the phone. Would you like to have dinner with me tonight or tomorrow and we can set the wheels in motion. I know you've made the right decision, Flora. I really do.'

It was Simon's death that had determined that decision. She had gone for a long ride on Hal, along the cliffs and up onto the moor, thinking about this monster that had, in their own small circle, killed Simon – for she remained as sure as she could be of anything that it had been suicide – destroyed Nigel Cowper's upright, harmless life and Catherine Morgan's bright young one, and led a small boy into running away. If she could keep that monster from taking any more from any of them, she wanted to do it passionately. She knew that; without any doubt at all.

Except that the moment she put the phone down, the doubts began to rise again. She crushed them determinedly. She had to hold firm. It was the only thing to do. Otherwise Lloyd's had won. And she just wouldn't let them. She just wouldn't.

Chapter 44

September to October, 1990

It just wasn't possible, was it? She couldn't be, could she? And if she was – well, was it good, or was it bad? Could she cope with it? Didn't she have enough to cope with already? What would everyone think? What would everyone say? Did it make things worse? Or did it make them better?

She had to know for sure. Then at least she could think properly and sensibly about it. Two days, they'd said. That was doing it properly. Which, of course, she wanted. She wasn't going to trust some over-the-counter rubbish.

Oh God. It just wasn't possible – was it? She couldn't be, could she?

Blue had gone on a two-day trip to Brussels; Lucinda had decided to take advantage of his absence to go and see Steve Durham, make a progress report. Now that she had given up work, it was much harder to do anything without Blue cross-questioning her about it; where had she been, who had she seen, why, what for; for some reason he probed very closely into her comings and goings, how long she had been out, how she had got there. It was beginning to drive her mad. Even her weekly classes with Betty Parsons seemed to arouse his suspicions: 'What exactly do you do there?' he would say, and when she tried to explain, would snort rather contemptuously and tell her it sounded like a lot of bollocks to him.

'Well, all I can say, Blue Horton, is that if you do pluck up the courage to stay with me while I have the baby,' for he was swiftly losing his enthusiasm for that particular aspect of fatherhood, 'then you'll understand. It means all the difference

618

between giving birth with dignity and staying in control and – and well, not.'

'Can't imagine it being that dignified anyway,' he said, 'not considering what's going on. I mean—'

'Oh, shut up,' said Lucinda. She felt increasingly irritable these days; she was sleeping very badly, her stomach felt permanently sore as if she was being kicked in it, which she supposed she was, she had chronic indigestion and quite often a headache as well.

Blue was very patient and sympathetic most of the time, even when she told him she couldn't have sex – or rather didn't want it, which was a pretty well chronic condition by now – but every so often when he was tired, when he had had a bad day at work, and life wasn't easy for him, with rocketing interest rates and the country tipping fast into a depression – 'Those effing politicians, they all say it's only a recession, they should try getting out, actually selling something, making some money, then they'd know what we was all up against' – then he would take it out on her, snapping if she said she was fed up, telling her she had nothing to be fed up about, complaining bitterly if supper wasn't ready the instant he walked into the house, and constantly telling her they should have moved, that it was like living in a bloody rabbit hutch and what did she think they were going to do for space when the baby came?

And he did have a point, Lucinda thought. The little house looked like the baby department of Peter Jones, with a pram, car seat and high chair stacked in the hall, the tiny room she had turned into a nursery only just big enough to take the frilled crib, the chest of drawers and the changing table; and the sleek white, chrome-trimmed bathroom was filled with packs of nappies, a baby bath, and another changing table.

'This thing that's coming's going to be the size of a cat,' he said one morning. 'How come it's requiring as much kit as a small football team? It's bloody ridiculous, Lucinda, and it's got to stop. Either we move in double-quick time or the baby has to make do with a lot less.'

'We can't move now,' said Lucinda, while thinking wistfully of the huge and comfortable houses she had rejected, with their nurseries and en suite baby bathooms, their pram cupboards and double garages, their sunny patios, their au pair flats and their huge kitchens – God, she was doing a lot for Nigel. 'It's much too late. I've only got about six weeks to go—'

'Thank God,' said Blue and walked out, slamming the door.

'How are you feeling then?' Steve Durham said as she walked into his office. 'You look wonderful.'

This was so patently untrue that Lucinda felt quite cross.

'I don't look wonderful, Steve, I look like some kind of two-legged hippo.'

'Nonsense,' he said, and grinned at her. 'And what's it like, being a lady of leisure?'

'A lady of leisure! Me! You must be joking! Oh, I see, you mean not working. It's horrible, Steve, I hate it. I'm bored to death half the time and the other half I'm frantically trying to get the washing dry or Blue's supper on the table. I'm always behind for some reason. I don't think I'm cut out for the domestic life.'

'Bit late,' he said, with a pointed look at her stomach. 'Anyway, we're nearly there – don't think there are going to be any problems. Your American friend wrote a very nice letter, very nice indeed, saying exactly what I asked him to. Want to see it?'

'No,' said Lucinda, 'I don't think so. It would just make me cry, thinking what I might be doing, running some chic gallery in the middle of Manhattan and earning mega-bucks for it.'

'Hmm . . .' said Steve Durham. He saw her glaring at him and gave her a quick smile. 'Course. But then you wouldn't be here, wouldn't have married Nigel, wouldn't be having Blue's baby.'

'You think he just made it up, don't you,' said Lucinda coldly, 'about what I was worth to him. Well, let me tell you, I was jolly successful in that gallery. All the dealers said so, and—' She fished in her bag for a tissue.

Steve looked at her nervously. 'Of course I don't think he made it up,' he said. 'You were obviously a huge asset to the place. Now, I've written back to your husband's solicitor, sorted out his questions, told him both clients are happy with it, and then we'll put it to the court, send off the consent order, and hopefully get it all done and dusted this side of Christmas. And then you can do what you like with it all. Now he has still got the farm, hasn't he?'

'Yes, he has. But it's got to go soon, he says.'

'Not too soon,' said Steve Durham, 'or this isn't going to wash so well. You had better point that out to him, Lucinda, and best not in writing, just give him a call. Say once it's all over, it'll be fine to go ahead; in fact, it'll make it all the more convincing. Now, do you want to have a little chat about setting up this charitable trust? Can't leave it too long.'

'Yes, I think we'd better,' said Lucinda wearily.

When she got home, her head was throbbing; she lay down on the bed and closed her eyes. This was exactly what she didn't need just now: complicated arrangements and the need to remember dozens of small important things. Like . . . golly, like she must ring Nigel. Tell him not to sell the farm yet, whatever he did.

She rang his office; no reply. What was he doing, out in the middle of the day – and where was that annoying secretary of his? She dialled the home number, the dear old 730 number and as it rang, was transported back there, to the hall where the phone sat, that great big hall with those lovely black and white tiles, the high ceiling, the mouldings, saw herself wandering into the drawing room with its beautiful fireplace, its tall windows, with the long looped-back curtains that she had made, space everywhere, lovely, cool, luxurious space – that would be a wonderful place to live after she had the baby – saw Nigel standing in the doorway, dear old quiet, adoring Nigel— Stop it, Lucinda! Whatever is the matter with you . . .

The answering machine cut in with Nigel's voice telling her very slowly that he was out at present and unable to take her call, but if she could be kind enough to leave a message he would respond as soon as possible, and then thanking her very courteously for calling.

'Hello, Nigel,' she said, 'it's Lucinda here. Hope you're well. I need to speak to you as soon as poss, so give me a call at home, either today or tomorrow.' And then she fell asleep.

*

It was terrible. And absolutely glorious. And how had she allowed herself to do this, to get into a full-blown, wonderfully brilliant affair; and worse than that to admit what she had known all along, of course, of course: that she was in love, in love for the first time, as she could now see it was. Proper love, heart-possessing, mind-engrossing, completely obsessing love. It was insane and dangerous and stupid, so stupid, and every time she tried to tell herself that next time would be the last, and every time she knew it wouldn't, that it couldn't be.

She wanted to see him so much that it was like some strange physical illness, she ached with wanting to see him, actually ached, her body felt as if it had been pushed and pulled about, and her scalp felt sore as if someone had been tugging at her hair, and her skin felt tender as if she hadn't slept, which she hadn't much.

She'd thrown caution not just to the wind, but into a reckless hurricane. She told lies to everyone: to her colleagues, to her children, to her husband, to her friends.

She had to see clients, she said, she had to attend late meetings, she had to visit her dentist, her doctor – if anything really went wrong with her health or her teeth, she thought, if she was in terrible pain or violently ill, it would be impossible to claim any further appointments and she would die of a ruptured appendix and it would serve her right. She was shocked at her own deviousness, calling Richard from the office just before she left to meet Joel, so that he wouldn't ring home and find her out, spinning elaborate tales of how she might have to see a journalist first thing, she wasn't sure, she'd call and let the office know, inventing complex meetings that might take place and might not, depending on whether or not the key people could attend. Jenny was pressed to babysit, for twice the money she knew she should pay her; Jan as well, in the name of friendship and old times. She told Jan – she knew she could trust her.

It wasn't just to go to bed with Joel, their meetings; sometimes it was just to snatch a coffee break, a drink after work, spending time together, talking, laughing, quite often in Debbie's case crying, it was as important as sex. The sex was amazing, flying, shouting, blazing, glorious sex; she couldn't quite believe how wonderful it could be, what her body was capable of, what it could do on its frantic, greedy journey to pleasure, and she would go into carnal trances, remembering things Joel had done or said in bed, remembering so fiercely that her body was pierced and fractured by it: and she would wonder too that what, after all, were fairly basic pieces of physical equipment could vary so in their accomplishments.

But it was Joel himself that she loved, Joel, who was funny and solemn and tender and crude and sweet and harsh, and loving and lovable. She learned as much about him from being with him, enjoying him, making love to him, as she did from his stories of his difficult childhood. Her own having been secure and easy, despite its dullness, she marvelled that someone who had gone through those traumas could have emerged so well-adjusted, so empathetic. He never used his childhood as an excuse for his bad behaviour, or even the breakdown of his first marriage: 'I'm a selfish sod,' he would say cheerfully, or, 'I was totally amoral – before you, that is,' or, 'You haven't seen a temper tantrum, till you've seen one of mine.'

Selfish, amoral, bad-tempered, she didn't care. She loved him, as he was, fiercely, unquestioningly: and tried not to look beyond the present. The dangerous, disgraceful, wonderful present.

The thing that had swung it, first swung her back into bed with him, was not that he had finished with Maggie, but something else, an unbelievable story that she had believed.

'Do you know when I realised I cared about you?' he had said at the first meeting, two days after he had come to her house. 'Really cared about you, I mean.'

'No. But I think you're going to tell me.'

'I am. When I was in the Bahamas, fresh from you, from enjoying you, I met this girl.'

'What girl?' she said almost crossly, putting down her wine glass.

'She's a model. Quite a famous one.'

'Called?'

'Bibi.'

623

'I've never heard of her,' she said, crosser still.

'OK. She was in *Vogue* this month, she told me.'

'And—'

'She came to my room.'

'Oh, right.' Why was she even bothering to sit here listening to this man, she wondered, this outstandingly shining example of a male chauvinist pig. What was she doing even sharing a sandwich with him, sitting in a wine bar with him, breathing the same air as him?

'Yes. And I asked her in.'

'Joel, I think I'll go, if you don't mind. I'm not finding this very attractive.'

'Don't,' he said. 'Please. There's a nice ending.'

'Really?'

'Really. We shared some champagne, she wasn't even staying in my hotel, I met her at the other place, she'd tracked me down . . .'

'Am I supposed to be impressed by this? That she fancied you so much?'

'I want you to be.'

'Oh, great.'

'And then she stood up and started taking her clothes off. Well, she didn't have much on – a sort of silk tunic thing and some trousers. That was it.'

'Oh really?'

'Yes. And she just stood there, totally sublime, this glorious colour all over, not a millimetre of white flesh anywhere – and you know what?'

'It was great, dare I suggest.' She stood up, glaring down at him; he reached up, took her hand.

'I told her to go away. Just go away. I thought of you, with those wonderful round firm little breasts, and that flat stomach of yours, how did you ever house all those babies there, and your gorgeous thick, black bush, and I just didn't want her. I was in a hotel room with a supermodel who was gagging for it, and I didn't want her. I wanted you. Now you can believe me or not, as you wish, but it's the truth, Debbie. How's that?'

'Let's say I've heard better seduction speeches,' she said, picked up her jacket and walked out.

*

He didn't follow her; on the way back to the office she bought *Vogue*. And found the pages with Bibi in them. Even a short piece about her, Bibi the glorious Italian who had Calvin Klein and Ralph Lauren and Karl Lagerfield outbidding one another for her, Bibi with her armpit-high legs and what they called her shank of black hair, and Debbie sat there at her desk, studying her and imagining her stripping off for Joel in his hotel room and him sending her away, and two things happened. One was that she found she believed him, for why else should he tell her such a story if it wasn't true? What would be the point? It would take an arrogance beyond all believing to imagine it would persuade someone into bed and Joel was not that arrogant; and the other was that she began to find it funny, started to laugh. And then she called him.

'I've been checking Bibi out,' she said. 'In *Vogue*.'

'And?'

'And – did you really send her away?'

'I did.'

'And was it really because of me?'

'It was. I think you're a hundred times lovelier, and sexier, and more lovable.'

'You're mad,' she said. 'Completely mad.'

'Maybe. Mad with love. Sounds very Shakespearean, doesn't it. Now, you going to meet me again? Like – tonight?'

'Yes,' she said. 'Tonight.'

That was when the lying had to begin.

The first weekend Richard came home, she was terrified. Would he be able to tell, would her body feel different, would he know it had moved and moulded itself round another, different man, would he suspect that her cries of pleasure were faked, would he be wary of her enthusiasm – which was simply to have it over and done with, quickly, while her mind was almost not looking and her senses were caught unawares.

In fact, it took time. He was strangely reluctant, said he was tired the first night, she had to go all through the next day, waiting, fretting, wanting to have it over, while he talked endlessly of the school and his delight in it, of Morag and her patience with him, of what they might do with the children, even of what she had been doing, how she was getting on without him. And that night, too, he fell asleep, made some half-joke about it. And then when he woke her in the morning, when she found his hands moving on her, felt his mouth on hers and knew there was no escape, she was still blessedly sleepy, her reactions dulled and it really wasn't so bad.

Joel was sullen and angry on the Monday when he saw her. 'I couldn't stop thinking about it,' he said. 'I tried and tried not to, and it was no good. I kept seeing you lying there, doing what you do to me—'

'I didn't,' she said briefly, 'not really. And this won't do, Joel, we'll go mad this way. It's a fact of our life at the moment, and there's nothing I can do about it and nothing you can do about it either. So – just try to stop it, OK?'

'Not OK, no,' he said. 'Not OK at all,' and for the first time he put the phone down on her and she sat staring at it and wondering if all adulterous wives had this to endure from their lovers and even if she would ever see him again. Which of course she did; he phoned, said he was sorry, said he had to see her. And the next time they made love he was somehow wary, holding back; it took him time to recover.

But she was right; there was nothing they could do about it. Absolutely nothing.

Annabel often wondered how she would have got through those first awful weeks without Florian. He was so considerate, so gentle, so completely different from what she would have expected. He didn't fuss much, just asked her every morning how she was, always bought her a *pain au chocolat* from the baker in Sloane Street on his way in, because it was her favourite, and then alternately cosseted her and teased her through the day. He didn't allow her to slack and indeed, once the first fortnight was over, pushed her quite hard; and she was grateful for that too. She was enough her mother's daughter to recognise the value of work as therapy. And then most evenings he bought her a drink on her way home, actually waiting for her if he finished before she did.

They would sit in a wine bar, gossiping lazily about the day; he had instigated a competition to see which of them had had the worse client; he invariably won, claiming the most outrageous behaviour.

'So there she was, darling, with her hand creeping towards my cock, pretending she was giving me a tip, and she was rather gorgeous. I could feel, you know, a problem coming on, and then there was Miki watching and I just fled and she complained that I'd never shown her the back. I tell you, Bel, nothing I'd like more than to show her my back, and to see hers for that matter, she has the most gorgeous little arse, but—'

'Florian, you're making it up.'

'I am not. So that's a good nine for me, and I really think only a four to you. I mean, what's a cup of spilled coffee? You can't cry over that.'

'I can when it's over my new white espadrilles – and she did it on purpose,' said Annabel staunchly.

'Rubbish. Anyway, only another month or so and you'll be styling! And you can be absolutely *vile* to that poor little new junior. He's very delicious, isn't he? I can't take my eyes off him.'

'Um ... yes,' said Annabel. She still found Florian's pretence of bisexual behaviour rather difficult to cope with.

'And how's your lovely little sister, out there in the blackboard jungle?'

Tilly had started at the local comprehensive; none of the London independent schools could take her, although Francis Holland had said they might have a place after Christmas; Annabel and Elizabeth had seen her off the first day in a state of great apprehension at what the pupils of Cromwell Road School would make of this hopelessly posh creature with her wide-blue-eyed innocence, and in love with her pony.

'She's been there now for two weeks, and she seems OK,' Annabel said. 'I keep asking her if she's had any problems and she looks at me vaguely and says no, it's fine. I think it's because she's in her own Tilly world, and she just gets on with it. She comes home with two girls from the estate, you know, and they seem to really like her. They came round the other evening, one's black and very skinny and the other's white and very fat, and they all sat watching telly and giggling together. Apparently she helps the skinny one – she's called Fallon – with her homework, because she's dyslexic. And the boys all shout and whistle at her, call her Princess Posho, but quite nicely. You can see they think she's rather gorgeous ....'

'Well, she is,' said Florian. 'I'd love to be her prince.'

'Well, you're not even to think about it,' said Annabel crossly.

'Darling, you can't stop me thinking about it. I promise to leave it there, for the time being. Now, how's your mum?'

'She's all right, I think. She's back at work, although coming home quite early, which is nice. She's so brave, Florian, she tries to be cheerful with us, but I hear her crying sometimes in her room. She's lost loads of weight, and I actually don't think she's very well; she's not eating much, says she feels nauseated, and she's quite often actually sick, poor Mummy.'

'Poor Mummy,' said Florian.

Lucinda woke up from her afternoon nap, it was getting dark; she looked at her watch: half-past seven. Winter was clearly on its way, she somehow hadn't noticed it approaching. Well, they were nearly halfway through October: and then, goodness, only four weeks or so and the baby would be here.

She felt a little apprehensive for a lot of the time now; she had reached the stage of pregnancy when the actual birth dominated her thoughts; she kept looking at her stomach and feeling the baby kicking and writhing about, and thinking how big it was and how small the exit available to it, and wondering how on earth it was going to get through. It seemed fairly impossible.

And she wasn't actually very brave, she knew. In spite of Mrs Parsons' encouraging words about the importance of control and relaxation through breathing techniques, she couldn't imagine herself being able to bear what was clearly going to be considerable pain: not without a lot of help anyway, in the form of anaesthesia.

The epidural she had notionally rejected, earlier in her pregnancy (better for the baby if you can manage without, she had averred, nothing more wonderful and exhilarating than a totally natural birth) being completely numb from the waist down, looked increasingly attractive now. The return of several girls to the classes, complete with still-thick waistlines and small wailing babies in slings, claiming that yes, it had been terribly painful, but it had also been absolutely wonderful, the most amazing experience of their lives, did little to reassure her. Her gynaecologist at the Princess Louise Hospital where she was having the baby had assured her that of course she could have an epidural if she wanted it, there would be no problem at all; but even he had said that Lucinda might be surprised to discover how well she could cope without one.

'It's not like ordinary pain, you see, it's more like very hard work, and it's got such a happy ending. And it's not constant, the contractions come and go; you have lots of time to rest in between, to gather your strength. I would advise you not to opt for the epidural too soon.'

Lucinda had dutifully agreed that she wouldn't; but she was beginning to think now that she would opt for it the moment the first contraction began. She realised as she struggled up from the bed that her almost chronic headache had got worse. In fact, it was awful. She would have to take something; she had been very good throughout her pregnancy, had hardly taken so much as an aspirin, but this was exceptional.

But – God, it was late, the shops would be shut; she'd have to drive to the big supermarket, get something there. It wouldn't matter to Blue, he'd said it would be at least eight, probably later, before he got back, and she'd got some steak for his supper, that she couldn't cook until he got home anyway . . .

She picked up her keys, and went out to her car.

Blue felt absolutely shattered when he finally reached Limehouse. These trips sounded all well and good, but they were bloody exhausting. Well, he'd got back sooner than he'd expected at least; he was hungry though, the food on the plane had been complete crap and the delicious lunch in Brussels a long time ago.

He paid off the cab, unlocked the front door and shouted to Lucinda that he was home: no reply. He looked in their bedroom wondering if she was asleep – she seemed to drop off at a moment's notice these days – and then went into the kitchen, dropping his briefcase in the middle of the hall. No sign of any cooking having been done: there were some potatoes scrubbed lying on the draining board, and what was clearly going to be a salad, but that was all. God, things were going from bad to worse. Sex was becoming a distant memory and although he understood the reason and even sympathised, it wasn't exactly ideal, and now it seemed food was going the same way. Where was she, and why hadn't she left a note, for God's sake.

The phone rang; he was about to pick it up and then decided against it; it might be Lucinda's mother, who had taken to calling her recently, and that was the last thing he needed, a strained conversation with the hideous old bat. How she had produced Lucinda, he would never know.

The answering machine would deal with it, and then if it was someone he wanted to talk to, he could pick up. Someone like Lucinda's best friend Katy, for instance, who he had got quite fond of, or even his own mother, who had also begun to ring Lucinda regularly. There was something about this baby business that set a kind of bush telegraph in motion among women.

But it wasn't Katy, and it wasn't his mother. It was Nigel.

Chapter 45

October, 1990

So she was: definitely. And she defnitely wasn't going to have it. For so many reasons. She told her nice gynaecolgist, Sarah Goodrich, when she went to see her to request a termination.

'But, Elizabeth – why, exactly?' Sarah said. 'Tell me your reasons. And how do you feel?'

'Dreadful,' she had said. 'Sick and so, so tired, all the time.'

'Of course. Goes with the territory, I'm afraid. You've forgotten.'

'I have not. And that's one of the reasons.'

'But that won't last.'

'The tiredness will. Sarah, I'm over forty. I'm not a girl.'

'Of course. But—'

'And that's another thing. Think of the risks – of a Downs baby especially. And all the other risks to my health. I can't afford that when the children need me. And I have to work, I'm the only source of income.'

'Elizabeth, I know that. Of course. But you do earn a good salary, or I imagine so, and you can afford a lot of help.'

'That's a matter of opinion. Sarah, I still don't know how it's happened.'

'Usual way, I imagine,' said Sarah with a slight smile.

'You know what I mean,' said Elizabeth, determined not to allow the mood to lighten.

'Yes, of course. Well, we took you off your high-dose pill because it was turning you into Samantha Fox, as I recall. And you had a short break from it then—'

'Yes, but that was before . . . well, before I got pregnant. And only a few days . . .'

'I realise that. But the changeover would still have been a

631

dangerous time, in terms of conception, that is. And you know what they say about pre-menopausal women.'

'No,' said Elizabeth, 'actually I don't.'

'It's an old wives' tale, that women around forty seem to have a big zoom in fertility. It's supposed to be nature giving you a last chance of motherhood. What I think is more likely is that it's women giving themselves, probably completely subconsciously, a last chance. Something has to explain all those afterthought babies.'

'Well, I certainly didn't want one,' said Elizabeth crossly, 'and you might have warned me.'

'Elizabeth! I couldn't possibly do such a thing, not seriously and in my capacity as a gynaecologist.'

'You could have about the pill. Anyway, I'm not having the baby.'

'Have you considered talking to the children about it?'

'No, I haven't. I want to have the termination and for them never to know. They're going to find it very distressing otherwise.'

'And how do you think they'd find it if you had the baby?'

'I'm pretty sure they'd find it very difficult. For a start, they would have to confront the fact that their father and I were still having sex. Teenagers find that almost unbearable as a thought. You know, nobody has sex over the age of thirty at the latest. And when it's your mother . . .'

'They might not feel like that. They might find it rather lovely. A positive and good thing to happen. Out of all the sorrow.'

'Sarah, I'm *not* going to have this baby. I don't know why you're so keen on the idea.'

'It's not so much that I'm keen for you to have it, it's that I think you're in no condition to decide not to. Your feeings are in chaos. And you know, terminations do cause depression. It won't help.'

'Oh, and having a baby, being exhausted and sick and not being able to work and looking hideous *will* help?'

'You won't look hideous, don't be ridiculous.'

'I will. To my colleagues I will, especially the younger ones – hideous and faintly ridiculous – and they're what matters. I won't have a devoted husband telling me I'm still beautiful to him, will I?' She was close to tears now, fumbling in her bag for a tissue.

Sarah handed her one. 'Here. Cup of tea?'

'No, thank you. It makes me sick. Maybe some water.'

'Here you are.' She filled a glass from the carafe on her desk. 'Look – please give it a bit more time, Elizabeth –'

'I don't have much time. I'm two months down the line. I'd rather just do it, get over it, get on with my life.'

'All right,' said Sarah with a sigh. 'I'll put things in motion. I could do it next week, would that suit you?'

'Not as well as this week, but—'

'Elizabeth, we have to get a psychiatrist's signature, you need health check-ups, all that sort of thing. Now – how about next Wednesday? And then you come in on the Monday to see Dr Young. He's our resident shrink.'

'Yes, I think that would be all right.' Elizabeth looked at her diary. 'As long as he isn't going to counsel me. Oh – no. Could it be Thursday? I've got a big meeting on Wednesday.'

'Sorry, can't do Thursday. How about Friday? That's my final offer.' She smiled rather too brightly at Elizabeth. 'Now do take care of yourself.'

'What for?' said Elizabeth rather briskly, and walked out of the office.

She had reached a stage of being violently angry with Simon. For dying. How could he have done it to her, how could he? Either on purpose, or by being careless. It was unforgivable. What she had wanted to do, what she knew she could do, was help him through the problems; he had robbed her of that, just left her alone, reproaching herself forever, knowing it was not enough. Bastard! If he walked in the door now, she'd be so angry with him. And then she thought of what it would be like if Simon did walk in the door, smiling, calling her name, giving her a kiss, suggesting a drink, suggesting they went out for supper, sighing when she said she couldn't, that she didn't have time, had work to do . . . How could she have done that, all those hundreds of times, refused to spend so much as two hours with him . . .

'Oh God,' said Elizabeth aloud, raising her arm to hail a taxi. 'Oh God . . .'

The anger was as much a reason as anything for not having the baby. She could see that in theory it would be lovely to have a child, a legacy of Simon, happiness coming out of the pain; but her anger was such that she didn't want that. It was too easy, too sentimental, she'd be struggling to cope when she shouldn't be struggling, the bastard had gone off without her, as he so often had, leaving her to manage without him. Why should she, why should she go through all that alone, the increasing discomfort of pregnancy, the insomnia – she could never sleep for the last three months or so, and then you certainly didn't sleep for at least three months after; how was she supposed to work through that? And to go through the birth – she always had terrible labours – and then to take the baby home on her own. Of course she could have help, but those first difficult exhausting weeks, when you were worried and sore and fretful and the baby got colic or wouldn't feed, or even when it was quiet, you needed someone then as well, to share it all with you, to say, 'There, there, never mind, it'll all be fine, you're just tired, and look, is that a smile? Think so. Let me get you another pillow. Are you sore, poor darling?' *No.* Those were not times to live through alone.

She was late for a meeting, and short with Peter Hargreaves when he made excuses for her; she felt sick and weary and altogether dreadfully unhappy.

Catherine knew it was terrible of her, but she was feeling increasingly resentful. Both her children were sublimely happy at their schools; Caroline had settled in as quickly as Freddie and they both had large circles of friends, who invited them for tea and for sleepovers, and to play at the weekends. Caroline's new best friend was called Jane-Anne and it was a name Catherine was coming to dread hearing. Jane-Anne dominated their lives: what Jane-Anne thought, what Jane-Anne said, what she liked to eat, what she liked to wear. Jane-Anne had a pony, and rode rather well; in fact, her pony was such a good one, Caroline informed Catherine one morning over breakfast, that Jane-Anne's father was considering letting her ride with him when he next went hunting.

Catherine struggled to display the excitement this inform-ation clearly required. 'Good gracious me. How wonderful.'

'He's got two horses, of course,' Caroline said, unconsciously echoing Jane-Anne.

'Why of course?'

'Well, he needs them,' said Caroline. 'You can't hunt on the same horse two days running and ideally not all day.'

'Oh I see,' Catherine said humbly.

It turned out that Jane-Anne's first pony was still kept in their stables and was very docile indeed; Jane-Anne's mother, a chatty rather sturdy lady, said that if Catherine wouldn't mind, they would be more than happy to give Caroline a few lessons on him.

'She seems terribly interested, and then the girls could come out with me sometimes, I'd love to take them. But I can see it might be worrying for you; why don't you come over one day after school and you can meet Dorcas – that's the pony – and see for yourself how quiet she is.'

'That's terribly kind of you,' said Catherine, thinking that she wouldn't have the faintest idea if a pony was quiet or not, 'but—'

'Good. Super. How about next Thursday? I'll pick the girls up from school and if you put a pair of old trousers in Caroline's school bag they'll do beautifully for now. Time to get her kitted out if she likes it – which I'm sure she will. Jolly plucky little thing, isn't she?'

Phyllis was very excited about all this. 'You do realise that Jane-Anne's father is actually the Honourable Mark Price, don't you? They are one of the oldest families in the county, and of course Mrs Price is extremely well connected too. It's wonderful that they've taken such a fancy to Caroline.'

Catherine said she hadn't realised, but she would bear it in mind in future. Freddie too had a best friend, the beaming and bespectacled Hutchings; she felt easier with Hutchings, indeed all the Hutchings. His father was a solicitor and his mother a rather worn-looking woman taking care of all the little Hutchings: there were three younger than Hutchings himself, and a fifth on the way. Mr Hutchings must earn a lot of money as a solicitor, Catherine thought. Mrs Hutchings, whose name was Miriam, was rather earnest and *Guardian*-reading, grew her own vegetables and believed in complementary medicine. She wasn't exactly a kindred spirit but Catherine was a lot more comfortable with her than with Mrs Jane-Anne. Or rather the Honourable Mrs Jane-Anne.

635

Freddie and Hutchings, whose first name was Martin, ('Only never call him that at school or even the gates, will you?' Freddie said rather sternly) shared several interests, including astronomy – 'He's got a super telescope' – and bird-watching, and would go off into the countryside together with their bird books and binoculars for hours at a time. Catherine had worried about it at first, used as she was to the perils of the city, but Miriam Hutchings said she really didn't need to be anxious, Martin had been going off on his own for almost two years now. 'He never goes far, just into the woods, or over those meadows, see, and he has to come home every two hours; he's got a watch and he's very reliable.'

It was all very lovely for them; but after the third Saturday in a row when she had seen nobody between the hours of nine and seven except for Phyllis and Dudley, Catherine was beginning to feel desperate and more lonely than she had ever been in her life.

She couldn't even go and see Lucinda, she couldn't be away for the length of time it took to drive to London and back; she had no new friends, unless you counted Miriam or the Hon. Mrs Jane-Anne, she couldn't go shopping because she didn't have any money. She read a lot, but there was a limit even to that; although she had become an expert on current affairs, devouring Dudley's *Telegraph* from front page to last, and her own *Daily Mail* which cheered her with its glamorous gossip. Only she longed for someone to discuss it all with: Thatcher's precarious position, Geoffrey Howe's resignation, Neil Kinnock at the Labour Conference being proclaimed Prime Minister in Waiting: and Princess Diana wowing Washington (with a rather unflattering new hairstyle) and George Michael's new girlfriend (a model called Zoe). She had tried to engage Miriam on Mrs Thatcher, and Mrs Jane-Anne on Princess Diana, but without success; they both seemed rather shocked that she had time to devote to such matters. And indeed she looked back in amazement now on her days working in London, when reading was an unimaginable luxury in terms of time.

She decided to take up gardening and asked Phyllis if she might have a patch to cultivate: Phyllis said she would have to ask Dudley, and together they showed her a patch the size of a rather small patio, totally overgrown and in almost permanent shade from the rhododendron bushes.

She spent quite a lot of time wandering round Shaftesbury, which was a charming town, with its steeply cobbled Gold Hill made famous in the Hovis advertisements; and hunted the antique shops for secondhand books, a hobby of hers from when she had lived in London before her marriage. She had thought that she might, if she could get hold of a few, do a bit of dealing in them, and in fact bore a set of early edition *Just William* books home one day in triumph.

'I thought I could restore them a bit,' she said, showing them to Phyllis, 'clean up the covers, and maybe sell them on, make a bit of a profit,' but Phyllis had been rather pinched about it, and said she didn't want the house turned into some kind of junk shop.

'It wouldn't be,' Catherine said stoutly. 'I'd just sell them to other, more specialist bookshops. There are a couple in Wells. I know it's bit of a trek but . . .' She persevered for a bit, but worrying about Phyllis's reaction rather robbed the whole thing of its pleasure.

About once a week Phyllis did invite her to meet some of her friends at various charity and coffee mornings, but as they were all (not surprisingly) old enough to be Catherine's mother, it wasn't exactly ideal. And very occasionally, if Phyllis and Dudley gave a dinner party they would invite her to join them; she didn't exactly enjoy them, but at least it wasn't sitting alone upstairs in her quarters while the children were asleep.

And so as autumn arrived and the evenings got darker and the children's new lives developed so happily, she looked at the years stretching out ahead of her and wondered what on earth might become of her.

She really should have taken Simon's advice, Lucinda thought, staring fretfully after Blue as he stalked out of the house, the door slammed behind him for the third time that week. But somehow, what with the sorrow of Simon's death, and feeling increasingly rotten, and then of course Virgil coming over and it seeming wise to keep that to herself, until he'd done what she'd asked, she hadn't felt able to face it.

Steve Durham and indeed Nigel himself had both asked her

repeatedly if she had discussed it with Blue, and she'd said rather vaguely that she hadn't yet, no, but she knew it would be fine, and more and more now, she found herself wondering what on earth was the point of upsetting him until she had to and the divorce came to a head. Not that she thought he would be upset; it was only window-dressing after all and he was so good-natured anyway . . .

But he wasn't any more, he was rather the reverse, tetchy and argumentative, and that evening she'd got back late, when he'd been to Brussels and Nigel had phoned, he'd been perfectly horrible.

'What the hell is going on?' he'd said. 'What are you doing, calling Nigel, asking him to ring you? What about, for fuck's sake!'

He was so cross she hadn't dared tell him not to swear, had just stood there staring at him, and then said, 'Well, it was about the divorce, obviously.'

'And why do you have to talk to him about the divorce? I thought that's what you were paying the solicitor for, paying a fucking fortune incidentally.'

'It was – it was just a detail,' she said. 'Steve wanted to know and I said I'd ask him, it was easier and—'

'Well, don't ask him about any more details,' he said, 'because I don't like it. I've nothing against that aristocratic waste of space that was once your husband—'

'Blue, he is not a waste of space, don't talk about him like that.'

'I'll talk about him how I like,' he said, 'and as I was saying, I've nothing against him. I just don't want him intruding into my life.'

'He is not intruding.'

'Oh really? I'd call it that. And finding you out of the house as well. I'd have thought you could at least have got a meal on the table for me.'

'I will get a meal on the table for you. You're much earlier than you said, and anyway, it's steak. I couldn't cook it till you were here.'

'Yes, all right, all right. Anyway, I call getting home to some cretinous message from Nigel asking you to call him back an intrusion.'

'Does he want me to call him back? When?'

That was a mistake. Blue stood up again, picked up his coat and said, 'You call him back whenever you like. I'm going out.'

She had spent a wretched evening waiting for his return; at ten o'clock he did walk in, looking at last slightly remorseful and said he was sorry and could they go to bed, please, he was exhausted; and when he started wanting sex, in spite of his exhaustion – she didn't think he could know what exhaustion was, actually – she made a monumental effort and responded, and actually it had been quite fun, getting round the problem of the bump. But she could see she was walking on very thin ice and in danger of upsetting him quite badly, and that this was not the time to get his agreement to what she was proposing.

So she had still said nothing and now Steve had phoned and said he was biking over a document at the end of the day for her to look at and agree to, and if it was all right with her he'd get it over to Nigel's solicitor and they should be in business.

Well, maybe it would be all right. Maybe she could get through the whole thing without ever clearing it with Blue. It wasn't as if it was going to affect him.

'Can't it wait a few more days?' she said, playing for time.

'It can in theory, but time is of the essence with this case and it's been going on much too long anyway. We don't want it looking suspicious, and if Nigel's really got to sell that farm within the next few weeks, which is what you said, then that's exactly how it will look.'

'Will it?'

'Yes, Lucinda, it will. Think about it.'

'Well, all right,' she said, 'but Steve, don't send it over this evening, make it tomorrow morning. I'm – well, I'm out this afternoon. I'll OK it straight away and get it back to you.'

God, she felt rotten this morning. So tired, and her head was really bad again. And her ankles were swollen, she looked hideous, and actually this morning so were her hands; her rings were cutting into her fingers. Her fat, pudgy, horrible fingers. She might try and get them off later, cool her hands down and use lots of soap. They really were rather uncomfortable.

'I'd love to have lunch with you, yes,' said Debbie, 'but I can't. I've got a meeting.'

'Drink after work?'

'Can't. I've used every excuse under the sun to Jenny, and she absolutely has to go home on time tonight, she's got a parents' evening at her children's school.'

'Could I come to supper?'

'No, of course you can't,' said Debbie sharply. She was learning that to give Joel an inch was to give him if not a mile, then several furlongs.

'Why not?'

'Joel, you know why not. What would the children say?'

'You could say that I'd come to see the house again. It would be true, after all.'

'I'm sorry, but you really can't.'

He put the phone down. She glared at it for a minute then picked it up and rang him back. 'This isn't fair.'

'What isn't fair?'

'Getting at me because I can't see you. It isn't my fault. You knew—'

'Yeah, yeah, I knew you were married and you had three children. You kept on saying it, like a bloody mantra.'

'Well, it's true.'

'I should have listened to you,' he said moodily.

'Yes, perhaps you should.'

'But what good would it have done me, Debbie? I'd still be in love with you.'

She was silent.

'It's bloody tough,' he said.

'I know. I do know and it's tough for me as well.'

'Not so tough.'

'Why not?'

'Because you call all the shots. I could be with you every evening, fuck you every night. Jesus, what a thought. What a bloody thought. Do you think we'll ever get there, Debbie?'

'No,' she said wearily, 'we won't. And don't even think about it.'

'So – you're telling me there is no light at the end of this extremely dark tunnel.'

'Joel, there can't be. You know. You know this is . . .'

'Yes?' he said. 'What is it? Do tell me, Debbie, I really want to know.'

She did know what it was; it was something that was throwing the rest of her life into increasing turmoil, it would

640

wreck what was left of her marriage, of whatever she had once felt for Richard, it was endangering her children's happiness, it was even harming her career. It was completely hopeless; it could end only in misery. And yet she would not have missed it, any of it, for anything. It was rich and rare, it was happiness of the most extreme kind, it was worth whatever it cost. She knew that, she didn't even have to ask herself. She often wondered, as she lay awake in the night, if she hadn't met Joel, hadn't gone through this violent emotional experience, how different she would be. She wouldn't know, after all, that what she had thought was happiness was some pale, contented shadow of it, wouldn't know that what she'd thought was love was merely a pleasant warm affection, she would just have gone muddling on, caring for her children, fond of her husband, feeling perfectly pleased with her life, with the modest gratification it threw at her.

She would not have been branded in this way, unmistakably and for always, so that she could never return to what had been, to that earlier Debbie with her straightforward life; she was changed for ever, and damaged for ever too; for as long as she lived, what she had known with Joel would be with her, and of her, and there was no escaping it.

'I must go,' she said, and rang off.

He did come round that evening, as she had feared he would; he was increasingly reckless, risking discovery, threatening her with the danger of it.

'I want us to be caught,' he said.

'That is so selfish,' she said, 'so wrong. You don't have anything to lose, it's all right for you.'

'But I do,' he said. 'If you go, I have everything to lose, everything I have. You don't seem to understand.'

'Go away,' she hissed at him now as he stood at the door, smiling, an official-looking briefcase under one arm. 'Just go away.'

'I won't take much of your time,' he said, 'I've come about the proposed development on the green. I've got details here – I hope we can rely on your support. If you'll just give me a few minutes, I can explain. Or if the kiddies are still up, I can come back later.'

'They're all in bed,' she said, fighting a smile, trying to close the door, 'but I don't really care about the development—'

'Oh, but you do,' he said, and before she even realised, he had put one foot in the door and slithered past her into the hall. 'Years of doorstepping taught me that.'

'Please go away.'

'I'm not going away. Sorry.'

'We can't – can't do anything now. Not with the children here.'

'Of course not,' he said, and his face was very serious as he looked at her. 'I don't need to make love to you, Debbie, I don't even need to talk to you, I just need to be with you. That's all. I don't know what you're doing, but if you're washing up, I'll watch you and if you're talking to a friend, I'll listen to you and if you're working, I'll help you. But please don't send me away, not yet. Please.'

And so she made him some tea, and after she had gone upstairs to check the children were all asleep, she went into the room where he was and shut the door and said, 'Oh Joel, I love you.'

'And I love you,' he said. 'And what are we going to do about it?'

'Nothing,' she said, 'absolutely nothing. And if you try and fight that, then I will have to do something about it, and it will all end much sooner. So don't.'

'I won't,' he said.

But she was terribly afraid he didn't mean it.

Chapter 46

October, 1990

God, Elizabeth thought. Now her skirts were getting tight. This was awful. She tugged at the buttons harder, managed to make them meet: and then looked at the undoubted rounding of tummy that promptly appeared beneath the waistband. It was ridiculous when – the – when what was in there was only the size of an orange pip. She supposed it was hormones, making her put on weight. Bloody hormones. God, they had a lot to answer for. Someone would notice soon, someone would put two and two together . . . Well, it was Friday today, she was off to see Dr Young on Monday, that would be a step nearer, and then it would only be four more days and it would be over. Sarah had booked her into the hospital, she'd made elaborate excuses to everyone, told Peter Hargreaves she was seeing someone about the inquest – he never queried anything she had to do in connection with Simon's death – told Annabel and Tilly she had to go out of Town for a client meeting. It would be fine. And she'd be home next day and Annabel would be working, and Tilly might well be going out with her new friends.

'We're going down the market, Mummy,' she would say, in her still-perfect accent, or, 'We're going up West, to Top Shop and that.'

Tilly had become extremely fond of Fallon, the black girl; she was very sweet, Elizabeth liked her. She had nice manners and was clearly inordinately grateful to Tilly for her help with her schoolwork; she lived with her mum and her five brothers and sisters in a two-bedroom flat in Pimlico.

'She has to share with the other girls, three of them in one room, can you imagine, Mummy, and of course she can't get

643

any work done, the TV's always on. I feel so sorry for her. She's doing much better with me helping her though, and being able to do her homework here; she's really pleased. The only thing is that Madison, that's my other friend, she's getting a bit jealous now so it's rather difficult.'

'It must be,' said Elizabeth carefully. This unlikely scenario of Tilly being idyllically happy at the comprehensive could all go very pear-shaped indeed if she started falling out with people. 'Why don't you ask Madison over on Sunday, just on her own, so you can spend some time with her?'

'No, I can't. She sees her mum Sundays.'

'Her mum? Who looks after her then?'

'Her dad and his girlfriend. His girlfriend is really nice, Madison says, always giving her clothes and stuff, only of course Madison can't get into them. She gets so upset about her size, I don't know how to help. She doesn't eat much, she says, she's just got funny hormones.'

'Oh really? So what does she have for lunch?'

'Chips,' said Tilly with a sublime lack of irony, 'but that's all, she goes down the chip shop and gets a bag and that's all she eats all day till she gets home. And then she has to get her own tea, because Lara, that's her dad's girlfriend, doesn't get home till late, and she says she doesn't have much then either. I feel so sorry for her, it's so unfair.'

'It is indeed,' said Elizabeth, with a flash of insight into the unfortunate Madison's loveless, uncared-for life. 'Well, maybe she could come over on Sunday evening, when she leaves her mum.' She thought of Tilly's friends at St Mary's, open-faced little girls, with loving, caring parents, beautifully dressed, carefully fed, with no greater worries than whether their ponies might be missing them during the term or whether they'd manage to pass Common Entrance, and felt a pang of sudden rage – rage seemed to rise in her rather easily these days – at the basic unfairness of the human condition.

'That's a good idea, we could watch a video. Thanks, Mum.' She gave her mother a kiss and danced off; she was much happier these days, at last beginning to come to terms with her father's death. She certainly didn't need the trauma of a new and demanding sibling and having to confront the reality of its conception.

God, she was going to be sick . . . She reached the cloak-room just in time, deposited the small amount of breakfast she had eaten down the lavatory and was coming out, wiping her streaming eyes, when she bumped into Annabel.

'Oh, hello, darling. I thought you'd gone.'

'No, not quite. You OK, Mum? Still being sick?'

'Yes. 'Fraid so. It's quite normal, the doctor says, when you're depressed. Your body gets into a state of turmoil, doesn't know what it's doing.'

'Is it? Poor you. It can't help. Let me get you a cup of tea.'

'No, thank you,' said Elizabeth, repressing a shudder. 'I'll just have some water.'

'OK, I'll get you that. Sit down in the kitchen for a bit. Come on.' She got a bottle of mineral water out of the fridge, handed her mother a glass. 'There you are. I need to talk to you tonight, about something. About Jamie, actually. Are you in?'

'Yes, I am. Might be a bit late . . .'

'Oh, that's all right. Florian and I are going for a drink with some friends of his. See you around eight-thirty, OK?'

'OK. Bye, darling.'

And she was gone. Just as well she was so wrapped up in her own life, thought Elizabeth wearily, sipping the water. Otherwise she just might start to notice – or even suspect – something.

'Lucinda, it's Mummy.' She sounded odd, strained, her rather booming voice softer than usual.

'Hello, Mummy. Everything all right?'

'No, I'm afraid not. Your – your father's had a stroke.'

'Oh God. When?'

'Earlier today.'

'And how – how bad is it?'

'We don't know yet. It could go either way. He's in hospital, they're doing tests. The great danger, apparently, is of a second stroke. Anyway, I wanted you to know.'

'Yes. Yes, of course. Oh Mummy, how dreadful. How do you feel?'

'Oh, all right. A bit . . . shocked, you know.'

'You must do. I'll come down. Straight away.'

'Lucinda, I don't know that that's a very good idea. The baby's due any minute.'

'No, it isn't. Not for another four weeks. Of course I want to come, see Daddy. I'll be there at lunchtime. Don't worry, I'm fine, had a check-up yesterday. Everything's completely tickety-boo. I'll just sort a few things out and come. I'll stay tonight, if that's OK.'

'All right. It will be very nice to see you. Susannah's coming over later and the boys this evening.'

'Good. Take care of yourself, won't you? Give my love to Daddy. Bye.'

She rang Blue; told him what had happened, that she was going down to Gloucestershire.

'I'll stay tonight at least. You don't mind, do you?'

'Course not. Stay as long as you need. Hope the old bugger's all right. Give him my best.'

Lucinda felt very upset; her father might have been frightful over Blue, might not even have been a particularly involved father; in fact, she could remember weeks going past, even before she went away to school, when she had hardly seen him; but he was still her father, and she still loved him. And it was terrible to think that he – well, both her parents – had reached such a stage in their lives. She had, rather foolishly she realised now, seen them as virtually immortal, when they were well into their sixties.

She packed a bag, left a note for Blue, telling him she loved him, and set off for Gloucestershire.

Half an hour later, a bike arrived, bearing an envelope addressed to Lucinda, and marked *Strictly private and confidential* and *Urgent*. When he found she wasn't there, as he had been assured she would be, the messenger cursed her, and then decided to push the letter through the door. It was only a letter and he hadn't been told to wait for a reply. It was marked urgent after all, and it wasn't his fault if the silly moo had decided not to wait in for him.

It would be a sort of rehearsal, Debbie thought. She would try and think of it like that. For the time when the term ended, the last seven weeks and four days of it and she would be going up to Scotland for good. Having said goodbye to Joel.

The thought of that was so frightful, that it sometimes actually made her cry. The thought of a life and a world without him, for the rest of her life. If you could call it life, that is . . . Oh Debbie, stop being so melodramatic! You'll be all right. Of course you will. Hearts mend, life goes on, the sun still rises and sets . . .

The children were terribly excited, especially Emma, who was planning on inspecting the stables and notionally placing her pony in it. And Alex had been told that several boys stayed at school for half-term, the ones whose parents were abroad, and he could meet them. They had packed their bags days ago, and were counting the hours.

Richard was tremendously excited too: 'I can't wait to show you everything. I know you're going to love it here. Rosgate is quite a good little town, you'll be fine for shopping, and the countryside is just glorious. I've done my best with the house, and Morag has been fantastic, given us lots of things like cast-off curtains – that sort of thing – keep us going till you can get it all to your liking.'

God save me from Morag's cast-offs, Debbie thought; even her curtains would be sturdy, and sturdily patterned: and then felt very ashamed of herself. Morag would certainly never commit adultery.

Having to take a whole week off work annoyed her terribly; she was frantically trying to build up her accounts, so that Anna was more likely to let her handle at least one from Scotland, and it was difficult enough finding time for Joel without losing five whole more days. But Anna was very accommodating; it was as if she was on Debbie's side in some strange way. Maybe she was sorry for her because of her husband's absence . . .

And then on the Friday afternoon, she came back to find Emma lying on the sofa, face ashen, with a bowl at her side, being sick at roughly ten-minute intervals.

'I'm so sorry,' Jenny said apologetically, 'It started just as we left school.'

'Oh Jenny, it's not your fault. How awful. Not in your car, I hope?'

'Well, yes, a bit,' said Jenny, 'but goodness, nothing a bit of hot water can't sort out. And actually,' she said, her voice lowering, 'I don't like the look of Rachel either. She—'

The door opened and Rachel appeared, equally ashen. She had hardly said, 'Mu-um,' when the inevitable happened.

'You can't take them up to Scotland like this,' said Jenny, rushing for a bowl. Somehow, even when all three children were vomiting in unison, Debbie felt wildly and absurdly happy.

It was a very nasty bug, going round all the schools in the area, the GP surgery confirmed.

'Both ends too,' said Debbie to Richard next morning. 'And, in fact, Emma's so bad I got the doctor in. She just lies there, white and listless, still throwing up endlessly; she must be terribly dehydrated.'

'And what did the doctor say?'

'Oh, that it was just D and V, to keep up her fluid intake, all the usual things. I'm so sorry, Richard, but—'

'Of course, of course,' he said. 'But when—'

'Well, I thought I'd see how they were on Monday. Then maybe we can rethink.'

'I hope so. I was looking forward to seeing you all so much and, of course, Morag will be so disappointed.'

'Sorry,' said Debbie humbly. He clearly felt it was her fault this had happened. She put the phone down and called Joel. 'I had to let you know. Only don't you dare come round.'

'I will.'

'You'll have to clear up sick if you do.'

'Maybe I won't,' he said hastily. He was, she had discovered, intensely squeamish.

Blue got in very late that night. He had taken advantage of Lucinda's absence to entertain some clients; after dinner at Langan's they went to Aspinalls and emerged into Curzon Street at two in the morning in a champagne-fuelled haze, several hundred pounds worse off, but in high spirits. They moved on to a club in Shepherd's Market called Amanda's where one of the girls did appalling things with customers' spectacles, but after half an hour there, Blue was tired and beginning to feel he should be at least on call for Lucinda. Her father might, after all, be worse. He had been irresistibly reminded of the old bugger and his heavily-rimmed spectacles while sitting at Amanda's.

He called a cab and directed it home to Limehouse; at least he wouldn't have to tiptoe around in case he woke Lucinda up. She was very good-natured about that sort of thing, but he still felt bad, especially at the moment, when she was so tired. He felt a pang of remorse as he contemplated her tiredness; he really hadn't been as nice to her as he should. Maybe he would even drive down to Gloucestershire himself in the morning, see how things were. He could stay in a hotel, after all, didn't have to put up with that freezing cold museum of a place.

As he walked in the door, he stepped on a letter, lying on the mat. *Strictly private and confidential*, it said, and *Urgent*. It was addressed to Lucinda. He turned it over, saw that it was from Stephen Durham, Solicitor, Regent Street W1 and decided he should open it. Obviously the lazy sod had finally pulled his finger out with the divorce proceedings. He was still hoping to persuade Lucinda to at least have a civil ceremony before the baby was born; no way did Blue Horton want his son and heir born illegitimate.

An hour later, having had a cold shower, and drunk a large jug of coffee, he was in the Ferrari, headed westwards out of the city, and not sure whether rage or grief was his dominant emotion.

Elizabeth woke early that Saturday morning; she felt very sad. She dreaded waking up, it was the worst moment of the day. Sometimes, emerging from happy dreams of Simon being alive, with her, smiling at her, she would lie for a moment or two in a sweet confusion before reality advanced towards her again. She wasn't sure which were worse, the sad days or the angry ones; at least when she was angry she felt some kind of energy. The sad ones were grey and listless, and every movement she had to make was an effort.

And this was a very, very sad one.

The conversation with Annabel the night before had been about Jamie: Jamie and the wretched engagement party that Frances Cartwright so wanted.

'She's suggesting early December, Mummy. I don't know how you'd feel about that. I know it's still a bit soon, but – well, it would be lovely for me. Especially as we probably can't have one here, or not for a while anyway.'

'Indeed not.'

'I mean, I hope you don't mind, but I sort of feel that Daddy would have wanted it. For me to be happy in some ways at least. It's not that I'm even beginning to get over it, Mummy, Daddy dying, of course—'

'I should hope not!' said Elizabeth with a sudden flash of anger, and then seeing Annabel's stricken expression, felt a dreadful remorse. 'Oh darling, I'm sorry, of course I know what you mean, and God knows the last thing I want is for you to be endlessly unhappy – I hope you realise that.'

'Of course I do. And I can see this party might seem a bit heartless. But—'

'But life must go on,' said Elizabeth firmly, 'of course. And Jamie's been very patient. I mean, he never really knew Daddy—'

'Oh, I so wish he had,' said Annabel. 'They'd have loved each other, don't you think?'

'Yes, I do.'

'Anyway, it did seem quite a nice idea. To go over for the party. And then we could maybe do something here after Christmas.'

'Fine. Lovely idea.' Christmas! How was she going to endure Christmas. Don't think about it, Elizabeth; one day at a time . . .

'Well, the main question after that is whether you'd like to come. Feel up to it, that is.'

'No,' said Elizabeth fiercely, 'absolutely I won't. I'm sorry, Annabel, but it's a long trip and to see a lot of people I don't know, stay in a strange house – no, it's out of the question.'

'Of course. Sorry. Totally understand. And Frances isn't exactly an easy person. Although I know you'd love some of them – Bif and Dana and Kathleen—'

'Annabel, no. I couldn't – I'm sorry. It would be so exactly the opposite of how it should be, and I don't think I'd be much of an asset anyway, bit of a spectre at the feast.'

'Oh Mummy, I'm sure you wouldn't be that, but I can see

how hard it would be for you. Um . . . would you think it was all right if Tilly came? And Toby? So they could meet the Cartwrights?'

'Of course it would. I think it would be very nice.'

'Jamie got on with them both so well, and—'

'Annabel, I said yes,' said Elizabeth wearily. 'Look, I'm sorry, darling, but I really do feel so tired, I think I might get an early night.'

'Yes, that's a good idea. Shall I bring you some supper up? An omelette or something like that, all soft and runny the way you like it.'

Eggs were the thing that most nauseated Elizabeth; the very thought of a runny omelette turned her stomach over.

'No, thanks,' she said, standing up. 'Honestly, I don't want anything. Something has gone terribly wrong with my appetite. Maybe just a cup of tea.' She could throw that away without Annabel knowing.

'Fine. I'll make you one. Thank you so much, Mummy.'

'What for?'

'For being so understanding. You're a star and I love you.'

'I love you too,' said Elizabeth.

But the next morning, thinking of how Annabel's engagement party ought to be: proud smiling parents, a roomful of friends from both generations, she could hardly breathe she felt so unhappy.

Or so sick. When Annabel looked in on her, before she went to work, she saw her rushing white-faced into the bathroom, holding a towel to her mouth.

'Right,' said Blue. 'Sit down.' He had woken her, banging on the door just after six, stalked into the hall, his face distorted with rage.

'Blue—'

'I said sit down. And tell me what the fuck this is about!'

'Blue – Mummy will hear.'

'I don't care what Mummy will hear. Or Daddy, or your fucking toffee-nosed brothers and sisters. Is he here as well? Your – your husband? I wouldn't be surprised.'

'Of course he's not here. What are you talking about, what is all this about?'

651

'This,' he said, getting the letter out of his pocket, waving it at her. 'This letter. Setting a few things out, making a few things clear.'

'Oh,' she said. 'That.' She went very white, and sat down, abruptly.

'Yes, this. This – document. Sent by your solicitor. I must have been insane, sending you to him. Completely insane. But at least it's cleared a few things up. Why you wouldn't agree to buying a house, why Nigel kept ringing you up. Jesus, you're disgusting. I cannot believe you'd have done this, Lucinda, while you're pregnant with my child. If it *is* my child – I'm beginning to doubt that as well. Is it Nigel's? Have you been seeing him all this time?'

'Of course I haven't. Don't be ridiculous. Of course it's your child. How could you even think such a thing?'

'Quite easily,' he said, 'having read what's written down here. How you don't feel totally confident about your new relationship, how you're not married yet, how you're living somewhere totally unsuitable, how you can't work because you're pregnant – nice one, Lucinda – how the thought of the house being held in trust for you is very reassuring for you under the circumstances. And I hadn't realised that you gave up your career to marry Nigel; what was that job at the publishers then? Charity work?'

'Blue, you don't—'

'Funny you never mentioned your move to New York before this either – and Jesus, what is this fantasy about the money you gave up to marry Nigel? The hundred thousand pounds?'

'It's not fantasy,' said Lucinda staunchly. 'If I'd gone to New York with Virgil I could easily have earned that in commission – his paintings go for millions.'

'Ah, Virgil. The poof. Nice little bit of fraud you've cooked up with him. I take my hat off to you, Lucinda, I must say. I didn't think you had it in you.'

She was silent.

'And where does Nigel come into all this? Poor sod, I feel almost sorry for him. I had no idea he'd – what does it say here – oh yes, put a brake on your career, severely limited your social life. So what were all those house parties and weddings and christenings you were going to practically all the bloody time when I first met you? Work? Part of your career at the gallery? And that his being so much older than you put an inevitable strain on your marriage and affected your personal life. Your personal life, God help me. Does that mean sex, Lucinda?'

'It was just something else that Steve suggested. He said it would help.'

'I see. Help who?'

'Help me get a good settlement.'

'Oh yes. And what is this settlement he's helping you to get?'

'Well, the house for a start.'

'The house! What do you need the house for? I'm buying you a house!'

'Yes, I know. But at the moment – oh, you don't understand.'

'I most certainly don't. You're hoping for some money as well, I suppose?'

'Well, yes. But—'

'What for, for fuck's sake? Don't I give you enough money?'

'Yes, of course you do. You're incredibly generous.'

'So why do you want more? I'm really struggling here, Lucinda.'

'Well, I don't, that's the whole point. Look, please, *please* let me explain.'

'I don't think I want you to explain, Lucinda. I don't think I want to hear anything from you ever again. I feel completely sickened by you. You can tear that nice little document up, you won't be needing it. A rather different one will be coming from me, in a very few days. And don't even think about coming to the house to get your stuff. Nigel will no doubt buy you anything you need. You still seem to have him wrapped very nicely round your finger.'

And he was gone; the Ferrari disappeared up the drive, the noise and the fumes lingering for a long time. Together with Blue's words . . .

'I'm so worried about my mother,' said Annabel fretfully.

'Of course you are,' said Florian. 'She must still be in a very bad way, poor lady. Is she sleeping all right?'

'I don't think so, although the doctor's given her some pills. But she cries a lot. I hear her, it's so awful and I don't know what to do.'

'Just be your lovely self,' said Florian, giving her a kiss. 'That's all you can do at the moment.'

'Yes, but she's not well. I mean, really not well. She keeps being sick. She says it's a symptom of depression – or she says the doctor says that. But I looked up depression in our medical book and it doesn't mention it.'

'Sweetie, everyone's different. If that's what the doctor says, I'm sure it's right.'

'Yes, I suppose so. But – well, it just upsets me. Every morning while I'm getting ready, I hear her. It's horrible. And she's so brave, just says it's nothing and goes off to work. God, I admire her. I think she's wonderful, I want to be just like her.'

'Fat chance of that with the Bostonians, darling,' said Florian snidely. He had taken a dislike to Jamie and even more to what he had heard of the rest of the Cartwrights. 'Brood mare you'll be, raising a dynasty.'

'Don't be silly, of course I won't. I'll do what I want. This is 1990, Florian, do try to remember that.'

'Not to the Cartwright family, from what I've heard. Now look, must dash. And try not to worry about your mama, she'll be fine. I've never met a lady with such courage.'

Just the same, Annabel went on worrying.

Tilly's new friend Fallon stayed at the house on Saturday night. The girls played music very loudly in Tilly's room and watched videos. It was rather nice, Annabel thought, to hear the house brought alive again; it had been terribly quiet lately. She walked into the kitchen in the morning and found them making eggy bread, a delight Fallon hadn't savoured before, apparently.

'Oh hi,' said Tilly. 'You've met Fallon, haven't you?'

'Of course. Hello, Fallon.'

'Hi,' said Fallon. She was rather beautiful, Annabel thought. She could be a model; and then hoped no one would suggest it to her, or not for at least three or four more years. 'This is a fab house,' she added.

'We won't have it much longer,' said Annabel. 'It's on the market and we're supposed to be looking for somewhere else, I expect Tilly's told you, but . . . well, our mother doesn't feel up to it. Last thing she needs at the moment.'

'Yeah, course,' said Fallon.

'Poor Mummy,' said Tilly, 'she was being sick this morning again. It must be so horrible, she's got enough to cope with without that.'

'My mum's sick every morning at the moment an' all,' said Fallon.

'Oh really?'

'Yeah. She's in the club again, and not too pleased about it, I can tell you.'

'What club?' said Tilly.

'Tilly!' said Annabel. 'You really are hopeless. It means she's pregnant.'

'Oh really?' said Tilly. 'How exciting. Well, Mummy certainly isn't that. You want grated cheese on this, Fallon? It's ever so nice.'

She wasn't looking at Annabel; if she had been, she would have seen her sister freeze in her tea-making and turn extremely pink, and then hurry out of the kitchen and upstairs to her room. Where she got out her diary and started rather feverishly leafing through it.

Chapter 47

October to November, 1990

Blue had spent the weekend in a state first of rage and then violent grief; he felt as if Lucinda had died.

He had loved her so much, and trusted her so completely; she had always seemed to him as transparently sweet and truthful as clear running water. How was it that she could possibly have been capable of cruel and devious behaviour, how could she have deceived him so savagely, lain in his arms, told him she loved him, smiled at him, sparkled for him, made his life totally and perfectly happy, while telling her solicitor in virtually the next breath that she was so unsure about the relationship that she required large sums of money and a house – and not any house, but the ex-marital home as it had been called in that document – by way of security for herself and her unborn child.

He spent the weekend either lying in bed or in a chair, having drunk himself to sleep, or driving very much too fast in the Ferrari on the ring roads of Greater London. Quite often he had to stop in a layby because tears blurred his eyes and he was unable to see properly. He felt literally haunted by images of Lucinda: Lucinda smiling at him that first evening, in her absurd Sloaney gear, Lucinda naked in bed with him the first time, that incredible body – so well camouflaged by the absurd gear – arching triumphantly as she came for him, Lucinda weeping when she told him she must go back to Nigel, Lucinda sweetly anxious when she told him she was pregnant, Lucinda giggling helplessly as he told her his filthy jokes, Lucinda taking his hand and placing it on her heaving stomach as their baby kicked and writhed around inside her. Their baby. Their son. The greatest achievement of his life without doubt. Only – and this thought was the most unbearable of all –

perhaps it wasn't his son. For if she was capable of creating that picture of their marriage, she was capable of anything.

He was at that moment parked in a layby off the A12; he buried his head in his arms on the Ferrari's steering wheel and wept.

By Monday morning, the girls had begun to recover, and were sitting up drinking lemon barley water and eating dry toast. Alex, however, was still vomiting. Debbie called the doctor again; he appeared slightly more concerned, took his pulse, and prescribed rehydration powders.

'Let me know if he's still bad tomorrow.'

She rang Richard again. 'We can't come, Richard, I'm sorry. Maybe you could come down. The children would so love to see you.'

'Debbie, I can't. I'm as disappointed as you all are, but there are children still at school here and I'm on duty till the end of the week. I'm really sorry. I hope you'll understand.'

'Of course I do. What a shame. Bye, Richard.' She put the phone down, smiling. God, she was a bitch.

By the evening the children were beginning to look more themselves; even Alex was sitting up and demanding unsuitable food like crisps, and the girls were squabbling limply. But they were still not well enough to make the long journey to Scotland.

'It's such a shame,' Debbie said to Flora that evening. She had rung to wish them a lovely week on Friday, and had been told the news. 'They were so excited and now they look dreadful; they need some good fresh air.'

'You could bring them down here,' said Flora thoughtfully. 'It's not nearly so far, and the weather's lovely. What about that? You've got the week off, haven't you?'

'Ye-es.'

'Well then, come. I'd love it. Better make the best of it, Debbie, the old place will soon be up for sale.'

'Oh Flora, no. How horrible for you.'

'Yes, it is rather. I've put it off and off, but Lloyd's are getting very heavy.'

'But – where will you go?' She found it hard to imagine Flora living anywhere else; she was part of that house, as much as the grey stone and the slate roof and the flagstone floor. It needed her to fill it with flowers and grasses and the smell of baking bread and woodsmoke; new owners just wouldn't do it right.

'I have no idea. I think I want to move right away. Somewhere where the few pennies I have left can go further. I certainly don't fancy living in a bungalow in Swansea, and anyway, I can't afford it. I might just get a tent and pay the new owners to let me camp in my – the meadow.'

She was very brave, Debbie thought. Most people would be railing against their fate.

'Anyway – want to come? I really would like it.'

Suddenly it seemed like a lovely idea; to be somewhere safe, away from the whole painful difficult thing, a break for a few days at least, with nothing more emotionally challenging to cope with than stopping the children from squabbling too much and trying not to mind when Flora acted as if the children were hers.

'We'd love to come, Flora,' she said. 'Thank you.'

Elizabeth hadn't liked Dr Young the psychiatrist at all. He had been brusque and rather dismissive of her; he had asked her exactly why she felt she couldn't have the baby, and she had told him she would have thought any fool could see that: her husband had just died, she had three children to take care of already, a full-time and demanding job.

She was also over forty, her health was suffering already through the pregnancy, and she was deeply worried about foetal abnormalities.

Dr Young clearly didn't like the implication that he was a fool. 'Plenty of women over forty have babies these days,' he said, 'and you seem pretty well to me. Statistically, you have a very good chance of having a completely healthy baby. And in any case, there are very good screening processes for abnormalities.'

'Yes, I do know that,' said Elizabeth, fighting a desire to lean across the desk and slap him – this wasn't like her, her hormones really were in freefall – 'and the one for Down's syndrome means a termination at twenty weeks if it's positive. That's hardly going to help me recover from my husband's death.'

'You wouldn't have to have a termination,' he said. 'Down's children are very lovable; raising them can be a wonderfully rewarding experience.'

'Oh, for God's sake,' said Elizabeth, 'haven't you been listening to a word I've said?'

'I think, Mrs Beaumont,' he said rather acidly, 'it is you who are not listening. But – yes, all right, I am prepared to recommend a termination for you. I would urge you to reconsider, just the same. Depression almost invariably results from the process and I really don't think you are in a fit state to make this decision. Do please take time out between now and Friday to make sure you know what you're doing.'

'Unfortunately I am unable to take time out,' said Elizabeth. 'I told you, I have a living to earn.'

And now she had Fiona Broadhurst coming to see her, wasting more of her time. She had agreed to see her to discuss something Fiona had said was important; she was regretting it now.

'I really won't keep you long, Mrs Beaumont.' Fiona Broadhurst smiled her rather distant smile. 'But I thought what I have to tell you was better dealt with by a meeting.'

'Fine,' said Elizabeth, 'but I only have half an hour.' She looked at her watch, to make the point.

'Of course. I understand. Now, I know you don't want to proceed with the lawsuit, you wrote and told me that, but I wonder if you realise that the group George Meyer was leading, together with your husband, has at least a chance of succeeding. Or so our QC feels.'

'Really? What would you say the odds are?'

'I'm a lawyer, Mrs Beaumont,' said Fiona Broadhurst. 'I don't bet. It would be wrong of me to mislead you in any way. But I did think you should know the chances were good.'

'Really? From everything I've heard and read, there is precious little chance of Lloyd's ever giving up a brass farthing.'

'Not quite true. Although it wasn't at all the same thing, and it was a while ago, there is a precedent for Lloyd's settling: over the Cameron Webb business – I expect you know about that?'

Elizabeth shook her head.

'Peter Cameron Webb and Peter Dixon, two very

prominent brokers at Lloyd's, were found guilty of fraud. Most particularly of diverting reinsurance premiums to themselves, thus leaving their Members without adequate cover. Writs were actually issued for their arrests, but they're out of the country now, living somewhere like Miami. Anyway, Lloyd's did make a substantial offer to the Members.' She paused. 'The group Mr Meyer has formed is now about a hundred strong. A large proportion of the Westfield Bradley Names – that's your late husband's main syndicate – have joined it. And we are not alone in this case. There is a vortex of them; at least four thousand Names, possibly many more, are at this precise moment forming action groups, and preparing writs.'

'Oh,' said Elizabeth. She felt rather surprised at this; she had somehow thought the lawsuit was little more than therapy for the beleaguered Names. She realised that for fully sixty seconds at least she hadn't given her pregnancy, Simon's death or even her job a moment's thought.

'But I actually think,' said Fiona Broadhurst, 'that you probably have more than enough stress to cope with. If I were you, I would feel exactly the same.'

'You would?'

'Of course I understand completely. I shall write you a letter, absolving you from any further involvement in the matter, and of course return the money your husband deposited with us for preliminary work. Minus your husband's share of any costs so far incurred.'

'Thank you,' said Elizabeth.

'Now, as you know, I had lunch with your husband, the day before he died.'

'Indeed? And?' What was she going to say? That Simon had made a pass at her? Not impossible.

'And he told me that he was still determined to go ahead. Although I had to tell him that some evidence he was rather excited about would not be admissible in court. He was disappointed about that.'

That would have been Joel Strickland's tapes, Elizabeth thought.

'And that seemed possibly quite important to me,' said Fiona.

'You mean, wanting to go ahead? As a gauge to his state of mind?'

'Yes. It seemed clear to me that he was still feeling very positive. He certainly didn't seem depressed. And of course I shall say that at the inquest. You know I've been called to make a statement?'

'I do. It was my impression too. Thank you for telling me.'

Not time wasted at all; Elizabeth felt much better suddenly.

'I need to see you,' said Joel. His voice was raw-edged. 'I need to talk to you. Properly. A real conversation.'

'Joel, you know I can't. I'm going down to Wales in the morning, the children are all quite sickly still, I can't get a babysitter tonight.'

'I'm sorry, but you're going to have to. This can't wait. *I* can't wait. I know you're going away tomorrow, that's exactly why I have to see you tonight. Before – well, before you see *him* again. OK?'

'But—'

'Debbie, please. It's so important.'

'Well, I'll see what I can do.' She rang Jan who, rather relishing the whole thing, said yes, of course, she'd babysit.

'It couldn't be better, there's some desperately exciting football match on, which Mike's been looking forward to for weeks. And I can catch up on my *Dynasty* videos. You won't be later than twelve though, will you? He gets a bit tetchy if I'm really late.'

'Twelve!' said Debbie. 'Of course not. Home by ten at the latest, I should think.'

'That won't give you much time.'

'Jan, this is not that sort of occasion. I swear.'

'Oh, OK,' said Jan. Debbie could hear the smile in her voice. 'If you say so.'

He had asked her to come to his flat. 'I can't talk about this in some cruddy bar.'

She agreed, 'But Joel, I can't be long, I really can't.'

'Yes, all right.'

'You know what I mean.'

661

'I know what you mean.'
'I'll wear my tightest knickers.'
'OK.'

Already the relationship was changing, she thought, driving through the dark November evening towards Clapham; was becoming less of a delicious treat, was taking in real life, real troubles. He had sounded very serious, almost strained; perhaps he had decided it wasn't worth it, worth all the agony of the waiting, the snatched meetings, the interrupted conversations. Perhaps he wanted to finish it. She shrank from the thought, while thinking that at least it would be over, resolved; she could start to recover, be living in the agony, rather than dreading it . . .

'Hi.' He was wearing jeans and a white shirt, was barefoot, he had obviously just had a shower; his hair was spiky and still wet. It was all she could do to keep herself from attacking him, unbuttoning his shirt, unzipping his fly . . . . She made do with a rather extended kiss, shutting the door behind her. He stood back and smiled at her.

'Phew. Please sit down. Would you like a drink?'
'No, thank you. I've got to drive and anyway, I kind of feel I need a clear head for this.'
'You kind of feel right. Just hang on – I'll make the coffee.'

He was fussy about coffee, about everything that was food or drink; the snobbery she had discovered that first evening – the Michelob beer, the gourmet-sandwiched picnic, the designer water was absolutely standard for him, he could no more have eaten a McDonald's meal than dog food. Good thing he didn't have any kids, she thought; and absurdly felt a pang of jealousy that one day he would, and with someone other than her.

'There. Enjoy.'
'Thank you.'
'Right,' he said, 'are you sitting comfortably?'
'Yes, thank you.'
'I'm getting sick of all this,' he said. 'Never knowing when we can meet, never having long enough for anything, never having a whole night together, sharing you with your family, trying not to think about sharing you with *him*.'

662

'Yes,' she said quietly. 'Yes, I thought it would be something like that.'

'It's just not – not good enough. I mean that in the most straightforward way. It's not good enough for us. For what we've got, what we feel. It was all right at first, but now I can't bear it. I love you too much, I want all of you. All the time.'

'But—'

'And how does it seem to you?' he said. He was looking rather fierce.

She swallowed, then said, 'The same. Of course. I'm not – not enjoying it so much. It's getting spoiled.'

'Exactly. The game's not worth the candle, all of a sudden. Here you are, totally perfect for me, what I've always wanted, the first woman I've ever properly trusted . . .'

'Trusted?'

'Yes. Well, except for my nan.' He grinned at her. 'Pretty big compliment that, Debbie, you know.'

'I do know.'

'You make me feel good about myself. I never had anyone do that before. And all the other girls, they – they want things. Things I can't – or don't want – to give them. You don't want anything.'

'Well, it wouldn't do me any good, would it?' she said, smiling, giving him a quick kiss. 'And anyway, I do want some things. Or one thing anyway.'

'I know. Which is great. And that's exactly what I mean really. You just want me, nothing else, not a slice of my life, not half my flat or . . . Oh, I'm probably not making a lot of sense.'

She was silent.

'Anyway, like I said, all I'm getting is wretched little snatches of you. So . . .' She braced herself, closed her eyes, unable to look at him while he said it, while he said the awful, hideous ugly thing '. . . So I've decided.'

'Yes?'

'Yes. I want you to marry me. I want you to divorce your husband and marry me.'

She was so shocked she felt as if he had hit her; the breath left her body, she felt light-headed and slightly sick. She swallowed, tried to speak, found she couldn't.

'I just have to, you see. I've got to have you. I'll never find anyone else, not who I love like I love you. And so I'm going to take you on. Well, I want to. And your children, and all the complicated baggage you'll bring with you. I don't know what sort of husband I'll make, but I'll be sweating blood, I'll try so hard.'

'Oh,' she said. And this time she didn't feel as if he had hit her, she still felt rather shocked, but sweetly so, contentedly so; listening to this amazing thing, that Joel loved her so much he wanted to marry her, and marry her children; he wanted to be with her for the rest of his life, and the rest of hers, and wondering what on earth she did or indeed what she was that made him want that, when he could have had hundreds of girls, cool, beautiful, uncomplicated girls, and she sat there still not speaking, not moving, wanting him to go on, to say more and if there was no more, to say it all over again.

'I can't quite believe I'm saying all this,' he said. 'I mean, I don't really believe in marriage at all. I really don't . . . . It's the last thing I want in theory. And especially taking on some other bloke's kids. But I thought if I just asked you to move in with me, it wouldn't be enough. I mean, anyone can say that. I had to show you how much I meant it.'

'Yes, I see,' she said.

'So . . . so do you have anything to say?'

'Well . . .' She stopped.

'Yes?'

'I can't think of anything to say,' she said, rather helplessly. 'Except of course what I want to say is yes, yes, yes and I'd love to marry you, too.'

'You would?'

'Of course I would. I can't believe you just said all that, and I feel completely and utterly knocked out by it.'

'Well, that's all right then, isn't it?' He sounded rather uncertain.

'No, Joel, it isn't. Because I can't.'

'Why not? Debbie, for Christ's sake why not! Just tell me!'

'Because I'm already married. And I don't have any reason not to be. Not really.'

'Yes, you do.'

'Joel, I don't.'

'So – let's take this from the top,' he said. 'And I'm trying, I'm trying very hard to keep calm here. I love you. You love me – or so you say. Or am I wrong?'

'No,' she said, 'you're not wrong. I do love you, I love you terribly.'

'OK. So here we are, the two of us, loving each other. We have earth-and sky-moving sex. We make each other happy. It's all pretty well perfect really.'

'But—'

'And you don't love your husband, you absolutely don't. He's dull, he's manipulative, he puts you down, he's not interested in you, not interested in what you do.'

'Joel, don't. Don't talk about Richard like that. You don't know him, and if I've said he is dull or manipulative, it was very wrong of me.'

'You haven't. You're very loyal about him, actually.'

'Loyal! I don't think he'd see it quite like that.'

'Well, I think you are. Anyway, we won't argue about him. We've got better things to do. Look, Debbie, I'm thirty-four years old now, and I have never wanted to get married. I've never wanted domesticity, I've certainly never wanted children. I'm ambitious and selfish and extravagant and, well – terrible husband material really. But for you I'll do it. I will take on your children – like I said, they seem rather jolly, and I would love, one day, for you to have my babies too.'

'Oh Joel.' Her eyes filled with tears.

'I can't quite believe I'm saying all this, you know,' he said again. 'All my friends who have wives and kids and money problems, and no time on their own, and can't even get out to go down the pub of an evening, I've always just thought, Poor sods, and thanked God it wasn't me in there. And now suddenly I want it to be. I don't understand it actually. I really, really don't. I mean, I'm sure some of it will be complete hell, and the kids'll resent me because I'm not their dad and all that stuff. And I really don't think we're all going to waltz off into the sunset together, but the thing is I'm ready for it, ready for the hell. Just because I love you. So – what do you say, Debbie? There must be something.'

'There is something,' she said, 'of course there is. I love you like that too. But . . .'

'But what? You wouldn't do it for me? Divorce him, all that stuff?'

'Joel, please. You've known about this for – I don't know how long.'

'Oh, hours,' he said, with a grin. 'Possibly even days.'

'Yes, well, exactly. You've got used to the idea. It's a complete shock to me, I would never have expected it, not in a million years, and I think it's so, so wonderful, and half of me wants to just stay here and never go back.'

'And the other half?'

'The other half is scared. Of all sorts of things. Walking away from everything I know, with all that that implies. I mean, it would be totally horrible, that whole divorce thing, you know, well, you don't—'

'I've sat in a few divorce courts,' he said.

'Not quite the same thing, as when it's you; some of my friends have been through it and it's hideous.'

'I wouldn't mind. Well, I would, but it'd be worth it. But if that's the problem, we don't have to do it. Not for a long time anyway – we could leave it. But that's exactly what I don't want, you see. I don't want ragged ends. I want it all neat and tidy. For you. Christ, remind me of this, Debbie, when we can't afford to share a bottle of beer.'

'I will,' she said. 'I promise. And God, it would be bad, you know, the kids being difficult, Richard hating me, Flora putting an evil spell on me.'

'You do see the worst of her, don't you?' he said. 'I thought she was great.'

'Yes, well, you wait till she's your ex-mother-in-law, or rather my ex-mother-in-law, and see how she is then. Anyway, I'd even risk that.'

'So – is that a yes?'

'No, it isn't a yes. It can't be. I need to think, terribly, terribly hard. It's not me and it's not you and it's not even Richard I have to consider. It's the children. They love him, they think he's wonderful—'

'They'd come to think I was wonderful too,' he said confidently.

'I don't think they would. Like you say, they'd resent you. And I'd feel so guilty all the time—'

666

'Listen,' he said. 'Let's look at our situations, shall we, our childhoods, yours and mine? Your parents were as dull as ditchwater, your life as a child was ditto, but I don't see you as a failure because of it. You've turned out a brilliant mother and a brilliant person. With a potentially brilliant career.'

'Joel, come on. Working for a half-baked PR outfit . . .'

'Yes, I know, but I've read some of those releases of yours. You're bloody good. You could do very well in Fleet Street. Or rather in Wapping or Holborn Circus or wherever. I absolutely bloody know you would. And as for me, that awful childhood I had – and am I in a psychiatric ward, or even severely disturbed? Not at all. Here I am, a charming and successful young man . . .'

'Joel,' she said, laughing.

'Well, it's true – and we could give your kids a much better life than either of us had. They'll be all right, Debbie, they'll survive. I mean, for just how long do you have to go on leading a rotten life in order not to upset your children?'

'For ever, probably,' she said soberly.

'Rubbish. It's your turn, Debbie. They'll be fine, you're not going to leave them in some Romanian orphanage. They can spend the holidays up there with Daddy, and they can live with us down here in termtime. And go to dreadful sink state schools, because that's what we both believe in.'

'Oh, do stop it.'

'I can't, Debbie. Please, please. Say yes.'

'All I can say,' she said, dizzy with longing to say it, knowing she mustn't, not yet, not for a long, long time, 'is definitely hopefully. Remember that? I told you, they say it in Gower, where Flora lives. That's all. For now. It'll have to do. I'm sorry. I need time.'

'Oh fuck,' he said sulkily, lighting a cigarette. He hardly ever smoked with her, he knew she hated it.

'Don't, Joel. Don't be angry. I can't help it, I have to do the – the right thing.'

'The right thing is to be with me.'

'Well, maybe. I want to be, more than anything in the world; that's all I have to say.'

'Oh, all right,' he said, and then looked at his watch. 'What time do you have to get back to your bloody responsibilities?'

'I said ten.'

'Ten! It's already nine.'

'I know. But,' she hesitated, 'Jan said she could actually stay till twelve.'

'Right.' He reached forward, put his hand inside her shirt, started to caress her breasts. 'I like this Jan. She sounds like a good egg.'

'She is a good egg.'

She moved nearer him, unbuttoning his shirt, slithering her hand down his jeans. She felt incredible, suddenly, wired, alive, every nerve on edge, on edge with wanting him.

'Bedroom then? Or in here?'

'I don't think I can wait,' she said, 'to get into the bedroom,' and then everything was confused, confused and amazing, and she could never remember feeling quite like this, even the first time with him; she seemed to feel everything at once, her whole body confused, not knowing what she was doing, only what she wanted, and they were lying on the floor, and he was in her and it was over almost before it had begun, only wonderfully and brilliantly so, and she was sobbing and shouting and laughing with it; and then he said as she quietened, 'Come on, let's go to bed now, do it properly.'

It was after twelve when she got home, exhausted, exhilarated, hardly knowing who she was or what she might do. She apologised to Jan, told her they had had a lot to talk about.

'Yeah, yeah,' Jan said, looking at her smudged mascara, her flushed face, her crumpled clothes. 'Lot of talking you've been doing.'

'We have actually,' said Debbie, with a desperate grab at dignity. 'A lot.'

'I'll believe you,' said Jan, 'millions wouldn't. Anyway, you're in luck, Hubby didn't phone. Mine did though, twice. I must go. You've been at a sales conference, if you happen to see him. See you in the morning. I want to hear all about it, by way of payment, OK?'

'OK,' said Debbie, 'some of it anyway. Some things you can't describe. Wouldn't you say?'

'Oh Debbie,' said Jan, 'if only I could remember not being able to describe it. You lucky cow.'

Steve Durham had been waiting in a state of increasing exasperation to hear from Lucinda. She knew how urgent the matter was, for God's sake. He wouldn't have biked the bloody document over to her if it hadn't been. She'd only had to sign it and send it back; how much of an administrative burden was that?

By the end of the Monday, he had had enough; he had called her repeatedly during the day and left messages; the matter was too important to leave unsettled. He supposed she might have gone into hospital, be having the baby even; but he needed to know. Cowper's solicitor had his own document ready and signed; having pushed this whole thing through at his own instigation, he now appeared and felt completely incompetent.

He decided to call Blue Horton at his office. It was he who had introduced him to Lucinda in the first place. More was the pity . . .

When he asked him if he knew what had happened to a document he had had delivered to the Horton household on Friday, and said that he was anxious to get it returned with Lucinda's signature, Blue delivered a pithy epithet to the effect that Steve could put his document up his arse and set light to it for all he cared, and told him to call Lucinda at her parents' house.

'And you can go after her for any money owing to you, incidentally. And tell her I said so.'

Steve Durham didn't feel he could ask him for the telephone number. Something must have gone extremely wrong with Lucinda; he wondered what, and felt a very brief pang of concern for her, before directing his attention to the far more important matter of who might actually pay his bill.

Elizabeth got home feeling completely exhausted. It had been, to put it mildly, a brute of a day. Culminating in Peter Hargreaves saying almost apologetically that he would be grateful if she could possibly do the Mercers' new range presentation on Monday. Monday! She wouldn't be at her best, to put it mildly.

'I know it's a lot to ask at the moment,' he said, 'but you

know how important it is. You said yourself it's virtually a repitch to keep the whole account.'

'Peter, I'll be there. Don't worry.'

And the estate agent had phoned to say that the Americans had come back with an even better offer and he really thought they should proceed.

'There's no chain, they've sold their house and—'

'Yes, but I haven't got anywhere to live.'

'I can get you somewhere you can rent for a few weeks, until you find a property. I really think you should take the offer, Mrs Beaumont. The market's not exactly buoyant at the moment.'

'I'll get back to you in the morning,' she said.

She walked into the drawing room, collapsed onto the sofa. And looked around the room and thought that among other things, the sheer hard work of moving would be incredible. Yes, the removal men would do all the packing, all the work, but she'd still have to sort through everything; apart from anything else, they wouldn't have room for half the furniture, there would be endless decisions to make, sales to organise. And she would have to deal with all Simon's stuff; she'd put that off day after day, hadn't even got rid of any of his clothes. She couldn't face it, couldn't face touching them, holding them, throwing – or giving – them away. It would seem so unbearably, unutterably final.

'Shit,' she said aloud. 'Shit!'

She heard the front door open and then Annabel calling her name.

'In the drawing room, darling.'

Annabel walked in; she looked very pale and tense.

'Are you all right, sweetheart? What's the matter?'

She saw her Annabel take a deep breath, then: 'It's not what's the matter with me, Mummy. It's what's the matter with you. Are you – well, are you pregnant?'

670

Chapter 48

November, 1990

It had been such a good idea, to come down here. She felt really relaxed for the first time for – well, she couldn't remember when. No phones ringing, nobody pressuring her, no need to tell lies, no elaborate planning or frantic clock-watching; it was just the best.

She did a lot of thinking: not the decisive sort, that would have been too difficult, just wonderfully self-indulgent thinking, and remembering. She lived and relived that evening, what Joel had said, the amazing shocked happiness of hearing it, and for the time being, that was enough. There would have to be decisions made and action taken, but not yet; she could put them away, lock them up, take them out when she felt strong enough. For now, she wanted simply to enjoy them, a few easily perfect days. She could never remember being so happy.

The weather had put in a last Herculean effort for them, and the day before, they had actually had a sort of picnic, a bit breezy to be sure, and only biscuits and a cake and a Thermos of tea, and they'd had to sit sheltering just in the lee of the big rocks at Mewslade, but still with the wonderful sense of being properly outdoors. She looked at the three of them, rosy again, eating for England – 'Or Wales,' as she said to Flora.

Flora was briskly brave about the house, full of plans. 'I'm thinking of going to Scotland,' she said. 'The Highlands. It's beautiful up there, even a bit like Gower, only more dramatic, and the weather won't be as nice, of course. I can get a nice little place for almost nothing.'

Debbie didn't like to ask her about the horses; she couldn't imagine Prince Hal travelling up to Scotland, but it might be possible, she supposed; and as for Boy . . .

'This is the first time Tilly hasn't been down for half-term,' Flora said rather sadly, clearly recognising her train of thought. 'She says she wants to stay close to her mother for a little longer, and she's got a lot of friends at her new school, apparently. Such a relief that's worked out so well.'

'Why shouldn't it?' said Debbie, feeling a stab of the old irritation.

'Well, it's a little different from what she's used to.'

'Doesn't mean it's worse. And children are very adaptable.'

'Debbie, darling, really! Tilly is used to extreme privilege and a very narrow social spectrum. She's unworldly to the point of absurdity; and to her new schoolmates, something of a joke, I would imagine. She could have been horribly teased, bullied even; I think it's little short of miraculous that she's adapted so well. A great credit to her. And she does actually like it there; she wrote me such a sweet funny letter about how the boys tease her rotten and call her posho, and what she does every weekend with her two best friends, Fallon and Madison. Extraordinary.'

'But don't you think it's awfully good for her,' said Debbie, 'seeing another side of life, mixing with real people? I mean, the sort of school she went to, it's so ridiculously privileged.'

'I think you and I are going to have to disagree on all this,' said Flora. 'It is good for her, of course, seeing the other side, but she won't get anything like as good an education.'

'How do you know that?'

'I read the papers, I look at the results. And she'll learn a lot of unattractive things – sex, far too early, drugs . . .'

'Flora, honestly,' said Debbie, and she was laughing now. 'Do you really think there aren't any drugs in independent schools?'

Flora looked at her in clear astonishment. 'Well, of course there aren't. What an absurd idea.'

Debbie gave up.

She didn't even think about contacting Joel; it would have revived all the difficulties, and the emotional discomfort; she just basked in her happiness. Richard had agreed to come down for the weekend. The thought of that was quite literally awful, she shrank from it, which was frightening in itself. But Flora was very pleased.

'The whole of my family together under this dear old roof,' she said, 'possibly for the last time.'

'Flora, don't say that.'

'I have to keep saying it,' said Flora, 'I have to learn to live with it.' And then she turned to Debbie and said – and Debbie had never been so surprised by anything, apart from Joel asking her to marry him – 'Debbie, I'd like your opinion on something. I'm desperate to discuss it, and there's no one else I trust. Simon is – well, gone – and I can't talk to Richard because it would affect him. It's about the house.' She was trying to be clever, she went on, but, 'I hope not too clever. I'm going to be completely honest with you, and rely on you to keep it to yourself.'

'Yes, of course I will.' Debbie was so curious, she would have agreed in that moment to take up hunting to keep Flora talking.

'It's a way of saving myself, and doing Lloyd's down. And I am a bit ashamed of it. That's the thing. It's not entirely honest.'

'As far as I can see,' Debbie said, 'nor are they.'

'True. Anyway, I've got a – a friend in the property business. It was his idea. His rather brilliant idea.'

Goodness, Debbie thought, this gets better; another man in Flora's life.

'Go on,' she said.

'All right. He buys my house – at its face value – with the land. Now the thing is, you can't build on Gower. It's all protected.'

'So . . .'

'Unless you have buildings. They can be in total rack and ruin – cottages, barns, stables – but as long as they're proper buildings, not just sheds, you can sometimes get permission to convert them into houses.'

'Ye-es.'

'Right. Now Colin's plan is that I go to Lloyd's, show them the contract, say I've sold my house and I need some money; how much are you going to take? It'll be most of it. I could maybe get a tiny flat somewhere.'

'Yes?' said Debbie again.

'But there'll be a second contract between the developer

and another company, guaranteeing it a substantial sum of money if planning is granted within three years. To build three houses there.'

'And your friend can get the planning consent?'

'Well, yes. He's pretty confident. He has all sorts of contacts.'

'And you'd have some link with this other company?'

'Good Lord, what an idea!' She grinned at Debbie. 'Well, I just – might. Not as a director or a shareholder, of course. Just – behind it, a beneficiary. It would be an offshore company, and this would be a joint-venture agreement with the developer. My friend says, and this is where things get a bit technical, it's some sort of piggy-backing agreement. Even if they investigated it, I wouldn't be there. It would mean I'd still have some money, quite a lot actually, and so I could afford to buy somewhere quite nice. I'd have to move, obviously. As I said, I'm thinking of Scotland, the Highlands. Apparently it's beautiful up there.' She was silent for a moment, then said, 'It's not Gower, of course. But at least I wouldn't have to be in some hovel somewhere.'

'Well,' said Debbie, 'that does sound very clever. I don't quite get the technical bit, but – well, yes. Very clever indeed. And, you know this person quite well, do you? I mean, you trust him?'

'Oh, absolutely, yes,' said Flora. 'He's not the shark you might be imagining. At all. We go to concerts together.'

As if that made it all right, Debbie thought, carefully not looking at her; as it would be if he had been at Eton or belonged to the right club.

'So, what do you think, Debbie? I'm not asking you what I should do, of course. I just wanted to – to talk about it. It's going round and round in my head and I'm beginning to feel as if I'm going mad.'

'Well, it is very clever,' said Debbie again. 'Your friend is clearly some sort of genius. And I like the thought of you being able to do Lloyd's down. They deserve all they get. Or all they don't get. And if it's foolproof, I mean you don't get caught or sent to prison or something – only joking, but you know what I mean – then yes. And presumably you could keep on riding, keep your horse and everything. So, why not?'

Flora met her eyes very levelly; they sat there looking at each other for quite a long time. Then: 'You don't actually think that, Debbie, do you? I hope I haven't shocked you.'

'No, of course you haven't. Like I say, it's a wonderful idea.'

'But – come on, Debbie, I can tell there's a but. This is exactly why I've told you. I want to discuss it and I want an honest reaction.'

'Well . . .' She looked at Flora and for the first time in their difficult relationship, felt they were on a completely level footing. 'Well, the thing is, Flora, I don't think it suits you.'

'Because it's dishonest?'

'No, of course not. No, it's because I – well, I . . .'

'Go on, please.'

'It's because I can't see you agreeing to anything that would mean ruining your meadow. And Broken Bay House, come to that. You'd never forgive yourself. At least, I don't think you would. Sorry, Flora.'

'Oh Debbie.' Flora looked at Debbie and then smiled at her, a very soft smile, and there were tears in her dark blue eyes. 'Oh my dear, how very wise you are. Thank you for that. I'm very grateful.'

There was a pause; then she said, and her tone was brusque, the familiar Flora again, 'Now let's not talk about it any more. Probably should never have told you.'

'Flora,' said Debbie, 'I'm awfully glad you did.'

Only two more days, and then she'd be feeling better. Well, she'd feel a bit worse, first, but then . . .

The atmosphere in the house was horrible; Annabel wasn't speaking to her. Tilly, clearly baffled for she had picked up on the hostility without having the faintest idea what it was about, was endeavouring earnestly to pour oil on the clearly troubled waters. Toby hadn't come home for half-term, but had gone to stay with his best friend Piers Wilson who lived in Herefordshire; she had actually been relieved when he asked her if he could go.

'Do you mind, Mum? I know I should be there with you, but this should be great, four of us are going and Wilson's father is going to organise a boys' shoot.'

Elizabeth understood; it was not heartlessness, it was a

complete inability to face the trauma, not that his father was dead, but of all that it entailed. Sooner or later he would have to, she supposed; but for the time being, she was of the opinion that if he could stay distant from it all until he felt emotionally stronger, the better it would be. She was comforted to hear from the chaplain at school that he had talked to him a little, and that he didn't believe there was a real problem. 'He just needs time. Let's try and give it to him, leave him be.'

But Annabel was facing the trauma, and a new one too, an incredibly hard one. If only Elizabeth could have kept it from her for just a few more days.

She had guilt now, to add to her rage and misery, and of course her ill-health. She had denied it at first that evening, had said, no, of course not; but Annabel was sharp-eyed and sharp-eared too; she could hear the lie in her mother's voice, see the slight avoidance in her eyes.

'Mum! Come on. Grief and depression don't make you throw up every morning regular as clockwork.'

'That's all you know,' said Elizabeth.

'Well, I think I do. And I tell you something else – your boobs have got bigger. I noticed the other day and I thought, well, lucky her, you know how we're all totally flat-chested in this family. And then, well, I began putting two and two together, or rather one and one, and making a rather surprising three. Come on, Mummy, admit it.'

'Well, all right. Yes, I am.'

'How absolutely lovely!' Annabel had said, staring at her, a little flushed now, but shining-eyed. 'You must be so pleased. I mean, I can see it's horrible being sick, but it won't last, will it, and then—'

'Annabel,' said Elizabeth gently, 'Annabel, my darling, I'm not going to have it.'

'What?' Her eyes, her face, her voice were all shocked. 'What, you mean you're going to have an abortion?'

'Yes. Yes, I am.'

'But you can't. It's so, so wrong. And this is Daddy's baby! What do you think he'd have said? Of course you can't.'

'I'm afraid I can. And I know it's Daddy's baby, but he isn't here, and I have to look after all of us and I can't have it, not possibly.'

'I can't believe I'm hearing this. Mummy, you've got to have it, you've simply got to. You can't kill your baby. It's the one good thing I've heard since – well, since Daddy died. It's lovely.'

'Sweetheart, I really can't. Just think for a bit . . .'

'I am thinking. Thinking of you ripping it out of you, killing it, what's left of Daddy—'

'Annabel, that's hysterical talk.'

'Why? Why is it?'

'Listen,' said Elizabeth patiently, 'I know it would be lovely, if everything else was the same. But it isn't. Daddy's died. I don't have him any more. I can't bring up a baby without his help. Not emotionally, not physically, not financially. It's impossible.'

'It is not impossible. You've got us, we'll help, we'll support you. It'll be wonderful.'

'Annabel, listen to me. You're all growing up.'

'So? We can be more use to you.'

'But my darling, you're going away. And I want you to be free to do what you want. To be with Jamie. Toby's going to university and anyway, can you imagine how he'd feel about it – the embarrassment for him, what would his friends think and say . . .'

'He'd be pretty cruddy if he thought like that,' said Annabel.

'No, he wouldn't. He'd be normal. And Tilly, well . . .'

'Tilly would be fantastic. Especially now she's at home all the time. Think what a lot she could do for you, and her friend Fallon, too; she seems to know all about babies.'

'Tilly is just beginning to grow up, Annabel. She doesn't want to be held back by a mother with a baby. And there's something else. I'm nearly forty-one. There are serious risks to having babies at my age – risks for the baby, that is. It could have all sorts of abnormalities. How would I cope with that? And risks to me, for that matter. It's a strain on any body, never mind a middle-aged one.'

'Oh rubbish!' said Annabel. 'You haven't got a middle-aged body – you look like you're about twenty-five.'

'Not gynaecologically, I don't. I'm sorry, and I would give anything to have spared you all this, but I really am not going to have this baby. I've got a termination booked for Friday and—'

677

'Well, don't expect me to look after you when you come home,' said Annabel. She stood up and glared at her mother. 'I would never have believed this of you. And I'm sure Daddy wouldn't either. I feel – I feel ashamed of you. Really ashamed.'

Lucinda's father was recovering. Slowly but steadily.

'I'm delighted with him,' the doctor told Mrs Worthington when she arrived on the Tuesday morning. 'His speech is returning and he's managed to eat some scrambled egg this morning, hasn't he, Nurse?'

'Yes, Doctor.'

'There's some impairment of movement down his right side, and the hand is decidedly a problem, but with stroke cases, it's the first forty-eight hours that matter. If we get lightening, as we call it, then the auspices are good.'

He patted her hand.

'Well done,' he said rather vaguely and was gone.

Lucinda received this piece of news rather listlessly; she had tried very hard, ever since Blue's departure, to be a good daughter and put her parents' problems first, but it was very difficult. She felt terribly unhappy and dreadfully anxious. Mercifully her mother, who had taken a sleeping pill the night before, hadn't heard anything of the drama and her sister had gone home for the night.

The only reference to Blue by her mother had been an acid comment that he didn't appear to be very interested in her husband's condition; Lucinda ignored this. Her two brothers asked after him and she told them he was away; her sister preferred to ignore Blue's existence altogether.

Which seemed to be what Blue was doing with hers, Lucinda thought sadly; she really didn't know what to do. She had tried ringing him twice and he had simply put the phone down. Steve Durham, when he had finally found her, reported a similar problem, without actually spelling out Blue's words. What was she supposed to do, how could she ever explain? He was hardly going to read a letter if she tried writing one, and certainly not believe what it said.

It was so dreadful and entirely her own fault; the story was so extremely unlikely, and even Steve had urged her to tell Blue what she was planning in good time. She must have been mad, she thought fretfully to herself, pacing up and down her parents' freezing cold house, wondering what she could do and even where she could go. She seemed to spend her life having to find some kind of refuge from her husbands. There were various friends who she knew would take her in; but the story of why she needed the taking in was so convoluted she could hardly even contemplate it.

What on earth was to become of her, she wondered, with a sigh that was a half-sob: divorced, pregnant, cast out by the father of her child, and with no money, no visible means of support. She didn't even have a job any more. She would be a statistic, in one of those *Daily Mail* articles about the complete moral collapse of the country.

Well, she could stay here for a bit, she supposed; it was cold and uncomfortable and her mother was driving her mad already, but it was a roof over her head and food in her stomach, and there was a month before the baby came – although it looked so enormous now she couldn't believe her body could possibly contain it for that long, and certainly not allow it to grow any more. And she certainly had to get back up to London before she had it, for in London stood not only the hospital with the wonderful promise of comfort that was the epidural, but Mrs Parsons and her inspiring and soothing presence.

'Oh Gertie,' she said to the small black and tan Dachshund that was her mother's rather unlikely choice of dog – she always said she was an antidote to Eric's three labradors – 'Gertie, what on earth am I going to do?'

And then she heard the phone ringing, and her mother answering it, and then heard her name being called.

'Lucinda, quickly, dear, come quickly.'

She thought something terrible must have happened, Blue must have taken an overdose or something, but, 'It's Nigel,' her mother said, handing her the phone, smiling at her in a rather arch way. 'He wants to speak to you, as soon as possible. And he asked so nicely about your father, please thank him from me.'

She clearly thought they were going to get together again, Lucinda thought, and that explained Blue's absence. She took

679

the phone and said, 'Hello, Nigel,' and then, as her mother hovered on the stairs, clearly hoping to hear more of a reconciliation, 'I'll take this in Daddy's study.'

'No need for that,' said Mrs Worthington, and went into the kitchen and slammed the door.

'Lucinda, hello. Are you all right?'

'Yes, Nigel, I'm fine. Thank you.'

'Good. Only I gather there's been a bit of a problem . . .'

'With the divorce? Oh Nigel, yes, there has. It's so totally awful, I should have listened to you, should have talked to Blue, told him what we were doing, but I kept putting it off, you know, and now he believes it all, all that rubbish about me feeling insecure and wanting the house and everything; he thinks I meant it and he won't listen to me, won't speak to me, and Steve Durham and I just don't know what to do.'

'Oh dear. Oh Lord,' said Nigel, and she could see him standing there in the hall taking this in, stooping slightly over the telephone table, frowning: and thought how sweet he was.

'I think I'd better go and see him,' Nigel said.

'What?' said Lucinda. 'You? Go and see Blue?'

'Yes, think so.'

'Nigel, you can't. He won't listen to you.'

'I don't see why not. I'm the only person who he will listen to, it seems to me.'

'I wouldn't be too sure,' said Lucinda. 'He's terribly angry with both of us.'

'Well, something's got to be done,' said Nigel. 'I mean, you want to get it settled, don't you, before . . . well, before the end of the month.'

Poor darling, she thought; he couldn't even bear to mention the baby, it hurt him so much.

'Well, yes, and you need the money, but—'

'Then I'll go this evening. Give me the address, Lucinda.'

'He might not be there. He might be out.'

'Well, I'll wait till he gets home.'

'Nigel, you might be waiting all night.'

'I really don't mind,' he said, 'and try not to worry too much, it'll be all right.'

He was such a gentleman, Lucinda thought, putting down the phone.

Blue was sitting down to a very large whisky when there was a knock at the door. He ignored it at first; but at the third time, he got up swearing and went to open it.

'Whatever you're selling—' he said, and stopped short. Nigel Cowper stood there, looking very determined, holding a very battered leather document case. 'Good God,' he said, 'you've got a nerve. Just fuck off, will you.'

'Absolutely not,' said Nigel. 'I need to come in and talk to you.'

'Well, you'll have to go on needing. And if you want her back, you're very welcome. You can tell her that with my compliments.'

'Of course I don't want her back,' said Nigel. 'Well, I do, but she wouldn't come. She doesn't want to be with me. She wants to marry you.'

'Yeah? So much that she feels – what was it? Oh yes, "unsure of our relationship". Wants to keep the house. Like fuck she wants to marry me.'

'There really is no need to be so offensive,' said Nigel. He flushed slightly. 'I've come to explain. Please let me in.'

'Look, mate,' said Blue, 'I don't want anyone here, anyone at all. Least of all you. That is, with the possible exception of your wife. So just piss off to whatever gentlemanly place you spend your evenings, and leave me in peace.'

'I'm not going to,' said Nigel. 'Not until I've explained. Not until you understand. Look, it really isn't how you think.'

'No? How do you work that out then?'

'I'll tell you if you let me in,' said Nigel slightly desperately. Blue opened the door fully and gestured into the living room. 'In there,' he said.

Nigel looked around with great interest; he could see it had all cost a lot of money, but it looked pretty dreadful to him. Deep, deep carpets, flashy chrome furniture, an enormous television, a music centre that filled up half a wall, a large glass coffee-table, a lot of very odd pictures – and not a book in sight. How did Lucinda stand it, what was she doing here? The only sign of her was some rather vulgar curtains and cushions, the sort she liked so much, all frilled and ruched; he had tried to steer her away from that sort of thing himself without success. At least they had – almost – suited the house in Cadogan Square. Here, surrounded by all this modern stuff, they looked appalling. Like a tailored suit, with ruffled revers.

'Very nice,' he said politely.

'Just get on with it,' said Blue.

'Yes. Well, the thing is, and I did tell Lucinda she should have told you this, the whole divorce thing is a – a sort of front.'

'A what? You mean she doesn't want a divorce at all?'

'Yes, of course she does. Very much. But – it's something her lawyer dreamed up. You know I'm dreadfully in hock to Lloyd's . . .'

'I had heard, yes.'

'Well . . .' Nigel tried to explain; about the charitable trust, how he would be one of the major trustees, how the house in Cadogan Square would be made over to Lucinda, mortgage free, and that she'd borrow against that to benefit the trust.

'Could be quite a lot of money. Or she might buy a second property, where I could live, and—'

'All right, all right. I get the drift. So Lloyd's won't be able to get hold of all this money of yours?'

'That's it in a nutshell.'

'Well, I don't know,' said Blue after a pause. 'Doesn't quite wash, to me. You could have done this anyway, couldn't you – set up all these trusts and things, without involving a divorce.'

'Well, no, not at all. The thing about a divorce is that it's legally binding and the case had to at least appear sound. She had to seem as if she really did need the money, that she had a right to it.'

There was a long silence. Blue sat staring at the blank television screen, clearly thinking.

'Right,' he said finally. 'Right, I get it. Very clever.'

'Oh good. So – is that all right then? You're quite clear? No more problem over Lucinda or – or anything.'

'Oh, I don't think I could say that,' said Blue. He looked at Nigel and his almost black eyes were very hard in his white face. 'Of course there's a problem. I'd never have believed it of her, that's the problem. It might not be as bad as I thought, but the fact remains she was prepared to say all that and she never told me about it, just went on plotting and conniving behind my back, with you and that arsehole Durham. Why the fuck couldn't she have talked to me about it?'

'Well, I think she was scared to,' said Nigel, 'quite honestly. Once it had got under way, you know? It was easier to leave it and think she'd tell you – later.'

'Very good of her,' said Blue, 'and how am I supposed ever to trust her now? The fact remains she's a deceitful, conniving little cow and—'

He didn't get any further; Nigel stood up and said, 'I really don't think you should talk about Lucinda like that.'

'Oh really? Would you like to tell me why not, you public-school ponce? I'd have thought you'd feel much the same about her.'

'Could you take that back, please?' said Nigel. He could feel the blood beginning to pound in his head.

'Take what back?'

'What you said about Lucinda. And me, for that matter.'

'I couldn't, actually. No. It was all true. Sorry. Old chap,' he added.

Something snapped in Nigel; the room seemed to have become rather dark, the only light thing in it was Blue Horton, sitting there on the sofa, looking up at him. He bent down, grabbed Blue by the tie and pulled him up to his feet.

'I said, take it back.'

'I can't,' said Blue, 'unfortunately. Like I said, it was true. She *is* a deceitful, conniving little cow and—'

He got no further; Nigel pulled back his fist and hit him very hard, an uppercut to the chin. Blue wasn't expecting it; if he had been, he would probably have ducked. Or fought back. As it was, he staggered backwards, hit his head against the coffee-table and sank, neatly and rather theatrically, onto the ground, his eyes closed. A trickle of blood began to seep down onto the beige carpet.

'Oh my God,' said Nigel, staring down at him. 'Oh my God.'

Chapter 49

November, 1990

Elizabeth walked into the house to the sound of weeping. Please God, don't let it be Annabel, she thought; and God, clearly answering her prayer, led her into the kitchen where Tilly was weeping, as only she could. Tilly had always been a champion weeper; not only did she weep loudly but an enormous amount of wetness was generated, as a waterfall of huge tears appeared and flowed down her cheeks. Annabel was with her, her arm round her; she looked at Elizabeth and her face froze.

'What is it?' said Elizabeth. 'Tilly, darling, whatever is the matter?'

'It's Fallon,' wailed Tilly.

'What about Fallon?' said Elizabeth, fearing that the bullying and the ostracising had finally begun.

But: 'She's so upset,' said Tilly, 'she cried all day; her mum's lost her baby – she's in hospital, she's really poorly, Fallon's there now . . .'

'Oh dear,' said Elizabeth, as calmly as she could. 'I'm so sorry.'

'Yeah, right,' said Annabel, 'you would be,' and walked out of the room.

Elizabeth looked after her and sighed, and then returned her attention to Tilly. 'Darling, don't cry. These things are usually for the best. It's nature's way of dealing with things. Most miscarriages are babies with something wrong with them.'

'No, no, you don't understand,' said Tilly, wiping her eyes. 'It wasn't a miscarriage, Fallon's dad hit her mum – punched her in the stomach, he was so angry about the new baby. How

684

horrible, don't you think? Madison is so afraid she's going to die. I just don't know how anybody could do that, Mummy, hit someone like that, kill a little baby on purpose. It's so, so wrong, don't you think?'

Half an hour later Elizabeth walked into Annabel's bedroom. She looked at her daughter rather awkwardly.

'I've decided to keep the baby,' she said. 'To have it. But you're bloody well going to have to help me, Annabel. I can't do it on my own.'

Annabel stared at her for a while, her face very serious. Then she got up and went over to her mother and put her arms round her.

'You won't have to,' she said, 'I promise.'

'Mummy, I've got to go to London.' Lucinda appeared in the kitchen looking wild-eyed. 'Blue's had a – a – an accident, he's in hospital.'

'What sort of accident?'

'Um, I'm not sure, but he's been hit on the head, been concussed. I'll go there now.'

'But, Lucinda – it's eight o'clock at night. You can't go driving off like that—'

'I've only got to drive up the M4 and it's practically still the rush hour,' said Lucinda. 'Don't be silly, Mummy, I'll be fine. I'll call you later.' And she was gone.

'If only she'd never met that wretched man,' said Mrs Worthington to Gertie.

Nigel was sitting in the Casualty Department of Barts when Lucinda rushed in. 'Where is he? Is there any news?'

'I think he's going to be all right,' said Nigel, 'he's gone for an X-ray. He's concussed. And he lost a fair bit of blood – you know how heads bleed. But – yes, they don't think it's very serious. He'd come round even before the ambulance arrived.'

'Thank goodness,' said Lucinda. 'Will they let me see him?'

'I should think so, when he comes back. They're talking about keeping him in overnight, whatever the X-ray shows.'

'What could it show?' said Lucinda fearfully.

'Well, I don't know. A clot or something. But he doesn't seem too bad; apparently he was swearing like a trooper in the ambulance.'

'He swears like a trooper wherever he is,' said Lucinda, 'but I would say that's a pretty good sign, yes. Oh Nigel, thank you for letting me know so quickly But – how exactly did it happen? I don't understand.'

'I hit him,' said Nigel simply.

Blue was brought back from X-ray about thirty minutes later and wheeled into a cubicle; a doctor and a nurse went in after him and pulled the curtains closed.

'Oh dear,' said Lucinda fretfully, 'it must be bad. I hope he hasn't got brain damage, Nigel. Or—'

'Lucinda, don't. I feel bad enough as it is.'

A nurse came over. 'You're with Mr Horton, I believe,' she said to Nigel.

'Yes, I am.'

'And I'm his – his wife,' said Lucinda. 'Is he all right? Can I see him?'

'I can't give you an answer to either question for a moment,' she said. 'Doctor is looking at the X-rays now. He seems not too bad, if his conversation is anything to go by.'

'Oh dear,' said Lucinda. 'I suppose he's swearing terribly?'

'Just a little.'

'I'm so sorry. How upsetting for you.'

'Oh, I've heard worse,' said the nurse cheerfully. She looked at Lucinda, taking in her condition. 'Er, you say you're his wife? He told us he was unmarried.'

'Well, I nearly am. Or nearly was, I should say,' she added with a sigh. 'Sorry, I'm not making a lot of sense. I've just driven up from the country. Bit tired.'

'Actually, she's *my* wife,' Nigel said. He sounded irritable, almost pompous. The nurse looked at the two of them and visibly gave up.

'When's the baby due?' she asked Lucinda, reverting to safer territory. 'Do you feel OK?'

'Not for another four weeks. Honestly, I'm fine . . . oh goodness, here's the doctor. How is he, Doctor? Is he going to be all right? And can I see him?'

The doctor looked at her rather wearily. 'He's going to be fine. He has a concussion but the bleeding was just from a surface wound. And yes, you can see him. But I don't want to send him home tonight, I'd like to keep him under observation.'

'Yes, of course,' said Lucinda. 'I understand. So – can I go in?'

'Well, if you really want to. I hope he'll be more polite to you than he was to us,' he added.

Lucinda put her head round the curtains. Blue was lying on his back with his eyes closed, a large bandage wound round his head.

'Just piss off, would you?' he said. 'I'm tired, I feel sick and I'm trying to get some bloody sleep. What is it with you people?'

Lucinda went over to him, picked up one of his hands and looked down at him. 'I'll piss off in a minute,' she said gently. 'I just wanted to make sure you were alive first.'

He turned to look at her. 'My God,' he said. 'Lucinda.'

'That's me. Glad you recognised me.'

'Of course I recognised you, you silly cow. I'm not in a fucking coma, although you'd think I was, the way they've been carrying on.'

'Blue, they're just trying to help, to look after you.'

'Yeah, yeah. They'd do it better by leaving me alone. Christ, my head hurts.' He closed his eyes again. 'That husband of yours can pack a bloody punch. Couldn't believe it.'

There was a note in his voice she couldn't at first analyse; then she realised what it was. Admiration.

'He learned to box at Eton,' she said. 'People are always surprised.'

Blue opened his eyes and looked at her rather hazily; then he half-smiled. 'Don't spoil it, Lucinda. I was just coming round to thinking he wasn't quite the idiot I'd thought.'

'Sorry. And – well, what were you thinking? I mean, do you – think about me? If anything?' she said, and she was so frightened she could literally hardly speak. And then the words came out in a rush, and she stood there, the tears running down her face, still holding his hand – at least he hadn't snatched it away from her. 'Blue, I'm so sorry, I know Nigel's tried to explain and I know how wrong of me it was not to tell you, but I do love you so, so much, I wouldn't have hurt you for the world, you must believe that, I'm just stupid, stupid and – thoughtless, and—'

'Just shut up, for Christ's sake,' he said, 'you silly cow.'

'Yes, all right,' she said humbly, 'but Blue, I really, really did—'

'I said shut, up.' And then he opened his eyes again, and looked at her very seriously, and she was afraid he was going to tell her to go away again. But: 'It's all right, Lucinda,' he said quite gently, 'I'll get over it in time. In time for the boy to be born, I daresay. How is he, by the way?' And he reached out and moved his hand tenderly over her stomach.

'He's fine. Oh Blue, darling Blue, I'm so, so relieved and thankful and—'

'I tell you something,' he said, and there was a new expression in his eyes as he looked at her, that she would have said came close to respect, 'that scheme you dreamed up between you. Bloody clever. Specially that stuff about the art gallery. Wouldn't have thought it of you, Lucinda. I'm well impressed, I can tell you that.'

'Impressed! Blue, I can't take any credit for it, you know, any at all . . .'

'Course you can,' he said. 'You're obviously not quite as feather-brained as I thought you were. Now give your old man a kiss . . .'

She bent down to kiss him and he kissed her back, quite thoroughly; he couldn't be too bad, she thought, if he could do that, his reflexes must be pretty all right . . .

The curtains were pulled back and the nurse's voice said, 'Mr Horton—'

'Just fuck off, would you?' said Blue.

Nigel accompanied Lucinda home. 'I think I should, the house is in a bit of a mess – it might upset you.'

'Crikey,' she said, looking at the scene – the blood on the carpet, an upturned chair, the heap of magazines on the coffee-table tipped onto the floor. 'It looks like robbery with violence. Oh Nigel, you are an angel. But I still don't understand, why did you hit him?'

'He insulted you,' said Nigel. His tone was mildly outraged again.

'Nigel! You know what?'

'What?'

'You really are a complete gentleman. And I didn't deserve you.'

'Oh, I don't know about that,' said Nigel.

Catherine had come up to London to see her solicitor and to do some early Christmas shopping. Her children, who seemed increasingly able to manage without her altogether, had been invited to stay with friends for the night; and she had twenty-four hours' glorious freedom. She phoned Lucinda to see if she could meet her at some point, only to be told that Blue was in hospital.

'He got knocked out,' Lucinda said, her voice shaky. 'I'll explain later. You couldn't come over, Catherine, could you? I'm a bit tired, and I'd love to see you.'

Catherine said she'd come straight away.

Lucinda was looking extremely tired; hardly surprising, Catherine thought, considering what she'd been through: her father's stroke, some row with Blue – she didn't expand on that – and a late-night spell in Casualty at Barts.

'But Nigel was so sweet, he looked after me. And he's been trying to clean up the carpet. He'll actually be back in a minute – he's just gone to return some machine he hired.'

'Nigel!' said Catherine.

'Yes. Goodness, you might as well know, he and Blue had a fight last night, and he knocked Blue out. Only don't say anything when he comes back, will you?'

'Of – of course not,' said Catherine. If Lucinda had told her Nigel had opened a gay strip-joint she could scarcely have been more surprised. 'He knocked Blue out?'

'Yes.'

'But why? I don't understand.'

'Oh, so silly. Blue said something Nigel didn't like about me and – oh, here he is now. Nigel, darling, You remember Catherine, don't you?'

'Of course I do,' said Nigel. He smiled at Catherine. 'In fact, we shared a very racy dining experience didn't we?'

'Yes, we did,' said Catherine. She was still trying to come to terms with the thought of gentle, vague Nigel knocking anybody out. Let alone Blue. He must be still very much in love with Lucinda, she thought, and felt a pang of sadness.

'Oh, did you?' said Lucinda. 'How lovely. Now let's all have some coffee and then I'm going to have to love you and leave you; the hospital just phoned and said I could go and collect Blue. I'm not sure I relish nursing him, but still . . . no choice, I'm afraid.'

'So how's country life?' asked Nigel as Lucinda disappeared into the kitchen.

'Lovely,' said Catherine, and then, 'Well, all right. Well, pretty awful, actually.'

'I'm sorry. That's a lovely part of the world.'

'It is, yes. But the people a bit less so. Specially the ones I live with.'

'Ah. Think I can imagine. Yes. Children like it?'

'They absolutely love it,' said Catherine.

'Well, that's the main thing. I mean, that's why you went, after all.'

'Yes. Indeed.'

'Good. Excellent. And children should live in the country, don't you think?'

'I suppose so,' said Catherine with a sigh.

Lucinda came back with the coffee-pot; she set it down on the glass coffee-table.

'The carpet does look miles better, Nigel,' she said. 'Well done.'

'That's all right. Least I could do.'

Catherine suddenly felt as if she was going to cry. She stood up abruptly; knocked the coffee-table, and the contents of the jug went all over the newly cleaned carpet. And although Lucinda and Nigel were both absolutely sweet about it, and Lucinda said she couldn't mind less, it was nothing compared to what might have happened, and Nigel said that there was plenty of carpet shampoo left, so it couldn't have been more convenient, as she drove away, she did start to cry and she was still very weepy as she joined the Westway, wondering what it must feel like to be Lucinda, who had two men in love with her and literally fighting over her, and trying not to mind too much that she was returning to her Jane Eyre existence. With not a single Mr Rochester anywhere in sight.

It would have been over now, Elizabeth thought, sitting toying with a piece of dry toast; she wouldn't have been pregnant any more, wouldn't be feeling sick, she'd have been on her way to feeling better.

All the good things that had resulted from her decision, Annabel's relief and happiness, Tilly's pink-faced delight, even Sarah, her gynaecologist's quiet, 'I do think that's wise,' were over now and she was facing the reality: of having a baby as a widow, of coping with it all on her own, of having no one to share it with – well, of course she did have the children, and that was lovely, and Annabel had been incredibly sweet, had even offered to cancel her trip to Boston. 'No need for that,' Tilly had said, clinging to her mother's hand. 'I'll look after Mummy. She'll be all right with me.'

But there would be no Simon to share the weariness, the anxiety, the trauma of the tests – like the amniocentesis she had insisted on, and even explained to the children and what it could mean; the discomfort of the later months, the labour; and then, worst of all, no Simon to share the joy with. It all seemed once again, and as she had known it would do, far too much to bear.

She had taken Peter Hargreaves into her confidence; he had rather surprisingly flushed and said how delighted he was for her, how wonderful that she would have this comfort. Comfort! this exhaustion, this loneliness, this struggle. But she managed to smile back and thank him.

'So – are you really all right to go on working?' he had said, and, 'Yes,' she told him, 'of course I'll be fine.'

'Well, you must let me know if you're not. Immediately. I'll do everything I can to help.'

'Thank you, Peter, I appreciate that. But I won't let you down.'

She hadn't told Toby yet; she was waiting till he came home next, rather than inform him over the phone or in a letter. It was difficult news for a sixteen-year-old boy, coping with his own raging hormones; he would be embarrassed, possibly shocked, and he would find it difficult to tell his friends. But he wouldn't be home for a couple of weeks. Which gave her time to rehearse it.

She really, really didn't want this baby: still. It was a burden, a brake on her recovery, and indeed on her. She didn't sit staring dreamily at her stomach as she had with the others, thinking how miraculous it all was; she sat thinking with foreboding how hard she would find it to cope with, to live with. She had changed her mind only because of the girls; because she could see that for them it would be dreadfully hurtful to think of their mother terminating a pregnancy, a pregnancy that would have resulted in a new sibling, the last legacy of their father. And it was going to take all her love for them to get her through it without resentment. She knew that maternal love was often labelled unconditional; the bearing of this child came very close to straining that. But – she could do it; and she would do it.

She suddenly stood up, experiencing a rather unfamiliar sensation; a shot of energy. Perhaps she was finally going to start feeling better. For a while at least.

She mustn't waste it; she would make a start on the sorting for the move; go through each room methodically, making lists, deciding what to take and what to sell, what furniture was clearly unsuitable for any house smaller than this one; perhaps just begin to have a look at Simon's clothes. His study, sorting that out, seemed to her beyond endurance; the desk was more or less untouched, still covered with bits of paper, lists, his diary; she hadn't even looked properly at his last emails, she felt she would be somehow sending yet more of him away if she disposed of any of it; it was so intensely personal, that room, and he was still sitting there, chatting, laughing, making arrangements, making a mess. Her own study in the house, crisply neat and ordered, had none of the charm of Simon's; where every inch of wall, every millimetre of surface was covered: in photographs, framed certificates, pictures the children had done, things they had made, postcards from friends from particularly interesting places. Old press cuttings, landmark invitations, other mementoes were pinned onto a huge cork board, several layers deep, letters and cards were piled high on the desk, together with jars of pencils and pens, three clocks all set at different times – one was London – she couldn't now remember the significance of the other two – two Filofax diaries, one desk-sized, one smaller: those she had looked at, fearing a blank, but they were reassuringly full of appointments weeks ahead of his death. The rest she hadn't even touched; she couldn't bear to disturb it.

But she could make a start on the rest ... Elizabeth had always had a rather quirky fondness for taking herself by surprise, as she put it; for getting disagreeable jobs done on the spur of the moment. This seemed to be exactly that occasion.

Two hours later, she was feeling very pleased with herself, having listed all the drawing-room furniture that must go, all the dining-room furniture – including the truly beautiful Queen Anne table that seated at least fourteen; that would be horrible, seeing that and all the dazzling dinner parties they had held round it consigned to history – and the things in the front hall. And then, as she stood at the bottom of the stairs, looking up, thinking she had earned a little lie-down, she suddenly felt that yes, she would start – just start – on his dressing room. It had to be done, it wasn't going to sort itself; nobody else could do it – it couldn't be so terribly bad, could it? And taking a deep breath, she walked up the stairs and into it. That in itself was hard: but she did it.

She started pulling down the suits, one by one: and of course it was terribly bad, for they exuded him, every one of them; she could see him in them, feel him in them, his dinner jacket smelled still, albeit slightly, of cigar smoke; some of his jackets even had stray hairs on the shoulders, and she sank onto the ground weeping, clutching them, longing for him as she would never have thought possible, longing for him to hold her, to talk to her, to smile at her, to tell her how lovely she looked, how good she felt, how much he loved her.

And after weeping, the now-familiar anger came back, and she stood up, dragging the other suits off their hangers now, raging at him for daring to die, for taking himself away from her, leaving her alone with this new, unwelcome burden; and as she reached and pulled and hurled them onto the ground, she suddenly realised there was a dull but unmistakable pain, stabbing deep within her, not constant, but spasmodic: and realised at once also what it meant. She was having a miscarriage.

Chapter 50

November, 1990

'Darling, I want to talk to you.' Florian handed Annabel her *pain au chocolat*. 'Properly, I mean. Can you come for a drink tonight?'

'Yes, of course. Sounds very serious. Have I done something naughty?'

'Sadly not, I fear. No, rather the reverse. I got you a *Daily Mirror* as well. Such a good paper, has the real news in, not all this nonsense about Maggie going or not going. I'm bored with that already, aren't you? And if she does go, at least we won't have to look at the bouffant any more. Although Hezza's got a fair old bouffant himself.'

'Florian, you're obsessed. Anyway, thanks for the pastry. And yes, tonight'll be fine.'

'How's your mum?'

'She's much better, thank you.' She hadn't told him about the baby yet; it was too soon, they were all still adjusting to it; her mother hadn't even told Toby.

'Right,' he said, as they settled into corner seats at the Royal Court bar. 'I've got some news. Very, very exciting news.'

'You've got a new girlfriend?'

'Nope.'

'You've got a new flat?'

'Nope. You're hopeless. You reduce everything to the personal, Annabel. This is about the real me, the professional me.'

'I didn't know that was the real you. OK. Miki's promoting you?'

'No. Better than that. No, darling, I'm going to set up on my own.'

695

'You're not!' She stared at him. 'Goodness. How exciting. How brave.'

'Indeed. And what a good name. *Florian*. I can see it now, can't you, in lovely Art Nouveau lettering over the door.'

'Where will the door be?'

'Oh, Fulham Road. Much cheaper than the West End, but up and coming faster than a schoolboy in a brothel.'

'Florian, that's so wonderful. How on earth did you get the money?'

'In the most boring way imaginable. I'd love to tell you it was a rich sugar mummy or something, but actually it was a merchant bank. With a small slug from me – some money my grandpa left.'

'Your grandpa!'

'Yes, I told you about him, he was the stockbroker.'

'Florian, you are such an old fraud. I heard you only the other day, banging on again about growing up on a council estate.'

'I know, I know, but the Home Counties are so bad for my image.'

'Well, anyway, I am just so impressed. Truly. So – when is all this going to happen?'

'In the New Year, I hope. Miki's been quite good about it; of course, I'm not allowed to breathe a word to the clients, or he'd have me for enticement faster than you could say blow job – I mean blow dry. Lot of work needed on the place, of course. Painting, all that stuff.'

'I'll help. It's the least I can do, after all you've done for me. But oh, Florian, I shall miss you.'

'Sweet of you. To offer to help, I mean. But if I have my way, you're not going to miss me. I want you to join me. Come as one of my stylists.'

'Me!'

Florian looked around. 'I don't see anyone else who I'd be asking. Yes, my darling, you. This is going to be a young, groovy place. I want young, groovy people. I think you'll just about qualify. Just.'

'Oh my God! Goodness. How absolutely amazing.'

'So . . . what do you say? Can I persuade you?'

'Don't be ridiculous. Of course you can. I'm over the moon.

It sounds fantastic. I'd love it, absolutely love it. Thank you so, so much.'

'My pleasure. Good, that's settled then. Miki won't like it, but there's nothing he can do. You're still only a junior. But under me, you'll become a star stylist – provided you do exactly what I say, of course. I wasn't too impressed with that cut you did last week on model night. Were you actually aiming for the freshly sheared look?'

'Oh shut up,' said Annabel. She knew it had been a good cut, Miki himself had said so. She was good at cutting, she knew; could somehow see a very clear shape carved out while the actual hair hung tangled and tousled in front of her. Before she had begun to work on it, could see how it could change a face and why. It seemed to her the most interesting part of hairdressing; even more than colour. Colour was fun, but less demanding somehow; except with the most avant garde clients, it was just highlights or roots or certainly at her level. She was due to qualify as a fully-fledged junior stylist in December; in a less starry salon it would have happened already, she knew.

'That's no way to speak to your boss,' said Florian. 'Anyway, give it a year or two, and we'll have Cool London fighting to get in the door. I think we should celebrate, don't you? Champagne?'

She sat sipping the champagne, feeling quite dizzy with excitement. A stylist! In a brand new salon that would undoubtedly get loads of publicity, Florian's contacts with the press were impressive. It would be absolutely fantastic. And he actually wanted her to join him, thought she was good enough.

She felt quite different suddenly, rather cool and very confident and grown-up. A success. Or a success-to-be. She had no doubt about it. It was hers for the taking. How pleased and proud her mother would be. And as for Jamie . . . And then found herself, as she did at the most unexpected times, weeping. Because her father too would have been pleased and proud. But she couldn't tell him. And she wanted to, so, so much.

She wasn't bleeding – well, hardly. Just a few spots. But the pain was still there; quite insistent, tugging away.

So – what should she do? Carry on with the sorting, with

697

lugging suits off hangers, cursing Simon the while? Or go and lie down and ring the doctor? She'd made this decision once; it wasn't fair.

Dr Rice, who had looked after the family for years, said he would come at once. 'Just go to bed and stay there. Put the door on the latch first, so you don't have to come downstairs to let me in. Any bleeding?'

'Only a bit. A tiny bit.'

'Good. I'll be there in about half an hour.'

She was actually in bed. Lying down, and staying there. And fearfully checking the bleeding, every few minutes. She felt rather near to tears and wished Annabel was there.

This wasn't fair. It really wasn't. And she'd only been sorting out Simon's suits, for God's sake. Not heaving stuff up and downstairs. Oh God, here came another pain. But – was it a bit less strong? It certainly wasn't any worse. And the doctor would be here soon and he'd give her a hormone injection which would hopefully stop the contractions. Which is what the pains were. Elizabeth knew all about threatened miscarriages; she'd had one with Tilly. And there was Tilly, alive and kicking, all thirteen years of her. She'd also had an actual miscarriage, of course. After Toby. But then she'd been doing all sorts of crazy things, flying to Canada for a conference, working round the clock . . . Simon hadn't actually said it served her right, but she had known it did.

She lay back, taking deep breaths, trying to relax. Come on, Dr Rice, what are you doing?

He arrived about ten minutes later, came running up the stairs.

'Hello, Elizabeth. How are you? I had no idea you were pregnant – you should have told me.'

'I know. I only saw my gynaecologist last week, what with everything, you know . . .'

'Of course. I can imagine. Very, very difficult for you. I'm so sorry, my dear. It can't be helping, however welcome in the long run. And how do you feel?'

'Awful,' said Elizabeth. 'Really awful, sicker than I ever was with the others.'

'What a shame. And now . . .?'

'Not too bad. Bit anxious.'

'What were you doing,' he asked, picking up her wrist, taking her pulse, 'when it started?'

'Oh, nothing much. Just – sorting out – sorting out . . .' She felt the sobs beginning to rise, crushed them, bit her lip. 'Just sorting out Simon's clothes, actually. And deciding what furniture to sell. The house is on the market, you see.'

'Elizabeth! Not very sensible.'

'I know, but—'

'You should be taking things easy. Especially at this stage. You know that.'

'Yes, but there's so much to do.'

'I daresay there is, but you must get other people to help you. It's essential. You want to keep this baby, don't you?'

'Yes,' she said, 'yes, of course I do.'

And realised in that moment that it was true. She did want to keep it, terribly badly.

Richard didn't come to Wales for the weekend. He phoned on Saturday morning and said it was essential he stayed at school. Morag had asked him to completely overhaul the timetable-ing for the second half of the term, a parent wanted to consult him about his son's chances in Common Entrance, another about some alleged bullying . . . There was no way he could suddenly disappear for two days, he told Debbie.

'It would lay too big a burden on Morag. She's absolutely exhausted, she needs my input and support . . .'

A few months earlier, Debbie would have argued, told him that his own family was just as important as the school, and that she needed his input and support as much as Morag. Things being what they were, she heaved a sigh of relief, said of course she understood, and then had to spend half an hour comforting the children, who all burst into tears. And if they cried because they weren't going to see him for a weekend, what hope for— Stop it, Debbie, don't. It's too soon to think like that.

Flora knew she must ring Colin, get it over; he had worked so hard on her behalf, was even risking his professional reputation, to a degree. She had wasted a lot of his time and possibly lost his goodwill. And – and she would still lose the house, even without his scheme. She couldn't really win either way.

She knew Debbie had been right: but the temptation lingered.

And then, the morning after Debbie and the children had gone, she woke early. It was a beautiful morning; the dawn was breaking over a frosty landscape, the grey slowly giving way to brilliant blue, sharp green. She stood at the window, staring across her meadow at the perfect view, at the cliffs, the great stretch of beach in both directions, the sea summer-blue. It was a totally unique view, 180 degrees of perfection. It was one of the main reasons she had bought the meadow; she had actually been buying the view. It was engraved on her heart, that view, an integral part of her life; she had always rather fancied the idea of dying at the dining-room window, dying happily, gazing at it.

And as she stood there, sipping her tea, she realised afresh that she could never bear to betray it, to give her signature – for that was what she was doing in essence – to three neat, four-bedroomed, three-bathroomed (two ensuite), centrally heated homes, with integral garages and perfectly square little gardens with perfectly mown grass, the waist-high flowers of summer ruthlessly crushed beneath strips of bright green turf.

This view would be changed, hopelessly for ever, it would become polite, manicured, parcelled up, and the occupants of the executive homes would only get a part of its glory. And would they care? Would they appreciate it? Would they look at it and see a storm coming, or the surf rolling in, or would they just think it was pretty and get on with mowing their lawns?

She stood there for a long time, thinking; until the tea was cold and some streaks of cloud had covered the sun, and at the end of it, it was really quite simple. She couldn't do it, couldn't betray it; it was impossible. She would sell the house because she had to, but to someone who would love it and care for it, and enjoy the meadow, and leave the buildings derelict and overgrown. She went into the hall and picked up the phone, so that she could tell Colin as soon as possible. She owed him that at least.

He was more upset than she had thought he would be, clearly found her explanation unsatisfactory.

'Of course, you must do what you think best, Flora. But

I imagined you had thought it all through a little more clearly.'

'Well, I have tried, of course. But . . . well, I'm sorry, Colin. I'm afraid I must have wasted a lot of your time.'

'Never mind about that,' he said, making it obvious that he felt she had. 'These things happen. I do hope you won't regret this, Flora. I mean, you're going to lose your house anyway, aren't you?'

'Yes,' she said, 'yes, I realise that, of course. But – well, Colin, there are just some things that one can't quite come to terms with. I'm sure it's happened to you?'

'Of course,' he said, and his voice was very cool. 'Right, I'll cancel the whole project then. If you're sure.'

'I am,' she said. 'Quite sure.' And put the phone down thinking that a degree of male pride had been injured, as well as time lost. She hoped he would forgive her. She would miss him if not. Well, miss their outings, at least.

'Mummy! Mummy, where are you?'

It was Annabel. Elizabeth called to her, 'Up here, darling. In my room.'

'I'll bring some tea.'

'OK.' She sat up, nervous even of doing that, blew her nose, hoped her face wasn't too ravaged. She had been crying again.

Annabel came in with two mugs of tea. 'Mummy, what are you doing in bed? Are you all right? What—'

'I hope so,' said Elizabeth carefully. 'I – think so.'

'Why? What's happened?'

'I – well, I've got a bit of a tummy ache. Doctor Rice came – he thinks it'll probably be all right; anyway, he sent me to bed.'

'You mean, you might be having a – a miscarriage? Oh no! Oh Mummy, does it hurt? What can I do? Shouldn't you be in hospital—'

'No, of course I shouldn't. Doctor Rice has given me a lovely hormone injection, which should make everything all right. I just have to stay here and rest completely for a few days . . .'

'Yes, I'll do everything, I promise.'

'And it really doesn't hurt – much. Hardly at all. In fact, it's getting better already, and I'm only bleeding a bit.' She hoped that was true, it had actually been increasing a bit, but then she had with Tilly, quite a lot, and . . .

'Oh God! Oh, if only I'd been here. What were you doing, for goodness sake?'

'Nothing. Honestly. Just making lists and things. About the furniture, what's got to go and all that sort of thing. Nothing stupid. I mean, I wasn't doing aerobics or anything. And the doctor is coming back later, to check me and . . . What are you doing, Annabel? Who are you ringing?'

'Florian,' said Annabel. She was pale and obviously anxious, but determinedly calm. 'To tell him I can't come out tonight.'

'Oh now, Annabel, that's ridiculous. I've only got to stay here in bed. I don't need nursing. I've got the phone, I'll be fine.'

'Mummy,' said Annabel, 'just shut up. I'm not going out. I want to stay here and make sure you're OK. It's only a stupid party, for God's sake. I don't even really want to go.'

'Well, all right. If you're sure,' said Elizabeth.

'I'm sure. Tilly won't be back till later, she and Fallon are going to the cinema. So just lie back and don't argue. Now I'm going to find you some more pillows, you don't look very comfortable.'

Elizabeth lay back, her eyes filling with tears, as she looked after Annabel. This was exactly what she hadn't wanted, this was exactly why she hadn't wanted the baby, the children's lives disrupted, *her* working life disrupted – for she clearly couldn't do a major presentation on Monday now, at very best she had to go and have a scan done, Dr Rice had said – being anxious and frightened as well as grieving. But it was all happening anyway; there was nothing she could do about it. And somehow, she could see quite clearly now, it would be worth it.

'You'd better hang on in there,' she said sternly in the direction of her stomach. 'I need you.'

And felt another twinge, more painful than the last, and wondered how she would bear it if she lost this baby now.

702

Chapter 51

November, 1990

The Sunday papers were full of it: impending drama, tragedy even, of crises and conspiracies, of stalking horses and wrestles for power. Elizabeth, lying free from pain but still anxious, still bleeding a little, read of the unthinkable, the almost unimaginable eventuality of the departure of Margaret Thatcher from the leadership of the Conservative Party and, even more unimaginably, at the instigation of someone other than herself.

Heseltine was on every front page, looking more handsome, more grim-faced, more filled with political gravitas in each one; he had written an open letter saying that Geoffrey Howe's departure from the Cabinet was potentially a crisis – and by implication that something very radical needed to be done. A great many bandwagons were being mounted, and a great many quotes given, largely by sources close to Mr Howe and Mr Heseltine. Some papers were lining up alternative leaders, all of them were examining Mrs Thatcher's achievements or lack of them, according to their politics.

It was all wonderfully distracting.

Joel, who had missed Debbie more than he would have believed possible, was quite relieved when Hugh Renwick phoned him halfway through the morning and asked him to do a piece for Monday's paper on the financial implications of Mrs Thatcher's possible departure.

'A lot of it's to do with finance, after all: Lawson's resignation last year, John Major no great shakes, terrible state of the economy, everyone going bust, negative equity, all that crap – and you could drag Heseltine's opposition to the Community

Charge into it as well. About fifteen hundred words, OK? Sorry about your Sunday.'

'It's fine.' It would give him something to do, something else to think about.

Until he had her back again.

'Blimey,' said Blue, 'I wonder if the old girl's finally going?'

'What old girl?' said Lucinda. 'More coffee?'

'Yes, please. Maggie. Could be on her way out.'

'Mrs Thatcher! Of course not. She'll leave Downing Street feet first.'

'Not so sure. They seem to be out to get her. Heseltine and that mob.'

'I rather like Michael Heseltine,' said Lucinda. 'He's awfully handsome.'

'Not a very good qualification for Prime Minister. Mind you, I always admired him, ever since he told her what for about Westland.'

'Did he?' said Lucinda vaguely.

'Yes, Anyway, there's more to him than that drip Major. Waste of space he is, in my view.'

'Is he?'

'Yeah. Christ. This country's in a right old mess at the moment . . .'

'Is it? Blue, I've been thinking. About Nigel.'

'Oh yeah? Got some new way of giving him even more money?'

'No. Something better than money.'

'Not much that's better than money, Lucy. What were you thinking of?'

'Love. All that sort of thing.'

'Look, I've been very magnanimous so far about this whole thing,' said Blue, 'but I don't want to hear any more about poor darling Nigel and how much you feel you want to help – OK?'

'Not *me* helping him, Blue. Not in that way, anyway. No. Catherine.'

'Catherine! What – the plain one?'

'She is not plain,' said Lucinda firmly, 'and I think she and Nigel could be rather good together. Don't you? They're both lonely, both in need of someone. What do you think?'

'You'll have to give me a bit of time to digest that, Lucinda. Blimey, my head hurts.'

'Shall I get you some more painkillers?'

'No, thanks. I've got something better than painkillers in mind. Come over here, give your old man a kiss.'

Lucinda was glad he felt better enough to contemplate sex; she only wished she did. Still, she had a lot of making up to him to do . . .

Catherine was sitting in her room, reading the paper; she wasn't sure how she felt about Mrs Thatcher's apparently imminent political demise. Comparatively liberal for her modestly suburban background, and indeed having been a socialist in her extreme youth, she had greatly disapproved of the market-driven, greed culture that Mrs Thatcher had supposedly created; but Frederick had been a great admirer, saying that she had made it possible to run an efficient business once more in the UK. Catherine had been born in the fifties, grown up in the hippy seventies, and been at her happiest in the eighties married to her successful husband. She had been perfectly happy to accept his judgement in all things, Thatcherism included; forced now to think for herself once more, she felt confused. Confused altogether, she thought, the treacherous tears threatening again; her life was one huge confusion, confusion and mess, and what was to become of her, alone and disregarded in this horrible house with these awful people and a complete lack of social life of any sort? She was like one of those Hindu women, forced to climb onto the funeral pyres of their husbands, their lives considered completely over.

'Mummy!'

'Yes, Caroline?'

'It's Jane-Anne's mummy. She wants me to go over for lunch. Can I, Mummy, please, please.'

Freddie was out for the day, working with Hutchings on their stamp collections; another endless lonely day stretched before her, the only chance of relief being fatty lamb – or overdone beef – with Phyllis and Dudley. It wasn't fair, it just—

'Yes, of course, darling. I'll come and speak to her.'

And climbing another inch up onto her notional funeral pyre she accepted the invitation for Caroline and pulled on her jeans, preparatory to driving her daughter over to the Honourable Jane-Annes.

Elizabeth was finding it very hard to concentrate on anything except what might be going on inside her – and what would be revealed the following morning when she went to have her scan.

'Toby just rang,' said Annabel, coming in with yet more tea.

'Toby? I thought he was killing things with his friend.'

'Yes, he was. But he's decided to come home tomorrow, for a day or two. Before he goes back to Eton. You haven't told him yet, have you?'

'No, of course not. I'm sure he'll be horrified.'

'Mum! Why ever?'

'Use your brain,' said Elizabeth briskly. 'I'm absolutely dreading his reaction.'

'Well, don't,' said Annabel. 'I'll deal with him. Promise.'

'Mrs Morgan?'

'Yes?' Catherine could see that Phyllis was hanging about in the hall, pretending to be sorting through the post; she turned her back on her, spoke into the wall, hoped her mother-in-law would take the hint. She didn't.

'Mrs Morgan, I do hope you don't mind my telephoning you.'

'No. No, of course not.' Mind? Being called by a man – a man who wasn't Dudley or one of the children's teachers – why should she mind, for heaven's sake? It was wonderful, the most exciting thing that had happened to her for months.

'We met last week, at the point-to-point. You were there with the Prices. Patrick Fisher . . .'

'Yes, I remember you, of course.'

'Good, good. Jolly day, wasn't it?'

It had been quite jolly. It had also been very cold and wet, and inevitably muddy, and her hands had been so frozen she'd dropped the mug of tea Mrs Jane-Anne had handed her, but they'd been so nice to her, both of them, and it had been quite interesting, watching the races, following the Prices as they

706

charged about in the mud, and certainly good to see Caroline so happy; at one point she had turned to her, radiant as the rain poured down her small face, and said, 'This is such fun,' and – well, compared to spending the day with Dudley and Phyllis, yes, it had been jolly. She remembered Patrick Fisher too; he'd been about fifty, jolly himself, a bit overweight with a rather red face, sitting on his shooting stick, dressed in a Barbour so old it was shiny and a checked cap on his head, the caricature of an English country gentleman.

She hauled herself back to the present. 'It was terrific fun, yes.'

'I'm having a few people over for drinks next Saturday evening, wondered if you'd like to come. Nothing too special, but it'd be good to see you. I remember you saying you hadn't met many people down here yet . . .'

If Phyllis hadn't still been hovering in the hall, Catherine would have sunk onto her knees there and then and offered up a prayer of thanksgiving. As it was she said, as coolly as she could manage, 'That would be lovely, thank you so much.'

'Good, good. Now I know you've been living in London, so you may find us rather boring . . .'

'Of course I won't,' said Catherine, thinking of the endless evenings alone in Fulham; he clearly saw her spending her time at one dazzling party after another.

'Hope not. Jolly good. About six. Now then, address is Musgrove Hall, Upton Stratton. I think you're quite near Gillingham, so you take the road to . . .'

She hardly heard what he said; she could find out later. She just stood there, listening to this angelic creature, actually issuing an invitation, not to her children but to her, a proper grown-up invitation.

Phyllis was clearly very put out. Catherine had to tell her, because she had to know if she could leave the children at home on Saturday evening.

'Yes, we will be in. You're going to drinks with Patrick Fisher? Well, I hope you enjoy it. He's very eccentric, of course.'

'Is he?'

'Well yes. Never married. I mean, there are stories . . . well, never mind.'

Catherine didn't ask about the stories, although Phyllis was clearly dying to share them.

'He seemed very nice,' she said. 'I met him at that point-to-point that the Prices took Caroline and me to last week, do you remember?'

'Yes, of course,' said Phyllis crossly. She had found the Honourable Prices inviting Catherine as well as Caroline to join them at the point-to-point almost intolerable.

'So, is it a nice house?' Catherine went on. 'What's it called – Musgrove . . .'

'Musgrove Hall,' said Phyllis more crossly still. 'Yes, it's very nice, I suppose – if you like that sort of thing. Freezing cold, of course, stone floors and so on, and the one time *we* went there, it looked as if it needed a jolly good clean to me.'

Why did they have to talk like that, Elizabeth wondered. Why? As if you were in some way mentally defective. Why couldn't they just say, 'Wait over there,' instead of, 'If you could just go over there for me,' or, 'Please put this on,' instead of 'Now could you just pop into this gown.' Always accompanied by that painfully bright smile.

It just made everything worse. And worse – rather than better – was what she was expecting. She felt better, for a start: that in itself was worrying. If she was still pregnant, why didn't she feel sick? She was still bleeding – only a tiny bit, but it was going on. And—

'Mrs Beaumont, would you like to come in now? Sorry about the designer outfit.'

She stood up. 'The what?'

'The robe. Not exactly Chanel, is it?'

'Mum,' hissed Annabel. 'Don't look so cross.' She had insisted on taking the morning off to come to the hospital. She said she didn't give a shit if Miki was annoyed or not. 'You're much more important. Don't argue.'

'Now, Mrs Beaumont, if you could just pop onto the bed for me, that's right, lovely. How are you feeling?' The nurse had an Australian accent; for some reason, it made things much worse.

'Fine, thank you.'

'That's great. What we like to hear. Now, I'm just going to rub this jelly stuff on your tummy – sorry, it's so cold. All right?'

'Yes, thank you. Fine.' What did she think, silly cow? That she was going to pass out with the shock of a bit of cold jelly?

'There. Not too bad, I hope. Now, have you had a scan before?'

'No, I haven't. They hadn't been invented when I had my other children.'

'And do you know how they work?'

'I – think so.'

'Right, well, I'll explain. This contraption here,' she waved what looked rather like a microphone at Elizabeth, 'is called a transducer, and not to get too technical, it emits and receives sound waves. Which convert into a two-dimensional image of whatever we want to see. In this case, your baby. So I'm just going to start now. If you look at that screen, Mrs Beaumont, you can see for yourself what's going on in your uterus. Now you are . . . let's see . . . nearly thirteen weeks, so Junior is about seven, maybe eight centimetres long, and you know he's in a kind of little watery sac—'

'I do, yes, thank you,' said Elizabeth. 'I do have three children already.'

'Three! Well, isn't that lovely. Girls or boys?'

'One boy, two girls.'

'How old are they?'

'They're all teenagers.'

'Teenagers? You don't look old enough to be the mother of teenagers.'

Smile, Elizabeth, come on, make an effort, she's very nice really.

'They must be so thrilled about this. Now, he's bobbing around in there . . . where is he? Can't see him. He must be playing hide and seek . . .'

She couldn't see him, silly bitch, because he – or she – wasn't there. He'd left her, dissatisfied with the accommodation, with the negative vibes she'd been sending down to him all these weeks. She clenched her fists.

'Right. Well, no luck that side, let's have a look over here . . . there's one of your ovaries, see, and there's the other one . . . come on, little feller, where are you?'

Elizabeth thought she might scream. No, more than that, she had to scream. She couldn't lie here, listening to this drivel, feeling so terrified and so despairing, any longer. She would just – just count to ten very slowly and then scream. She shut her eyes; the radiographer, silent now, was moving the transducer over her stomach. Her flat, clearly empty stomach. *Eight . . . nine . . . ten.* She opened her mouth, took a deep breath. Instead of a scream coming out, she heard a long, loud groan, a groan of despair.

'Mrs Beaumont?' The girl's face was etched with concern. 'Are you all right? Are you in pain? I'm so sorry—'

'No, I'm not in pain,' said Elizabeth, and her voice sounded odd, rather low still and breathless. 'I just want this useless wasteful procedure to end.'

'No, you don't. This is going to tell us all sorts of important things about your baby.'

Yes, like it's dead.

'Mrs Beaumont, it isn't wasteful at all, honestly. And if you just open your eyes and look now – there, see – there he is, bobbing around like crazy. I'd say you've got a real little footie player there . . .'

'Oh, my God. My God.' Suddenly the Australian accent was the most wonderful sound in the world, and the girl's podgy face rather beautiful. 'So, you mean, you mean it's still – still there?'

'Of course it's still there. Set to stay for the duration, I'm sure. Is that pretty girl out there one of your daughters?'

'Yes, she is.'

'Do you want me to get her in, show her her baby brother? Or sister, of course, let's not be too sexist here.'

'Oh, would you, could you? That'd be so kind,' said Elizabeth.

And for a full five minutes, she and Annabel sat transfixed and tearful, clutching one another's hands and staring at the flickering image on the black screen, watching the baby, Simon's final legacy to them: and sharing a sense of huge relief and happiness mixed inevitably with intense sadness and loss.

'Now you've got to be sensible, Elizabeth,' said Sarah Goodrich. 'You've been lucky.'

'I know,' she said humbly.

'I want you to stay in bed for twenty-four hours after the

710

bleeding's completely stopped. And then you must take at least a week off, just pottering around at home. All right?'

'Yes, all right.'

'Good. And you keep an eye on your mum,' she said sternly to Annabel. 'Don't let her start heaving furniture about or doing some early Christmas shopping – OK?'

'Absolutely OK,' said Annabel. 'I'll stay home for a bit, tie her to the bed.'

'Good girl.'

'Annabel, darling, there's no need.'

'Mum! Just shut up will you. *I'm* in charge now. First time ever,' she said to Sarah, and grinned. 'I'm really looking forward to it.'

711

Chapter 52

Well, that was a bad start. She'd managed to persuade Nigel to invite Catherine to a drinks party; in fact, his sad, bloodhoundy eyes had quite lit up at the suggestion, and then it turned out that Catherine was going to another on the very same day. Which was excellent, of course, Lucinda thought, it was wonderful that she was making friends down there, but: 'Gosh, how annoying,' Catherine said. 'I'd much rather go to Nigel's. Talk about all the buses coming along at once. But I can't change it, unfortunately.'

'Of course not. Well, never mind.'

'Look, I'm coming up next week to do some Christmas shopping and I could at least see *you*. My children are never here,' she said, sounding halfway between pleased and cross, 'always sleeping in other people's houses, and who could blame them? I would too if I could.'

'Well, come and sleep in mine,' Lucinda said. 'I'd love it. I'm so fed up.'

'I just might. But won't Blue mind?'

'Not a bit.'

Lucinda put the phone down and sighed. It had been such a perfect occasion to get them together. And she could hardly ask him and Lucinda to cosy little drinks at their house. Blue had been very sweet, ever since the fight, but there was a limit even to his indulgence, and she could see that that would probably be it.

'Well, I'm sorry, Jamie, but you'll just have to postpone it. Yes, I can see that's difficult and I'm sure your mother won't be—

Yes, I know that. But this is really, really important. My mother's pregnant, for God's sake, and she's just nearly lost the baby. I really can't come rushing over there in a couple of weeks. What? Well, yes, I would say another two weeks after that would probably be OK. It would still be only early December . . . sorry? Yes, well, I can't see that would matter terribly, it could be a Christmas and engagement party combined. Oh, wouldn't she? Oh dear. Jamie, I am sorry but you must see how difficult it is for me as well. And if Tilly and Toby are going to come too, well, Mummy'd be alone. What about after Christmas? Like January. How would that be? Nicer in a way and – yes, of course I want to get properly engaged, but I've promised to look after my mother and I want to look after my mother and at this precise moment that's the most important thing! It's very hard for her, you know and – oh, for fuck's sake, Jamie. I can't take any more of this . . .'

'I just put the phone down on him,' she said to Tilly later. 'He's so selfish, couldn't see how much it mattered, and went on and on about what a lot of work it would be for his mother, unscrambling everything and reinviting everyone. I mean, what's that, compared to a baby?'

'I could look after Mummy,' said Tilly, 'I'd love to.'

'Tilly, you couldn't, things might go really wrong again; it would be too much for you, and I promised Mummy right at the beginning that I'd be there for her, and I'm not going to break that promise.'

'I don't want to go over there anyway,' said Tilly. 'At least, I don't think so. They sound so scary.'

'They are a bit,' said Annabel, 'and Mrs Cartwright is the scariest of all. Or maybe it's Mr Cartwright. Anyway, if Jamie thinks some stupid party is going to be more important than Mummy's baby, he's got another think coming, as Daddy used to say. Oh Tilly, don't cry, I'm sorry.'

'It's all right,' said Tilly, wiping her streaming eyes while fresh tears flowed on, apparently unstoppable. 'I'm sorry too, it's just that I miss him so much, it's like a huge hole in me somewhere and you know, I keep thinking such stupid things, like he always said I'd be taller than all of you, and I am, at the moment, I s'pose Toby'll catch up; anyway, the day I realised that, I thought, I must go and tell Daddy – and then I thought, I can't tell him, can't tell him anything, ever again. And he used to say, "I wish you didn't go away to school, how would you like to go to day school?" – and here I am doing it, and he doesn't know that either, and oh . . . Annabel, why did he have to do it?'

'Do what?'

'Oh, sorry. I mean, why did he have to take the boat out that day?'

'I don't know,' said Annabel. 'I guess he was bored and fed up, and he thought it would cheer him up. And then there was this storm, and—'

'Annabel, tell me truthfully,' Tilly said. 'Do you think he did it on purpose?'

'Of course not,' said Annabel staunchly. 'He wouldn't do anything so selfish and so mean to us. He just wouldn't. I'm quite, quite sure.'

But she wasn't sure; none of them could be.

Jamie rang back; he said he was terribly sorry, that he hadn't meant to be selfish, that of course Elizabeth and her baby were much the most important thing and that yes, his mother thought January would be a better idea.

'We can wait if you can,' he said.

'I can wait. Well, I can't, but I have to. I'll enjoy it much more. How is your mother?'

'She's fine. She sends her love. She says to tell you she's writing to your mother. About the baby. It must be making her feel so much better.'

'Well, yes and no,' said Annabel cautiously. 'I think she's pretty scared. Of coping on her own, you know.'

'I guess so. Well, better go, this is costing Dad a fortune. Love you.'

'Love you too,' said Annabel, 'lots and lots. Jamie . . .'

'Yes?'

'Sorry, this is going to cost your dad another fortune. Jamie, could you – that is, would you like to – come here for Christmas? It was Mummy's suggestion, and it would be so nice for me and for all of us. This Christmas is going to be difficult and—'

714

There was a silence, then Jamie said, 'Well, it would be lovely, of course. And thank you for the invitation. I'll – well, I'll have to talk to my parents. Christmas is pretty sacred here; we have terrific family traditions, you know, and—'

'Most families do,' said Annabel briskly. 'Well, think about it, Jamie. Bye now.'

She rang off; if Jamie thought she was going to spend the next fifty years or whatever having Christmas with his family and not hers he – well he really did have another think coming . . .

'Debbie, it's Joel. What the fuck are you playing at? It's Thursday, and I haven't seen you for over a week. What are you trying to do to me?'

'I'm not trying to do anything to you. I'm just – just thinking.'

'Well, stop it. Or at least, don't think on your own. Let me help.'

'Joel, I can't see you. Not for a few more days. I really can't. I'm – I'm sorry.' And she put the phone down.

She'd thought she was doing all right, clearing her head of him, in order properly to face the future, and decide what she was going to do. She was managing without him, after all. If she could manage a week, she could manage another. And then another . . . One day at a time. That was what alcoholics did.

But hearing his voice was agony, a bit like pulling off a scab. Or having the first drink. Just like having the first drink. Suddenly she couldn't resist it. She had to see him. She just had to. While she could.

She rang him back. 'I'll see what I can do,' she said, 'babysitting wise. Tonight.'

'I love you,' he said. Nothing else. Just, 'I love you.'

'I love you too.'

She changed her mind almost hourly about what she was going to do; the arguments came and went. She had a right to happiness: she had no right to happiness, it was the ultimate me-decade concept, born of navel-gazing. The children would get over it: the children would never get over it, they'd have hang ups for the rest of their lives. Richard didn't need her:

Richard did need her, or at any rate, his life needed her. She'd be so unhappy, behave so appallingly if she gave Joel up, nobody would benefit at all: she wouldn't stay so unhappy, she'd get over it, you got over everything in time, and she'd start behaving well again. Or as well as she had ever behaved.

It was so awful that at times it was quite funny; it was only as she was driving over to Clapham to see Joel that evening that she found herself giggling helplessly, so engrossed had she been in a *Wuthering Heights* scenario, where she was fading away from some terrible illness and Joel arrived at the door and carried her in his arms up to a mountain top to gaze her last on some dazzling view that they had both adored: only of course they had never shared any dazzling views, only a few bars, a couple of restaurants and Joel's flat, so where would he carry her to? The only dazzling views she could think of were in Gower; and bloody Flora would insist on coming with them to point out the colour of the gorse or the sound of the skylarks . . .

'You look cheerful,' he said, as he opened the door. 'What isn't the matter?'

'I was just imagining I was dying,' said Debbie, giving him a quick kiss, 'in your arms, with Flora at our side.'

'Sounds fun,' he said. 'Any other ideas like that?'

'Well, I don't suppose you could wait till the children are grown up?' she said, as he handed her a glass of wine. 'In ten or fifteen years, like in Pinter's *Betrayal* – you know?'

'That was five years actually, and I do know and I couldn't. I couldn't live without you for that long. Or rather share you for that long. I'd go mad. Next?'

'Well, how about Richard going off into the sunset with Morag?'

'Excellent. Is that likely, do you think?'

'Well, he is obsessed with her. Talks of nothing else. But – I don't think she's wife material for him. Sadly.'

'Debbie, how about you get your kit off. Maybe when you're lying down you'll be able to think more clearly.'

Afterwards as she lay helpless and shaken in his arms, she knew she couldn't live without him, however much unhappiness she might wreak. And then later, driving home again, she knew she had to. Sated with him, worn out with love, it was easy to know

716

that, in the early dark dawn, alone in her bed, she could see once more that it was completely impossible.

'Oh God,' she said aloud. 'God help me.' And started to cry.

Toby had been told about the baby – by Annabel. He had reacted exactly as Elizabeth had predicted: he was embarrassed, shocked, almost morose. He managed to come and congratulate her, while looking firmly at the carpet as he spoke, but she could see he was finding it almost impossibly difficult. He had gone back to school, clearly with relief, barely even able to kiss her goodbye.

'Stupid wanker,' Tilly said, as his glowering face disappeared into the train. Her still-perfect accent made her comment somehow all the more powerful.

'Tilly, that's not a nice word,' said Elizabeth.

'Good. He doesn't deserve nice words. He's a complete pig. What does it mean, by the way?' she added. 'Madison says it a lot, but I don't like to ask her.'

Annabel was shocked by his reaction and talked to Florian about it.

'It doesn't exactly help poor Mummy.'

'Darling, do use what tiny brain you've got. It's hideous for him. One minute he's got two parents, nice and straight-forward, doing what parents have to do – like wait on him and supply him with money; the next his dad's gone and he finds himself the only male in a clucky household, coping with the information that his mother was having sex with his father when they were both old enough to know better, and possibly even worse, the one thing he's been warned about, being inefficient about contraception. And knowing he ought to appear pleased, when he wants to throw up. Horrible. Poor lad. Leave him be, he'll come to terms with it in time. I'll maybe speak to him when he comes home for Christmas.'

'You know,' said Annabel, 'I just don't know what I'd do without you, Florian.'

As Elizabeth sat at her desk, writing a conference speech and feeling better and stronger than she had for months, she had a call from the Coroner's office. The date for the inquest had

717

been set: for the second week in January. January! So long after Simon's death. It would inevitably threaten her fragile recovery. The pain was no less, the loneliness un-eased; at times it was greater, but familiarity with it had taught her at least how to live with it. She knew about waking to it each morning, that those two or three early dreadful hours had to be got through; knew about the onset of the anger, followed by the remorse; knew her new pain of not being able to share the baby with him. Their shock value at least was diminished; the days when she stood gasping with pain as some new aspect of the grief besieged her, seemed to be over. She was at least surviving; surviving and functioning, doing her job, coping with her family, and that was all she could hope for, for the foreseeable future. Even the sale of the house, due to be completed two weeks before Christmas, seemed to be manageable.

But the thought of going into the exact circumstances of his death: that was truly terrifying. What would emerge on that unimaginable day, as witnesses came before the Coroner? She might perhaps hear things that she had not known, be questioned herself about her last hours with Simon, hear him referred to as 'the deceased', see her children freshly assaulted by it all. And – worst of all – there was the verdict. What if it was suicide – as seemed increasingly likely to her, considering all the facts, how would they endure that, that awful, ugly, somehow aggressive act?

She tried to tell herself it didn't change anything; but she knew it did, it changed it into something official, diminished their ability to tell themselves that of course he wouldn't have done it, that of course he would have turned to them for hope and for comfort.

Brave as she was, tough as she was, Elizabeth Beaumont really didn't know how she was going to face it.

Chapter 53

November to December, 1990

Well, was this really worse than being at home with the children? Catherine wondered. She had been at Musgrove Hall for over an hour now, and she could have been invisible for all the notice people took of her.

Patrick had been very nice and welcoming when she arrived, inevitably one of the first. 'Sorry, lot of the guests have been out hunting today, sure to make them a bit late. Still, jolly nice to see you. Gin? Or whisky? Or there's sherry, of course. Your shout.'

It all reminded Catherine of her childhood; of growing up with people who offered gin and tonic or sherry. But that had been over thirty years ago; had life changed so little in the country? Clearly it had. She settled for a gin and tonic, thinking that it would make her slightly less drunk and she could move onto just tonic; and then followed Patrick into the freezing cold room that he described as the drawing room.

It lacked the comforts of any normal drawing room: no carpets, no curtains, just stone flags on the floor – she'd have to be careful not to drop anything on that, she thought, clutching her glass more tightly – and shutters at the windows, and the stone fireplace contained a rather feeble log fire, but it was unarguably beautiful.

She felt rather under-dressed in her black trousers and silk shirt; the two women who were already there both wore what she also remembered from her childhood, cocktail dresses. Wherever could you still buy such things, stiffly-skirted, three-quarter-sleeved, scoop-necked dresses – one in dark velvet, one in heavy silk; the perfect background for strings of what were inevitably real pearls, and large brooches.

'Right now, this is Pattie Smithers and her husband Paul, and this is Mo Cummings, and this useless-looking fellow is Mr Mo, as we call him.'

'Don't you dare,' said Mr Mo, holding out a clammy hand to Catherine. 'Mike Cummings.'

'And this is Catherine Morgan, only been here for a couple of months. These are all neighbours, my dear. Catherine's from London, so she's used to all sorts of excitement. I told her she'd find us pretty dull . . .'

'Oh no, not at all,' said Catherine. 'It was London that was dull. I—'

'Husband away, is he?' said Pattie, interrupting her. She looked rather fierce.

'No, he's – that is, I'm a widow.' She smiled nervously at Pattie.

'Oh, sorry to hear that.' She appeared neither embarrassed by what would have seemed to many a considerable social gaffe, nor in the least sorry for Catherine. 'So where do you live?'

'Oh, over at Gillingham. I'm – well, I'm living with my parents-in-law. At the moment. And with my—'

'Gillingham, eh? said Mo, her brow briefly furrowed. 'No, don't know anyone there. Do they shoot?'

'Er, no. No, they don't.'

'Hunt?'

'No. 'Fraid not.'

'Shame. Well, jolly nice to meet you. Ah Sally, lovely to see you,' and she beamed at a third cocktail-dressed lady with an even redder face. 'Good day?'

'Oh terrific, we found almost at once, and—'

And Catherine was spoken to no more.

Every so often, Patrick would clearly remember her, feel he must do something about her; drag her from one group and over to another. He was really very sweet, Catherine thought gratefully. He was trying hard. But he must be regretting his decision, as she seemed to be nothing but a burden to him. And very hard work.

The talk was entirely of hunting and shooting; no one had so far mentioned fishing, but she felt that was inevitable. The drink was very slow to materialise; she supposed it was harder to remix gin and tonic than pour glasses of wine. The good news was that she was still stone cold sober. And stone cold, come to that.

The only other topic of conversation was Mrs Thatcher and her downfall; the general consensus seemed to be that Heseltine deserved to be strung up for setting the whole thing in motion.

'Met him once,' someone said, 'couldn't stand him. Bit of a cad. And that hair . . .'

'Well, at least he's been to a decent school,' said someone else. 'Suppose we got Major. Dreadful fellow.'

'Hurd'd be all right,' said a completely bald man, wearing a kilt with his tweed jacket. 'Not exactly charismatic, but—'

'I say, Geoffrey old chap, long word for you,' said Patrick. 'Catherine, do you know any of these dreadful politicians, as you live in London?'

Bless him, Catherine thought, he really wants to include me. 'Well, I once met Neil Kinnock,' she said tentatively, anxious to be worthy of his efforts, 'but he—'

'Kinnock? The Welsh Windbag? Only thing I can say for him is he's doing a pretty good job, keeping the Labour lot out,' said Geoffrey. 'How on earth did you meet him?'

They clearly saw it as a piece of inexplicable misfortune. Catherine started to explain that he had come to her children's school, realised that must indicate being in the state system and therefore even worse, and said, with a glance at her watch, that goodness, she really had to be getting home, she hadn't realised how late it was. As it said 7.25 p.m. she could see it wasn't very convincing.

Patrick, however, appeared to find it perfectly acceptable. Clearly party regulations, like everything else, were different in the country.

'I'll come and see you off,' he said. 'Hope you enjoyed it?'

'Gosh, yes, it was great fun,' said Catherine. 'Thank you so much.'

'Oh, not at all. Very nice to have you here. Breath of fresh air, someone new you know, not just the old crowd. Still, they're a pretty good lot, as you'll discover. Well, see you again soon, I hope. Goodbye, Catherine.'

'Goodbye, Patrick. And thank you again.'

She was in the car, actually putting it into reverse when he reappeared, banging on the window. She wound it down.

'You going to the point-to-point at Trister on Saturday?'

'Um – no.'

'Ah. Prices not going, perhaps?'

'They don't always take me,' said Catherine carefully.

'No, no, stupid of me. Well – look. I'm going. Should be quite a good one. Would you like to come with me?'

'Oh, gosh.' Catherine felt rather confused. Was this a date? If so, did she want to accept? He might be very sweet, but he wasn't exactly her type. And although she'd enjoyed the last point-to-point, it had been largely due to its novelty value. On the other hand, it would be lovely to be out. Except of course . . .

'It's so kind of you,' she said, 'and I'd love to. But I'm afraid I'll probably have to bring the children.'

'Oh, that's all right. Seemed rather a jolly little thing, your daughter. Yes, yes, the more the merrier. I'll come and pick you up, if you like. Expect I can find the place.'

'Oh no, don't do that,' said Catherine, appalled to think what he and Phyllis and Dudley might make of one another. 'We'll come over to you. It'll be easier. And shall I bring the picnic?'

'Oh – that's jolly kind. No, don't bother, Mrs P will do that.'

'Then let me add to it. I'll make a cake. For – for sort of teatime.'

'Capital,' he said. 'Very good of you. See you on Saturday then.' And he banged twice on the car roof to indicate that she was to leave.

If Mrs Bennet had been her mother, Catherine thought, looking back at Musgrove Hall in all its Jacobean splendour, she'd be getting quite excited.

Debbie felt she had grown two heads. Or at least two lives. There was the familiar one, where she was a good wife and mother, much concerned with, and involved in, her children's lives: she delivered them to school every morning, neatly uniformed – much more neatly than in the old days – and well-breakfasted, their homework done and their projects well in order; after which she proceeded to her job, where she worked hard, and did rather well, five days a week now, three of them finishing at three so she could collect the children. And then proceeded home, where she did the housework and the washing and entertained the children's friends and spoke to her absent husband on the phone, reassuring him that all was well, and asking him how his new job was going: and then at night she went to bed fairly early, in order to begin the next, well-ordered day.

And then there was the other, secret life: the one in which she lied and deceived and invented meetings and set up fake interviews and spent half her housekeeping money on babysitters, and drove across London, her heart racing, her body dissolving with desire, in order to meet her lover: to spend precious, rapturous hours with him, talking to him, laughing with him, making love with him, and all the time refusing to consider the future, and how fast it was rushing towards her.

The indecision had got so bad, she couldn't endure it; with a ruthlessness that surprised her, she set it aside, learned to live not so much with it, as without it. If Joel pressed her in any way, she simply told him not to. 'What matters is now, us being together, me loving you, you loving me; us just enjoying each other – why spoil it till we have to?'

For it would have to be spoiled, and for many people, including herself; it followed as the night the day. There was no happy ending to this story, no crock of gold, and indeed the end of the rainbow was shrouded in rain; but while it lasted, it was spell-binding and full of joy.

And the fact that the weeks dwindled from seven to six to five to ... God, only four ... made her all the more determined to stay within that spell.

It was not all sweetness and light, of course. Joel sometimes grew angry, often impatient, demanding a decision, upbraiding her for failing to commit herself.

'I can't do more, for Christ's sake. I've asked you to marry me – why won't you answer? What else can I do?'

'Nothing,' she would say, kissing him, holding him, 'nothing at all. Let me be, let it be, something will happen, something will settle it. Please, Joel, please wait.'

The rows were worse on the weekends that Richard was coming home: when Joel raged and stormed and told her she was cowardly and fraudulent and cruel too, and that if she wouldn't make her decision, then he would do it for her. She went through those weekends (only two of them since half-term, thank God) in a state of complete terror: terror of Richard growing suspicious, of the children revealing how often she went out, of Joel arriving on the doorstep, of – and this was by far the most stressful – of Richard making love to her. Which he did. How she got through that, she never afterwards knew; she simply shut her eyes and thought not of England but of her work. That alone was neutral enough; she would compose press releases in her head, plan meetings, even think what she might wear on the Monday morning. The amazing thing was that he never seemed to notice.

And Monday came in due course, after what seemed like an eternity, mostly of stories about the wonders of Morag and the joys of the new job, and she returned with a sigh of welcome to her two lives.

Only she knew, deep within the heart of her, at the centre of both the lives, that she did have to make the decision and she had to make it alone.

'Please, please Mr Clark can you hurry it up?' said Lucinda, looking fretfully at her consultant over her vast stomach. 'I'm going to burst, I think. I can't stand it any longer. Can't I be induced or something?'

'No, you can't. Induction for social reasons is a thing of the past, I'm very glad to say. You're not even due till next Thursday. First babies are generally late. And the head isn't engaged yet.'

'It must be.'

'It isn't. It's still quite high. I should say you've got a good week to go. At least.' He patted the stomach, beamed at her. 'I know it's a bore, but try to be patient. They come when they're good and ready.'

'Yes, but I don't think he ever will be.'

'Course he will. Give him a chance. Or her. And don't worry, if you go more than two weeks overdue, then we will bring you in. Promise.'

'Oh, all right.' She sighed. 'These Braxton Hicks thingies don't mean much then.'

'Not a lot. Just getting your uterine muscles into trim. What does the inestimable Mrs Parsons have to say about them?'

'She says just about the same. And she says I'll be able to tell when they mean business.'

'You certainly will.' He beamed at her. 'Quite confident about it all, are you?'

'No, I'm absolutely petrified. You have got good stocks of epidural, haven't you?'

He laughed. 'We have, don't worry. But obviously, the further into labour you can get without it, the better. For your baby, that is.'

'I'm more worried about me,' said Lucinda, 'just at the moment.'

She took a cab home; Blue was already there, looking slightly apprehensive.

'You're early,' she said.

'Yeah, I know. Easy day. What'd the doc say, Lucy?'

'Oh dear. He said probably another week or even two. I think I'll go mad.'

'No, you won't. Poor you. I got your supper ready for you, by the way.'

'Blue, you're so sweet.'

He looked slightly shamefaced. 'Yeah, well, it's only Chicken Chernobyl. From Marks and Sparks.'

'I wish you wouldn't call it that.'

'What, Marks and Sparks?'

'No, Chicken Chernobyl. It's so – so insensitive.'

'Sorry.'

'Anyway, I do appreciate it. Thank you.'

'You sit down, put your feet up, I'll bring it in.'

As she sat there, trying to imagine ever having a flat stomach again, the phone rang. It was Catherine. She'd got the children sorted for Monday: would Lucinda still like a visit?

'Oh, yes. So, so much. Come over here as soon as you can; as soon as you're shopped out.'

'All right. Golly, Phyllis is calling me. Better go. Bye, Lucinda.'

Blue came in with a tray, complete with Lucinda's best linen napkins and a small vase with a rose in it. She looked at him suspiciously.

'Blue, what are you up to?'

'Nothing. Aren't I allowed to show what a romantic I am?'

'No, because you're not. What's going on? Come on, tell me.'

'Well, few of the lads are going over to Paris on Monday. Just for the day. Bit of a pre-Christmas jolly. I said I wouldn't go, of course. Said the baby was due.'

'Well, it is.'

'Yeah, but you said – well, obviously I wouldn't dream of going. Not if it's imminent.'

'It isn't. Blue, you are such a bad liar. You'd better go.'

'Really? You don't mind?'

'Not too terribly,' said Lucinda with a sigh. 'It might even bring it on.'

'In that case I'll certainly go. It really is only for the day. And we're going by private plane – a client do. So all you've got to do is call me—'

'In Paris?'

'That's the one. On my mobile phone. And I'll be back before you can say contraction. Anyway, they did say in that fact sheet you gave me, from that woman – wosser name?'

'Mrs Parsons. You mean after the fathers' evening that you suddenly found you couldn't attend?'

'Lucy, I was working.'

'Yes, I know. Very few of the other fathers are unemployed. Actually.'

'Sorry.'

'It's OK. I know how you're dreading the whole thing. Not like me, of course.'

'I'm not exactly dreading it, Lucinda. I'm just a bit squeamish. Faint at the sight of blood, that sort of thing.'

'Yes, well, it's a good thing I don't, isn't it? Oh, this is a stupid conversation.'

'Sorry, but I do remember it said first labours take a pretty long time. At least twelve hours, most of them. Usually more. So as long as you ring me the minute you get a twinge, I can be home two hours later, max.'

'Two hours?'

'Yeah. We're going from City Airport. But honestly, Lucy, I swear I won't go, if you don't want me to.'

'You go,' said Lucinda, 'it's fine. Probably the last time you'll be able to go out for ages. You're not going out to Christmas parties and leaving me holding the baby. So, like I said, it's fine. But if you switch your mobile phone off, and I need you, I warn you I'll never speak to you again. I'll – I'll go back to Nigel. Now I'd like a glass of wine, please.'

'You're not supposed to drink, you know that.'

'I'm sorry, but you've just announced that you're going to Paris three days before our baby's due. I think that entitles me to a nice glass of claret. Mr Clark says it's good for expectant mothers, red wine. It relaxes them and he should know.'

'Smooth bugger,' said Blue, who rather disliked the silver-tongued Mr Clark. But he poured her a glass just the same. He didn't want her getting into a bad mood. It happened rather easily these days.

Lucinda didn't tell him about Catherine coming; the guiltier he felt, the better.

Nigel's company was limping towards closure; if he got hold of John Major, he thought, he'd give him a very strong piece of his mind about what Major swore was a recession and which was clearly a full-scale depression. The company had a small factory in Yeovil which, it was becoming increasingly obvious, should be closed down. It was running at catastrophically low production levels, and was costing him more than it earned. He decided he should bite the bullet, go down the next Friday and break the news himself. A lot of people did that sort of thing at long distance, of course, let a spokesman break the news; but Nigel regarded that as pretty ungentlemanly. Besides, his grandfather had opened the factory; it was a family affair. And probably the nearest he'd ever come to having children now, he thought. He felt particularly low just at the moment.

Looking at the map, it occurred to him that he wouldn't be so very far away from Gillingham, which was where Catherine now lived. If Lucinda had been right, she was pretty lonely and might appreciate a visit. Although maybe not so lonely now, as she hadn't been able to come to his party last Saturday, which had disappointed him quite a bit. She was such a sweet girl, and pretty too, in a pale and interesting way. And he liked her children a lot. He'd give her a ring, see what she said. Perhaps they could all go out to lunch together on Saturday.

Catherine was very sorry, she said, but she was going out on Saturday. 'To a point-to-point. With a – a friend.'

'Oh, shame. Well, never mind. Just an idea. Another time.' Only he didn't know when he'd be down in this part of the world again: probably never.

'I don't suppose,' said Catherine tentatively, 'you'll still be down here on Sunday?' She didn't want to frighten him off, appear too keen; but she did like him so much, and it seemed silly to lose the opportunity to meet.

'No 'fraid not,' said Nigel, and then, because he really rather wanted to know, without being sure why, he said, 'This friend of yours, does she live in Gillingham as well?'

Catherine hesitated, then said, 'No, but quite near.'

At least it was a woman. Not a man. That was something.

'Well, nice to talk to you, Catherine. Some other time perhaps.'

'Yes.'

He obviously wasn't really interested in her; otherwise he would have hung around till Sunday. Or suggested Saturday evening. Damn. He was so nice, so gentle, and although he was very English, he was in a different league altogether from Patrick and his friends. More civilised, somehow, more . . . Catherine, do pull yourself together. You're going out with one man; just be grateful for that. And don't start crying for the moon. Neither of them's going to ask you to marry them, for goodness sake.

It was fairly horrible, telling the people at the factory that he had to close it. Nigel looked round it, at the old-fashioned, noisy shop-floor, most of which was empty of both people and machinery, remembering the time his father had brought him all those years ago when it had been working at full capacity and how excited and proud he had felt. Well, it was over now. Sadly, terribly over.

He took everyone out for a few drinks at the pub, and then a few key people for a pub meal in Yeovil. They were all very good about it, said they'd been expecting it, swapped stories about the old days. There was hardly anybody young there.

He told them he'd arrange as much redundancy money as he could, left them for a rather dismal commercial hotel, and woke up next morning feeling suicidal. If only he could have seen Catherine, she would have cheered him up. And God, she'd had far worse troubles than this. Suddenly it seemed worth waiting at least till Saturday evening. Maybe they could go out for a drink or something. He could mooch around during the day, maybe visit Wells or somewhere like that – he'd always wanted to see the Cathedral. He'd got her address from Lucinda, it should be quite easy to find. He ate a fairly disgusting breakfast and set off for Wells, where he enjoyed the Cathedral and indeed the rest of his day, then drove back to Gillingham and parked in the lane by the Morgan seniors' hideous house – he was a little shocked by its hideousness, but told himself Catherine could hardly be blamed for it – to wait for her return from the day with her girlfriend.

And then drove away, even more shocked, and indeed saddened, after a very large and mud-spattered Range Rover had pulled into the drive and disgorged not only Catherine and Freddie, but Caroline, fast asleep and carried in the arms of its equally large and mud-spattered male driver.

Chapter 54

Flora could never remember disliking anyone as much as the crass, sharp-suited lad who arrived on Monday morning complete with tape measure and clipboard, and who held out his hand – a limp, clammy hand, sporting a large gold ring, and said, 'Very nice property, Mrs Fielding. Very nice indeed.'

'Thank you. I like it.'

'I'm sure. Still, not very convenient, these old places, are they? I can imagine why you want to get rid of it. Moving into something smaller, I suppose, nearer the shops?'

'I'm getting rid of it, as you put it, purely through financial necessity,' said Flora, resisting with great difficulty the temptation to send him away again, 'and I do assure you I have no desire to be near any shops.'

'Oh really? Right. Well, shall we just have a quick look round together, and then I can get on with the measuring up. My word, people must have been smaller then – the doorways are very low, aren't they? Bit of woodworm in that frame, let's give it the old key test –' he thrust a key deep into the frame round the front door and riddled it round '– yes, thought so, look at that – see? Completely rotten, I'd say, might need fixing. Or taken into consideration in the price, if we find any more. Now this is the kitchen, funny old range that – coal-fired, is it? Hard work, I'd imagine, and does it run the central heating?'

'It does not,' said Flora.

'So – what does then? Gas?'

'Nothing runs it. There is no central heating.'

'Ah. Right.' He wrote something down on his board, underlined it twice. 'Righty-ho. And this is the lounge? Lovely windows, aren't they, and what a view. Now that's a real selling point, Mrs Fielding, I can tell you that. Worth several hundreds, that view.'

'Really?'

'Yes, really.' He misread her tone. 'You'd be surprised, views really matter to people. Specially in the country.'

'I probably wouldn't,' she said icily, 'be surprised, I mean.'

'No, indeed. Wood-burning, is it, the old stove?'

'It is, yes.'

'And those shutters. When did you last have those looked at?'

'We look at them most days,' said Flora, 'and thence to the view.'

'Of course. But I meant have them checked for worm, because I'm afraid – yes . . . Dear oh dear. Lot of woodworm in this house – Rentokil would have a field day. Okey dokey. Dining room. Yes. More problems there, with those doors. Still, nice room. And what would we call this? TV room?'

'We call it the family room,' said Flora wearily. 'As you may notice, there is no television in it.'

'Oh, no. Well, big selling-point, separate TV room. Mind if I call it that in the particulars?'

'Yes, I do. Very much. Now perhaps we could go upstairs.'

'Right you are. And then I'll take the old measurements.'

Flora sat at the kitchen table as he did that, trying to concentrate on *The Times* crossword, and feeling, for the first time since she had had the initial letter from Lloyd's, truly defeated.

'Hello, Lucinda, how are you?'

'Oh, all right. You know.'

It was so unlike her to sound down, Catherine felt quite alarmed. 'You're not – not . . .'

'God, no such luck. Just fed up. I'm so looking forward to seeing you, Catherine, having a chat. Blue's in Paris and—'

'Paris!' For the umpteenth time, Catherine wondered what on earth Lucinda saw in Blue, how she could have left Nigel for him; Nigel would never have gone off to Paris the week before the baby was due, he'd have been there, with her every moment, caring for her, worrying about her.

'Yes, but it's all right, only for a day. He'll be back tonight,

731

sooner if I need him. 'Fraid I won't though. But do come, Catherine, as soon as you can. I feel awfully odd.'

'Well, OK. I've got to do a bit more shopping, haven't got anything for Phyllis yet. I'm in Selfridges – there must be something there, and then I'll come right over.'

'So, how long do you think you'll be?' She sounded almost desperate.

'Let me see, about . . . an hour and a half. That should do it. Yes, by – let's see – four.'

'OK. I'll try and stay sane. Got any tips, for starting labour?'

'They do say hot baths.'

'Yes. Mrs Parsons says that. And castor oil. Well, I could try the bath.'

'Well, don't have it too hot. Or wait till I get there, OK? When will Blue be back?'

'Oh, quite late. He just rang, said the client wants to have dinner there. An early one, of course. I've been so bad-tempered and horrid to him all weekend, I think he'd stay the week if he could.'

'I'm sure you haven't,' said Catherine, who found it impossible to imagine Lucinda being horrid. 'Just hang on, and I'll be there by four.'

'OK. Thanks.'

Lucinda did, as she had told Catherine, feel terribly odd. Not physically so much as mentally; she felt rather confused, restless, she couldn't settle to anything, kept pacing about the house, picking things up and putting them away – in rather unlikely places, she suddenly realised, looking at Blue's underpants neatly folded in the desk drawer.

The phone rang: 'Lucinda?'

'Oh – Nigel. Oh, how lovely to hear your voice. How are you?'

'I'm all right. Bit depressed. Had to tell them I was closing the factory down this weekend, winding up the company. Golly, Lucinda, I'll need that money of – of –'

'Yours,' said Lucinda firmly. 'All yours. There isn't any news, is there?'

'Not from my end. That's why I rang you actually, to see if you had heard anything.'

'Not yet, no. But Steve says he's totally confident. Don't worry. Um – do you want to come round, have a cup of tea, see if I can cheer you up. I've got some crumpets.'

Nigel felt rather choked suddenly; she had always got him crumpets or scones, every week, and had served them with Little Scarlet strawberry jam or Coopers Oxford Marmalade for Sunday tea. Bloody Horton. Why couldn't he have left her alone . . .

'Oh, I don't know,' he said.

'Please, Nigel, I'd so love to see you. I'm terribly bored and lonely. And fed up with waiting for this baby. Catherine's coming too. We can have a tea party.'

'Catherine? Ah, yes,' said Nigel, thinking of his lonely vigil at the bottom of the Morgans' drive, and its unsatisfactory outcome.

'Yes. She's up here Christmas shopping.'

Nigel hesitated, then he said, 'Well, it does sound quite nice. I'm at a bit of a loose end, actually.'

'Good. How long will you be? Because I was about to have a bath . . .'

'Oh, about an hour.'

'That's exactly what Catherine said. Good. I'll have the kettle on.'

Nigel and Catherine actually arrived at the same time; they smiled rather awkwardly at each other as they approached Lucinda's house from opposite directions.

'Hello, Nigel.'

'Hello, Catherine. You're looking well. Country life must agree with you.'

'The life maybe,' said Catherine with a sigh. 'Not sure about the people.'

'But you are making some friends?'

'Sort of. I suppose.'

Nigel thought of the large male figure, cradling the small girl in his arms so tenderly, and felt irritated.

'Well – shall we go in?' he said.

Lucinda was very pink-faced, her hair damp; she was wearing a towelling bathrobe, and her bump looked enormous. Nigel tried to avert his eyes.

733

'How lovely,' she said. 'I am just so pleased to see you both. Sorry, got a bit carried away with my bath. I'll just go and get dressed and then we can all have tea. Catherine, darling, put the kettle on, would you? And Nigel, you can find the crumpets. I feel rather perky all of a sudden. I shall enjoy our party.'

'Crumpets!' said Catherine. 'I love crumpets. We used to have them every Saturday for tea. With Little Scarlet strawberry jam. Frederick's favourite – mine too.'

'How extraordinary,' said Nigel, staring at her.

'What?'

'Oh, nothing.'

Half an hour later, they were all munching crumpets when the phone rang.

'Hello? What? Oh Blue, you are so hopeless. How could you have let it do that? He's let his phone run down,' she said to the others. 'What? Oh, just a couple of friends, popped in for tea. Some people are concerned about me, you see, want to keep me company in my hours of need. Well, thanks for ringing anyway. And no, I'm not in labour. Which is lucky for you, I'd say. So, yes, you keep ringing me, since I can't ring you, all right? At least every hour. Bye. And don't come home drunk.'

'Where is he then?' said Nigel.

'He's in Paris. On a pre-Christmas jolly.'

'Paris!' said Nigel. 'I say, that's a bit hard, isn't it?'

'Oh, not really. He'll be back tonight. Not late either – they went by private plane.'

What sort of husband, thought Nigel, looking at her tenderly, went to Paris when his baby was due? And had to be told not to get drunk. What did she see in him, for goodness sake – what? If it had been his baby, he wouldn't have left her side for the whole nine months. It didn't occur to him that that was precisely the sort of behaviour that had driven her into Blue's arms.

'Now,' said Lucinda briskly, 'more tea, anyone? I'll go and fill the kettle. I – goodness. Golly. What a mess. I didn't spill all that, did I?'

'No,' said Catherine calmly, looking at the large pool of

water that had formed underneath Lucinda, 'your waters just broke. The hot bath must have done the trick.'

'Oh my God,' said Lucinda. 'How amazing. This is it. But I don't feel anything at all. No pain, I mean.'

'It doesn't always start straight away,' said Catherine. 'Mine broke in the greengrocer's when I had Caroline. It was so embarrassing. I just walked home and went into labour about three hours later.'

'We were told we should go straight into hospital,' Lucinda said, 'because there's a risk of infection.'

'Better – better go then,' said Nigel. He had been staring petrified at the pool of water and Lucinda's face. She was flushed and her eyes were very bright; she looked feverish. 'Shall I call an ambulance?'

'You could try,' said Catherine, 'it's the rush hour so they'll take a while, I should think. Where are you having it, Lucinda?'

'The Princess Louise, in Weymouth Street. Bit of a trek, but surely an ambulance should get through. Anyway, I think I'll ring Mr Clark.'

'Who's he?'

'My obstetrician. Such a sweetie. Goodness, this is so exciting. It's not nearly as bad as I thought.'

'It might get a little worse,' said Catherine carefully. 'Um – shall I ring?'

'Yes, please. The number's by the phone. And my little bag's all packed, so I'll just go and get that. How lucky you were both here. Oh goodness, we must tell Blue. No, we can't, can we? The phone being out of order and everything, silly him. Tell you what, I'll leave a message on the answering machine for him. Then he'll know to get back.'

She was babbling rather; it was as if she was slightly drunk, Nigel thought. He felt absolutely terrified, half-expecting the baby to suddenly emerge as Lucinda stood there.

'Let's get on with it,' he said.

Catherine rang the ambulance number; after an incredibly long time (or so it seemed), someone answered and said they would try and get one out immediately, but they were experiencing serious delays.

'Traffic's shocking. How often are the contractions?'

'There aren't any,' said Catherine.

'No sign of any at all?'

'No. Nothing. Her waters have broken.'

'Just broken?'

'Yes, about five minutes ago.'

There was a silence; then the voice said, 'Where are you?'

'Limehouse.'

'Bit of a way. Is this her first baby?'

'Yes.'

'And absolutely no contractions?'

'Absolutely not.'

'I wouldn't normally suggest this, but I honestly think you'd be better bringing her in by car. The traffic's bad going out in that direction, but it's more or less OK coming in. So – just set off, I'm sure you'll do better that way.'

'OK,' said Catherine, 'we're on our way. But what shall we do if – if things start hotting up?'

'Unless she's one of the tiny percentage of women who have their babies in one hour flat, just keep driving. Tell your hospital you're coming so they know to expect you. Good luck.'

They went out into the street; Nigel's Volvo, square and reassuring, stood waiting for them.

'You get in the back,' Catherine said to Lucinda, 'and I'll mapread.'

'Oh, no need for that,' said Lucinda. 'I'll tell you the best way to go. I'd rather you sat next to me, Catherine, held my hand. This is rather fun, I'm enjoying it.'

'Good,' said Catherine, 'that's as it should be. Off we go, Nigel.'

Nigel was shaking so much he could hardly turn the ignition key.

They were just going over Holborn Viaduct when Lucinda gave a small yelp.

Catherine looked at her. 'Contraction?'

'Yes, think so. Wasn't very bad though.'

'OK. We need two more.'

'Surely it'll take longer than that?' Lucinda's teeth were beginning to chatter.

'Of course it will, you idiot. But that means we can time

736

them. Oh dear, traffic ahead looks awful. Know any back ways, Nigel?'

'We could try cutting up to Theobalds Row. Might be better.'

'OK, do that. All right, Lucinda?'

'Absolutely fine.'

They were driving down towards Gower Street when Lucinda yelped again; Catherine looked at her watch.

'That was quick. I mean, after the last one.'

'Was it?'

'Yes. About five minutes. Keep going, Nigel.'

'I'm doing my best,' he said. He sounded very shaky.

Another contraction came in five minuutes; it lasted about thirty seconds.

'You're fine,' said Catherine. 'They're very short.'

'They may be short, but they're not exactly sweet,' said Lucinda. 'It quite hurt, that one. Maybe I should do my breathing. How are we doing, Nigel?'

'Fine. Much better. Don't worry, soon have you there.'

But the journey took another half-hour, and by the time they did arrive, Lucinda was having contractions every three minutes.

'Thank God,' she said as Nigel pulled up in front of the hospital. 'I'll just— No, here comes another one – wait, I can't walk while it's going on.'

A traffic warden advanced on the car: a stout wasp of a woman with a hard face and mean little eyes.

'You can't wait here,' she said.

'I'm afraid we're going to have to,' said Catherine. 'This lady is in labour.'

'Oh yes?' said the warden. 'D'you think I've never heard that one before?'

'I have no idea. Anyway, we need to help her in.'

'Sorry,' said the woman, 'you're on a double yellow, I have to issue a ticket.'

Nigel suddenly got out of the car. 'Don't you dare even talk about issuing tickets,' he said, 'when this lady is in labour. Where is your humanity? Just leave us alone, go on, go away.' He made shooing gestures with his arm; rather as if he was seeing a dog off.

737

'You her husband then?' said the warden.

'Yes, actually,' said Nigel. 'I am.'

To everyone's amazement she nodded, then uttered a sort of sniff and moved on.

'You're so masterly, Nigel,' said Lucinda, and then doubled over again and said, 'Ouch.'

'I'll go and get help,' said Catherine.

Everything happened rather quickly after that; a nurse appeared with a wheelchair and Lucinda was helped into it.

'Thank you so m—' she said, and then her face distorted with pain as another contraction hit her.

'How often are these coming?' the nurse asked Catherine as they wheeled her in.

'Every three minutes.'

'Three! That's pretty quick. When did she start?'

'Just now,' said Lucinda, 'on Holborn Viaduct. But it seems to be happening quite quickly.' She smiled her radiant smile. 'So aren't I lucky? But I'd like to get the epidural going. Is Mr Clark here?'

'Not yet. But he's on his way.'

Nigel looked at them both hopefully. 'Should I – should I go and park the car?'

'Yes,' said Catherine, 'but then mind you come back. We need you.'

'Is he the husband?' said the nurse, looking after Nigel's tall gangly figure.

'Yes. But he's not— Oh God, here comes another. This is quite – Oh dear, oh Catherine – quite painful. Hold my hand, will you.'

Nigel tried to park quickly, but it was very difficult. It was the first real week of the Christmas rush and the whole of the area was jammed with cars. Every car park was full and all the single yellow lines were taken. He found a rather small space on some double yellows and managed to get into it. He felt rather anxious about getting clamped and then wondered how on earth he could be worrying about parking fines when Lucinda was having a baby.

738

'I'll just go and check Lucinda's all right,' said Blue. He had just had a third champagne cocktail; they were sitting in the bar of the George V Hotel in Paris, having had an extremely long and drunken lunch in the Crillon. They were all flushed, unsteady, slurred of speech, shaky of hand.

'Remember where the phone is?' asked Charlie.

'Course.'

They watched him weaving off; some very chic Parisians drew aside from him, severe Gallic disdain on their faces.

'Silly old fool,' said Charlie affectionately. 'I think one more of these all round and then—'

Blue reappeared wild-eyed. 'We've got to go,' he said. 'Now.'

Nigel and Catherine sat in the corridor outside Lucinda's room at the hospital. Various people came and went; an atmosphere of great urgency prevailed.

'She's obviously going like the clappers,' said Catherine. 'Don't look so frightened, Nigel, it's much better that way.'

'Is it?'

'Yes, of course.'

A nurse came out of the room. Catherine stood up. 'We're with Mrs Cowper. Any news?'

'Not yet. But she's doing very well. Mr Clark has just arrived. I'm Sister Johns. Are you her husband?' she said to Nigel.

'Yes, but—'

'Good, good. We'll have you in, in a minute – just doing some checks and so on. Don't worry, you won't miss anything important – promise.'

'But—'

'I said you won't miss it,' she repeated, patting his hand. 'Sorry, here's the anaesthetist now.'

They both disappeared into the room. Nigel looked at Catherine. He was white and wild-eyed.

'I won't – that is, they won't—'

'Of course not. Nigel, just explain. It'll be fine.'

'Yes, but they don't seem to listen.'

'They will – I'll help. Oh goodness . . .'

A rather loud groan came from the room; followed by another.

'Oh God,' said Nigel. He grabbed Catherine's hand. 'This is awful.'

'Nigel, it's quite normal. Don't worry, she'll be fine. It does make you make noises. Lots of people swear. I did.'

'I'm sure Lucinda won't.'

Another groan.

'Oh, poor Lucinda. Why don't they help her?'

'I'm sure they are. If that was the anaesthetist, they'll have the epidural rigged up in no time. Lucky her – they hadn't been invented when I had mine.'

A large, rather handsome man came hurrying along the corridor, wearing a three-piece suit and a bow tie, and disappeared into the room.

'That must be Mr Clark,' hissed Catherine to Nigel.

'How do you know?'

'That's what expensive gynaecologists look like. All of them.'

Sister Johns put her head out of the door. 'Mr Cowper, you can come in now. Quickly, or you're going to miss the big moment. She's doing wonderfully well.'

'But – but –' Nigel was very green now. 'I'm not – that is . . .'

'You'll be fine,' she said. 'Don't worry. Best moment of your life, I promise. Besides, she needs you. Nurse!' she called into the room. 'Have you got a gown for Mr Cowper?'

'Yes, I have. Tell him to get a move on, she wants to push.'

There was a loud wail of pain from the room.

'No, I can't,' said Nigel. He sat down, put his head in his hands. 'I really can't. I feel sick.'

'Mr Cowper, do pull yourself together.' Sister sounded quite stern.

'The thing is,' said Catherine quickly, 'he's not – not the father.'

'Oh. Oh, I see.' Sterner still. 'Well, where is the father?'

'On a plane somewhere,' said Catherine.

Another wail: long and low, followed by Lucinda's voice telling someone very loudly to fuck off. Nigel looked very shocked.

'Told you,' said Catherine. 'That's a very good sign. She's nearly there.'

'She does need some support though,' said Sister. 'She keeps asking if Blue's arrived. I assumed it was Mr Cowper.'

'Could – could I come in?' said Catherine.

'What's your name? I could ask her.' She reappeared. 'She says she'd love you to come in. You'd better stay here and keep quiet,' she said severely to Nigel, as if it was he making all the noise, not Lucinda.

Catherine went into the room; Lucinda held out her arms to her. 'Catherine, Catherine, I'm so pleased to s— Oh shit. Shit! This is fucking agony. Tell them to give me an epidural, for God's sake. They won't.'

'We can't,' said Mr Clark. 'It's far too late. Wouldn't work in time now. Here comes another one. Push, Lucinda, push hard . . . head down on your chest . . . that's right. Good girl. Few more of those and you'll be there.'

'I wish I was there,' said Lucinda. 'I wish I was anywhere. How did you do this twice, Catherine, how— Oh God. God. Shit. *He-elp!*'

It seemed to Nigel to be going on for ever: the groans, the yells, heavy panting, like a terrified dog: how could he have even considered putting Lucinda through this? And where was Horton? Where was he when she needed him?

Blue was on a plane somewhere over the Channel, silent with terror. Occasionally he said, quite quietly, that if the fucking pilot didn't get the fucking plane to City Airport in the next ten minutes, he'd fucking sue him; but apart from that he said nothing, just sat berating himself, wondering how, why, he could possibly have done this awful thing, abandoned Lucinda, leaving her alone in her hour of greatest need. God, he was a shit, a bastard. What had she done, for God's sake, to deserve him? If she was all right, if the baby waited for him to arrive, he'd join a fucking monastery. No, that wouldn't do any good, he had to support them both. He looked down at the darkness, beginning now to break up into pinpricks of light. England at last. So – within an hour? Maybe. Surely he'd be in time – surely. That woman – what was her name, Mrs Something – said first babies often took up to twenty-four hours to arrive. Probably nothing much was happening yet; probably she was just lying there, doing those bloody breathing exercises she had demonstrated to him – why hadn't he concentrated harder on what she was saying? – and he'd be there before anything really happened.

'If you don't get this fucking thing to fucking City Airport, I'll fucking sue you,' he said for the fourth time in half an hour.

'Blue, calm down, mate,' said Charlie. 'She'll be fine.'

'You don't know that,' said Blue. 'Anything might be happening, anything.'

'Come on Lucinda, once more. PUSH.' Mr Clark was looking very stern. 'And again . . . go on, harder, harder, come on, this is why it's called labour, you know . . . Now – good, good – right, big deep breath and nearly there . . . There we are. Yes! You've done it! Let's just – well done. There she is. A beautiful little girl.'

'A girl! Oh, how lovely. Oh, Blue will be so cross. Serve him right, just serve him right. Look, Catherine, look, isn't she lovely, aren't I clever, aren't we all clever; thank you so, so much, Mr Clark, sorry I swore at you. Oh, look at her, look at her great big blue eyes . . . Come here, let me hold you, you beautiful, beautiful little thing . . .'

Catherine went out of the room to tell Nigel the news and to reassure him that all was well; he was still sitting holding his head in his hands.

'Nigel, it's OK. She's fine, absolutely fine. And so's the baby – a little girl – absolutely beautiful.'

'I thought – I thought she was going to die,' he said. 'I couldn't bear it.'

And as she stood there, tearful herself, Catherine realised that Nigel was weeping, great tears rolling down his cheeks which in his turmoil he kept wiping away with his tie.

He's still in love with her, she thought, with a sense of desperate sadness. Still in love with her, and he always, always will be.

Chapter 55

December, 1990

The house still wasn't sold. Maybe that was going to save her; maybe she'd have to stay another term, or maybe the children should go up and start at their new schools without her, or—

'I think the best thing would be to let the house,' Richard said, his voice rather crackly on the phone – it made her feel crackly too, crackly and cranky, unable to order her thoughts, to respond with any kind of sense. 'I'm sure we'd get a fairly good rent for it, and it's not as if we've got to pay for the one up here. Talk to the agent, Debbie, would you – see what he thinks. This has all gone on long enough.'

But it hadn't, of course; it hadn't gone on nearly long enough. She could have done with another lifetime of it going on, for all its problems.

'You don't think,' she said, 'that I should stay down here on my own for a few weeks? We could reduce the price, after all, if it really doesn't matter so much. I just think empty houses never sell.'

'You haven't been listening, Debbie. It won't be empty. It'll be let.'

'But who will show people round? Not the tenants, surely.'

'No, of course not. The agent. Hopefully the same agent, then he can dovetail the sale and the letting together. Morag says other people have done something similar when they've moved up here, with great success. But don't even think about not coming up, Debbie. I couldn't stand another term without you. I really do need you here, for professional as well as personal reasons. And you know, Morag's been terribly patient, given me every help and support, but I don't think she would wear another term. And besides, she wants you up here too,

743

working with her as well as me. She's looking forward to welcoming you; she's a very warm, and almost motherly person.'

'Ah.' Even if she did go, even if she said goodbye to Joel, even if she became the most perfectly behaved and honourable wife in Christendom, even if her own virtue allowed her peace, and in due course happiness, how in the name of everything terrible was she to endure sharing her life with Morag?

Maurice Crane had finally returned to work at Jenkins & Jenkins. His leg had taken longer to heal than expected, and as everyone kept reminding him, he wasn't as young as he had been. Maurice found this more than a little irritating, although he had to admit that being back in the office was actually rather nice. He did immediately feel younger, in fact. The girls all made a great fuss of him, and although he had become a dab hand at the big crossword in the *Telegraph* and had finally read the complete works of Dickens, his brain felt ready for a change. Or rather, a return to its old haunts.

On the third day, Roger Spence the Managing Director of Jenkins & Jenkins, called him into his office. Rather nervous, wondering if his absence had been too long, whether he was going to be eased out, Maurice straightened his tie, brushed down his jacket and went along the corridor.

'Ah, Maurice. Good to have you back. Feeling completely yourself again, are you?'

'Yes, thank you, Mr Spence. I never thought to say this, but I was really missing the old place. Only thing is, instead of looking forward to my retirement, I'm now rather dreading it.'

'Well, you've got a few years yet, haven't you?'

'Four,' said Maurice, feeling more nervous still; clearly Mr Spence was leading up to an early-retirement package.

'Now, one of your clients was a Mr Simon Beaumont, wasn't he?'

'Indeed, Mr Spence.'

'As I expect you know, he was drowned, just about the time you had your accident.'

'Yes. Most regrettable. Such a charming man.'

'He was. But – apparently, there is to be an inquest.'

744

'Oh, really?'

'Yes. Although it was probably an accident, there were circumstances which could be interpreted as being sufficient to drive him to suicide.'

'I'm very sorry to hear that.'

'Yes, he'd lost an awful lot of money from Lloyd's, had to sell everything, even lost his job, poor chap. Now the Coroner's office has been making various enquiries; investigating the actual state of his finances, whether he had further debts and so on and so forth.'

'Oh dear.'

'Now, because you were the executive in charge of his policies, I have to ask you if you received any instructions from him, over the course of the past – what? – six months. Any changes made, any extra policies taken out, that sort of thing.'

'Ah. Yes.' Maurice Crane looked at his well-shone shoes. 'Yes, I see.' His voice was slightly hesitant.

Roger Spence looked at him sharply. 'Do I take it that means yes, you did hear from him?'

Maurice Crane sighed. 'Like George Washington,' he said, 'I cannot tell a lie. I was hoping not to be asked such a question, that I might remain silent. I think Mr Washington would have found that acceptable.'

'I think, Maurice,' said Roger Spence wearily, 'that you'd better tell me what you're talking about.'

Maurice Crane did so; and was told later in the day that he must make a statement and would probably be called as a witness at Simon Beaumont's inquest.

He went home feeling depressed and rather guilty.

Jamie wrote Annabel a long letter, declining her invitation to spend Christmas with the Beaumonts: *I would have loved it, of course, but Mother is very protective about our family Christmas. The matriarch in her comes out.* Comes out! thought Annabel. It doesn't seem very well hidden to me. *I'm hoping that next year you may be here, spending it with us. But we can talk on the day and I do send you and your brother and sister and your mother, of course, our very best wishes for a happy day. Or as happy as it could be, under the circumstances. Do you have any plans? I'd love to hear them.*

And then, darling Annabel, it will be January and you'll be here for our engagement party. You haven't told me yet how many of you will be able to join us. But actually as long as you're there, that's all that will matter to me . . . Love, love, love you, Jamie

Annabel sat for a long time, holding the letter, staring out of the window. She was thinking not of Jamie, but of Christmas. It was going to be totally hideous. Life was altogether rather grim. They were moving in another week; the house had been stripped of all the large furniture, and walls that had worn pictures for years and rooms that had sheltered tables and chairs and wardrobes and tallboys all looked not only empty, but oddly shabby. It was horrible.

The house they were renting in Fulham, painted, furnished and carpeted throughout in shades of beige, completely bland and modern, was not an ideal setting for Christmas.

Their mother was feeling well now, and almost restored to her normal energetic self, but she was very thin – apart from a very neat little bump – and her face was pale and drawn. Tilly spent a great deal of time weeping over Boy and his imminent departure from her life, the news broken to her by a distressed Flora, who now had the house on the market, and wasn't even getting on so well with Fallon and Madison, who couldn't be informed of the cause of her grief and were beginning to find it boring. Toby was breaking up in a few days; he was still edgy and down, and clearly found his mother's pregnancy deeply embarrassing. The only bright spot on the horizon was the new salon and her role there, her job title of Stylist – Young Clients, which she'd agreed on with Florian, and the sheer joy of him wanting her there.

'Got a minute, Joel?' Hugh Renwick's large figure loomed in his doorway.

'Yeah, sure.'

'Like a word. Maybe after conference?'

'Fine.' Now what?

'She's so beautiful, so bl— absolutely perfect,' said Blue. He was gazing intently into his daughter's face as she took her sixth meal of the day. 'I still can't get over it.'

'Can't get over what?'

'Well, you know, the whole thing really. It's a blooming miracle. Nine months earlier there's a bit of how's yer father and then – boom. A new person.'

'I know. Haven't we done well? Here, take her a minute, I want to get more comfy.'

Blue took the baby rather gingerly. 'You look like your mum,' he said to her, 'you know that?'

'She does, doesn't she? Everyone says so. You don't mind, do you?'

'Course not. Think if she looked like me.'

'Well, it would be fine if she'd been a boy. There, that's better. I'll have her back. Come on, precious, back to the milking parlour.'

'The what?'

'It's what you call the place where they milk cows every day.'

'They haven't half changed,' said Blue, looking at the mountainous objects that had replaced Lucinda's rather neat round breasts.

'Just as well. Blue, give me those tissues, would you. Thank you. How are things at work?'

She had ordered him back to work on the second day, finding his restless, nervous presence the opposite of what she wanted; and his undoubtedly genuine remorse had become extremely irritating.

'Look, Blue,' she had said as he embarked on yet another round of, 'How could I have done that to you,' and, 'How are you ever going to forgive me?' – 'It's all right. It happened. I said you could go, it was just as much down to me as to you. Just stop going on about it. We've got more important things to think about. Our new responsibilities.'

'You're an angel, Lucinda,' said Blue, kissing her tenderly. 'An absolute angel.'

'I know,' she said, smiling sweetly, and kissed him back. Her plans for herself and the baby were actually the opposite of angelic, but he didn't have to know that.

'Now,' she said, 'I've been thinking. We're coming home tomorrow, Little Miss and me – we must settle on a name for her, Blue.'

'Yes, I know.'

So far, they had been unable to agree on anything: so sure had they both been that the baby was going to be William John. They had ranged from the popular Jade ('over my dead body,' said Lucinda), to the esoteric Annunciata ('you must be bleedin' joking') and taken in the plain Janes and Annas and Carolines ('she's much too pretty') and the fashionably floral, Daisy and Lily and Rose ('because she's my little flower,' said Blue tenderly).

'But anyway, yes, you can come and get me at two o'clock and then we'll be home together, a proper little family. Isn't it totally lovely?'

'It is.'

'But – you know something? I just don't know how we're going to manage in that house.'

'You've noticed. Lucy, I've been telling you that for months.'

'Yes, I know and I'm sorry, but at least you know why. Now I had one idea,' said Lucinda, and her eyes sparkled at him.

'Yeah? Look, I'm sure she's smiling.'

'No, I think it's only wind. Golly, there's a lot coming out the other end, did you hear that?' She giggled. 'She farts as loudly as you do. Now you might not like my idea . . .'

'Not your mother? Please, please, not your mother's—'

'Well, she did offer. And there is lots of room.'

'Lucy, no.'

'Now you did promise, Blue. To make it up to me. For – not being here, you know.'

There was an endless silence while a series of violent and rather obvious emotions chased one another across Blue's face; then he said, dragging the words out of himself, clearly with an enormous effort, 'Yes. All right.'

'Or,' said Lucinda, 'we could go to Nigel's house. Well, my house actually.'

'What? Lucinda, I can't live there, I just can't.'

'It wouldn't be for long. Just till we put it into this trust thingy. I asked Steve if he thought it was a good idea, and he said brilliant, gave the whole thing a bit of credence.'

'When did you ask him?' said Blue suspiciously.

'Yesterday – I rang him. And there's something else. I think I'm going to have to get a maternity nurse.'

'What's that? I've told you, Lucinda, I'm not having any nannies.'

'A maternity nurse is not a nanny,' said Lucinda firmly. 'She comes for about six weeks or so, until the baby starts sleeping through the night. So you can recover properly. I just think we need the help. And we can't fit her into Limehouse. And the other house is empty – it's not as if Nigel would be there. He's found a flat in Sloane Street to rent; he says the house is just impossibly big, and he feels lonelier and lonelier in it. Poor darling Nigel. I do wish he and Catherine could ... well, anyway, the house is empty, it's mine in any case, and I think we should go and live there for a bit. It would be so easy.'

'For you maybe. What do you think I'm going to feel like, moving into your ex's place, sleeping in his bed, all that stuff. I can't do it, Lucy, I really can't – sorry.'

'Well, it'll have to be Mummy then. Oh Blue, and I thought ... I thought ...' She started to cry.

Blue hastily went over to her, handed her some tissues. 'Don't cry, Lucinda, it's – it's all right, we'll manage somehow. Can't you get these maternity people to come in just for the day?'

'Don't be silly,' said Lucinda, blowing her nose. 'The whole point is having her there at night. No, we'll have to go down to my parents'. Maybe you could stay in Limehouse if the journey's too bad.'

There was a silence, then: 'Lucinda, I'm not having us separated. I'm not leaving you and the baby, when I've just got you both. I just – oh, all right. Yes. As long as it's not for long. We'll move into that mausoleum. But I'm having a new bed.'

'Oh Blue, thank you. Thank you so much. Of course you – we, I hope – can have a new bed. And the minute I'm feeling better, we can have a new house. Oh, you're an angel. I love you, I love you so much. It'll all be so easy – we can just drive there tomorrow and move in.'

'Yeah, OK,' said Blue wearily.

'Now you'll have to put a bit of time in, moving our stuff. Or rather the baby's stuff. I think we should use the small room next to – to the main bedroom for a nursery, what do you think?'

'I don't know,' he said, looking very sulky. 'I've never set foot in the bloody place, how could I—'

'Of course. I'd forgotten. Sorry. Well, you'll love it, honestly. And you know, lots of those houses we looked at are still on the market. I checked up on that as well.'

'How?'

'I phoned the agents, how do you think?'

'What, even the one in Chislehurst – with the indoor pool?'

'Even that one,' said Lucinda. 'Now . . .' She reached for a pen and a piece of paper.

'Lucinda, be careful, you nearly dropped the baby then.'

'Of course I didn't. You mustn't molly-coddle her, Blue, it's—' She stopped. 'Goodness! Maybe we could call her Molly? Molly! How do you like that? I think it's divine.'

'I – well, it's quite nice, I suppose. Look, I don't care what you say, Lucinda, that baby is smiling.'

'She obviously likes the idea of her new name. Go on, Blue, say you like it. I love it.'

'It'll do,' he said, taking the baby, stroking her small head. 'It'll certainly do.'

'And if you like, we can make Rose her second name. Molly Rose. Molly Rose Horton. How do you like that?'

'Fine,' he said. 'Absolutely fine. Quite like it, actually.' He smiled down at his daughter. 'Hello, Molly Rose.'

The baby farted loudly again.

'There – you see? It's the only way she can show her approval at the moment. And now you'd better get going on moving all her stuff. We haven't got long.'

'How do I get a key?' he said.

'I've still got one,' she said, fishing the key Nigel had given her the day before out of her bag. 'Here you are. And I'll make a list, to help you.'

When he had gone, she looked down at the baby. 'Well, that wasn't too difficult, was it?' she said. 'And how lucky, Uncle Nigel having the key with him yesterday. And I tell you something else, Molly Rose, there is no way I'm going to go and live in Chislehurst. But we won't have to. Silly lot, they are, men. When you're older I'll tell you exactly how to deal with them. Now, do you want to come back into the milking parlour, or . . .?'

But Molly Rose was already fast asleep.

'Flora? This is Colin.'

'Oh – Colin. How nice.'

'Yes. Well, I hope so.'

He sounded slightly stiff. Even so, he had phoned. She'd half-feared she'd never see him again.

'I'm – I'm sorry if I over-reacted the other day. I was—'

'Colin, you didn't. You *under*-reacted: lots of people would have beaten me up.'

'I hope not.' His tone was quite shocked. 'Anyway, I admire you really, Flora. Admire your integrity. And feel a little ashamed of my own lack of it.'

'Colin!' Flora suddenly saw things very clearly, that he had actually had to bend his own principles to help her, that it went against his own rather honest grain. She felt a lump in her throat. 'Colin, I shall never, ever cease to be grateful to you, for what you were willing to do for me. I do thank you from the bottom of my heart. And I feel very bad indeed for wasting so much of your extremely valuable time. Why don't you come to supper tonight and I'll cook one of your favourites. How about some nice Welsh Black beef?'

'That – that would be very nice,' he said, 'and there's something I want to discuss with you. Something I was going to ask you a while back.'

'Yes?'

'I wondered – well, that is, I thought . . . I mean, I wondered how you'd feel about us – that is . . .'

'Colin, whatever is it you're trying to say?'

'Well, I wondered how you'd feel about us going to Salzburg together this summer. For the festival.'

'Colin, I'd love that. Absolutely love it. You know I would. Why should I feel anything but pleasure?'

'Well, you know,' he said. 'I mean, some people might think – well . . .'

'What might they think?' said Flora. She felt absurdly near to tears. 'They'd think what a very, very kind man you were and how lucky I was not only to be going, but going with you.'

'Oh. Well, that's marvellous.' She could hear his pleasure, even hear his smile. 'In that case I'll book it all up then, the whole thing – flights, hotels, everything. Er, separate rooms, of course,' he added quickly.

'Of course,' said Flora, even more quickly.

Suddenly, even losing the house seemed less dreadful.

There was something wrong: Debbie could feel it. Joel wasn't properly – there. Distracted and distant, even as he made love to her: silent afterwards.

'What is it?' she said. 'What's the matter?'

'Oh, nothing,' he said, and his voice was cool. 'I mean, it's just great, you know, what's happening to me at the moment.'

'What do you mean?'

'I mean, I'm so much in love with you I've asked you and not only you, your three bloody kids, to marry me, and all I get is being told to wait. While you think. My whole life on hold, while Debbie Fielding thinks. Can't work properly, can't make any plans, everything based on the next time you might be able to see me, and all the time fucking terrified in case you say no and go off to bloody Scotland. What do you *think's* the bloody matter, Debbie, do tell me. I'd love to get your angle on it.'

She was silent; her heart thudding so loudly she felt he must be able to hear it, but she couldn't find any words. She sat up in the bed, started pulling on her shirt.

'What am I to make of it, your behaviour, your inability to decide what to do? How am I supposed to believe you love me, when you throw this pile of shit at me. I'm fucking fed up with it, you know that? Even with fucking, as a matter of fact. It's all so bloody – futile. You arrive, you say you love me, we have sex, you say you haven't decided yet, you go again. I can't stand it much longer, you know.'

'You won't have to,' she said, very low. 'In two weeks, term ends, and—'

'Well, that's very good news, isn't it?' he said, and he was up and pacing round the room now, staring at her, his face dark. 'Very encouraging. Term ends. Your husband comes home. That'll be the end of it, of us. Unless – and it seems increasingly unlikely – unless you deign to say yes, you will marry me, and leave him; unless these protestations of love of yours actually turn out to mean something, instead of just being rather pretty words. Why don't you go home now, Debbie, right now, and don't come back until you've made your mind up.'

752

And confronted by the reality of it, of losing him, of saying goodbye to him, Debbie started to cry.

'Oh, for God's sake,' he said, 'I've had enough of your tears, more than enough. They don't seem to mean anything very much, they're just – just . . .'

'Something's happened, hasn't it?' said Debbie. 'Something's changed. You're not just fed up, it's something else – something you haven't told me.'

'Well, yes, there is. I – I didn't want to tell you until you'd made up your mind. I felt it wasn't fair. But – well, I suppose you know me too well for that.'

'I suppose I do.'

As she did; and as he knew her, every tiny piece of her, not just her body, not even just her senses and how perfectly and exquisitely to arouse them, but her brain, how it worked, what it did, where it went. It was almost frightening: that they should be so close, after so short a time, when Richard, who she had been married to for ten years, whose children she had borne, was still in some ways an unknown quantity. The Richard who could decide to move to Scotland, for instance, uproot his family, disrupt all their lives without consulting her, the Richard to whom Morag was a beacon of perfection, the Richard who could deceive her, lie to her even . . .

She came back to Joel with an effort. 'So – what is it?'

'I've been offered a job. In New York.'

'New York.' It didn't mean anything to her at first; anything at all. Just as, at first, a cut – even a burn – doesn't hurt: and then the pain comes.

'Yes. Running our New York office. It would be fun, and it would be a huge step up for me.'

'God. How amazing. How – how absolutely amazing. I'm so – so happy for you, Joel, so proud of you, I – I –' She realised she was crying again. She had no idea why, really, except that the pain had started.

'I'm sorry,' he said, 'I was so determined not to tell you. It's too much to put on you.'

'What do you mean?'

'I mean that of course you can't come to New York. If we're together. It would be out of the question.'

'Yes,' she said very quietly. 'Yes, of course I couldn't.'

'So, you'd be making your decision on the wrong basis.'

'Would I?' She felt dizzy; her brain didn't seem to be functioning.

'Well, yes. I think so. You'd know you were changing my career. Stopping me from doing what I wanted to do.' He smiled, rather awkwardly. 'It suddenly struck me that this must seem rather déjà vu to you. I mean, it's a bit the same, isn't it, as Richard going to Scotland.'

'No,' she said, thinking about it. 'No, it isn't. You've made me your prime consideration. You've put me before the decision. He dragged me along after it, in its wake.' She started to cry again, went into his arms, clung to him. 'Oh Joel, I love you, so much, I don't know how to bear it. I'm so, so sorry that I've been so useless. That I am so useless and selfish.'

'You're not,' he said, 'not useless, anyway. Come here.' He sat down on the bed, held out his arms. 'Come and be useful. I love you so much too. Do you think I want to go away to New York without you? Do you think I want to leave you here, far away from me? I dread it already – if it has to happen. I'm just hoping and praying to a God I have no time for, as you know, that it won't.'

He bent his head, started to kiss her breasts, very gently, moving his mouth over them. She shivered, partly with fear, partly with wanting him.

'I can't imagine being without you now,' he said. 'I can't begin to envisage what a chasm there would be, or how I could begin to fill it. Whatever I said before, I—'

And: 'Joel,' she said, still awed at her realisation of the extraordinary difference in the way she was to him and the way she was to Richard, reaching out to touch his face, 'it's all right. You won't have to fill it, I promise. I want to be with you, I want to marry you, if you'll still have me.'

'What?'

'I said, I wanted to be with you. Please. I'm sorry I've been so long making the decision.'

'Oh God,' he said, 'oh, thank God.' And she felt something splash onto her hand, and realised he was weeping.

Chapter 56

December, 1990

Elizabeth had received a list of names from the Coroner's office, of the people who would be giving evidence at the inquest. It was alarmingly lengthy, and some of the names slightly unexpected. It was going to be a very long and dreadful day, but apparently it was most unlikely to run into a second. Looking at the list, she didn't share their confidence.

There was at least no need for the people from France to come over; the Coroner's Officer, she had been told, would read out the medical reports from France, the results of the post mortem, the pathology, the official reason for Simon's death.

There would also be a statement from his doctor in London – what would that be about? – and there would be a summary, apparently of his recent history, and his financial position. John Fraser, their solicitor, would be attending. His boss at Graburn & French would also be called. Good, thought Elizabeth. I hope he can't sleep, thinking about it all. I hope he's dreading this even more than I am.

And then came a long list of the people who had seen him, or spoken to him, the day before: 'Not a lot of men, are there, Simon?' said Elizabeth aloud. 'Nothing new there.' Catherine Morgan, Lucinda Cowper, Flora Fielding, Fiona Broadhurst – it sounded like the roll call at a girls' school – followed by Joel Strickland. Why would he be involved, she wondered, and then remembered the article. David Green would be called, of course; and then there would be a technical report on the yacht, on its general seaworthiness, and another from an expert on lifebelts.

And then there was a name that made no sense to her at all,

a name she simply didn't know. Maurice Crane, an executive at Jenkins & Jenkins, insurance brokers. That worried her: quite a lot. Of course, she had spoken to several people there, and they had all been most helpful, over the life policy and so on, but who was Maurice Crane, and why had he got to make a statement?

The whole thing loomed over her life, casting a huge, heavy shadow. A shadow she had to walk through. And it was a way off yet; it would be many weeks still before it was over.

There were other shadows too: Christmas, how were they going to get through Christmas, the four of them, alone in this house that wasn't home? She could hardly bear to think about it, about the forced jollity – for they would have to try, *she* would have to try – the aching void where Simon should have been, the celebrations all around them. She even considered suggesting they went away, to a hotel, abroad even; but felt that would be even worse, to be among strangers who didn't know, didn't understand.

Well, it would end. Everything ended. She looked down at the small neat mound, beginning to grow a little now, that was her baby, and stroked it tenderly. Next year, it would be there, and that would make it better: a small piece of happy, laughing oblivion to their grief, and then she thought, as she often did, how sad it was that the child would never know the lovely, charming, generous man who had created him, and what a dreadful loss that was. Somehow they must keep Simon alive, all of them; somehow they must explain him, the essence of him, for this, the last of his children. It was almost more important than anything.

Catherine was also dreading Christmas. Phyllis and Dudley had told her they always had Christmas dinner at the Golf Club, and that she and the children would be very welcome; she almost felt that warming up some cooked turkey on her gas ring would be preferable. She was still pushing the whole thing as far back in her mind as she could when the Jane-Annes asked her if they would all like to go there.

'Jane-Anne would love it,' Kate Price said, 'and so would the boys. We've got masses of family coming – you'd be so welcome. And Patrick always comes round in the evening –

loves his charades. You and he have become rather friendly, I believe,' she added, winking at Catherine.

Which they had; but friendship was clearly all he had in mind. Thinking of her Mrs Bennet moments, Catherine now felt rather silly; but it was just the same a relief. He was sweet and kind and rather amusing in his bluff way; but he was the opposite of sexy.

And anyway, she was in love with Nigel.

Dear, bumbling, perfectly-natured Nigel, with his bloodhound eyes and his oddly jaunty walk, and his sweet smile and his rather desperate honesty. Nigel was good: good through and through. And she loved him through and through. The only problem was, he didn't seem to be in love with her . . . So – what was the point of wishing he did, and crying for the moon? He was still in love with Lucinda.

Oh well. Enough of that, Catherine. The invitation touched her immensely; she also savoured the uncharitable thought of how much it would annoy Phyllis and Dudley, to think of her spending Christmas with the Honourable Prices.

A sort of peace had descended on Debbie. Even the suggestion that they might all spend Christmas with Flora, which she acceded to with some misgivings, couldn't shatter it. She still had moments of complete panic, but released now from the anguish of indecision, she felt she could at least look forward, although the view was not pleasant.

She had to tell Richard. She had to tell the children. She had to tell Flora, or at least, let Richard tell Flora. At the very thought of that, she literally shook. Finally, Richard had to tell Morag. It seemed to her not impossible that Morag would decide to find someone else to run the school, another family man, with a more amenable wife.

The house still had to be sold; or she supposed it would. Richard was hardly going to let her live in it on her own. They had to decide where the children would go to school, whether they went up to Scotland with him, or stayed in West London with her. In which case she'd need the house.

Decisions had to be taken about decisions. Who would decide on where the children lived and when? And would the children have a say in where they spent the term-time – always supposing their father stayed in Scotland? It was all very ugly.

The children and Richard and Flora, however, had no idea about the ugliness; they were safely encased in a shiny rainbow-coloured bubble. Debbie stood outside that bubble, looking in, and knew she had to burst it, had to tell them all these horrible things and contemplated what it would do to them. Her husband would be hurt almost beyond endurance, his fragile self-esteem further diminished. Her children would be grieving and shocked, the absolute security within which they had grown up shattered forever. Their loyalty would be strained, they would find it terribly difficult. They would quite possibly think they hated her and would certainly tell her so. They would certainly hate Joel. And the joyful, intense way that she and Joel loved one another would also be damaged, dragged through the dirt of real life.

All these things she knew must happen; all these things she was afraid of. And all these things were worth her being with Joel for the rest of their lives. She had decided, after discussing it with Joel very carefully, that they shouldn't be told until after Christmas. It would be too horrible for them to bear, Christmas made dreadfully unhappy: what child deserved that? The carols, the Nativity plays, the presents, the tree, the fairy-lights, the stockings, the surprises, the secrets: all revealed as miserable fakes, like the smiling old man coming down the chimney bringing them what they most wanted while his reindeer pawed the night sky. She couldn't do it; they couldn't do it.

And Joel, happily patient, agreed. He had turned down the New York job 'for personal reasons', had suggested various other people to Hugh Renwick, who told him he was a fool. Joel agreed that he very probably was.

And with only two days left until Richard came home, the two of them seized and savoured whatever time they could find.

Flora had just got back from taking Tilly to Swansea Station to catch the London train when the phone call came.

They had had a perfect three days together: the four of them – Tilly and Boy and she and Hal. Flora had found a buyer for Hal – 'Honestly, darling, she couldn't be better,' invited Tilly

758

down to spend a last weekend with Boy; hoping it would somehow ease her grief, or at least give her some outstandingly happy memories. The weather had been wonderful, brilliant and frosty, and they had ridden every corner of Gower; along the beaches, over Rhossili Down, along Cefn Bryn, through the woods at Parkmill to Three Cliffs Bay and up to the storybook ruins of Pennard Castle high above the sea. Mostly they walked slowly and chatted, long rambling conversations, about things horsey, Flora telling Tilly about her childhood, about her pony and how he had been sent away at the beginning of the war, about childhood gymkhanas where she had won lots of rosettes – 'magical!' – and others where she had won none – 'total humiliation' – her first cross-country event – 'terrifying' – her first ride out to hounds – 'so, so exciting'.

She spoke of the horses she had owned, from the small Shetland she could scarcely get her legs across, to her beloved Prince Hal, a present from William for her fortieth birthday. How all her memories were linked to her horses. How the best thing about getting home from boarding school was the rush to see her horse 'and the smell, that lovely smell – to me that means happiness'. How she had consoled herself after disastrous dances, where no one had asked her to dance – 'I can't believe that, Flora'; 'It's true' – with a midnight visit to the stables, or at bad exam results – 'also true, I just never did any work' – with the most dangerous rides she could think of.

She told Tilly that she had lost lots of babies, after she had had Richard, and that riding out across the hills was the most healing thing she could do, and that after William had died she could lose her grief entirely for a few hours with long fierce gallops along the beach.

'If only Mummy could ride,' Tilly had said, 'but you know, I think work does the same for her, it heals her somehow; everyone keeps saying she should take time out, specially with the baby, but it would be disastrous for her.'

Tilly talked too, of her first pony, 'a lovely part-Arab, far too good for me; bit of Daddy-madness – he had to go back'; a small Welsh cob mare – 'she was so patient'; and then, of course, the wonder of Boy – 'another bit of Daddy-madness really, but at least I could ride him' – on her tenth birthday.

But there was an underlying sadness to her, as she talked;

and on the last night she started to cry. 'It's not just Boy, Flora, it's because he's so much part of Daddy to me, that sounds so stupid but you know what I mean; Daddy wanted me to have him and he was so proud of me and my riding, which is pretty pathetic really as you know, and I feel I'll be saying goodbye to both of them when Boy goes, and I can't bear it, I just can't.'

She cried for a long time in Flora's arms, and then went quietly to bed; in the morning, pale and subdued, she dressed for her return to London and went out to the stables on her own. Flora watched her, as she put her thin arms round Boy's neck and rested her head against his nose; watched Boy pushing his head into her, while rooting hopefully for Polo mints, and then she ran her fingers through his mane and kissed his nose, and a very short time later she came in again, her small face white and set and said, 'Can we go now, quickly?' And she had got into the car, her face turned determinedly away from the stables, fiddling with her seat belt, doing up her buttons, and breathing rather fast; and as they turned onto the road, she said, 'Right. Well, that was all lovely, Flora, thank you,' and smiled at her – a quick, brilliant smile – and then cried all the way to Swansea as if her heart would break.

Flora drove back slowly, stopped at the small supermarket in Bishopston for a few things and, as she pulled into the yard at home, thought more savagely than she had for some time of Lloyd's and their power to wreck lives. The phone was ringing as she opened the front door, and she almost didn't answer it. It was that awful estate agent, no doubt, to say he had more people wanting to view the house; the advertisement, published the previous Saturday with its absurdly small photograph, reducing Broken Bay House to something the size of the bungalows that littered the property pages, had had a poor response so far. For which she was profoundly, if foolishly, grateful.

'Mrs Fielding? Mrs William Fielding?' The voice was not Welsh, it was rather grand English.

'Yes.'

'Good morning, Mrs Fielding, this is Bernard Edmund-Jones from Harris and Harris, solicitors. Of Cardiff.'

Who on earth were Harris & Harris? Not her solicitors, not the one she and William had used; she'd never heard of them.

'Yes?'

'May I speak with Mr Fielding, please?'

'I'm very sorry,' said Flora, 'but I'm afraid you can't. He died six years ago.'

'I'm sorry to hear that. Very sorry. Well, then I shall have to discuss the matter with you.'

'Which matter, Mr Edmund-Jones?'

'I have just seen the advertisement for Broken Bay House.'

'Oh yes?' Obviously he wanted to buy it; and he did sound a much more appropriate inhabitant than Mr and Mrs Davies from Llandeilo.

'Mrs Fielding, I'm sorry, but you can't sell that house. It doesn't belong to you; it's not yours to sell.'

Chapter 57

December, 1990

'Well, this is it.'

'Yes, 'fraid so.'

'I shall miss these,' Joel bent to kiss her breasts, 'and this,' moving lower. 'Take care of it all, won't you?'

'Of course I will. And it's not for long. After all.'

'It will seem long.'

'Yes, I know. But then next time we're together, it'll be so different. It'll be proper.'

'I don't know if I want to be properly together with you. I've enjoyed improper.'

'Well, me too. But—'

'You won't forget about me over Christmas, will you?'

'Probably,' she said, smiling and thinking she could never, ever forget him, even if she never saw him again; he was imprinted on her, part of her now, part of her thinking and her doing, there as she woke and talked and worked and played with her children and drove her car and cooked and shopped and drifted off to sleep at night: whether he was with her or not.

'Well, I'll try not to forget you,' he said. 'But it won't be easy.'

She looked at her watch. 'I must go.'

'I know.'

She hated these times, getting up, dressing, leaving him when she longed to stay, driving home too fast, suddenly fearful for the children who she was betraying, even as she betrayed their father.

'Love you. And thank you so, so much for my present.'

It was a mobile phone; he said it might not seem very romantic, but it meant they could hear each other's voices whenever they wanted. 'And it'll help, maybe on the day. You can call me just as often as you like.'

'But don't you dare use it over Christmas.'

'I can't promise that, I'm afraid. Too much to ask.'

'I won't take it then. I'll leave it behind.'

'Well, that's really sensible. Oh Debbie, I love you too. And see you on the twenty-seventh.'

That was the day they had agreed she would return to London to join him, the day she would break the news, leaving Richard and the children to be comforted by Flora.

'The twenty-seventh. Definitely hopefully.'

'Don't say that, Joel. Just – definitely.'

'Just definitely.'

Flora sat waiting in what was called by Harris & Harris 'the outer office', and indeed there was no other word to describe the rather shabby mahoganied grandeur of the room; it was certainly not 'Reception', just as the lady who looked as if she had been there since it was built could not possibly be described as a receptionist.

Flora felt very nervous as she waited to be called in by Mr Edmund-Jones, for he had refused to elaborate on his rather cryptic statement – 'This is not a matter to be discussed on the telephone' – but had agreed that she should drive over to Cardiff that afternoon to see him.

Was she to be evicted? Was there some demon landlord she had had no idea about, waiting to take over the house? Had it been sold over her head, without her knowledge? Would she find herself standing on the South Gower Road within hours, penniless as well as homeless? Would she wander over the moors, like Jane Eyre, cold and hungry . . .

'Mrs Fielding, Mr Edmund-Jones will see you now. Do follow me.'

Flora followed her into Mr Edmund-Jones's office, which was even shabbier and more mahoganied, and even grander, with bulging walls which clearly defied any safety order, lined with books and files, and a window so dirty that even the brilliant early-afternoon sun had trouble finding its way in.

Mr Edmund-Jones stood up to greet her. He had the white hair and almost transparent skin of the very old, and the hand

763

he held out to her was bony and etched with large brown freckles, the nails long and yellowing. He wore striped trousers and a black jacket, and a slightly grubby Old Wykehamist tie. He smiled at her, showing some surprisingly good teeth, and gestured to the chair in front of his desk.

'How do you do, Mrs Fielding. Do please sit down. May I offer you some refreshment? Some tea, or perhaps coffee – we find some of our younger clients prefer coffee these days . . .'

So I'm a younger client, Flora thought; the idea was at once both pleasing and intriguing.

'I'd prefer tea,' she said, 'thank you.'

'Good, good. Mrs Andrews, tea for two if you please, and do bring in the Dundee cake.'

Mrs Andrews withdrew and for a very long time there was no sign of either tea or Dundee cake; Flora wondered if she might have forgotten.

'Well, now,' said Mr Edmund-Jones, 'I expect you have some questions for me.'

'I do,' said Flora. 'Indeed, I do.'

'Please do go ahead.'

'Well, obviously and most importantly, if I don't own Broken Bay House, who does?'

'A trust. The beneficiary of which is your grandson,' said Mr Edmund-Jones. His tone was at the same time surprised and slightly impatient, as if he would not have expected quite so crass a question. 'As you really should know.'

'My – my grandson!' Flora said. Alexander, with his skinny legs and knock knees, his floppy brown hair, and his rather high-pitched ten-year-old voice: how could he possibly own Broken Bay House?

'Yes, indeed. I do apologise for not realising your husband had died.'

'Thank you.'

'I really should study the obituary notices. Somehow there's never time. I'm so sorry, Mrs Fielding. Such a charming man.'

'Well, thank you. Yes, indeed he was. But how, why, isn't the house mine? I don't understand.'

'Because you're a female,' said Mr Edmund-Jones, his bloodshot eyes almost sympathetic as he looked at her.

'I'm a female?'

'Indeed.'

'Well, yes, I do realise that, of course' – God, this was an absurd conversation – 'but why does that mean I can't own the house?'

'Mrs Fielding, Broken Bay House is a male entail.'

'A what?'

'It's held in trust for the eldest grandson's first grandson. I know you have a grandson, because your husband told me.'

'Oh,' said Flora. She felt rather dizzy. 'So – so what happens to the house?'

'Well, nothing very much,' said Mr Edmund-Jones. 'Ah, Mrs Andrews, tea. How nice. Perhaps you would be Mother, Mrs Fielding?'

She smiled at him rather weakly, and poured out the tea. He nodded approvingly as she added the milk.

'So nice to see it properly done. My mother always divided people into Mifs and non-Mifs.'

'She did?' said Flora. Any minute now a white rabbit would surely run through the office.

'Indeed, Milk In First. Not the right way at all. Cake, Mrs Fielding?'

'Er, no thank you,' said Flora. The cake looked as dusty as the office.

'Very well. Now, what did you ask me?'

'What might happen next.'

'As I said, nothing very much. I imagine your grandson is quite young?'

'He's ten.'

'Yes, I see. Well, unless you and he are on very bad terms, I would expect him to allow you to remain there, until your demise. On his reaching twenty-one, the entail passes the house to him, subject to it passing on his death to *his* eldest grandson. Your grandson will be entitled to live there for his lifetime. If he dies without a grandson, it will pass to the eldest living male in the family succession . . .' He pulled out a file from one of his drawers.

'It's all in here,' he said, leafing through the tattered, yellow pages. 'Fascinating story. Would make a rather good film, I always thought. Began with the first owner of the house, John Fielding, who had it built in 1780. John had had a bit of a ne'er-do-well son called David, a gambler, and John was afraid that he might try to sell the house at some point in the future to pay his debts. So he set up an entailed settlement cutting out David and leaving everything in trust for David's son, John's grandson, and thereafter to each eldest grandson, thus ensuring that the house could never be sold or bequeathed; only *designated*. That is what is meant by a male entail, and we as trustees hold it for your grandson.'

'But I have to sell the house,' said Flora, slightly desperately. 'I have considerable debts to Lloyd's of London. They are insisting on it.'

'Well, I'm afraid that is their misfortune,' said Mr Edmund-Jones. 'Lloyd's can't lay a finger on Broken Bay House. It belongs to the trust. They will have to – what is that rather vulgar modern expression – ah yes, they will have to whistle for their money. Dreadful business, that. I have several clients who have been completely ruined by it.'

'So – sorry to go back over this and I must seem very stupid to you, but does this mean I can stay in the house? That it can't be taken away from me.'

'Well, unless, as I say, you and your grandson are on bad terms. In which case, after his reaching his majority, he could ask you to leave. Insist on it, in fact. But I presume that is not the case.'

An image rose before Flora's eyes of Alexander curled up on the battered kitchen sofa beside her, saying sleepily, 'You're a really great granny, you know.'

'I don't think so,' she said. 'No.'

The first thing she did when she got home was pour herself a very large whisky. Then she sat down at the telephone and dialled not Richard's number or even Debbie's but the Beaumonts'.

Elizabeth answered it. 'Oh, hello, Flora. How nice to hear from you. Thank you so much for your note.'

'Not at all. Such lovely news. How are you feeling? Tired, I expect.'

'Yes, I am a bit.'

'Is Tilly there?'

'No, she's not, I'm afraid. She's out with her friends. Is there something wrong with Boy, or—'

766

'There is absolutely nothing wrong with Boy. He's never looked better. No, I would very much like to speak to Tilly, that's all.'

'Well,' said Elizabeth briskly, 'I could be trusted with a message, you know. And if you'll excuse me, I must cut this conversation short; we are being packed up tomorrow, ready for our move the following day. I'm sorting out my clothes even now. So—'

'Elizabeth,' said Flora, 'I know this must be hugely annoying for you, but I do desperately want to tell Tilly this news myself. It's so important to – to both of us. Perhaps you could ask her to ring me when she gets in. Will she be very long?'

'I have no idea, I'm afraid.' Elizabeth's tone was cool still. 'But not late, no. She has to be in by ten at the latest.'

'Then – could you please ask her to ring me? As soon as you possibly can?'

'Yes, all right,' said Elizabeth. 'As soon as I possibly can.'

Irritating woman, she thought, returning to her packing. She just had to control everything! Including the imparting of news to other people's children. But – Simon had been very fond of her, and she had done a lot for Tilly. God, she was tired. She'd be lucky to stay awake until ten at this rate. Maybe she should leave a note out for Tilly, in case. It was only eight.

And thus it was that she went to bed early, leaving a note on the hall table for Tilly; and Tilly burst into her bedroom just after ten, her eyes shining, her pale face flushed, great tears welling in her large blue eyes, and woke her as she drifted into oblivion – and now she'd have trouble getting back to sleep, bloody, bloody Flora Fielding . . .

'Mummy, Mummy, the most wonderful thing. Flora can stay in her house, and Boy can stay with her! Some peculiar legal thing. Isn't that amazing? Isn't that just totally amazing?'

And Elizabeth was forced to admit that it was indeed totally amazing.

A lot of it had to be guesswork. She pieced the story together, with the help of such solid facts as Mr Edmund-Jones was able to supply, and with her rather more intimate knowledge of

William. He had, of course, told her quite early in their relationship – before their marriage, indeed – that the house had been in the family ever since it had been built, and that 'it always will be'.

She hadn't asked why; it seemed obvious – it was a nice thought that it would be passed down from generation to generation. He had never explained anything further, and certainly never mentioned a trust, but that was William, in every way. He had been quite a lot older than her, twenty-five years older, and very old-fashioned in all his attitudes. Flora, marrying him at the age of nineteen, highly unconventional herself, had been kept in the dark about many things, including his income and his financial status.

He had loved her very much, but he had always made it plain that because she was a woman, she did not need – and indeed should not ask for – knowledge of his affairs. She had occasionally asked him about his investments, and of course forced him to explain about Lloyd's to her, including the involvement of the dreadful Trafford Smythe, but even then he had been not so much secretive as protective of his status. Just as he did not expect her to discuss her housekeeping or maternal problems with him, he did not expect to discuss his financial ones with her.

They did not use Harris & Harris as their day-to-day solicitors; a firm in Swansea had handled all their affairs. The will had been absolutely straightforward, and everything had been bequeathed to her; he often said that he must revise it, but he had died so suddenly that any plans he might have had were not incorporated.

She also wondered if he had not entirely trusted her when they were first married: however much he loved her. She was to him an entirely unknown entity, young, bohemian, hugely impulsive; he might have decided she should not be given too much information about his affairs, feared that she might meet someone younger one day and divorce him, her pockets nicely lined. And any revelations would have become more difficult to make as the years went by, as the lack of trust had to be confessed to.

And of course there was another explanation for a possible lack of trust, she thought soberly, staring into the darkness; she had always hoped and indeed had been fairly sure that he had never known of it, but what if he had? She felt a stab of remorse and then of fear; and then crushed them both. Set it aside, Flora, she told herself. As you did then.

He must have planned to tell Richard at some point – which of course would have meant telling her; but Alexander had only been four when William had died – with a suddenness that had not only shocked everyone, but had removed any opportunity for the setting in order of his affairs.

She roamed the house for a while, smiling, savouring it, savouring it remaining hers; she hadn't realised the depth of her dread at leaving it until it was removed. She leaned on the gate overlooking her meadow, and stood there a long time, careless of the cold, drinking in the great expanse of sea and sky; and then, went out to the yard and told the horses. They took the news calmly. And then she went indoors and stood at the dining-room window in a state of joyful excitement, looking down at the sea and waiting impatiently for Tilly's call.

Tilly had been one of her first thoughts; that she and Boy need not be parted. There was no way she could have allowed Elizabeth to tell her; it was rarely granted to human beings to grant perfect happiness themselves, and she intended to make the very most of it.

Blue was a man in love. He often wondered what on earth he had thought about or talked about before Molly Rose had been born. Lucinda, of course, and then, in descending order: his work, and his sundry expensive toys like the Ferrari and his Jet-Ski; but none of them had even begun to occupy his mind in this all-consuming way.

He thought of her the moment he woke up in the morning, leaping out of bed to go and gaze at her before she woke – or, more frequently, while the maternity nurse fed her or changed her, for she was an early riser – and last thing at night, as he drifted off to sleep, while listening anxiously for her cries which he was convinced the nurse wouldn't hear.

The maternity nurse, whose name was Maureen Gardener neither liked nor approved of Blue Horton; she found him not only vulgar – 'not at all our usual sort of father' she said to her friends in the park in the afternoons – but also extremely troublesome, constantly questioning her about what she was doing to Molly Rose, whether that was the best thing, taking her out of the nursery when she wasn't there, fretting over an imaginary rash or a prolonged snuffle, and generally making it impossible for her to do her job. Mrs Cowper was charming, of course, absolutely the breed of mother Miss Gardener understood – 'although I do find their relationship rather hard to understand' – and she had mentioned to her several times that she felt it would be better if Mr Horton stayed out of the nursery, except when invited in. The unspoken words 'and properly dressed' hung in the air.

'Oh, I'm so sorry, Miss Gardener,' Lucinda said, her eyes large blue pools of sympathy, 'but he is so terribly excited about the baby, he's never had one before, of course, and I really think he might become very difficult if I tell him to leave her alone.'

Miss Gardener was tempted to say that *she* might become very difficult if Mr Horton didn't leave her and Molly Rose alone, but she didn't.

Lucinda could never remember being so happy. People always said that, of course, and she had had other periods of great happiness in her life, most recently when she and Blue had first lived together, but this was so stupendously different from anything she had ever known that it quite took her breath away. She had been warned so many times, by people in her ante-natal classes, by her mother and her sister, by friends, by magazine articles – even by Mr Clark, that she would have a let-down, that she would feel tired and sore and depressed, that she might have trouble with feeding, that she would be desperate for sleep: but she experienced none of those things. She glided through the days, and indeed the weeks in a haze of absolute contentment. She recovered physically with extraordinary speed, and was going out for walks with Blue and the baby only a week after the birth, and even did some Christmas shopping – 'not that going to Harvey Nichols was exactly arduous'. She had so much milk that she was able to express bottle after bottleful, which made the night feeds much easier for Miss Gardener, and Molly Rose was absurdly well-behaved, slithering off her mother's breast with a loud burp when she was sated and thus into a deep sleep. Colic was a word which didn't enter her small lexicon; she cried so rarely that when she did, everyone remarked upon it, and even if she was awake, lay contentedly squinting at the mobiles which hung above her cot and her pram. Nor did she favour the behaviour pattern best known to babies of sleeping peacefully all day and commencing to scream at around six o'clock in the evening until far into the night; she lay, squinting happily, or slept peacefully on.

She was also extremely pretty, the sort of baby strangers voluntarily admire; and a few days before Christmas she did unarguably smile properly for the first time. They knew it was a smile and not wind because Lucinda screamed to Blue to come and see, and although she had stopped, she did it again quite quickly. It was the usual rather uncertain, wobbly smile, the small face almost surprised by it; but a smile it was.

'She is clearly quite incredibly advanced,' said Lucinda, 'and you are right to be so proud of her, Blue.'

'Aren't you proud too?' he said and, 'Yes,' said Lucinda, 'of course I am. Oh look – look, Blue, here it comes again!' And indeed it did, and repeatedly throughout the evening until, quite exhausted by all her efforts, Molly Rose fell asleep.

'Isn't that lovely? What a wonderful Christmas present,' said Lucinda. 'I just don't think I want anything else ever again.'

'That's a pity,' said Blue, ''cos I got you this. Better take it back then.'

'This' was a small blue Tiffany box, tied up with a white ribbon. 'Don't you dare,' said Lucinda, snatching it from him, and then: 'Oh Blue,' gazing into it at a diamond eternity ring, 'Blue, I must have been terribly good in a former life to deserve you. And Molly Rose, of course.'

Nigel was going to stay with his Norfolk relatives for Christmas; the prospect was profoundly depressing, but he could see no alternative, apart from spending it alone in his new flat. At least it would remove him physically from the same square mile of Blue Horton and Lucinda; he would still inevitably think of them uncomfortably often, but there would be no danger of his almost bumping into them, as had happened one dreadful afternoon in Knightsbridge. He had rushed into the doorway of Russell & Bromley and studied the shoes rather intently until they had both passed, but it had upset him a lot.

Once the divorce was through, he felt he could at least begin to look forward. The revenue from letting the house would be considerable. He still felt a degree of disquiet about the whole plan – it wasn't quite the sort of thing he had been brought up to think one did, and what his father would have had to say about it he could scarcely begin to contemplate. But he would be clearing over half of his debt to Lloyd's, and whenever he felt particularly bad, he thought of poor Gillian Thompson and several of the other tragic people featured in Joel Strickland's article, and found his conscience eased. And there was Catherine Morgan, of course: her experiences had been dreadful. Who would have dreamed that the conduct of a company that had been so generally assumed to be upright and gentlemanly, could have led people into such distress and indeed, danger?

Nigel sighed. He was doing it again – thinking of Catherine; he tried very hard to keep her out of his thoughts. And failed.

She was so – so sweet. Not many young women these days could be described as sweet, as far as Nigel could see, but Catherine could. In an old-fashioned, totally unselfconscious way. Sweet and gentle and really rather brave: leaving London and her friends, moving to a place where she knew no one, where she would have no independence, to live with what sounded like the most dreadful people: and all to ensure her children's happiness.

He had considered inviting her and the children up for a day before Christmas, perhaps to see a show, but every time he plucked up the courage, approached the phone even, he saw that picture of the three of them going into the house, little Caroline in that other man's arms, and decided against it. He wasn't risking his heart a second time.

Leaving the house hadn't actually been as dreadful as Elizabeth had expected. It had hurt, of course; it brought back exquisitely painful happy memories, of Simon's excited phone call when he had first found it, of their viewing of it, of moving in with one small child and one quite large bump, of the happy family years there, of parties, of fun.

But it held others too, she realised, as she pulled the door behind her for the last time and stood waiting for the pain to hit her; of suspicion and loneliness, of rejection and a sense of personal failure, of bitterness and even at times despair. Simon was so much a part of that house, with all the contradictory experiences of living with him, being married to him, and it might be easier now, in some ways at least, to say goodbye to him, to accept that he was gone.

She had seen a house that she liked very much: smaller, of course, but charming in its own way, early Victorian, in Little Venice, close to the canal, with lovely light, tall rooms, the street overhung with trees and a quiet green garden. She could see her new life being lived there, for it was large enough for the older children to lead their lives and entertain their friends, while small enough to contain her and the baby without a sense of being surrounded with too much space. And far enough away from The Boltons not to feel haunted by the past. She had shown it to the children; they had all liked it, bagged rooms, staked out their territories.

The rented place was all right; they would survive Christmas in it, and then in the New Year, the inquest would soon be behind them for better or for worse. They had discussed Christmas very honestly, had agreed it was just something to get through, that they could do it together.

'I think we should go to church,' Annabel had said rather unexpectedly, 'on Christmas morning, give the day a focus,' and having gone through the obligatory protests, the other two had agreed.

They would have scruffy lunch, Tilly said, and supper in the evening. 'Maybe even beef or something,' said Toby, 'not turkey and all that.'

'Yes, good idea,' said Tilly, 'but I do want crackers. We can't have Christmas without crackers. And stockings.'

'Stockings, of course,' said Elizabeth. 'But I want one too.'

'Self self self with you, isn't it?' said Annabel, giving her a hug. 'Never think of us having to find things for you. OK, just this once.'

And then, a week before the day, she came home and said, 'Mummy, say no at once, but Florian wondered if he could come round in the evening on Christmas Day. Just for some champagne and a chat. He's such a brilliant chatter, and I think it would be nice, give the evening a lift. Only if everyone agrees, obviously.'

'Obviously we agree,' said Tilly. 'Don't we, Toby?'

'Suppose so,' said Toby, sounding sulky. But he did manage to smile; he actually rather liked Florian. He had street cred and Toby longed for that beyond anything.

So it wouldn't be too bad. They'd get through it. As they were getting through all the rest.

Toby was much more relaxed about the baby now; he would still have preferred it not to have happened, but he had stopped being unable to look at his mother, or to mention it. The change had been wrought not by Florian, but by Fallon. Fallon was becoming day by day increasingly beautiful: she had had her wild hair cropped short – by Florian, who had met her one night at the house and begged her to allow him to do it – and it clung to her head like a small black cap. She was tall, almost as tall as Tilly, and very slender, and she had begun to wear rather eccentric clothes, bought from secondhand stalls in Kensington Market – long floating skirts and loose silk blouses, rainbow-coloured sweaters and large floppy hats. Her voice was gorgeous, low and husky, and she had a deep, rather dirty laugh. Toby thought she was wonderful and had even asked her out, but as Fallon said to Tilly, there was no way she could go out with someone who looked and dressed and talked like Toby.

'No offence, Til, but I'd be a laughing stock.'

But she did like him and they had many long conversations over the kitchen table; and one of the things she said to him was that he must be well pleased about the baby.

Whereupon Toby had gone scarlet in the face and opened another bottle of beer and lit one of the cigarettes that Elizabeth had forbidden in the house.

'What's the matter? Did I say something I shouldn't?'

'No,' said Tilly, 'but he doesn't really like the idea.'

'Why on earth not?' said Fallon. 'I mean, there's all the noise, I suppose, and the stink from the nappies and that, but you're not here that much, so you can't complain. And I'm sure your mum will keep it nice. But they're good fun, babies are. I

774

should know, we got enough of them.'

'Yes, but you're a girl,' said Toby after a long silent struggle to find some words.

'You noticed! Well done. Yeah, I know, but what if it's a boy? You can be its – what d'you call it, Tilly, you're good at words – something about a model.'

'Role model?' said Tilly.

'Yeah, role model. You'll be the only male in this house, and he won't half need you. You can take him off, go to the football together, all that stuff. Nah, it'll be great. Me little brother misses me big one something awful.'

'What's happened to him?' said Tilly.

'Oh, Dean's gone to live with Ron – that's our oldest brother,' she explained to Toby. 'Dean is a lot better off with 'im 'cos he doesn't like my mum's latest boyfriend at all. Well, none of us do. But poor little Darren, he's quite lost without Dean. Nearest thing to a dad he's got.'

'Yes, I see,' said Toby, and then, smiling at Fallon rather awkwardly, 'Well, I hadn't thought of it like that.'

'No,' said Fallon, looking at him almost pityingly, 'I don't suppose you had. Can I have a puff of that, Toby?'

And they sat there, sharing the cigarette and chatting while Tilly endured an agony of anxiety that her mother might suddenly appear.

Which she wouldn't; for Elizabeth had come downstairs in search of a cup of tea, caught the whiff of cigarette smoke, heard Fallon's unmistakable voice and Toby's laugh, and decided the best thing she could do was creep back upstairs and pretend ignorance of all of it. Certainly until the morning.

Flora was acutely excited about Christmas. To be spending it at Broken Bay, the future safe: it was truly too good to be true.

She went into a fever of cooking and planning and decorating and shopping; and when Debbie and the children arrived, on the evening of 22 December, ahead of Richard, the house looked so beautiful, hung with holly and with ivy garlands, every windowsill set with candles, a huge tree in the hall, they burst into spontaneous applause.

Debbie looked very strained, Flora thought; she did too much, worked too hard. She would try to give her a happy

Christmas, a rest, try not to annoy her, not to be bossy.

She had written to Richard about the house; explaining that it was safe, that she could stay there 'as long as Alexander allows!', telling the story of the first John Fielding, saying that she had known nothing of the entail, and that she had no idea why Alexander and not Richard would be the next guardian, as she put it, of the house.

Richard would find it difficult, she knew; he was stiff and proud, just as William had been, but he had to know; and he seemed to have taken it well, wrote back a generous letter – but she felt there was more to come. What pleased her far more was that Debbie had rung to congratulate her, sounding genuinely pleased.

Richard was coming down directly from Scotland; he had a lot of administration to do at the end of term – 'reports to write, plans for next term' – and he and Morag needed a few days of quiet together to accomplish it: 'She's worn out, but she won't give in, of course.'

The children were in a state of acute excitement, decorating their rooms, deciding where best to hang their stockings, foraging for holly and locking themselves into rooms with much giggling while they wrapped presents. It was all totally idyllic, Flora thought, the sort of Christmas people dreamed of.

'You've made a wonderfully happy family, Debbie,' she said, as they walked out on the moor, the children running ahead, shouting. 'It can't always have been easy. Well done.'

Debbie said nothing; looking at her sharply, Flora saw that her eyes had filled with tears. Some instinct told her to pretend not to have noticed, and to change the subject. She hoped the marriage wasn't going wrong again; she had allowed herself to think things were better, she had no reason for that, except that at half-term Debbie had seemed much happier. But she was fearful for her happiness in Scotland with the much-revered Morag.

Later, she said, rather casually, that she had a friend coming to supper on the following evening. 'I hope you don't mind, Debbie, but it's quite a longstanding arrangement and Richard will be very late.'

'Of course I don't mind,' said Debbie, 'and anyway, I've got to go and meet Richard at Cardiff Airport. Who is she, your friend? Have I met her before?'

'It's not a she,' said Flora, 'and no, you haven't. His name is Colin Peterson – the one who was helping me with the sale of the house, remember?'

'Oh – yes,' said Debbie. 'Of course.'

Flora was clearing the table very busily; if the notion hadn't been completely ridiculous, Debbie would have thought she was blushing.

She was getting through it; hour by hour, day by day. She did her best to close her mind to the events of the twenty-seventh, when she would talk to Richard, to the dreadful repercussions that would ensue, but she mostly failed; it overshadowed everything she did.

They would stand there, all of them, happy and smiling in the Christmas house, and one by one they would be pushed into a kind of torture chamber, and she would turn the key. And then have to listen to their screams, unable to help them.

She had never doubted, for all her remorse and fear, that it was the right thing to do, that she almost had no choice; but the fact remained that it would be very traumatic.

And Flora congratulating her on her happy family as she had today made her feel even more like a murderess, like Lady Macbeth or Lucrezia Borgia. How could she do it to them? What right did she have? She didn't know, and she had no right; she only knew she had to do it. She had passed the point of no return in her head; there was no turning back.

She hadn't spoken to Joel; they had agreed it was better that way.

'We'll have the rest of our lives to talk,' he had said. 'I'll just leave you in peace.'

Some peace.

She drove over to Cardiff to collect Richard from the airport, feeling queasy. How was she going to endure this? How was she going to pretend for – what – three more endless days? How was she going to smile at him, talk to him, express interest, affection, let him make love to her . . .

Stop it, Debbie. You've got to. Just do it.

The temptation to ring Joel for a shot of courage was almost overwhelming: but she resisted. It would make things worse: far worse.

She stood there, in Arrivals, looking at all the happy, lucky people waiting for people they loved to come home for Christmas, watched them greeting one another, hugging, kissing, walking away with their arms round each other . . .

'Debs, hello. Lovely to see you. Let me give you a hug.'

Well, that was all right. She could handle a hug. Just . . .

'Lovely to see you too,' she said. 'How are you?'

'A bit shattered. We've been working flat out, Morag and I. There's so much still to learn, you know. And she's incredibly patient with me.'

'Good, I'm glad. How was your flight?'

'OK. Bit late leaving, as you know.'

'Yes. Luckily, I'd phoned to check. So I've even had a quarter of a supper. What about you? Your mum's keeping something for you.'

'Good. I need it. How is my mother?'

'She's fine,' said Debbie, leading the way to the car. 'So happy about the house.'

'She must be. What an extraordinary story, isn't it?'

'Quite extraordinary. Our little Alexander, a landowner.'

'Yes, well, that does seem rather absurd,' Richard said stiffly. So there would be trouble to come. Quite clearly.

'Anyway, I must tell you,' Debbie said, 'oh look – there's the car – yes, I must tell you, your mother's got an admirer.'

'She's what?' Richard had been putting his luggage into the boot; he froze and turned to stare at Debbie. 'What sort of admirer?'

'The usual sort. A man, you know. Clearly interested in her – devoted actually, I'd say.'

'Devoted? Some man devoted to my mother?'

'Yes. Don't look so disapproving, it's lovely for her.'

'Well, I don't know what to say. Who – who is he?'

'Not sure. Some kind of property developer, I think. He had been advising her over the sale of the house. Obviously he's thrilled about the way things have turned out for her. I rather like him. Anyway, he may still be there when we get back. He said he'd like to meet you.'

'But – what's he like? I mean, is he an old man? I don't

778

understand why she's never mentioned him.'

'I think because she was embarrassed,' said Debbie, doing up her seat belt – thank God they had so much to talk about. 'She was talking coyly about a friend and stuff like that, and when she had to tell me the friend was a him, she got very flustered. Anyway, when he arrived, it was perfectly obvious they were very fond of each other.'

'What sort of fond?'

'Oh Richard, I don't know! They go to concerts together. He's her sort of age, I suppose, and the most surprising thing about him is that he's not like the people she usually has as friends. I mean, he's – well, you know, a bit naff.'

'No, I don't know,' said Richard. He sounded irritable. 'What do you mean?'

'Well, he's not what I'd have expected. His clothes are a bit odd, for a start. I mean, he had a really weird cardigan on, sort of striped ... And he's not exactly posh, bit North Country. He's perfectly sweet. He's called Colin.'

'But – do you think it's serious? Debbie, do look what you're doing, there's a lorry coming towards us.'

'I did see it.' She controlled herself with an effort. 'I don't know if it's serious, I mean, I presume they're not planning to get married. Or—'

'If you're going to drive in the outside lane, you really should speed up a bit. It's dangerous.'

Why did she always forget the way he did this? She pulled sharply over to the inside lane. 'Better?'

'Yes. Anyway, you were saying – about this man?'

'He's called Colin. Colin Peterson. You can meet him and judge for yourself. Like I said, I really liked him.'

The other Debbie would have added, 'You probably won't,' but she was determined not to sound crabby. She owed him three good days. And the children. Three really happy days. And then ...

'Well, I do think she could have told us,' Richard said.

'There's nothing to tell. In her mind, anyway. He's a friend, OK? Now there's—'

'Debbie, please get into fifth gear. Surely you can hear the engine labouring?'

Debbie pulled up onto the hard shoulder and got out.

He stared at her. 'What's the matter?'

'You drive. Please. I can't cope with this.' She was close to tears: all her good resolutions gone.

'Look,' he said, 'I'm exhausted, I've only just got off a plane, for heaven's sake—'

'Just shut up, will you? If you can't say anything nice, don't say anything at all. Let's just get home. And then you can ask Colin yourself what his intentions are.'

He didn't say another word all the way to Gower; and when they reached the house, Colin's car was gone.

Flora came out to meet them.

'Hello, darling. Lovely to see you. Happy Christmas.'

'Yes, it all looks wonderful. You've excelled yourself, Mother.'

'Well, I've had lots of help. Good trip? Come along in, I've saved you some casserole.'

'Thank you, that was kind. Are the children all asleep?'

'Emma's still awake. She wants to see you.'

They went into the hall; a small thunderbolt in a nightdress hurled itself at Richard.

'Daddy! Oh, I've missed you so much!'

'I've missed you too, darling.'

This is why it's so dreadful, Debbie thought, staring at the two of them, Richard lifting Emma up, kissing her, her small arms winding round his neck. This is why I know I'm so wicked. This is what I've got to destroy.

She felt so bad, she drank two large glasses of wine in the time it took Richard to eat a very small supper, Emma on his knee. And was vaguely aware of Flora watching her. She was a sharp old bird, didn't miss much. Oh God. God help me.

As if He would, a wicked woman like her.

They went quite early up to bed; Emma had fallen asleep and Richard carried her up, put her in her bed.

Braced for sex, Debbie was spared. Richard kissed her, said he was sorry, but he was completely exhausted, and turned out the light. She lay there, looking at his back, listening to his snores, thanking God for the reprieve. And tomorrow, to quote her favourite heroine, was another day.

Chapter 58

December, 1990

She had watched herself go through it, hour by hour, smiling, opening parcels, saying thank you, singing carols, eating turkey, drinking too much, playing charades, watching Rachel this time fall asleep on her father's knee, putting the children to bed. And then sitting with Richard and Flora, drinking still more, listening while they talked and reminisced and didn't seem to notice how quiet she was.

To bed, then; where Richard made love to her. She got through it somehow.

'Lovely Christmas,' he said, turning away from her. 'Thank you.' And fell asleep. How could he not know? How could he not tell?

But – tomorrow was Boxing Day. And then soon, soon it would be over. The worst would be over.

For her at any rate.

Amazingly, through it all, she had still felt not one shred of doubt. She knew she was doing the right thing.

Boxing Day was cold and brilliant, frost spangling the grass and the holly hedge.

'Isn't it lovely?' said Flora. 'You know what we ought to do. Walk the Worm.'

'Oh ye-es!' the children all shouted at once. They had only done it once, walked along the sometime peninsula, sometime island of Worm's Head, the great stretch of land that stuck out over a mile from Rhossili Bay. Named the Worm, because it looked like a dragon, lying there in the water (*wurm* being Old English for dragon), it was one of the great walks of Gower: children particularly loved it, and loved looking at it when the

781

tide was in and saying, 'We were walking there yesterday.' But it could be dangerous, if not enough time was allowed for tides; and today it would be icy cold.

'I – really don't think . . .' said Debbie doubtfully.

'Now, Debbie,' said Flora briskly, 'you know we always have this discussion' – hardly a discussion, Debbie thought, a one-sided lecture – 'and it's always fine. The children are growing up, they're wonderful walkers,' she paused, for a notional 'thanks to me', 'and it's a beautiful day. Let's look at the tides, anyway. Richard, what do you think?'

'I think it would be fun,' he said. His expression as he looked at Debbie was chilly; she was doing what he most hated in front of his mother, being over-protective.

'Good. Now let's see . . . ah yes. Low tide at one-thirty. So we'd be absolutely fine.'

'Don't forget it gets dark at half-past four,' said Debbie.

'I hadn't,' said Flora, 'and I had no intention of going as late as one-thirty. You know the tides allow us five clear hours. In fact, we could take a picnic.'

'A picnic!' said Debbie, and this time she was laughing. 'Flora, it's freezing out there.'

But, 'Ye-es!' shouted the children again. Debbie gave up.

The phone rang; Flora answered it.

'Colin! How lucky that you rang. What? Well, because I thought you might like to join us. We're going on a picnic – yes, I know it's freezing, but look at the sun – on the Worm. Then you could meet Richard, and – Oh, all right. What? Oh, that's a good idea. Yes, come and meet us, park at Rhossili and walk along towards the Worm. At about four. No, let's say three-thirty. Debbie, my daughter-in-law, is anxious about the tides. And the light, of course. Then we can come back here for tea. Fine. What? Yes, I will.' She smiled at Debbie. 'Colin said to tell you how much he enjoyed meeting you, and how he was looking forward to seeing you again today.'

'Well – good,' said Debbie, 'and I'll look forward to seeing him.' Thinking that when she did, they'd be back, warm and safe, not stranded on the icy rocks. And it would be the end of the last day. Their last day as a family.

They set out along the grassy cliff walk that led to the sea;

the children ran ahead, shouting and laughing.

'They're having a lovely time,' Debbie said, and meant it.

'Of course. Now, Richard, you take the rucksack, and then I can help Rachel over the Causeway. Are you all right, Debbie?'

'Yes, I'm fine. Thank you.'

It would be all right; they'd have loads of time and she'd already said bravely she didn't want them to go as far as the Devil's Causeway, the treacherous narrow high walkway that had to be crossed to reach the last quarter of the Worm. Richard, to her surprise, agreed.

'It is too far, in the cold. And I don't want to have to carry anyone back.'

Flora slightly scornfully agreed.

The sun was still high and the sky brilliant as they set out across what was known as the causeway; not exactly a causeway at all, Debbie thought, just a difficult scramble across rocks and stones. Emma danced ahead, chattering to her father, Rachel held her grandmother's hand, Alex walked more slowly with Debbie. Every so often, Richard or Emma would turn and shout, 'Come on!'

'Don't take any notice,' Debbie said, 'and don't let them hurry you.'

'I won't.'

They had their picnic on the grassy plateau just above the causeway; Flora had put some soup in a big Thermos jug and they dipped French bread into it, and then ate cheese sandwiches and tomatoes. It was idyllic, but in spite of the sun and the blue sky, it was very cold; a sharp wind had blown up, and Richard looked around almost anxiously.

'We'd better get on,' he said. 'Don't want to risk anything.'

'Dear oh dear,' said Flora, 'you townies!'

They set off again, Richard and Emma walking with Debbie and Alex now. Flora stomped ahead, her long rainbow-coloured scarf blowing in the wind, holding Rachel's hand. They slowly drew ahead; Debbie watching anxiously for signs of flagging from Rachel. She was awfully little, Debbie thought, only six; this was a big journey for her. She said so to Richard.

'Oh Debs, don't be silly. She's a very good little walker and—'

'I'd feel happier if you were with them,' said Debbie stubbornly, 'so if Rachel does start flagging you can insist on coming back.'

'Oh, all right,' he said. 'Coming, Al?'

'No, thanks,' said Alex; he had become rather pale and quiet.

She watched till Richard and Emma had caught the others up, then said, 'Alex, you don't have to do this. We can wait here for them, if you like.'

He shook his head. 'Granny'll think I'm feeble,' he said.

'Which won't matter one bit. Well, just say if you really start to get tired. Remember, every inch we walk, we have to walk back again.'

'Yes, all right.' He looked up at her and smiled, his gap-toothed little-boy smile. 'It's nice to be with Dad, isn't it, Mum?'

For you, not for me; for me it's horrible; everything about him hurts me – his voice, his face, the way he talks to me, just the way he isn't who I want him to be.

'It is, indeed.'

'Soon we'll be with him all the time again. It'll be great, Mum, won't it?'

Soon we won't be with him all the time. It won't be great and you'll be very unhappy.

'Yes, it will, love. Really great. Now, shall we try and catch them up, or—'

'Mum.' He stopped walking. 'I feel a bit sick. Sorry.'

'Don't be sorry, Alex, you can't help it. Although I did tell you not to eat so much of Granny's ice cr—Oh, Al.'

He was very sick suddenly, there on the grass. Standing trying to comfort him, clean him up, looking after the others, too far ahead now to hear her call, Debbie wondered what she should do.

'Just stay there quietly,' she said to Alex. 'I'll go and tell them what's happened.'

'No! Don't leave me! I'm scared.'

'Lovely, there's no need to be scared. I'll only be ten minutes.'

'You might be longer. I can't see them any more.'

'Oh, it's too bad,' said Debbie, feeling a wave of rage. 'They could have waited for us. It's just not fair.'

784

'Yes, and look, Mum. It's getting sort of misty.'

This was true; the sea mist that the wind blew in and onto Gower was descending, grey and wet and scary; it wasn't thick like a fog – you could see perfectly well where you were going: for about 200 yards or so. But – no further. And it had certainly blanked out the rest of their party.

'Well, all right, I won't leave you. But what do you think we should do? Just sit here – or start going back? I think we should just wait.'

'OK, but it's getting jolly cold.'

'Here,' said Debbie, taking off her scarf, one of Flora's thick long ones that she had borrowed. 'Wrap this round you. It'll help. I'm sure they'll be here in about half an hour at the most.'

'Half an hour! Mum, that's too long.'

'Well, I can't help that,' said Debbie, resisting the temptation to tell him he had wanted to come on this stupid crazy bloody outing. 'It'll soon pass. We'll sing some songs.'

'OK,' said Alex with a sigh.

'Where are they?' said Flora. 'And however did they get so far behind?'

'God knows,' said Richard. He felt anxious now as well as irritated. And he felt irritated with everyone, with Flora for proposing this absurd walk, with himself for not resisting her, with Debbie for not keeping up with them, even with Emma who was whining now, saying she was cold, she wanted to go back. Only Rachel was still dancing ahead, like some small island creature, turning to beckon to them through the mist every few minutes.

'Oh, very well,' said Flora, 'we'd better turn back. Come on, Rachel, everybody wants to go home.'

'Everybody but us' hung in the air; Rachel stood still, her hands on her hips, clearly cross.

'Come on, Rachel. We've lost Mummy and Alex, we have to go back.'

'That's their fault. I don't want to go back.'

'Well, you've got to,' said Richard.

'No!'

'Rachel!'

'No. It's so fun being here.'

'Look,' said Flora, 'you go back, Richard, with Emma. Rachel and I'll go a bit further. Don't worry, we won't go near the Devil's Causeway. But she's enjoying it so much and it seems a shame to cut it short now.'

'Well, it's getting terribly misty,' said Richard.

'Richard! It's only a mist. You know these things as well as I do. They come and go – it'll be sunny again in half an hour.'

'It's also getting late. It's half-past two, well past low tide.'

'Yes, and with at least two hours when it's completely safe to cross. Look, we'll just go a bit further and then we'll turn round and catch you up. Well, we'll meet you on the Rhossili side. That'd be best. All right?'

'Yes, all right,' said Richard, 'but do be careful.'

'All right, all right,' said Flora. 'You sound like your father.'

'I don't consider that such a bad thing,' said Richard slightly stiffly, and turned away with Emma.

Flora was quite right; in half an hour, the mist had gone again and the winter sunshine was back. As Richard and Emma reached the place where they had had lunch, they saw Debbie and Alex sitting and singing.

'What happened to you then?' said Richard. 'Why didn't you keep up?'

'Alex was sick and felt rotten,' said Debbie. 'We had to sit down and wait. Anyway, where are the others?'

'Oh, Mother decided to take Rachel on a bit, she was enjoying it so much. They'll be here soon.'

'Hope so. Can we start to cross?'

'Yes, she said we should meet her on the other side of the causeway.'

'Good. I can't wait to get back. I hate this walk, it frightens me. And I think I was right. Actually. What with the mist and the cold, and—'

'Yes, all right, all right. Come on then, let's get started.'

'I don't like leaving them here,' said Debbie, looking over her shoulder. 'I wish you hadn't agreed to them going on, Richard.'

'Debbie, you just said you wanted to get onto the mainland. Let's go. They'll be fine.'

They reached the other side safely, although rather slowly; it took almost three-quarters of an hour. Alex was feeling sick again, and kept stopping, and the mist had made the rocks more slippery. Both children fell over several times.

'God, I'll be glad to get safely back to the house,' said Debbie, as they navigated the last hundred yards. 'I'm exhausted.'

'So am I,' said Alex plaintively.

'Well, you can have a rest now. Let's go up the hill a bit, then we can watch them coming.'

They went rather slowly up the cliff path, found a place to sit and settled down to wait.

'I'm thirsty,' said Alex.

'So am I,' said Emma.

'Well, you'll have to wait,' said Richard. 'The café's shut, this time of year.'

He sounded harsher than usual; Debbie wondered why, then saw he was looking down into Rhossili Bay.

'The tide's coming in quite fast now,' he said, almost as if it didn't matter.

'Hello!'

It was Colin Peterson, dressed in a virginally new waxed coat and matching cap. And Hunter wellies so new they positively gleamed. His voice was incredibly welcome; he was so sensible, so – so normal. What did he want to get mixed up with Flora for, Debbie wondered.

'Hello, Colin. How nice to see you. This is Richard, Richard, this is Colin Peterson.'

'How do you do,' said Richard rather shortly. 'Sorry I missed you the other night.'

'I was sorry too. But very pleased to meet you now. And this must be Alex.'

'Yes. And Emma you met.'

'I did indeed. How are you, Emma?'

'All right,' said Emma. 'We've just had a picnic.'

'Only your grandmother would have a picnic on a day like this,' said Colin.

Too right, Debbie thought. And where is she? Where is their grandmother – and where is my youngest child?

'So where is she, the redoubtable Mrs Fielding?'

'Oh, just coming,' said Richard. 'She'll be here any minute, I should think.'

Only she wasn't just coming. There was no sign of her, of either of them. And she would certainly be more than a minute.

Afterwards, none of them could think why they hadn't gone back onto the Worm earlier. It seemed so obviously the thing to do. But – they didn't. Somehow, because they were doing what they had all agreed, and because they all felt so totally confident that Flora would appear, waving, her long scarf blowing in the wind, it continued to seem sensible. Long after it wasn't sensible at all.

It was Debbie who cracked first. 'Where are they? Where are they?' Her voice an unexploded scream. 'What are they doing? Why don't they come? What's happened?'

The children looked at her, alarmed; until that moment they had been cheerfully playing 'Spot the Flora, first one gets a prize'. It had been Colin's idea; he was clearly getting worried himself, but determined not to show it.

The tide was rushing in, up the beach; in ten minutes, Debbie thought, it would be lapping at those stones, those bloody stones, all of which had to be crossed before Rachel was safe. It wouldn't be easy. God, it was all happening so fast, the wind was creating cross-currents, the sea was getting up; it was horrible – her worst nightmare.

'I'm going back,' said Richard, suddenly standing up. 'Something must have happened.'

'I'll come with you.'

'No, you won't. It's dangerous. I might get stuck there, and someone has to stay with the children.'

'I can do that,' said Colin. 'No, better still, I'll come with you, Richard. Debbie can stay with the children.'

'OK,' said Debbie, her teeth chattering with fright and cold. 'Thank you.' She would rather have gone, anything would be better than just sitting here helplessly, but she could see their chances were better than hers.

'Be careful, Daddy,' said Emma cheerfully. She and Alex were mercifully unaware of the real danger.

'I will.'

Richard and Colin started running down the path; Colin's new cap blew off, was tossed out on the wind. Debbie watched it slowly descending into the dark grey sea, a hideous omen of what might come. Suppose they were already in that sea, Flora and Rachel? Suppose Flora had decided to explore some cliff path? It was more than likely, stupid bloody woman. Suppose Rachel was hanging on desperately to some rock. Suppose—

'I hope they'll be all right,' said Alex.

'So do I. Colin is so nice,' said Emma.

'Of course they will,' said Debbie. 'They'll be fine.' She started making bargains with God; if they got out of this, if Rachel came back to her safely, she'd give up work, she'd never see Joel again, she'd train as a teacher, she'd have sex with Richard every night—

'There they are,' said Alex suddenly. 'Look!'

'Oh, thank God, thank God,' said Debbie, even then thinking fearfully of her bargains.

But then: 'It's not them,' said Emma. 'There's only one.'

'No,' said Debbie, straining her eyes into the light. 'No, it can't be.'

'Mummy, it is. It's Rachel – I think. Yes, look . . .'

Well, it was Rachel. Not Flora alone, thank God. But how would she manage? She was so tiny; how had she got this far alone? But the men would reach her, surely, before the tide really came in.

She was waving now furiously, trying to attract their attention; she must be so frightened, Debbie thought, so terribly frightened, she was just a dot out there, a solitary dot, moving dreadfully slowly . . . why? Don't be ridiculous, Debbie, she's being careful not to slip, as she'd been told so many times, better she comes slowly.

'Daddy's coming, darling!' she shouted, while knowing it was totally impossible that Rachel could hear her. 'Don't worry, they're on their way.'

She looked down the cliff path, realised that Richard and Colin might not even have seen her, from their lower viewpoint, and shouted again to tell them, but the wind blew her voice away from them as well.

'Stay there,' she said to the children. 'I'm just going down to the rocks, to tell Daddy and Colin. Don't worry, I'll be back in no time.'

'Don't go, Mummy, please.'

'I must. I promise I won't go far.'

She reached the bottom of the path, waved, shouted, but they didn't hear her. She wondered if she should go after them, but decided it would be silly, someone had to be with the children. *And someone not be drowned* came the thought unbidden into her head; she crushed it with all the determination she had and went back up the cliff, to watch as Richard and Colin began to work their way, agonisingly slowly, across the causeway. The water was already creeping up over the stones.

'Oh God,' she said, for Richard had slipped, fallen heavily; it took him what seemed a long time to get up again, and Colin came back to help him. This was terrible, awful. He seemed to have hit his head; she could see him wiping his forehead, look at his hand, obviously at blood. He sat down very gingerly, took something from Colin, a handkerchief she supposed, dabbed at his head.

'Get on, get on!' she screamed into the wind, unheard. 'Your head doesn't matter. Nothing matters except Rachel, don't waste time!'

And then Richard slowly stood up, said something to Colin, and together they recommenced their journey. Having lost a lot of precious time.

It was very difficult to make out what was happening from where Debbie and the children were sitting. It was extraordinary how distance distorted perception. At times, Rachel seemed to be going in the wrong direction, moving away from her: surely that couldn't be right. But maybe it was; maybe she could see the tide coming in, had decided to go back. She was so little, Debbie thought, looking at her, and so vulnerable in the pink anorak she had begged for and the pink wellingtons, a tiny little girl, just six years old: battling now all alone with the sea and the tide and the wind. How could she have left her, trusted Flora to look after her, how, how?

Richard appeared to be halfway across now, and the water was well over his feet; he had boots on, but they were slippery in the water and he kept sliding sideways, just managing to right himself each time. But for how long, she wondered fearfully, and what would happen when the water came over his boots, filled them: which it would, in a few more minutes, another clutch of waves. At least he had seen Rachel now, was waving at her, and she was waving back, apparently cheerful. God, she was brave.

Colin was moving doggedly forwards too, in fact rather more confidently than Richard; he was almost level with him now. But what could they do? How could they bring a small child over, once the water was thigh-high, waist-high – chest-high on her, as it would be, and it would be dangerous, fast-running.

'Oh Emma,' she said aloud, unable any longer to pretend everything was all right. 'Oh God.'

Emma looked at her. 'Do you think we should get help?' she said.

Richard was actually quite scared. He knew these seas and this crossing, he had grown up near it, knew the dangers. But Rachel was only about 200 yards away, and still clear of the water; she should stay there, he saw with sudden clarity, stay on that side. It was perfectly safe there, someone would help, the inshore lifeboat at Port Eynon would rescue them; and he began to wave at her, to try to indicate that she should go back up onto the Worm. But she misunderstood, of course, waved again quite cheerfully; she had no real idea of the danger she was in. He went on towards her; at least he could see properly, the late-afternoon sun was brilliant, it helped, made it seem just a little less frightening.

He heard a shout, saw Colin had caught him up; he was being pretty brave, the old chap, he didn't look exactly robust, silly really, he hoped he wasn't going to fall over, create more problems. Although he'd been pretty grateful for his help when he fell. His head was bleeding quite hard; large drops of blood fell steadily from his wound into the water, but he felt nothing, no pain, only the awful fear.

Colin was actually showing no signs of falling over, he was making rather impressive progress, picking his way across the higher stretches of the causeway, steadily and confidently. He grinned at Richard as he drew level with him. 'We're doing OK, I'd say,' he said. 'Nearly there.'

'Hardly,' said Richard. 'But we should be with Rachel in five minutes now. Where the hell is my mother?'

'God knows,' said Colin and then, managing a half-smile, 'And it's possible that even He isn't sure. So we're agreed, we'll go back up onto the Worm?'

'Yes. Rachel,' he shouted, 'go back, go back!'

And this time she did hear him, but shook her head and shouted something in reply, her light child's voice useless against the wind.

'Plucky little soul,' said Colin. 'Look, if we go over onto that side there, look, it's a bit higher and dryer, we'll get to her sooner. See? Come on.'

He was right; it was higher and dryer. But Rachel was not coming that way, she had chosen the central route and her small pink wellingtons were already half-covered in water. She looked horribly vulnerable. And then she stopped still, for the rainbow scarf had become unleashed, was blowing away, and she grabbed at it, almost losing her balance in the process, and it blew away into the wind.

'I'll go down and head her off,' said Richard. 'You carry on up to the Worm.'

'No, no, I'll keep with you. We could both be needed. Oh – shit.'

Richard, surprised even in his anxiety that Colin should swear, looked behind him for the reason, and saw a wave suddenly break over the rocks and rush towards Rachel.

She was knocked flying by it; Debbie could see. It wasn't that it was particularly big, it was just very fast-running and forceful. An adult would have found it a considerable assault. Screaming with fear herself, she watched in gut-wrenching terror as the small pink figure struggled to right itself, only to be knocked sideways again.

'Do something! Do something!' she shouted to anyone or thing who might be able to hear her, and to help, but Richard and Colin were too far from her to hear and from Rachel to reach. And God seemed to have turned away.

Flora surfaced again to find Rachel gone.

She had forbidden her to leave, had insisted, through the pain that kept blacking her out, that they should stay together, but Rachel had argued vociferously that she should go, that she could get help. It wasn't even a temptation to let her try, it was too dangerous, the tide would be rushing in now; when it went down again, people would be able to find them, they would be rescued. They might even be rescued before that; if Richard had the sense to get help, to ring the police, they would send the lifeboat out, or even the helicopter. But they must stay together, she told Rachel, wrapping the rainbow scarf round her to try and keep her warmer; it would be cold and dark and boring but they would get through it, they would sing songs and play games and they would be rescued. But the third time she had blacked out, for longer than before, Rachel had simply been gone when she surfaced again.

And then there had been terror; absolute terror; for she could see, when she hauled herself painfully, so painfully and slowly onto her feet, hanging onto the rock to support herself, to keep the weight off the leg that she knew was broken, that the tide was coming over the causeway; and any chance of Rachel getting across now was being removed, yard by dreadful yard.

She had sunk down again then, weeping with remorse as well as terror, for her arrogance in insisting she and Rachel went on, her folly in suggesting the outing at all, her stubbornness in refusing to listen to the voice of caution and commonsense that was Debbie's. And decided that however great the pain, and impossible-seeming the task, she must make her way at least as far as she was able, so that she might have a chance of calling Rachel back, of stopping her in her dangerous quest.

She looked about her for something to support her, a stick of some kind; she could see nothing remotely suitable, and thought with regret as well as guilt of her sneering at the walking stick that Colin always brought with him. What she would give for that now?

And then a few yards away, she saw a large piece of driftwood: that would do, that would do very well. But she had to get to it. Hopping was too dangerous, she would fall again;

crawling would be easier. And so inch by agonising inch, she crawled towards the piece of wood, every movement of the broken leg agony, the other one cut and scratched by the stones, her hands too. But she went on. It might be fruitless, but she had to do it, just in the hope, the faint hope that she might find Rachel, might be able to stop her going further. She could do nothing else; and if she failed, then at least she would have tried.

Dusk was settling now, removing the colour from everything: and it was terribly cold. The sky was clear, which meant a bitterly cold night; if they didn't come and find her, if she had to stay there until the morning, might she die of hypothermia? No, of course not. Don't be absurd, Flora. People survive stranded on mountains for nights on end. You'll just be cold, and serve you right . . . Ah, now here she was, at the driftwood; if she could just lie on her side, propped on one elbow, and get a good grip on it, use it almost as a lever, she should be able to haul herself up. And yes, she could, she was rising on it, very slowly, little by little, up on the good knee now, she was nearly there, yes, she was upright . . . and just before the wood slipped again and she went down with a scream of pain, she saw that the water had completely covered the causeway and that Rachel could well have drowned in it, and she was alone as she had never been in her life before, alone and experiencing a fear that was far worse than any pain she had ever known.

Still on the cliff path, and in a scene she knew would be carved into her consciousness for ever, Debbie watched Rachel surface for the second time, saw her small arm reach out of the water, her desperate, supplicating pink arm, and thought she really could watch this no longer, it was beyond endurance; and then saw, incredulous, that Richard, up almost to his waist now in water, had managed somehow to grab Rachel's foot – *don't let her boot come off, don't, don't* – and then her leg, and draw her towards him, and lift her clear of the water and into his arms, and then turn and take Colin's outstretched hand, haul himself beside him up onto a rock; and then the pair of them, Richard holding Rachel, made their way slowly and with great difficulty away from the rushing water, and Colin climbed up onto the grass and reached down and took Rachel from Richard and appeared to be setting her down on the ground. And then they all froze into invisibility as dusk settled relentlessly down.

And then Emma said again, as she had said what seemed a lifetime earlier: 'Mummy, don't you think we should get help?'

There was an emergency phone on the cliff top: next to a sign that said *Danger*; how could she possibly not have remembered it was there, she thought, running towards it. She should be shot, or forcibly drowned, but somehow it had been wiped out by the drama and the fear; she lifted it, gasped out her message.

They looked down at the lifeless little figure on the ground: only for a moment, but it seemed forever, fearing she was drowned, for she had shipped in a lot of water, or concussed by the nasty gash on her head from the rocks. Then Richard dropped to his knees beside her, turned her on her front, with her head sideways, sobbing like a small child himself, started kneading away at her back, hoping to get her lungs working. 'I think she's OK,' said Colin. 'I mean, she's breathing, her pulse is quite strong, she's quite a good colour even,' and then suddenly there was the wonderfully unpleasant sound of Rachel vomiting up a lot of water, and then she looked up at them and said, 'We have to fetch Granny, we think she's broken her leg,' and then she started to cry and Richard cradled her in his arms, saying, 'It's all right, you're safe now,' and, 'No, no,' she sobbed, 'it's Granny's favourite scarf. I've lost it, she'll be so cross.'

Flora surfaced again to feel her hand being rubbed very gently, and her hair stroked tenderly back from her face; she thought she must be hallucinating, and opened her eyes with an enormous effort – for even that seemed to cause pain in her leg – to see Colin Peterson looking down at her, and to hear him saying in his wonderfully level voice, 'You really are an extremely silly woman' – and replying in a whisper, 'I know, I know, I'm sorry,' and then remembering and saying, 'Rachel . . .' her heart clutched with fear, and Colin telling her, 'She's

fine, she's cold and wet, but she's fine. Rachel? Over here –
your granny's over here.'

And by the time the wonderful rescue helicopter had
arrived, summoned by Debbie's call, Rachel at least was
cheerful, if cold, sitting by her grandmother and telling her
everything was going to be all right, and that she was terribly
sorry, but she'd lost her rainbow scarf.

'I think I can just about forgive you,' Flora said.

Chapter 59

December, 1990

Joel, back in London after a rather unsatisfactory Christmas with friends in Kent, had slept badly – and woke to the realisation that today, life properly began. It was 27 December, the day on which Debbie was telling her husband that she was going to leave him: and then she would drive to London to be with him.

He was not expecting her to arrive radiantly happy, nor that they would then spend an idyllic evening in one another's arms contemplating their future together; she would be desperately upset, remorseful, guilt-ridden, and quite possibly even hostile to him. It was a horrible thing that lay ahead of her. He felt wrenched with sympathy, concern, and even some guilt of his own for her; and he wished suddenly that he could be nearer her when she had done it, and that she didn't have to make the endless drive up to London alone. And then he realised that there was no reason indeed why he should not drive down, maybe to Cardiff, and meet her there. It had to be better for her: and so he would do it. He couldn't imagine indeed why he hadn't thought of it before; the only problem was how to let her know.

A phone call was dangerous, even today. Even on her mobile. Anyone might pick it up. But – oh, what the hell? It was worth the risk. And she surely wouldn't leave it lying around . . . not on the twenty-seventh.

He dialled her number: it rang and rang. *Come on, Debbie, come on. I want to hear your voice, I want to tell you I'm coming to get you.*

The phone moved cumbersomely onto the messaging service; Joel decided it was safe. Richard was such a dinosaur, he would hardly know mobile phones existed, so he certainly wouldn't be familiar with the mechanics of picking up messages.

'It's me. Good luck today. See you soon, definitely hopefully. Ring me. I'll come to Cardiff to meet you. Love you.'

Colin was sitting by Flora's bed in Swansea Hospital the next morning, as she lay still groggy from her ordeal and the general anaesthetic that had been necessary to set and pin her broken leg.

She turned her head towards him. Her voice was unnaturally faint.

'Could you ask if I can have a cup of tea? I'll die of caffeine withdrawal at this rate.'

'I'll try. What about some more water?'

'I don't want water, I'm sick of the beastly stuff. I want something warm and comforting. Please, Colin, do ask.'

'Yes, very well. But I don't think they'll agree. They didn't half an hour ago. They kept saying you'd been so sick last night.'

'Yes, well, this is this morning. And I feel fine.'

She felt far from fine, but it was not just the pain from her leg that was troubling her, it was a sense of dreadful shame and remorse. She had been solely responsible for risking the lives of her entire family, had very nearly caused the death by drowning of her youngest granddaughter; she had distressed her daughter-in-law almost beyond endurance; she was a stupid, arrogant woman, and if she never saw any of them again, if they turned against her and never allowed the children into her house, never mind her care, it would be absolutely fair and just and she would have no right to complain or even question it. Why was she like this? What drove her, what convinced her that *she* was right and everyone else wrong? Why couldn't she listen properly to people instead of simply hearing what they said and ignoring it? Somehow she must learn, even at this late stage in her life, and somehow she must do penance for this dreadful thing she had done. But how? What was she to do about herself, her overbearing, wilful self? And who would help her to do it?

Colin reappeared, smiling rather nervously. 'I'm sorry, Flora. They say in another hour . . .'

'Another hour? That's ridiculous. I'm asking for a cup of tea, not a glass of brandy.' And then she thought that this at least would be a beginning, an acceptance of a judgement of someone other than herself. 'I suppose I'll have to wait then,' she said, and then found herself weeping.

Colin was alarmed; he pulled his chair up to the bed and produced a very large, very clean handkerchief with his initial on it, which he passed her.

'It's the anaesthetic,' he said. 'Upsets all your emotions, everyone knows that. There, there, the tea'll be here soon.'

'No, Colin, that's not why I'm crying. I'm crying because I'm so ashamed of myself, I feel so wretched about what I did. It was so wrong of me, I should have known better, and—'

'No,' he said, taking her hand, 'you mustn't feel like that. You were only trying to give your family a nice day.'

'No, Colin, that's not true. I could have given them a nice day perfectly well by hiking over the Bryn, or in Oxwich Woods. But I have to – to sort of show off, to be reckless, to pooh-pooh people's anxieties. It's a terrible way to behave, it's no wonder Debbie doesn't like me.'

'Doesn't she like you?' he asked in genuine surprise.

'No, she never has. And it's entirely my fault. I was never very friendly to her, and I've made it worse over the years, being so domineering and bossy—'

'Flora—'

'Colin, don't interrupt.'

'Sorry.'

'And she's just grown to hate me – and who could blame her? I was the same with William, you know – I always had to know best. He was a very careful, rather fussy person, and I used to be so high-handed with him, ignore his wishes half the time – ride out without my hat, for instance . . .'

'That doesn't sound too bad.'

'But it was, because every time I went riding he was in agonies of worry, thinking I'd be thrown. It wouldn't have hurt me to wear a hat. And I used to tease him about his financial carefulness too; do you know, he had never ever been overdrawn in his entire life, not by so much as a fiver. I was always trying to persuade him to be a bit bolder, take a few risks, buy shares . . .'

'Going into Lloyd's was hardly careful,' said Colin mildly.

'Oh, but it was, or so he thought. It was his one bit of speculation and he went into it so carefully, examining all the history, went over and over it with the dreadful Trafford Smythe, who he was so sure he could trust, making sure there hadn't been a lot of big claims – and there hadn't, of course, as you know, except that one in the sixties. Oh no, he can't be blamed for that. If anyone could, it's me.'

She was crying harder now; Colin looked rather wildly round for help in the form of a nurse or a doctor who could distract her, and saw a nurse bearing down on them with a cup of tea.

'There you are,' she said to Flora, putting it down. 'Little sips, mind. Now what are you upsetting yourself for – you'll send your blood pressure up. Come on, lovely, drink your tea like a good girl, there, that's right.'

Ten minutes later, Flora lay back obediently, having duly taken the prescribed little sips, and submitting to being called 'lovely' and 'a good girl' without complaint. It wasn't easy, but she did it. It was a start, after all, on the making of a new humble, docile Flora. In time it might get easier.

'Why don't you have a little sleep,' said Colin, picking up on the hospital turn of phrase and she did suddenly feel very tired and closed her eyes.

The last thing she thought, as she smiled at him and thanked him for coming in, was that his clothes were particularly dreadful this morning: a light-green polo-neck sweater in the style favoured by Mr Val Doonican, with contrasting blue stripes, and some ready-creased trousers. The funny thing was though that it actually didn't seem to matter in the very least.

Richard walked into the kitchen; it was eight o'clock, unusually late for him to get up. Debbie was sitting in the kitchen with Rachel on her lap, trying to keep her quiet as the doctor had said she should, and reading aloud from *James and the Giant Peach*.

'You all right?' he asked.

'Yes, I'm fine.' She looked very white and drawn.

'Good.' He smiled at her. 'You were so fantastic last night, Debbie. Thank you.'

She looked at him. 'What for?'

'Being so – so great. Especially to my mother. I really appreciated it. It can't have been easy.'

'Was I? I can't remember much about it.'

'Of course you were. Not a word of reproach.'

'Well, you know. Not a lot of choice really. And she was in a terrible state.'

She had been, poor Flora; in fearful pain, until they gave her the morphine injection and even then it had still obviously been agonising. But she had insisted on talking to Debbie as she lay in Casualty, waiting to be seen by the orthopaedic surgeon.

'I know you've got enough to worry about with Rachel, but if you could see her, just for a minute, please,' Richard said.

They had all rendezvous-ed at Swansea Hospital; the helicopter that had picked them all up, Richard, Rachel, Colin and Flora, had radioed the police at Reynoldston, where Debbie was waiting. She would never forget that moment, she knew, for as long as she lived – being told they were all safe, that Flora had a broken leg, but that the others were just wet and cold. The policeman had insisted on driving her over to Swansea, said she wasn't fit to drive, that she'd had a terrible shock, and indeed, she was shivering violently as she sat in the back, one arm round each child, Alex goggle-eyed at being in a police car, and one moreover that was going extremely fast with its blue light on . . .

Debbie had been touched by that, and said so. 'Well,' said the Sergeant, twinkling at her in the mirror, 'you want to get there as fast as you can, don't you? Must be terribly worried.'

They'd rushed into Casualty, and Rachel had shot into her arms, kissing her, saying, 'Mummy, Mummy, the helicopter was so exciting, it made a huge wind and we looked down and we could see all of Gower.'

She was showing no apparent signs of distress – 'That may come later' the doctor had said in a low voice, after putting a couple of butterfly stitches in the gash on her forehead.

Richard had appeared, kissed Debbie on the cheek and

asked her if she was all right, more tenderly than she could remember for some time.

'Of course I'm all right. What about you, Richard? You're soaked, and what about your head? That looks nasty.'

'No, it's fine, couple of stitches'll fix it, they said.'

'And I should have brought you some dry clothes – how stupid of me.'

'No, no,' he said. 'They're getting me some hospital pyjamas.'

'Pyjamas? You're not having to stay here, are you?' For some reason, she didn't want him to; she wanted him home.

'No, of course not. But it's all they've got in the way of dry clothes. That's what Rachel's wearing – hospital pyjies, didn't you notice?'

'No,' she said humbly, wondering what sort of mother she was, not even thinking of bringing warm clothes for her nearly-drowned child. 'No, I only noticed that she was alive. Sorry.'

'It's OK. She is. Very much so.'

'Where's Colin?'

'Oh, in that cubicle. He got a gash on his arm, they're just cleaning it up, checking him over. They thought he might show some ill-effects, but he seemed fine, said he'd enjoyed it. He was bloody wonderful, Debbie, don't know what I'd have done without him.'

'I know, I could see. Bless him. So – where's your mum?'

That was when he'd asked her to see Flora.

She'd looked dreadful, white and hollow-eyed with pain, but totally lucid.

'I just had to say something to you, Debbie,' she said, 'before they took me away. I said I wouldn't go until I'd seen you.'

'How – how are you?'

'I'm all right. Leg hurts a bit. But – I owe you an enormous apology. I am deeply and terribly ashamed of myself. I should never have done it, insisted we went, when I knew you were anxious, and as for putting Rachel in such danger . . .'

'Well, I'm sure it wasn't deliberate,' said Debbie carefully.

'That part wasn't, of course. I simply slipped; misjudged a gap in the rocks, went down with a bit of a bang. And I insisted she stayed with me, of course; only I conked out a couple of times and she took the law into her own hands, and when I came round the last time, she was gone. Plucky little thing. Oh Debbie, I'm not even going to ask you to forgive me, I'm sure you never can, but I do want you to know that I am completely remorseful—'

'Of course I forgive you,' said Debbie, 'don't be silly. It was – well it was an accident. Anyway, Richard shouldn't have left the two of you, shouldn't have agreed. It was stupid of him, he must bear some of the blame.'

'Oh, but I was fairly bombastic about it,' said Flora, 'pretty well insisted he went.'

'Oh Flora, that's rubbish. Richard is thirty-five years old. He can stand up for himself. Look, I've got to go, Rachel needs to be got home, given some food and the others too. I'll see you tomorrow. But please don't feel so bad. Everyone's all right, that's all that matters. Bye now.'

She kissed her mother in law and left. She was feeling odd, very odd indeed. She supposed it was the shock.

But this morning and if it was indeed shock, then that was only part of it. She did sleep, greatly to her surprise: a heavy, haunted sleep, filled with images of rushing water and darkness and the sound of screaming and terrible fear. But at least it was sleep. What she woke to was different and she knew what it was, and it was a revelation so inescapable and so dreadful that she couldn't face it, tried to push it away, to keep herself safe from it. Only she couldn't; it was impossible. It pursued her as she got up and went downstairs into the kitchen, and made herself a cup of tea and sat at the table staring unseeingly into the dark morning, thinking of what today would have held, and knowing that it could do so no longer. She couldn't leave Richard, not today, not tomorrow, not ever; however much she wanted to, however much she loved Joel.

Richard was who she belonged to; because he was the father of her children, their children. That was all there was to it. Together they had done this amazing thing, this amazing and yet totally unexceptional thing; they had created three people, three small people, totally dependent on them emotionally and physically. As she was in turn dependent on them.

They were the centre of her life, the core of herself, and she had known as she watched Rachel in the water yesterday, possibly lost to her forever, that nothing was as important, as precious as they were, and had thought too that if anything had happened to any of them, she would truly want to die.

There was a bond between her and Richard that was steely-strong, and it had been created by those children; they might be at odds with one another over many, many things, but in their love for the children they were not at odds at all, they were as one, absolutely concerned, completely together. And the thought of what that meant to her was so horrible, so painful that she sat there, bent over, clutching her stomach, her eyes closed, fighting down the tears. She couldn't start to cry, because that would do it, would defeat her, she mustn't, she couldn't and she fought them off, pacing the kitchen, her arms still folded in front of her, but the tears were stronger than any resolve she might have and finally they broke through, great waves of weeping, each larger and more painful than the last. She would not be driving to London this evening, to start her new, joyful life; she would not be telling Richard she was going; she would not be telling Richard anything at all, except that lunch was ready, or the children wanted to play some game or other, or that there was some football on the television . . . And at the terrible, aching banality of recognising that, of looking down the drab, love-starved years, she gasped aloud with pain. And then because the kitchen, the walls of the house could no longer contain her, she put on a coat and a pair of Flora's boots and walked out into the garden, down into Flora's meadow, and paced round and round it, sobbing loudly, and once or twice she screamed, the sound mingling with the cries of the seagulls and the crash of the sea. And then she went finally indoors, exhausted, and lay quietly on the kitchen sofa, to contemplate her new, dutiful life: and to try and dredge the strength from somewhere to telephone Joel and try to explain.

Joel went shopping. He wanted everything to be as perfect as possible for Debbie when she arrived. He had already put fresh sheets on the bed, cleaned the bathroom and the kitchen and filled every vase he possessed with the best post-

Christmas flowers he could find. He had bought her some presents too, silly things that he knew she would love, some white lace briefs from Knickerbox (she only liked white pants, said colours were tacky), a tape of Madonna doing the songs from *Dick Tracy*, a video of *Back to the Future*, a box of Ferrero Rocher chocolates which she always declared naff and then consumed in vast quantities; and a framed photograph of the two of them giggling, taken by his delayed-action camera. All designed to make her laugh, make her relax, make her glad to be with him. He bought supper too; she would probably say she wasn't hungry, but it would be awful if she wanted something. Some smoked salmon, some bread and some Brie, so ripe it was ready to walk out of the flat. And some champagne. Of course.

He took his mobile phone with him, but it didn't ring. When he got back, there was still no message on the answerphone. Well, it was early; only eleven, she had probably hardly started to talk to Richard. Or, as the children were there, maybe hadn't started. But she had promised that she would do so by lunchtime, that she would ask Flora to take the children for a walk, so they wouldn't have to wait until the evening.

He sat down and read the papers, including an article by himself which he found rather fascinating, about the implications of the Depression – and then wondered if it was too early to have a drink. It was Christmas after all; and a glass of wine might make him feel less jittery. But then if she wanted to meet him in Cardiff, he had to be very sober. He made himself a jug of coffee instead. Strong coffee. And sat down again, by the telephone, and tried not to look at the clock.

'Richard, I'm going to pop out for a bit, if you don't mind. I feel like a breath of fresh air.'

'Shall I come with you?'

'No! That is, it'll mean getting everyone into their coats and stuff and it looks like it's going to rain. I just thought I'd stretch my legs. Is that all right?'

'Yeah, OK. And then we can have lunch when you get back. I've found some soup in the freezer, thought we could have that.'

'Good idea.'

'I've got rather a dab hand at making soup myself. Morag's given me a couple of recipes. She's a marvellous cook—'

Suddenly, she could stand it no longer. 'Richard, I don't want to be rude, but I'm getting just a tiny bit tired of hearing about Morag's virtues. I'm sorry. Could we give them a rest for a day or two, do you think?' She had meant it to sound lighthearted, funny even; it came out heavy and almost bitter.

He looked at her, surprised. 'Oh, all right. Sorry,' he said, rather more patiently than she would have expected. Perhaps he was trying to make allowances, after the events of yesterday. 'Thanks. Right – well, won't be long.'

She walked out to the car as briskly as she could, in case he was watching her. Every step was a huge effort, she had to literally force herself along, one foot after another.

She got into the car, drove up onto the South Gower Road . . . back towards Penmaen and then Reynoldston and so up to Cefn Bryn. The mobile reception on Gower was very poor, she had discovered; you had to be at one of the highest points to be sure of getting any reception at all, and even then you could get cut off mid-sentence. She had considered using a public phone, but the thought of having this terrible conversation with Joel from a stinking call box – they all seemed to smell these days, a mixture of beer and pee – with other people quite possibly watching, or even banging impatiently on the glass, was horrendous. Maybe she could find a phone in a pub: that would be better, less smelly at least; but then she might see someone in the pub she knew . . . No, the mobile was the best option. She looked at her watch. God! It was half-past one. Joel would be expecting to have heard from her by now; would be sitting there – she pictured him in the flat, thinking about her, happily and confidently, or perhaps a little anxiously by now – and wondered what he was wearing, jeans probably and a white shirt, and no doubt bare feet, he never wore shoes in the house, and she had to close her eyes briefly, so awful was the contemplation of what she could have had, and that was now barred to her.

A new wave of grief hit her; it seemed to come in waves, it was like the pain of childbirth and she thought she must wait for it to pass, cry, release some more of It before she started to speak to him. She couldn't break down mid-sentence. She had to be very, very strong. Stronger than she'd ever been in her life.

This was awful. Still nothing and it was half-past one. No, it was twenty to two. What was she doing? Keep calm, Joel, she's probably still talking to the bugger, it was never going to be a quick conversation. But she had promised to call him by one; it had been one of her promises to him. 'I swear, just so you'll know everything's all right. Even if we haven't quite finished. All right?' It had comforted him, that timetable; he had been able to get through the morning, less anxious, less impatient.

But she – and it – had failed him now.

He'd just wait till two and then he'd really have to ring. Ring her mobile, not the house, obviously. He sat down, watched racing on the television; anything to take his mind off the crawling clock. It crawled on, and at two o'clock he dialled her number.

She was standing by then on the moorland of Cefn Bryn, had parked the car and taken her mobile out of her bag. And seen she had a message: from him, about meeting her in Cardiff. The sound of his voice was almost too much: for a moment she would have gone, left everyone and everything behind her, but then she pulled the broken pieces of herself together again. She must do it quickly, before he set out for Cardiff. What if he already had? How would she be able to resist that, knowing he was less than an hour's drive away? She stood there, gazing down at the lovely stretch of wooded bay that was Oxwich, and as she did so, her phone rang and it was him.

'Oh, hello,' she said, amazed that she could sound so ordinary, so cool; and then interrupted him as he started to talk and said, 'Joel, I'm not coming.' Just like that.

'Can we go and see Granny?' said Rachel.

'Of course we can. Tomorrow.'

'Why tomorrow? I want to go today. I'm sure she'd like that. And I'm worried about her.'

'So am I,' said Emma.

'So am I,' said Alex.

'Rachel, Daddy's just got back from seeing Granny,' said Debbie. 'She's fine. He told you.'

'But that was ages ago. She might be worse. She might be lonely. Why can't we?'

'Emma—' Debbie stopped. Why not? It was something to do, it was moving around, distraction . . .

'Well, maybe I could take you. Daddy's very busy. Go and see what he thinks.'

Emma came back, beaming. 'He says it's a good idea. But he can't come.'

'That's all right then,' said Debbie. 'Let's go. Quick, into the car.'

They stared at her; grown-ups usually spent hours getting ready to do anything, even going into another room to play a game.

'What – now?' said Alex.

'Now,' she said, and she could hear the desperation in her own voice. 'Yes, now.'

She really wasn't fit to drive. She felt rather as if she was drunk: drunk and exhausted and coming down with some horrible illness, all at the same time. She couldn't think either; couldn't think how to get to Swansea, even had trouble getting the car into gear. She stopped at the top of the drive, looking at the headlights of the traffic streaming along, wondering if this was actually such a good idea. But anything was better than sitting in that room, hurting, hurrying out of it every now and again to go upstairs or outside, to cry. This was good, it was moving around, shifting the pain about, making it briefly more bearable. The traffic blurred; she had been about to move forward, had to slam on the brakes until the view cleared again.

'You all right, Mum?' said Alex.

'Yes. Yes, I'm fine. Sorry. Just – just getting a cold, I think, that's all. Right. Off we go.'

He'd been so angry, that had been the worst thing. Not sympathetic, not understanding, not comforting, not even upset, just coldly, icily angry.

'Right,' he had said. 'Well, thank you for telling me. I

suppose I should have known. Known better. Goodbye, Debbie.'

And her mobile had gone dead. And she stood there, staring at the sky, trying to bear it; and then walked for a while, stomping along in the cold, the sheep and wild ponies which roamed the Bryn pausing in their grass-chomping to look at her, so much noise did she make, wailing and moaning like a madwoman. And then finally she felt strong enough to return to the car and go back to the life that had claimed her so irrevocably.

'Darlings!' Flora held out her arms. 'How lovely. What a surprise! How are you, Rachel, how's your poor head?'

'It's fine,' said Rachel, and then clearly mindful of all the spoiling it had already brought her, said, 'Well, it's quite sore.'

'Like my leg. Quite sore.'

'When can you come home?' said Alex.

'Oh, not for a couple of days. I've got to be able to get myself around first. They're going to bring me some crutches tomorrow, see how I get on. The minute I can sprint down the ward on them, they'll let me go.'

'Sprint!' said Alex. 'I don't think so, Granny.'

'Oh, I don't know. You just watch me. Debbie, dear, are you all right?'

'Yes,' said Debbie, 'yes, I'm fine. Thank you. Must – must just go to the loo. Is there one near?'

'In the corridor, just outside the ward look, down there.'

'Back in a minute.'

She looked appalling, Flora thought, white and tense, and she had clearly been crying. Maybe she'd had a row with Richard; maybe it was just shock. She smiled at the children. 'Well, what an adventure we had, didn't we? Never let Granny take you on the Worm again.'

'Of course we will,' said Alex. 'We love the Worm. It's fun.'

'Well, quite fun,' said Rachel. She seemed very cheerful; obviously not seriously affected, saved by the blessed resilience of childhood. Unlike her mother, Flora thought, looking at Debbie coming back now, managing to smile.

'So, what have you been doing today?' she said.

'Not much,' said Rachel. 'It's boring without you.'

809

'Thanks, Rachel,' said Debbie.

'Sorry, Mummy. But it is.'

'How's Colin?' said Emma. 'I liked him, he was so kind.'

'He is, very kind,' said Flora, 'and I'm glad you like him. He's coming in later. You might see him.'

'Excuse me,' said Debbie suddenly, and hurried out of the ward again.

'I don't think she's very well,' said Emma, looking after her. 'She seems to have a terrible cold, poor Mummy, her eyes and her nose are all red.'

'No, they're not.'

'Rachel, they are. She was trying to be brave and not cry after lunch, but I could tell . . .'

God, Flora thought, she's been seriously traumatised by this and no wonder. How on earth are she and I ever to become friends now?

'I can hear a phone,' said Alex.

'A phone? Can't be.'

'Well, it is. Listen . . .'

'Honestly,' said Emma scornfully, 'you're just hearing things – oh no, I heard it then too. Sounds as if it's under the bed.'

'Might be Mum's new mobile she got from work,' said Alex. 'Here, give me her bag. No, it's stopped. I wonder if . . .' He started rummaging in Debbie's bag.

'Alex,' said Flora, 'you shouldn't do that, handbags are private things.'

'How can it be private? It's always open. Here it is. I wonder if there's a message.'

'How on earth do you know about mobile phones?' said Flora. She felt rather impressed.

'My friend's dad's got one, he was showing me it the other day. It's just like Mum's. It's really good, you know. It doesn't just make calls, and take messages, you can find out about the traffic on it and share prices.'

'What?' said Flora. 'That's incredible.'

'I know. Anyway, yes, she's got a message, let's see who that was. Dad probably . . .' He looked up at his mother who was coming back to Flora's bedside, smiling determinedly. 'Mum, your phone just rang, you've got a message.' He was listening, looking mildly puzzled; then he said, 'Mum, who's Joel?'

And Flora watched as Debbie's face changed, went first white then very flushed, and she snatched the phone from Alex and ran away again, out to the corridor: but Flora could still just see her, and she was holding the phone and listening very, very intently and then she switched it off and leaned against the wall, her hand held over her eyes. It was quite a long time before she came back.

'Poor Mummy,' said Emma, 'you do look so sad, and why are you crying? Is it because your cold is so bad?'

'Yes, I – I think so,' said Debbie, and her voice was thick with tears. 'Children, we must go.'

'You've only just come,' said Flora, 'don't be ridiculous. Now you three, I want you to go exploring. See if you can find yourselves some drinks or some sweets. There are some machines on the ground floor, quite near where you came in, and on the third floor as well, I think. Take my purse, there's lots of change in it, and you can buy two things each. All right?'

'Ye-es!'

'Flora, they'll get lost,' said Debbie, blowing her nose. 'I really don't think that's a good idea.'

'Debbie,' said Flora firmly, 'if they can survive a picnic on the Worm in midwinter and being cut off by the tide, they can survive a walk round a hospital. Children, if you get lost, just ask a nurse or a doctor where Ward Six is, all right? And don't leave the hospital.'

'We won't.'

They rushed off; Debbie sat staring after them, too overcome now even to pretend not to cry, tears streaming down her face.

'Debbie,' said Flora gently, 'why don't you tell me what the matter is. It'll help you.'

'I can't.'

'Of course you can. And if it's anything like I think, then let me tell you, I won't be shocked, which is obviously what you're thinking. Not in the least. In fact, if it is what I think, let me tell you I've been through it myself.'

It had been so different, listening to that message. So different from listening to him before, being cold and angry and hostile. She had played it three times, unwilling to let it go.

811

'Debbie, it's Joel. I'm sorry about earlier, about being so angry. You must do what you think is right, and I'll try to understand and do what you want. New York is probably a good idea, yes. I don't think I could bear to be in the same city as you and not be with you . . . But I want you to know I love you, so much, and that this time with you has been perfect. Absolutely perfect.' A pause and then, his voice shaking, 'Bye, Debbie. Remember I love you.'

She felt she could cope now, bear it now. It would go on hurting, but it wouldn't be quite as bad.

'I'm sorry,' she said to Flora. 'Can I have one of those tissues?'

'Of course.' She passed her the box. 'Now do you want to tell me? I promise you it'll help.'

Debbie shook her head. 'I can't. I really can't. It wouldn't be fair.'

'Not fair to who?'

'You. And – and Richard.'

'Ah, so I'm right. Well, there's no need to tell me, of course. Certainly not now. Maybe another time – whenever you want to. Or not at all.' She reached out, stroked Debbie's hand very gently. 'But – you are staying? Staying with us?'

Debbie nodded helplessly. How did she know this, how could she?

'Good. I'm glad. It's the children who bear the brunt of these things. And as I said to you the other day, you've made such a happy family. Really happy. Those children are the greatest credit to you.'

Debbie nodded again. 'I've tried to,' she said.

'And you've succeeded. Debbie, listen. I more than anyone know how difficult Richard must be to live with. He's exactly like his father. Demanding and possessive. My wings were clipped quite severely in the early years. I longed to do more with my work, my photography, but William wouldn't hear of it. It was unbearably hard at times.'

Debbie stared at her. 'I thought – I always thought . . .'

'That I thought my son was wonderful? Yes, well I do, of course. And I also know he's good and kind and totally devoted to you all. But I'm not one of those blind mothers. I can see how he is, very clearly.' She paused, then said, 'It's going to be very hard for you. I know exactly how hard, in fact. It will hurt like hell. Bit like childbirth, I thought. Comes in waves.'

'Oh my God,' said Debbie, staring at her. 'That's what I thought too. Exactly.'

'Well, there you are. You see, I do understand. But it does end. Finally. And in a way you don't even want it to. You feel disloyal, mending, starting to forget. But you will, I promise you, you won't be able to help yourself. Things, little things at first, will start to work on you.'

'Will they?'

'Yes, of course. You just have to be patient. Put up with it. Because it will be worth it. I promise you that.'

Debbie sat there, gazing at her, feeling as if someone had given her a powerful drug, feeling suddenly able to go on.

'You're wonderful,' she said finally, 'and I'm so, so sorry I've been – been—'

'Oh, now don't let's start on all that,' said Flora. 'I'm just glad that finally I can be useful to you. Now listen, Debbie, if I were you, I'd tell Richard you don't want to go to Scotland. That you *won't* go.'

'What? But Flora, I have to. I—'

'You don't have to,' said Flora briskly. 'And it really would be too much to bear. At the moment, anyway. You need your friends, you need your work. And you *don't* need that dreadful woman, Morag whatever her name is.'

'Have you met her?'

'No, I haven't. But I don't need to. I can tell how ghastly she is. You just tell Richard you can't go. That he can stay there if he likes but you can't.'

'He'll be terribly angry,' said Debbie. 'Angry and upset. And it will ruin his career. No, Flora, I have to go. It's – well, it's one of the reasons I – I . . .' Her eyes filled again.

'At least tell him you need another term in London. Don't rush up there. I'll talk to him, if you like, put my two penn'orth in.'

'Would you?'

'Of course. I can get him thinking, to see what it's going to do to you. It was very selfish of him, putting you into that completely impossible position. He should have consulted you from the beginning. I felt very ashamed of him over that,

Debbie, and of myself. I really thought I should have done a better job with him. Insensitive, overbearing behaviour! But – he does have great virtues, as I said . . .'

'Yes, of course he does. Of course. And I do love him very much, really.'

'I know. Oh, now the children are back, and they've got Colin. How nice. Here, blow your nose again. Colin, how sweet of you to come again. Children, how did you get on?'

'Very well,' said Emma. 'We found two machines, and we've got Smarties, look, and Coca Cola cans and Mars Bars. And Mummy, this is for you, to cheer you up. It's your favourite, peppermint cream. Is that all right, Granny, do you mind?'

'Terribly,' said Flora, smiling at her.

'Oh Emma,' said Debbie, holding out her arms, enclosing her daughter in them, burying her face in her shining hair. 'Thank you. Thank you so, so much.'

'I love you, Mummy,' said Emma, looking up at her and then resting her head against her. 'I don't like it when you're sad.'

And Debbie remembered Flora's words, and thought that perhaps this was the first, the very first of the little things she had promised her would come.

'Come on, children,' she said. 'Let's leave Granny and Colin in peace.'

'But Mum—'

'No, I mean it. Granny's very tired, and Colin wants some time to talk to her before visiting time ends. Give her a kiss, and thank her for the sweets.'

She watched her children, dearer to her than anything in the world, worth all of it, all the pain, watched them kiss their grandmother, suddenly and surprisingly dear to her too; she bent down and kissed Flora herself and said, 'I don't know how to thank you. But – thank you.'

'You are thanking me,' said Flora simply, 'by staying with us. I couldn't bear you to have gone.'

Those words stayed with Debbie and comforted her, over and over again, in the weeks that followed.

Chapter 60

January, 1991

'Right. This is it. You look beautiful.'

'Thank you. You don't look so bad yourself.'

He didn't either: in his dinner jacket – would she ever be able to call it a tux? – his fair hair, newly trimmed, smoothly back, his blue eyes filled with love as he looked at her.

'Thanks for that. Excited?'

'So excited.'

And she was: what girl wouldn't be, the centre of attention, admired, exclaimed over, her engagement party about to begin? And the Cartwrights had all been so sweet to her: even Frances had been really sensitive about her father: 'We were so sorry, we could hardly bear it for you,' and about her mother not coming: 'Of course she mustn't come, she has enough to cope with, and besides, the flight might be dangerous for her. We would have loved to have her with us, but – we understand.'

And they did seem to: all of them. Dana had been especially sweet, tears in her eyes as she hugged Annabel, telling her she could talk about it if she wanted, but she would 'just totally understand' if she didn't. She really liked Dana; she was her favourite Cartwright, apart from Jamie. Well, she wasn't actually a Cartwright, of course.

But the others had been lovely too, obviously genuinely sympathetic; it did make her feel rather bad about her mother not coming. She had been invited, of course, and they had discussed it carefully and Elizabeth had offered to go. Although: 'I'd rather not, darling, to be honest. I feel my situation is a little odd, what with one thing and another.'

'Mummy, what's odd about it?'

'Well, first I'm a widow, a fairly new one, and strangers will find that difficult, clearly it has to be addressed, but then does everyone at the party come and sympathise with me one by one? Which would be very kind, of course, but not exactly easy for me. Or them. And then I'm pregnant. At the age of forty. And, well, added to being a widow, people will find that very hard to cope with, socially I mean. But I will come if you want me to. You've been so wonderful, I couldn't have got through without you. I feel I owe you.'

'Mummy, if you don't want to come, I truly don't want you to. I'd just be worried about you, in all sorts of ways. And I know they'll understand, and they are hard work, you know, and not exactly our sort of people.'

Even as she said that, Annabel felt a pang of disloyalty. She crushed it; they weren't and that was all there was to it. Even Jamie, in lots of ways. But Jamie was young and they were in love and they would work things out. That was one of the reasons for getting married, bringing your two lives together, making them both work.

'Let me know if you change your mind,' Elizabeth said. 'Frances Cartwright has written me the sweetest letter about it. She does sound very nice, Annabel.'

'She is nice,' said Annabel staunchly. 'Very nice.'

She felt more in love with Jamie than ever; he had been so over the moon about her arrival and he seemed to have got even better-looking. And he was so excited about the engagement, about showing her off to everyone.

'Especially my friends, they can't wait to meet you. Do you know, I already chose my supporters.'

'Your what?'

'My – Oh, I don't know what you call them in England. They kind of – of support you. Take you out on your stag night, welcome people to the church, make sure everything goes well at the reception . . .'

'Oh, you mean ushers,' said Annabel. 'Jamie, you can't have chosen them already.'

'Well, I have. I know it's a way off, but I can't help it. I haven't exactly told them yet, although I have asked Taylor – I've told you about Taylor, Taylor Ruffin, we were at Harvard together, and at school come to that – I've told him I want him to be my best man.'

'But . . .' Annabel felt a rush of panic, 'but Jamie, we're not getting married for at least eighteen months, are we?'

'Annabel, sweetheart, those eighteen months will just fly. I remember when Kathleen was marrying Joe, one minute we were reading the engagement announcement, the next we were doing the table plans.'

'How is Kathleen?' said Annabel, playing for time.

'She's just fine. Feeling really well now. Mother's so excited, she has the nursery decorated already—'

'What, at Kathleen's house?' This seemed a little excessive, even for Frances.

'No, no, here. She's expecting to have the baby here a lot. Obviously. She's using Kathleen's old room for it.'

'Yes, I see,' said Annabel.

After dinner, the night before the party, she and Dana were sitting in the snug as they called it, their shoes kicked off, watching a terrible old movie. Jamie and Bif were ensconced with their father in his study discussing some case they were all involved in.

Dana glanced at her. 'Looking forward to tomorrow?'

'So much, yes.'

'Good. We all certainly are,' said Dana. There was a silence, then: 'I'm really loving you being in this family,' said Dana. 'You're so – refreshing.'

'Am I?'

'Yes. It's not just because you're young, your attitudes are so good.'

'In what way?'

'Oh, hard to say exactly. I just feel you're not going to let them turn you into a Cartwright. Did I just say that? I did not.'

'OK, you didn't,' said Annabel, and grinned at her.

'It was the champagne talking. But – you know. They're pretty formidable. You've no idea what a hard time I'm getting over this baby thing.'

'What baby thing?'

'They think I should have a baby. All of them. Including Bif.'

'And you don't want one?'

817

'No. Not yet, I don't. I'm just getting to where my work's interesting, you know? I have my own caseload, it's great. Why should I give it all up to look after some squalling brat?' She sighed. 'I'm sorry. Not your problem. And very disloyal of me.'

'I don't see why you have to,' said Annabel. 'Give it all up, I mean. My mother didn't.'

'No. I remember you saying that. Tell me about her, she sounds great.'

'She is great.'

'She must have had such a tough time,' said Dana, her large brown eyes clouded with sympathy. 'Not just your dad dying, but being pregnant, and carrying on with everything. I mean, is she OK? It must have been so hard on you, Annabel, as well.'

'Just a bit. But we've got so close over it, Mummy and me. We help pick up each other's pieces. Some days she's worse, some days I am. She's really upset about the inquest now. It's only another few weeks.'

'Inquest? There has to be an inquest? Why?'

'Well, because Daddy's death was linked to an accident. And because there's some doubt over whether it really was an accident or – or well, suicide.'

Her voice shook. Dana turned to her, put her arm round her.

'How truly horrible for you. And for her. I'm so sorry.'

'Yes, it is very horrible. Of course, we all would so love it to be established as an accident. It would be so, so much nicer for us all, so much more hopeful. But how could it be proved now? It's so terrible to think of Daddy being in such despair it wasn't worth going on.'

'Poor you,' said Dana. 'Poor all of you.' She seemed genuinely upset.

'Anyway,' Annabel said, determined not to let the evening slide into gloom, 'my mother always worked. Right through three pregnancies, three babies. And now a fourth, of course.'

'I know, but – well, I guess your dad must have been pretty remarkable. To agree to that.'

'I suppose he was,' said Annabel. 'I mean, we had nannies, and so on. But it was more that he was so supportive and so proud of her, never complained if she was out or away at conferences. God, he was special. Oh dear.' Her eyes had filled with tears. 'Sorry, Dana, I guess it's a bit of an emotional occasion, what with one thing and another.'

'Of course. I understand.'

'Thank you. But really, if you want to work, nobody these days should have to stop working just because they have a child. It's – it's archaic. I certainly won't.'

'Well, good for you,' said Dana. She didn't look exactly convinced.

'Have you discussed it with Bif?'

'Annabel, we've stopped discussing it even. He's so opposed to mothers working, he says they should stay home with their children. And to an extent I do agree, of course. In an ideal world. But then not all of us are ideal people, are we?'

'No, I suppose not. That's what Mummy always said: she'd have been so miserable staying at home, we'd have been miserable too, so it was better for everyone that she worked.'

'And – how do you feel about it, now that you're grown? Do you have terrible complexes?'

'Oh, terrible,' said Annabel with a grin. 'So terrible that I intend to do exactly the same thing.'

'Did you discuss this with Jamie?'

'Not yet. It seemed slightly premature. But I will.'

'Let me know what happens, won't you?' said Dana. 'I might even hide in the closet while you talk to him.'

She smiled brilliantly, but Annabel felt she was actually close to desperation. Which provided yet another pang of panic.

It was bad without Annabel; Elizabeth hated it. They had grown very close since Simon's death and especially since the pregnancy; she missed her daughter terribly and began to wish she had been braver, gone to Boston.

Tilly was sweet, of course, and she loved her to distraction, was enjoying her being at day school, but she was still very young for her age, and caught up with her new schoolfriends – and that was a love affair which seemed to be going on and on, thank goodness. And Toby – well, he was a boy of sixteen with all the preoccupations of that age, girls, music, his appearance; she knew in a way he missed Simon more than any of them, needed male companionship. He had found himself in a household of women and it was far from ideal; she was deeply thankful he was away at school.

Certainly, neither of them could possibly replace Annabel as a companion for her. Well, she had to get used to it. She wasn't going to have her for ever. Far from for ever; maybe another two years at the most and then she'd be off to Boston. For the rest of her life. Whenever Elizabeth thought about that, she felt sick. It wasn't just that she was going to miss Annabel so much, she wasn't at all sure it was what Annabel ought to be doing. The Cartwright family – well, the Cartwright family senior – from everything Annabel had told her, was out of touch, overbearing, possessive. Annabel was a free spirit, and she was ambitious; she wasn't ready to be buried alive by in-laws and their traditional American customs.

Elizabeth had genuinely liked Jamie, when he came to stay, had thought he was sweet, and he was clearly completely devoted to Annabel: but he wasn't exactly a New Man, as the expression seemed to be.

In her role as student of demographics – the better to communicate professionally with all sectors of society – Elizabeth had learned of the New Man with great interest. Caring and concerned, unafraid of displaying emotion – 'in touch with his feminine side' was the ludicrous phrase – anxious to play his part in rearing his children, in no way a classic Alpha-type male, he sounded to her distinctly suspect and unsexy. Although Simon had displayed much of the New Man's behaviour – he had been totally involved with his children and concerned for her, and he had never minded showing emotion if he felt it strongly enough – he had also been an absolutely classic Alpha male.

Jamie, however, was rather different. His role model, clearly his father, and still most clearly an Alpha Plus male, had been held up all his life as the ideal; to tell Jamie he could rock a baby to sleep, or play supporting role to a wife now and again would be to preach a serious heresy. And she feared for Annabel with him, Annabel and her future; but there was no way she could ever tell her so. Annabel would accuse her of all sorts of heinous crimes, of jealousy and possessiveness, of exerting control. So what could she do?

She missed Simon in a hundred, a thousand ways, but she

was beginning to realise that one of the worst was having no one to discuss the children with. It was very hard.

The party passed in a glorious blur, of endless people wanting to talk to her, telling her how thrilled they were to meet her and how wonderful that she was going to marry Jamie; of Mr Cartwright's amazing speech, saying how charming and beautiful she was, and how happy they were to be welcoming her into the family; of hearing again and again Frances telling people she felt she was gaining a daughter and in no way losing a son; of Jamie's face flushed with pride as she made her own little speech – she wasn't sure about this and she could see from Frances's face that she felt it was a little forward of her, that if anyone else spoke it should have been Jamie. But she really wanted to do it, to thank everyone for coming, and the Cartwrights for being so wonderfully welcoming and kind, and how excited she and Jamie were about the future . . . and in the end nobody seemed to mind.

Jamie made a speech too, after that, full of references to 'my fiancée' (much cheering) and 'my future wife' (even more).

There was an amazing buffet supper; used as she was to her parents' sophisticated entertaining, she was still impressed by it, by the imaginativeness of the food and its presentation; and then there was a disco for the younger guests, and she danced endlessly with Jamie and all his friends, most of whom she liked very much, while thinking they did mostly seem rather young, much younger than Jamie, although of course they weren't.

And then later still, when most of the guests had left, all telling Jamie what an incredibly lucky guy he was, she sat with the family and chatted easily and happily, and conducted a bit of a post mortem about the party, and she went over to Mr Cartwright and put her arms round his neck and kissed him, and thanked him for the party, and for making such a wonderful speech, and then she moved on to Frances and kissed her and thanked her too.

And finally, they all went to bed; and Jamie joined her after the requisite thirty minutes and made the most perfect love to her, and she fell asleep in his arms, thinking she really must be the luckiest girl in the world.

Chapter 61

January, 1991

'Mummy?'

Elizabeth went out into the hall, gave her daughter a hug, said it was lovely to have her back; and then realised she was crying, quite quietly.

'Annabel, darling, what is it? Are you just sad at leaving him, or—'

'No. No, it's not that.' She got out a very soggy-looking tissue, blew her nose, tried to smile. 'Can we go and talk?'

'Of course. Don't worry, there's nobody here. Tilly's out, she felt bad not being here when you got back, but it's Madison's birthday and I said I thought that was more important.'

'Of course. Oh dear, I wish I was thirteen again. Mummy . . .' She stopped, swallowed hard. 'We're not engaged any more.'

'What? But Annabel, you went over to get engaged. How, why—?'

'Yes. But look,' she held out her left hand. Her bare left hand, with no Shreve, Crump & Low diamond on it. 'I gave it back to him. It's over. Almost before it began.'

'This is an occasion for strong liquor,' said Elizabeth firmly, 'for me if not for you. Just this once. Want one?'

'Yes. Glass of wine might be nice.'

'So – begin at the beginning,' said Elizabeth, as they sat down. 'God, these sofas are uncomfortable. How lovely it will be to get into our own house.'

'Yes, it will. 'Fraid you're going to have to put up with me a bit longer though.'

'That's fine But why? What's happened to you?'

'You, I think,' said Annabel simply. 'You being my mother and, just possibly, Dad being my dad.'

It had begun the day before; they had been having lunch alone and she'd finally told Jamie about her job at the salon.

'Can you imagine, Jamie, I'll be a stylist in the smartest, coolest salon in London. I can't believe it. Aren't you proud of me?'

'Well yes,' he said, and his voice had been rather flat. 'Yes, it's wonderful. Well done.'

She'd said, just slightly sadly, that he didn't sound very excited, and he'd said of course he was, but . . . 'You know what you always say, Mummy, that nothing counts before the *but* . . . but he sees my career now as being married to him, moving to Boston, having a family in due course. And I said yes, I saw it like that too, but still having a career. And he said that was not what he'd envisaged for us at all. And I said why not, that was what Dana wanted.'

That had been a big mistake; he'd gone rather pink and said Dana was causing Bif a lot of unhappiness, that he was desperate for children and she refused to have any.

'Jamie, that's nonsense,' Annabel had said. 'I've talked to her myself and she does want to have babies, she just doesn't want to give up her job. That's all. I told her about Mummy, about how she's made it work . . .'

'Dana discussed it with you?' he said, and his voice was rather harsh suddenly. 'What's it got to do with you?'

'Well, she's going to be my sister-in-law, I really like her, she obviously was upset about it . . .'

'Annabel,' Jamie said, 'that is between Bif and Dana, not you.'

'But if she can work and have a baby, why shouldn't she?'

'Because Bif doesn't want that. Because he feels she should be at home with the children. And I agree with him.'

'You don't think she – or I – could do both?'

'No, I don't. What Bif does, what I do come to that, is very gruelling and stressful. We work long hours and at the end of the day we need to come home to – to –'

'To what, Jamie?' She could feel a tight spring of anger beginning to uncoil.

'Well, to a well-run household, and a – a –'

'A little woman in a pinny? Jamie, come on, you can't think that's right.' She'd been so sure he was teasing she began to

823

tease him back. 'Barefoot, pregnant and in the kitchen, is that how you think we should be, us wives? With a gleaming house and a dinner ready to leap out of the oven? Sorry, Jamie, you've got the wrong girl if—'

'Don't be ridiculous,' he said. 'Of course I haven't.'

'Phew. For a moment I thought you meant all that rubbish.'

And then there had been a silence; and then he said, 'I did.'

After that, things had got quite bad, she said; they'd had a real row, with him shouting at her and telling her she didn't appear to know what marriage and commitment meant, and her shouting at him and telling him he didn't appear to know what the real world was like, and certainly not what she was like, that she would never agree to be a Stepford Wife, her sole aim to please and look after her man. Surely he couldn't expect that? And if he did, then they shouldn't be together.

'Don't you see, Jamie, if I was like that, you wouldn't love me. I'm me, you love me, not some figment of your imagination, not a carbon copy of your mother—'

He said they should leave his mother out of it, and that he hoped Annabel wasn't criticising her; she said of course she wasn't, but that Frances was another generation, a generation that saw things differently.

'Well, I'm afraid I don't,' Jamie had said. 'I don't think something so fundamental is susceptible to fashion.'

'Fashion! You think women having careers is a fashion!'

'No, but women having children and careers is. I'm sure it won't last, it doesn't work. Why do you think the divorce figures have shot up? Why children are growing up undisciplined and undirected? Why there's so much juvenile crime?'

'Jamie,' Annabel said, 'please be very careful what you say. I'm one of those undisciplined, undirected children. I grew up in a family where children and careers were absolutely compatible. My parents weren't divorced and we're not juvenile criminals.'

He'd pulled back a bit then, said he was sorry, and they'd gone home and everyone had been there, and they'd pretended everything was all right; but that night she'd slept alone – or rather not slept. 'I just lay there, going over and over

824

it in my head, thinking how important it was to me, knowing his attitude was wrong, and this morning, when he took me to the airport, I said that unless he would promise to acknowledge that my career was important, agree to my working when we had children, I didn't want to marry him. And – he said he couldn't do that. So I took off the ring and said goodbye to him and went through to Departures without even kissing him. I felt quite brave at the time,' she added, 'but scared now. Oh Mummy, I do love him so much, but – I can't marry him, can I? Not if he really feels like that?'

'No,' said Elizabeth, very gently, 'I don't think you can. But maybe he doesn't, not really.'

'What do you mean?'

'Darling, he's very young. They're obviously a powerful clan. He's been brainwashed all his life. It's going to take him a while to learn to see things differently.'

Annabel shook her head. 'I don't think he ever will. You've no idea how stubborn he was being. They are all the same, so different from us. Poor Dana is in despair.'

'Well, I still think you might be able to work it out.'

'How? When he's always, always with them! It's them he's married to, them and the firm. I actually said, it was one of my suggestions for us being together a bit more, why didn't he come to London for a year – his father has loads of contacts in London – and he said it was the most absurd idea, that he worked for Cartwrights and nobody else, and that if I wanted us to be together then I should move over there, right away. Tell me I've done the right thing, Mummy, please.'

Elizabeth hesitated. This was a minefield. The slightest step in the wrong direction could be fatal.

'I'm very proud of you for having the strength of your convictions, Annabel. And to be honest, I had been afraid the Cartwrights were overwhelming you rather. I can see now they weren't, so that's very important. And yes, it is something you have to work out between you. Some kind of compromise . . .'

'We won't be working anything out,' said Annabel. 'It's over.'

'Well, I think that's a terrible pity. He loves you, very much, and you love him.'

'But Mummy, I can't believe you're talking like this. It's against everything you've ever taught me, that having a career you love is as important as having a husband you love. You and Daddy made it work and—'

'Yes, we did,' said Elizabeth, 'but the cost was very high at times. It was very hard on both of us. Daddy was wonderful, but I know there were many times when he would have longed for a Frances Cartwright waiting at home for him, asking him about his day.'

'Of course he wouldn't. You wouldn't have been you and he wouldn't have loved you.'

'I know that. All I'm saying is, it isn't easy. As hard for him to cope with as staying at home would be on you. You have to recognise that, in your discussions with Jamie.'

'There won't be any discussions,' said Annabel. 'They're over. I told you, I've given the ring back.'

'I know. But he might come round, might think about it more carefully. Shake off some of the brainwashing.'

She shook her head. 'He won't. He's totally stubborn.'

'Well, we'll see. I'm sorry, sweetheart.'

'Are you?' Annabel's face was quite hard as she looked at her mother. 'I thought you'd be totally on my side. You seem to be talking more like the Cartwrights, telling me I ought to give in to him.'

'Darling, of course I'm not. I'm just saying it's not a black and white issue. That's all. I—'

'What?'

'Oh, nothing.'

Just for a moment she had considered telling Annabel the other side of the story of her marriage: the affairs, the unhappiness, the anxiety. All resulting to a degree from her blinkered view of life and her crushing determination to do it all, have it all. But she couldn't: it would mean destroying the image Annabel had of her father, her perfect, liberated, sympathetic, ahead-of-his-time father. Who she had loved so much.

'Come on,' she said, 'you look terribly tired. Go on up to bed, and I'll bring you some tea. How would that be? And if Tilly comes in, I'll tell her you're asleep. You don't want to have to tell her about it as well, do you?'

'No,' said Annabel. 'No, I suppose not. But I'll have to, won't I? And an awful lot of other people. Oh dear.'

She started to cry again; Elizabeth cuddled her for a while, and then sent her up to bed and went into the kitchen to make the tea. She felt very sorry and sad for Annabel, but also rather relieved. Not that she had broken off the engagement, but that she needn't worry about her daughter so much. Annabel knew exactly what she was doing; she could take care of herself. Whatever happened.

Three days before the inquest, Robert Jeffries at the Coroner's office telephoned Elizabeth at home. He said he hoped she was well, and not feeling too anxious about it all; and he asked her if she had any questions.

'No, not really, except what time should we be there?'

'We begin at nine-thirty. So – anything between nine and nine-fifteen, I would suggest. You'll have your children with you, I believe?'

'Yes, all three of them.'

'We don't have wonderful facilities, but I can take you to one of the waiting rooms, and if you come early enough, I can show you the court, where you'll be sitting and so on, before everyone arrives. It helps if it's familiar. Er . . . I have to warn you that there may be some press there.'

'Press! But why, how horrible! Do they have to be, can't you stop them?'

'I'm afraid not, Mrs Beaumont. Inquests are open courts, and the press can attend if they wish. Likewise members of the public. The thing is, in this case, your husband was well-known and his death was reported in the papers. As was his funeral, of course. The article, the famous one that young man wrote, featured him quite largely as well, so – yes, I'm afraid they may well be there, the press. I'm so sorry. Now we have a very nice Coroner, a Doctor Holden. Very kind and calm, and he's very experienced, been a Coroner for thirty years, and he's very good at keeping things moving.'

'Moving?'

'Yes. People can get bogged down in detail, you see. Doctor Holden won't allow that. You'll like him, I know.'

'Will I meet him?'

'Oh certainly you will, yes. If not before the inquest, then certainly afterwards. Now there's one other thing. You'll give evidence first, which I imagine you'll prefer. Get it over.'

'Yes,' said Elizabeth. 'Er – what sort of things will he ask me?'

'Oh, he'll want you to confirm that you identified your husband. All you'll have to say is yes. That's a formality, of course, but it's legally necessary. We have your statement already, so a lot of what he asks you will refer to that, how you thought your husband was, his mental state, whether he had any medical problems, whether he'd said anything to you that indicated he might be considering taking his own life.'

'I see. Well, thank you, Mr Jeffries. Thank you so much. I'll see you on Wednesday.'

'Indeed. Just ring the doorbell when you get there if it's closed, and I'll let you in.'

How was she going to get through this: how?

Debbie was dreading the inquest. It wasn't the inquest itself, of course, although that wasn't going to be the best fun; it was the thought that Joel might be there. Probably would be there. He'd been pretty involved with Simon over the article, which had been published, after all, only a couple of days before he'd died. She would be sitting in the same room as he was, contained by the same walls, breathing the same air . . . How was she going to bear it? How was she not going to smile at him, speak to him – it was horrendous. And she was just beginning to feel better. A little better.

It had worked, Flora's plan. She had told Debbie to be very straightforward about it, just say that she was very sorry, but she really couldn't go up to Scotland for another term.

'Of course he'll be furious, but he'll get over it. And if he's very bad, then I'll talk to him. OK?'

'Thank you, Flora. Thank you very much.'

He *had* been very bad, most unusually shouting at her, rather than moving into icy rage: what would he say to Morag, how could he do the job for another term on his own, what about the various schools the children were supposed to have left, and the house, supposing they sold the house? And how did he know she wouldn't do this next term, and the next and the next?

'You don't know,' she said calmly to this last, 'except that I give you my word I won't. You'll have to trust me on it, Richard, I can't do more.'

She said the schools wouldn't be a problem: she'd already rung them, to check, and they'd all said they'd be happy to keep the children for another term, that although they'd filled Alex's place, it was such a tiny class – only fifteen – they could easily accommodate him. Ironically, the state school was more awkward. 'Well, they're not going to benefit financially, are they?' said Flora with a twinkle. But in the end they said yes too, but that this would have to be Rachel's last term, there was a big new intake in the spring.

Anna was over the moon at hearing that Debbie could stay for another three months at Know How; she hadn't managed to replace her, nor had she properly worked out which of the accounts Debbie could do from Scotland. Which just left Morag – who had been very upset, Richard said, but marvellous just the same, and understanding too.

He imparted this information over supper, having had a long conversation with her; Debbie and Flora, who had come home that day, tried not to look at one another, but became helplessly overwhelmed with giggles.

'I don't see what's so funny,' Richard said rather stiffly, and Flora said through streaming eyes, 'Richard, you are obsessed with that woman. If you could only hear yourself. Do give us, particularly poor Debbie, a break. I'm sure Morag is magnificent in every way, but she does make us ordinary mortals feel terribly inferior.'

She winked at Debbie as she said this; she exploded afresh and then said, 'I'm sorry, Richard, but it's true, we feel we simply can't compete with Morag.' And then realised as she hurried out of the room, before he saw her giggling again, that she hadn't thought of Joel for at least ten minutes, and that laughing like that with Flora had been quite wonderfully enjoyable. Enjoyable! When she had never thought to enjoy anything again. Another little thing to tick off. She was surviving. She would survive.

But not if she had to see Joel. Maybe, as he was in New York, he wouldn't have to go. But if he did, how would she get through it? How?

Annabel wondered if even now she should offer to make a statement. Only if she did, it wouldn't exactly help. She would be saying that she had upset her father the night before the accident, by telling him she might want to have her wedding in Cape Cod, not in London. She discussed it with her mother, who said she really didn't think it would add anything to the proceedings. 'Daddy's hardly likely to go and deliberately fall over the side of a boat because you're not getting married in the garden.'

'No, I suppose not. Oh dear. And now I'm not getting married at all.'

She had told Florian that; he was delighted.

'He just wasn't for you, darling. I knew it. You were never cut out to be a corporate wife. Just stick to doing their hair.'

She had heard nothing from Jamie; she had been right about him, then. Pig-headed, arrogant – a true Cartwright. She was well shot of him. She didn't even feel that bad. Except first thing in the morning. And last thing at night. And pretty often in between as well. She had more or less stopped crying. Well, she was doing it slightly less often. She'd get over it; she knew she would. She'd be fine. She'd be successful. *Not* a corporate wife. And when she was the first woman to own a chain of hairdressing salons, she'd be able to write to him and tell him. And it would be totally, totally worth it.

The day before the inquest, Elizabeth felt restless, nervy, couldn't concentrate. Peter Hargreaves, thinking it might help, had taken her out to lunch, but she picked at the food, pushed it round her plate, and even found drinking a little of the superb white Burgundy he had ordered an effort.

'I'm sorry, Peter. I just can't think about anything else.'

'Poor you. Understandable. Would you like me to come? Moral support and all that?'

'Oh no, thank you. It's sweet of you, but I think we're best on our own.' She sighed. 'Poor Peter. I haven't been much use to you lately, have I? What with one thing and another. And now this.' She patted her stomach. 'I'm surprised you haven't put me out to grass.'

'Elizabeth,' he said, 'I've employed you through three

babies. Here and at Sky Waterton. I can't believe this time's going to be any different. You've done a lot of your best work immediately post-natally.'

'I have?'

'Yes. Proving yourself, I suppose. No doubt you will again, although I'd like you to take a bit more time off.'

'Like how much?'

'Well, I think you were away for ten days after you had Annabel. Three weeks with Toby. And an outrageous month with Tilly. Don't look at me like that – I got HR to check it out. So, this time, why not give yourself a break. Take six weeks. Go on, you know you want to.'

'Actually,' said Elizabeth rather soberly, 'I might not. It's going to be terribly terribly different. Without Simon.' And to her huge embarrassment she burst into tears. 'Sorry,' she said, 'sorry, Peter.'

'Don't be silly,' he said, passing her a clean napkin from an adjoining table. 'I rather like it. Proves to me you're human. I never really believed it before.'

Several people phoned her that afternoon to check she was all right, and to wish her well. David Green, of course, who was coming up and staying with them. Catherine, sweet Catherine and equally sweet Lucinda, who said she was desperately nervous and sure she was going to get everything wrong.

'Lucinda,' said Elizabeth, laughing in spite of herself, 'there's nothing to get wrong. You've just got to answer their questions.'

'Yes, I know. And I never can. I've told people I don't know where Cadogan Square is, when I'm standing in it, by my own front door. Honestly, I'm that bad. But I'll do my best. Lots of love, Elizabeth. See you tomorrow.'

Flora phoned, said she must try not to worry. 'It'll soon be over now. We had to have one for William, you know.'

'Why?'

'Well, he died within twenty-four hours of admission to hospital. It was dreadful, of course, but it lacked reality in a strange way. They're much less formal than a normal court, less frightening.'

'Flora, I'm so sorry. What a ghastly thing.'

'Oh, not really. One survives what one has to, don't you think?'

'I suppose so. Now – how are you going to get up here?'

'Oh, my friend Colin is driving me. He's got a very sleek Jaguar, very low to the ground, I can get in and out of it perfectly easily.'

'I'd have liked you to stay,' said Elizabeth, 'but we're living in a shoe box. I expect Tilly's told you.'

'Oh, my dear, don't be absurd. Colin has booked us into the Savoy. We'll be fine.'

Separate rooms, I hope, thought Elizabeth; and yearned as she so often did, to be able to share this delicious thought with Simon.

And Joel Strickland phoned her.

'Elizabeth, hello. I just wanted to call and say I will be there tomorrow. And that I hope you're not feeling too bad.'

'That's kind. Well, I'm dreading it, of course. It won't be exactly a cheerful experience.'

'Of course not. But that was the other thing I wanted to say – these things are much less forbidding than you might think. I've been to dozens of them in my capacity of tabloid reporter. I mean, clearly it won't be easy for you, but there's something about Coroners; they're so calm and make things seem so normal. I think it might not be quite as bad as you're expecting.'

'Yes, someone else said much the same thing,' said Elizabeth doubtfully. 'Flora Fielding – I think you met her.'

'Yes, I did,' he said, and there was an odd silence. 'And her daughter-in-law. I believe she's going to be there.'

'Yes, she is.'

Another silence, then, 'And is your lovely daughter going to be there?'

'All the children are.'

'That's brave of them,' he said, 'but then I suppose they would be. They've got brave genes. Please give Annabel my love.'

He was a charmer, she thought: charming and thoughtful. She did hope he had a nice wife or girlfriend.

*

And then she got the worst phone call: from Martin Dudley at Graburn & French.

'Ah, Elizabeth,' he said, 'looking forward to seeing you tomorrow. I'll do my best to explain.'

'Explain what?' asked Elizabeth politely.

'Well, you know, how what happened was entirely down to contractual obligations, nothing personal, nothing to do with Simon's performance. I loathed having to do it, but I had no choice. I'm sure Simon understood that.'

'I don't think he did actually,' said Elizabeth, 'but it doesn't make much difference now, does it? Goodbye, Martin. Nice of you to call.'

In fact, she thought, looking at the telephone as she put it down, Simon's ejection from Graburn & French was fairly unlikely to have driven him to suicide. But there was no doubt that in most people's opinion, and certainly that of the Coroner, it must have been a factor. And thought yet again that a verdict of suicide, or at best an open verdict, seemed increasingly and horribly likely. There just wasn't enough evidence to make it anything else.

The 2.30 p.m. British Airways flight from Barbados was an hour late getting in; it was after five when Felicity Parker Jones got away from the airport, and it took an hour and a half for her taxi to navigate the rush-hour traffic around Gatwick and to reach her house near Westdean in Sussex. By which time all the local shops were shut.

Felicity was starving; she made it a rule never to eat on planes, but the fish pie in her freezer was not an attractive colour and her housekeeper had most inconsiderately been taken to hospital with suspected appendicitis. Felicity decided to go to the Sailing Club to eat. There was always something good on the menu; and she really wasn't particularly tired. She got out her car – it was a Golf, and it always started, even after months of languishing in the garage – and turned it in the direction of Chichester, thinking as she always did how nice it was to be back in England.

She got quite a welcome; she was a bit of a heroine in the Club, and very popular, especially with the men, being both attractive and a superb sailor. She sat down in the bar for a pre-supper gin and tonic.

'Good trip?' someone asked.

'Super. Wonderful sailing. Bought myself a new baby, actually. Forty-footer. Very pleased with her. God, it's a beautiful place. Now, is David Green about? I really want to ask him something.'

'No, he's gone up to London,' said Brian Thomas, the Club Secretary, 'with Andy Peasmarsh. They're both giving evidence at this inquest tomorrow.'

'What inquest?' said Felicity, reaching out for a handful of roasted peanuts.

'Simon Beaumont's. You did know he died, didn't you – drowned – dreadful tragedy?'

'Yes, of course. Someone sent me a cutting from the paper. I was quite upset, I have to say. But why on earth are they having an inquest?'

'Well, given all the circumstances, it could be suicide, apparently. His financial situation and so on. Nobody can say for sure, of course.'

Felicity sat staring at him for a moment or two, and then she stood up; she looked rather pale beneath her tan.

'I can say for sure,' she said, 'at least I think I can. I must try and get hold of David Green. It's really rather important.'

Chapter 62

January, 1991

Debbie woke very early: feeling violently sick. This was going to be tough. Very tough. But – Flora would be there. She would manage. Somehow. She hoped.

She got up and went over to the window; it was still dark. Thank God Richard had gone back to Scotland; she would never have managed this with him asking her when she was going and how she was going to get there, and why was she so worried about it.

She'd asked Flora if she'd like to come and stay the night before, but Flora had refused.

'Sweet of you, Debbie darling, but Colin is coming too and – well, we're staying at the Savoy. Between you and me, I think he wants to impress me. So I'm letting him. But I'll see you there.' And then she said, very casually, 'I wondered who else might be giving evidence. Do you know?'

'No idea,' said Debbie quickly, 'apart from Simon's harem – you and me and Lucinda and so on.'

'I don't think I'd do very well in a harem, with you two competing for the Sultan's attention,' said Flora, and laughed.

Hating herself, Debbie took a lot of trouble over her appearance. She told herself it was because it was an important occasion and she would be the centre of the court's attention, albeit briefly. She didn't want to look tatty, she wanted them to take what she had to say seriously. And then she remembered Joel telling her, when they had discussed the inquest, that people often came to such events looking extraordinarily different: 'The last one I went to,' he'd said, 'there was a lady about Flora's age, all done up in furs and diamonds, and a funny old chap who was a plumber wearing his overalls.'

Just the same she washed her hair, put on a new shirt from Gap under her black suit, and spent more time than she would have normally done on her make-up.

'You look nice, Mummy,' said Emma, as Debbie gave them their breakfast. 'Going out to lunch?'

'No. I'm going to that thing called a court – remember I told you? I've got to give evidence.'

'Gosh,' said Alex, 'like Rumpole, you mean?'

'A bit like that,' said Debbie. 'Now eat your breakfast. Jenny's going to collect you all from school, as I may be late.'

'I've got used to you *not* being late,' said Rachel, giving her a hug. 'It's much nicer.'

Another little thing. They were becoming more frequent. She was going to need them all today.

Flora had been up for two hours before joining Colin for breakfast. She had to do her physiotherapy exercises, take her painkillers, wash herself – how she longed for a bath – and then dress. It all took forever. She sank exhausted onto the dressing-table stool to do her hair, wondering if she actually had the strength. And then told herself not to be ridiculous. As if she had anything to complain about: compared with poor Elizabeth and her children – and just possibly Debbie. She was aware that Joel Strickland might be there; and she was fearful for Debbie's fragile recovery. Odd how she had taken Debbie's part entirely in this; she supposed because she had been through it herself and understood it in its entirety, from temptation to conclusion. She would be all right; they would all be all right. Especially if Richard made a bit of an effort. She had had one conversation with him; and intended to have more. She loved him dearly, but he wasn't always very sensitive. Just like his father.

She twisted her hair into its high knot and swung herself on her crutch out into the corridor.

Elizabeth also woke up early. She lay quietly, in the rather small bed, thinking of the last time she had seen Simon, in a rather larger bed, and how he had told her he loved her, and how happy she had been all the following day. For the last time in her life, as far as she could see.

'Oh Simon,' she said aloud, 'why did you have to do it to us? Why, why, why couldn't you stay and let us help you?'

She felt a stab of the old anger and was pleased: that was the way to get through today, she thought, being angry with him. If a verdict of suicide or an open verdict was brought in she would never forgive him: never.

She heard Annabel moving about next door, saw the light go on, on the landing, then heard the lavatory door slam, followed by a muffled sob. She cried a lot in the morning, poor little thing: it was a bad time to be unhappy. Elizabeth certainly knew that.

She felt surprised that there had been nothing, no word, no call from Jamie; she had thought more of him than that. Annabel had said (unprompted) that she hadn't expected to hear from him, but Elizabeth knew she was lying.

They arrived at the court just after nine, the four of them in a car that Peter Hargreaves, ever thoughtful, had provided: Annabel quiet and quite calm, Tilly visibly trembling, Toby determinedly stiff upper-lipped.

It was a lovely day; Elizabeth wondered if it helped, and decided it didn't. Dark storm clouds would be more appropriate. The building was brick-built with a large wooden door, probably Edwardian, Elizabeth thought – why was she noticing such things? – in a wide, tree-lined street just behind the Brompton Road. A small crowd was already waiting outside.

Elizabeth didn't recognise any of them and felt panicked. Who were they? Why were they interested, strangers as they were, in her husband's death?

She rang the brass bell as instructed by Mr Jeffries. He appeared immediately, smiled his wonderfully calm, reassuring smile.

'Good morning, Mrs Beaumont. And what a good one it is. Now you must be . . .'

'Annabel,' said Annabel, 'and this is my brother Toby, and my sister Tilly.'

'Welcome, all of you. Now, if you would like to come along to the waiting room, I can fetch you some coffee.'

'Thank you,' said Elizabeth, 'how kind. And – who are all those people outside, Mr Jeffries?'

'Oh, don't worry about them. Few journalists, maybe a couple of hangers-on. Now why don't you have a look at the courtroom, while there's nobody here?' He led them along a corridor which opened into a large square hall: and through a door, which he opened with a flourish.

'Come in,' he said.

'Goodness,' said Annabel, speaking for all of them. 'It's rather – rather nice.' Somehow they hadn't expected this: a light, high-ceilinged room, with rows of seats, rather pew-like; a large Edwardian fireplace, tall, vaulted windows, and very nice brass wall-lights. Set higher than the rest of the room was the Coroner's bench.

'Now this is where the family – where you – will sit,' said Mr Jeffries, indicating the front two rows. 'And here the press, and that is the witness box, over there. Everone else just settles themselves down. Friends probably behind you, officials of various kinds, doctors and so on, over there. There's plenty of room, as you can see. Now, do you have any questions?'

'No, I don't think so,' said Elizabeth, 'except – do you have a loo?'

She had already been three times since breakfast; how did babies play quite such havoc with the bladder?

They drank their coffee in the waiting room and heard the noise-level rising as more people arrived. Elizabeth could hear Flora's clipped, rather musical tones, Lucinda's absurdly Sloane Ranger vowels (and Blue's rather different, equally strong ones), Martin Dudley's boom, and then Debbie Fielding's rather sweet, less posh voice, very subdued.

And then they were ushered in by Mr Jeffries, and the courtroom was suddenly full of familiar faces, people Elizabeth knew; it was rather like a wedding, she thought, and felt absurdly that she should rush round greeting people, admiring their hats, or even that she should say a quick prayer for the right verdict . . .

They sat in the family pew, the girls on either side of her, Tilly still shaking, hanging onto her hand as if it was a lifeline, Annabel staring calmly in front of her, Toby glaring at his feet.

And then, 'Rise, please,' Mr Jeffries said, and the Coroner, Dr Holden, Elizabeth could see his name on a plaque in front of the bench, came in from the side, mounted the steps to the bench, nodded briefly to them and they all sat down again.

It had begun.

Dr Holden had an extraordinarily nice voice, that was the first thing Elizabeth noticed; educated, well-modulated, and very clear without being in the least loud. It was going to help, that voice. He had fair, gently greying hair, and was wearing an extremely well-cut grey pinstriped suit. He could have been one of their neighbours in The Boltons.

He smiled very briefly in her direction and then said, 'We are considering today the death of a man by drowning. If we may start, Mr Jeffries?'

Mr Jeffries walked over to the witness box and took the oath. Somehow, in the pleasing half-informality of the court, she hadn't expected that, hadn't expected all the stuff about Almighty God and the truth the whole truth and nothing but . . .

He picked up a sheaf of notes and started to read from it.

'The deceased was identified as Simon Gerald Beaumont . . .' It gave her a start, that Gerald; she had always forgotten it, it didn't suit him, it had been his father's name. His sweet father, who had been so proud of him; thank God he wasn't there, didn't have to endure this, what his son had done to them all . . . concentrate, Elizabeth, for God's sake. 'Simon Gerald Beaumont, aged forty-seven years. He was born on May the seventeenth, 1943, and he lived at number seventeen Bolton Place, London SW7. His body was found on the French coast, at Gravelines, near Calais, on August the twenty-sixth, where a post mortem was performed and the cause of death stated as drowning. A dry drowning – that is to say, one where the water reaches the top of the trachea and closes it, shortly after which the heart stops.'

She hadn't realised that, it sounded rather bizarre. 'The deceased was identified initially in France by his passport, which had remained in the pocket of his trousers, and later by his widow, Mrs Elizabeth Beaumont. His body was brought to England and taken to the mortuary at the Kensington and Fulham Hospital.

'Until shortly before his death, Mr Beaumont had been

employed as a Board Director of Graburn and French, Merchant Bankers, and—'

She was losing concentration already. It just didn't seem relevant, was nothing to do with her. The Body had nothing to do with Simon, or The Deceased; it was all very odd. Mr Jeffries was continuing to read from his statement; a report from Toxicology stated that blood samples contained alcohol and analgesic, consistent with perhaps one or two glasses of wine and one or two paracetamol . . . insufficient to cause any loss of consciousness; there was indication of a blow to the back of the head, probably from the boom; the deceased had been wearing a life-jacket but it was not inflated; there was no indication of foul play; the boat, a twenty-two-foot Seal, was found intact the following day adrift in the Channel. Mr Beaumont had apparently been fit and well and in good spirits the day before his death.

Dr Holden leaned forward. 'Thank you, Mr Jeffries. Perhaps we can hear now from Mrs Elizabeth Beaumont. Mr Jeffries, would you read Mrs Beaumont's statement?'

This was how they did it, she was discovering; they read out a statement you had given, perhaps weeks earlier, and then you were questioned on it as if they didn't quite believe you. Or it. She listened as Mr Jeffries told the court that she had identified Simon's body and where, that a visit from the police had informed her of his death by drowning, that he had been in good spirits the day before . . . again she found it hard to concentrate.

'And now, Mrs Beaumont,' Dr Holden said in his beautifully courteous voice, 'would you please go to the witness box.'

Suddenly it was all real again: real and terrifying. She felt sick, she felt panicky, her mouth dry, her head spinning. She stood up and stared at Dr Holden, and couldn't move.

'Mrs Beaumont are you all right?'

For a long time, it seemed, in that courtroom there was silence: everyone looking at her. She could see the mass of faces, some kindly, some concerned, some shocked, some embarrassed. She realised that in spite of carefully dressing in a looser jacket, her pregnancy must be obvious: she was nearly five months now and without the taut stomach muscles of her twenties to help conceal it. She felt absurdly foolish, desperately alone; the full horror of her situation hit her suddenly. Here she was, alone in a courtroom, widowed, pregnant, giving evidence about her husband. Her late husband. Who had abandoned her, abandoned her to this.

And then she saw Annabel looking up at her, standing up too, taking her hand; and Tilly also standing, putting her arm round her waist, and strength soared back into her.

'Yes,' she said, with a quick smile at her two daughters. 'Yes, I'm perfectly all right. Thank you.'

She walked over to the witness box; Mr Jeffries gave her some water. She sipped it gratefully, and then put her hand on the Bible.

'I swear by Almighty God,' she began, and heard her own voice growing in confidence, and when she had finished, Dr Holden smiled at her, and she felt as if she had just done something extremely difficult, passed some tricky exam. Which she supposed, in a way, she had.

'Would you like to sit down while you give your evidence, Mrs Beaumont?' Mr Holden said, and, 'No,' she said, 'no, I'm perfectly all right now, thank you.'

'Very well. I see you live now at 14 Kensington Avenue, and you are employed by Hargreaves Harris and Osborne, who are . . .' he paused, looked at his notes . . . 'advertising agents.'

'Yes, that's correct.'

'And what is your position there?'

'I'm the Managing Director.'

'I see.' She was aware of him reacting to that; he looked up, just slightly surprised, and then smiled at her briefly – and it made her feel better, that reaction, slightly less vulnerable somehow, that she could still impress – and then went back to his notes.

'Now, you have moved from Bolton Place, I see. Could you tell us the reason for that?'

'Yes. We were forced to sell our house.'

'For financial reasons?'

'Yes. We lost a lot of money at Lloyd's and—'

'And – was the house already on the market on August the twenty-first?'

'Yes, it was.'

'Was your husband distressed by that? By being forced to sell the family home?'

'Of course. We both were.'

'Thank you. Now, it was you who identified your late husband's body?'

'Yes, it was.'

'And you last saw him alive on the evening of August the twentieth. Perhaps you could tell us about that.'

'I came home very late; Simon was half-asleep. I had been working on a presentation.'

'A presentation? Could you tell us what that is?'

'It's an advertising term. It describes work that you present to a client, work that will promote a product.'

'I see. And did you have any kind of conversation that evening?'

'Not really, no. We were both terribly tired. We went to sleep.' *After making love; after making this baby. The last thing he did for me.*

'And did he tell you where he was going in the morning?'

'No, he didn't. But he left me a note, to say he had gone sailing. That he'd be back probably that same night, but quite late.'

'You didn't actually see him that morning?'

'No.'

'And – did he often go sailing? During the week?'

'He often went sailing, he loved it. He had a sailing boat of his own once, but he had had to sell it. And not usually during the week, no, but he had recently lost his job, he had been dismissed by the bank he had worked for, for twenty-five years, and—'

'Yes, we will come to that. So it was not anything out of the ordinary that he went sailing?'

'Not at all, no.'

'And was he a competent sailor?'

'Very competent. He had won many races, had many trophies.'

'And had he been depressed during the days leading up to August the twentieth?'

She hesitated. 'Not exactly depressed. That wasn't his style. But – he was worried.'

'About?'

'Well, he had lost a great deal of money at Lloyd's, as I said. And he had lost his job. We were selling the house. It wasn't a situation likely to make him very cheerful.'

'Was he inclined to be depressed?'

'Not at all, I told you. He met life head on, always had; he was meeting this head on—'

'He wasn't undergoing any treatment for anxiety or depression?'

'No, of course not. As I said, he wasn't inclined to be depressed.'

'And were there other changes to your lifestyle recently?'

'Well, yes. We had a house in Sussex, which we sold over a year ago.'

'Would you describe your marriage as happy, Mrs Beaumont? Forgive me for asking.'

'Very happy,' said Elizabeth firmly. She felt suddenly acutely aware of her bump.

'Thank you. And your own employment was perfectly stable, was it? There was no question of your losing your job?'

'No, there wasn't.'

'You have quite a large family. Three children at public school . . .'

'Only two when Simon died. Our older daughter had been working for a while.'

'I see. Still, even two is expensive.'

'Well yes. But I could pay the fees. He wasn't worried about that.'

'Now, I see that your husband was involved in a lawsuit with Lloyd's?'

'He would have been, yes. It hadn't begun.'

'That must have been expensive.'

'Yes, indeed. We were planning to invest some of the proceeds of the house in it.'

'So you were supportive of him in that, were you, Mrs Beaumont?'

'Yes, eventually. I felt at first it meant further risk, but I came to see that if we gave the money to Lloyd's, they would continue to demand more, ad infinitum. Better to let them sue us, we thought.'

843

'I see. Thank you, Mrs Beaumont. You may sit down. I would now like to hear from Mr Beaumont's GP.'

God, she was fantastic, thought Annabel, with a rush of pride: she felt like cheering, stood up and gave her mother a hug. Elizabeth smiled at her rather uncertainly, and sat down, gratefully taking the glass of water that someone had handed her.

Dr Rice's evidence was swiftly over: Simon had been in excellent health, was exceptionally fit for his age, and had an extremely well-adjusted and optimistic outlook on life. He had never prescribed anything more for him than an occasional course of antibiotics, and certainly never any anti-depressants, or even sleeping pills. He had last seen him a year earlier for an annual check-up; he had passed it 20/20.

'Thank you, Dr Rice. Mr Martin Dudley, please.'

Dudley was self-righteous even in his statement; on his questioning, more so. He hadn't wanted to terminate Simon's employment but had been forced to do it by the terms of his contract. Mr Beaumont was about to be involved in a lawsuit against Lloyd's and possibly to become bankrupt, and therefore could not remain as a director of the bank. Yes, Mr Beaumont had been quite clear about this, had understood it. He had taken the news well.

'You make it sound as if he was grateful to you,' said Dr Holden, rather briskly. 'I'm sure it couldn't have been all sweetness and light. Were there no harsh words uttered at all? May I remind you that you are under oath, Mr Dudley.'

Elizabeth wanted to climb up onto the bench and hug him.

Dudley looked deeply embarrassed. Then he said, 'As I recall, Mr Beaumont did say he thought perhaps I could have tried to find a way round the problem.'

'I see. Any other exchange?'

'He – well, he was rather outspoken on the matter. He was quite – quite offensive.'

'What exactly did he say? I would like the exact words, Mr Dudley, if you can recall them.'

'He – he called me a miserable, mean, cowardly bastard,' said Dudley with extreme reluctance.

'Anything else?'

'No. Well, he said he hoped I didn't think this was going to finish him. I said of course not.'

'Did that not occur to you, though?'

'No. He was a very self-confident, competent person.'

'I see. And then?'

'And then he left my office. And indeed the building. We never saw him again.'

'Thank you, Mr Dudley. You may sit down.' He watched Dudley return to his place then said, 'Well now, where do we go from here?' He looked out at the court, his handsome face thoughtful. I bet he wanted to be an actor, Elizabeth thought.

'I think we should hear from the people who saw him in the two or three days before his death. Could we begin with Mrs Lucinda Cowper.'

They were all wonderful, Simon's girls. They all said he had been amazingly cheerful, considering how extensive his worries were. He was fantastic, Lucinda said, 'So brave and upbeat and good.'

'Did you see a lot of Mr Beaumont?' asked Dr Holden. 'I mean, was he a good friend of yours?'

'Oh yes, terribly good. We had lunch sometimes, and before I had the baby—'

'The baby?'

'Yes, I've just had a baby. Well, about six weeks ago.'

'I see. Now you are still married, Mrs Cowper?'

'Well, yes I am, but the baby . . .' God, she was making a hash of this. She'd known she would.

'I think I'd better start again,' she said. Her blue eyes were huge and earnest. 'Sorry. I was married, to someone who had also lost a lot of money at Lloyd's, that's how I met Simon – Mr Beaumont – but the father of my baby is – was . . .' There was a pause, while she wondered exactly what to say; she had an awful feeling Dr Holden thought it might be Simon. 'The father of my baby is that gentleman over there,' she pointed at Blue, who half-stood up, as if ready to acknowledge any applause. 'It was a rather difficult time, you can imagine, but whenever I was a bit down, I used to ring Simon for a chat, and he always cheered me up. He cheered us all up.'

'And did Mrs Beaumont know about these chats?' asked Dr Holden. He was clearly very taken with Lucinda.

'Yes, of course she did. Well obviously I didn't ring her up and tell her about every single one, but we all had connections with Lloyd's. And we met at Ascot, things like that.'

'I see,' said Dr Holden. He was clearly struggling now not to laugh.

'Anyway, I felt a bit bad because Simon wanted to have lunch with me, the day before – the day before . . . Oh dear.' She stopped, wiped her eyes. 'And I felt a bit bad because I couldn't. But he said, "Let's do it next week," and he said he'd ring me and fix it.'

'But he didn't set a date then?'

'No. No, he didn't.'

'Thank you, Mrs Cowper.'

Catherine was next; she said he'd been really kind and good to her, he'd got her a job at the bank which had saved her bacon. Dr Holden asked her to explain how at this point – 'but when he was fired, they fired me too. He was very upset about that,' she added.

'In what way?'

'Well, he enjoyed being able to help people. It was important to him. And that day, the day before the accident, he came to see me with a big bunch of flowers, to say he was sorry.'

'Sorry that you'd been fired?'

'Yes.'

'Although not by him?'

'Well, no, but he felt responsible. He took it all on himself, rather.'

There was a silence, while Dr Holden made a note.

Where was he, Debbie wondered in an agony of tension. Maybe he wasn't coming at all, maybe he was already in New York and hadn't got to come . . . God, this was awful. Horrible. Maybe if she was called soon – and it looked as if she might be – she could escape before he arrived. Was that allowed? Were you allowed to leave before the verdict? Were you allowed to be late? She was sure you weren't. Every time the door opened, her heart quite literally seemed to stop.

God, oh God—

'Could we hear now from Mrs Deborah Fielding?'

Well, at least she hadn't got to stand there, giving evidence with him watching her. Listening to her. She'd be able to speak, to think; just the same, she was shaking violently as she put her hand on the Bible, swore the oath.

She listened to her statement. A statement from someone very calm and competent. Who would have guessed that someone had been caught up in a kind of madness – reckless, lying, dangerous, adoring madness? Ready to jettison her husband, her family, everything she had? Who would think it, looking at her now, composed, careful, neatly dressed?

'Mrs Fielding.' The Coroner smiled at her; he was quite handsome, she supposed, in a middle-aged sort of way. Not unlike Simon, actually. Not unlike the Simon she had so resolutely disliked until she came actually to love him. Love him for his kindness, his patience with her, his interest in what she did, his wise counsel. Not as she had loved Joel, of course, but loved him just the same. And he was gone, and the last thing she had said to him had been brusque and even dismissive. 'Mrs Fielding. Perhaps you can tell us exactly how you came to know Mr Beaumont?'

'Yes.' Her voice was faint now, faint with fright. The door was opening. She . . . no, it was all right, it was yet another carafe of water being passed to someone – Flora this time, thank God, thank God. 'I met him through my mother-in-law,' she said, her voice firmer now. 'I got very fond of him and he was very, very kind to me.'

'In what way?'

'He advised me on my career.'

'Really? But he was a banker and you are a' – pause – 'a public relations executive.'

'Yes, I know. But he was imaginative and clever, and he loved helping people. He was sort of a family friend,' she added. 'I used to see him when he went to Wales with his daughter, to stay with my mother-in-law. She was looking after a horse for them.'

Oh, and he introduced me to my lover. I forgot to mention that. Who might walk through the door any minute now.

847

'Yes, I see. And I believe you saw him very soon after he had been fired from the bank.'

'Yes, that's right. I offered to buy him a drink.'

'*You* offered to buy *him* a drink? An interesting way round.'

'Not at all. He'd bought me drinks from time to time, and I felt it was my turn.'

'Yes, I see. Well, that was very generous of you. And how did you find Mr Beaumont on that occasion?'

'Well, he was slightly anxious, but full of plans. He was going to mount this lawsuit, you know, and—'

'Indeed. Now, this was some time before he went on that fateful sail, wasn't it?'

'Yes. A couple of weeks.'

'And did you see him after that?'

'I spoke to him several times. Including the day before he died.'

'And how was he that day?'

'Well . . .' she hesitated. 'He was a bit subdued.'

'Could you define subdued?'

'He was less – less cheery than usual. But far from depressed.'

'And what was the purpose of his phone call?'

'Oh, just to have a chat. He was at a bit of a loose end. And to ask me to lunch.'

'Really? And did you agree?'

'I said I couldn't, that day.' She'd said worse than that, she'd said she was too busy to talk. Suppose that had done it? Suppose it had been that, that had tipped the balance? 'But he said another time, maybe next week. He said he'd be very much around.'

'Right. Well, thank you, Mrs Fielding. And now I see we have another Mrs Fielding. Mrs Flora Fielding.' He looked at Flora as she stood up, assisted by Colin. 'Are you able to get up into the witness box, Mrs Fielding?'

'I most certainly am.'

She heaved herself across the court on her crutches and was helped up into the box. She stood there looking magnificent in her blue velvet jacket. That she'd worn the very first time she'd met Simon; she'd worn it deliberately, in his memory, the better not to let him down.

'May I tell you before you ask me any questions,' she said, having taken the oath, 'the last thing I said to Simon Beaumont was, did nothing ever get him down? And he said, "Not much".'

'The procedure of the court is for *me* to ask the questions, Mrs Fielding,' Dr Holden said briskly, 'which you are required to answer. Please observe that.'

'Very well.'

'Now – how was his mood that afternoon? When you had the lunch referred to in your statement.'

'Well, he was very upset. Briefly,' she added hastily, 'and more angry than anything.'

'Why was that, do you think?'

'He'd been involved in getting this lawsuit together. Against Lloyd's. It was only in the planning stages, but he was trying to gather evidence . . .'

'Ah yes. I see we have a statement from Miss Broadhurst, of Evans Dixon Campbell. Perhaps we should hear from her next. Anyway, was this evidence forthcoming?'

'No, it wasn't. I felt my Members' Agent at Lloyd's might be able to provide some information that would be helpful. But he couldn't.'

'I see. And Mr Beaumont had set great store on this information, had he?'

'He was very hopeful about it, yes.'

'So, would you say he was very disappointed?'

'Well yes. Yes, I would.'

'How did you and he meet, Mrs Fielding?'

'At a Lloyd's meeting. Or to be precise, a meeting of Members of our main syndicate at Lloyd's. We became friends; I was able to look after one of his daughters' horses at my house in Wales.'

'He must have been very grateful.'

'He was indeed.'

'So you were a victim of Lloyd's? Yes, of course you were. And – forgive me, have you come out of it unscathed?'

'No, not really. My house has been saved by a legal loophole. A trust fund, set up by my late husband. But at that point, I did think I would lose it. Mr Beaumont was very upset about that also.'

'Why particularly?'

'Well, because of the horse. His daughter's horse, which was being stabled by me. I clearly couldn't keep him in a flat in Swansea.'

'Indeed not,' Dr Holden twinkled at her, and then said more soberly, 'So – more unhappiness, more worry for Mr Beaumont.'

'Well yes, but I'm sure he would have worked something out. He was a very, very resourceful person.'

'I'm sure. Let me just ask you again, when you parted on that afternoon, was he visibly upset?'

'Well, he was,' said Flora, 'but as I told you, he was still in positive mood.'

'Thank you, Mrs Fielding. You may sit down.'

She'd failed him; been less helpful in her evidence even than Lucinda. She felt terrible; she'd made a complete hash of it, barging in like that, speaking before she should have done, bossing everyone about as usual, even the Coroner. And damaging Simon's cause. She felt suddenly near to tears and nudged Colin to give her a handkerchief. He looked at her alarmed as she wiped her eyes; such weakness was very unusual.

Fiona Broadhurst took the stand. She looked very self-assured, very cool. She really isn't Simon's type, Elizabeth thought. But – good legs. So not really surprising Simon had taken her to lunch at the Caprice. To discuss the lawsuit.

'Do you frequently go to lunch at the Caprice with clients, Miss Broadhurst?' Dr Holden smiled at her, an almost conspiratorial smile. He likes her, Elizabeth realised, likes what she represents, literally law and order. Like him, she knows what's what.

'No, not very often. But Mr Beaumont was very generous—'

'Despite being virtually penniless?'

'I don't think being penniless changes a personality,' said Fiona coolly.

'It seems not. Go on.'

'He wanted to tell me something important, he said.'

'Was it a pleasant occasion?'

'Yes, very pleasant.'

'And what did he want to tell you?'

'That he had what he hoped was some evidence – tape-recorded evidence. I had to tell him it wouldn't satisfy a court, as the person talking didn't know he was being recorded – although a judge might consider the contents as background evidence.'

'Indeed,' said Dr Holden. 'Quite correct.'

Fiona Broadhurst gave him a very cold look.

'And how did Mr Beaumont take this news?'

'He was very upset.'

'In what way?'

'He seemed rather shaken. His confidence had obviously taken a beating.'

God, thought Elizabeth, this isn't helping – we don't want to hear this.

'We've heard a lot about this confidence of Mr Beaumont's. You are the first person to imply today that it might have been shattered.'

She was silent.

'So then what happened?'

'As I told you, he said he still wanted to go ahead with the lawsuit.'

'And was he – disappointed about your reaction to his news?'

'I would say so, yes.'

'Very?'

'Yes.'

'I see. And did you discuss it any further after that?'

'No, we didn't. He said he would tell the others involved himself. And then we talked of other matters.'

'Legal matters?'

'No. More general ones.'

'And – there were no other conversations in the restaurant that day? No one came up to the table?'

'Well . . .' She paused, pushed back an imaginary lock of hair.

'Do go on, Miss Broadhurst. Do I take it that there were?'

'Well, I went to take a phone call, outside in the street. And as I came back, I saw him talking to someone.'

'Just exchanging a greeting?'

'No. They were – she was . . .'

'She? This was a lady?'

'Yes, it was.'

'A young lady?'

'I would say she was in her late thirties, early forties. She gave him a card, and then she went back to her table and they didn't meet again.'

Elizabeth felt herself tauten: the old familiar fear surfacing.

'He didn't tell you who she was?'

'No.'

'Thank you, Miss Broadhurst.'

He turned his brief, charming smile on the court.

'So – here is a man with good reason to be depressed, a man who logic tells us should be depressed, and yet who, by all accounts, was not depressed at all. Very admirable. He was obviously a very strong character indeed.'

He paused, as if to convey deep thought on the matter, then said, 'I think we should take a break now, stretch our legs. I would also like to hear evidence from the journalist, Mr Strickland. Has he arrived yet? I know he was going to be late.'

How could they say his name like that, Debbie wondered, give this desperately crucial information about him while sounding perfectly normal? How could she still be sitting here calmly, looking up at the bench, when she wanted to jump up and down and scream?

'I'm told he's on his way now, Doctor Holden. Hopefully within the next half-hour . . .'

Definitely hopefully, thought Debbie, almost his last words to me, the last time we were together. They shouldn't be using those words here, they belong to us.

'He was out of London last night, working in Liverpool, and the train was very badly delayed.'

'How very unusual,' said Dr Holden with a smile. 'Thank you. Well then, let us reconvene in fifteen minutes exactly.'

Mr Jeffries said, 'All rise,' and Dr Holden stepped down from the bench and disappeared, and life briefly became itself again.

852

Toby was very angry. 'He's just setting out to trip everyone up, make them say Dad was depressed when he wasn't.'

'I know,' said Elizabeth wearily. *Who was that woman who gave Simon her card? On the last afternoon of his life. How dare he? How dare she, indeed . . .*

'And I don't see why. What's the point?'

'Point of what?' *Not Her, not Her, surely, surely . . .*

'Making out he was depressed?'

'I don't know, Toby. I don't think he is really. He's just trying to get as much information as he can.'

'No, he isn't. He keeps saying things like—'

'Toby, please! Don't go on and on about it. Let's go back to the waiting room.'

Annabel slipped her arm through her mother's. 'You're doing so well, Mummy, so well.'

'And a lot of use it is too,' said Elizabeth bitterly. 'God, I want the loo again. Come with me, darling?'

Debbie left the courtroom, went to one of the officials.

'I've given my evidence,' she said. 'Is it all right if I go now?'

'I should think so. I'll go and ask Mr Jeffries.'

Be quick, Mr Jeffries, please be quick. I have to get away from here before . . . before . . .

'Yes, that's fine. Is there a number where we can get you if we really need you? Very unlikely, but . . . you're not leaving London, are you?'

'No, I'm not, and I have a mobile phone. The number's here, look, on my card.'

'Right, well, I'll give that to them but I don't suppose we'll need it. Thank you for coming, my dear.'

She started to run down the corridor; she'd have to say goodbye to Flora later, phone Elizabeth, hear the verdict, but she had to get away now, at once, quickly, before . . .

She shot out of the door into the brilliant sunshine; slightly dazzled by it, she saw a taxi had pulled up across the street. No, no, please no – yes, yes, please yes.

He stood there, ten yards away from her, perhaps less, stock still, just looking at her. And she stood, stock still also, frozen in time and fear and longing, looking at him.

Who she loved more than anything in the world – except, except – who she had wept over, longed for, dreamed of – literally, night after night – remembered him loving her with such force it shook her physically at times, wanted it still so, so much. There, standing there, real, hers for the asking. And she stepped off the kerb and started to walk across the road towards him as if compelled by something outside herself, and he did the same, their eyes fixed on one another, held absolutely, her own filled with tears.

And she might even then have gone, forgotten all her brave good resolutions, gone with him, into happiness; but the cab hooted and the cabbie shouted, 'Another fiver mate, please,' and he turned briefly to look at him, and as he did so her strength, her own will came back to her, and she ran, ran faster in her high heels than she would have thought possible, gasping, fighting for breath, away from him, away from all of it, terrified that he would follow her, speak to her, touch her, longing for him to follow her, speak to her, touch her.

Only he didn't; and after five minutes she felt safe, and walked on very fast for what seemed a long time and then found she was in a McDonald's – and sank down on a chair and sat staring, staring out of the door, still afraid he would come in; and then she started to cry, quite gently, when she realised he wouldn't.

'You all right, love?' said a stout middle-aged lady, who was working her way through two bags of chips.

'Yes,' said Debbie. 'Yes, I think so, thank you.'

'Had a row with your boyfriend? Don't let it upset you, darlin' – they're never worth it.'

'Oh, but they are,' said Debbie, trying to smile at her and failing entirely. 'Some of them are.'

'Well, if he is, he'll be back. You look all in, love – want a sip of my coffee?'

'Oh no, thank you. Well – yes.'

It seemed to seep right into her veins, that coffee, slowly returning her to some kind of normality. Sad, aching normality; but she could see she had travelled further than she had thought since that dreadful last conversation with him, staring down at the sea.

'Thank you,' she said, 'so much.'

'That's all right, love. Don't you fret. Like I say, they're all the same.'

'This one wasn't,' said Debbie, wiping her streaming eyes. 'Honestly. But I will try not to fret.'

And she left McDonald's and went out and crossed the road towards a tube station. She would go home now quickly, get her car and then collect the children from school, hug them, talk to them, take them to the park. They were what she needed now: more than anything in the world.

That's all right, love. Don't you fret, I like I say, they're all the same.

This one wasn't,' said Debbie, wiping her streaming eyes. 'Honestly, but I will try not to fret.'

And she left McDonald's and went out and crossed the road towards a tube station ... she must move now quickly, get her car and then collect the children from school, hug them, talk to them, take them to the park. They were what she needed now, more than anything in the world.

Chapter 63

January, 1991

Joel had given his evidence: Elizabeth felt close to despair. It had been yet another story of disappointment; of Simon's excitement, of his conviction that Joel had delivered him the smoking gun: only to be told by Fiona Broadhurst that it was of little use.

Joel was very pale, she had noticed; he looked very shaken as he walked into the court. Obviously the trauma of being late, of the delayed train, had taken its toll. As he sat down again, he very briefly buried his face in his hands. And then sat back, smiled at her and at Annabel, but rather wearily, and fixed his eyes very firmly on the witness box.

The next witness was David Green; and his session in the box took a long time. Every detail from when Simon arrived at the Sailing Club 'later than he said he would – about half-past ten or even eleven' to when he had untied David's boat around an hour later, saying he would be back in five or six hours.

'And how was he?' Dr Holden asked. 'How was his state of mind?'

'Extremely cheerful. Almost excited, I'd say.'

'Really?'

'Yes, indeed. He insisted on ordering a bottle of champagne which he shared with me before he went off.'

'He didn't tell you why he was excited?'

'No, he didn't.'

'Would you say he was in any way *over*-excited?'

Elizabeth felt Toby stiffen, put her hand over his and pressed it gently.

'No,' David Green said. 'He was just as he always was when he was feeling particularly cheerful.'

'And he was sailing your boat, Mr Green? You'd lent it to him?'

'That is correct.'

'Are you in the habit of lending your boat to people?'

'From time to time, yes. Especially to Simon. He had been very upset when the *Lizzie* had to go, naturally, and I said if he was ever desperate for a sail, he could take mine.'

'Which was called?'

'*Princess Charming*. She's a Seal, a twenty-two-footer.'

'And did he say where he was going?'

'He said he had wondered briefly about going over to France, and staying the night there if necessary, at a small hotel in Saint Vaast, a few miles south of Cherbourg, that we often use, but that as he had a lot to do, he'd almost certainly be back by evening.'

'And when he left, the weather was good?'

'Yes, it was. Fine, with a lovely breeze. The last thing he said to me was,' he paused, blew his nose, looked apologetically at Elizabeth: '"This is going to be a perfect sail. One for the archives". That was an expression he often used.'

A pause; then Dr Holden said, 'And what of the weather forecast? I believe you people have access to a rather sophisticated form of these things.'

'There were warnings of fairly stiff breezes mid-Channel. Nothing to worry about, just enough to make things a bit more exciting.'

'I see. So then he went straight off?'

'More or less. I walked him over to *Princess Charming* on her mooring. He had his lifejacket with him, actually put it on while I told him a couple of things about the boat.'

'Yes, we are to hear later about the lifejacket conundrum. What things did you want to tell Mr Beaumont about your yacht?'

'Oh, that I'd had a new radio fitted – ship-to-shore variety, that is – showed him how it worked. Basically it was a modern version of the one I'd had before.'

'He wouldn't have a problem with it?'

'Good Lord no. And I said there were some beers stashed away in the locker, if he wanted them. Oh, and he asked me if there were any paracetamol in the locker, that he had a bit of a headache. I told him he shouldn't drink champagne at break-fast time, and he said it was a good idea to drink champagne any time. And then – well, then he said – he said goodbye.'

'What were his exact words, Mr Green?'

'He said, "Cheerio, David, and thanks again. Wish me luck".'

'Why do you think he wanted you to wish him luck?'

'I have no idea.'

'Was that something he often said?'

'When we were racing, yes, Not normally, no.'

'So why do you think he said it?'

'I think he was just excited, looking forward to the day, dying to get out there . . .' His voice tailed away.

'Right. And when did you first suspect something was wrong?'

'Well, I was vaguely uneasy when he didn't come back at sundown. And there had been reports of a really nasty squall in the Channel. It happens out there, comes out of nowhere.'

'But you weren't worried about him, even then?'

'Not at first, no. I thought he'd probably decided to stay the night in France after all.'

'Did you try to make contact with the boat?'

'I did, yes. As the evening went on, I radioed constantly, but there was no reply, of course. And if he had docked in France, he wouldn't have heard it anyway. So I was a little worried, but not seriously. As I say, Simon was a superb sailor. There were very few situations he couldn't have dealt with.'

No, thought Elizabeth, don't say that, please don't say that.

'But of course one never knows how bad these squalls are going to get. And a Seal isn't a very big boat really. The *Lizzie*, that is to say Simon's boat, was a Contessa, quite a bit bigger, and he was used to sailing her, so he could have found himself in more trouble than he might have expected.'

'Yes, I see. And then, when did you get the first report that your boat had been found?'

'Not until the following morning. A fisherman reported it. It was just drifting, south of Calais; the mast was slightly damaged, but otherwise it was completely unharmed.'

'And did you think, immediately, that Mr Beaumont must have had an accident?'

'Yes, I'm afraid I did. In fact, I felt quite sure. So I called the emergency services and . . .'

Dr Holden called another break after that: an hour for lunch.

Elizabeth and her children were brought sandwiches, and more coffee, while everyone else went off to find food. Except Joel Strickland; he stayed, sitting quietly, in the other, larger waiting room. Annabel saw him when she went in search of more coffee.

'Hi, Joel, nice to see you. You OK?'

'Oh – yes. Yes, thanks.' He appeared to be only half with her, his mind elsewhere. After a moment or two he smiled at her and said with an obvious effort, 'Is your mum all right?'

'I think so. She's holding herself together with safety pins. She'll be better when it's over. Obviously we're all praying for a misadventure verdict. It will help her so much. But – not sure we'll get it. Somehow the evidence that it might be . . . well – not misadventure, is stacking up. Which will be very hard for her. For all of us, really.'

'Of course.' He sighed heavily, forced a smile at her. 'Well, we must all just hope. He's a good bloke, Holden. Very thorough.'

'Too thorough, if you ask me. He seems to keep almost prompting people to say Daddy was worried, depressed.'

'No, no, he's not. That's how they take evidence at these things – very, very methodically. No stone unturned and all that. All they're looking for is facts; there's no question of any blame being attached to anyone.'

'You missed the best bit,' she said with a grin, 'talking of blame. He sort of ticked off the Chairman of Graburn and French. For firing Daddy. He did it really well, just made some quite sarcastic comments. It was great.'

'I'd like to have heard that,' said Joel. 'Well, nice to see you, Annabel.'

As if it was nice to see anyone at the moment. Even stunningly beautiful girls like Annabel. He wanted to be with a girl who wasn't really beautiful at all, who was small and a bit too skinny, with mousey brown hair and pale, pale skin and huge brown eyes, and a smile that could light up England, when it came, which it didn't unless she really meant it . . .

Flora appeared in the doorway. 'Hello, Joel. So glad you got here. How are you?'

'Oh, I'm fine. Yes. Thanks. I'm off to New York in a couple of weeks. To run the *News* office there.'

'Oh, how marvellous. What fun. So good for one, a complete change of scene. It gives such a boost.'

'Well, hope so.'

'You missed Debbie,' she said. 'She had to rush away.'

'Debbie?' he said.

'Debbie, yes, Joel. She's been a bit – low recently. But I think she's beginning to feel a little better now. She's been very brave,' she added. 'I've been so proud of her. And so sorry for her too.'

'Er – yes.'

She smiled at him suddenly, a very sweet smile, reached out and patted his hand. 'Goodbye, Joel. Take care of yourself. Enjoy New York. You will, I promise you. Even if you don't think it now.'

'Goodbye, Mrs Fielding.'

'Flora, please. Well, I'd better get back. My escort will think I've done a runner. Let's hope for a good verdict. A correct one, that is.'

'Yes, indeed. And – thank you.'

What had she been on about, he wondered, watching her hobble off on her crutches. Was she trying to tell him she knew? That she understood? Surely not. But – it was possible. She was an amazingly nice woman. He'd always tried to persuade Debbie of that. And then because even thinking of Debbie that much was excruciatingly painful, he went out of the building and walked very fast down the street. He found a pub, downed half a pint of Michelob – would he ever be able to hear that word again without wanting to start blubbing – and then went back to the court.

'Now Mr Phillips. You're from the Royal Yachting Association and, as I understand it, something of an expert on lifejackets. Mr Beaumont's was not inflated when he was found. Does this mean that his jacket failed him? That it was faulty?'

'No, certainly not. It was a non-automatic type. That means, you have to pull a cord to inflate it. A lot of people don't like them, don't trust them: but then an equal number don't like the automatic sort.'

'Why would that be?'

'Well, they can be unreliable. They have a habit of over-inflating if they get wet, in heavy weather for instance, and once inflated they become very cumbersome.'

'But safer?'

'If you go overboard, yes, providing they work. As I said, you can't always rely on them.'

'Have you examined the lifejacket Mr Beaumont was wearing?'

'I have, sir, yes.'

'And was it faulty in any way?'

'Absolutely not. It just hadn't inflated.'

'And what could explain that, do you think?'

'Well, my theory would be that Mr Beaumont had this blow to the back of his head from the boom – they come at you very hard, booms do – and he would be momentarily stunned.'

'But why should the boom be swinging about? I thought it was central to the control of the boat.'

'Of course it is. But Mr Beaumont had clearly run into this storm, worse than he had anticipated; it's a lot to handle on your own. You've only got to get out of control for a few seconds, you know. Everything goes haywire very quickly. So he'd have got hit on the head, fallen into what would have been pretty rough water, and it's easy to imagine that he wouldn't have been able to find the cord. Underwater, as it were.'

'Yes, I see. Have you heard of other instances of people not opening these lifejackets?'

'It's unusual. But it does happen, yes.'

'And why do you think people continue to use them?'

'As I said, the automatic variety can be cumbersome. And unreliable.'

'I see. Thank you, Mr Phillips. I—'

The door of the court had opened and a clerk came in, spoke under his breath to Mr Jeffries.

Mr Jeffries followed him outside and shortly afterwards, and

861

looking distinctly ruffled, reappeared with a note which he passed up to Dr Holden.

Dr Holden read the note, clearly more than once, nodded to Mr Jeffries, who issued the now familiar exhortation to them all to rise. Which they did, and Dr Holden left the bench and indeed the courtroom, having announced a short break. The whole thing was a bit like a courtroom drama on television – as Annabel whispered to Elizabeth.

There seemed little point leaving the courtroom; they all remained, talking in rather hushed voices. Elizabeth was reminded once again of being in church, and the day swinging yet again in and out of reality. She felt very tired suddenly, tired and depressed. There had been very little evidence that seemed to be strong enough to secure a verdict of misadventure. And Toby was right; Dr Holden *did* seem to be persisting in a view that Simon's cheerfulness was forced, even slightly manic, his efforts to help people like Catherine interfering and manipulative – and a subsequent loss of control over events humiliating – and his last wonderful day out sailing a rather theatrical gesture in the face of a growing personal despair. And who was to say it was not? Who could say it was not? Only Simon himself, and he was not there to do it. This entirely foolish observation threatened to make her cry again; she made the excuse that she needed the loo and slipped out and along the corridor to the Ladies. As she went in, a woman was coming out: blonde, tanned, rather glamorous-looking. What was she doing there, Elizabeth wondered. She had nothing to do with their case; maybe she was involved with a subsequent one. Or was a lawyer. Or even a witness, come in to make a statement.

She sighed, looked after the woman, who was tall and very slim, and thought that before she was anything like slim and glamorous herself again she had to get a great deal fatter and a great deal less glamorous. Well, it was too late now.

She went into the Ladies and locked the door.

Only a minute or so after she returned to the courtroom, proceedings recommenced; with some very tedious evidence on yachts and their sea-worthiness, which lasted for about half an hour. How much more of this could she take? Did it really have to last so long? Surely––

862

'I would now like to hear from Mr Maurice Crane,' Dr Holden said, 'of Jenkins and Jenkins, insurance brokers. Mr Jeffries, could we have Mr Crane's statement, please, and Mr Crane, would you please go into the witness box . . .'

For some reason the statement didn't mean anything to Elizabeth. Maybe she was just exhausted, maybe growing numb with it all; she just heard Mr Jeffries reading out Mr Crane's statement, that he was employed at Jenkins & Jenkins as an insurance executive, that Mr Simon Beaumont had been one of his clients, how he had consulted him on the morning of 20 August about his insurance policies . . . she had the feeling something crucial had been said, but couldn't think what it exactly was . . .

'So, Mr Crane, you were quite possibly one of the last people to speak to Mr Beaumont?'

'Yes, sir.'

'And he telephoned you in your office. Do clients often telephone you about your policies?'

'Yes, sir. If it's something that requires an immediate answer.'

'Yes, I see. And Mr Beaumont telephoned you to ask you what, exactly?'

'It was about . . . about . . .' He stopped, cleared his throat.

'Please go on, Mr Crane.'

'It was about his life policy.'

'His life policy?' said Dr Holden. As if such a thing could be of no interest whatsoever.

'Indeed yes.'

The full importance of this slithered into Elizabeth's consciousness. Simon's life policy. He had telephoned Maurice Crane about it the morning he went out for his last sail. Because – well, obviously because . . .

'And what exactly did he ask you, Mr Crane?'

'He asked me if his life policy was – well, safe.'

'Safe? You mean was it still viable? That is what I could not ascertain from your statement.'

'Well, not exactly viable, no.'

'Then what was the purpose of this question?'

'He was concerned that in the event of his death, the policy might not benefit his wife and family. That it might go to Lloyd's, as part of his estate.'

863

There was an absolute silence in the courtroom. Nobody moved, nobody looked at anyone else. Down in the street, Elizabeth could hear a police siren wailing, and a lot of cars hooting and a burglar alarm going off somewhere, and she thought that she would never be able to hear such things for the rest of her life without reliving that moment. That moment when she knew, for a fact, that Simon must have gone out deliberately that morning, to drown. To leave her forever and not tell her about it. He had told her he loved her, made love to her indeed, and then left her for all eternity. The bastard, the absolute bastard.

'And what did you tell him, Mr Crane?'

'I told him that the policy was in trust for his wife. That Lloyd's couldn't touch it. Ever. That it was safe. As I said earlier.'

'I see. And was that the end of your conversation?'

'Yes, sir. He thanked me, he was a very courteous gentleman always, and then rang off.'

'And what time was this?'

'About half-past ten, sir.'

'So, shortly before Mr Beaumont arrived at the Sailing Club. Did he sound in any way distressed or anxious, Mr Crane?'

'No, sir. I would say he sounded more excited than anything.'

'Excited! I think that was how Mr Green described Mr Beaumont's mood as well. Thank you, Mr Crane.' Dr Holden paused. 'That would have concluded the evidence. However, we have another witness, who has arrived unexpectedly, with some new facts about Mr Beaumont's last day. I have agreed that we should hear it.'

And into the court, mounting the steps to the box, came a blonde woman, wearing what the initiated could see was a Chanel suit, and the uninitiated could just see was a very nice one, in pink tweed, the lapels in slightly lighter pink silk, the hemline just above the knee to show superb legs. She was tanned, and her long blond sun-streaked hair was held back loosely with a black ribbon, her shoes were brilliant pink, and extremely high-heeled, and as she looked round the court, her eyes finally settling on Elizabeth and the children, she gave the touch of a smile.

'Miss Parker Jones, thank you for coming today. Mr Jeffries, perhaps you would read Miss Parker Jones's statement.'

And so they learned that Felicity Parker Jones was a divorcée, that she lived in East Sussex, that she had spent the last four months sailing in Barbados, and that she had met Simon Beaumont several times at various regattas and sailing events. That she had actually sailed with him on several occasions; and that she had seen him on that fateful last morning and that they had met at the St George Hotel, Arundel, to discuss a proposition. She had heard that he had drowned, but no more details, and had not realised that there was to be an inquest until she arrived back in England the evening before.

'So, Miss Parker Jones, you last saw Mr Beaumont before that, on the twentieth of August. Where was that?'

'At the Caprice restaurant.'

So that was who it was, Elizabeth thought, but not Her, please don't let this be Her, this over-confident, tough looking woman.

'He was having lunch with someone and we talked briefly. He told me he was no longer employed and I said I could have a proposition for him. As I was leaving for Barbados the next day, we agreed we should talk sooner rather than later. He told me that he was going down to Chichester the following morning, and we arranged to meet at the Saint George Hotel in Arundel, as I said in my statement.'

You bastard, Simon. You knew you were going to meet her, and you didn't tell me. Just went off and didn't tell me. Well, a lifelong habit dies hard.

'And what was Mr Beaumont's mood when you met him that morning, Miss Parker Jones? Was he cheerful, buoyant?'

'Very cheerful. And pretty buoyant, yes. Of course, I knew about the Lloyd's thing, everyone at the Sailing Club did; it was so terrible when he had to sell the *Lizzie*, but of course he wasn't the only one – lots of friends have gone under. Simon always seemed to me to be taking it so much better than most people; he was so – so positive about it, and—'

Keep going, Miss Parker Jones. This is better, much more helpful. I might even forgive you at this rate and him as well.

'Now Miss Parker Jones, this proposition. Would you like to enlarge on it?'

'Oh yes, of course. I've got two yachts, one I keep in Barbados – just a cheap little thing, well, you know – and then another, much bigger one which I joint-own with my father. He always does the Atlantic Rally in it.'

'The Atlantic Rally, could you tell us what that's about?'

'It's a race from the Canaries to Saint Lucia.'

'I see. That's quite a long way, I would think.'

'Yes. It can take anything from two weeks to a month. It's a great race, any size of boat can enter, from twenty-seven to fifty-five feet. It's very exciting, and huge fun. Anyway, we were looking for a fourth crew member. I asked Simon Beaumont if he'd like to join us.'

'I see. Tell us about this race, Miss Parker Jones. When does it take place?'

'In November.'

'And it's a favourite, is it, in the sailing calendar?'

'Yes, it is.'

'And – is it dangerous?'

'Well, it's like all sailing – it can be. On the other hand, it sometimes isn't dangerous at all. It's all down to the weather.'

'I see. And what would most people's reaction be, to being invited to crew in such a race?'

'Well, I think I could say that most people would be thrilled.'

'And was Mr Beaumont thrilled?'

'Absolutely. He said it had given him a real motive for going on, getting the better of bloody Lloyd's, all that sort of thing. Yes. But—'

'But?'

'Well, he said he must talk it over with his wife, obviously. That he would do so that night, and let me know.'

'Did he say anything else?'

Such a silence there was then: time itself seemed not just to stand still but to freeze.

Lucinda gripped Blue's hand; Flora, Colin's; Annabel, her mother's. Fiona Broadhurst held her hands together as if in prayer; Catherine bit her lip so tightly that afterwards it was quite swollen. Every eye, every muscle of every face, was concentrated on Felicity Parker Jones.

'Well, then he said that one thing would be very important as the race was potentially dangerous, and that was his life policy. He would need to check it out, make sure that the money was safe for the family, that Lloyd's couldn't take it. He said his wife would obviously need to be reassured on that point. And he said he might as well do it straight away, so that at least was out of the way . . .'

Half an hour later, Dr Holden finished his summing up. And then he said, and he looked at Elizabeth and smiled, just very briefly, before he said it, 'On the evidence before me,' and then he paused, 'I am satisfied that this death came about by misadventure . . .'

Elizabeth burst into tears.

Much, much later that evening, when Elizabeth had gone exhausted – but happily – to bed, and Toby had gone out with his friends and Tilly with hers, and the phone had finally stopped ringing, and Annabel was sitting in the kitchen, trying to concentrate on a very tedious old film, and wondering if she would ever feel properly happy again, there was a knock at the door. She thought it must be Tilly, having forgotten her key as she so often did, and went to open it, mildly – no not mildly, very – irritated.

'You really are a complete idiot,' she said, as she pulled it open.

'I know I am,' said a voice: speaking rather humbly. Only it wasn't Tilly. It was Jamie. Jamie, looking slightly pale but very determined, in the light of the porch. 'Do you think I could possibly come in?' he said. 'I need to talk to you about something.'

And as she stood there, only half-able to believe he wasn't some figment of her imagination, he said, 'Annabel, I've left Boston. I've left Cartwright and Partners. I told Dad if working for the firm meant living in some kind of fifties time-warp, then it wasn't for me. I can work here as a lawyer, for God's sake. I love you and I want you to have a career if you want one, and I want to marry you. If you'll still have me.'

And Annabel, amazed and moved beyond anything at this demonstration of courage and determination, and indeed of love, said she most certainly would and that yes, he had better come in.

'I told Dad, all I wanted was to come to London to work for a year, so we could spend some time together, get our lives sorted out, that there was no earthly reason why not, the firm hardly depended on me, and that you had your career to consider as well. And of course he said your career should be taking care of me and our children, and I told him you felt you could work *and* do that, and he said he didn't want anyone in the family who felt that way.'

'I see,' said Annabel, wondering if she would ever be able to speak with civility to Philip Cartwright again.

'Yes. So I said I was going to come over and see you anyway, for a week or so, that we had to talk, and that was when he got really angry and said he didn't want me back in the firm if I came at all.' At this, his voice faltered; clearly this was equivalent to a small child being told he would lose all his toys if he didn't eat up his dinner.

'But you did, just the same.'

'Yes, I did,' he said staunchly, and she thought that nobody who hadn't spent time with the Cartwrights could ever know what courage that had required. And realised also how much he must love her.

'Oh Jamie,' she said, 'I love you so, so much. And I'm sure your dad doesn't mean it. And if he does, I can think of a dozen firms that would be thrilled to have you join them. Mummy knows lots of lawyers.'

'Really?'

'Really. Now try and calm down, have a little more Jack Daniel's and let me tell you what happened at my dad's inquest today. It was truly amazing . . .'

'Oh God,' he said. 'I forgot, I'm so sorry.'

'Don't be. Just listen.'

Epilogue

She made the most extraordinarily beautiful bride. Everyone said so. The blessing had been lovely, and as everyone also said, virtually indistinguishable from the marriage service proper: she had swept down the aisle in a cloud of white silk and pink roses and happiness, to join her fiancé who was so over-whelmed by this vision that he walked up to greet her. His best man, fearing things were going to get out of hand rather earlier than he had expected, followed him and led him swiftly back to his proper place.

There was an exceptionally large group of bridesmaids and page-boys, including the bride's nieces and nephews, and the children of friends, but none so excited and proud as Caroline Morgan who, when she heard she had been granted this great honour, dropped the glass of Ribena she was holding onto her grandmother's spotless white carpet, where it managed to form a stain of disproportionate size. Her mother reflected rather sadly that she had clearly inherited more of her own genes than the ones responsible for Caroline's brown eyes and hair, and that her pretty hands – also an inheritance – were going to drop a great many more things before very long.

The chief bridesmaid, Miss Molly Rose Horton, wasn't actually up to most of her duties, and certainly not capturing the heart of the best man, but she did succeed in looking absolutely ravishing, carried in the arms of Catherine Morgan, who had, after all, been present at her birth, beaming toothlessly on the congregation, wearing a dress made of the same material and as closely as possible in the same style as her mother's and, her large blue eyes wide with wonderment, watched as her parents exchanged their vows.

The bride's mother, not as happy as she had been at her daughter's last wedding, nevertheless had smiled graciously at the congregation as she entered the church on the arm of her youngest son, and at her husband as he rejoined her after giving the bride away himself.

There was a sharp social divide in the church; the bride's side brayed, as Blue put it afterwards, while the groom's whooped; the only visual difference was that the morning suits on the left were a lot older and shabbier than those on the right: and many of the whoopers were not in morning dress at all, but rather sharply cut suits.

Lucinda had carefully chosen hymns that everyone would know – 'It's like listening to *Songs of Praise*,' Mrs Worthington hissed to her elder daughter – and Lucinda and Blue left the church smiling with such patent joy it made even Mr Worthington smile back; Blue was carrying Molly Rose who by now had fallen so thoroughly into the spirit of the thing that she performed her latest trick, which was waving, to all and sundry, greatly encouraged by all and sundry waving back.

Mr Worthington found himself actually rather enjoying having Mrs Horton on his arm; she was a pretty woman anyway, and dressed entirely in varying shades of pink, the skirt of her dress being short enough to reveal some very good legs; she put Mrs Worthington, in her rather weary wedding navy, distinctly in the shade. Mrs Worthington took Mr Horton's arm rather gingerly, as if it might suddenly sting her, but when he told her in a stage whisper that he thought Lucinda was a dead ringer for her mum ('May God forgive me,' he said, recounting this later to Mrs Horton), she inclined her head to him graciously and started smiling almost as broadly as Molly Rose.

The reception was at the Hortons' new home, a large and impressive mansion in St George's Hill, Surrey; Lucinda had managed to steer Blue away from Chislehurst, but she could see that unless she made some concessions, she was going to find herself unmarried again, and that she should bid farewell to any ideas of Georgian or even Victorian houses in London.

The mansion, called Hedges on account of some splendidly tall and thick beech hedges which surrounded it, was one of St George's finest, boasting not only a swimming pool, a three-acre garden and six bedrooms all with ensuite bathrooms, but what the estate agents described as 'a small ballroom'. This, extended by a large marquee, formed the reception area; where the bridal party stood in line to receive their guests. Of which there were two hundred and twenty.

Flora, accompanied by Colin, was greatly enjoying herself. She was wearing a silk dress in darkest blue, with an embroidered red silk coat over it, a red hat with a display of osprey feathers that would not have disgraced the Queen Mother, and some very high-heeled red boots. Colin was wearing a morning suit that was not as new as he would have liked; he was all set to have one specially made for the wedding, but Flora had managed to persuade him against it.

'That one is so nice,' she said, pointing to the one hanging in his dressing room, to which he had summoned her, the better to discuss the matter. 'Why do you want to get a new one?'

Colin said the old one was at least ten years old, and he really thought the occasion demanded something a bit more special, as he put it; he'd been to a wedding recently where one of the guests had had the lapels of his coat piped in a much lighter grey, to match his trousers. Flora hoped he hadn't noticed her shudder and told him that she really thought his old one was fine and that he should leave such refinements to the bridal party. Colin rather reluctantly agreed, but said that at least he would get a new top hat – which sounded perfectly safe except that he had had a dark red band put round it, to match his waistcoat.

They had had a rather good lunch on the way to the wedding, and she was already feeling slightly tipsy; that, combined with the sunshine and the emotion of the day, and her own great new happiness, suddenly overwhelmed her and she reached up to kiss Colin.

'You look very, very nice,' she said. 'Really handsome.'

'Well, thank you,' he said, 'and you look absolutely beautiful. You must bring that outfit to Salzburg. Not long now.'

'No, indeed,' she said. 'And that reminds me, Colin, there's something I wanted to say to you about Salzburg.'

'Ye-es?' He looked rather wary.

She smiled and kissed him again. 'It's all right,' she said. 'All I wanted to say was, could you change the booking slightly?'

'I'll try,' he said, 'although it might be difficult. What would you like me to change?'

'Well,' she said, smiling at him and thinking how even the hat wasn't too bad, 'I really would rather we weren't in separate rooms. If it's all right with you.'

Annabel Beaumont was attracting a lot of attention. Dressed in a sliver of palest blue silk, with extremely high-heeled silver sandals, her hair scooped back in a waterfall of curls, she looked almost as ravishing as the bride herself: indeed, Lucinda hissed at her as she embraced her in the receiving line, she made her feel like a fat old bat.

'Lucinda, I don't think so. You look about seventeen, maybe a bit younger, doesn't she, Jamie? Lucinda, this is my fiancé, Jamie Cartwright.'

'Oh, how lovely to meet you' Lucinda cried. 'Blue, darling, this is Jamie, Annabel's totally handsome fiancé – he's a lawyer from the States, you know; lucky you to be married to a lawyer, Annabel – wish I'd been, saved me a lot of trouble.'

And Jamie kissed Lucinda's hand and shook Blue's and said how extremely generous of them to have invited him to their wedding, and Annabel thought not for the first time how charming he was, and how he really was rather like her father.

Jamie was still an associate of Cartwright & Partners, but he was to move to London for a year, to work for a firm in Lincoln's Inn with which Cartwrights had an agreement. After that, he and Annabel had agreed, they would decide together where they would settle permanently. This had not been arrived at without difficulty.

Elizabeth had managed not to display any great surprise at Jamie's presence in the house the day after the inquest and kept carefully out of the whole thing for the next twenty-four hours, merely greeting Jamie with affection and some well-hidden relief. Later, when she was told that Jamie and his father had made up their quarrel, and that Jamie was going to be allowed to spend a year in London she was more relieved still, and any anxiety she had felt for Annabel joining the Cartwright clan considerably diminished.

'The old bugger actually said,' Annabel told her, 'that he

could see Jamie was going to be an excellent lawyer, having demonstrated an ability to stay cool in a – a stand-off situation. And Jamie's going to work for some firm where all the partners are his best friends.'

'Well, it's lovely,' said Elizabeth carefully, 'and I'm very happy for you. The only thing I would say, darling, and it's nothing to do with me, is that you must make some concessions too.'

'Mummy,' said Annabel indignantly, 'do you think I'm stupid or something? Of course I will.' Adding that if Jamie thought she was going to move to Boston when she had Florian's salon to work in, then he had better change his mind pretty quickly.

'Annabel,' said Elizabeth warningly, and Annabel looked very discomfited and said, 'Well, not till we're married anyway.'

And now Jamie was in London for a year, and they were looking for a flat – 'But very, very near, Mummy, I promise you. You don't have to worry.'

'I'm not worried,' said Elizabeth, while thinking that this was what she had predicted would happen when she had agreed to have the baby, and that Annabel's life would of course take precedence over hers, and that that was precisely what she wanted for her.

Elizabeth was not at the wedding; she had been invited, of course, but as she was now eight and a half months' pregnant she said it wasn't the most tempting prospect, and that she was sure Lucinda would understand and forgive her.

Every day now she felt happier; stronger, more able to cope with what was a fairly daunting future. She had found a nanny, a stalwart Scottish girl called Tess, who was clearly going to fit into the household extremely well – not least in that she was very pretty and Toby approved of her. Elizabeth had insisted that they all interview her; and Tess had liked that very much, said she always knew there would be trouble when she'd only been allowed to meet the mother.

Nigel was not at the wedding either; Lucinda knew he wouldn't come, nor even want to, but she felt that he would be very hurt if he wasn't invited, and so sent him one of the somewhat excessive invitations. He had looked at it through

873

slightly blurred eyes while wondering even then how Lucinda could have become the sort of person who added pink ribbons to a wedding invitation, but after that he did feel much better, as she had known he would, and put it on his fireplace along with some more sober ones. He ordered a pair of bay trees for a present, to be delivered to the house on the day of the wedding, and then found it surprisingly easy to regard the whole thing with equanimity.

He supposed Catherine would be at the wedding; unless of course she was in Somerset with this man. If he hadn't feared rejection so, he might even now have tried to see her. But it was all a bit depressing.

He tried to think what he might do with the day. In the end he decided to stay in London; he had a few houses to look at – one in particular, a pretty little terrace house in Ovington Street. That would be a positive thing to do on such a day, and then maybe he'd have dinner at his club. The day would pass, although it wouldn't be exactly pleasant, and then – well, then what? A lifetime of bachelorhood, he supposed. There were worse things. At least you could do what you wanted.

Toby was at the wedding, and looking forward rather desperately to the wedding breakfast when Fallon was arriving, to help in the kitchen. Lucinda had told Tilly she could bring a couple of friends if she liked, and Tilly had asked both Fallon and Madison, but Madison, who was very shy anyway, said that it would be too much of a temptation with her diet – at Tilly's instigation she had joined Weight Watchers, and already lost two stone – and Fallon said she'd feel like some kind of freak at a fair, unless Tilly could find her something she could actually do. It turned out that the caterers were two short on the washing-up front, and Tilly had volunteered Fallon: 'And then we can maybe have a bit of a bop at the end of the evening.'

Fallon said pigs could maybe fly, 'And certainly not with that brother of yours, bet he's a sight on the dance floor.'

Tilly told her rather stiffly not to be so rude, and Fallon, who genuinely adored Tilly, told her not to be so silly and that actually she thought Toby was pretty good-looking really, and if he'd only unstarch his neck and learn to speak properly, he could look quite fit.

Debbie and Richard weren't at the wedding; they had hardly known Lucinda. In any case, Debbie couldn't have gone as it was a Friday and Friday was the day she wrote and filed her copy for the *Daily News*.

Joel had done something wonderful for Debbie, before he left the *News*; he had taken Nicky Holt out to lunch and asked her if she 'or one of your mates in that silly business of yours' could possibly give Debbie a chance to do some writing.

'Debbie Fielding! She's a PR,' said Nicky witheringly. 'You fancy her or something, Joel?'

Joel said of course not, but he just had a hunch she was rather talented. 'She writes really nicely and she's funny and she's just desperate for a break. Please, Nicky! I'll buy you dinner at the Pierre next time you come to New York.'

'You do fancy her, don't you?' said Nicky curiously. 'Yeah, OK, I'll try and think of something. I'm setting up a panel testing various products each week – how'd that be?'

'Great,' said Joel.

And Debbie, managing somehow to function more or less normally – how did she do that, how, when she felt increasingly she was going mad – was telephoned one morning by Nicky and asked if she would like to join her panel of guinea pigs. 'I'll only want about two hundred words each week – could you manage that, d'you think?'

'Of course I could,' said Debbie. 'I'd love to.' And within four weeks, she had so impressed Nicky, her two hundred words being much sharper and funnier and better composed than any of the others, that Nicky asked her if she'd like to extend her testing to various health clubs and spas – 'that sort of thing'.

She was now writing a regular review – literally a column running down the right-hand side of Nicky's Monday pages, of such places, some in London, some outside; she turned up incognito, stayed a day and then delivered copy so well-honed, and so coolly to the point that within weeks she had a modest fan-mail. Nothing could have soothed her pain, eased her loneliness, restored her sense of optimism more efficiently and quickly than that column. She could even listen to Richard telling her how wonderful Morag was without wanting to scream. And the best thing of all was that when she moved to Scotland in the spring, she could just carry on doing it. It meant being away overnight once a week, but that was wonderful; she told Richard it was the least he could do for her, and slightly to her surprise he agreed without any argument. She wondered if Flora, her newest and greatest ally, had anything to do with it, and decided she probably did.

She still missed Joel with a savageness that was physically painful, she still cried at least once a day; she still woke up from dreams that he was there, but she was surviving. The first dreadful days, when it had hurt so much she was actually frightened, had passed; she managed, from time to time to enjoy things, her children, her job, the contemplation of her lovely new house. And one day, she could see, she would be properly happy again.

Elizabeth hadn't mentioned a terrible headache to Annabel as she left for the wedding; or a feeling of distinct dizziness to Tilly when she came to kiss her goodbye, and obviously neither of these things to Toby. She knew if she did, they would all have refused to leave her. But once they had gone – soon after midday, for they all had much to do, not least Annabel who was assisting Florian on the bridal hair – she phoned Mr Taylor, her obstetrician and reported these things to him.

Within thirty minutes she was in a private ambulance on her way to the Princess Diana Hospital, where a rather worryingly large committee was waiting for her, headed by Mr Taylor, looking stern.

'I think,' he said, after checking her blood pressure, and both their heartbeats, 'it's time we got that baby out. Your blood pressure is extremely high, you're only two weeks away from term, and there's no earthly reason not to really. I'm going to do a section, so we don't waste any more time.'

'Oh God,' said Elizabeth, feeling fear literally clasping her heart, longing for Simon more than she could ever remember. 'Oh Mr Taylor, is it going to be all right?'

'Of course it is,' he said. 'The baby's heartbeat is extremely strong. It just wants to get out. Now try to keep calm, I'm going to get that blood pressure down a bit, and we'll do it late afternoon. You haven't had any lunch, have you?'

'No. Breakfast though. And a cup of tea about – oh, about one.' Her mouth felt very dry; she was shaking violently, her teeth chattering. 'I – I want –' she said, and then started to cry, for she knew she couldn't have what she wanted, what every woman in labour wants, her husband with her.

Mr Taylor was very sweet; he sat down beside her, took her hand and said, 'You're going to be fine, Elizabeth, just fine. And so is your baby. Now, is there anyone you'd like to have with you, who could come and be with you for a bit?'

And, 'No,' she said, and that made her cry harder than ever, her alone-ness spelled out by that small, awful word. 'The children are all at a wedding and I don't want to spoil their day.'

Mr Taylor looked at her and smiled. 'Elizabeth Beaumont,' he said, 'you are a trouper. World Class. And you'll just have to make do with me.'

Nigel was about to have a bath when the florist phoned. They were simply devastated, but it appeared that the pair of bay trees, destined for Weybridge that afternoon, had not after all been delivered.

'Well, do it now,' he said, and they replied that they couldn't because their drivers had all gone home; and would the morning do?

He had been about to say yes, when he thought he really did want them to arrive that day, he had envisaged them at the entrance to the marquee, had indeed written that on the card, giving him some kind of presence there, and thought then that it would only take him an hour at the most to drive them over himself; no need to go in, or to announce that he was there, he could deliver them and then drive away. And when the trees arrived by taxi at his flat, in square white wooden tubs with large white bows tied around the trees – 'We might remove those, I think,' he said to the totally disinterested cab driver, 'bit vulgar' – he put them in the back of his Volvo and set out for Weybridge.

Catherine wasn't sure if she was enjoying the wedding or not. Of course it was all very lovely, and the idea of having Molly Rose as the chief bridesmaid was enchanting, and Lucinda looked gorgeous and so did the garden and the house and the marquee; and the string quartet was playing the most delicious music, and everyone was being very nice to her, and Caroline and Freddie had both been extremely good – although they were now being slightly less good and haring about the garden shrieking with Lucinda's nephews and nieces – but the fact remained that she did feel very lonely. Again.

The wedding was accentuating that, rather. Everyone was in couples, not just the young ones; she had looked at the table-plan and it was very sweet, Lucinda had put her on the top table, but the fact still remained that sitting on one side she had Mr Horton Senior, who did look like a lot of fun, she had to say, and on the other, Lucinda's younger brother, who was also charming, but like all the other men at the wedding, was married.

Halfway through the reception, and before the meal, she began to feel tearful, and decided to go for a walk round the garden. She was looking rather hopelessly for Freddie and Caroline and consequently not at where she was going; and managed to walk straight into one of the waiters, his tray laden with glasses of wine.

Catherine looked down at her pale pink suit, now liberally spattered with red, tried not to cry and fled up to the room where she had got ready. She would just have to change; she had a linen dress with her, it was hardly festive and a bit creased, but it was at least all one colour and didn't smell like a winery.

She put it on, trying to keep positive – all would be lost if she gave in to self-pity now – and was just reapplying her make-up when she saw in the drive what looked remarkably like Nigel's Volvo. And not only did it look like it, it *was* Nigel's Volvo, and what was more, he was getting out of it and removing first one and then a second bay tree from the boot and handing them over to a man in charge of the gate.

Catherine watched him, as he looked up at the house rather wistfully, all on his own, as she was, not dressed in wedding finery as she no longer was, and knew with absolutely clarity what she had to do. She leaned out of the window and waved and shouted, 'Nigel! Nigel, wait!' He didn't hear her.

She raced out of the room, down the stairs, out of the door and down the drive, through the gate: to see the Volvo moving away, quite fast down the tree-lined road.

'Oh Nigel – oh God, no,' she said, and because it really did seem like more than she could bear, she sank onto her haunches and started to cry, her head buried in her arms.

And then suddenly she heard him say, 'Catherine? Isn't it?' and he must have reversed up the road, for she looked up and saw him, leaning out of the window, clearly very concerned.

And, 'Oh yes, it is, it is Catherine,' she said, grief and relief making her stupid; and he got out of the car and came across to her and squatted beside her and put his arm round her.

'Whatever is it? What's the matter?' he said, and she really started crying then, sobbing quite loudly, and he stood up and helped her up too and led her across to his car and put her into it and drove very slowly down the road, away from the house and the noise and the curious eyes.

'Now then,' he said finally, pulling into the kerb and turning off the engine. 'Now then, tell me what the matter is. Thank goodness I spotted you. I can't bear to see you like this, Catherine, I really can't. Has someone upset you?'

And Catherine looked at him, at his face, even more mournful than usual, his pale-blue eyes full of concern for her, and said – because she had to know that first – 'Nigel, are you – are you still in love with Lucinda?'

And when he said, Good Lord, no, no he wasn't, not at all, thank goodness – although he was still very, very fond of her, of course – she said, 'Because you see, I think . . .' God, this took courage, huge courage, she felt terrible, so scared, and so foolish, but it was her last chance, she knew, and a chance she wanted so much, 'Nigel, I think I – I might be in love with you.'

And after that it all became very simple.

At roughly the same moment, Mr Taylor was stroking Elizabeth's hair back gently from her face as she surfaced from the anaesthetic, and smiling down at her – really he thought he might be a little in love with her himself – and telling her that she had a very fine and extremely noisy new son.

The meal had been wonderful, the speeches very funny – especially Charlie's – and the dancing had begun, when the maitre d' walked up to Lucinda who was chattering at one of the tables, and whispered something in her ear.

Whereupon she said, 'Oh my God!' and began looking wildly round the room. And then ran over to Toby, who was the only member of the Beaumont family she could see, and who was dancing, really rather badly, she thought, with a ravishing black girl, who was dancing rather well, and said, 'Toby, Toby, she's had it, your mother's had her baby, it's a boy!'

And was alarmed to see Toby standing first stock-still, completely emotionless, and then bite his lip and his blue eyes, so like his father's, fill with tears.

And then he punched the air with his fist and shouted, 'Yesss!!' and Tilly came rushing over and Annabel too, and they all three stood there, hugging one another, crying and laughing at the same time. And then Annabel said, 'We must go to her at once, can someone get us a cab?' and the maitre d' said he would, right away.

When they had gone, Lucinda, quite tearful herself, suddenly said, 'Has anyone seen Catherine? She wasn't even at the dinner, I hope she's all right.'

'Oh yes, sorry,' said Caroline, 'we were meant to tell you. She's gone off with Nigel to have dinner, she hopes you won't mind. She'll be back later.'

'Nigel!' said Lucinda. 'My goodness, how wonderful.'

And, 'Blimey,' said Blue, 'any more dramas at this wedding and I'm going to the office, get a bit of peace and quiet.'

In their mother's room at the hospital, Annabel and Toby and Tilly stood by her bed, smiling down at her as she said sleepily, 'Didn't we do well?'

'You did, Mummy,' said Annabel, and, 'Darling Mummy,' said Tilly, and, 'It's great,' said Toby. 'I'm really pleased.' And then the nurse brought the baby in, still yelling. 'I'm afraid he's going to be a rather noisy addition to the household,' Elizabeth said, taking him in her arms – and they all gazed at him, in absolute awe, and Tilly spoke for them all when she said, quietly but quite happily, 'How pleased Daddy would be.'

'He would indeed,' said Elizabeth, and she said it quite happily too.

*

They left not long after that, for she was very tired, and the baby wouldn't settle; promising to come back in the morning.

'You know what?' said Annabel, as they sat in the kitchen, toasting the baby in tea. 'I just had a rather good thought.'

'What's that then?' said Toby.

'Those beastly people didn't beat us, did they, not any of us. They didn't win. We did.'

Have you read every

PENNY VINCENZI?